The Editor

RICHARD J. DUNN is Professor Emeritus of English at the University of Washington, where he has taught since 1967. His publications include the Norton Critical Editions of *Wuthering Heights* and *Jane Eyre; Approaches to Teaching Dickens's David Copperfield; David Copperfield: An Annotated Bibliography; The English Novel: Twentieth-Century Criticism, Defoe to Hardy;* and *Oliver Twist: Whole Heart and Soul*. He is the author of many articles on the Brontës, Dickens, Tennyson, and Carlyle.

W. W. NORTON & COMPANY, INC.
Also Publishes

ENGLISH RENAISSANCE DRAMA: A NORTON ANTHOLOGY
edited by David Bevington et al.

THE NORTON ANTHOLOGY OF AFRICAN AMERICAN LITERATURE
edited by Henry Louis Gates Jr. and Nellie Y. McKay et al.

THE NORTON ANTHOLOGY OF AMERICAN LITERATURE
edited by Nina Baym et al.

THE NORTON ANTHOLOGY OF CHILDREN'S LITERATURE
edited by Jack Zipes et al.

THE NORTON ANTHOLOGY OF DRAMA
edited by J. Ellen Gainor, Stanton B. Garner Jr., and Martin Puchner

THE NORTON ANTHOLOGY OF ENGLISH LITERATURE
edited by M. H. Abrams and Stephen Greenblatt et al.

THE NORTON ANTHOLOGY OF LITERATURE BY WOMEN
edited by Sandra M. Gilbert and Susan Gubar

THE NORTON ANTHOLOGY OF MODERN AND CONTEMPORARY POETRY
edited by Jahan Ramazani, Richard Ellmann, and Robert O'Clair

THE NORTON ANTHOLOGY OF POETRY
edited by Margaret Ferguson, Mary Jo Salter, and Jon Stallworthy

THE NORTON ANTHOLOGY OF SHORT FICTION
edited by R. V. Cassill and Richard Bausch

THE NORTON ANTHOLOGY OF THEORY AND CRITICISM
edited by Vincent B. Leitch et al.

THE NORTON ANTHOLOGY OF WORLD LITERATURE
edited by Sarah Lawall et al.

THE NORTON FACSIMILE OF THE FIRST FOLIO OF SHAKESPEARE
prepared by Charlton Hinman

THE NORTON INTRODUCTION TO LITERATURE
edited by Alison Booth and Kelly J. Mays

THE NORTON READER
edited by Linda H. Peterson and John C. Brereton

THE NORTON SAMPLER
edited by Thomas Cooley

THE NORTON SHAKESPEARE, BASED ON THE OXFORD EDITION
edited by Stephen Greenblatt et al.

For a complete list of Norton Critical Editions, visit
www.wwnorton.com/college/English/nce_home.htm

A NORTON CRITICAL EDITION

Emily Brontë

WUTHERING HEIGHTS

THE 1847 TEXT
BACKGROUNDS AND CONTEXTS
CRITICISM

FOURTH EDITION

Edited by

RICHARD J. DUNN

UNIVERSITY OF WASHINGTON

W • W • NORTON & COMPANY • *New York* • *London*

This title is printed on permanent paper containing 30 percent post-consumer waste recycled fiber.

Printed in the United States of America.

The text of this book is composed in Fairfield Medium
with the display set in Bernhard Modern.
Composition by PennSet, Inc.
Manufacturing by The Maple-Vail Book Manufacturing Group.

Library of Congress Cataloging-in-Publication Data

Brontë, Emily, 1818–1848.
Wuthering Heights : the 1847 text, backgrounds and criticism / Emily Brontë ; edited by Richard J. Dunn.— 4th ed.
p. cm.— (A Norton critical edition)
Includes bibliographical references.

ISBN 0-393-97889-3 (pbk.)

1. Triangles (Interpersonal relations)—Fiction. 2. Rejection (Psychology)—Fiction. 3. Yorkshire (England)—Fiction. 4. Rural families—Fiction. 5. Foundlings—Fiction. 6. Brontë, Emily, 1818–1848. Wuthering heights. I. Dunn, Richard J., 1938– II. Title.

PR4172.W7 2002b
823'.8—dc21 2002026531

W. W. Norton & Company, Inc., 500 Fifth Avenue, New York, N.Y. 10110
www.wwnorton.com

W. W. Norton & Company Ltd., Castle House, 75/76 Wells Street, London W1T 3QT

5 6 7 8 9 0

Contents

Preface to the Fourth Edition

William M. Sale, Jr.'s first Norton Critical Edition of *Wuthering Heights* in 1962 was a pioneering effort that established a reliable text, provided backgrounds and contexts, and recovered selected reviews and criticism. For the second edition ten years later, he replaced several of the critical essays with newer ones and added brief commentary of his own concerning the relationship of Emily Brontë's earlier Gondal poems and her novel. For the third edition in 1990, the first after Sale's death, I retained his textual and explanatory notes and much of the background material, but rearranged it and added materials to distinguish between the composition, publication, and reception of the first edition and the one edited by Charlotte Brontë in 1850.

Because biographical, textual, and critical and cultural studies of the past quarter of a century have provided more and better information about the Brontës and their times, we can better situate Emily's novel among those of her sisters and also better understand the cultural context of someone reading the 1847 or 1850 editions of *Wuthering Heights*. This edition's selective bibliography provides a guide to the Brontë scholarship which has made possible the fourth Norton Critical Edition of *Wuthering Heights*. I give primacy to the 1847 edition, because given both the independence of Emily's mind and art and the qualifications Charlotte's edition made to the work, it is helpful to read *Wuthering Heights* first as it appeared in 1847 and then to deal with it as edited and promoted by the then better-known Charlotte.

Editions of *Wuthering Heights*, 1847–1850

Although we know that Emily Brontë received proofs and corrected them to some extent, her publisher, Thomas Newby, produced a disappointing first edition, flawed by obvious typographical errors, eccentric paragraphing, and much inconsistency in punctuation. Although no comment by Emily on the finished product remains, it is reasonable to assume she shared Charlotte Brontë's disgust with the Newby edition. Pleased with her own publishers, Charlotte complained to them that although Newby had proof-sheets by the beginning of August 1847, he "shuffles, gives his word and breaks it," and that her "relatives have suffered from exhausting delay and procrastination." After receiving copies of the Newby edition that fall, she reported that "The books [both *Wuthering Heights* and *Agnes Grey*] are not well got up—they abound in errors of the press," particularly, "The orthography & punctuation of the books are mortifying to a degree—almost all the errors that were corrected in the proof-sheets appear intact in what should have been the fair copies. If Mr. Newby always does business in this way, few authors would like to have him for their publisher a second time."[1]

American editions of *Jane Eyre*, *Wuthering Heights*, and *Agnes Grey* appeared in 1848. There was no international copyright, and the Brontës had not authorized the American editions. Thus textual variants in the first American edition have no authority. The American editions, however, did lead to reviews which came to the Brontës' attention.

Wuthering Heights would not have gained stature and even remained in print for many years had not *Jane Eyre* been such an instant and continuing sensation. Charlotte's novel was published by Smith, Elder in October 1847. In December of the same year, Thomas Newby printed only 250 of the promised 350 copies of the volumes containing *Wuthering Heights* and *Agnes Grey*. Reviewers were convinced that *Jane Eyre* was by far the superior work, but thanks in part to Newby's unscrupulous and insinuative promotion of the other two novels, there was rampant speculation that the pseudonyms, Currer, Ellis, and Acton Bell, were those of a single author or, possibly, of a combination of brother(s) and sister(s). The 1848 New York edition attributed *Wuthering Heights* to "The Author of 'Jane Eyre'," and a Boston edition of the same year simply indicated it was "Edited by Currer Bell" (which had been the wording on the title-page of the first British edition of *Jane Eyre* the year before).

Confused and misled though the public had been in the late 1840s about the authorship of these works, it is evident that Emily's and Anne's fictions rode the coattails or skirts (depending on whether they were seen as male or female writing) of *Jane Eyre*. In 1848, Charlotte, while Emily and Anne were yet alive, persuaded her own publisher to reissue the sisters' *Poems* that two years earlier Aylott and Jones had published but which had sold only two copies. The Smith, Elder reissue of the poems and their 1850 *Wuthering Heights and Agnes Grey . . . A New Edition Revised, With A Biographical Notice of the Authors, A Selection from Their Literary Re-*

1. Margaret Smith, ed. *The Letters of Charlotte Brontë*. Vol. I. Oxford: Clarendon Press, 1995. 561, 575, 590.

mains, and a Preface by Currer Bell were direct consequences of *Jane Eyre*'s success.

As editor of her late sisters' work, Charlotte addressed a number of issues concerning *Wuthering Heights* and Emily. This was her opportunity to correct the many textual errors of the first edition and to introduce more of Emily's poetry, which she also heavily edited. In her biographical notice she intended to end much of the confusion about the Bell pseudonyms (although she did not state the Brontë surname), and in her preface she replied to the most hostile and echoed the most favorable earlier reviews of the 1847 *Wuthering Heights*. Although Emily lived only a year after the publication of *Wuthering Heights*, she was aware of the novel's reception, and in her writing desk were found excerpts of five reviews. Also, Charlotte brought to her attention comments from *The North American Review* in 1848. Unfortunately, we have no inkling of what she thought about these or of whether she might had seen other comments she did not retain.

Recovering a *Wuthering Heights* Text

As is the case with the number plans, proofs, and letters of Charles Dickens, modern editors of nineteenth-century fiction often can track closely a book's conception, composition, and revision. Such is not possible for *Wuthering Heights*. The problem, as noted above, is that nothing remains directly from Emily's hand and we are left with an error-riddled first edition. Modern editors have scant information upon which to construct a copy-text. A later section of this Norton Critical Edition provides Charlotte's 1850 biographical statement and preface and also the poems she selected to present as a sampling of Emily's literary remains. These are important early and intimate responses to much of the negative reception of the first edition, but textually critical modern editors can grant no authority to the 1850 edition because they are unable to determine what awareness Charlotte had of her sister's intentions —whether she had manuscript or proof corrections.

In the "Textual Commentary" for the 1963, 1972, and 1990 Norton Critical Editions of *Wuthering Heights*, William M. Sale, Jr. described the kind of textual errors attributable to Emily's publisher, Newby, as "typographical; . . . letters are transposed and out of alignment; ellipsis dots are sometimes used in place of dashes; hyphens are occasionally omitted at the ends of lines when words are divided." He realized that some of these are "hard to account for except as a consequence of Newby's ignorance or carelessness," but he also granted that, with no surviving manuscript or corrected proof for the Newby edition, it is impossible to determine "the degree to which printer and author should share in the responsibility for the state of the text."

For her 1976 Clarendon *Wuthering Heights*, Hilda Marsden likewise chose the Newby edition as copy-text, but made numerous emendations to avoid "reproducing the orthography and punctuation which Charlotte deplored."[2] Like Sale, Marsden corrected "the punctuation and other examples where . . . wrong, misleading, irritating, or disconcerting to the reader" (xxxii). The Sale and Marsden texts differ little in substance, but careful comparison of their corrections to the 1847 text indicates some different choices about how best to address their concerns for the modern reader. These choices certainly reflect Sale's primary concern for American readers and Marsden's for British ones.

This fourth Norton Critical Edition of *Wuthering Heights* reproduces, with only a few exceptions, the text Sale established for the first two Norton editions (1963, 1972) and which I used again in the third Norton Critical Edition (1990). Each of those editions contained a number of textual notes, which I have not included this time, because my purpose has been to make the 1847 text as accessible as possible and, in the "Backgrounds and Contexts" section of this novel, to describe the nature and impact of Charlotte's 1850 edition. To collate Sale's and Marsden's work or even to reprint the textual variants Sale himself listed in the first three editions would provide, primarily in accidentals, scores of variant editorial choices that document the impossibility of arriving at a truly authentic text. Any reader needing to review the textual issues in detail, including the changes in spelling and punctuation made by Charlotte Brontë in 1850, should consult both the 1990 Sale-Dunn Third Norton Critical Edition and the 1976 Marsden Clarendon Edition.

In this text, I have silently corrected what appear to have been a few errors by Sale in dealing with the 1847 edition, and in a few places I have cancelled Sale's changes in punctuation to favor those of the first edition. For example, in Chapter V, Nelly Dean speaks of Catherine Earnshaw as "a wild, wick slip," and Sale, assuming this to be Newby's error, corrected the wording to "a wild, wicked slip." Although the *Oxford English Dictionary* cites "wick" as a variant of "wicked," it also shows the word to be a Northern term for "quick," which better fits the context. The major differences in punctuation between the Sale and Marsden texts concern terminal punctuation. Sale generally shortened sentences, eliminating more of the original dashes, ellipses, and semicolons than did Marsden. Following the first edition punctuation retained by Marsden, I have

2. Marsden, Hilda and Ian Jack, eds. *Wuthering Heights*. Oxford: Clarendon Press, 1976. xxv.

chosen to restore dashes within a few key speeches where this punctuation signifies fragmentary expressions of characters under the great stress of often inexplicable states of mind or heart. Such is the case in Catherine's efforts to give Nelly "a feeling of how I feel" (Ch. IX), Heathcliff's account of his experiences at the grave of Catherine (Ch. XXIX), and Nelly's admission of her fear of ghosts (Ch. XXXIV).

I have expanded and revised all the explanatory footnotes for this edition, based upon the needs of recent generations of college-level readers. In passages heavy with North-of-England dialect, footnotes in earlier editions glossed selected terms, and students have objected to having their reading interrupted by such notes. To ease this, I have now translated the passages of dialect, which, according to their ear for the regionalisms, readers may take or leave.

Headnotes to the "Backgrounds and Contexts" and "Criticism" sections of this edition make clear the rationale for selection. The objective is to provide the reader with reliable information about the composition, production, and reception of the 1847 and 1850 texts and to supply samples of contemporary critical commentary and approaches to *Wuthering Heights*. New to this edition are Edward Chitham's commentary on the composition of the novel; critical excerpts from Sandra Gilbert and Susan Gubar, *The Madwoman in the Attic*; and from Martha Nussbaum's "*Wuthering Heights*: The Romantic Ascent." As with much nineteenth-century fiction, film versions of *Wuthering Heights* have proliferated. Thus, this edition includes Lin Haire-Sargeant's essay on the portrayal of Heathcliff in the major film adaptations.

To acknowledge all who have contributed to this edition would demand reprinting a number of class lists naming the many students who continue to be fascinated and sometimes repulsed by this novel. In recent years I have urged them to take a cue from J. Hillis Miller, who describes the reader as "the last surviving consciousness enveloping all these other consciousnesses, one inside the other. The reader is condemned . . . to keep the book open and at the same time to close its covers once and for all, so it may be forgotten, or so it may be read once more, this time definitively" (see "*Wuthering Heights*: Repetition and the 'Uncanny' "). For the support of colleagues among faculty and staff at the University of Washington, advisers and contributors to this edition, and particularly growing numbers of readers in my close family, I am most grateful.

Seattle, Washington RICHARD J. DUNN

The Text of
WUTHERING HEIGHTS

Chapter I

1801.—I have just returned from a visit to my landlord—the solitary neighbour that I shall be troubled with. This is certainly a beautiful country! In all England, I do not believe that I could have fixed on a situation so completely removed from the stir of society. A perfect misanthropist's heaven—and Mr. Heathcliff and I are such a suitable pair to divide the desolation between us. A capital fellow! He little imagined how my heart warmed towards him when I beheld his black eyes withdraw so suspiciously under their brows, as I rode up, and when his fingers sheltered themselves, with a jealous resolution, still further in his waistcoat, as I announced my name.

"Mr. Heathcliff?" I said.

A nod was the answer.

"Mr. Lockwood, your new tenant, sir. I do myself the honour of calling as soon as possible after my arrival, to express the hope that I have not inconvenienced you by my perseverance in soliciting the occupation of Thrushcross Grange: I heard, yesterday, you had had some thoughts ..."

"Thrushcross Grange is my own, sir," he interrupted, wincing, "I should not allow any one to inconvenience me, if I could hinder it—walk in!"

The "walk in," was uttered with closed teeth and expressed the sentiment, "Go to the Deuce!". Even the gate over which he leant manifested no sympathizing movement to the words, and I think that circumstance determined me to accept the invitation: I felt interested in a man who seemed more exaggeratedly reserved than myself.

When he saw my horse's breast fairly pushing the barrier, he did pull out his hand to unchain it, and then sullenly preceded me up the causeway, calling, as we entered the court—

"Joseph, take Mr. Lockwood's horse; and bring up some wine."

"Here we have the whole establishment of domestics, I suppose," was the reflection, suggested by this compound order. "No wonder the grass grows up between the flags, and cattle are the only hedgecutters."

Joseph was an elderly, nay, an old man, very old, perhaps, though hale and sinewy.

"The Lord help us!" he soliloquized in an undertone of peevish displeasure, while relieving me of my horse: looking, meantime, in my face so sourly that I charitably conjectured he must have need of divine aid to digest his dinner, and his pious ejaculation had no reference to my unexpected advent.

Wuthering Heights is the name of Mr. Heathcliff's dwelling. "Wuthering" being a significant provincial adjective, descriptive of the atmospheric tumult to which its station is exposed in stormy weather. Pure, bracing ventilation they must have up there, at all times, indeed: one may guess the power of the north wind, blowing over the edge, by the excessive slant of a few stunted firs at the end of the house; and by a range of gaunt thorns all stretching their limbs one way, as if craving alms of the sun. Happily, the architect had foresight to build it strong: the narrow windows are deeply set in the wall, and the corners defended with large jutting stones.

Before passing the threshold, I paused to admire a quantity of grotesque carving lavished over the front, and especially about the principal door, above which, among a wilderness of crumbling griffins and shameless little boys, I detected the date "1500," and the name "Hareton Earnshaw." I would have made a few comments, and requested a short history of the place from the surly owner, but his attitude at the door appeared to demand my speedy entrance, or complete departure, and I had no desire to aggravate his impatience, previous to inspecting the penetralium.

One step brought us into the family sitting-room, without any introductory lobby or passage: they call it here "the house" preeminently. It includes kitchen and parlour, generally, but I believe at Wuthering Heights the kitchen is forced to retreat altogether into another quarter; at least I distinguished a chatter of tongues, and a clatter of culinary utensils deep within; and I observed no signs of roasting, boiling, or baking about the huge fire-place; nor any glitter of copper saucepans and tin cullenders on the walls. One end, indeed, reflected splendidly both light and heat from ranks of immense pewter dishes, interspersed with silver jugs and tankards, towering row after row, in a vast oak dresser, to the very roof. The latter had never been underdrawn: its entire anatomy lay bare to an inquiring eye, except where a frame of wood laden with oatcakes, and clusters of legs of beef, mutton, and ham, concealed it. Above the chimney were sundry villainous old guns, and a couple of horse-pistols, and, by way of ornament, three gaudily-painted canisters disposed along its ledge. The floor was of smooth, white stone; the chairs, high-backed, primitive structures, painted green, one or two heavy black ones lurking in the shade. In an arch under the dresser, reposed a huge, liver-coloured bitch pointer surrounded by a swarm of squealing puppies, and other dogs haunted other recesses.

The apartment and furniture would have been nothing extraordinary as belonging to a homely, northern farmer, with a stubborn countenance, and stalwart limbs set out to advantage in knee-breeches and gaiters. Such an individual, seated in his arm-chair, his mug of ale frothing on the round table before him, is to be seen in any circuit of five or six miles among these hills, if you go at the right time, after dinner. But Mr. Heathcliff forms a singular contrast to his abode and style of living. He is a dark-skinned gypsy in aspect, in dress and manners a gentleman, that is, as much a gentleman as many a country squire: rather slovenly, perhaps, yet not looking amiss with his negligence, because he has an erect and handsome figure—and rather morose. Possibly, some people might suspect him of a degree of under-bred pride; I have a sympathetic chord within that tells me it is nothing of the sort: I know, by instinct, his reserve springs from an aversion to showy displays of feeling—to manifestations of mutual kindliness. He'll love and hate, equally under cover, and esteem it a species of impertinence to be loved or hated again—No, I'm running on too fast—I bestow my own attributes over-liberally on him. Mr. Heathcliff may have entirely dissimilar reasons for keeping his hand out of the way when he meets a would-be acquaintance, to those which actuate me. Let me hope my constitution is almost peculiar: my dear mother used to say I should never have a comfortable home, and only last summer I proved myself perfectly unworthy of one.

While enjoying a month of fine weather at the sea-coast, I was thrown into the company of a most fascinating creature, a real goddess in my eyes, as long as she took no notice of me. I "never told my love" vocally;[1] still, if looks have language, the merest idiot might have guessed I was over head and ears: she understood me at last, and looked a return—the sweetest of all imaginable looks. And what did I do? I confess it with shame—shrunk icily into myself, like a snail; at every glance retired colder and farther; till, finally, the poor innocent was led to doubt her own senses, and, overwhelmed with confusion at her supposed mistake, persuaded her mamma to decamp.

By this curious turn of disposition I have gained the reputation of deliberate heartlessness, how undeserved, I alone can appreciate.

I took a seat at the end of the hearthstone opposite that towards which my landlord advanced, and filled up an interval of silence by attempting to caress the canine mother, who had left her nursery and was sneaking wolfishly to the back of my legs, her lip curled up, and her white teeth watering for a snatch.

My caress provoked a long, guttural gnarl.

"You'd better let the dog alone," growled Mr. Heathcliff in unison, checking fiercer demonstrations with a punch of his foot. "She's not accustomed to be spoiled—not kept for a pet."

1. Viola, explaining woman's love for man, speaks of one "who never told her love,/ But let concealment, like a worm in th' bud,/ Feed upon her damask cheek." *Twelfth Night* 2.4.110–12. Lockwood not only exaggerates his romantic disappointment but renders it ironic, because he is in fact "telling" readers of his love.

Then, striding to a side-door, he shouted again—

"Joseph!"

Joseph mumbled indistinctly in the depths of the cellar, but gave no intimation of ascending; so his master dived down to him, leaving me *vis-à-vis* the ruffianly bitch and a pair of grim, shaggy sheep dogs, who shared with her a jealous guardianship over all my movements.

Not anxious to come in contact with their fangs, I sat still; but, imagining they would scarcely understand tacit insults, I unfortunately indulged in winking and making faces at the trio, and some turn of my physiognomy so irritated madam, that she suddenly broke into a fury and leapt on my knees. I flung her back, and hastened to interpose the table between us. This proceeding roused the whole hive. Half-a-dozen four-footed fiends, of various sizes and ages, issued from hidden dens to the common centre. I felt my heels and coat-laps peculiar subjects of assault; and, parrying off the larger combatants as effectually as I could with the poker, I was constrained to demand, aloud, assistance from some of the household in re-establishing peace.

Mr. Heathcliff and his man climbed the cellar steps with vexatious phlegm. I don't think they moved one second faster than usual, though the hearth was an absolute tempest of worrying and yelping.

Happily, an inhabitant of the kitchen made more dispatch; a lusty dame, with tucked-up gown, bare arms, and fire-flushed cheeks, rushed into the midst of us flourishing a frying-pan; and used that weapon, and her tongue, to such purpose, that the storm subsided magically, and she only remained, heaving like a sea after a high wind, when her master entered on the scene.

"What the devil is the matter?" he asked, eyeing me in a manner that I could ill endure after this inhospitable treatment.

"What the devil, indeed!" I muttered. "The herd of possessed swine could have had no worse spirits in them than those animals of yours, sir.[2] You might as well leave a stranger with a brood of tigers!"

"They won't meddle with persons who touch nothing," he remarked, putting the bottle before me, and restoring the displaced table. "The dogs do right to be vigilant. Take a glass of wine?"

"No, thank you."

"Not bitten, are you?"

"If I had been, I would have set my signet on the biter."

Heathcliff's countenance relaxed into a grin.

2. Luke 8.27–34 is the story of the man called Legion, because he was beset by many devils. Through Christ's intercession, the demons were transferred to a herd of swine.

"Come, come," he said, "you are flurried, Mr. Lockwood. Here, take a little wine. Guests are so exceedingly rare in this house that I and my dogs, I am willing to own, hardly know how to receive them. Your health, sir!"

I bowed and returned the pledge, beginning to perceive that it would be foolish to sit sulking for the misbehaviour of a pack of curs: besides, I felt loath to yield the fellow further amusement, at my expense, since his humour took that turn.

He—probably swayed by prudential considerations of the folly of offending a good tenant—relaxed a little, in the laconic style of chipping off his pronouns and auxiliary verbs, and introduced what he supposed would be a subject of interest to me, a discourse on the advantages and disadvantages of my present place of retirement.

I found him very intelligent on the topics we touched; and, before I went home, I was encouraged so far as to volunteer another visit to-morrow.

He evidently wished no repetition of my intrusion. I shall go, notwithstanding. It is astonishing how sociable I feel myself compared with him.

Chapter II

Yesterday afternoon set in misty and cold. I had half a mind to spend it by my study fire, instead of wading through heath and mud to Wuthering Heights.

On coming up from dinner, however (N. B. I dine between twelve and one o'clock; the housekeeper, a matronly lady taken as a fixture along with the house, could not, or would not comprehend my request that I might be served at five.)—on mounting the stairs with this lazy intention, and stepping into the room, I saw a servant-girl on her knees, surrounded by brushes and coal-scuttles, and raising an infernal dust as she extinguished the flames with heaps of cinders. This spectacle drove me back immediately; I took my hat, and, after a four miles' walk, arrived at Heathcliff's garden gate just in time to escape the first feathery flakes of a snow shower.

On that bleak hilltop the earth was hard with a black frost, and the air made me shiver through every limb. Being unable to remove the chain, I jumped over, and, running up the flagged causeway bordered with straggling gooseberry bushes, knocked vainly for admittance, till my knuckles tingled and the dogs howled.

"Wretched inmates!" I ejaculated, mentally, "you deserve perpetual isolation from your species for your churlish inhospitality. At least, I would not keep my doors barred in the day time. I don't care—I will get in!"

So resolved, I grasped the latch and shook it vehemently. Vinegar-faced Joseph projected his head from a round window of the barn.

"Whet are ye for?" he shouted. "T' maister's dahn i' t' fowld. Goa rahnd by th' end ut' laith, if yah went tuh spake tull him."[1]

"Is there nobody inside to open the door?" I hallooed, responsively.

"They's nobbut t' missis; and shoo'll nut oppen't an ye mak yer flaysome dins till neeght."[2]

"Why? cannot you tell her who I am, eh, Joseph?"

"Nor-ne me! Aw'll hae noa hend wi't,"[3] muttered the head vanishing.

The snow began to drive thickly. I seized the handle to essay another trial, when a young man, without coat, and shouldering a pitchfork, appeared in the yard behind. He hailed me to follow him, and, after marching through a wash-house and a paved area containing a coal-shed, pump, and pigeon cote, we at length arrived in the large, warm, cheerful apartment where I was formerly received. It glowed delightfully in the radiance of an immense fire, compounded of coal, peat, and wood; and near the table, laid for a plentiful evening meal, I was pleased to observe the "missis," an individual whose existence I had never previously suspected.

I bowed and waited, thinking she would bid me take a seat. She looked at me, leaning back in her chair, and remained motionless and mute.

"Rough weather!" I remarked. "I'm afraid, Mrs. Heathcliff, the door must bear the consequence of your servants' leisure attendance: I had hard work to make them hear me!"

She never opened her mouth. I stared—she stared also. At any rate, she kept her eyes on me, in a cool, regardless manner, exceedingly embarrassing and disagreeable.

"Sit down," said the young man, gruffly. "He'll be in soon."

I obeyed; and hemmed, and called the villain Juno, who deigned, at this second interview, to move the extreme tip of her tail, in token of owning my acquaintance.

"A beautiful animal!" I commenced again. "Do you intend parting with the little ones, madam?"

"They are not mine," said the amiable hostess more repellingly than Heathcliff himself could have replied.

"Ah, your favourites are among these!" I continued, turning to an obscure cushion full of something like cats.

"A strange choice of favourites," she observed scornfully.

1. "What do you want? . . . The master's down at the [sheep] fold. Go around by the end of the barn if you want to speak to him."
2. "There's no one but the missus; and she'll not open it if you make your dreadful noises until night."
3. "Not me! I'll have no hand in it."

Unluckily, it was a heap of dead rabbits. I hemmed once more, and drew closer to the hearth, repeating my comment on the wildness of the evening.

"You should not have come out," she said, rising and reaching from the chimney-piece two of the painted canisters.

Her position before was sheltered from the light; now, I had a distinct view of her whole figure and countenance. She was slender, and apparently scarcely past girlhood: an admirable form, and the most exquisite little face that I have ever had the pleasure of beholding: small features, very fair; flaxen ringlets, or rather golden, hanging loose on her delicate neck; and eyes—had they been agreeable in expression, they would have been irresistible. Fortunately for my susceptible heart, the only sentiment they evinced hovered between scorn and a kind of desperation, singularly unnatural to be detected there.

The canisters were almost out of her reach; I made a motion to aid her; she turned upon me as a miser might turn if any one attempted to assist him in counting his gold.

"I don't want your help," she snapped, "I can get them for myself."

"I beg your pardon," I hastened to reply.

"Were you asked to tea?" she demanded, tying an apron over her neat black frock, and standing with a spoonful of the leaf poised over the pot.

"I shall be glad to have a cup," I answered.

"Were you asked?" she repeated.

"No," I said, half smiling. "You are the proper person to ask me."

She flung the tea back, spoon and all, and resumed her chair in a pet, her forehead corrugated, and her red under-lip pushed out, like a child's, ready to cry.

Meanwhile, the young man had slung onto his person a decidedly shabby upper garment, and, erecting himself before the blaze, looked down on me from the corner of his eyes, for all the world as if there were some mortal feud unavenged between us. I began to doubt whether he were a servant or not; his dress and speech were both rude, entirely devoid of the superiority observable in Mr. and Mrs. Heathcliff; his thick, brown curls were rough and uncultivated, his whiskers encroached bearishly over his cheeks, and his hands were embrowned like those of a common labourer. Still his bearing was free, almost haughty, and he showed none of a domestic's assiduity in attending on the lady of the house.

In the absence of clear proofs of his condition, I deemed it best to abstain from noticing his curious conduct, and, five minutes afterwards, the entrance of Heathcliff relieved me, in some measure, from my uncomfortable state.

"You see, sir, I am come according to promise!" I exclaimed, assuming the cheerful; "and I fear I shall be weather-bound for half an hour, if you can afford me shelter during that space."

"Half an hour?" he said, shaking the white flakes from his clothes; "I wonder you should select the thick of a snow-storm to ramble about in. Do you know that you run a risk of being lost in the marshes? People familiar with these moors often miss their road on such evenings, and, I can tell you, there is no chance of a change at present."

"Perhaps I can get a guide among your lads, and he might stay at the Grange till morning—could you spare me one?"

"No, I could not."

"Oh, indeed! Well, then, I must trust to my own sagacity."

"Umph."

"Are you going to mak th' tea?" demanded he of the shabby coat, shifting his ferocious gaze from me to the young lady.

"Is *he* to have any?" she asked, appealing to Heathcliff.

"Get it ready, will you?" was the answer, uttered so savagely that I started. The tone in which the words were said revealed a genuine bad nature. I no longer felt inclined to call Heathcliff a capital fellow.

When the preparations were finished, he invited me with—

"Now, sir, bring forward your chair." And we all, including the rustic youth, drew round the table, an austere silence prevailing while we discussed our meal.

I thought, if I had caused the cloud, it was my duty to make an effort to dispel it. They could not every day sit so grim and taciturn, and it was impossible, however ill-tempered they might be, that the universal scowl they wore was their every day countenance.

"It is strange," I began in the interval of swallowing one cup of tea and receiving another, "it is strange how custom can mould our tastes and ideas; many could not imagine the existence of happiness in a life of such complete exile from the world as you spend, Mr. Heathcliff; yet, I'll venture to say, that, surrounded by your family, and with your amiable lady as the presiding genius over your home and heart—"

"My amiable lady!" he interrupted, with an almost diabolical sneer on his face. "Where is she—my amiable lady?"

"Mrs. Heathcliff, your wife, I mean."

"Well, yes—Oh! you would intimate that her spirit has taken the post of ministering angel, and guards the fortunes of Wuthering Heights, even when her body is gone. Is that it?"

Perceiving myself in a blunder, I attempted to correct it. I might have seen there was too great a disparity between the ages of the parties to make it likely that they were man and wife. One was about forty, a period of mental vigour at which men seldom cherish the delusion of being married for love, by girls: that dream is reserved for the solace of our declining years. The other did not look seventeen.

Then it flashed upon me—"The clown at my elbow, who is drinking his tea out of a basin and eating his bread with unwashed hands, may be her husband. Heathcliff, junior, of course. Here is the consequence of being buried alive: she has thrown herself away upon that boor, from sheer ignorance that better individuals existed! A sad pity—I must beware how I cause her to regret her choice."

The last reflection may seem conceited; it was not. My neighbour struck me as bordering on repulsive. I knew, through experience, that I was tolerably attractive.

"Mrs. Heathcliff is my daughter-in-law," said Heathcliff, corroborating my surmise. He turned, as he spoke, a peculiar look in her direction, a look of hatred, unless he has a most perverse set of facial muscles that will not, like those of other people, interpret the language of his soul.

"Ah, certainly—I see now; you are the favoured possessor of the beneficent fairy," I remarked, turning to my neighbour.

This was worse than before: the youth grew crimson, and clenched his fist with every appearance of a meditated assault. But he seemed to recollect himself, presently, and smothered the storm in a brutal curse, muttered on my behalf, which, however, I took care not to notice.

"Unhappy in your conjectures, sir!" observed my host; "we neither of us have the privilege of owning your good fairy; her mate is dead. I said she was my daughter-in-law, therefore, she must have married my son."

"And this young man is—"

"Not my son, assuredly!"

Heathcliff smiled again, as if it were rather too bold a jest to attribute the paternity of that bear to him.

"My name is Hareton Earnshaw," growled the other; "and I'd counsel you to respect it!"

"I've shown no disrespect," was my reply, laughing internally at the dignity with which he announced himself.

He fixed his eye on me longer than I cared to return the stare, for fear I might be tempted either to box his ears, or render my hilarity audible. I began to feel unmistakably out of place in that pleasant family circle. The dismal spiritual atmosphere overcame, and more than neutralized the glowing physical comforts round me; and I resolved to be cautious how I ventured under those rafters a third time.

The business of eating being concluded, and no one uttering a word of sociable conversation, I approached a window to examine the weather.

A sorrowful sight I saw: dark night coming down prematurely, and sky and hills mingled in one bitter whirl of wind and suffocating snow.

"I don't think it possible for me to get home now, without a guide," I could not help exclaiming. "The roads will be buried already; and, if they were bare, I could scarcely distinguish a foot in advance."

"Hareton, drive those dozen sheep into the barn porch. They'll be covered if left in the fold all night; and put a plank before them," said Heathcliff.

"How must I do?" I continued, with rising irritation.

There was no reply to my question; and, on looking round, I saw only Joseph bringing in a pail of porridge for the dogs, and Mrs. Heathcliff, leaning over the fire, diverting herself with burning a bundle of matches which had fallen from the chimney-piece as she restored the tea-canister to its place.

The former, when he had deposited his burden, took a critical survey of the room, and, in cracked tones, grated out—

"Aw woonder hagh yah can faishion tuh stand thear i' idleness un' war, when all on 'em's goan aght! Bud yah're a nowt, and it's noa use talking—yah'll niver mend uh yer ill ways; bud goa raight tuh t' divil, like yer mother afore ye!"[4]

I imagined, for a moment, that this piece of eloquence was addressed to me; and, sufficiently enraged, stepped towards the aged rascal with an intention of kicking him out of the door.

Mrs. Heathcliff, however, checked me by her answer.

"You scandalous old hypocrite!" she replied. "Are you not afraid of being carried away bodily, whenever you mention the devil's name? I warn you to refrain from provoking me, or I'll ask your abduction as a special favour. Stop, look here, Joseph," she continued, taking a long, dark book from a shelf. "I'll show you how far I've progressed in the Black Art[5]—I shall soon be competent to make a clear house of it. The red cow didn't die by chance; and your rheumatism can hardly be reckoned among providential visitations!"

"Oh, wicked, wicked!" gasped the elder, "may the Lord deliver us from evil!"

4. "I wonder how you can bring yourself to stand there in idleness and worse, when all of them have gone out! But you're a nothing, and there's no use talking—you'll never mend your bad ways; but go right to the devil, like your mother before you."

5. Necromancy: the art of performing wonderful feats by supernatural means, with assistance from the powers of evil. The otherwise imperceptive Lockwood here realizes Cathy is countering Joseph with a little witch's "mock malignity."

"No, reprobate! you are a castaway—be off, or I'll hurt you seriously! I'll have you all modelled in wax and clay; and the first who passes the limits I fix, shall—I'll not say what he shall be done to —but, you'll see! Go, I'm looking at you!"

The little witch put a mock malignity into her beautiful eyes, and Joseph, trembling with sincere horror, hurried out praying and ejaculating "wicked" as he went.

I thought her conduct must be prompted by a species of dreary fun; and, now that we were alone, I endeavoured to interest her in my distress.

"Mrs. Heathcliff," I said, earnestly, "you must excuse me for troubling you—I presume, because, with that face, I'm sure you cannot help being good-hearted. Do point out some landmarks by which I may know my way home. I have no more idea how to get there than you would have how to get to London!"

"Take the road you came," she answered, ensconcing herself in a chair, with a candle, and the long book open before her. "It is brief advice, but as sound as I can give."

"Then, if you hear of me being discovered dead in a bog, or a pit full of snow, your conscience won't whisper that it is partly your fault?"

"How so? I cannot escort you. They wouldn't let me go to the end of the garden-wall."

"*You!* I should be sorry to ask you to cross the threshold, for my convenience, on such a night," I cried. "I want you to *tell* me my way, not to *show* it; or else to persuade Mr. Heathcliff to give me a guide."

"Who? There is himself, Earnshaw, Zillah, Joseph, and I. Which would you have?"

"Are there no boys at the farm?"

"No, those are all."

"Then it follows that I am compelled to stay."

"That you may settle with your host. I have nothing to do with it."

"I hope it will be a lesson to you, to make no more rash journeys on these hills," cried Heathcliff's stern voice from the kitchen entrance. "As to staying here, I don't keep accommodations for visitors; you must share a bed with Hareton, or Joseph, if you do."

"I can sleep on a chair in this room," I replied.

"No, no! A stranger is a stranger, be he rich or poor—it will not suit me to permit any one the range of the place while I am off guard!" said the unmannerly wretch.

With this insult my patience was at an end. I uttered an expression of disgust, and pushed past him into the yard, running against Earnshaw in my haste. It was so dark that I could not see the means of exit, and, as I wandered round, I heard another specimen of their civil behaviour amongst each other.

At first, the young man appeared about to befriend me.

"I'll go with him as far as the park," he said.

"You'll go with him to hell!" exclaimed his master, or whatever relation he bore. "And who is to look after the horses, eh?"

"A man's life is of more consequence than one evening's neglect of the horses; somebody must go," murmured Mrs. Heathcliff, more kindly than I expected.

"Not at your command!" retorted Hareton. "If you set store on him, you'd better be quiet."

"Then I hope his ghost will haunt you; and I hope Mr. Heathcliff will never get another tenant, till the Grange is a ruin!" she answered sharply.

"Hearken, hearken, shoo's cursing on 'em!"[6] muttered Joseph, towards whom I had been steering.

He sat within earshot, milking the cows by the aid of a lantern which I seized unceremoniously, and, calling out that I would send it back on the morrow, rushed to the nearest postern.

"Maister, maister, he's staling t' lantern!" shouted the ancient, pursuing my retreat. "Hey, Gnasher! Hey, dog! Hey, Wolf, holld him, holld him!"

On opening the little door, two hairy monsters flew at my throat, bearing me down and extinguishing the light, while a mingled guffaw, from Heathcliff and Hareton, put the copestone on my rage and humiliation.

Fortunately, the beasts seemed more bent on stretching their paws, and yawning and flourishing their tails, than devouring me alive; but they would suffer no resurrection, and I was forced to lie till their malignant masters pleased to deliver me: then hatless, and trembling with wrath, I ordered the miscreants to let me out—on their peril to keep me one minute longer—with several incoherent threats of retaliation that, in their indefinite depth of virulency, smacked of King Lear.[7]

The vehemence of my agitation brought on a copious bleeding at the nose, and still Heathcliff laughed, and still I scolded. I don't know what would have concluded the scene had there not been one person at hand rather more rational than myself, and more benevolent than my entertainer. This was Zillah, the stout housewife, who at length issued forth to inquire into the nature of the uproar. She thought that some of them had been laying violent hands on me,

6. "She's putting a curse on him."
7. The allusion may be to Lear's passion for vengeance: "I will do such things— / What they are, yet I know not, but they shall be / The terrors of the earth." *King Lear* 2.4.280–83.

and, not daring to attack her master, she turned her vocal artillery against the younger scoundrel.

"Well, Mr. Earnshaw," she cried, "I wonder what you'll have agait[8] next! Are we going to murder folk on our very door-stones? I see this house will never do for me—look at t' poor lad, he's fair choking! Wisht, wisht! you mun'n't[9] go on so—come in, and I'll cure that. There now, hold ye still."

With these words she suddenly splashed a pint of icy water down my neck, and pulled me into the kitchen. Mr. Heathcliff followed, his accidental merriment expiring quickly in his habitual moroseness.

I was sick exceedingly, and dizzy and faint; and thus compelled, perforce, to accept lodgings under his roof. He told Zillah to give me a glass of brandy, and then passed on to the inner room, while she condoled with me on my sorry predicament, and having obeyed his orders, whereby I was somewhat revived, ushered me to bed.

Chapter III

While leading the way upstairs, she recommended that I should hide the candle, and not make a noise, for her master had an odd notion about the chamber she would put me in, and never let anybody lodge there willingly.

I asked the reason.

She did not know, she answered; she had only lived there a year or two; and they had so many queer goings on, she could not begin to be curious.

Too stupified to be curious myself, I fastened my door and glanced round for the bed. The whole furniture consisted of a chair, a clothes-press, and a large oak case, with squares cut out near the top, resembling coach windows.

Having approached this structure, I looked inside, and perceived it to be a singular sort of old-fashioned couch, very conveniently designed to obviate the necessity for every member of the family having a room to himself. In fact, it formed a little closet, and the ledge of a window, which it enclosed, served as a table.

I slid back the panelled sides, got in with my light, pulled them together again, and felt secure against the vigilance of Heathcliff, and every one else.

The ledge, where I placed my candle, had a few mildewed books piled up in one corner; and it was covered with writing scratched on the paint. This writing, however, was nothing but a name repeated in all kinds of characters, large and small—*Catherine Earn-*

8. A-going.
9. "Hush, hush, you must not . . ."

shaw, here and there varied to *Catherine Heathcliff*, and then again to *Catherine Linton*.

In vapid listlessness I leant my head against the window, and continued spelling over Catherine Earnshaw—Heathcliff—Linton, till my eyes closed; but they had not rested five minutes when a glare of white letters started from the dark, as vivid as spectres—the air swarmed with Catherines; and rousing myself to dispel the obtrusive name, I discovered my candle wick reclining on one of the antique volumes, and perfuming the place with an odour of roasted calf-skin.

I snuffed it off, and, very ill at ease under the influence of cold and lingering nausea, sat up, and spread open the injured tome on my knee. It was a Testament, in lean type, and smelling dreadfully musty: a fly-leaf bore the inscription—"Catherine Earnshaw, her book," and a date some quarter of a century back.

I shut it, and took up another, and another, till I had examined all. Catherine's library was select, and its state of dilapidation proved it to have been well used, though not altogether for a legitimate purpose; scarcely one chapter had escaped a pen and ink commentary—at least, the appearance of one—covering every morsel of blank that the printer had left.

Some were detached sentences; other parts took the form of a regular diary, scrawled in an unformed, childish hand. At the top of an extra page, quite a treasure probably when first lighted on, I was greatly amused to behold an excellent caricature of my friend Joseph, rudely yet powerfully sketched.

An immediate interest kindled within me for the unknown Catherine, and I began, forthwith, to decypher her faded hieroglyphics.

"An awful Sunday!" commenced the paragraph beneath. "I wish my father were back again. Hindley is a detestable substitute—his conduct to Heathcliff is atrocious—H. and I are going to rebel—we took our initiatory step this evening.

"All day had been flooding with rain; we could not go to church, so Joseph must needs get up a congregation in the garret; and, while Hindley and his wife basked downstairs before a comfortable fire—doing anything but reading their Bibles, I'll answer for it—Heathcliff, myself, and the unhappy plough-boy were commanded to take our Prayer-books, and mount. We were ranged in a row, on a sack of corn, groaning and shivering, and hoping that Joseph would shiver too, so that he might give us a short homily for his own sake. A vain idea! The service lasted precisely three hours; and yet my brother had the face to exclaim, when he saw us descending—

" 'What, done already?'

"On Sunday evenings we used to be permitted to play, if we did not make much noise; now a mere titter is sufficient to send us into corners!

" 'You forget you have a master here,' says the tyrant. 'I'll demolish the first who puts me out of temper! I insist on perfect sobriety and silence. Oh, boy! was that you? Frances, darling, pull his hair as you go by; I heard him snap his fingers.'

"Frances pulled his hair heartily and then went and seated herself on her husband's knee; and there they were, like two babies, kissing and talking nonsense by the hour—foolish palaver that we should be ashamed of.

"We made ourselves as snug as our means allowed in the arch of the dresser. I had just fastened our pinafores together, and hung them up for a curtain, when in comes Joseph, on an errand from the stables. He tears down my handywork, boxes my ears, and croaks—

" 'T' maister nobbut just buried, and Sabbath nut oe'red, und t' sahnd uh't gospel still i' yer lugs, and yah darr be laiking! shame on ye! sit ye dahn, ill childer! they's good books eneugh if ye'll read 'em; sit ye dahn, and think uh yer sowls!'[1]

"Saying this, he compelled us so to square our positions that we might receive, from the far-off fire, a dull ray to show us the text of the lumber he thrust upon us.

"I could not bear the employment. I took my dingy volume by the scroop,[2] and hurled it into the dog-kennel, vowing I hated a good book.

"Heathcliff kicked his to the same place.

"Then there was a hubbub!

" 'Maister Hindley!' shouted our chaplain. 'Maister, coom hither! Miss Cathy's riven th' back off "Th' Helmet uh Salvation," un' Heathcliff's pawsed his fit intuh t' first part uh "T' Brooad Way to Destruction!" It's fair flaysome ut yah let 'em goa on this gait. Ech! th' owd man ud uh laced 'em properly—bud he's goan!'[3]

"Hindley hurried up from his paradise on the hearth, and seizing one of us by the collar, and the other by the arm, hurled both into the back-kitchen, where, Joseph asseverated, 'owd Nick' would fetch us as sure as we were living; and, so comforted, we each sought a separate nook to await his advent.

1. "The master not but just buried, and Sunday just past, and the sound of the gospel still in your ears, and you dare be playing! shame on you! sit down, bad children, there's good books enough if you'll read them; sit yourselves down, and think of your souls!"
2. The back of the cover of a book.
3. "Miss Cathy's torn the back off . . . and Heathcliff's made a hole by putting his foot on the first part of . . . It's just dreadful of you to let them go on in this way. Oh, the old man would have punished them properly, but he's dead!" [The damage is to apparently fictionally titled tracts of the sort fit for Sunday reading.]

"I reached this book, and a pot of ink from a shelf, and pushed the house-door ajar to give me light, and I have got the time on with writing for twenty minutes; but my companion is impatient and proposes that we should appropriate the dairy woman's cloak, and have a scamper on the moors, under its shelter. A pleasant suggestion—and then, if the surly old man come in, he may believe his prophesy verified—we cannot be damper, or colder, in the rain than we are here."

* * * * *

I suppose Catherine fulfilled her project, for the next sentence took up another subject; she waxed lachrymose.

"How little did I dream that Hindley would ever make me cry so!" she wrote. "My head aches, till I cannot keep it on the pillow; and still I can't give over. Poor Heathcliff! Hindley calls him a vagabond, and won't let him sit with us, nor eat with us any more; and, he says, he and I must not play together, and threatens to turn him out of the house if we break his orders.

"He has been blaming our father (how dared he?) for treating H. too liberally; and swears he will reduce him to his right place—"

I began to nod drowsily over the dim page; my eye wandered from manuscript to print. I saw a red ornamented title—"Seventy Times Seven, and the First of the Seventy-First. A Pious Discourse delivered by the Reverend Jabes Branderham, in the Chapel of Gimmerden Sough." And while I was, half consciously, worrying my brain to guess what Jabes Branderham would make of his subject, I sank back in bed, and fell asleep.

Alas, for the effects of bad tea and bad temper! what else could it be that made me pass such a terrible night? I don't remember another that I can at all compare with it since I was capable of suffering.

I began to dream, almost before I ceased to be sensible of my locality. I thought it was morning, and I had set out on my way home, with Joseph for a guide. The snow lay yards deep in our road; and, as we floundered on, my companion wearied me with constant reproaches that I had not brought a pilgrim's staff, telling me I could never get into the house without one, and boastfully flourishing a heavy-headed cudgel, which I understood to be so denominated.

For a moment I considered it absurd that I should need such a weapon to gain admittance into my own residence. Then, a new idea flashed across me. I was not going there; we were journeying to hear the famous Jabes Branderham preach from the text—"Seventy Times Seven"; and either Joseph, the preacher, or I had committed the "First of the Seventy-First," and were to be publicly exposed and excommunicated.[4]

We came to the chapel. I have passed it really in my walks, twice or thrice; it lies in a hollow, between two hills—an elevated hollow, near a swamp, whose peaty moisture is said to answer all the purposes of embalming on the few corpses deposited there. The roof has been kept whole hitherto, but, as the clergyman's stipend is only twenty pounds per annum, and a house with two rooms, threatening speedily to determine into one, no clergyman will undertake the duties of pastor, especially as it is currently reported that his flock would rather let him starve than increase the living by one penny from their own pockets. However, in my dream, Jabes had a full and attentive congregation: and he preached—good God—what a sermon! Divided into *four hundred and ninety* parts, each fully equal to an ordinary address from the pulpit, and each discussing a separate sin! Where he searched for them, I cannot tell; he had his private manner of interpreting the phrase, and it seemed necessary the brother should sin different sins on every occasion.

They were of the most curious character—odd trangressions that I never imagined previously.

Oh, how weary I grew. How I writhed, and yawned, and nodded, and revived! How I pinched and pricked myself, and rubbed my eyes, and stood up, and sat down again, and nudged Joseph to inform me if he would *ever* have done!

I was condemned to hear all out; finally, he reached the "*First of the Seventy-First*." At that crisis, a sudden inspiration descended on me; I was moved to rise and denounce Jabes Branderham as the sinner of the sin that no Christian need pardon.

"Sir," I exclaimed, "sitting here, within these four walls, at one stretch, I have endured and forgiven the four hundred and ninety heads of your discourse. Seventy times seven times have I plucked up my hat and been about to depart—Seventy times seven times have you preposterously forced me to resume my seat. The four hundred and ninety-first is too much. Fellow martyrs, have at him! Drag him down, and crush him to atoms, that the place which knows him may know him no more!"

"*Thou art the Man!*" cried Jabes, after a solemn pause, leaning over his cushion. "Seventy times seven times didst thou gapingly contort thy visage—seventy times seven did I take counsel with my

4. Matthew 18.21–35 is the text Branderham exploits by relishing his procrastinated opportunity for retribution. Christ's words, when asked about forgiveness, were "I will not say unto thee, Until seven times seven: but, Until seven times seventy."

soul—Lo, this is human weakness; this also may be absolved! The First of the Seventy-First is come. Brethren, execute upon him the judgment written! Such honour have all His saints!"

With that concluding word, the whole assembly, exalting their pilgrim's staves, rushed round me in a body, and I, having no weapon to raise in self-defence, commenced grappling with Joseph, my nearest and most ferocious assailant, for his. In the confluence of the multitude, several clubs crossed; blows, aimed at me, fell on other sconces. Presently the whole chapel resounded with rappings and counter-rappings. Every man's hand was against his neighbour; and Branderham, unwilling to remain idle, poured forth his zeal in a shower of loud taps on the boards of the pulpit, which responded so smartly that, at last, to my unspeakable relief, they woke me.

And what was it that had suggested the tremendous tumult, what had played Jabes's part in the row? Merely the branch of a fir tree that touched my lattice, as the blast wailed by, and rattled its dry cones against the panes!

I listened doubtingly an instant; detected the disturber, then turned and dozed, and dreamt again; if possible, still more disagreebly than before.

This time, I remembered I was lying in the oak closet, and I heard distinctly the gusty wind, and the driving of the snow; I heard, also, the fir-bough repeat its teasing sound, and ascribed it to the right cause; but it annoyed me so much, that I resolved to silence it, if possible; and, I thought, I rose and endeavoured to unhasp the casement. The hook was soldered into the staple, a circumstance observed by me when awake, but forgotten.

"I must stop it, nevertheless!" I muttered, knocking my knuckles through the glass, and stretching an arm out to seize the importunate branch: instead of which, my fingers closed on the fingers of a little, ice-cold hand!

The intense horror of nightmare came over me; I tried to draw back my arm, but the hand clung to it, and a most melancholy voice sobbed—

"Let me in—let me in!"

"Who are you?" I asked, struggling, meanwhile, to disengage myself.

"Catherine Linton," it replied, shiveringly (why did I think of *Linton?* I had read *Earnshaw* twenty times for Linton). "I'm come home, I'd lost my way on the moor!"

As it spoke, I discerned, obscurely, a child's face looking through the window. Terror made me cruel; and, finding it useless to attempt shaking the creature off, I pulled its wrist on to the broken pane, and rubbed it to and fro till the blood ran down and soaked the bed-clothes: still it wailed, "Let me in!" and maintained its tenacious gripe, almost maddening me with fear.

"How can I?" I said at length. "Let *me* go, if you want me to let you in!"

The fingers relaxed, I snatched mine through the hole, hurriedly piled the books up in a pyramid against it, and stopped my ears to exclude the lamentable prayer.

I seemed to keep them closed above a quarter of an hour, yet, the instant I listened again, there was the doleful cry moaning on!

"Begone!" I shouted, "I'll never let you in, not if you beg for twenty years!"

"It's twenty years," mourned the voice, "twenty years, I've been a waif for twenty years!"

Thereat began a feeble scratching outside, and the pile of books moved as if thrust forward.

I tried to jump up, but could not stir a limb; and so yelled aloud, in a frenzy of fright.

To my confusion, I discovered the yell was not ideal. Hasty footsteps approached my chamber door; somebody pushed it open, with a vigorous hand, and a light glimmered through the squares at the top of the bed. I sat shuddering yet, and wiping the perspiration from my forehead: the intruder appeared to hesitate, and muttered to himself.

At last, he said in a half-whisper, plainly not expecting an answer—

"Is any one here?"

I considered it best to confess my presence, for I knew Heathcliff's accents, and feared he might search further, if I kept quiet.

With this intention, I turned and opened the panels. I shall not soon forget the effect my action produced.

Heathcliff stood near the entrance, in his shirt and trousers, with a candle dripping over his fingers, and his face as white as the wall behind him. The first creak of the oak startled him like an electric shock: the light leaped from his hold to a distance of some feet, and his agitation was so extreme that he could hardly pick it up.

"It is only your guest, sir," I called out, desirous to spare him the humiliation of exposing his cowardice further. "I had the misfortune to scream in my sleep, owing to a frightful nightmare. I'm sorry I disturbed you."

"Oh, God confound you, Mr. Lockwood! I wish you were at the—" commenced my host, setting the candle on a chair, because he found it impossible to hold it steady.

"And who showed you up to this room?" he continued, crushing his nails into his palms, and grinding his teeth to subdue the maxillary convulsions. "Who was it? I've a good mind to turn them out of the house this moment!"

"It was your servant, Zillah," I replied, flinging myself on to the floor, and rapidly resuming my garments. "I should not care if you did, Mr. Heathcliff; she richly deserves it. I suppose that she wanted to get another proof that the place was haunted, at my expense. Well, it is—swarming with ghosts and goblins! You have reason in shutting it up, I assure you. No one will thank you for a doze in such a den!"

"What do you mean?" asked Heathcliff, "and what are you doing? Lie down and finish out the night, since you *are* here; but, for heaven's sake! don't repeat that horrid noise. Nothing could excuse it, unless you were having your throat cut!"

"If the little fiend had got in at the window, she probably would have strangled me!" I returned. "I'm not going to endure the persecutions of your hospitable ancestors again. Was not the Reverend Jabes Branderham akin to you on the mother's side? And that minx, Catherine Linton, or Earnshaw, or however she was called—she must have been a changeling—wicked little soul! She told me she had been walking the earth these twenty years: a just punishment for her mortal transgressions, I've no doubt!"

Scarcely were these words uttered, when I recollected the association of Heathcliff's with Catherine's name in the book, which had completely slipped from my memory till thus awakened. I blushed at my inconsideration; but, without showing further consciousness of the offence, I hastened to add—

"The truth is, sir, I passed the first part of the night in—" here, I stopped afresh—I was about to say "perusing those old volumes;" then it would have revealed my knowledge of their written, as well as their printed contents; so, correcting myself, I went on—"in spelling over the name scratched on that window-ledge. A monotonous occupation, calculated to set me asleep, like counting, or—"

"What *can* you mean by talking in this way to *me!*" thundered Heathcliff with savage vehemence. "How—how *dare* you, under my roof—God! he's mad to speak so!" And he struck his forehead with rage.

I did not know whether to resent this language, or pursue my explanation; but he seemed so powerfully affected that I took pity and proceeded with my dreams, affirming I had never heard the appellation of "Catherine Linton" before, but reading it often over produced an impression which personified itself when I had no longer my imagination under control.

Heathcliff gradually fell back into the shelter of the bed as I spoke, finally sitting down almost concealed behind it. I guessed, however, by his irregular and intercepted breathing, that he struggled to vanquish an access of violent emotion.

Not liking to show him that I heard the conflict, I continued my toilette rather noisily, looked at my watch, and soliloquized on the length of the night—

"Not three o'clock yet! I could have taken oath it had been six. Time stagnates here—we must surely have retired to rest at eight!"

"Always at nine in winter, and always rise at four," said my host, suppressing a groan, and, as I fancied, by the motion of his shadow's arm, dashing a tear from his eyes.

"Mr. Lockwood," he added, "you may go into my room; you'll only be in the way, coming downstairs so early; and your childish outcry has sent sleep to the devil for me."

"And for me, too," I replied. "I'll walk in the yard till daylight, and then I'll be off; and you need not dread a repetition of my intrusion. I am now quite cured of seeking pleasure in society, be it country or town. A sensible man ought to find sufficient company in himself."

"Delightful company!" muttered Heathcliff. "Take the candle, and go where you please. I shall join you directly. Keep out of the yard, though; the dogs are unchained, and the house—Juno mounts sentinel there, and—nay, you can only ramble about the steps and passages—but, away with you! I'll come in two minutes."

I obeyed, so far as to quit the chamber; when, ignorant where the narrow lobbies led, I stood still, and was witness, involuntarily, to a piece of superstition on the part of my landlord, which belied, oddly, his apparent sense.

He got on to the bed and wrenched open the lattice, bursting, as he pulled at it, into an uncontrollable passion of tears.

"Come in! come in!" he sobbed. "Cathy, do come. Oh, do—*once* more! Oh! my heart's darling, hear me *this* time—Catherine, at last!"

The spectre showed a spectre's ordinary caprice; it gave no sign of being; but the snow and wind whirled wildly through, even reaching my station, and blowing out the light.

There was such anguish in the gush of grief that accompanied this raving, that my compassion made me overlook its folly, and I drew off, half angry to have listened at all, and vexed at having related my ridiculous nightmare, since it produced that agony, though *why*, was beyond my comprehension.

I descended cautiously to the lower regions and landed in the back-kitchen, where a gleam of fire, raked compactly together, enabled me to rekindle my candle.

Nothing was stirring except a brindled, grey cat, which crept from the ashes and saluted me with a querulous mew.

Two benches, shaped in sections of a circle, nearly enclosed the hearth; on one of these I stretched myself, and Grimalkin[5] mounted the other. We were both of us nodding, ere any one invaded our retreat; and then it was Joseph shuffling down a wooden ladder that vanished in the roof, through a trap: the ascent to his garret, I suppose.

He cast a sinister look at the little flame which I had enticed to play between the ribs, swept the cat from its elevation, and bestowing himself in the vacancy, commenced the operation of stuffing a three-inch pipe with tobacco; my presence in his sanctum was evidently esteemed a piece of impudence too shameful for remark. He silently applied the tube to his lips, folded his arms, and puffed away.

I let him enjoy the luxury, unannoyed; and after sucking out the last wreath, and heaving a profound sigh, he got up, and departed as solemnly as he came.

A more elastic footstep entered next, and now I opened my mouth for a "good morning," but closed it again, the salutation unachieved; for Hareton Earnshaw was performing his orisons, *sotto voce*, in a series of curses directed against every object he touched, while he rummaged a corner for a spade or shovel to dig through the drifts. He glanced over the back of the bench, dilating his nostrils, and thought as little of exchanging civilities with me as with my companion, the cat.

I guessed by his preparations that egress was allowed, and leaving my hard couch, made a movement to follow him. He noticed this, and thrust at an inner door with the end of his spade, intimating by an inarticulate sound, that there was the place where I must go, if I changed my locality.

It opened into the house, where the females were already astir, Zillah, urging flakes of flame up the chimney with a colossal bellows, and Mrs. Heathcliff, kneeling on the hearth, reading a book by the aid of the blaze.

She held her hand interposed between the furnace-heat and her eyes, and seemed absorbed in her occupation; desisting from it only to chide the servant for covering her with sparks, or to push away a dog, now and then, that snoozled its nose over-forwardly into her face.

I was surprised to see Heathcliff there also. He stood by the fire, his back towards me, just finishing a stormy scene to poor Zillah, who ever and anon interrupted her labour to pluck up the corner of her apron, and heave an indignant groan.

"And you, you worthless—" he broke out as I entered, turning to

5. An old she-cat, but the term applies also to a jealous or imperious old woman.

his daughter-in-law, and employing an epithet as harmless as duck, or sheep, but generally represented by a dash[6]—"there you are at your idle tricks again! The rest of them do earn their bread—you live on my charity! Put your trash away, and find something to do. You shall pay me for the plague of having you eternally in my sight—do you hear, damnable jade?"

"I'll put my trash away, because you can make me, if I refuse," answered the young lady, closing her book, and throwing it on a chair. "But I'll not do anything, though you should swear your tongue out, except what I please!"

Heathcliff lifted his hand, and the speaker sprang to a safer distance, obviously acquainted with its weight.

Having no desire to be entertained by a cat-and-dog combat, I stepped forward briskly, as if eager to partake the warmth of the hearth, and innocent of any knowledge of the interrupted dispute. Each had enough decorum to suspend further hostilities: Heathcliff placed his fists, out of temptation, in his pockets; Mrs. Heathcliff curled her lip and walked to a seat far off, where she kept her word by playing the part of a statue during the remainder of my stay.

That was not long. I declined joining their breakfast, and, at the first gleam of dawn, took an opportunity of escaping into the free air, now clear and still, and cold as impalpable ice.

My landlord hallooed for me to stop, ere I reached the bottom of the garden, and offered to accompany me across the moor. It was well he did, for the whole hill-back was one billowy, white ocean, the swells and falls not indicating corresponding rises and depressions in the ground: many pits, at least, were filled to a level; and entire ranges of mounds, the refuse of the quarries, blotted from the chart which my yesterday's walk left pictured in my mind.

I had remarked on one side of the road, at intervals of six or seven yards, a line of upright stones, continued through the whole length of the barren: these were erected, and daubed with lime, on purpose to serve as guides in the dark, and also, when a fall, like the present, confounded the deep swamps on either hand with the firmer path: but, excepting a dirty dot pointing up here and there, all traces of their existence had vanished; and my companion found it necessary to warn me frequently to steer to the right or left, when I imagined I was following, correctly, the windings of the road.

We exchanged little conversation, and he halted at the entrance of Thrushcross park, saying, I could make no error there. Our

6. He is referring to the convention of leaving parts of epithets blank (d——n). In her preface to the 1850 *WH*, Charlotte Brontë noted Emily's frankness: "A large class of readers . . . will suffer greatly from the introduction of words printed with all their letters, which it has become the custom to represent by the initial and final letter only—a blank line filling the interval."

adieux were limited to a hasty bow, and then I pushed forward, trusting to my own resources, for the porter's lodge is untenanted as yet.

The distance from the gate to the Grange is two miles: I believe I managed to make it four, what with losing myself among the trees, and sinking up to the neck in snow, a predicament which only those who have experienced it can appreciate. At any rate, whatever were my wanderings, the clock chimed twelve as I entered the house; and that gave exactly an hour for every mile of the usual way from Wuthering Heights.

My human fixture and her satellites rushed to welcome me; exclaiming, tumultuously, they had completely given me up: everybody conjectured that I perished last night; and they were wondering how they must set about the search for my remains.

I bid them be quiet, now that they saw me returned, and, benumbed to my very heart, I dragged upstairs, whence, after putting on dry clothes, and pacing to and fro thirty or forty minutes, to restore the animal heat, I am adjourned to my study, feeble as a kitten, almost too much so to enjoy the cheerful fire and smoking coffee which the servant has prepared for my refreshment.

Chapter IV

What vain weather-cocks we are! I, who had determined to hold myself independent of all social intercourse, and thanked my stars that, at length, I had lighted on a spot where it was next to impracticable—I, weak wretch, after maintaining till dusk a struggle with low spirits and solitude, was finally compelled to strike my colours; and, under pretence of gaining information concerning the necessities of my establishment, I desired Mrs. Dean, when she brought in supper, to sit down while I ate it, hoping sincerely she would prove a regular gossip, and either rouse me to animation, or lull me to sleep by her talk.

"You have lived here a considerable time," I commenced; "did you not say sixteen years?"

"Eighteen, sir; I came, when the mistress was married, to wait on her; after she died, the master retained me for his house-keeper."

"Indeed."

There ensued a pause. She was not a gossip, I feared, unless about her own affairs, and those could hardly interest me.

However, having studied for an interval, with a fist on either knee, and a cloud of meditation over her ruddy countenance, she ejaculated—

"Ah, times are greatly changed since then!"

"Yes," I remarked, "you've seen a good many alterations, I suppose?"

"I have: and troubles too," she said.

"Oh, I'll turn the talk on my landlord's family!" I thought to myself. "A good subject to start—and that pretty girl-widow, I should like to know her history: whether she be a native of the country, or, as is more probable, an exotic that the surly *indigenae*[1] will not recognise for kin."

With this intention I asked Mrs. Dean why Heathcliff let Thrushcross Grange, and preferred living in a situation and residence so much inferior.

"Is he not rich enough to keep the estate in good order?" I enquired.

"Rich, sir!" she returned. "He has, nobody knows what money, and every year it increases. Yes, yes, he's rich enough to live in a finer house than this, but he's very near—close-handed; and, if he had meant to flit to Thrushcross Grange, as soon as he heard of a good tenant he could not have borne to miss the chance of getting a few hundreds more. It is strange people should be so greedy, when they are alone in the world!"

"He had a son, it seems?"

"Yes, he had one—he is dead."

"And that young lady, Mrs. Heathcliff, is his widow?"

"Yes."

"Where did she come from originally?"

"Why, sir, she is my late master's daughter; Catherine Linton was her maiden name. I nursed her, poor thing! I did wish Mr. Heathcliff would remove here, and then we might have been together again."

"What, Catherine Linton!" I exclaimed, astonished. But a minute's reflection convinced me it was not my ghostly Catherine. "Then," I continued, "my predecessor's name was Linton?"

"It was."

"And who is that Earnshaw, Hareton Earnshaw, who lives with Mr. Heathcliff? are they relations?"

"No; he is the late Mrs. Linton's nephew."

"The young lady's cousin, then?"

"Yes; and her husband was her cousin also—one, on the mother's—the other, on the father's side. Heathcliff married Mr. Linton's sister."

"I see the house at Wuthering Heights has 'Earnshaw' carved over the front door. Are they an old family?"

1. Natives.

"Very old, sir; and Hareton is the last of them, as our Miss Cathy is of us—I mean, of the Lintons. Have you been to Wuthering Heights? I beg pardon for asking; but I should like to hear how she is!"

"Mrs. Heathcliff? She looked very well, and very handsome; yet, I think, not very happy."

"Oh dear, I don't wonder! And how did you like the master?"

"A rough fellow, rather, Mrs. Dean. Is not that his character?"

"Rough as a saw-edge, and hard as whinstone! The less you meddle with him the better."

"He must have had some ups and downs in life to make him such a churl. Do you know anything of his history?"

"It's a cuckoo's,[2] sir—I know all about it, except where he was born, and who were his parents, and how he got his money, at first. And Hareton has been cast out like an unfledged dunnock! The unfortunate lad is the only one, in all this parish, that does not guess how he has been cheated!"

"Well, Mrs. Dean, it will be a charitable deed to tell me something of my neighbours—I feel I shall not rest, if I go to bed; so, be good enough to sit and chat an hour."

"Oh, certainly, sir! I'll just fetch a little sewing, and then I'll sit as long as you please. But you've caught cold; I saw you shivering, and you must have some gruel to drive it out."

The worthy woman bustled off; and I crouched nearer the fire; my head felt hot, and the rest of me chill: moreover, I was excited, almost to a pitch of foolishness, through my nerves and brain. This caused me to feel, not uncomfortable, but rather fearful, as I am still, of serious effects from the incidents of today and yesterday.

She returned presently, bringing a smoking basin, and a basket of work; and, having placed the former on the hob, drew in her seat, evidently pleased to find me so companionable.

Before I came to live here, she commenced, waiting no further invitation to her story, I was almost always at Wuthering Heights, because my mother had nursed Mr. Hindley Earnshaw, that was Hareton's father, and I got used to playing with the children. I ran errands too, and helped to make hay, and hung about the farm ready for anything that anybody would set me to.

One fine summer morning—it was the beginning of harvest, I remember—Mr. Earnshaw, the old master, came downstairs, dressed for a journey; and, after he had told Joseph what was to be done during the day, he turned to Hindley, and Cathy, and me—

2. The reference is to the cuckoo's practice of laying its eggs in other birds' nests (a way of characterizing Heathcliff as an interloper).

for I sat eating my porridge with them—and he said, speaking to his son—

"Now, my bonny man, I'm going to Liverpool, today. What shall I bring you? You may choose what you like; only let it be little, for I shall walk there and back; sixty miles each way, that is a long spell!"

Hindley named a fiddle, and then he asked Miss Cathy; she was hardly six years old, but she could ride any horse in the stable, and she chose a whip.

He did not forget me, for he had a kind heart, though he was rather severe, sometimes. He promised to bring me a pocketful of apples and pears, and then he kissed his children good-bye, and set off.

It seemed a long while to us all—the three days of his absence—and often did little Cathy ask when he would be home. Mrs. Earnshaw expected him by supper-time, on the third evening; and she put the meal off hour after hour; there were no signs of his coming, however, and at last the children got tired of running down to the gate to look. Then it grew dark; she would have had them to bed, but they begged sadly to be allowed to stay up; and, just about eleven o'clock, the door-latch was raised quietly and in stept the master. He threw himself into a chair, laughing and groaning, and bid them all stand off, for he was nearly killed—he would not have such another walk for the three kingdoms.

"And at the end of it, to be flighted[3] to death!" he said, opening his great-coat, which he held bundled up in his arms, "See here, wife; I was never so beaten with anything in my life; but you must e'en take it as a gift of God, though it's as dark almost as if it came from the devil."

We crowded round, and, over Miss Cathy's head, I had a peep at a dirty, ragged, black-haired child; big enough both to walk and talk—indeed, its face looked older than Catherine's—yet, when it was set on its feet, it only stared round, and repeated over and over again some gibberish that nobody could understand. I was frightened, and Mrs. Earnshaw was ready to fling it out of doors: she did fly up—asking how he could fashion to bring that gipsy brat into the house, when they had their own bairns to feed and fend for? What he meant to do with it, and whether he were mad?

The master tried to explain the matter; but he was really half dead with fatigue, and all that I could make out, amongst her scolding, was a tale of his seeing it starving, and houseless, and as good as dumb in the streets of Liverpool, where he picked it up and inquired for its owner. Not a soul knew to whom it belonged, he

3. Frightened.

said, and his money and time being both limited, he thought it better to take it home with him at once, than run into vain expenses there; because he was determined he would not leave it as he found it.

Well, the conclusion was that my mistress grumbled herself calm; and Mr. Earnshaw told me to wash it, and give it clean things, and let it sleep with the children.

Hindley and Cathy contented themselves with looking and listening till peace was restored; then, both began searching their father's pockets for the presents he had promised them. The former was a boy of fourteen, but when he drew out what had been a fiddle, crushed to morsels in the great-coat, he blubbered aloud, and Cathy, when she learnt the master had lost her whip in attending on the stranger, showed her humour by grinning and spitting at the stupid little thing, earning for her pains a sound blow from her father to teach her cleaner manners.

They entirely refused to have it in bed with them, or even in their room, and I had no more sense, so I put it on the landing of the stairs, hoping it might be gone on the morrow. By chance, or else attracted by hearing his voice, it crept to Mr. Earnshaw's door and there he found it on quitting his chamber. Inquiries were made as to how it got there; I was obliged to confess, and in recompense for my cowardice and inhumanity was sent out of the house.

This was Heathcliff's first introduction to the family. On coming back a few days afterwards, for I did not consider my banishment perpetual, I found they had christened him "Heathcliff"; it was the name of a son who died in childhood, and it has served him ever since, both for Christian and surname.

Miss Cathy and he were now very thick; but Hindley hated him, and to say the truth I did the same; and we plagued and went on with him shamefully, for I wasn't reasonable enough to feel my injustice, and the mistress never put in a word on his behalf when she saw him wronged.

He seemed a sullen, patient child, hardened, perhaps, to ill-treatment: he would stand Hindley's blows without winking or shedding a tear, and my pinches moved him only to draw in a breath, and open his eyes as if he had hurt himself by accident, and nobody was to blame.

This endurance made old Earnshaw furious when he discovered his son persecuting the poor, fatherless child, as he called him. He took to Heathcliff strangely, believing all he said (for that matter, he said precious little, and generally the truth) and petting him up far above Cathy, who was too mischievous and wayward for a favourite.

So, from the very beginning, he bred bad feeling in the house;

and at Mrs. Earnshaw's death, which happened in less than two years after, the young master had learnt to regard his father as an oppressor rather than a friend, and Heathcliff as a usurper of his parent's affections and his privileges, and he grew bitter with brooding over these injuries.

I sympathised a while, but, when the children fell ill of the measles and I had to tend them, and take on me the cares of a woman at once, I changed my ideas. Heathcliff was dangerously sick, and while he lay at the worst he would have me constantly by his pillow; I suppose he felt I did a good deal for him, and he hadn't wit to guess that I was compelled to do it. However, I will say this, he was the quietest child that ever nurse watched over. The difference between him and the others forced me to be less partial. Cathy and her brother harassed me terribly; *he* was as uncomplaining as a lamb, though hardness, not gentleness, made him give little trouble.

He got through, and the doctor affirmed it was in a great measure owing to me, and praised me for my care. I was vain of his commendations, and softened towards the being by whose means I earned them, and thus Hindley lost his last ally; still I couldn't dote on Heathcliff, and I wondered often what my master saw to admire so much in the sullen boy who never, to my recollection, repaid his indulgence by any sign of gratitude. He was not insolent to his benefactor; he was simply insensible, though knowing perfectly the hold he had on his heart, and conscious he had only to speak and all the house would be obliged to bend to his wishes.

As an instance, I remember Mr. Earnshaw once bought a couple of colts at the parish fair, and gave the lads each one. Heathcliff took the handsomest, but it soon fell lame, and when he discovered it, he said to Hindley—

"You must exchange horses with me; I don't like mine, and if you won't I shall tell your father of the three thrashings you've given me this week, and show him my arm, which is black to the shoulder."

Hindley put out his tongue, and cuffed him over the ears.

"You'd better do it at once," he persisted, escaping to the porch (they were in the stable); "you will have to, and if I speak of these blows, you'll get them again with interest."

"Off, dog!" cried Hindley, threatening him with an iron weight, used for weighing potatoes and hay.

"Throw it," he replied, standing still, "and then I'll tell how you boasted that you would turn me out of doors as soon as he died, and see whether he will not turn you out directly."

Hindley threw it, hitting him on the breast, and down he fell, but staggered up immediately, breathless and white, and had not I prevented it he would have gone just so to the master, and got full revenge by letting his condition plead for him, intimating who had caused it.

"Take my colt, gipsy, then!" said young Earnshaw. "And I pray that he may break your neck; take him, and be damned, you beggarly interloper! and wheedle my father out of all he has, only afterwards show him what you are, imp of Satan—And take that, I hope he'll kick out your brains!"

Heathcliff had gone to loose the beast, and shift it to his own stall. He was passing behind it, when Hindley finished his speech by knocking him under its feet, and without stopping to examine whether his hopes were fulfilled, ran away as fast as he could.

I was surprised to witness how coolly the child gathered himself up, and went on with his intention, exchanging saddles and all, and then sitting down on a bundle of hay to overcome the qualm which the violent blow occasioned, before he entered the house.

I persuaded him easily to let me lay the blame of his bruises on the horse; he minded little what tale was told since he had what he wanted. He complained so seldom, indeed, of such stirs as these, that I really thought him not vindictive—I was deceived completely, as you will hear.

Chapter V

In the course of time, Mr. Earnshaw began to fail. He had been active and healthy, yet his strength left him suddenly; and when he was confined to the chimney-corner he grew grievously irritable. A nothing vexed him, and suspected slights of his authority nearly threw him into fits.

This was especially to be remarked if any one attempted to impose upon, or domineer over, his favourite: he was painfully jealous lest a word should be spoken amiss to him, seeming to have got into his head the notion that, because he liked Heathcliff, all hated, and longed to do him an ill-turn.

It was a disadvantage to the lad, for the kinder among us did not wish to fret the master, so we humoured his partiality; and that humouring was rich nourishment to the child's pride and black tempers. Still it became in a manner necessary; twice, or thrice, Hindley's manifestations of scorn, while his father was near, roused the old man to a fury. He seized his stick to strike him, and shook with rage that he could not do it.

At last, our curate (we had a curate then who made the living answer by teaching the little Lintons and Earnshaws, and farming his bit of land himself)—he advised that the young man should be sent to college, and Mr. Earnshaw agreed, though with a heavy spirit, for he said—

"Hindley was naught, and would never thrive as where he wandered."

I hoped heartily we should have peace now. It hurt me to think the master should be made uncomfortable by his own good deed. I fancied the discontent of age and disease arose from his family disagreements, as he would have it that it did; really, you know, sir, it was in his sinking frame.

We might have got on tolerably, notwithstanding, but for two people, Miss Cathy and Joseph, the servant; you saw him, I dare say, up yonder. He was, and is yet, most likely, the wearisomest, self-righteous pharisee that ever ransacked a Bible to rake the promises to himself, and fling the curses on his neighbours. By his knack of sermonizing and pious discoursing, he contrived to make a great impression on Mr. Earnshaw, and the more feeble the master became, the more influence he gained.

He was relentless in worrying him about his soul's concerns, and about ruling his children rigidly. He encouraged him to regard Hindley as a reprobate; and, night after night, he regularly grumbled out a long string of tales against Heathcliff and Catherine; always minding to flatter Earnshaw's weakness by heaping the heaviest blame on the last.

Certainly, she had ways with her such as I never saw a child take up before; and she put all of us past our patience fifty times and oftener in a day: from the hour she came downstairs, till the hour she went to bed, we had not a minute's security that she wouldn't be in mischief. Her spirits were always at high-water mark, her tongue always going—singing, laughing, and plaguing everybody who would not do the same. A wild, wick[1] slip she was—but she had the bonniest eye, and sweetest smile, and lightest foot in the parish; and, after all, I believe she meant no harm; for when once she made you cry in good earnest, it seldom happened that she would not keep you company, and oblige you to be quiet that you might comfort her.

She was much too fond of Heathcliff. The greatest punishment we could invent for her was to keep her separate from him: yet she got chided more than any of us on his account.

In play, she liked, exceedingly, to act the little mistress; using her hands freely, and commanding her companions: she did so to me, but I would not bear slapping and ordering; and so I let her know.

Now, Mr. Earnshaw did not understand jokes from his children: he had always been strict and grave with them; and Catherine, on

1. North England variant of quick (lively); *OED* cites it in Elizabeth Gaskell's *Mary Barton* (1848).

her part, had no idea why her father should be crosser and less patient in his ailing condition, than he was in his prime.

His peevish reproofs wakened in her a naughty delight to provoke him; she was never so happy as when we were all scolding her at once, and she defying us with her bold, saucy look, and her ready words; turning Joseph's religious curses into ridicule, baiting me, and doing just what her father hated most, showing how her pretended insolence, which he thought real, had more power over Heathcliff than his kindness; how the boy would do *her* bidding in anything, and *his* only when it suited his own inclination.

After behaving as badly as possible all day, she sometimes came fondling to make it up at night.

"Nay, Cathy," the old man would say, "I cannot love thee; thou'rt worse than thy brother. Go, say thy prayers, child, and ask God's pardon. I doubt thy mother and I must rue that we ever reared thee!"

That made her cry, at first; and then, being repulsed continually hardened her, and she laughed if I told her to say she was sorry for her faults, and beg to be forgiven.

But the hour came, at last, that ended Mr. Earnshaw's troubles on earth. He died quietly in his chair one October evening, seated by the fire-side.

A high wind blustered round the house, and roared in the chimney: it sounded wild and stormy, yet it was not cold, and we were all together—I, a little removed from the hearth, busy at my knitting, and Joseph reading his Bible near the table (for the servants generally sat in the house then, after their work was done). Miss Cathy had been sick, and that made her still; she leant against her father's knee, and Heathcliff was lying on the floor with his head in her lap.

I remember the master, before he fell into a doze, stroking her bonny hair—it pleased him rarely[2] to see her gentle—and saying—

"Why canst thou not always be a good lass, Cathy?"

And she turned her face up to his, and laughed, and answered—

"Why cannot you always be a good man, father?"

But as soon as she saw him vexed again, she kissed his hand, and said she would sing him to sleep. She began singing very low, till his fingers dropped from hers, and his head sank on his breast. Then I told her to hush, and not stir, for fear she should wake him. We all kept as mute as mice a full half-hour, and should have done so longer, only Joseph, having finished his chapter, got up and said that he must rouse the master for prayers and bed. He stepped

2. Exceedingly.

forward, and called him by name, and touched his shoulder, but he would not move—so he took the candle and looked at him.

I thought there was something wrong as he set down the light; and seizing the children each by an arm, whispered them to "frame upstairs, and make little din—they might pray alone that evening—he had summut to do."[3]

"I shall bid father good-night first," said Catherine, putting her arms round his neck, before we could hinder her.

The poor thing discovered her loss directly—she screamed out—

"Oh, he's dead, Heathcliff! he's dead!"

And they both set up a heart-breaking cry.

I joined my wail to theirs, loud and bitter; but Joseph asked what we could be thinking of to roar in that way over a saint in heaven.

He told me to put on my cloak and run to Gimmerton for the doctor and the parson. I could not guess the use that either would be of, then. However, I went, through wind and rain, and brought one, the doctor, back with me; the other said he would come in the morning.

Leaving Joseph to explain matters, I ran to the children's room; their door was ajar, I saw they had never laid down, though it was past midnight; but they were calmer, and did not need me to console them. The little souls were comforting each other with better thoughts than I could have hit on; no parson in the world ever pictured heaven so beautifully as they did, in their innocent talk; and, while I sobbed and listened, I could not help wishing we were all there safe together.

Chapter VI

Mr. Hindley came home to the funeral; and—a thing that amazed us, and set the neighbours gossiping right and left—he brought a wife with him.

What she was, and where she was born he never informed us; probably, she had neither money nor name to recommend her, or he would scarcely have kept the union from his father.

She was not one that would have disturbed the house much on her own account. Every object she saw, the moment she crossed the threshold, appeared to delight her; and every circumstance that took place about her, except the preparing for the burial, and the presence of the mourners.

I thought she was half silly, from her behaviour while that went on; she ran into her chamber, and made me come with her, though

3. ". . . go upstairs, and make little noise—they might pray alone that evening—he had something to do."

I should have been dressing the children; and there she sat shivering and clasping her hands, and asking repeatedly—

"Are they gone yet?"

Then she began describing with hysterical emotion the effect it produced on her to see black; and started, and trembled, and, at last, fell a weeping—and when I asked what was the matter? answered, she didn't know; but she felt so afraid of dying!

I imagined her as little likely to die as myself. She was rather thin, but young, and fresh complexioned, and her eyes sparkled as bright as diamonds. I did remark, to be sure, that mounting the stairs made her breathe very quick, that the least sudden noise set her all in a quiver, and that she coughed troublesomely sometimes: but I knew nothing of what these symptoms portended, and had no impulse to sympathize with her. We don't in general take to foreigners here, Mr. Lockwood, unless they take to us first.

Young Earnshaw was altered considerably in the three years of his absence. He had grown sparer, and lost his colour, and spoke and dressed quite differently; and, on the very day of his return, he told Joseph and me we must thenceforth quarter ourselves in the back-kitchen, and leave the house for him. Indeed, he would have carpeted and papered a small spare room for a parlour; but his wife expressed such pleasure at the white floor, and huge glowing fire-place, at the pewter dishes, and delf-case, and dog-kennel, and the wide space there was to move about in, where they usually sat, that he thought it unnecessary to her comfort, and so dropped the intention.

She expressed pleasure, too, at finding a sister among her new acquaintance, and she prattled to Catherine, and kissed her, and ran about with her, and gave her quantities of presents, at the beginning. Her affection tired very soon, however, and when she grew peevish, Hindley became tyrannical. A few words from her, evincing a dislike to Heathcliff, were enough to rouse in him all his old hatred of the boy. He drove him from their company to the servants, deprived him of the instructions of the curate, and insisted that he should labour out of doors instead, compelling him to do so, as hard as any other lad on the farm.

Heathcliff bore his degradation pretty well at first, because Cathy taught him what she learnt, and worked or played with him in the fields. They both promised fair to grow up as rude as savages, the young master being entirely negligent how they behaved, and what they did, so they kept clear of him. He would not even have seen after their going to church on Sundays, only Joseph and the curate reprimanded his carelessness when they absented themselves, and that reminded him to order Heathcliff a flogging, and Catherine a fast from dinner or supper.

But it was one of their chief amusements to run away to the moors in the morning and remain there all day, and the after-punishment grew a mere thing to laugh at. The curate might set as many chapters as he pleased for Catherine to get by heart, and Joseph might thrash Heathcliff till his arm ached; they forgot everything the minute they were together again, at least the minute they had contrived some naughty plan of revenge; and many a time I've cried to myself to watch them growing more reckless daily, and I not daring to speak a syllable for fear of losing the small power I still retained over the unfriended creatures.

One Sunday evening, it chanced that they were banished from the sitting-room, for making a noise, or a light offence of the kind, and when I went to call them to supper, I could discover them nowhere.

We searched the house, above and below, and the yard and stables; they were invisible; and, at last, Hindley in a passion told us to bolt the doors, and swore nobody should let them in that night.

The household went to bed; and I, too anxious to lie down, opened my lattice and put my head out to hearken, though it rained, determined to admit them in spite of the prohibition, should they return.

In a while, I distinguished steps coming up the road, and the light of a lantern glimmered through the gate.

I threw a shawl over my head and ran to prevent them from waking Mr. Earnshaw by knocking. There was Heathcliff, by himself; it gave me a start to see him alone.

"Where is Miss Catherine?" I cried hurriedly. "No accident, I hope?"

"At Thrushcross Grange," he answered, "and I would have been there too, but they had not the manners to ask me to stay."

"Well, you will catch it!" I said, "you'll never be content till you're sent about your business. What in the world led you wandering to Thrushcross Grange?"

"Let me get off my wet clothes, and I'll tell you all about it, Nelly," he replied.

I bid him beware of rousing the master, and while he undressed, and I waited to put out the candle, he continued—

"Cathy and I escaped from the wash-house to have a ramble at liberty, and getting a glimpse of the Grange lights, we thought we would just go and see whether the Lintons passed their Sunday evenings standing shivering in corners, while their father and mother sat eating and drinking, and singing and laughing, and burning their eyes out before the fire. Do you think they do? Or reading sermons, and being catechised by their man-servant, and set to learn a column of Scripture names, if they don't answer properly?"

"Probably not," I responded. "They are good children, no doubt, and don't deserve the treatment you receive, for your bad conduct."

"Don't you cant, Nelly," he said. "Nonsense! We ran from the top of the Heights to the park, without stopping—Catherine completely beaten in the race, because she was barefoot. You'll have to seek for her shoes in the bog to-morrow. We crept through a broken hedge, groped our way up the path, and planted ourselves on a flower-plot under the drawing-room window. The light came from thence; they had not put up the shutters, and the curtains were only half closed. Both of us were able to look in by standing on the basement,[1] and clinging to the ledge, and we saw—ah! it was beautiful—a splendid place carpeted with crimson, and crimson-covered chairs and tables, and a pure white ceiling bordered by gold, a shower of glass-drops hanging in silver chains from the centre, and shimmering with little soft tapers. Old Mr. and Mrs. Linton were not there. Edgar and his sister had it entirely to themselves; shouldn't they have been happy? We should have thought ourselves in heaven! And now, guess what your good children were doing? Isabella—I believe she is eleven, a year younger than Cathy—lay screaming at the farther end of the room, shrieking as if witches were running red hot needles into her. Edgar stood on the hearth weeping silently, and in the middle of the table sat a little dog shaking its paw and yelping, which, from their mutual accusations, we understood they had nearly pulled in two between them. The idiots! That was their pleasure! to quarrel who should hold a heap of warm hair, and each begin to cry because both, after struggling to get it, refused to take it. We laughed outright at the petted things, we did despise them! When would you catch me wishing to have what Catherine wanted? or find us by ourselves, seeking entertainment in yelling, and sobbing, and rolling on the ground, divided by the whole room? I'd not exchange, for a thousand lives, my condition here, for Edgar Linton's at Thrushcross Grange—not if I might have the privilege of flinging Joseph off the highest gable, and painting the house-front with Hindley's blood!"

"Hush, hush!" I interrupted. "Still you have not told me, Heathcliff, how Catherine is left behind?"

"I told you we laughed," he answered. "The Lintons heard us, and with one accord, they shot like arrows to the door; there was silence, and then a cry, 'Oh, mamma, mamma! Oh, papa! Oh, mamma, come here. Oh, papa, oh!' They really did howl out, something in that way. We made frightful noises to terrify them still

1. The raised stonework around the house foundation. There is just such a basement outside the main floor of Ponden Hall, one of the possible models for Thrushcross Grange.

more, and then we dropped off the ledge, because somebody was drawing the bars, and we felt we had better flee. I had Cathy by the hand, and was urging her on, when all at once she fell down.

" 'Run, Heathcliff, run!' she whispered. 'They have let the bulldog loose, and he holds me!'

"The devil had seized her ankle, Nelly; I heard his abominable snorting. She did not yell out—no! She would have scorned to do it, if she had been spitted on the horns of a mad cow. I did, though; I vociferated curses enough to annihilate any fiend in Christendom, and I got a stone and thrust it between his jaws, and tried with all my might to cram it down his throat. A beast of a servant came up with a lantern, at last, shouting—

" 'Keep fast, Skulker, keep fast!'

"He changed his note, however, when he saw Skulker's game. The dog was throttled off, his huge, purple tongue hanging half a foot out of his mouth, and his pendant lips streaming with bloody slaver.

"The man took Cathy up; she was sick, not from fear, I'm certain, but from pain. He carried her in; I followed, grumbling execrations and vengeance.

" 'What prey, Robert?' hallooed Linton from the entrance.

" 'Skulker has caught a little girl, sir,' he replied, 'and there's a lad here,' he added, making a clutch at me, 'who looks an out-and-outer![2] Very like, the robbers were for putting them through the window, to open the doors to the gang after all were asleep, that they might murder us at their ease. Hold your tongue, you foul-mouthed thief, you! you shall go to the gallows for this. Mr. Linton, sir, don't lay by your gun!'

" 'No, no, Robert!' said the old fool. 'The rascals knew that yesterday was my rent-day; they thought to have me cleverly. Come in; I'll furnish them a reception. There, John, fasten the chain. Give Skulker some water, Jenny. To beard a magistrate in his stronghold, and on the Sabbath, too! Where will their insolence stop? Oh, my dear Mary, look here! Don't be afraid, it is but a boy—yet the villain scowls so plainly in his face, would it not be a kindness to the country to hang him at once, before he shows his nature in acts, as well as features?'

"He pulled me under the chandelier, and Mrs. Linton placed her spectacles on her nose and raised her hands in horror. The cowardly children crept nearer also, Isabella lisping—

" 'Frightful thing! Put him in the cellar, papa. He's exactly like

2. A total scoundrel, one who lives by out-and-out lies. Dickens said that he did not know what to make of "such an out-and-outer" as *Oliver Twist*'s Fagin. *The Letters of Charles Dickens*, ed. Madeline House and Graham Storey, Oxford: Clarendon Press, 1965, I, 441.

the son of the fortune-teller that stole my tame pheasant. Isn't he, Edgar?'

"While they examined me, Cathy came round; she heard the last speech, and laughed. Edgar Linton, after an inquisitive stare, collected sufficient wit to recognise her. They see us at church, you know, though we seldom meet them elsewhere.

" 'That's Miss Earnshaw!' he whispered to his mother, 'and look how Skulker has bitten her—how her foot bleeds!'

" 'Miss Earnshaw? Nonsense!' cried the dame, 'Miss Earnshaw scouring the country with a gipsy! And yet, my dear, the child is in mourning—surely it is—and she may be lamed for life!'

" 'What culpable carelessness in her brother!' exclaimed Mr. Linton, turning from me to Catherine. 'I've understood from Shielders' (that was the curate, sir) 'that he lets her grow up in absolute heathenism. But who is this? Where did she pick up this companion? Oho! I declare he is that strange acquisition my late neighbour made in his journey to Liverpool—a little Lascar, or an American or Spanish castaway.'

" 'A wicked boy, at all events,' remarked the old lady, 'and quite unfit for a decent house! Did you notice his language, Linton? I'm shocked that my children should have heard it.'

"I recommenced cursing—don't be angry, Nelly—and so Robert was ordered to take me off—I refused to go without Cathy; he dragged me into the garden, pushed the lantern into my hand, assured me that Mr. Earnshaw should be informed of my behaviour, and bidding me march directly, secured the door again.

"The curtains were still looped up at one corner; and I resumed my station as spy, because, if Catherine had wished to return, I intended shattering their great glass panes to a million fragments, unless they let her out.

"She sat on the sofa quietly. Mrs. Linton took off the grey cloak of the dairy maid which we had borrowed for our excursion, shaking her head, and expostulating with her, I suppose; she was a young lady and they made a distinction between her treatment and mine. Then the woman servant brought a basin of warm water, and washed her feet; and Mr. Linton mixed a tumbler of negus, and Isabella emptied a plateful of cakes into her lap, and Edgar stood gaping at a distance. Afterwards, they dried and combed her beautiful hair, and gave her a pair of enormous slippers, and wheeled her to the fire, and I left her, as merry as she could be, dividing her food between the little dog and Skulker whose nose she pinched as he ate; and kindling a spark of spirit in the vacant blue eyes of the Lintons—a dim reflection from her own enchanting face—I saw they were full of stupid admiration; she is so immeasurably superior to them—to everybody on earth, is she not, Nelly?"

"There will more come of this business than you reckon on," I answered, covering him up and extinguishing the light. "You are incurable, Heathcliff, and Mr. Hindley will have to proceed to extremities, see if he won't."

My words came truer than I desired. The luckless adventure made Earnshaw furious. And then Mr. Linton, to mend matters, paid us a visit himself on the morrow; and read the young master such a lecture on the road he guided his family, that he was stirred to look about him, in earnest.

Heathcliff received no flogging, but he was told that the first word he spoke to Miss Catherine should ensure a dismissal; and Mrs. Earnshaw undertook to keep her sister-in-law in due restraint, when she returned home; employing art, not force—with force she would have found it impossible.

Chapter VII

Cathy stayed at Thrushcross Grange five weeks, till Christmas. By that time her ankle was thoroughly cured, and her manners much improved. The mistress visited her often, in the interval, and commenced her plan of reform by trying to raise her self-respect with fine clothes and flattery, which she took readily: so that, instead of a wild, hatless little savage jumping into the house, and rushing to squeeze us all breathless, there alighted from a handsome black pony a very dignified person with brown ringlets falling from the cover of a feathered beaver, and a long cloth habit which she was obliged to hold up with both hands that she might sail in.

Hindley lifted her from her horse, exclaiming delightedly—

"Why, Cathy, you are quite a beauty! I should scarcely have known you—you look like a lady now. Isabella Linton is not to be compared with her, is she, Frances?"

"Isabella has not her natural advantages," replied his wife, "but she must mind and not grow wild again here. Ellen, help Miss Catherine off with her things. Stay, dear, you will disarrange your curls—let me untie your hat."

I removed the habit, and there shone forth beneath, a grand plaid silk frock, white trousers, and burnished shoes; and, while her eyes sparkled joyfully when the dogs came bounding up to welcome her, she dare hardly touch them lest they should fawn upon her splendid garments.

She kissed me gently—I was all flour making the Christmas cake, and it would not have done to give me a hug—and then she looked round for Heathcliff. Mr. and Mrs. Earnshaw watched anxiously their meeting, thinking it would enable them to judge, in some measure, what grounds they had for hoping to succeed in separating the two friends.

Heathcliff was hard to discover, at first. If he were careless and uncared for, before Catherine's absence, he had been ten times more so, since.

Nobody but I even did him the kindness to call him a dirty boy, and bid him wash himself, once a week; and children of his age seldom have a natural pleasure in soap and water. Therefore, not to mention his clothes, which had seen three months' service in mire and dust, and his thick uncombed hair, the surface of his face and hands was dismally beclouded. He might well skulk behind the settle, on beholding such a bright, graceful damsel enter the house, instead of a rough-headed counterpart to himself, as he expected.

"Is Heathcliff not here?" she demanded, pulling off her gloves, and displaying fingers wonderfully whitened with doing nothing, and staying indoors.

"Heathcliff, you may come forward," cried Mr. Hindley, enjoying his discomfiture and gratified to see what a forbidding young blackguard he would be compelled to present himself. "You may come and wish Miss Catherine welcome, like the other servants."

Cathy, catching a glimpse of her friend in his concealment, flew to embrace him; she bestowed seven or eight kisses on his cheek within the second, and then stopped, and drawing back, burst into a laugh, exclaiming—

"Why, how very black and cross you look! and how—how funny and grim! But that's because I'm used to Edgar and Isabella Linton. Well, Heathcliff, have you forgotten me?"

She had some reason to put the question, for shame and pride threw double gloom over his countenance, and kept him immovable.

"Shake hands, Heathcliff," said Mr. Earnshaw, condescendingly; "once in a way, that is permitted."

"I shall not!" replied the boy, finding his tongue at last, "I shall not stand to be laughed at, I shall not bear it!"

And he would have broken from the circle, but Miss Cathy seized him again.

"I did not mean to laugh at you," she said, "I could not hinder myself. Heathcliff, shake hands, at least! What are you sulky for? It was only that you looked odd. If you wash your face and brush your hair, it will be all right. But you are so dirty!"

She gazed concernedly at the dusky fingers she held in her own, and also at her dress, which she feared had gained no embellishment from its contact with his.

"You needn't have touched me!" he answered, following her eye and snatching away his hand. "I shall be as dirty as I please, and I like to be dirty, and I will be dirty."

With that he dashed head foremost out of the room, amid the merriment of the master and mistress, and to the serious disturbance of Catherine, who could not comprehend how her remarks should have produced such an exhibition of bad temper.

After playing lady's maid to the new-comer, and putting my cakes in the oven, and making the house and kitchen cheerful with great fires befitting Christmas eve, I prepared to sit down and amuse myself by singing carols, all alone, regardless of Joseph's affirmations that he considered the merry tunes I chose as next door to songs.

He had retired to private prayer in his chamber, and Mr. and Mrs. Earnshaw were engaging Missy's attention by sundry gay trifles bought for her to present to the little Lintons, as an acknowledgment of their kindness.

They had invited them to spend the morrow at Wuthering Heights, and the invitation had been accepted, on one condition: Mrs. Linton begged that her darlings might be kept carefully apart from that "naughty, swearing boy."

Under these circumstances I remained solitary. I smelt the rich scent of the heating spices; and admired the shining kitchen utensils, the polished clock, decked in holly, the silver mugs ranged on a tray ready to be filled with mulled ale for supper; and, above all, the speckless purity of my particular care—the scoured and well-swept floor.

I gave due inward applause to every object, and then I remembered how old Earnshaw used to come in when all was tidied, and call me a cant lass,[1] and slip a shilling into my hand, as a Christmas box; and from that I went on to think of his fondness for Heathcliff, and his dread lest he should suffer neglect after death had removed him; and that naturally led me to consider the poor lad's situation now, and from singing I changed my mind to crying. It struck me soon, however, there would be more sense in endeavouring to repair some of his wrongs than shedding tears over them. I got up and walked into the court to seek him.

He was not far; I found him smoothing the glossy coat of the new pony in the stable, and feeding the other beasts, according to custom.

"Make haste, Heathcliff!" I said, "the kitchen is so comfortable—and Joseph is upstairs; make haste, and let me dress you smart before Miss Cathy comes out, and then you can sit together, with

1. Lively girl.

the whole hearth to yourselves, and have a long chatter till bed-time."

He proceeded with his task and never turned his head towards me.

"Come—are you coming?" I continued. "There's a little cake for each of you, nearly enough; and you'll need half an hour's donning."

I waited five minutes, but getting no answer left him. Catherine supped with her brother and sister-in-law: Joseph and I joined at an unsociable meal seasoned with reproofs on one side and sauciness on the other. His cake and cheese remained on the table all night for the fairies. He managed to continue work till nine o'clock, and then marched dumb and dour to his chamber.

Cathy sat up late, having a world of things to order for the reception of her new friends: she came into the kitchen, once, to speak to her old one, but he was gone, and she only stayed to ask what was the matter with him, and then went back.

In the morning, he rose early; and, as it was a holiday, carried his ill-humour onto the moors, not re-appearing till the family were departed for church. Fasting and reflection seemed to have brought him to a better spirit. He hung about me for a while, and having screwed up his courage, exclaimed abruptly—

"Nelly, make me decent, I'm going to be good."

"High time, Heathcliff," I said, "you *have* grieved Catherine; she's sorry she ever came home, I dare say! It looks as if you envied her, because she is more thought of than you."

The notion of *envying* Catherine was incomprehensible to him, but the notion of grieving her he understood clearly enough.

"Did she say she was grieved?" he inquired, looking very serious.

"She cried when I told her you were off again this morning."

"Well, *I* cried last night," he returned, "and I had more reason to cry than she."

"Yes, you had the reason of going to bed with a proud heart and an empty stomach," said I. "Proud people breed sad sorrows for themselves. But, if you be ashamed of your touchiness, you must ask pardon, mind, when she comes in. You must go up and offer to kiss her, and say—you know best what to say, only do it heartily, and not as if you thought her converted into a stranger by her grand dress. And now, though I have dinner to get ready, I'll steal time to arrange you so that Edgar Linton shall look quite a doll beside you: and that he does. You are younger, and yet, I'll be bound, you are taller and twice as broad across the shoulders—you could knock him down in a twinkling: don't you feel that you could?"

Heathcliff's face brightened a moment; then it was overcast afresh, and he sighed.

"But, Nelly, if I knocked him down twenty times, that wouldn't make him less handsome, or me more so. I wish I had light hair and a fair skin, and was dressed and behaved as well, and had a chance of being as rich as he will be!"

"And cried for mamma, at every turn," I added, "and trembled if a country lad heaved his fist against you, and sat at home all day for a shower of rain. O, Heathcliff, you are showing a poor spirit! Come to the glass, and I'll let you see what you should wish. Do you mark those two lines between your eyes; and those thick brows, that instead of rising arched, sink in the middle; and that couple of black fiends, so deeply buried, who never open their windows boldly, but lurk glinting under them, like devil's spies? Wish and learn to smooth away the surly wrinkles, to raise your lids frankly, and change the fiends to confident, innocent angels, suspecting and doubting nothing, and always seeing friends where they are not sure of foes. Don't get the expression of a vicious cur that appears to know the kicks it gets are its desert, and yet hates all the world, as well as the kicker, for what it suffers."

"In other words, I must wish for Edgar Linton's great blue eyes, and even forehead," he replied. "I do—and that won't help me to them."

"A good heart will help you to a bonny face, my lad," I continued, "if you were a regular black; and a bad one will turn the bonniest into something worse than ugly. And now that we've done washing, and combing, and sulking—tell me whether you don't think yourself rather handsome? I'll tell you, I do. You're fit for a prince in disguise. Who knows but your father was Emperor of China, and your mother an Indian queen, each of them able to buy up, with one week's income, Wuthering Heights and Thrushcross Grange together? And you were kidnapped by wicked sailors, and brought to England. Were I in your place, I would frame high notions of my birth; and the thoughts of what I was should give me courage and dignity to support the oppressions of a little farmer!"

So I chattered on; and Heathcliff gradually lost his frown, and began to look quite pleasant, when, all at once, our conversation was interrupted by a rumbling sound moving up the road and entering the court. He ran to the window, and I to the door, just in time to behold the two Lintons descend from the family carriage, smothered in cloaks and furs, and the Earnshaws dismount from their horses—they often rode to church in winter. Catherine took a hand of each of the children, and brought them into the house, and set them before the fire, which quickly put colour into their white faces.

I urged my companion to hasten now, and show his amiable humour, and he willingly obeyed; but ill luck would have it that, as he opened the door leading from the kitchen on one side, Hindley opened it on the other. They met, and the master, irritated at seeing him clean and cheerful, or, perhaps, eager to keep his promise to Mrs. Linton, shoved him back with a sudden thrust, and angrily bade Joseph "keep the fellow out of the room—send him into the garret till dinner is over. He'll be cramming his fingers in the tarts, and stealing the fruit, if left alone with them a minute."

"Nay, sir," I could not avoid answering, "he'll touch nothing, not he—and, I suppose, he must have his share of the dainties as well as we."

"He shall have his share of my hand, if I catch him downstairs again till dark," cried Hindley. "Begone, you vagabond! What! you are attempting the coxcomb, are you? Wait till I get hold of those elegant locks—see if I won't pull them a bit longer!"

"They are long enough already," observed Master Linton, peeping from the door-way; "I wonder they don't make his head ache. It's like a colt's mane over his eyes!"

He ventured this remark without any intention to insult; but Heathcliff's violent nature was not prepared to endure the appearance of impertinence from one whom he seemed to hate, even then, as a rival. He seized a tureen of hot apple-sauce, the first thing that came under his gripe, and dashed it full against the speaker's face and neck—who instantly commenced a lament that brought Isabella and Catherine hurrying to the place.

Mr. Earnshaw snatched up the culprit directly and conveyed him to his chamber, where, doubtless, he administered a rough remedy to cool the fit of passion, for he reappeared red and breathless. I got the dish-cloth, and, rather spitefully, scrubbed Edgar's nose and mouth, affirming it served him right for meddling. His sister began weeping to go home, and Cathy stood by, confounded, blushing for all.

"You should not have spoken to him!" she expostulated with Master Linton. "He was in a bad temper, and now you've spoilt your visit, and he'll be flogged—I hate him to be flogged! I can't eat my dinner. Why did you speak to him, Edgar?"

"I didn't," sobbed the youth, escaping from my hands, and finishing the remainder of the purification with his cambric pocket-handkerchief. "I promised mamma that I wouldn't say one word to him, and I didn't!"

"Well, don't cry!" replied Catherine, contemptuously. "You're not killed—don't make more mischief—my brother is coming—be quiet! Give over, Isabella! Has anybody hurt *you*?"

"There, there, children—to your seats!" cried Hindley, bustling in. "That brute of a lad has warmed me nicely. Next time, Master Edgar, take the law into your own fists—it will give you an appetite!"

The little party recovered its equanimity at sight of the fragrant feast. They were hungry after their ride, and easily consoled, since no real harm had befallen them.

Mr. Earnshaw carved bountiful platefuls; and the mistress made them merry with lively talk. I waited behind her chair, and was pained to behold Catherine, with dry eyes and an indifferent air, commence cutting up the wing of a goose before her.

"An unfeeling child," I thought to myself, "how lightly she dismisses her old playmate's troubles. I could not have imagined her to be so selfish."

She lifted a mouthful to her lips; then she set it down again: her cheeks flushed, and the tears gushed over them. She slipped her fork to the floor, and hastily dived under the cloth to conceal her emotion. I did not call her unfeeling long, for I perceived she was in purgatory throughout the day, and wearying to find an opportunity of getting by herself, or paying a visit to Heathcliff, who had been locked up by the master, as I discovered on endeavouring to introduce to him a private mess of victuals.

In the evening we had a dance. Cathy begged that he might be liberated then, as Isabella Linton had no partner; her entreaties were vain, and I was appointed to supply the deficiency.

We got rid of all gloom in the excitement of the exercise, and our pleasure was increased by the arrival of the Gimmerton band, mustering fifteen strong: a trumpet, a trombone, clarionets, bassoons, French horns, and a bass viol, besides singers. They go the rounds of all the respectable houses, and receive contributions every Christmas, and we esteemed it a first-rate treat to hear them.

After the usual carols had been sung, we set them to songs and glees. Mrs. Earnshaw loved the music, and so they gave us plenty.

Catherine loved it too; but she said it sounded sweetest at the top of the steps, and she went up in the dark; I followed. They shut the house door below, never noting our absence, the place was so full of people. She made no stay at the stairs' head, but mounted farther, to the garret where Heathcliff was confined, and called him. He stubbornly declined answering for a while; she persevered, and finally persuaded him to hold communion with her through the boards.

I let the poor things converse unmolested, till I supposed the songs were going to cease, and the singers to get some refreshment: then, I clambered up the ladder to warn her.

Instead of finding her outside, I heard her voice within. The little monkey had crept by the skylight of one garret, along the roof, into the skylight of the other, and it was with the utmost difficulty I could coax her out again.

When she did come, Heathcliff came with her; and she insisted that I should take him into the kitchen, as my fellow-servant had gone to a neighbour's to be removed from the sound of our "devil's psalmody," as it pleased him to call it.

I told them I intended, by no means, to encourage their tricks; but as the prisoner had never broken his fast since yesterday's dinner, I would wink at his cheating Mr. Hindley that once.

He went down; I set him a stool by the fire, and offered him a quantity of good things; but he was sick and could eat little, and my attempts to entertain him were thrown away. He leant his two elbows on his knees, and his chin on his hands, and remained wrapt in dumb meditation. On my inquiring the subject of his thoughts, he answered gravely—

"I'm trying to settle how I shall pay Hindley back. I don't care how long I wait, if I can only do it, at last. I hope he will not die before I do!"

"For shame, Heathcliff!" said I. "It is for God to punish wicked people; we should learn to forgive."

"No, God won't have the satisfaction that I shall," he returned. "I only wish I knew the best way! Let me alone, and I'll plan it out: while I'm thinking of that, I don't feel pain."

But, Mr. Lockwood, I forget these tales cannot divert you. I'm annoyed how I should dream of chattering on at such a rate; and your gruel cold, and you nodding for bed! I could have told Heathcliff's history, all that you need hear, in half-a-dozen words.

Thus interrupting herself, the housekeeper rose, and proceeded to lay aside her sewing; but I felt incapable of moving from the hearth, and I was very far from nodding.

"Sit still, Mrs. Dean," I cried, "do sit still, another half hour! You've done just right to tell the story leisurely. That is the method I like; and you must finish in the same style. I am interested in every character you have mentioned, more or less."

"The clock is on the stroke of eleven, sir."

"No matter—I'm not accustomed to go to bed in the long hours. One or two is early enough for a person who lies till ten."

"You shouldn't lie till ten. There's the very prime of the morning gone long before that time. A person who has not done one half his day's work by ten o'clock runs a chance of leaving the other half undone."

"Nevertheless, Mrs. Dean, resume your chair; because to-morrow I intend lengthening the night till afternoon. I prognosticate for myself an obstinate cold, at least."

"I hope not, sir. Well, you must allow me to leap over some three years; during that space Mrs. Earnshaw—"

"No, no, I'll allow nothing of the sort! Are you acquainted with the mood of mind in which, if you were seated alone, and the cat licking its kitten on the rug before you, you would watch the operation so intently that puss's neglect of one ear would put you seriously out of temper?"

"A terribly lazy mood, I should say."

"On the contrary, a tiresomely active one. It is mine, at present, and, therefore, continue minutely. I perceive that people in these regions acquire over people in towns the value that a spider in a dungeon does over a spider in a cottage, to their various occupants; and yet the deepened attraction is not entirely owing to the situation of the looker-on. They *do* live more in earnest, more in themselves, and less in surface change, and frivolous external things. I could fancy a love for life here almost possible; and I was a fixed unbeliever in any love of a year's standing. One state resembles setting a hungry man down to a single dish on which he may concentrate his entire appetite, and do it justice; the other, introducing him to a table laid out by French cooks. He can perhaps extract as much enjoyment from the whole, but each part is a mere atom in his regard and remembrance."

"Oh! here we are the same as anywhere else, when you get to know us," observed Mrs. Dean, somewhat puzzled at my speech.

"Excuse me," I responded; "you, my good friend, are a striking evidence against that assertion. Excepting a few provincialisms of slight consequence, you have no marks of the manners that I am habituated to consider as peculiar to your class. I am sure you have thought a great deal more than the generality of servants think. You have been compelled to cultivate your reflective faculties, for want of occasions for frittering your life away in silly trifles."

Mrs. Dean laughed.

"I certainly esteem myself a steady, reasonable kind of body," she said, "not exactly from living among the hills and seeing one set of faces, and one series of actions, from year's end to year's end; but I have undergone sharp discipline which has taught me wisdom; and then, I have read more than you would fancy, Mr. Lockwood. You could not open a book in this library that I have not looked into, and got something out of also, unless it be that range of Greek and Latin, and that of French—and those I know one from another: it is as much as you can expect of a poor man's daughter."

"However, if I am to follow my story in true gossip's fashion, I had better go on; and instead of leaping three years, I will be content to pass to the next summer—the summer of 1778, that is, nearly twenty-three years ago."

Chapter VIII

On the morning of a fine June day, my first bonny little nursling, and the last of the ancient Earnshaw stock, was born.

We were busy with the hay in a far-away field, when the girl that usually brought our breakfasts came running, an hour too soon, across the meadow and up the lane, calling me as she ran.

"Oh, such a grand bairn!" she panted out. "The finest lad that ever breathed! But the doctor says missis must go; he says she's been in a consumption these many months. I heard him tell Mr. Hindley: and now she has nothing to keep her, and she'll be dead before winter. You must come home directly. You're to nurse it, Nelly—to feed it with sugar and milk, and take care of it, day and night. I wish I were you, because it will be all yours when there is no missis!"

"But is she very ill?" I asked, flinging down my rake, and tying my bonnet.

"I guess she is; yet she looks bravely," replied the girl, "and she talks as if she thought of living to see it grow a man. She's out of her head for joy, it's such a beauty! If I were her, I'm certain I should not die. I should get better at the bare sight of it, in spite of Kenneth. I was fairly mad at him. Dame Archer brought the cherub down to master, in the house, and his face just began to light up, when the old croaker steps forward, and, says he—'Earnshaw, it's a blessing your wife has been spared to leave you this son. When she came, I felt convinced we shouldn't keep her long; and now, I must tell you, the winter will probably finish her. Don't take on, and fret about it too much, it can't be helped. And besides, you should have known better than to choose such a rush of a lass!' "[1]

"And what did the master answer?" I enquired.

"I think he swore—but I didn't mind him, I was straining to see the bairn," and she began again to describe it rapturously. I, as zealous as herself, hurried eagerly home to admire, on my part, though I was very sad for Hindley's sake; he had room in his heart only for two idols—his wife and himself: he doted on both, and adored one, and I couldn't conceive how he would bear the loss.

When we got to Wuthering Heights, there he stood at the front door; and, as I passed in, I asked, how was the baby?

"Nearly ready to run about, Nell!" he replied, putting on a cheerful smile.

"And the mistress?" I ventured to inquire, "the doctor says she's—"

1. Slender, delicate as a reed.

"Damn the doctor!" he interrupted, reddening. "Frances is quite right—she'll be perfectly well by this time next week. Are you going upstairs? will you tell her that I'll come, if she'll promise not to talk? I left her because she would not hold her tongue; and she must—tell her Mr. Kenneth says she must be quiet."

I delivered this message to Mrs. Earnshaw; she seemed in flighty spirits, and replied merrily—

"I hardly spoke a word, Ellen, and there he has gone out twice, crying. Well, say I promise I won't speak; but that does not bind me not to laugh at him!"

Poor soul! Till within a week of her death that gay heart never failed her; and her husband persisted doggedly, nay, furiously, in affirming her health improved every day. When Kenneth warned him that his medicines were useless at that stage of the malady, and he needn't put him to further expense by attending her, he retorted—

"I know you need not—she's well—she does not want any more attendance from you! She never was in a consumption. It was a fever; and it is gone—her pulse is as slow as mine now, and her cheek as cool."

He told his wife the same story, and she seemed to believe him; but one night, while leaning on his shoulder, in the act of saying she thought she should be able to get up to-morrow, a fit of coughing took her—a very slight one. He raised her in his arms; she put her two hands about his neck, her face changed, and she was dead.

As the girl had anticipated, the child Hareton fell wholly into my hands. Mr. Earnshaw, provided he saw him healthy, and never heard him cry, was contented, as far as regarded him. For himself, he grew desperate; his sorrow was of that kind that will not lament. He neither wept nor prayed—he cursed and defied—execrated God and man, and gave himself up to reckless dissipation.

The servants could not bear his tyrannical and evil conduct long: Joseph and I were the only two that would stay. I had not the heart to leave my charge; and besides, you know, I had been his foster sister, and excused his behaviour more readily than a stranger would.

Joseph remained to hector over tenants and labourers, and because it was his vocation to be where there was plenty of wickedness to reprove.

The master's bad ways and bad companions formed a pretty example for Catherine and Heathcliff. His treatment of the latter was enough to make a fiend of a saint. And, truly, it appeared as if the lad *were* possessed of something diabolical at that period. He delighted to witness Hindley degrading himself past redemption; and became daily more notable for savage sullenness and ferocity.

I could not half tell what an infernal house we had. The curate dropped calling, and nobody decent came near us, at last, unless Edgar Linton's visits to Miss Cathy might be an exception. At fifteen she was the queen of the country-side; she had no peer, and she did turn out a haughty, headstrong creature! I own I did not like her after her infancy was past; and I vexed her frequently by trying to bring down her arrogance; she never took an aversion to me, though. She had a wondrous constancy to old attachments; even Heathcliff kept his hold on her affections unalterably, and young Linton, with all his superiority, found it difficult to make an equally deep impression.

He was my late master; that is his portrait over the fireplace. It used to hang on one side, and his wife's on the other; but hers has been removed, or else you might see something of what she was. Can you make that out?

Mrs. Dean raised the candle, and I discerned a soft-featured face, exceedingly resembling the young lady at the Heights, but more pensive and amiable in expression. It formed a sweet picture. The long light hair curled slightly on the temples; the eyes were large and serious; the figure almost too graceful. I did not marvel how Catherine Earnshaw could forget her first friend for such an individual. I marvelled much how he, with a mind to correspond with his person, could fancy my idea of Catherine Earnshaw.

"A very agreeable portrait," I observed to the housekeeper. "Is it like?"

"Yes," she answered; "but he looked better when he was animated; that is his every day countenance; he wanted spirit in general."

Catherine had kept up her acquaintance with the Lintons since her five weeks' residence among them; and as she had no temptation to show her rough side in their company, and had the sense to be ashamed of being rude where she experienced such invariable courtesy, she imposed unwittingly on the old lady and gentleman, by her ingenious cordiality; gained the admiration of Isabella, and the heart and soul of her brother—acquisitions that flattered her from the first, for she was full of ambition, and led her to adopt a double character without exactly intending to deceive anyone.

In the place where she heard Heathcliff termed a "vulgar young ruffian," and "worse than a brute," she took care not to act like him; but at home she had small inclination to practise politeness that would only be laughed at, and restrain an unruly nature when it would bring her neither credit nor praise.

Mr. Edgar seldom mustered courage to visit Wuthering Heights openly. He had a terror of Earnshaw's reputation, and shrunk from encountering him, and yet he was always received with our best attempts at civility: the master himself avoided offending him, knowing why he came, and if he could not be gracious, kept out of the way. I rather think his appearance there was distasteful to Catherine; she was not artful, never played the coquette, and had evidently an objection to her two friends meeting at all; for when Heathcliff expressed contempt of Linton, in his presence, she could not half coincide, as she did in his absence; and when Linton evinced disgust and antipathy to Heathcliff, she dare not treat his sentiments with indifference, as if depreciation of her playmate were of scarcely any consequence to her.

I've had many a laugh at her perplexities and untold troubles, which she vainly strove to hide from my mockery. That sounds ill-natured—but she was so proud, it became really impossible to pity her distresses, till she should be chastened into more humility.

She did bring herself, finally, to confess, and confide in me. There was not a soul else that she might fashion into an adviser.

Mr. Hindley had gone from home, one afternoon, and Heathcliff presumed to give himself a holiday on the strength of it. He had reached the age of sixteen then, I think, and without having bad features or being deficient in intellect, he contrived to convey an impression of inward and outward repulsiveness that his present aspect retains no traces of.

In the first place, he had, by that time, lost the benefit of his early education: continual hard work, begun soon and concluded late, had extinguished any curiosity he once possessed in pursuit of knowledge, and any love for books or learning. His childhood's sense of superiority, instilled into him by the favours of old Mr. Earnshaw, was faded away. He struggled long to keep up an equality with Catherine in her studies and yielded with poignant though silent regret: but he yielded completely; and there was no prevailing on him to take a step in the way of moving upward, when he found he must, necessarily, sink beneath his former level. Then personal appearance sympathised with mental deterioration; he acquired a slouching gait, and ignoble look; his naturally reserved disposition was exaggerated into an almost idiotic excess of unsociable moroseness; and he took a grim pleasure, apparently, in exciting the aversion rather than the esteem of his few acquaintance.

Catherine and he were constant companions still, at his seasons of respite from labour; but he had ceased to express his fondness for her in words, and recoiled with angry suspicion from her girlish caresses, as if conscious there could be no gratification in lavishing such marks of affection on him. On the before-named occasion he came into the house to announce his intention of doing nothing, while I was assisting Miss Cathy to arrange her dress: she had not reckoned on his taking it into his head to be idle, and imagining she would have the whole place to herself, she managed, by some means, to inform Mr. Edgar of her brother's absence, and was then preparing to receive him.

"Cathy, are you busy, this afternoon?" asked Heathcliff. "Are you going anywhere?"

"No, it is raining," she answered.

"Why have you that silk frock on, then?" he said. "Nobody coming here, I hope?"

"Not that I know of," stammered Miss, "but you should be in the field now, Heathcliff. It is an hour past dinner time; I thought you were gone."

"Hindley does not often free us from his accursed presence," observed the boy. "I'll not work any more to-day, I'll stay with you."

"O, but Joseph will tell," she suggested. "You'd better go!"

"Joseph is loading lime on the farther side of Pennistow Crag; it will take him till dark, and he'll never know."

So saying he lounged to the fire, and sat down. Catherine reflected an instant, with knitted brows—she found it needful to smooth the way for an intrusion.

"Isabella and Edgar Linton talked of calling this afternoon," she said, at the conclusion of a minute's silence. "As it rains, I hardly expect them; but they may come, and if they do, you run the risk of being scolded for no good."

"Order Ellen to say you are engaged, Cathy," he persisted. "Don't turn me out for those pitiful, silly friends of yours! I'm on the point, sometimes, of complaining that they—but I'll not—"

"That they what?" cried Catherine, gazing at him with a troubled countenance. "Oh, Nelly!" she added petulantly, jerking her head away from my hands, "you've combed my hair quite out of curl! That's enough, let me alone. What are you on the point of complaining about, Heathcliff?"

"Nothing—only look at the almanack on that wall." He pointed to a framed sheet hanging near the window, and continued—

"The crosses are for the evenings you have spent with the Lintons, the dots for those spent with me—do you see? I've marked every day."

"Yes—very foolish; as if I took notice!" replied Catherine in a peevish tone. "And where is the sense of that?"

"To show that I *do* take notice," said Heathcliff.

"And should I always be sitting with you?" she demanded, growing more irritated. "What good do I get? What do you talk about? You might be dumb or a baby for anything you say to amuse me, or for anything you do, either!"

"You never told me before that I talked too little, or that you disliked my company, Cathy!" exclaimed Heathcliff in much agitation.

"It is no company at all, when people know nothing and say nothing," she muttered.

Her companion rose up, but he hadn't time to express his feelings further, for a horse's feet were heard on the flags, and, having knocked gently, young Linton entered, his face brilliant with delight at the unexpected summons he had received.

Doubtless Catherine marked the difference between her friends as one came in, and the other went out. The contrast resembled what you see in exchanging a bleak, hilly, coal country, for a beautiful fertile valley; and his voice and greeting were as opposite as his aspect. He had a sweet, low manner of speaking, and pronounced his words as you do: that's less gruff than we talk here, and softer.

"I'm not come too soon, am I?" he said, casting a look at me. I had begun to wipe the plate, and tidy some drawers at the far end in the dresser.

"No," answered Catherine. "What are you doing there, Nelly?"

"My work, Miss," I replied. (Mr. Hindley had given me directions to make a third party in any private visits Linton chose to pay.)

She stepped behind me and whispered crossly, "Take yourself and your dusters off! When company are in the house, servants don't commence scouring and cleaning in the room where they are!"

"It's a good opportunity, now that master is away," I answered aloud: "he hates me to be fidgetting over these things in his presence. I'm sure Mr. Edgar will excuse me."

"I hate you to be fidgetting in *my* presence," exclaimed the young lady imperiously, not allowing her guest time to speak. She had failed to recover her equanimity since the little dispute with Heathcliff.

"I'm sorry for it, Miss Catherine!" was my response; and I proceeded assiduously with my occupation.

She, supposing Edgar could not see her, snatched the cloth from my hand, and pinched me, with a prolonged wrench, very spitefully on the arm.

I've said I did not love her, and rather relished mortifying her vanity, now and then; besides, she hurt me extremely, so I started up from my knees, and screamed out—

"O, Miss, that's a nasty trick! you have no right to nip me, and I'm not going to bear it!"

"I didn't touch you, you lying creature!" cried she, her fingers tingling to repeat the act, and her ears red with rage. She never had power to conceal her passion, it always set her whole complexion in a blaze.

"What's that, then?" I retorted, showing a decided purple witness to refute her.

She stamped her foot, wavered a moment, and then, irresistibly impelled by the naughty spirit within her, slapped me on the cheek a stinging blow that filled both eyes with water.

"Catherine, love! Catherine!" interposed Linton, greatly shocked at the double fault of falsehood and violence which his idol had committed.

"Leave the room, Ellen!" she repeated, trembling all over.

Little Hareton, who followed me everywhere, and was sitting near me on the floor, at seeing my tears commenced crying himself, and sobbed out complaints against "wicked Aunt Cathy," which drew her fury on to his unlucky head: she seized his shoulders, and shook him till the poor child waxed livid, and Edgar thoughtlessly laid hold of her hands to deliver him. In an instant one was wrung free, and the astonished young man felt it applied over his own ear in a way that could not be mistaken for jest.

He drew back in consternation. I lifted Hareton in my arms, and walked off to the kitchen with him, leaving the door of communication open, for I was curious to watch how they would settle their disagreement.

The insulted visitor moved to the spot where he had laid his hat, pale and with a quivering lip.

"That's right!" I said to myself. "Take warning and begone! It's a kindness to let you have a glimpse of her genuine disposition."

"Where are you going?" demanded Catherine, advancing to the door.

He swerved aside and attempted to pass.

"You must not go!" she exclaimed energetically.

"I must and shall!" he replied in a subdued voice.

"No," she persisted, grasping the handle; "not yet, Edgar Linton—sit down; you shall not leave me in that temper. I should be miserable all night, and I won't be miserable for you!"

"Can I stay after you have struck me?" asked Linton.

Catherine was mute.

"You've made me afraid, and ashamed of you," he continued; "I'll not come here again!"

Her eyes began to glisten and her lids to twinkle.

"And you told a deliberate untruth!" he said.

"I didn't!" she cried, recovering her speech. "I did nothing deliberately—Well, go, if you please—get away! And now I'll cry—I'll cry myself sick!"

She dropped down on her knees by a chair and set to weeping in serious earnest.

Edgar persevered in his resolution as far as the court; there he lingered. I resolved to encourage him.

"Miss is dreadfully wayward, sir!" I called out. "As bad as any marred child[2]—you'd better be riding home, or else she will be sick, only to grieve us."

The soft thing looked askance through the window: he possessed the power to depart, as much as a cat possesses the power to leave a mouse half killed, or a bird half eaten.

Ah, I thought, there will be no saving him—He's doomed, and flies to his fate!

And so it was; he turned abruptly, hastened into the house again, shut the door behind him; and, when I went in a while after to inform them that Earnshaw had come home rabid drunk, ready to pull the old place about our ears (his ordinary frame of mind in that condition), I saw the quarrel had merely effected a closer intimacy—had broken the outworks of youthful timidity, and enabled them to forsake the disguise of friendship, and confess themselves lovers.

Intelligence of Mr. Hindley's arrival drove Linton speedily to his horse, and Catherine to her chamber. I went to hide little Hareton, and to take the shot out of the master's fowling piece, which he was fond of playing with in his insane excitement, to the hazard of the lives of any who provoked, or even attracted his notice too much; and I had hit upon the plan of removing it, that he might do less mischief, if he did go the length of firing the gun.

Chapter IX

He entered, vociferating oaths dreadful to hear; and caught me in the act of stowing his son away in the kitchen cupboard. Hareton was impressed with a wholesome terror of encountering either his wild beast's fondness or his madman's rage; for in one he ran a chance of being squeezed and kissed to death, and in the other of being flung into the fire, or dashed against the wall; and the poor thing remained perfectly quiet wherever I chose to put him.

"There, I've found it out at last!" cried Hindley, pulling me back by the skin of the neck, like a dog. "By Heaven and Hell, you've sworn between you to murder that child! I know how it is, now, that he is always out of my way. But, with the help of Satan, I shall make you swallow the carving knife, Nelly! You needn't laugh; for I've just crammed Kenneth, head-downmost, in the Blackhorse marsh; and two is the same as one—and I want to kill some of you, I shall have no rest till I do!"

"But I don't like the carving knife, Mr. Hindley," I answered; "it has been cutting red herrings. I'd rather be shot, if you please."

"You'd rather be damned!" he said, "and so you shall. No law in

2. Spoiled child.

England can hinder a man from keeping his house decent, and mine's abominable! open your mouth."

He held the knife in his hand, and pushed its point between my teeth: but, for my part, I was never much afraid of his vagaries. I spat out, and affirmed it tasted detestably—I would not take it on any account.

"Oh!" said he, releasing me, "I see that hideous little villain is not Hareton: I beg your pardon, Nell. If it be, he deserves flaying alive for not running to welcome me, and for screaming as if I were a goblin. Unnatural cub, come hither! I'll teach thee to impose on a good-hearted, deluded father. Now, don't you think the lad would be handsomer cropped? It makes a dog fiercer, and I love something fierce—get me a scissors—something fierce and trim! Besides, it's infernal affectation—devilish conceit it is—to cherish our ears: we're asses enough without them. Hush, child, hush! well, then, it is my darling! wisht, dry thy eyes—there's a joy; kiss me; what! it won't? kiss me, Hareton! Damn thee, kiss me! By God, as if I would rear such a monster! As sure as I'm living, I'll break the brat's neck."

Poor Hareton was squalling and kicking in his father's arms with all his might, and redoubled his yells when he carried him upstairs and lifted him over the banister. I cried out that he would frighten the child into fits, and ran to rescue him.

As I reached them, Hindley leant forward on the rails to listen to a noise below, almost forgetting what he had in his hands.

"Who is that?" he asked, hearing some one approaching the stair's foot.

I leant forward also, for the purpose of signing to Heathcliff, whose step I recognized, not to come further; and, at the instant when my eye quitted Hareton, he gave a sudden spring, delivered himself from the careless grasp that held him, and fell.

There was scarcely time to experience a thrill of horror before we saw that the little wretch was safe. Heathcliff arrived underneath just at the critical moment; by a natural impulse, he arrested his descent, and setting him on his feet, looked up to discover the author of the accident.

A miser who has parted with a lucky lottery ticket for five shillings, and finds next day he has lost in the bargain five thousand pounds, could not show a blanker countenance than he did on beholding the figure of Mr. Earnshaw above. It expressed, plainer than words could do, the intensest anguish at having made himself the instrument of thwarting his own revenge. Had it been dark, I dare say, he would have tried to remedy the mistake by smashing Hareton's skull on the steps; but we witnessed his salvation; and I was presently below with my precious charge pressed to my heart.

Hindley descended more leisurely, sobered and abashed.

"It is your fault, Ellen," he said, "you should have kept him out of sight; you should have taken him from me! Is he injured anywhere?"

"Injured!" I cried angrily, "If he's not killed, he'll be an idiot! Oh! I wonder his mother does not rise from her grave to see how you use him. You're worse than a heathen—treating your own flesh and blood in that manner!"

He attempted to touch the child, who, on finding himself with me, sobbed off his terror directly. At the first finger his father laid on him, however, he shrieked again louder than before, and struggled as if he would go into convulsions.

"You shall not meddle with him!" I continued, "He hates you—they all hate you—that's the truth! A happy family you have; and a pretty state you're come to!"

"I shall come to a prettier, yet, Nelly!" laughed the misguided man, recovering his hardness. "At present, convey yourself and him away. And, hark you, Heathcliff! clear you too, quite from my reach and hearing. I wouldn't murder you to-night, unless, perhaps, I set the house on fire; but that's as my fancy goes—"

While saying this he took a pint bottle of brandy from the dresser, and poured some into a tumbler.

"Nay, don't!" I entreated, "Mr. Hindley, do take warning. Have mercy on this unfortunate boy, if you care nothing for yourself!"

"Any one will do better for him than I shall," he answered.

"Have mercy on your own soul!" I said, endeavouring to snatch the glass from his hand.

"Not I! on the contrary, I shall have great pleasure in sending it to perdition, to punish its Maker," exclaimed the blasphemer. "Here's to its hearty damnation!"

He drank the spirits, and impatiently bade us go; terminating his command with a sequel of horrid imprecations, too bad to repeat or remember.

"It's a pity he cannot kill himself with drink," observed Heathcliff, muttering an echo of curses back when the door was shut. "He's doing his very utmost; but his constitution defies him. Mr. Kenneth says he would wager his mare, that he'll outlive any man on this side Gimmerton, and go to the grave a hoary sinner; unless some happy chance out of the common course befall him."

I went into the kitchen and sat down to lull my little lamb to sleep. Heathcliff, as I thought, walked through to the barn. It turned out, afterwards, that he only got as far as the other side the settle, when he flung himself on a bench by the wall, removed from the fire, and remained silent.

I was rocking Hareton on my knee, and humming a song that began—

"It was far in the night, and the bairnies grat,
The mither beneath the mools heard that,"[1]

when Miss Cathy, who had listened to the hubbub from her room, put her head in, and whispered—

"Are you alone, Nelly?"

"Yes, Miss," I replied.

She entered and approached the hearth. I, supposing she was going to say something, looked up. The expression of her face seemed disturbed and anxious. Her lips were half asunder as if she meant to speak; and she drew a breath, but it escaped in a sigh, instead of a sentence.

I resumed my song, not having forgotten her recent behaviour.

"Where's Heathcliff?" she said, interrupting me.

"About his work in the stable," was my answer.

He did not contradict me; perhaps he had fallen into a doze.

There followed another long pause, during which I perceived a drop or two trickle from Catherine's cheek to the flags.

Is she sorry for her shameful conduct? I asked myself. That will be a novelty, but she may come to the point as she will—I shan't help her!

No, she felt small trouble regarding any subject, save her own concerns.

"Oh, dear!" she cried at last. "I'm very unhappy!"

"A pity," observed I. "You're hard to please—so many friends and so few cares, and can't make yourself content!"

"Nelly, will you keep a secret for me?" she pursued, kneeling down by me, and lifting her winsome eyes to my face with that sort of look which turns off bad temper, even when one has all the right in the world to indulge it.

"Is it worth keeping?" I inquired, less sulkily.

"Yes, and it worries me, and I must let it out! I want to know what I should do. To-day, Edgar Linton has asked me to marry him, and I've given him an answer. Now, before I tell you whether it was a consent, or denial, you tell me which it ought to have been."

"Really, Miss Catherine, how can I know?" I replied. "To be sure, considering the exhibition you performed in his presence this afternoon, I might say it would be wise to refuse him: since he asked you after that, he must either be hopelessly stupid or a venturesome fool."

1. "It was late in the night, and the little ones wept, / The mother in the grave heard that,"

"If you talk so, I won't tell you any more," she returned, peevishly, rising to her feet, "I accepted him, Nelly. Be quick, and say whether I was wrong!"

"You accepted him? then, what good is it discussing the matter? You have pledged your word, and cannot retract."

"But, say whether I should have done so—do!" she exclaimed in an irritated tone, chafing her hands together, and frowning.

"There are many things to be considered before that question can be answered properly," I said sententiously. "First and foremost, do you love Mr. Edgar?"

"Who can help it? Of course I do," she answered.

Then I put her through the following catechism: for a girl of twenty-two, it was not injudicious.

"Why do you love him, Miss Cathy?"

"Nonsense, I do—that's sufficient."

"By no means; you must say why."

"Well, because he is handsome, and pleasant to be with."

"Bad," was my commentary.

"And because he is young and cheerful."

"Bad, still."

"And because he loves me."

"Indifferent, coming there."

"And he will be rich, and I shall like to be the greatest woman of the neighbourhood, and I shall be proud of having such a husband."

"Worst of all! And now, say how you love him."

"As everybody loves—You're silly, Nelly."

"Not at all—Answer."

"I love the ground under his feet, and the air over his head, and everything he touches, and every word he says—I love all his looks, and all his actions, and him entirely, and altogether. There now!"

"And why?"

"Nay—you are making a jest of it; it is exceedingly ill-natured! It's no jest to me!" said the young lady, scowling, and turning her face to the fire.

"I'm very far from jesting, Miss Catherine," I replied. "You love Mr. Edgar, because he is handsome, and young, and cheerful, and rich, and loves you. The last, however, goes for nothing. You would love him without that, probably; and with it, you wouldn't, unless he possessed the four former attractions."

"No, to be sure not—I should only pity him—hate him, perhaps, if he were ugly, and a clown."

"But there are several other handsome, rich young men in the world; handsomer, possibly, and richer than he is. What should hinder you from loving them?"

"If there be any, they are out of my way—I've seen none like Edgar."

"You may see some; and he won't always be handsome, and young, and may not always be rich."

"He is now; and I have only to do with the present—I wish you would speak rationally."

"Well, that settles it—if you have only to do with the present, marry Mr. Linton."

"I don't want your permission for that—I *shall* marry him; and yet you have not told me whether I'm right."

"Perfectly right; if people be right to marry only for the present. And now, let us hear what you are unhappy about. Your brother will be pleased; the old lady and gentleman will not object, I think; you will escape from a disorderly, comfortless home into a wealthy, respectable one; and you love Edgar, and Edgar loves you. All seems smooth and easy—where is the obstacle?"

"*Here!* and *here!*" replied Catherine, striking one hand on her forehead, and the other on her breast. "In whichever place the soul lives—in my soul, and in my heart, I'm convinced I'm wrong!"

"That's very strange! I cannot make it out."

"It's my secret; but if you will not mock at me, I'll explain it; I can't do it distinctly—but I'll give you a feeling of how I feel."

She seated herself by me again: her countenance grew sadder and graver, and her clasped hands trembled.

"Nelly, do you never dream queer dreams?" she said, suddenly, after some minutes' reflection.

"Yes, now and then," I answered.

"And so do I. I've dreamt in my life dreams that have stayed with me ever after, and changed my ideas; they've gone through and through me, like wine through water, and altered the colour of my mind. And this is one—I'm going to tell it—but take care not to smile at any part of it."

"Oh! don't, Miss Catherine!" I cried. "We're dismal enough without conjuring up ghosts and visions to perplex us. Come, come, be merry, and like yourself! Look at little Hareton—*he's* dreaming nothing dreary. How sweetly he smiles in his sleep!"

"Yes; and how sweetly his father curses in his solitude! You remember him, I dare say, when he was just such another as that chubby thing—nearly as young and innocent. However, Nelly, I shall oblige you to listen—it's not long; and I've no power to be merry to-night."

"I won't hear it, I won't hear it!" I repeated, hastily.

I was superstitious about dreams then, and am still; and Catherine had an unusual gloom in her aspect, that made me dread something from which I might shape a prophecy, and foresee a fearful catastrophe.

She was vexed, but she did not proceed. Apparently taking up another subject, she recommenced in a short time.

"If I were in heaven, Nelly, I should be extremely miserable."

"Because you are not fit to go there," I answered. "All sinners would be miserable in heaven."

"But it is not for that. I dreamt, once, that I was there."

"I tell you I won't harken to your dreams, Miss Catherine! I'll go to bed," I interrupted again.

She laughed, and held me down, for I made a motion to leave my chair.

"This is nothing," cried she; "I was only going to say that heaven did not seem to be my home; and I broke my heart with weeping to come back to earth; and the angels were so angry that they flung me out, into the middle of the heath on the top of Wuthering Heights; where I woke sobbing for joy. That will do to explain my secret, as well as the other. I've no more business to marry Edgar Linton than I have to be in heaven; and if the wicked man in there had not brought Heathcliff so low, I shouldn't have thought of it. It would degrade me to marry Heathcliff now; so he shall never know how I love him; and that, not because he's handsome, Nelly, but because he's more myself than I am. Whatever our souls are made of, his and mine are the same, and Linton's is as different as a moonbeam from lightning, or frost from fire."

Ere this speech ended, I became sensible of Heathcliff's presence. Having noticed a slight movement, I turned my head, and saw him rise from the bench, and steal out, noiselessly. He had listened till he heard Catherine say it would degrade her to marry him, and then he stayed to hear no farther.

My companion, sitting on the ground, was prevented by the back of the settle from remarking his presence or departure; but I started, and bade her hush!

"Why?" she asked, gazing nervously round.

"Joseph is here," I answered, catching, opportunely, the roll of his cartwheels up the road; "and Heathcliff will come in with him. I'm not sure whether he were not at the door this moment."

"Oh, he couldn't overhear me at the door!" said she. "Give me Hareton, while you get the supper, and when it is ready ask me to sup with you. I want to cheat my uncomfortable conscience, and be convinced that Heathcliff has no notion of these things. He has not, has he? He does not know what being in love is?"

"I see no reason that he should not know, as well as you," I returned; "and if *you* are his choice, he'll be the most unfortunate creature that ever was born! As soon as you become Mrs. Linton, he loses friend, and love, and all! Have you considered how you'll bear the separation, and how he'll bear to be quite deserted in the world? Because, Miss Catherine—"

"He quite deserted! we separated!" she exclaimed, with an accent of indignation. "Who is to separate us, pray? They'll meet the fate of Milo![2] Not as long as I live, Ellen—for no mortal creature. Every Linton on the face of the earth might melt into nothing, before I could consent to forsake Heathcliff. Oh, that's not what I intend—that's not what I mean! I shouldn't be Mrs. Linton were such a price demanded! He'll be as much to me as he has been all his lifetime. Edgar must shake off his antipathy, and tolerate him, at least. He will when he learns my true feelings towards him. Nelly, I see now, you think me a selfish wretch, but, did it never strike you that if Heathcliff and I married, we should be beggars? whereas, if I marry Linton, I can aid Heathcliff to rise, and place him out of my brother's power."

"With your husband's money, Miss Catherine?" I asked. "You'll find him not so pliable as you calculate upon: and, though I'm hardly a judge, I think that's the worst motive you've given yet for being the wife of young Linton."

"It is not," retorted she, "it is the best! The others were the satisfaction of my whims; and for Edgar's sake, too, to satisfy him. This is for the sake of one who comprehends in his person my feelings to Edgar and myself. I cannot express it; but surely you and everybody have a notion that there is, or should be, an existence of yours beyond you. What were the use of my creation if I were entirely contained here? My great miseries in this world have been Heathcliff's miseries, and I watched and felt each from the beginning; my great thought in living is himself. If all else perished, and *he* remained, I should still continue to be; and, if all else remained, and he were annihilated, the Universe would turn to a mighty stranger. I should not seem a part of it. My love for Linton is like the foliage in the woods. Time will change it, I'm well aware, as winter changes the trees—my love for Heathcliff resembles the eternal rocks beneath—a source of little visible delight, but necessary. Nelly, I *am* Heathcliff—he's always, always in my mind—not as a pleasure, any more than I am always a pleasure to myself—but, as my own being—so, don't talk of our separation again—it is impracticable; and—"

She paused, and hid her face in the folds of my gown; but I jerked it forcibly away. I was out of patience with her folly!

"If I can make any sense of your nonsense, Miss," I said, "it only

2. An athlete devoured by wild beasts when the tree he was trying to uproot bound him.

goes to convince me that you are ignorant of the duties you undertake in marrying; or else that you are a wicked, unprincipled girl. But trouble me with no more secrets. I'll not promise to keep them."

"You'll keep that?" she asked, eagerly.

"No, I'll not promise," I repeated.

She was about to insist, when the entrance of Joseph finished our conversation; and Catherine removed her seat to a corner, and nursed Hareton, while I made the supper.

After it was cooked, my fellow servant and I began to quarrel who should carry some to Mr. Hindley; and we didn't settle it till all was nearly cold. Then we came to the agreement that we would let him ask, if he wanted any, for we feared particularly to go into his presence when he had been some time alone.

"Und hah isn't that nowt comed in frough th' field, be this time? What is he abaht? girt eedle seeght!"[3] demanded the old man, looking round for Heathcliff.

"I'll call him," I replied. "He's in the barn, I've no doubt."

I went and called, but got no answer. On returning, I whispered to Catherine that he had heard a good part of what she said, I was sure; and told how I saw him quit the kitchen just as she complained of her brother's conduct regarding him.

She jumped up in a fine fright, flung Hareton onto the settle, and ran to seek for her friend herself, not taking leisure to consider why she was so flurried, or how her talk would have affected him.

She was absent such a while that Joseph proposed we should wait no longer. He cunningly conjectured they were staying away in order to avoid hearing his protracted blessing. They were "ill eneugh for ony fahl manners," he affirmed. And, on their behalf, he added that night a special prayer to the usual quarter of an hour's supplication before meat, and would have tacked another to the end of the grace, had not his young mistress broken in upon him with a hurried command that he must run down the road, and, wherever Heathcliff had rambled, find and make him re-enter directly!

"I want to speak to him, and I *must*, before I go upstairs," she said. "And the gate is open, he is somewhere out of hearing; for he would not reply, though I shouted at the top of the fold as loud as I could."

Joseph objected at first; she was too much in earnest, however, to suffer contradiction; and at last he placed his hat on his head, and walked grumbling forth.

Meantime, Catherine paced up and down the floor, exclaiming—

"I wonder where he is—I wonder where he *can* be! What did I

3. "And why has no one come in from the field by now? What is he doing, that great idle sight?"

say, Nelly? I've forgotten. Was he vexed at my bad humour this afternoon? Dear! tell me what I've said to grieve him. I do wish he'd come. I do wish he would!"

"What a noise for nothing!" I cried, though rather uneasy myself. "What a trifle scares you! It's surely no great cause of alarm that Heathcliff should take a moonlight saunter on the moors, or even lie too sulky to speak to us, in the hay-loft. I'll engage he's lurking there. See if I don't ferret him out!"

I departed to renew my search; its result was disappointment, and Joseph's quest ended in the same.

"Yon lad gets war un war!" observed he on re-entering. "He's left th' yate ut t' full swing, and Miss's pony has trodden dahn two rigs uh corn, un plottered through, raight o'er intuh t' meadow! Hahsomdiver, t' maister 'ull play t' divil to-morn, and he'll do weel. He's patience itsseln wi' sich careless, offald craters—patience itsseln, he is! Bud he'll nut be soa allus—yah's see, all on ye! Yah mumn't drive him aht uf his heead fur nowt!"[4]

"Have you found Heathcliff, you ass?" interrupted Catherine. "Have you been looking for him, as I ordered?"

"Aw sud more likker look for th' horse," he replied. "It 'ud be tuh more sense. Bud Aw can look for norther horse, nur man uf a neeght loike this—as black as t' chimbley! und Hathecliff's noan t' chap tuh coom ut *maw* whistle—happen he'll be less hard uh hearing wi' *ye!*"[5]

It *was* a very dark evening for summer: the clouds appeared inclined to thunder, and I said we had better all sit down; the approaching rain would be certain to bring him home without further trouble.

However, Catherine would not be persuaded into tranquillity. She kept wandering to and fro, from the gate to the door, in a state of agitation which permitted no repose; and at length took up a permanent situation on one side of the wall, near the road, where, heedless of my expostulations, and the growling thunder, and the great drops that began to plash around her, she remained, calling at intervals, and then listening, and then crying outright. She beat Hareton, or any child, at a good, passionate fit of crying.

About midnight, while we still sat up, the storm came rattling over the Heights in full fury. There was a violent wind, as well as

4. "That lad gets worse and worse . . . He's left the gate wide open, and Miss's pony has trodden down two rows of grain, and scrambled into the meadow. However, the master will be devilishly angry tomorrow, and he'll do well. He's patience itself with such careless, worthless creatures—patience itself, he is! But he'll not be so always—you'll see, all of you! You must not drive him out of his head for no reason!"

5. "I should like better to look for the horse . . . It would make more sense. But I can look for neither horse, nor man on a night like this—as black as a chimney! And Heathcliff's not someone to come at my whistle—but he'll be less hard of hearing with you."

thunder, and either one or the other split a tree off at the corner of the building; a huge bough fell across the roof, and knocked down a portion of the east chimney-stack, sending a clatter of stones and soot into the kitchen fire.

We thought a bolt had fallen in the middle of us, and Joseph swung onto his knees, beseeching the Lord to remember the Patriarchs Noah and Lot;[6] and, as in former times, spare the righteous, though he smote the ungodly. I felt some sentiment that it must be a judgment on us also. The Jonah, in my mind, was Mr. Earnshaw, and I shook the handle of his den that I might ascertain if he were yet living. He replied audibly enough, in a fashion which made my companion vociferate more clamorously than before that a wide distinction might be drawn between saints like himself, and sinners like his master. But the uproar passed away in twenty minutes, leaving us all unharmed, excepting Cathy, who got thoroughly drenched for her obstinacy in refusing to take shelter, and standing bonnetless and shawl-less to catch as much water as she could with her hair and clothes.

She came in and lay down on the settle, all soaked as she was, turning her face to the back, and putting her hands before it.

"Well, Miss!" I exclaimed, touching her shoulder; "you are not bent on getting your death, are you? Do you know what o'clock it is? Half-past twelve. Come! come to bed; there's no use waiting longer on that foolish boy—he'll be gone to Gimmerton, and he'll stay there now. He guesses we shouldn't wake[7] for him till this late hour; at least, he guesses that only Mr. Hindley would be up; and he'd rather avoid having the door opened by the master."

"Nay, nay, he's noan at Gimmerton!" said Joseph. "Aw's niver wonder, bud he's at t' bothom uf a bog-hoile. This visitation worn't for nowt, und Aw wod hev ye tuh look aht, Miss—yah muh be t' next. Thank Hivin for all! All warks togither for gooid tuh them as is chozzen and piked aht froo' th' rubbidge![8] Yah knaw whet t' Scripture ses—"

And he began quoting several texts; referring us to the chapters and verses where we might find them.

I, having vainly begged the wilful girl to rise and remove her wet

6. Noah and Lot respectively survived flood and fire and brimstone; the part of the Jonah story Nelly refers to is the ill luck he brought shipmates when he tried to flee God's directive. Jonah 1.

7. Wait up.

8. "No, no, he's not at Gimmerton. . . . It would not surprise me if he were at the bottom of a bog-hole. This visitation was not for nothing, and I would have to look out, Miss—you may be the next. Thank Heaven for all! All works together for good to them who are chosen and picked from out of the rubbish!" The allusion is to Romans 8.28: "And we know that all things work together for good to them that love God, to them who are the called according to his purpose."

things, left him preaching and her shivering, and betook myself to bed with little Hareton, who slept as fast as if every one had been sleeping round him.

I heard Joseph read on a while afterwards; then I distinguished his slow step on the ladder, and then I dropt asleep.

Coming down somewhat later than usual, I saw, by the sunbeams piercing the chinks of the shutters, Miss Catherine still seated near the fire-place. The house door was ajar, too; light entered from its unclosed windows; Hindley had come out, and stood on the kitchen hearth, haggard and drowsy.

"What ails you, Cathy?" he was saying when I entered; "you look as dismal as a drowned whelp. Why are you so damp and pale, child?"

"I've been wet," she answered reluctantly, "and I'm cold, that's all."

"Oh, she is naughty!" I cried, perceiving the master to be tolerably sober. "She got steeped in the shower of yesterday evening, and there she has sat the night through, and I couldn't prevail on her to stir."

Mr. Earnshaw stared at us in surprise. "The night through," he repeated. "What kept her up, not fear of the thunder, surely? That was over, hours since."

Neither of us wished to mention Heathcliff's absence, as long as we could conceal it; so I replied, I didn't know how she took it into her head to sit up; and she said nothing.

The morning was fresh and cool; I threw back the lattice, and presently the room filled with sweet scents from the garden; but Catherine called peevishly to me—

"Ellen, shut the window. I'm starving!"[9] And her teeth chattered as she shrunk closer to the almost extinguished embers.

"She's ill," said Hindley, taking her wrist, "I suppose that's the reason she would not go to bed. Damn it! I don't want to be troubled with more sickness here. What took you into the rain?"

"Running after t'lads, as usuald!" croaked Joseph, catching an opportunity, from our hesitation, to thrust in his evil tongue.

"If Aw wur yah, maister, Aw'd just slam t' boards i' their faces, all on 'em, gentle and simple! Never a day ut yah're off, but yon cat uh Linton comes sneaking hither; and Miss Nelly shoo's a fine lass! shoo sits watching for ye i' t' kitchen; and as yah're in at one door, he's aht at t' other; und, then, wer grand lady goes a coorting uf hor side! It's bonny behaviour, lurking amang t' fields, after twelve ut' night, wi that fahl, flaysome divil uf a gipsy, Heathcliff! They think *Aw'm* blind; but Aw'm noan, nowt ut t' soart! Aw seed young

9. Freezing.

Linton, boath coming and going, and Aw seed *yah*" (directing his discourse to me), "yah gooid fur nowt, slattenly witch! nip up und bolt intuh th' hahs, t' minute yah heard t' maister's horse fit clatter up t' road."[1]

"Silence, eavesdropper!" cried Catherine. "None of your insolence before me! Edgar Linton came yesterday, by chance, Hindley; and it was *I* who told him to be off, because I knew you would not like to have met him as you were."

"You lie, Cathy, no doubt," answered her brother, "and you are a confounded simpleton! But never mind Linton, at present. Tell me, were you not with Heathcliff last night? Speak the truth, now. You need not be afraid of harming him: though I hate him as much as ever, he did me a good turn a short time since, that will make my conscience tender of breaking his neck. To prevent it, I shall send him about his business this very morning; and after he's gone, I'd advise you all to look sharp, I shall only have the more humour for you!"

"I never saw Heathcliff last night," answered Catherine, beginning to sob bitterly: "and if you do turn him out of doors, I'll go with him. But, perhaps, you'll never have an opportunity—perhaps, he's gone." Here she burst into uncontrollable grief, and the remainder of her words were inarticulate.

Hindley lavished on her a torrent of scornful abuse, and bid her get to her room immediately, or she shouldn't cry for nothing! I obliged her to obey; and I shall never forget what a scene she acted, when we reached her chamber. It terrified me. I thought she was going mad, and I begged Joseph to run for the doctor.

It proved the commencement of delirium; Mr. Kenneth, as soon as he saw her, pronounced her dangerously ill; she had a fever.

He bled her, and he told me to let her live on whey and water-gruel, and take care she did not throw herself downstairs, or out of the window; and then he left, for he had enough to do in the parish where two or three miles was the ordinary distance between cottage and cottage.

Though I cannot say I made a gentle nurse, and Joseph and the master were no better; and though our patient was as wearisome and headstrong as a patient could be, she weathered it through.

1. "If I were you, master, I'd just slam the doors in their faces, all of them, gentle and simple. [There's] not a day when you're away but that cat Linton doesn't come sneaking here, and Miss Nelly she's a fine lass! She sits waiting for you in the kitchen, and while you are in at one door, he's out at the other; and, then, our grand lady goes a courting on her side. It's some good behavior, lurking among the fields with that foul, dreadful devil of a gypsy, Heathcliff! They think I'm blind; but I'm not, nothing of the sort! I saw young Linton, both coming and going, and I saw you . . . you good-for-nothing, slovenly witch! Jump up and run into the house the minute you heard the master's horse's feet clatter up the road."

Old Mrs. Linton paid us several visits, to be sure, and set things to rights, and scolded and ordered us all; and when Catherine was convalescent, she insisted on conveying her to Thrushcross Grange: for which deliverance we were very grateful. But the poor dame had reason to repent of her kindness; she and her husband both took the fever, and died within a few days of each other.

Our young lady returned to us, saucier and more passionate, and haughtier than ever. Heathcliff had never been heard of since the evening of the thunder-storm, and, one day, I had the misfortune, when she had provoked me exceedingly, to lay the blame of his disappearance on her (where indeed it belonged, as she well knew). From that period, for several months, she ceased to hold any communication with me, save in the relation of a mere servant. Joseph fell under a ban also; he *would* speak his mind, and lecture her all the same as if she were a little girl; and she esteemed herself a woman, and our mistress, and thought that her recent illness gave her a claim to be treated with consideration. Then the doctor had said that she would not bear crossing much, she ought to have her own way; and it was nothing less than murder, in her eyes, for any one to presume to stand up and contradict her.

From Mr. Earnshaw and his companions she kept aloof; and tutored by Kenneth, and serious threats of a fit that often attended her rages, her brother allowed her whatever she pleased to demand, and generally avoided aggravating her fiery temper. He was rather *too* indulgent in humouring her caprices; not from affection, but from pride, he wished earnestly to see her bring honour to the family by an alliance with the Lintons, and, as long as she let him alone, she might trample us like slaves for ought he cared!

Edgar Linton, as multitudes have been before and will be after him, was infatuated; and believed himself the happiest man alive on the day he led her to Gimmerton chapel, three years subsequent to his father's death.

Much against my inclination, I was persuaded to leave Wuthering Heights and accompany her here. Little Hareton was nearly five years old, and I had just begun to teach him his letters. We made a sad parting, but Catherine's tears were more powerful than ours. When I refused to go, and when she found her entreaties did not move me, she went lamenting to her husband and brother. The former offered me munificent wages; the latter ordered me to pack up. He wanted no women in the house, he said, now that there was no mistress; and as to Hareton, the curate should take him in hand, by and by. And so I had but one choice left, to do as I was ordered. I told the master he got rid of all decent people only to run to ruin a little faster; I kissed Hareton good-bye; and, since then, he has been a stranger, and it's very queer to think it, but I've no doubt he has completely forgotten all about Ellen Dean and that he was ever more than all the world to her, and she to him!

At this point of the housekeeper's story, she chanced to glance towards the time-piece over the chimney; and was in amazement on seeing the minute-hand measure half-past one. She would not hear of staying a second longer. In truth, I felt rather disposed to defer the sequel of her narrative myself: and now that she is vanished to her rest, and I have meditated for another hour or two, I shall summon courage to go, also, in spite of aching laziness of head and limbs.

Chapter X

A charming introduction to a hermit's life! Four weeks' torture, tossing and sickness! Oh, these bleak winds, and bitter, northern skies, and impassable roads, and dilatory country surgeons! And, oh, this dearth of the human physiognomy, and, worse than all, the terrible intimation of Kenneth that I need not expect to be out of doors till spring!

Mr. Heathcliff has just honoured me with a call. About seven days ago he sent me a brace of grouse—the last of the season. Scoundrel! He is not altogether guiltless in this illness of mine; and that I had a great mind to tell him. But, alas! how could I offend a man who was charitable enough to sit at my bedside a good hour, and talk on some other subject than pills and draughts, blisters and leeches?

This is quite an easy interval. I am too weak to read, yet I feel as if I could enjoy something interesting. Why not have up Mrs. Dean to finish her tale? I can recollect its chief incidents, as far as she had gone. Yes, I remember her hero had run off, and never been heard of for three years; and the heroine was married. I'll ring; she'll be delighted to find me capable of talking cheerfully.

Mrs. Dean came.

"It wants twenty minutes, sir, to taking the medicine," she commenced.

"Away, away with it!" I replied; "I desire to have—"

"The doctor says you must drop the powders."

"With all my heart! Don't interrupt me. Come and take your seat here. Keep your fingers from that bitter phalanx of vials. Draw your knitting out of your pocket—that will do—now continue the history of Mr. Heathcliff, from where you left off, to the present day. Did he finish his education on the Continent, and come back a gentleman? or did he get a sizer's place at college? or escape to America, and earn honours by drawing blood from his foster country? or make a fortune more promptly, on the English highways?"

"He may have done a little in all these vocations, Mr. Lockwood; but I couldn't give my word for any. I stated before that I didn't know how he gained his money; neither am I aware of the means he took to raise his mind from the savage ignorance into which it was sunk; but, with your leave, I'll proceed in my own fashion, if you think it will amuse and not weary you. Are you feeling better this morning?"

"Much."

"That's good news."

I got Miss Catherine and myself to Thrushcross Grange; and to my agreeable disappointment, she behaved infinitely better than I dared to expect. She seemed almost over-fond of Mr. Linton; and even to his sister, she showed plenty of affection. They were both very attentive to her comfort, certainly. It was not the thorn bending to the honeysuckles, but the honeysuckles embracing the thorn. There were no mutual concessions; one stood erect, and the others yielded; and who *can* be ill-natured and bad-tempered, when they encounter neither opposition nor indifference?

I observed that Mr. Edgar had a deep-rooted fear of ruffling her humour. He concealed it from her; but if ever he heard me answer sharply, or saw any other servant grow cloudy at some imperious order of hers, he would show his trouble by a frown of displeasure that never darkened on his own account. He, many a time, spoke sternly to me about my pertness; and averred that the stab of a knife could not inflict a worse pang than he suffered at seeing his lady vexed.

Not to grieve a kind master, I learnt to be less touchy; and, for the space of half a year, the gunpowder lay as harmless as sand, because no fire came near to explode it. Catherine had seasons of gloom and silence, now and then: they were respected with sympathizing silence by her husband, who ascribed them to an alteration in her constitution, produced by her perilous illness, as she was never subject to depression of spirits before. The return of sunshine was welcomed by answering sunshine from him. I believe I may assert that they were really in possession of deep and growing happiness.

It ended. Well, we *must* be for ourselves in the long run; the mild and generous are only more justly selfish than the domineering—and it ended when circumstances caused each to feel that the one's interest was not the chief consideration in the other's thoughts.

On a mellow evening in September, I was coming from the garden with a heavy basket of apples which I had been gathering. It had got dusk, and the moon looked over the high wall of the court, causing undefined shadows to lurk in the corners of the numerous projecting portions of the building. I set my burden on the house steps by the kitchen door, and lingered to rest and draw in a few more breaths of the soft, sweet air; my eyes were on the moon, and my back to the entrance, when I heard a voice behind me say—

"Nelly, is that you?"

It was a deep voice, and foreign in tone; yet there was something in the manner of pronouncing my name which made it sound familiar. I turned about to discover who spoke, fearfully, for the doors were shut, and I had seen nobody on approaching the steps.

Something stirred in the porch; and moving nearer, I distinguished a tall man dressed in dark clothes, with dark face and hair. He leant against the side, and held his fingers on the latch, as if intending to open for himself.

"Who can it be?" I thought. "Mr. Earnshaw? Oh, no! The voice has no resemblance to his."

"I have waited here an hour," he resumed, while I continued staring; "and the whole of that time all round has been as still as death. I dared not enter. You do not know me? Look, I'm not a stranger!"

A ray fell on his features; the cheeks were sallow, and half covered with black whiskers; the brows lowering, the eyes deep set and singular. I remembered the eyes.

"What!" I cried, uncertain whether to regard him as a worldly visitor, and I raised my hands in amazement. "What! you come back? Is it really you? Is it?"

"Yes, Heathcliff," he replied, glancing from me up to the windows, which reflected a score of glittering moons, but showed no lights from within. "Are they at home—where is she? Nelly, you are not glad—you needn't be so disturbed. Is she here? Speak! I want to have one word with her—your mistress. Go, and say some person from Gimmerton desires to see her."

"How will she take it?" I exclaimed. "What will she do? The surprise bewilders me—it will put her out of her head! And you *are* Heathcliff? But altered! Nay, there's no comprehending it. Have you been for a soldier?"

"Go, and carry my message," he interrupted impatiently; "I'm in hell till you do!"

He lifted the latch, and I entered; but when I got to the parlour where Mr. and Mrs. Linton were, I could not persuade myself to proceed.

At length, I resolved on making an excuse to ask if they would have the candles lighted, and I opened the door.

They sat together in a window whose lattice lay back against the wall, and displayed, beyond the garden trees and the wild green park, the valley of Gimmerton, with a long line of mist winding nearly to its top (for very soon after you pass the chapel, as you may have noticed, the sough that runs from the marshes joins a beck which follows the bend of the glen). Wuthering Heights rose above this silvery vapour; but our old house was invisible—it rather dips down on the other side.

Both the room and its occupants, and the scene they gazed on, looked wondrously peaceful. I shrank reluctantly from performing my errand, and was actually going away, leaving it unsaid, after having put my question about the candles, when a sense of my folly compelled me to return, and mutter—

"A person from Gimmerton wishes to see you, ma'am."

"What does he want?" asked Mrs. Linton.

"I did not question him," I answered.

"Well, close the curtains, Nelly," she said; "and bring up tea. I'll be back again directly."

She quitted the apartment; Mr. Edgar inquired carelessly, who it was?

"Some one the mistress does not expect," I replied. "That Heathcliff, you recollect him, sir, who used to live at Mr. Earnshaw's."

"What, the gipsy—the plough-boy?" he cried. "Why did you not say so to Catherine?"

"Hush! you must not call him by those names, master," I said. "She'd be sadly grieved to hear you. She was nearly heart-broken when he ran off; I guess his return will make a jubilee to her."

Mr. Linton walked to a window on the other side of the room that overlooked the court. He unfastened it, and leant out. I suppose they were below, for he exclaimed, quickly—

"Don't stand there, love! Bring the person in, if it be any one particular."

Ere long, I heard the click of the latch, and Catherine flew upstairs, breathless and wild, too excited to show gladness; indeed, by her face, you would rather have surmised an awful calamity.

"Oh, Edgar, Edgar!" she panted, flinging her arms round his neck. "Oh, Edgar, darling! Heathcliff's come back—he is!" And she tightened her embrace to a squeeze.

"Well, well," cried her husband, crossly, "don't strangle me for that! He never struck me as such a marvellous treasure. There is no need to be frantic!"

"I know you didn't like him," she answered, repressing a little the intensity of her delight. "Yet, for my sake, you must be friends now. Shall I tell him to come up?"

"Here?" he said, "into the parlour?"

"Where else?" she asked.

He looked vexed, and suggested the kitchen as a more suitable place for him.

Mrs. Linton eyed him with a droll expression—half angry, half laughing at his fastidiousness.

"No," she added, after a while; "I cannot sit in the kitchen. Set two tables here, Ellen; one for your master and Miss Isabella, being gentry; the other for Heathcliff and myself, being of the lower orders. Will that please you, dear? Or must I have a fire lighted elsewhere? If so, give directions. I'll run down and secure my guest. I'm afraid the joy is too great to be real!"

She was about to dart off again; but Edgar arrested her.

"*You* bid him step up," he said, addressing me; "and, Catherine, try to be glad, without being absurd! The whole household need not witness the sight of your welcoming a runaway servant as a brother."

I descended and found Heathcliff waiting under the porch, evidently anticipating an invitation to enter. He followed my guidance without waste of words, and I ushered him into the presence of the master and mistress, whose flushed cheeks betrayed signs of warm talking. But the lady's glowed with another feeling when her friend appeared at the door; she sprang forward, took both his hands, and led him to Linton; and then she seized Linton's reluctant fingers and crushed them into his.

Now fully revealed by the fire and candlelight, I was amazed, more than ever, to behold the transformation of Heathcliff. He had grown a tall, athletic, well-formed man, beside whom my master seemed quite slender and youth-like. His upright carriage suggested the idea of his having been in the army. His countenance was much older in expression and decision of feature than Mr. Linton's; it looked intelligent, and retained no marks of former degradation. A half-civilized ferocity lurked yet in the depressed brows and eyes full of black fire, but it was subdued; and his manner was even dignified, quite divested of roughness, though too stern for grace.

My master's surprise equalled or exceeded mine: he remained for a minute at a loss how to address the ploughboy, as he had called him. Heathcliff dropped his slight hand, and stood looking at him coolly till he chose to speak.

"Sit down, sir," he said, at length. "Mrs. Linton, recalling old times, would have me give you a cordial reception, and, of course, I am gratified when anything occurs to please her."

"And I also," answered Heathcliff, "especially if it be anything in which I have a part. I shall stay an hour or two willingly."

He took a seat opposite Catherine, who kept her gaze fixed on him as if she feared he would vanish were she to remove it. He did not raise his to her often; a quick glance now and then sufficed; but it flashed back, each time more confidently, the undisguised delight he drank from hers.

They were too much absorbed in their mutual joy to suffer embarrassment. Not so Mr. Edgar; he grew pale with pure annoyance, a feeling that reached its climax when his lady rose, and stepping across the rug, seized Heathcliff's hands again, and laughed like one beside herself.

"I shall think it a dream to-morrow!" she cried. "I shall not be able to believe that I have seen, and touched, and spoken to you once more—and yet, cruel Heathcliff! you don't deserve this welcome. To be absent and silent for three years, and never to think of me!"

"A little more than you have thought of me!" he murmured. "I heard of your marriage, Cathy, not long since; and, while waiting in the yard below, I meditated this plan: just to have one glimpse of your face, a stare of surprise, perhaps, and pretended pleasure; afterwards settle my score with Hindley; and then prevent the law by doing execution on myself. Your welcome has put these ideas out of my mind; but beware of meeting me with another aspect next time! Nay, you'll not drive me off again. You were really sorry for me, were you? Well, there was cause. I've fought through a bitter life since I last heard your voice, and you must forgive me, for I struggled only for you."

"Catherine, unless we are to have cold tea, please to come to the table," interrupted Linton, striving to preserve his ordinary tone, and a due measure of politeness. "Mr. Heathcliff will have a long walk, wherever he may lodge to-night; and I'm thirsty."

She took her post before the urn; and Miss Isabella came, summoned by the bell; then, having handed their chairs forward, I left the room.

The meal hardly endured ten minutes. Catherine's cup was never filled, she could neither eat nor drink. Edgar had made a slop in his saucer, and scarcely swallowed a mouthful.

Their guest did not protract his stay that evening above an hour longer. I asked, as he departed, if he went to Gimmerton?

"No, to Wuthering Heights," he answered, "Mr. Earnshaw invited me when I called this morning."

Mr. Earnshaw invited *him!* and *he* called on Mr. Earnshaw! I pondered this sentence painfully after he was gone. Is he turning out a bit of a hypocrite, and coming into the country to work mischief under a cloak? I mused—I had a presentiment, in the bottom of my heart, that he had better have remained away.

About the middle of the night, I was wakened from my first nap by Mrs. Linton gliding into my chamber, taking a seat on my bedside, and pulling me by the hair to rouse me.

"I cannot rest, Ellen," she said by way of apology. "And I want some living creature to keep me company in my happiness! Edgar is sulky, because I'm glad of a thing that does not interest him. He refuses to open his mouth, except to utter pettish, silly speeches; and he affirmed I was cruel and selfish for wishing to talk when he was so sick and sleepy. He always contrives to be sick at the least cross! I gave a few sentences of commendation to Heathcliff, and he, either for a headache or a pang of envy, began to cry: so I got up and left him."

"What use is it praising Heathcliff to him?" I answered. "As lads they had an aversion to each other, and Heathcliff would hate just as much to hear him praised—it's human nature. Let Mr. Linton alone about him, unless you would like an open quarrel between them."

"But does it not show great weakness?" pursued she. "I'm not envious: I never feel hurt at the brightness of Isabella's yellow hair, and the whiteness of her skin; at her dainty elegance, and the fondness all the family exhibit for her. Even you, Nelly, if we have a dispute sometimes, you back Isabella, at once; and I yield like a foolish mother—I call her a darling, and flatter her into a good temper. It pleases her brother to see us cordial, and that pleases me. But they are very much alike; they are spoiled children, and fancy the world was made for their accommodation; and, though I humour both, I think a smart chastisement might improve them, all the same."

"You're mistaken, Mrs. Linton," said I. "They humour you: I know what there would be to do if they did not! You can well afford to indulge their passing whims, as long as their business is to anticipate all your desires. You may, however, fall out, at last, over something of equal consequence to both sides; and then those you term weak are very capable of being as obstinate as you!"

"And then we shall fight to the death, shan't we, Nelly?" she returned laughing. "No! I tell you, I have such faith in Linton's love that I believe I might kill him, and he wouldn't wish to retaliate."

I advised her to value him the more for his affection.

"I do," she answered, "but he needn't resort to whining for trifles. It is childish; and, instead of melting into tears because I said that Heathcliff was now worthy of any one's regard, and it would honour the first gentleman in the country to be his friend, he ought to have said it for me, and been delighted from sympathy. He must get accustomed to him, and he may as well like him. Considering how Heathcliff has reason to object to him, I'm sure he behaved excellently!"

"What do you think of his going to Wuthering Heights?" I inquired. "He is reformed in every respect, apparently—quite a Christian—offering the right hand of fellowship to his enemies all round!"

"He explained it," she replied. "I wondered as much as you. He said he called to gather information concerning me, from you, supposing you resided there still; and Joseph told Hindley, who came out and fell to questioning him of what he had been doing, and how he had been living; and finally, desired him to walk in. There were some persons sitting at cards; Heathcliff joined them; my brother lost some money to him; and, finding him plentifully supplied, he requested that he would come again in the evening, to which he consented. Hindley is too reckless to select his acquaintance prudently; he doesn't trouble himself to reflect on the causes he might have for mistrusting one whom he has basely injured. But Heathcliff affirms his principal reason for resuming a connection with his ancient persecutor is a wish to install himself in quarters at walking distance from the Grange, and an attachment to the house where we lived together, and likewise a hope that I shall have more opportunities of seeing him there than I could have if he settled in Gimmerton. He means to offer liberal payment for permission to lodge at the Heights; and doubtless my brother's covetousness will prompt him to accept the terms; he was always greedy, though what he grasps with one hand, he flings away with the other."

"It's a nice place for a young man to fix his dwelling in!" said I. "Have you no fear of the consequences, Mrs. Linton?"

"None for my friend," she replied. "His strong head will keep him from danger; a little for Hindley, but he can't be made morally worse than he is; and I stand between him and bodily harm. The event of this evening has reconciled me to God and humanity! I had risen in angry rebellion against providence. Oh, I've endured very, very bitter misery, Nelly! If that creature knew how bitter, he'd be ashamed to cloud its removal with idle petulance. It was kindness for him which induced me to bear it alone: had I expressed the agony I frequently felt, he would have been taught to long for its alleviation as ardently as I. However, it's over, and I'll take no revenge on his folly; I can afford to suffer anything, hereafter! Should the meanest thing alive slap me on the cheek, I'd not only turn the other, but I'd ask pardon for provoking it; and, as a proof, I'll go make my peace with Edgar instantly. Goodnight—I'm an angel!"

In this self-complacent conviction she departed; and the success of her fulfilled resolution was obvious on the morrow: Mr. Linton had not only abjured his peevishness (though his spirits seemed still subdued by Catherine's exuberance of vivacity), but he ventured no objection to her taking Isabella with her to Wuthering Heights in the afternoon; and she rewarded him with such a summer of sweetness and affection in return, as made the house a paradise for several days; both master and servants profiting from the perpetual sunshine.

Heathcliff—Mr. Heathcliff I should say in future—used the liberty of visiting at Thrushcross Grange cautiously, at first: he seemed estimating how far its owner would bear his intrusion. Catherine, also, deemed it judicious to moderate her expressions of pleasure in receiving him; and he gradually established his right to be expected.

He retained a great deal of the reserve for which his boyhood was remarkable, and that served to repress all startling demonstrations of feeling. My master's uneasiness experienced a lull, and further circumstances diverted it into another channel for a space.

His new source of trouble sprang from the not anticipated misfortune of Isabella Linton evincing a sudden and irresistible attraction towards the tolerated guest. She was at that time a charming young lady of eighteen; infantile in manners, though possessed of keen wit, keen feelings, and a keen temper, too, if irritated. Her brother, who loved her tenderly, was appalled at this fantastic preference. Leaving aside the degradation of an alliance with a nameless man, and the possible fact that his property, in default of heirs male, might pass into such a one's power, he had sense to comprehend Heathcliff's disposition—to know that, though his exterior was altered, his mind was unchangeable, and unchanged. And he dreaded that mind; it revolted him; he shrank forebodingly from the idea of committing Isabella to its keeping.

He would have recoiled still more had he been aware that her attachment rose unsolicited, and was bestowed where it awakened no reciprocation of sentiment; for the minute he discovered its existence, he laid the blame on Heathcliff's deliberate designing.

We had all remarked, during some time, that Miss Linton fretted and pined over something. She grew cross and wearisome, snapping at and teasing Catherine continually, at the imminent risk of exhausting her limited patience. We excused her to a certain extent, on the plea of ill health—she was dwindling and fading before our eyes. But one day, when she had been peculiarly wayward, rejecting her breakfast, complaining that the servants did not do what she told them; that the mistress would allow her to be nothing in the house, and Edgar neglected her; that she had caught a cold with the doors being left open, and we let the parlour fire go out on purpose to vex her; with a hundred yet more frivolous accusations, Mrs. Linton peremptorily insisted that she should get to bed; and, having scolded her heartily, threatened to send for the doctor.

Mention of Kenneth caused her to exclaim, instantly, that her health was perfect, and it was only Catherine's harshness which made her unhappy.

"How can you say I am harsh, you naughty fondling?" cried the mistress, amazed at the unreasonable assertion. "You are surely losing your reason. When have I been harsh, tell me?"

"Yesterday," sobbed Isabella, "and now!"

"Yesterday!" said her sister-in-law. "On what occasion?"

"In our walk along the moor; you told me to ramble where I pleased, while you sauntered on with Mr. Heathcliff!"

"And that's your notion of harshness?" said Catherine, laughing. "It was no hint that your company was superfluous; we didn't care whether you kept with us or not; I merely thought Heathcliff's talk would have nothing entertaining for your ears."

"Oh, no," wept the young lady; "you wished me away, because you knew I liked to be there!"

"Is she sane?" asked Mrs. Linton, appealing to me. "I'll repeat our conversation, word for word, Isabella; and you point out any charm it could have had for you."

"I don't mind the conversation," she answered. "I wanted to be with—"

"Well!" said Catherine, perceiving her hesitate to complete the sentence.

"With him; and I won't be always sent off!" she continued, kindling up. "You are a dog in the manger, Cathy, and desire no one to be loved but yourself!"

"You are an impertinent little monkey!" exclaimed Mrs. Linton, in surprise. "But I'll not believe this idiocy! It is impossible that you can covet the admiration of Heathcliff—that you can consider him an agreeable person! I hope I have misunderstood you, Isabella?"

"No, you have not," said the infatuated girl. "I love him more than ever you loved Edgar; and he might love me if you would let him!"

"I wouldn't be you for a kingdom, then!" Catherine declared, emphatically—and she seemed to speak sincerely. "Nelly, help me to convince her of her madness. Tell her what Heathcliff is—an unreclaimed creature, without refinement, without cultivation; an arid wilderness of furze and whinstone. I'd as soon put that little canary into the park on a winter's day as recommend you to bestow your heart on him! It is deplorable ignorance of his character, child, and nothing else, which makes that dream enter your head. Pray don't imagine that he conceals depths of benevolence and affection beneath a stern exterior! He's not a rough diamond—a pearl-containing oyster of a rustic; he's a fierce, pitiless, wolfish man. I never say to him, 'Let this or that enemy alone, because it would be ungenerous or cruel to harm them'; I say, 'Let them alone, because *I* should hate them to be wronged': and he'd crush you, like a sparrow's egg, Isabella, if he found you a troublesome charge. I know he couldn't love a Linton; and yet he'd be quite capable of marrying your fortune and expectations. Avarice is growing with him a besetting sin. There's my picture; and I'm his friend—so much so, that had he thought seriously to catch you, I should, perhaps, have held my tongue, and let you fall into his trap."

Miss Linton regarded her sister-in-law with indignation.

"For shame! for shame!" she repeated, angrily. "You are worse than twenty foes, you poisonous friend!"

"Ah! you won't believe me, then?" said Catherine. "You think I speak from wicked selfishness?"

"I'm certain you do," retorted Isabella; "and I shudder at you!"

"Good!" cried the other. "Try for yourself, if that be your spirit; I have done, and yield the argument to your saucy insolence."

"And I must suffer for her egotism!" she sobbed, as Mrs. Linton left the room. "All, all is against me; she has blighted my single consolation. But she uttered falsehoods, didn't she? Mr. Heathcliff is not a fiend; he has an honourable soul, and a true one, or how could he remember her?"

"Banish him from your thoughts, Miss," I said. "He's a bird of bad omen; no mate for you. Mrs. Linton spoke strongly, and yet I can't contradict her. She is better acquainted with his heart than I, or any one besides; and she never would represent him as worse than he is. Honest people don't hide their deeds. How has he been living? how has he got rich? why is he staying at Wuthering Heights, the house of a man whom he abhors? They say Mr. Earnshaw is worse and worse since he came. They sit up all night together continually; and Hindley has been borrowing money on his land, and does nothing but play and drink: I heard only a week ago—it was Joseph who told me—I met him at Gimmerton."

" 'Nelly,' he said, 'we's hae a Crahnr's 'quest enah, at ahr folks. One on 'em's a'most getten his finger cut off wi' hauding t' other froo' sticking hisseln loike a cawlf. That's maister, yah knaw, ut's soa up uh going tuh t'grand 'sizes. He's noan feard uh t' Bench uh judges, norther Paul, nur Peter, nur John, nor Mathew, nor noan on 'em, nut he! He fair like's—he langs tuh set his brazened face agean 'em! And yon bonny lad Heathcliff, yah mind, he's a rare un! He cau girn a laugh, as weel's onybody at a raight divil's jest. Does he niver say nowt of his fine living amang us, when he goas tuh t' Grange? This is t' way on't—up at sun-dahn; dice, brandy, cloised shutters, und can'le lught till next day, at nooin—then, t'fooil gangs banning un' raving tuh his cham'er, makking dacent fowks dig thur fingers i' thur lugs fur varry shaume; un' the' knave, wah, he carn cahnt his brass, un' ate, un' sleep, un' off tuh his neighbour's tuh gossip wi' t' wife. I' course, he tells Dame Catherine hah hor father's goold runs intuh his pocket, and her fathur's son gallops dahn t' broad road, while he flees afore tuh oppen t' pikes.'[1] Now, Miss Linton, Joseph is an old rascal, but no liar; and, if his account of Heathcliff's conduct be true, you would never think of desiring such a husband, would you?"

"You are leagued with the rest, Ellen!" she replied. "I'll not listen to your slanders. What malevolence you must have to wish to convince me that there is no happiness in the world!"

Whether she would have got over this fancy if left to herself, or persevered in nursing it perpetually, I cannot say; she had little time to reflect. The day after, there was a justice-meeting at the next town; my master was obliged to attend; and Mr. Heathcliff, aware of his absence, called rather earlier than usual.

Catherine and Isabella were sitting in the library, on hostile terms, but silent. The latter, alarmed at her recent indiscretion, and the disclosure she had made of her secret feelings in a transient fit of passion; the former, on mature consideration, really offended with her companion; and, if she laughed again at her pertness, inclined to make it no laughing matter to *her*.

She did laugh as she saw Heathcliff pass the window. I was sweeping the hearth, and I noticed a mischievous smile on her lips. Isabella, absorbed in her meditations, or a book, remained till the door opened, and it was too late to attempt an escape, which she would gladly have done had it been practicable.

"Come in, that's right!" exclaimed the mistress, gaily, pulling a chair to the fire. "Here are two people sadly in need of a third to

1. "Nelly," he said, "We're to have a coroner's inquest [soon] enough, at our house. One of them almost had his finger cut off from holding the other from sticking himself as one would kill a calf. That's master, you know, it's therefore to be going to the grand assizes [sessions of county court]. He's not afraid of the bench of judges, neither Paul, nor Peter, nor John, nor Matthew, nor any of them, not he! He much likes—he longs to set his brazened face against them! And yon good lad Heathclilff, you note, he's a rare one. He can show his teeth in laughing as well as anyone at a true devil's jest. Does he never say anything about his fine living with us, when he goes to the Grange? This is the way of it—up at sundown; dice, brandy, closed shutters, and candlelight till next day, at noon—then, the fool goes cursing and raving to his chamber, making decent folks dig their fingers in their ears for shame; and the knave, why, he can count his money, and eat, and sleep, and go off to his neighbors to gossip with the wife. As he does so, he tells Miss Catherine how her father's gold runs into his pocket, and [how] her father's son gallops down the broad road [to destruction], while he runs ahead to open the toll gates [to hasten Hindley to his ruin]." Matthew 7 begins with the warning, "Judge not, that ye be not judged," and it notes that "broad is the way, that leadeth to destruction."

thaw the ice between them, and you are the very one we should both of us choose. Heathcliff, I'm proud to show you, at last, somebody that dotes on you more than myself. I expect you to feel flattered. Nay, it's not Nelly; don't look at her! My poor little sister-in-law is breaking her heart by mere contemplation of your physical and moral beauty. It lies in your own power to be Edgar's brother! No, no, Isabella, you shan't run off," she continued, arresting, with feigned playfulness, the confounded girl who had risen indignantly. "We were quarrelling like cats about you, Heathcliff; and I was fairly beaten in protestations of devotion and admiration; and, moreover, I was informed that if I would but have the manners to stand aside, my rival, as she will have herself to be, would shoot a shaft into your soul that would fix you for ever, and send my image into eternal oblivion!"

"Catherine," said Isabella, calling up her dignity, and disdaining to struggle from the tight grasp that held her, "I'd thank you to adhere to the truth and not slander me, even in joke! Mr. Heathcliff, be kind enough to bid this friend of yours release me: she forgets that you and I are not intimate acquaintances, and what amuses her is painful to me beyond expression."

As the guest answered nothing, but took his seat, and looked thoroughly indifferent what sentiments she cherished concerning him, she turned, and whispered an earnest appeal for liberty to her tormentor.

"By no means!" cried Mrs. Linton in answer. "I won't be named a dog in the manger again. You *shall* stay: now then, Heathcliff, why don't you evince satisfaction at my pleasant news? Isabella swears that the love Edgar has for me is nothing to that she entertains for you. I'm sure she made some speech of the kind, did she not, Ellen? And she has fasted ever since the day before yesterday's walk, from sorrow and rage that I despatched her out of your society, under the idea of its being unacceptable."

"I think you belie her," said Heathcliff, twisting his chair to face them. "She wishes to be out of my society now, at any rate!"

And he stared hard at the object of discourse, as one might do at a strange repulsive animal, a centipede from the Indies, for instance, which curiosity leads one to examine in spite of the aversion it raises.

The poor thing couldn't bear that; she grew white and red in rapid succession, and, while tears beaded her lashes, bent the strength of her small fingers to loosen the firm clutch of Catherine, and perceiving that as fast as she raised one finger off her arm, another closed down, and she could not remove the whole together, she began to make use of her nails, and their sharpness presently ornamented the detainer's with crescents of red.

"There's a tigress!" exclaimed Mrs. Linton, setting her free, and shaking her hand with pain. "Begone, for God's sake, and hide your vixen face! How foolish to reveal those talons to *him*. Can't you fancy the conclusions he'll draw? Look, Heathcliff! they are instruments that will do execution—you must beware of your eyes."

"I'd wrench them off her fingers, if they ever menaced me," he answered brutally, when the door had closed after her. "But what did you mean by teasing the creature in that manner, Cathy? You were not speaking the truth, were you?"

"I assure you I was," she returned. "She has been pining for your sake several weeks; and raving about you this morning, and pouring forth a deluge of abuse, because I represented your failings in a plain light for the purpose of mitigating her adoration. But don't notice it further. I wished to punish her sauciness, that's all. I like her too well, my dear Heathcliff, to let you absolutely seize and devour her up."

"And I like her too ill to attempt it," said he, "except in a very ghoulish fashion. You'd hear of odd things, if I lived alone with that mawkish, waxen face; the most ordinary would be painting on its white the colours of the rainbow, and turning the blue eyes black, every day or two; they detestably resemble Linton's."

"Delectably," observed Catherine. "They are dove's eyes—angel's!"

"She's her brother's heir, is she not?" he asked, after a brief silence.

"I should be sorry to think so," returned his companion. "Half-a-dozen nephews shall erase her title, please Heaven! Abstract your mind from the subject, at present. You are too prone to covet your neighbour's goods: remember *this* neighbour's goods are mine."

"If they were *mine*, they would be none the less that," said Heathcliff, "but though Isabella Linton may be silly, she is scarcely mad; and, in short, we'll dismiss the matter, as you advise."

From their tongues, they did dismiss it; and Catherine, probably, from her thoughts. The other, I felt certain, recalled it often in the course of the evening; I saw him smile to himself—grin rather—and lapse into ominous musing whenever Mrs. Linton had occasion to be absent from the apartment.

I determined to watch his movements. My heart invariably cleaved to the master's, in preference to Catherine's side; with reason, I imagined, for he was kind, and trustful, and honourable: and she—she could not be called the *opposite*, yet she seemed to allow herself such wide latitude that I had little faith in her principles, and still less sympathy for her feelings. I wanted something to happen which might have the effect of freeing both Wuthering Heights and the Grange of Mr. Heathcliff, quietly, leaving us as we had been prior to his advent. His visits were a continual nightmare to me; and, I suspected, to my master also. His abode at the Heights was an oppression past explaining. I felt that God had forsaken the stray sheep there to its own wicked wanderings, and an evil beast prowled between it and the fold, waiting his time to spring and destroy.

Chapter XI

Sometimes, while meditating on these things in solitude, I've got up in a sudden terror, and put on my bonnet to go see how all was at the farm; I've persuaded my conscience that it was a duty to warn him how people talked regarding his ways; and then I've recollected his confirmed bad habits, and, hopeless of benefiting him, have flinched from re-entering the dismal house, doubting if I could bear to be taken at my word.

One time I passed the old gate, going out of my way, on a journey to Gimmerton. It was about the period that my narrative has reached—a bright, frosty afternoon, the ground bare, and the road hard and dry.

I came to a stone where the highway branches off on to the moor at your left hand; a rough sand-pillar, with the letters W. H. cut on its north side, on the east, G., and on the south-west, T. G. It serves as guide-post to the Grange, and Heights, and village.

The sun shone yellow on its grey head, reminding me of summer; and I cannot say why, but all at once, a gush of child's sensations flowed into my heart. Hindley and I held it a favourite spot twenty years before.

I gazed long at the weather-worn block; and, stooping down, perceived a hole near the bottom still full of snail-shells and pebbles, which we were fond of storing there with more perishable things; and, as fresh as reality, it appeared that I beheld my early playmate seated on the withered turf, his dark, square head bent forward, and his little hand scooping out the earth with a piece of slate.

"Poor Hindley!" I exclaimed, involuntarily.

I started—my bodily eye was cheated into a momentary belief that the child lifted its face and stared straight into mine! It vanished in a twinkling; but, immediately, I felt an irresistible yearning to be at the Heights. Superstition urged me to comply with this impulse. Supposing he should be dead! I thought—or should die soon!—supposing it were a sign of death!

The nearer I got to the house the more agitated I grew; and on catching sight of it, I trembled every limb. The apparition had outstripped me; it stood looking through the gate. That was my first idea on observing an elf-locked, brown-eyed boy setting his ruddy countenance against the bars. Further reflection suggested this must be Hareton, *my* Hareton, not altered greatly since I left him, ten months since.

"God bless thee, darling!" I cried, forgetting instantaneously my foolish fears. "Hareton, it's Nelly—Nelly, thy nurse."

He retreated out of arm's length, and picked up a large flint.

"I am come to see thy father, Hareton," I added, guessing from the action that Nelly, if she lived in his memory at all, was not recognised as one with me.

He raised his missile to hurl it; I commenced a soothing speech, but could not stay his hand. The stone struck my bonnet; and then ensued, from the stammering lips of the little fellow, a string of curses, which, whether he comprehended them or not, were delivered with practised emphasis, and distorted his baby features into a shocking expression of malignity.

You may be certain this grieved more than angered me. Fit to cry, I took an orange from my pocket, and offered it to propitiate him.

He hesitated, and then snatched it from my hold, as if he fancied I only intended to tempt and disappoint him.

I showed another, keeping it out of his reach.

"Who has taught you those fine words, my barn,"[1] I inquired. "The curate?"

"Damn the curate, and thee! Gie me that," he replied.

"Tell us where you got your lessons, and you shall have it," said I. "Who's your master?"

"Devil daddy," was his answer.

"And what do you learn from Daddy?" I continued.

He jumped at the fruit; I raised it higher. "What does he teach you?" I asked.

"Naught," said he, "but to keep out of his gait.[2] Daddy cannot bide me, because I swear at him."

"Ah! and the devil teaches you to swear at Daddy?" I observed.

"Aye—nay," he drawled.

"Who then?"

"Heathcliff."

I asked if he liked Mr. Heathcliff?

"Aye!" he answered again.

Desiring to have his reasons for liking him, I could only gather the sentences—"I known't—he pays Dad back what he gies to me—he curses Daddy for cursing me—he says I mun do as I will."

1. *Barn* [bairn]: child.
2. Way.

"And the curate does not teach you to read and write, then?" I pursued.

"No, I was told the curate should have his ——[3] teeth dashed down his —— throat, if he stepped over the threshold. Heathcliff had promised that!"

I put the orange in his hand, and bade him tell his father that a woman called Nelly Dean was waiting to speak with him, by the garden gate.

He went up the walk, and entered the house; but, instead of Hindley, Heathcliff appeared on the door stones, and I turned directly and ran down the road as hard as ever I could race, making no halt till I gained the guide post, and feeling as scared as if I had raised a goblin.

This is not much connected with Miss Isabella's affair; except that it urged me to resolve further on mounting vigilant guard, and doing my utmost to check the spread of such bad influence at the Grange, even though I should wake a domestic storm by thwarting Mrs. Linton's pleasure.

The next time Heathcliff came, my young lady chanced to be feeding some pigeons in the court. She had never spoken a word to her sister-in-law for three days; but she had likewise dropped her fretful complaining, and we found it a great comfort.

Heathcliff had not the habit of bestowing a single unnecessary civility on Miss Linton, I knew. Now, as soon as he beheld her, his first precaution was to take a sweeping survey of the housefront. I was standing by the kitchen window, but I drew out of sight. He then stept across the pavement to her, and said something: she seemed embarrassed, and desirous of getting away; to prevent it, he laid his hand on her arm. She averted her face; he apparently put some question which she had no mind to answer. There was another rapid glance at the house, and supposing himself unseen, the scoundrel had the impudence to embrace her.

"Judas! Traitor!" I ejaculated. "You are a hypocrite too, are you? A deliberate deceiver."

"Who is, Nelly?" said Catherine's voice at my elbow. I had been over-intent on watching the pair outside to mark her entrance.

"Your worthless friend!" I answered warmly; "the sneaking rascal yonder. Ah, he has caught a glimpse of us—he is coming in! I wonder will he have the art to find a plausible excuse for making love to Miss, when he told you he hated her?"

Mrs. Linton saw Isabella tear herself free, and run into the garden; and a minute after, Heathcliff opened the door.

3. By use of blanks for curses, Nelly, even more than Lockwood, spares the ears of her listener. See Chapter III, note 6.

I couldn't withhold giving some loose to my indignation; but Catherine angrily insisted on silence, and threatened to order me out of the kitchen, if I dared be so presumptuous as to put in my insolent tongue.

"To hear you, people might think *you* were the mistress!" she cried. "You want setting down in your right place! Heathcliff, what are you about, raising this stir? I said you must let Isabella alone! —I beg you will, unless you are tired of being received here, and wish Linton to draw the bolts against you!"

"God forbid that he should try!" answered the black villain. I detested him just then. "God keep him meek and patient! Every day I grow madder after sending him to heaven!"

"Hush!" said Catherine, shutting the inner door. "Don't vex me. Why have you disregarded my request? Did she come across you on purpose?"

"What is it to you?" he growled. "I have a right to kiss her, if she chooses, and you have no right to object. I'm not *your* husband: *you* needn't be jealous of me!"

"I'm not jealous *of* you," replied the mistress, "I'm jealous *for* you. Clear your face, you shan't scowl at me! If you like Isabella, you shall marry her. But do you like her? Tell the truth, Heathcliff! There, you won't answer. I'm certain you don't!"

"And would Mr. Linton approve of his sister marrying that man?" I inquired.

"Mr. Linton should approve," returned my lady decisively.

"He might spare himself the trouble," said Heathcliff; "I could do as well without his approbation. And as to you, Catherine, I have a mind to speak a few words now, while we are at it. I want you to be aware that I *know* you have treated me infernally—infernally! Do you hear? And if you flatter yourself that I don't perceive it, you are a fool; and if you think I can be consoled by sweet words you are an idiot; and if you fancy I'll suffer unrevenged, I'll convince you of the contrary, in a very little while! Meantime, thank you for telling me your sister-in-law's secret. I swear I'll make the most of it. And stand you aside!"

"What new phase of his character is this?" exclaimed Mrs. Linton, in amazement. "I've treated you infernally—and you'll take revenge! How will you take it, ungrateful brute? How have I treated you infernally?"

"I seek no revenge on you," replied Heathcliff less vehemently. "That's not the plan. The tyrant grinds down his slaves and they don't turn against him, they crush those beneath them. You are welcome to torture me to death for your amusement, only allow me to amuse myself a little in the same style, and refrain from insult, as much as you are able. Having levelled my palace, don't erect a hovel and complacently admire your own charity in giving me that for a home. If I imagined you really wished me to marry Isabella, I'd cut my throat!"

"Oh, the evil is that I am *not* jealous, is it?" cried Catherine. "Well, I won't repeat my offer of a wife: it is as bad as offering Satan a lost soul. Your bliss lies, like his, in inflicting misery. You prove it. Edgar is restored from the ill-temper he gave way to at your coming; I begin to be secure and tranquil; and you, restless to know us at peace, appear resolved on exciting a quarrel. Quarrel with Edgar, if you please, Heathcliff, and deceive his sister; you'll hit on exactly the most efficient method of revenging yourself on me."

The conversation ceased. Mrs. Linton sat down by the fire, flushed and gloomy. The spirit which served her was growing intractable: she could neither lay nor control it. He stood on the hearth, with folded arms, brooding on his evil thoughts; and in this position I left them to seek the master, who was wondering what kept Catherine below so long.

"Ellen," said he, when I entered, "have you seen your mistress?"

"Yes, she's in the kitchen, sir," I answered. "She's sadly put out by Mr. Heathcliff's behaviour: and, indeed, I do think it's time to arrange his visits on another footing. There's harm in being too soft, and now it's come to this—" And I related the scene in the court, and, as near as I dared, the whole subsequent dispute. I fancied it could not be very prejudicial to Mrs. Linton, unless she made it so afterwards, by assuming the defensive for her guest.

Edgar Linton had difficulty in hearing me to the close. His first words revealed that he did not clear his wife of blame.

"This is insufferable!" he exclaimed. "It is disgraceful that she should own him for a friend, and force his company on me! Call me two men out of the hall, Ellen. Catherine shall linger no longer to argue with the low ruffian—I have humoured her enough."

He descended, and bidding the servants wait in the passage, went, followed by me, to the kitchen. Its occupants had recommenced their angry discussion; Mrs. Linton, at least, was scolding with renewed vigour; Heathcliff had moved to the window, and hung his head, somewhat cowed by her violent rating apparently.

He saw the master first, and made a hasty motion that she should be silent; which she obeyed, abruptly, on discovering the reason of his intimation.

"How is this?" said Linton, addressing her; "what notion of propriety must you have to remain here, after the language which has been held to you by that blackguard? I suppose, because it is his ordinary talk, you think nothing of it—you are habituated to his baseness, and, perhaps, imagine I can get used to it too!"

"Have you been listening at the door, Edgar?" asked the mistress, in a tone particularly calculated to provoke her husband, implying both carelessness and contempt of his irritation.

Heathcliff, who had raised his eyes at the former speech, gave a sneering laugh at the latter, on purpose, it seemed, to draw Mr. Linton's attention to him.

He succeeded; but Edgar did not mean to entertain him with any high flights of passion.

"I have been so far forbearing with you, sir," he said, quietly; "not that I was ignorant of your miserable, degraded character, but I felt you were only partly responsible for that; and Catherine wishing to keep up your acquaintance, I acquiesced—foolishly. Your presence is a moral poison that would contaminate the most virtuous: for that cause, and to prevent worse consequences, I shall deny you, hereafter, admission into this house, and give notice, now, that I require your instant departure. Three minutes' delay will render it involuntary and ignominious."

Heathcliff measured the height and breadth of the speaker with an eye full of derision.

"Cathy, this lamb of yours threatens like a bull!" he said. "It is in danger of splitting its skull against my knuckles. By God, Mr. Linton, I'm mortally sorry that you are not worth knocking down!"

My master glanced towards the passage, and signed me to fetch the men: he had no intention of hazarding a personal encounter.

I obeyed the hint; but Mrs. Linton, suspecting something, followed, and when I attempted to call them, she pulled me back, slammed the door to, and locked it.

"Fair means!" she said, in answer to her husband's look of angry surprise. "If you have not the courage to attack him, make an apology, or allow yourself to be beaten. It will correct you of feigning more valour than you possess. No, I'll swallow the key before you shall get it! I'm delightfully rewarded for my kindness to each! After constant indulgence of one's weak nature, and the other's bad one, I earn, for thanks, two samples of blind ingratitude, stupid to absurdity! Edgar, I was defending you and yours; and I wish Heathcliff may flog you sick, for daring to think an evil thought of me!"

It did not need the medium of a flogging to produce that effect on the master. He tried to wrest the key from Catherine's grasp; and for safety she flung it into the hottest part of the fire; whereupon Mr. Edgar was taken with a nervous trembling, and his countenance grew deadly pale. For his life he could not avert that access of emotion: mingled anguish and humiliation overcame him completely. He leant on the back of a chair, and covered his face.

"Oh, heavens! In old days this would win you knighthood!" exclaimed Mrs. Linton. "We are vanquished! we are vanquished!

Heathcliff would as soon lift a finger at you as the king would march his army against a colony of mice. Cheer up, you shan't be hurt! Your type is not a lamb, it's a sucking leveret."

"I wish you joy of the milk-blooded coward, Cathy!" said her friend. "I compliment you on your taste: and that is the slavering, shivering thing you preferred to me! I would not strike him with my fist, but I'd kick him with my foot, and experience considerable satisfaction. Is he weeping, or is he going to faint for fear?"

The fellow approached and gave the chair on which Linton rested a push. He'd better have kept his distance: my master quickly sprang erect, and struck him full on the throat a blow that would have levelled a slighter man.

It took his breath for a minute; and, while he choked, Mr. Linton walked out by the back door into the yard, and from thence, to the front entrance.

"There! you've done with coming here," cried Catherine. "Get away, now; he'll return with a brace of pistols, and half a dozen assistants. If he did overhear us, of course, he'd never forgive you. You've played me an ill turn, Heathcliff! But go—make haste! I'd rather see Edgar at bay than you."

"Do you suppose I'm going with that blow burning in my gullet?" he thundered. "By Hell, no! I'll crush his ribs in like a rotten hazel-nut, before I cross the threshold! If I don't floor him now, I shall murder him sometime, so, as you value his existence, let me get at him!"

"He is not coming," I interposed, framing a bit of a lie. "There's the coachman, and the two gardeners; you'll surely not wait to be thrust into the road by them! Each has a bludgeon, and master will, very likely, be watching from the parlour windows to see that they fulfil his orders."

The gardeners and coachman *were* there; but Linton was with them. They had already entered the court. Heathcliff, on second thoughts, resolved to avoid a struggle against three underlings; he seized the poker, smashed the lock from the inner door, and made his escape as they tramped in.

Mrs. Linton, who was very much excited, bid me accompany her upstairs. She did not know my share in contributing to the disturbance, and I was anxious to keep her in ignorance.

"I'm nearly distracted, Nelly!" she exclaimed, throwing herself on the sofa. "A thousand smiths' hammers are beating in my head! Tell Isabella to shun me—this uproar is owing to her; and should she or any one else aggravate my anger at present, I shall get wild. And, Nelly, say to Edgar, if you see him again to-night, that I'm in danger of being seriously ill. I wish it may prove true. He has startled and distressed me shockingly! I want to frighten him. Besides, he might come and begin a string of abuse, or complainings; I'm certain I should recriminate, and God knows where we should end! Will you do so, my good Nelly? You are aware that I am no way blameable in this matter. What possessed him to turn listener? Heathcliff's talk was outrageous, after you left us; but I could soon have diverted him from Isabella, and the rest meant nothing. Now, all is dashed wrong by the fool's-craving to hear evil of self that haunts some people like a demon! Had Edgar never gathered our conversation, he would never have been the worse for it. Really, when he opened on me in that unreasonable tone of displeasure, after I had scolded Heathcliff till I was hoarse for *him*, I did not care, hardly, what they did to each other, especially as I felt that, however the scene closed, we should all be driven asunder for nobody knows how long! Well, if I cannot keep Heathcliff for my friend, if Edgar will be mean and jealous, I'll try to break their hearts by breaking my own. That will be a prompt way of finishing all, when I am pushed to extremity! But it's a deed to be reserved for a forlorn hope; I'd not take Linton by surprise with it. To this point he has been discreet in dreading to provoke me; you must represent the peril of quitting that policy, and remind him of my passionate temper, verging, when kindled, on frenzy. I wish you could dismiss that apathy out of your countenance, and look rather more anxious about me!"

The stolidity with which I received these instructions was, no doubt, rather exasperating, for they were delivered in perfect sincerity; but I believed a person who could plan the turning of her fits of passion to account, beforehand, might, by exerting her will, manage to control herself tolerably even while under their influence; and I did not wish to "frighten" her husband, as she said, and multiply his annoyances for the purpose of serving her selfishness.

Therefore I said nothing when I met the master coming towards the parlour; but I took the liberty of turning back to listen whether they would resume their quarrel together.

He began to speak first.

"Remain where you are, Catherine," he said, without any anger in his voice, but with much sorrowful despondency. "I shall not stay. I am neither come to wrangle, nor be reconciled; but I wish just to learn whether, after this evening's events, you intend to continue your intimacy with—"

"Oh, for mercy's sake," interrupted the mistress, stamping her foot, "for mercy's sake, let us hear no more of it now! Your cold blood cannot be worked into a fever; your veins are full of ice-water, but mine are boiling, and the sight of such chillness makes them dance."

"To get rid of me, answer my question," persevered Mr. Linton. "You *must* answer it; and that violence does not alarm me. I have found that you can be as stoical as any one, when you please. Will you give up Heathcliff hereafter, or will you give up me? It is impossible for you to be *my* friend and *his* at the same time; and I absolutely *require* to know which you choose."

"I require to be let alone!" exclaimed Catherine, furiously. "I demand it! Don't you see I can scarcely stand? Edgar, you—you leave me!"

She rung the bell till it broke with a twang: I entered leisurely. It was enough to try the temper of a saint, such senseless, wicked rages! There she lay dashing her head against the arm of the sofa, and grinding her teeth, so that you might fancy she would crash them to splinters!

Mr. Linton stood looking at her in sudden compunction and fear. He told me to fetch some water. She had no breath for speaking.

I brought a glass full; and, as she would not drink, I sprinkled it on her face. In a few seconds she stretched herself out stiff, and turned up her eyes, while her cheeks, at once blanched and livid, assumed the aspect of death.

Linton looked terrified.

"There is nothing in the world the matter," I whispered. I did not want him to yield, though I could not help being afraid in my heart.

"She has blood on her lips!" he said, shuddering.

"Never mind!" I answered, tartly. And I told him how she had resolved, previous to his coming, on exhibiting a fit of frenzy.

I incautiously gave the account aloud, and she heard me, for she started up—her hair flying over her shoulders, her eyes flashing, the muscles of her neck and arms standing out preternaturally. I made up my mind for broken bones, at least; but she only glared about her for an instant, and then rushed from the room.

The master directed me to follow; I did, to her chamber door; she hindered me from going farther by securing it against me.

As she never offered to descend to breakfast next morning, I went to ask whether she would have some carried up.

"No!" she replied, peremptorily.

The same question was repeated at dinner and tea; and again on the morrow after, and received the same answer.

Mr. Linton, on his part, spent his time in the library, and did not inquire concerning his wife's occupations. Isabella and he had had an hour's interview, during which he tried to elicit from her some sentiment of proper horror for Heathcliff's advances; but he could make nothing of her evasive replies, and was obliged to close the examination unsatisfactorily; adding, however, a solemn warning, that if she were so insane as to encourage that worthless suitor, it would dissolve all bonds of relationship between herself and him.

Chapter XII

While Miss Linton moped about the park and garden, always silent, and almost always in tears; and her brother shut himself up among books that he never opened—wearying, I guessed, with a continual vague expectation that Catherine, repenting her conduct, would come of her own accord to ask pardon, and seek a reconciliation—and while *she* fasted pertinaciously, under the idea, probably, that at every meal, Edgar was ready to choke for her absence, and pride alone held him from running to cast himself at her feet, I went about my household duties, convinced that the Grange had but one sensible soul in its walls, and that lodged in my body.

I wasted no condolences on Miss, nor any expostulations on my mistress, nor did I pay attention to the sighs of my master, who yearned to hear his lady's name, since he might not hear her voice.

I determined they should come about as they pleased for me; and though it was a tiresomely slow process, I began to rejoice at length in a faint dawn of its progress, as I thought at first.

Mrs. Linton, on the third day, unbarred her door; and having finished the water in her pitcher and decanter, desired a renewed supply, and a basin of gruel, for she believed she was dying. That I set down as a speech meant for Edgar's ears; I believed no such thing, so I kept it to myself, and brought her some tea and dry toast.

She ate and drank eagerly; and sank back on her pillow again, clenching her hands and groaning.

"Oh, I will die," she exclaimed, "since no one cares anything about me. I wish I had not taken that."

Then a good while after I heard her murmur—

"No, I'll not die—he'd be glad—he does not love me at all—he would never miss me!"

"Did you want anything, ma'am?" I enquired, still preserving my external composure, in spite of her ghastly countenance and strange exaggerated manner.

"What is that apathetic being doing?" she demanded, pushing the thick entangled locks from her wasted face. "Has he fallen into a lethargy, or is he dead?"

"Neither," replied I; "if you mean Mr. Linton. He's tolerably well, I think, though his studies occupy him rather more than they ought; he is continually among his books, since he has no other society."

I should not have spoken so, if I had known her true condition, but I could not get rid of the notion that she acted a part of her disorder.

"Among his books!" she cried, confounded. "And I dying! I on the brink of the grave! My God! does he know how I'm altered?" continued she, staring at her reflection in a mirror, hanging against the opposite wall. "Is that Catherine Linton? He imagines me in a pet—in play, perhaps. Cannot you inform him that it is frightful earnest? Nelly, if it be not too late, as soon as I learn how he feels, I'll choose between these two: either to starve at once—that would be no punishment unless he had a heart—or to recover and leave the country. Are you speaking the truth about him now? Take care. Is he actually so utterly indifferent for my life?"

"Why, ma'am," I answered, "the master has no idea of your being deranged; and, of course, he does not fear that you will let yourself die of hunger."

"You think not? Cannot you tell him I will?" she returned. "Persuade him—speak of your own mind—say you are certain I will!"

"No, you forget, Mrs. Linton," I suggested, "that you have eaten some food with a relish this evening, and to-morrow you will perceive its good effects."

"If I were only sure it would kill him," she interrupted, "I'd kill myself directly! These three awful nights, I've never closed my lids—and oh, I've been tormented! I've been haunted, Nelly! But I begin to fancy you don't like me. How strange! I thought, though everybody hated and despised each other, they could not avoid loving me—and they have all turned to enemies in a few hours. *They* have, I'm positive; the people *here*. How dreary to meet death, surrounded by their cold faces! Isabella, terrified and repelled, afraid to enter the room, it would be so dreadful to watch Catherine go. And Edgar standing solemnly by to see it over; then offering prayers of thanks to God for restoring peace to his house, and going back to his *books!* What, in the name of all that feels, has he to do with *books*, when I am dying?"

She could not bear the notion which I had put into her head of Mr. Linton's philosophical resignation. Tossing about, she increased her feverish bewilderment to madness, and tore the pillow with her teeth; then raising herself up all burning, desired that I would open the window. We were in the middle of winter, the wind blew strong from the northeast, and I objected.

Both the expressions flitting over her face, and the changes of her moods, began to alarm me terribly; and brought to my recollection her former illness, and the doctor's injunction that she should not be crossed.

A minute previously she was violent; now, supported on one arm, and not noticing my refusal to obey her, she seemed to find childish diversion in pulling the feathers from the rents she had just made, and ranging them on the sheet according to their different species: her mind had strayed to other associations.

"That's a turkey's," she murmured to herself; "and this is a wild-duck's; and this is a pigeon's. Ah, they put pigeons' feathers in the pillows—no wonder I couldn't die! Let me take care to throw it on the floor when I lie down. And here is a moor-cock's; and this—I should know it among a thousand—it's a lapwing's. Bonny bird; wheeling over our heads in the middle of the moor. It wanted to get to its nest, for the clouds touched the swells, and it felt rain coming. This feather was picked up from the heath, the bird was not shot; we saw its nest in the winter, full of little skeletons. Heathcliff set a trap over it, and the old ones dare not come. I made him promise he'd never shoot a lapwing after that, and he didn't. Yes, here are more! Did he shoot my lapwings, Nelly? Are they red, any of them? Let me look."

"Give over with that baby-work!" I interrupted, dragging the pillow away, and turning the holes towards the mattress, for she was removing its contents by handfuls. "Lie down and shut your eyes, you're wandering. There's a mess! The down is flying about like snow!"

I went here and there collecting it.

"I see in you, Nelly," she continued, dreamily, "an aged woman—you have grey hair, and bent shoulders. This bed is the fairy cave under Penistone Crag, and you are gathering elf-bolts to hurt our heifers;[1] pretending, while I am near, that they are only locks of wool. That's what you'll come to fifty years hence; I know you are not so now. I'm not wandering: you're mistaken, or else I should believe you really *were* that withered hag, and I should think I *was* under Penistone Crag, and I'm conscious it's night, and there are two candles on the table making the black press shine like jet."

"The black press? where is that?" I asked. "You are talking in your sleep!"

"It's against the wall, as it always is," she replied. "It *does* appear odd—I see a face in it!"

"There is no press in the room, and never was," said I, resuming my seat, and looping up the curtain that I might watch her.

"Don't *you* see that face?" she enquired, gazing earnestly at the mirror.

And say what I could, I was incapable of making her comprehend it to be her own; so I rose and covered it with a shawl.

"It's behind there still!" she pursued, anxiously. "And it stirred. Who is it? I hope it will not come out when you are gone! Oh! Nelly, the room is haunted! I'm afraid of being alone!"

1. Shots (bolts) by fairies at cattle. Earlier, when Nelly is stoned by young Hareton (Ch. XI), his "string of curses" and "shocking expression of malignity" suggest that he acts under the agency of an evil spirit (*OED* mentions that shepherds and cowherds are often exposed to the effects of elf-bolts).

I took her hand in mine, and bid her be composed, for a succession of shudders convulsed her frame, and she *would* keep straining her gaze towards the glass.

"There's nobody here!" I insisted. "It was *yourself*, Mrs. Linton; you knew it a while since."

"Myself," she gasped, "and the clock is striking twelve! It's true, then; that's dreadful!"

Her fingers clutched the clothes, and gathered them over her eyes. I attempted to steal to the door with an intention of calling her husband; but I was summoned back by a piercing shriek. The shawl had dropped from the frame.

"Why, what *is* the matter?" cried I. "Who is coward now? Wake up! That is the glass—the mirror, Mrs. Linton; and you see yourself in it, and there am I too, by your side."

Trembling and bewildered, she held me fast, but the horror gradually passed from her countenance; its paleness gave place to a glow of shame.

"Oh, dear! I thought I was at home," she sighed. "I thought I was lying in my chamber at Wuthering Heights. Because I'm weak, my brain got confused, and I screamed unconsciously. Don't say anything; but stay with me. I dread sleeping, my dreams appal me."

"A sound sleep would do you good, ma'am," I answered; "and I hope this suffering will prevent your trying starving again."

"Oh, if I were but in my own bed in the old house!" she went on bitterly, wringing her hands. "And that wind sounding in the firs by the lattice. Do let me feel it—it comes straight down the moor—do let me have one breath!"

To pacify her, I held the casement ajar, a few seconds. A cold blast rushed through; I closed it, and returned to my post.

She lay still now, her face bathed in tears. Exhaustion of body had entirely subdued her spirit; our fiery Catherine was no better than a wailing child!

"How long is it since I shut myself in here?" she asked, suddenly reviving.

"It was Monday evening," I replied, "and this is Thursday night, or rather Friday morning, at present."

"What! of the same week?" she exclaimed. "Only that brief time?"

"Long enough to live on nothing but cold water and ill-temper," observed I.

"Well, it seems a weary number of hours," she muttered doubtfully; "It must be more. I remember being in the parlour after they had quarrelled; and Edgar being cruelly provoking, and me running into this room desperate. As soon as ever I had barred the door, utter blackness overwhelmed me, and I fell on the floor. I couldn't explain to Edgar how certain I felt of having a fit, or going raging mad, if he persisted in teasing me! I had no command of tongue, or brain, and he did not guess my agony, perhaps; it barely left me sense to try to escape from him and his voice. Before I recovered sufficiently to see and hear, it began to be dawn; and, Nelly, I'll tell you what I thought, and what has kept recurring and recurring till I feared for my reason. I thought as I lay there with my head against that table leg, and my eyes dimly discerning the grey square of the window, that I was enclosed in the oak-panelled bed at home; and my heart ached with some great grief which, just waking, I could not recollect. I pondered, and worried myself to discover what it could be; and, most strangely, the whole last seven years of my life grew a blank! I did not recall that they had been at all. I was a child; my father was just buried, and my misery arose from the separation that Hindley had ordered between me and Heathcliff. I was laid alone, for the first time, and, rousing from a dismal doze after a night of weeping, I lifted my hand to push the panels aside: it struck the table-top! I swept it along the carpet, and then memory burst in—my late anguish was swallowed in a paroxysm of despair. I cannot say why I felt so wildly wretched—it must have been temporary derangement, for there is scarcely cause. But, supposing at twelve years old, I had been wrenched from the Heights, and every early association, and my all in all, as Heathcliff was at that time, and been converted at a stroke into Mrs. Linton, the lady of Thrushcross Grange, and the wife of a stranger; an exile, and outcast, thenceforth, from what had been my world. You may fancy a glimpse of the abyss where I grovelled! Shake your head as you will, Nelly, *you* have helped to unsettle me! You should have spoken to Edgar, indeed you should, and compelled him to leave me quiet! Oh, I'm burning! I wish I were out of doors—I wish I were a girl again, half savage, and hardy, and free; and laughing at injuries, not maddening under them! Why am I so changed? why does my blood rush into a hell of tumult at a few words? I'm sure I should be myself were I once among the heather on those hills. Open the window again wide, fasten it open! Quick, why don't you move?"

"Because I won't give you your death of cold," I answered.

"You won't give me a chance of life, you mean," she said sullenly. "However, I'm not helpless yet, I'll open it myself."

And sliding from the bed before I could hinder her, she crossed the room, walking very uncertainly, threw it back, and bent out, careless of the frosty air that cut about her shoulders as keen as a knife.

I entreated, and finally attempted to force her to retire. But I soon found her delirious strength much surpassed mine (she *was* delirious, I became convinced by her subsequent actions, and ravings).

There was no moon, and everything beneath lay in misty darkness; not a light gleamed from any house, far or near; all had been extinguished long ago; and those at Wuthering Heights were never visible—still she asserted she caught their shining.

"Look!" she cried eagerly, "that's my room, with the candle in it, and the trees swaying before it; and the other candle is in Joseph's garret. Joseph sits up late, doesn't he? He's waiting till I come home that he may lock the gate. Well, he'll wait a while yet. It's a rough journey, and a sad heart to travel it; and we must pass by Gimmerton Kirk, to go that journey! We've braved its ghosts often together, and dared each other to stand among the graves and ask them to come. But Heathcliff, if I dare you now, will you venture? If you do, I'll keep you. I'll not lie there by myself; they may bury me twelve feet deep, and throw the church down over me, but I won't rest till you are with me. I never will!"

She paused, and resumed with a strange smile, "He's considering—he'd rather I'd come to him! Find a way, then! not through that Kirkyard. You are slow! Be content, you always followed me!"

Perceiving it vain to argue against her insanity, I was planning how I could reach something to wrap about her, without quitting my hold of herself, for I could not trust her alone by the gaping lattice, when, to my consternation, I heard the rattle of the door-handle, and Mr. Linton entered. He had only then come from the library; and, in passing through the lobby, had noticed our talking and been attracted by curiosity, or fear, to examine what it signified at that late hour.

"Oh, sir!" I cried, checking the exclamation risen to his lips at the sight which met him, and the bleak atmosphere of the chamber. "My poor mistress is ill, and she quite masters me; I cannot manage her at all; pray, come and persuade her to go to bed. Forget your anger, for she's hard to guide any way but her own."

"Catherine ill?" he said, hastening to us. "Shut the window, Ellen! Catherine! why—"

He was silent; the haggardness of Mrs. Linton's appearance smote him speechless, and he could only glance from her to me in horrified astonishment.

"She's been fretting here," I continued, "and eating scarcely anything, and never complaining; she would admit none of us till this evening, and so we couldn't inform you of her state, as we were not aware of it ourselves, but it is nothing."

I felt I uttered my explanations awkwardly; the master frowned. "It is nothing, is it, Ellen Dean?" he said sternly. "You shall account more clearly for keeping me ignorant of this!" And he took his wife in his arms, and looked at her with anguish.

At first she gave him no glance of recognition—he was invisible to her abstracted gaze. The delirium was not fixed, however; having weaned her eyes from contemplating the outer darkness, by degrees she centred her attention on him, and discovered who it was that held her.

"Ah! you are come, are you, Edgar Linton?" she said, with angry animation. "You are one of those things that are ever found when least wanted, and when you are wanted, never! I suppose we shall have plenty of lamentations, now—I see we shall—but they can't keep me from my narrow home out yonder, my resting place where I'm bound before spring is over! There it is, not among the Lintons, mind, under the chapel-roof; but in the open air with a head-stone, and you may please yourself, whether you go to them, or come to me!"

"Catherine, what have you done?" commenced the master. "Am I nothing to you, any more? Do you love that wretch, Heath—"

"Hush!" cried Mrs. Linton. "Hush, this moment! You mention that name and I end the matter instantly, by a spring from the window! What you touch at present, you may have; but my soul will be on that hilltop before you lay hands on me again. I don't want you, Edgar; I'm past wanting you. Return to your books. I'm glad you possess a consolation, for all you had in me is gone."

"Her mind wanders, sir," I interposed. "She has been talking nonsense the whole evening; but, let her have quiet and proper attendance, and she'll rally. Hereafter, we must be cautious how we vex her."

"I desire no further advice from you," answered Mr. Linton. "You knew your mistress's nature, and you encouraged me to harass her. And not to give me one hint of how she has been these three days! It was heartless! Months of sickness could not cause such a change!"

I began to defend myself, thinking it too bad to be blamed for another's wicked waywardness!

"I knew Mrs. Linton's nature to be headstrong and domineering," cried I; "but I didn't know that you wished to foster her fierce temper! I didn't know that, to humour her, I should wink at Mr. Heathcliff. I performed the duty of a faithful servant in telling you, and I have got a faithful servant's wages! Well, it will teach me to be careful next time. Next time you may gather intelligence for yourself!"

"The next time you bring a tale to me, you shall quit my service, Ellen Dean," he replied.

"You'd rather hear nothing about it, I suppose, then, Mr. Linton?" said I. "Heathcliff has your permission to come a-courting to Miss, and to drop in at every opportunity your absence offers, on purpose to poison the mistress against you?"

Confused as Catherine was, her wits were alert at applying our conversation.

"Ah! Nelly has played traitor," she exclaimed, passionately. "Nelly is my hidden enemy. You witch! So you do seek elf-bolts to hurt us! Let me go, and I'll make her rue! I'll make her howl a recantation!"

A maniac's fury kindled under her brows; she struggled desperately to disengage herself from Linton's arms. I felt no inclination to tarry the event; and, resolving to seek medical aid on my own responsibility, I quitted the chamber.

In passing the garden to reach the road, at a place where a bridle hook is driven into the wall, I saw something white moved irregularly, evidently by another agent than the wind. Notwithstanding my hurry, I stayed to examine it, lest ever after I should have the conviction impressed on my imagination that it was a creature of the other world.

My surprise and perplexity were great to discover, by touch more than vision, Miss Isabella's springer, Fanny, suspended by a handkerchief, and nearly at its last gasp.

I quickly released the animal, and lifted it into the garden. I had seen it follow its mistress upstairs, when she went to bed, and wondered much how it could have got out there, and what mischievous person had treated it so.

While untying the knot round the hook, it seemed to me that I repeatedly caught the beat of horses' feet galloping at some distance; but there were such a number of things to occupy my reflections that I hardly gave the circumstance a thought, though it was a strange sound, in that place, at two o'clock in the morning.

Mr. Kenneth was fortunately just issuing from his house to see a patient in the village as I came up the street; and my account of Catherine Linton's malady induced him to accompany me back immediately.

He was a plain, rough man; and he made no scruple to speak his doubts of her surviving this second attack, unless she were more submissive to his directions than she had shown herself before.

"Nelly Dean," said he, "I can't help fancying there's an extra cause for this. What has there been to do at the Grange? We've odd reports up here. A stout, hearty lass like Catherine does not fall ill for a trifle; and that sort of people should not either. It's hard work bringing them through fevers, and such things. How did it begin?"

"The master will inform you," I answered; "but you are acquainted with the Earnshaws' violent dispositions, and Mrs. Linton caps them all. I may say this; it commenced in a quarrel. She was struck during a tempest of passion with a kind of fit. That's her account, at least; for she flew off in the height of it, and locked herself up. Afterwards, she refused to eat, and now she alternately raves and remains in a half dream, knowing those about her, but having her mind filled with all sorts of strange ideas and illusions."

"Mr. Linton will be sorry?" observed Kenneth, interrogatively.

"Sorry? He'll break his heart should anything happen!" I replied. "Don't alarm him more than necessary."

"Well, I told him to beware," said my companion, "and he must bide the consequences of neglecting my warning! Hasn't he been thick with Mr. Heathcliff lately?"

"Heathcliff frequently visits at the Grange," answered I, "though more on the strength of the mistress having known him when a boy, than because the master likes his company. At present, he's discharged from the trouble of calling; owing to some presumptuous aspirations after Miss Linton which he manifested. I hardly think he'll be taken in again."

"And does Miss Linton turn a cold shoulder on him?" was the doctor's next question.

"I'm not in her confidence," returned I, reluctant to continue the subject.

"No, she's a sly one," he remarked, shaking his head. "She keeps her own counsel! But she's a real little fool. I have it from good authority that last night (and a pretty night it was!) she and Heathcliff were walking in the plantation at the back of your house, above two hours; and he pressed her not to go in again, but just mount his horse and away with him! My informant said she could only put him off by pledging her word of honour to be prepared on their first meeting after that: when it was to be, he didn't hear, but you urge Mr. Linton to look sharp!"

This news filled me with fresh fears; I outstripped Kenneth, and ran most of the way back. The little dog was yelping in the garden yet. I spared a minute to open the gate for it, but instead of going to the house door, it coursed up and down snuffing the grass, and would have escaped to the road, had I not seized and conveyed it in with me.

On ascending to Isabella's room, my suspicions were confirmed: it was empty. Had I been a few hours sooner, Mrs. Linton's illness might have arrested her rash step. But what could be done now? There was a bare possibility of overtaking them if pursued instantly. *I* could not pursue them, however; and I dare not rouse the family, and fill the place with confusion; still less unfold the business to my master, absorbed as he was in his present calamity, and having no heart to spare for a second grief!

I saw nothing for it but to hold my tongue, and suffer matters to take their course; and Kenneth being arrived, I went with a badly composed countenance to announce him.

Catherine lay in a troubled sleep; her husband had succeeded in soothing the access of frenzy; he now hung over her pillow, watching every shade, and every change of her painfully expressive features.

The doctor, on examining the case for himself, spoke hopefully to him of its having a favourable termination, if we could only preserve around her perfect and constant tranquillity. To me, he signified the threatening danger was not so much death, as permanent alienation of intellect.

I did not close my eyes that night, nor did Mr. Linton; indeed, we never went to bed; and the servants were all up long before the usual hour, moving through the house with stealthy tread, and exchanging whispers as they encountered each other in their vocations. Every one was active but Miss Isabella; and they began to remark how sound she slept. Her brother too asked if she had risen, and seemed impatient for her presence, and hurt that she showed so little anxiety for her sister-in-law.

I trembled lest he should send me to call her; but I was spared the pain of being the first proclaimant of her flight. One of the maids, a thoughtless girl, who had been on an early errand to Gimmerton, came panting upstairs, open-mouthed, and dashed into the chamber, crying—

"Oh, dear, dear! What mun[2] we have next? Master, master, our young lady—"

"Hold your noise!" cried I hastily, enraged at her clamorous manner.

"Speak lower, Mary—What is the matter?" said Mr. Linton. "What ails your young lady?"

"She's gone, she's gone! Yon' Heathcliff's run off wi' her!" gasped the girl.

"That is not true!" exclaimed Linton, rising in agitation. "It cannot be—how has the idea entered your head? Ellen Dean, go and seek her—it is incredible—it cannot be."

As he spoke he took the servant to the door, and then repeated his demand to know her reasons for such an assertion.

"Why, I met on the road a lad that fetches milk here," she stammered, "and he asked whether we weren't in trouble at the Grange.

1. Must.

I thought he meant for Missis's sickness, so I answered, yes. Then, says he, 'They's somebody gone after 'em, I guess?' I stared. He saw I knew naught about it, and he told how a gentleman and lady had stopped to have a horse's shoe fastened at a blacksmith's shop, two miles out of Gimmerton, not very long after midnight! and how the blacksmith's lass had got up to spy who they were: she knew them both directly. And she noticed the man—Heathcliff it was, she felt certain, nob'dy could mistake him, besides—put a sovereign in her father's hand for payment. The lady had a cloak about her face; but having desired a sup of water, while she drank, it fell back, and she saw her very plain. Heathcliff held both bridles as they rode on, and they set their faces from the village, and went as fast as the rough roads would let them. The lass said nothing to her father, but she told it all over Gimmerton this morning."

I ran and peeped, for form's sake, into Isabella's room: confirming, when I returned, the servant's statement. Mr. Linton had resumed his seat by the bed; on my re-entrance, he raised his eyes, read the meaning of my blank aspect, and dropped them without giving an order, or uttering a word.

"Are we to try any measures for overtaking and bringing her back?" I inquired. "How should we do?"

"She went of her own accord," answered the master; "she had a right to go if she pleased. Trouble me no more about her. Hereafter she is only my sister in name, not because I disown her, but because she has disowned me."

And that was all he said on the subject; he did not make a single inquiry further, or mention her in any way, except directing me to send what property she had in the house to her fresh home, wherever it was, when I knew it.

Chapter XIII

For two months the fugitives remained absent; in those two months, Mrs. Linton encountered and conquered the worst shock of what was denominated a brain fever. No mother could have nursed an only child more devotedly than Edgar tended her. Day and night, he was watching, and patiently enduring all the annoyances that irritable nerves and a shaken reason could inflict; and, though Kenneth remarked that what he saved from the grave would only recompense his care by forming the source of constant future anxiety—in fact, that his health and strength were being sacrificed to preserve a mere ruin of humanity—he knew no limits in gratitude and joy when Catherine's life was declared out of danger; and hour after hour he would sit beside her, tracing the gradual return to bodily health, and flattering his too sanguine hopes with the illusion that her mind would settle back to its right balance also, and she would soon be entirely her former self.

The first time she left her chamber was at the commencement of the following March. Mr. Linton had put on her pillow, in the morning, a handful of golden crocuses; her eye, long stranger to any gleam of pleasure, caught them in waking, and shone delighted as she gathered them eagerly together.

"These are the earliest flowers at the Heights!" she exclaimed. "They remind me of soft thaw winds, and warm sunshine, and nearly melted snow. Edgar, is there not a south wind, and is not the snow almost gone?"

"The snow is quite gone down here, darling," replied her husband, "and I only see two white spots on the whole range of moors. The sky is blue, and the larks are singing, and the becks and brooks are all brim full. Catherine, last spring at this time, I was longing to have you under this roof; now, I wish you were a mile or two up those hills; the air blows so sweetly, I feel that it would cure you."

"I shall never be there, but once more!" said the invalid; "and then you'll leave me, and I shall remain for ever. Next spring you'll long again to have me under this roof, and you'll look back and think you were happy to-day."

Linton lavished on her the kindest caresses, and tried to cheer her by the fondest words; but, vaguely regarding the flowers, she let the tears collect on her lashes and stream down her cheeks unheeding.

We knew she was really better, and, therefore, decided that long confinement to a single place produced much of this despondency, and it might be partially removed by a change of scene.

The master told me to light a fire in the many-weeks-deserted parlour, and to set an easy-chair in the sunshine by the window; and then he brought her down, and she sat a long while enjoying the genial heat, and, as we expected, revived by the objects round her, which, though familiar, were free from the dreary associations investing her hated sick-chamber. By evening, she seemed greatly exhausted; yet no arguments could persuade her to return to that apartment, and I had to arrange the parlour sofa for her bed, till another room could be prepared.

To obviate the fatigue of mounting and descending the stairs, we fitted up this, where you lie at present, on the same floor with the parlour; and she was soon strong enough to move from one to the other, leaning on Edgar's arm.

Ah, I thought myself, she might recover, so waited on as she was. And there was double cause to desire it, for on her existence depended that of another; we cherished the hope that in a little while

Mr. Linton's heart would be gladdened, and his lands secured from a stranger's gripe, by the birth of an heir.

I should mention that Isabella sent to her brother, some six weeks from her departure, a short note, announcing her marriage with Heathcliff. It appeared dry and cold; but at the bottom was dotted in with pencil an obscure apology, and an entreaty for kind remembrance and reconciliation, if her proceeding had offended him; asserting that she could not help it then, and being done, she had now no power to repeal it.

Linton did not reply to this, I believe; and, in a fortnight more, I got a long letter, which I considered odd coming from the pen of a bride just out of the honeymoon. I'll read it, for I keep it yet. Any relic of the dead is precious, if they were valued living.

DEAR ELLEN, it begins.

I came last night to Wuthering Heights, and heard, for the first time, that Catherine has been, and is yet, very ill. I must not write to her, I suppose, and my brother is either too angry or too distressed to answer what I send him. Still, I must write to somebody, and the only choice left me is you.

Inform Edgar that I'd give the world to see his face again—that my heart returned to Thrushcross Grange in twenty-four hours after I left it, and is there at this moment, full of warm feelings for him, and Catherine! *I can't follow it, though*—(those words are underlined)—they need not expect me, and they may draw what conclusions they please; taking care, however, to lay nothing at the door of my weak will or deficient affection.

The remainder of the letter is for yourself alone. I want to ask you two questions: the first is—

How did you contrive to preserve the common sympathies of human nature when you resided here? I cannot recognise any sentiment which those around share with me.

The second question, I have great interest in; it is this—

Is Mr. Heathcliff a man? If so, is he mad? And if not, is he a devil? I shan't tell my reasons for making this inquiry; but I beseech you to explain, if you can, what I have married—that is, when you call to see me; and you must call, Ellen, very soon. Don't write, but come, and bring me something from Edgar.

Now, you shall hear how I have been received in my new home, as I am led to imagine the Heights will be. It is to amuse myself that I dwell on such subjects as the lack of external comforts; they never occupy my thoughts, except at the moment when I miss them. I should laugh and dance for joy, if I found their absence was the total of my miseries, and the rest was an unnatural dream!

The sun set behind the Grange, as we turned on to the moors; by that, I judged it to be six o'clock; and my companion halted half-an-hour, to inspect the park, and the gardens, and, probably, the place itself, as well as he could; so it was dark when we dismounted in the paved yard of the farmhouse, and your old fellow-servant, Joseph, issued out to receive us by the light of a dip candle. He did it with a courtesy that redounded to his credit. His first act was to elevate his torch to a level with my face, squint malignantly, project his under-lip, and turn away.

Then he took the two horses, and led them into the stables; reappearing for the purpose of locking the outer gate, as if we lived in an ancient castle.

Heathcliff stayed to speak to him, and I entered the kitchen—a dingy, untidy hole; I dare say you would not know it, it is so changed since it was in your charge.

By the fire stood a ruffianly child, strong in limb and dirty in garb, with a look of Catherine in his eyes and about his mouth.

"This is Edgar's legal nephew," I reflected—"mine in a manner; I must shake hands, and—yes—I must kiss him. It is right to establish a good understanding at the beginning."

I approached, and, attempting to take his chubby fist, said—

"How do you do, my dear?"

He replied in a jargon I did not comprehend.

"Shall you and I be friends, Hareton?" was my next essay at conversation.

An oath, and a threat to set Throttler on me if I did not "frame off,"[1] rewarded my perseverance.

"Hey, Throttler, lad!" whispered the little wretch, rousing a half-bred bull-dog from its lair in a corner. "Now, wilt tuh be ganging?"[2] he asked authoritatively.

Love for my life urged a compliance; I stepped over the threshold to wait till the others should enter. Mr. Heathcliff was nowhere visible; and Joseph, whom I followed to the stables and requested to accompany me in, after staring and muttering to himself, screwed up his nose and replied—

"Mim! mim! mim! Did iver Christian body hear owt like it? Minching un' munching! Hah can Aw tell whet ye say?"[3]

"I say, I wish you to come with me into the house!" I cried, thinking him deaf, yet highly disgusted at his rudeness.

"Nor nuh me! Aw getten summut else to do,"[4] he answered, and

1. Be gone.
2. Will you be going?
3. "Mim" is affectedly prim speech. Did ever a Christian hear anything like it? Miming and mouthing! How can I understand you?"
4. "Not me! I'm getting something else to do."

continued his work, moving his lantern jaws meanwhile, and surveying my dress and countenance (the former a great deal too fine, but the latter, I'm sure, as sad as he could desire) with sovereign contempt.

I walked round the yard, and through a wicket, to another door, at which I took the liberty of knocking, in hopes some more civil servant might shew himself.

After a short suspense, it was opened by a tall, gaunt man, without neckerchief, and otherwise extremely slovenly; his features were lost in masses of shaggy hair that hung on his shoulders; and *his* eyes, too, were like a ghostly Catherine's, with all their beauty annihilated.

"What's your business here?" he demanded, grimly. "Who are you?"

"My name *was* Isabella Linton," I replied. "You've seen me before, sir. I'm lately married to Mr. Heathcliff; and he has brought me here—I suppose by your permission."

"Is he come back, then?" asked the hermit, glaring like a hungry wolf.

"Yes—we came just now," I said; "but he left me by the kitchen door; and when I would have gone in, your little boy played sentinel over the place, and frightened me off by the help of a bull-dog."

"It's well the hellish villain has kept his word!" growled my future host, searching the darkness beyond me in expectation of discovering Heathcliff; and then he indulged in a soliloquy of execrations, and threats of what he would have done had the "fiend" deceived him.

I repented having tried this second entrance, and was almost inclined to slip way before he finished cursing, but ere I could execute that intention, he ordered me in, and shut and re-fastened the door.

There was a great fire, and that was all the light in the huge apartment, whose floor had grown a uniform grey; and the once brilliant pewter dishes, which used to attract my gaze when I was a girl, partook of a similar obscurity, created by tarnish and dust.

I inquired whether I might call the maid, and be conducted to a bed-room? Mr. Earnshaw vouchsafed no answer. He walked up and down, with his hands in his pockets, apparently quite forgetting my presence; and his abstraction was evidently so deep, and his whole aspect so misanthropical, that I shrank from disturbing him again.

You'll not be surprised, Ellen, at my feeling particularly cheerless, seated in worse than solitude on that inhospitable hearth, and remembering that four miles distant lay my delightful home, containing the only people I loved on earth; and there might as well be the Atlantic to part us, instead of those four miles: I could not overpass them!

I questioned with myself—where must I turn for comfort? and —mind you don't tell Edgar, or Catherine—above every sorrow beside, this rose pre-eminent—despair at finding nobody who could or would be my ally against Heathcliff!

I had sought shelter at Wuthering Heights, almost gladly, because I was secured by that arrangement from living alone with him; but he knew the people we were coming amongst, and he did not fear their intermeddling.

I sat and thought a doleful time; the clock struck eight, and nine, and still my companion paced to and fro, his head bent on his breast, and perfectly silent, unless a groan or a bitter ejaculation forced itself out at intervals.

I listened to detect a woman's voice in the house, and filled the interim with wild regrets and dismal anticipations, which, at last, spoke audibly in irrepressible sighing and weeping.

I was not aware how openly I grieved, till Earnshaw halted opposite, in his measured walk, and gave me a stare of newly awakened surprise. Taking advantage of his recovered attention, I exclaimed—

"I'm tired with my journey, and I want to go to bed! Where is the maid-servant? Direct me to her, as she won't come to me!"

"We have none," he answered; "you must wait on yourself!"

"Where must I sleep, then?" I sobbed—I was beyond regarding self-respect, weighed down by fatigue and wretchedness.

"Joseph will show you Heathcliff's chamber," said he; "open that door—he's in there."

I was going to obey, but he suddenly arrested me, and added in the strangest tone—

"Be so good as to turn your lock, and draw your bolt—don't omit it!"

"Well!" I said. "But why, Mr. Earnshaw?" I did not relish the notion of deliberately fastening myself in with Heathcliff.

"Look here!" he replied, pulling from his waistcoat a curiously constructed pistol, having a double-edged spring knife attached to the barrel. "That's a great tempter to a desperate man, is it not? I cannot resist going up with this, every night, and trying his door. If once I find it open, he's done for! I do it invariably, even though the minute before I have been recalling a hundred reasons that should make me refrain: it is some devil that urges me to thwart my own schemes by killing him. You fight against that devil, for love, as long as you may; when the time comes, not all the angels in heaven shall save him!"

I surveyed the weapon inquisitively; a hideous notion struck me. How powerful I should be possessing such an instrument! I took it from his hand, and touched the blade. He looked astonished at the expression my face assumed during a brief second. It was not horror, it was covetousness. He snatched the pistol back, jealously; shut the knife, and returned it to its concealment.

"I don't care if you tell him," said he. "Put him on his guard, and watch for him. You know the terms we are on, I see; his danger does not shock you."

"What has Heathcliff done to you?" I asked. "In what has he wronged you to warrant this appalling hatred? Wouldn't it be wiser to bid him quit the house?"

"No," thundered Earnshaw; "should he offer to leave me, he's a dead man: persuade him to attempt it, and you are a murderess! Am I to lose *all*, without a chance of retrieval? Is Hareton to be a beggar? Oh, damnation! I *will* have it back; and I'll have *his* gold too; and then his blood; and hell shall have his soul! It will be ten times blacker with that guest than ever it was before!"

You've acquainted me, Ellen, with your old master's habits. He is clearly on the verge of madness—he was so last night, at least. I shuddered to be near him, and thought on the servant's ill-bred moroseness as comparatively agreeable.

He now recommenced his moody walk, and I raised the latch, and escaped into the kitchen.

Joseph was bending over the fire, peering into a large pan that swung above it; and a wooden bowl of oatmeal stood on the settle close by. The contents of the pan began to boil, and he turned to plunge his hand into the bowl; I conjectured that this preparation was probably for our supper, and, being hungry, I resolved it should be eatable; so, crying out sharply, "*I'll* make the porridge!" I removed the vessel out of his reach, and proceeded to take off my hat and riding habit. "Mr. Earnshaw," I continued, "directs me to wait on myself: I will. I'm not going to act the lady among you, for fear I should starve."

"Gooid Lord!" he muttered, sitting down, and stroking his ribbed stockings from the knee to the ankle. "If they's tuh be fresh ortherings—just when Aw getten used tuh two maisters, if Aw mun hev a *mistress* set o'er my heead, it's loike time tuh be flitting. Aw niver *did* think tuh say t' day ut Aw mud lave th' owld place—but Aw daht it's nigh at hend!"[5]

This lamentation drew no notice from me; I went briskly to work, sighing to remember a period when it would have been all merry fun, but compelled speedily to drive off the remembrance. It racked

5. "Good Lord! . . . If there's to be new orders—just when I'm getting used to two masters, if I must have a mistress set over my head, it's a good time to be fleeing. I never did think to say the day that I must leave the old place—but I doubt [not] it's near at hand."

me to recall past happiness, and the greater peril there was of conjuring up its apparition, the quicker the thible[6] ran round, and the faster the handfuls of meal fell into the water.

Joseph beheld my style of cookery with growing indignation.

"Thear!" he ejaculated. "Hareton, thah willut sup thy porridge tuh neeght; they'll be nowt bud lumps as big as maw nave. Thear, agean! Aw'd fling in bowl un all, if Aw wer yah! Thear, pale t' guilp off, un' then yah'll hae done wi't. Bang, bang. It's a marcy t' bothom isn't deaved aht!"[7]

It *was* rather a rough mess, I own, when poured into the basins; four had been provided, and a gallon pitcher of new milk was brought from the dairy, which Hareton seized and commenced drinking and spilling from the expansive lip.

I expostulated, and desired that he should have his in a mug; affirming that I could not taste the liquid treated so dirtily. The old cynic chose to be vastly offended at this nicety; assuring me, repeatedly, that "the barn was every bit as gooid" as I, "and every bit as wollsome,"[8] and wondering how I could fashion to be so conceited; meanwhile, the infant ruffian continued sucking; and glowered up at me defyingly, as he slavered into the jug.

"I shall have my supper in another room," I said. "Have you no place you call a parlour?"

"*Parlour!*" he echoed, sneeringly, "*parlour!* Nay, we've noa *parlours*. If yah dunnut loike wer company, they's maister's; un' if yah dunnut loike maister, they's us."[9]

"Then I shall go upstairs," I answered; "shew me a chamber!"

I put my basin on a tray, and went myself to fetch some more milk.

With great grumblings, the fellow rose and preceded me in my ascent: we mounted to the garrets, he opening a door, now and then, to look into the apartments we passed.

"Here's a rahm," he said, at last, flinging back a cranky board on hinges. "It's weel eneugh tuh ate a few porridge in. They's a pack uh corn i' t' corner, thear, meeterly clane; if yah're feared uh muckying yer grand silk cloes, spread yer hankerchir ut t' top on't."[1]

6. A smooth stick for stirring broth or porridge.
7. "Hareton, you will not eat your porridge tonight; there will be nothing but bad lumps as big as my fist. There, again! I'd throw in bowl and all, if I were you! There, cool the iron pot off, and then you will be done with it. Bang, bang. It's a mercy the bottom isn't broken!"
8. Healthy.
9. "No, we've no parlor. If you don't like our company, there's master's; and if you don't like master's, there's ours."
1. "Here's a room . . . It's good enough to eat some porridge in. There's a sack of grain in the corner, there, fairly clean; and if you are afraid of dirtying your fine silk clothes, spread your handkerchief on the top of it."

The "rahm" was a kind of lumber-hole smelling strong of malt and grain; various sacks of which articles were piled around, leaving a wide, bare space in the middle.

"Why, man!" I exclaimed, facing him angrily, "this is not a place to sleep in. I wish to see my bed-room."

"*Bed-rume!*" he repeated, in a tone of mockery. "Yah's see all t' *bed-rumes* thear is—yon's mine."

He pointed into the second garret, only differing from the first in being more naked about the walls, and having a large, low, curtainless bed, with an indigo-coloured quilt, at one end.

"What do I want with yours?" I retorted. "I suppose Mr. Heathcliff does not lodge at the top of the house, does he?"

"Oh! it's Maister *Hathecliff's* yah're wenting?" cried he, as if making a new discovery. "Couldn't ye uh said soa, at onst? un then, Aw mud uh telled ye, 'baht all this wark, ut that's just one yah cannut sea—he allas keeps it locked, un' nob'dy iver mells on't but hisseln."[2]

"You've a nice house, Joseph," I could not refrain from observing, "and pleasant inmates; and I think the concentrated essence of all the madness in the world took up its abode in my brain the day I linked my fate with theirs! However, that is not to the present purpose—there are other rooms. For heaven's sake, be quick, and let me settle somewhere!"

He made no reply to this adjuration; only plodding doggedly down the wooden steps, and halting before an apartment which, from that halt and the superior quality of its furniture, I conjectured to be the best one.

There was a carpet, a good one; but the pattern was obliterated by dust; a fire-place hung with cut paper, dropping to pieces; a handsome oak-bedstead with ample crimson curtains of rather expensive material and modern make. But they had evidently experienced rough usage; the valances hung in festoons, wrenched from their rings, and the iron rod supporting them was bent in an arc on one side, causing the drapery to trail upon the floor. The chairs were also damaged, many of them severely; and deep indentations deformed the panels of the walls.

I was endeavouring to gather resolution for entering, and taking possession, when my fool of a guide announced—

"This here is t' maister's."

My supper by this time was cold, my appetite gone, and my patience exhausted. I insisted on being provided instantly with a place of refuge, and means of repose.

2. "Couldn't you have said so, at once? And then, I might have told you without all this work, and that's just one [room] you cannot see—he always keeps it locked, and nobody ever meddles in it but himself."

"Whear the divil—" began the religious elder. "The Lord bless us! The Lord forgie us! Whear the *hell* wold ye gang? ye marred, wearisome nowt! Yah seen all bud Hareton's bit uf a cham'er. They's nut another hoile tuh lig dahn in i' th' hahse!"[3]

I was so vexed, I flung my tray and its contents on the ground; and then seated myself at the stairs-head, hid my face in my hands, and cried.

"Ech! ech!" exclaimed Joseph. "Weel done, Miss Cathy! weel done, Miss Cathy! Hahsiver, t' maister sall just tum'le o'er them brocken pots, un' then we's hear summut; we's hear hah it's tuh be. Gooid-fur-nowt madling! yah desarve pining froo this tuh Churstmas, flinging t' precious gifts uh God under fooit i' yer flaysome rages! Bud Aw'm mista'em if yah shew yer sperrit lang. Will Hathecliff bide sich bonny ways, think ye? Aw nobbut wish he muh cotch ye i' that plisky. Aw nobbut wish he may."[4]

And so he went scolding to his den beneath, taking the candle with him, and I remained in the dark.

The period of reflection succeeding this silly action compelled me to admit the necessity of smothering my pride, and choking my wrath, and bestirring myself to remove its effects.

An unexpected aid presently appeared in the shape of Throttler, whom I now recognised as a son of our old Skulker; it had spent its whelphood at the Grange, and was given by my father to Mr. Hindley. I fancy it knew me: it pushed its nose against mine by way of salute, and then hastened to devour the porridge, while I groped from step to step, collecting the shattered earthenware, and drying the spatters of milk from the banister with my pocket-handkerchief.

Our labours were scarcely over when I heard Earnshaw's tread in the passage; my assistant tucked in his tail, and pressed to the wall; I stole into the nearest doorway. The dog's endeavour to avoid him was unsuccessful, as I guessed by a scutter downstairs, and a prolonged, piteous yelping. I had better luck. He passed on, entered his chamber, and shut the door.

Directly after, Joseph came up with Hareton, to put him to bed. I had found shelter in Hareton's room, and the old man, on seeing me, said—

"They's rahm fur boath yah un yer pride, nah, Aw sud think i' th'

3. "The Lord forgive us. Where the hell would you go, you spoiled, wearisome nothing! You have seen all except Hareton's bit of a chamber. There's no other hole to lie down in in the house."

4. "Well done, Miss Cathy . . . Howsoever, the master shall just tumble over those broken pots, and we'll hear something; we'll hear how it's to be. Good-for-nothing blockhead. [Andrew Wright's *English Dialect Dictionary* cites this passage in defining "madling"]. You deserve [to be] pining about this until Christmas, flinging the precious gifts of God underfoot in your terrible rage. But I'm mistaken if you show your spirit long. Do you think Heathcliff will put up with such behavior? I only hope that he may catch you in that rage. I only wish he may."

hahse. It's empty; yah muh hev it all tuh yerseln, un Him as allas maks a third, i' sich ill company!"[5]

Gladly did I take advantage of this intimation; and the minute I flung myself into a chair, by the fire, I nodded, and slept.

My slumber was deep and sweet, though over far too soon. Mr. Heathcliff awoke me; he had just come in, and demanded, in his loving manner, what I was doing there?

I told him the cause of my staying up so late—that he had the key of our room in his pocket.

The adjective *our* gave mortal offence. He swore it was not, nor ever should be mine; and he'd—but I'll not repeat his language, nor describe his habitual conduct; he is ingenious and unresting in seeking to gain my abhorrence! I sometimes wonder at him with an intensity that deadens my fear: yet, I assure you, a tiger or a venomous serpent could not rouse terror in me equal to that which he wakens. He told me of Catherine's illness, and accused my brother of causing it; promising that I should be Edgar's proxy in suffering, till he could get a hold of him.

I do hate him—I am wretched—I have been a fool! Beware of uttering one breath of this to any one at the Grange. I shall expect you every day—don't disappoint me!

ISABELLA.

Chapter XIV

As soon as I had perused this epistle, I went to the master, and informed him that his sister had arrived at the Heights, and sent me a letter expressing her sorrow for Mrs. Linton's situation, and her ardent desire to see him; with a wish that he would transmit to her, as early as possible, some token of forgiveness by me.

"Forgiveness!" said Linton. "I have nothing to forgive her, Ellen. You may call at Wuthering Heights this afternoon, if you like, and say that I am not *angry*, but I'm *sorry* to have lost her: especially as I can never think she'll be happy. It is out of the question my going to see her, however; we are eternally divided; and should she really wish to oblige me, let her persuade the villain she has married to leave the country."

"And you won't write her a little note, sir?" I asked, imploringly.

"No," he answered. "It is needless. My communication with Heathcliff's family shall be as sparing as his with mine. It shall not exist!"

5. "There's room for both you and your pride, now, I should think in the house. It's empty; you may have it all to yourself, and Him [God] who always makes a third in such ill company."

Mr. Edgar's coldness depressed me exceedingly; and all the way from the Grange I puzzled my brains how to put more heart into what he said, when I repeated it; and how to soften his refusal of even a few lines to console Isabella.

I dare say she had been on the watch for me since morning: I saw her looking through the lattice, as I came up the garden causeway, and I nodded to her; but she drew back, as if afraid of being observed.

I entered without knocking. There never was such a dreary, dismal scene as the formerly cheerful house presented! I must confess that, if I had been in the young lady's place, I would, at least, have swept the hearth and wiped the tables with a duster. But she already partook of the pervading spirit of neglect which encompassed her. Her pretty face was wan and listless; her hair uncurled, some locks hanging lankly down, and some carelessly twisted round her head. Probably she had not touched her dress since yester evening.

Hindley was not there. Mr. Heathcliff sat at a table, turning over some papers in his pocket-book; but he rose when I appeared, asked me how I did, quite friendly, and offered me a chair.

He was the only thing there that seemed decent, and I thought he never looked better. So much had circumstances altered their positions, that he would certainly have struck a stranger as a born and bred gentleman, and his wife as a thorough little slattern!

She came forward eagerly to greet me; and held out one hand to take the expected letter.

I shook my head. She wouldn't understand the hint, but followed me to a sideboard, where I went to lay my bonnet, and importuned me in a whisper to give her directly what I had brought.

Heathcliff guessed the meaning of her manœuvres, and said—

"If you have got anything for Isabella, as no doubt you have, Nelly, give it to her. You needn't make a secret of it; we have no secrets between us."

"Oh, I have nothing," I replied, thinking it best to speak the truth at once. "My master bid me tell his sister that she must not expect either a letter or a visit from him at present. He sends his love, ma'am, and his wishes for your happiness, and his pardon for the grief you have occasioned; but he thinks that after this time, his household, and the household here, should drop intercommunication, as nothing good could come of keeping it up."

Mrs. Heathcliff's lip quivered slightly, and she returned to her seat in the window. Her husband took his stand on the hearthstone, near me, and began to put questions concerning Catherine.

I told him as much as I thought proper of her illness, and he extorted from me, by cross-examination, most of the facts connected with its origin.

I blamed her, as she deserved, for bringing it all on herself; and ended by hoping that he would follow Mr. Linton's example, and avoid future interference with his family, for good or evil.

"Mrs. Linton is now just recovering," I said; "she'll never be like she was, but her life is spared, and if you really have a regard for her, you'll shun crossing her way again. Nay, you'll move out of this country entirely; and that you may not regret it, I'll inform you Catherine Linton is as different now from your old friend Catherine Earnshaw, as that young lady is different from me! Her appearance is changed greatly, her character much more so; and the person who is compelled, of necessity, to be her companion, will only sustain his affection hereafter by the remembrance of what she once was, by common humanity, and a sense of duty!"

"That is quite possible," remarked Heathcliff, forcing himself to seem calm, "quite possible that your master should have nothing but common humanity, and a sense of duty to fall back upon. But do you imagine that I shall leave Catherine to his *duty* and *humanity*? and can you compare my feelings respecting Catherine, to his? Before you leave this house, I must exact a promise from you, that you'll get me an interview with her: consent, or refuse, I *will* see her! What do you say?"

"I say, Mr. Heathcliff," I replied, "you must not—you never shall, through my means. Another encounter between you and the master would kill her altogether!"

"With your aid that may be avoided," he continued, "and should there be danger of such an event—should he be the cause of adding a single trouble more to her existence—why, I think, I shall be justified in going to extremes! I wish you had sincerity enough to tell me whether Catherine would suffer greatly from his loss. The fear that she would restrains me: and there you see the distinction between our feelings. Had he been in my place, and I in his, though I hated him with a hatred that turned my life to gall, I never would have raised a hand against him. You may look incredulous, if you please! I never would have banished him from her society, as long as she desired his. The moment her regard ceased, I would have torn his heart out, and drank his blood! But, till then—if you don't believe me, you don't know me—till then, I would have died by inches before I touched a single hair of his head!"

"And yet," I interrupted, "you have no scruples in completely ruining all hopes of her perfect restoration, by thrusting yourself into her remembrance, now, when she has nearly forgotten you, and involving her in a new tumult of discord and distress."

"You suppose she has nearly forgotten me?" he said. "Oh, Nelly! you know she has not! You know as well as I do, that for every thought she spends on Linton, she spends a thousand on me! At a most miserable period of my life, I had a notion of the kind; it haunted me on my return to the neighbourhood last summer, but only her own assurance could make me admit the horrible idea again. And then, Linton would be nothing, nor Hindley, nor all the dreams that ever I dreamt. Two words would comprehend my future—*death* and *hell*; existence, after losing her, would be hell.

"Yet I was a fool to fancy for a moment that she valued Edgar Linton's attachment more than mine. If he loved with all the powers of his puny being, he couldn't love as much in eighty years as I could in a day. And Catherine has a heart as deep as I have; the sea could be as readily contained in that horse-trough, as her whole affection be monopolized by him. Tush! He is scarcely a degree dearer to her than her dog, or her horse. It is not in him to be loved like me: how can she love in him what he has not?"

"Catherine and Edgar are as fond of each other as any two people can be!" cried Isabella, with sudden vivacity. "No one has a right to talk in that manner, and I won't hear my brother depreciated in silence!"

"Your brother is wondrous fond of you too, isn't he?" observed Heathcliff scornfully. "He turns you adrift on the world with surprising alacrity."

"He is not aware of what I suffer," she replied. "I didn't tell him that."

"You have been telling him something, then—you have written, have you?"

"To say that I was married, I did write—you saw the note."

"And nothing since?"

"No."

"My young lady is looking sadly the worse for her change of condition," I remarked. "Somebody's love comes short in her case, obviously—whose I may guess; but, perhaps, I shouldn't say."

"I should guess it was her own," said Heathcliff. "She degenerates into a mere slut! She is tired of trying to please me, uncommonly early. You'd hardly credit it, but the very morrow of our wedding, she was weeping to go home. However, she'll suit this house so much the better for not being over nice, and I'll take care she does not disgrace me by rambling abroad."

"Well, sir," returned I, "I hope you'll consider that Mrs. Heathcliff is accustomed to be looked after and waited on; and that she has been brought up like an only daughter, whom every one was ready to serve. You must let her have a maid to keep things tidy about her, and you must treat her kindly. Whatever be your notion of Mr. Edgar, you cannot doubt that she has a capacity for strong attachments, or she wouldn't have abandoned the elegancies, and comforts, and friends of her former home, to fix contentedly, in such a wilderness as this, with you."

"She abandoned them under a delusion," he answered, "picturing in me a hero of romance, and expecting unlimited indulgences from my chivalrous devotion. I can hardly regard her in the light of a rational creature, so obstinately has she persisted in forming a fabulous notion of my character, and acting on the false impressions she cherished. But, at last, I think she begins to know me. I don't perceive the silly smiles and grimaces that provoked me at first; and the senseless incapability of discerning that I was in earnest when I gave her my opinion of her infatuation, and herself. It was a marvellous effort of perspicacity to discover that I did not love her. I believed, at one time, no lessons could teach her that! And yet it is poorly learnt; for this morning she announced, as a piece of appalling intelligence, that I had actually succeeded in making her hate me! A positive labour of Hercules, I assure you! If it be achieved, I have cause to return thanks. Can I trust your assertion, Isabella? Are you sure you hate me? If I let you alone for half-a-day, won't you come sighing and wheedling to me again? I dare say she would rather I had seemed all tenderness before you; it wounds her vanity, to have the truth exposed. But I don't care who knows that the passion was wholly on one side, and I never told her a lie about it. She cannot accuse me of showing one bit of deceitful softness. The first thing she saw me do, on coming out of the Grange, was to hang up her little dog; and when she pleaded for it the first words I uttered were a wish that I had the hanging of every being belonging to her, except one: possibly she took that exception for herself. But no brutality disgusted her. I suppose she has an innate admiration of it, if only her precious person were secure from injury! Now, was it not the depth of absurdity—of genuine idiocy—for that pitiful, slavish, mean-minded brach[1] to dream that I could love her? Tell your master, Nelly, that I never, in all my life, met with such an abject thing as she is. She even disgraces the name of Linton; and I've sometimes relented, from pure lack of invention, in my experiments on what she could endure, and still creep shamefully cringing back! But tell him, also, to set his fraternal and magisterial heart at ease, that I keep strictly within the limits of the law. I have avoided, up to this period, giving her the slightest right to claim a separation; and, what's more, she'd thank nobody for dividing us. If she desired to go she might: the nuisance of her presence outweighs the gratification to be derived from tormenting her!"

1. Bitch-hound.

"Mr. Heathcliff," said I, "this is the talk of a madman, and your wife, most likely, is convinced you are mad; and, for that reason, she has borne with you hitherto: but now that you say she may go, she'll doubtless avail herself of the permission. You are not so bewitched, ma'am, are you, as to remain with him of your own accord?"

"Take care, Ellen!" answered Isabella, her eyes sparkling irefully; there was no misdoubting by their expression, the full success of her partner's endeavours to make himself detested. "Don't put faith in a single word he speaks. He's a lying fiend, a monster, and not a human being! I've been told I might leave him before; and I've made the attempt, but I dare not repeat it! Only, Ellen, promise you'll not mention a syllable of his infamous conversation to my brother or Catherine. Whatever he may pretend, he wishes to provoke Edgar to desperation: he says he has married me on purpose to obtain power over him; and he shan't obtain it—I'll die first! I just hope, I pray, that he may forget his diabolical prudence, and kill me! The single pleasure I can imagine is to die, or to see him dead!"

"There—that will do for the present!" said Heathcliff. "If you are called upon in a court of law, you'll remember her language, Nelly! And take a good look at that countenance—she's near the point which would suit me. No, you're not fit to be your own guardian, Isabella, now; and I, being your legal protector, must retain you in my custody, however distasteful the obligation may be. Go upstairs; I have something to say to Ellen Dean in private. That's not the way—upstairs, I tell you! Why, this is the road upstairs, child!"

He seized, and thrust her from the room; and returned muttering—

"I have no pity! I have no pity! The more the worms writhe, the more I yearn to crush out their entrails! It is a moral teething, and I grind with greater energy, in proportion to the increase of pain."

"Do you understand what the word pity means?" I said, hastening to resume my bonnet. "Did you ever feel a touch of it in your life?"

"Put that down!" he interrupted, perceiving my intention to depart. "You are not going yet. Come here now, Nelly: I must either persuade or compel you to aid me in fulfilling my determination to see Catherine, and that without delay. I swear that I meditate no harm; I don't desire to cause any disturbance, or to exasperate or insult Mr. Linton; I only wish to hear from herself how she is, and why she has been ill; and to ask if anything that I could do would be of use to her. Last night, I was in the Grange garden six hours, and I'll return there to-night; and every night I'll haunt the place, and every day, till I find an opportunity of entering. If Edgar Linton meets me, I shall not hesitate to knock him down, and give him enough to ensure his quiescence while I stay. If his servants oppose me, I shall threaten them off with these pistols. But wouldn't it be better to prevent my coming in contact with them, or their master? And you could do it so easily! I'd warn you when I came, and then you might let me in unobserved, as soon as she was alone, and watch till I departed, your conscience quite calm: you would be hindering mischief."

I protested against playing that treacherous part in my employer's house; and besides, I urged the cruelty and selfishness of his destroying Mrs. Linton's tranquillity, for his satisfaction.

"The commonest occurrence startles her painfully," I said. "She's all nerves, and she couldn't bear the surprise, I'm positive. Don't persist, sir! or else, I shall be obliged to inform my master of your designs, and he'll take measures to secure his house and its inmates from any such unwarrantable intrusions!"

"In that case, I'll take measures to secure you, woman!" exclaimed Heathcliff; "you shall not leave Wuthering Heights till to-morrow morning. It is a foolish story to assert that Catherine could not bear to see me; and as to surprising her, I don't desire it: you must prepare her—ask her if I may come. You say she never mentions my name, and that I am never mentioned to her. To whom should she mention me if I am a forbidden topic in the house? She thinks you are all spies for her husband. Oh, I've no doubt she's in hell among you! I guess by her silence, as much as any thing, what she feels. You say she is often restless, and anxious-looking—is that a proof of tranquillity? You talk of her mind being unsettled. How the devil could it be otherwise, in her frightful isolation. And that insipid, paltry creature attending her from *duty* and *humanity*! From *pity* and *charity*! He might as well plant an oak in a flowerpot, and expect it to thrive, as imagine he can restore her to vigour in the soil of his shallow cares! Let us settle it at once; will you stay here, and am I to fight my way to Catherine over Linton and his footmen? Or will you be my friend, as you have been hitherto, and do what I request? Decide! Because there is no reason for my lingering another minute, if you persist in your stubborn ill-nature!"

Well, Mr. Lockwood, I argued and complained, and flatly refused him fifty times; but in the long run he forced me to an agreement. I engaged to carry a letter from him to my mistress; and should she consent, I promised to let him have intelligence of Linton's next absence from home, when he might come, and get in as he was able. I wouldn't be there, and my fellow servants should be equally out of the way.

Was it right or wrong? I fear it was wrong, though expedient. I thought I prevented another explosion by my compliance; and I thought, too, it might create a favourable crisis in Catherine's mental illness: and then I remembered Mr. Edgar's stern rebuke of my carrying tales; and I tried to smooth away all disquietude on the subject, by affirming, with frequent iteration, that that betrayal of trust, if it merited so harsh an appellation, should be the last.

Notwithstanding, my journey homeward was sadder than my journey thither; and many misgivings I had, ere I could prevail on myself to put the missive into Mrs. Linton's hand.

But here is Kenneth; I'll go down, and tell him how much better you are. My history is *dree*[2] as we say, and will serve to wile away another morning.

Dree, and dreary! I reflected as the good woman descended to receive the doctor; and not exactly of the kind which I should have chosen to amuse me. But never mind! I'll extract wholesome medicines from Mrs. Dean's bitter herbs; and firstly, let me beware of the fascination that lurks in Catherine Heathcliff's brilliant eyes. I should be in a curious taking if I surrendered my heart to that young person, and the daughter turned out a second edition of the mother!

Chapter XV[1]

Another week over—and I am so many days nearer health, and spring! I have now heard all my neighbour's history, at different sittings, as the housekeeper could spare time from more important occupations. I'll continue it in her own words, only a little condensed. She is, on the whole, a very fair narrator and I don't think I could improve her style.

In the evening, she said, the evening of my visit to the Heights, I knew, as well as if I saw him, that Mr. Heathcliff was about the place; and I shunned going out, because I still carried his letter in my pocket, and didn't want to be threatened, or teased any more.

I had made up my mind not to give it till my master went some where, as I could not guess how its receipt would affect Catherine. The consequence was, that it did not reach her before the lapse of three days. The fourth was Sunday, and I brought it into her room after the family were gone to church.

There was a man-servant left to keep the house with me, and we generally made a practice of locking the doors during the hours of service; but on that occasion the weather was so warm and pleasant that I set them wide open, and, to fulfil my engagement, as I knew

2. Sad.
1. Chapters are numbered consecutively in this Norton Critical Edition, but in the 1847 edition, this was the first chapter of the second volume.

who would be coming, I told my companion that the mistress wished very much for some oranges, and he must run over to the village and get a few, to be paid for on the morrow. He departed, and I went upstairs.

Mrs. Linton sat in a loose, white dress, with a light shawl over her shoulders, in the recess of the open window, as usual. Her thick, long hair had been partly removed at the beginning of her illness, and now she wore it simply combed in its natural tresses over her temples and neck. Her appearance was altered, as I had told Heathcliff, but when she was calm, there seemed unearthly beauty in the change.

The flash of her eyes had been succeeded by a dreamy and melancholy softness; they no longer gave the impression of looking at the objects around her; they appeared always to gaze beyond, and far beyond—you would have said out of this world. Then, the paleness of her face—its haggard aspect having vanished as she recovered flesh—and the peculiar expression arising from her mental state, though painfully suggestive of their causes, added to the touching interest which she wakened, and—invariably to me, I know, and to any person who saw her, I should think—refuted more tangible proofs of convalescence and stamped her as one doomed to decay.

A book lay spread on the sill before her, and the scarcely perceptible wind fluttered its leaves at intervals. I believe Linton had laid it there, for she never endeavoured to divert herself with reading, or occupation of any kind, and he would spend many an hour in trying to entice her attention to some subject which had formerly been her amusement.

She was conscious of his aim, and in her better moods endured his efforts placidly, only showing their uselessness by now and then suppressing a wearied sigh, and checking him at last with the saddest of smiles and kisses. At other times, she would turn petulantly away, and hide her face in her hands, or even push him off angrily; and then he took care to let her alone, for he was certain of doing no good.

Gimmerton chapel bells were still ringing; and the full, mellow flow of the beck in the valley came soothingly on the ear. It was a sweet substitute for the yet absent murmur of the summer foliage, which drowned that music about the Grange when the trees were in leaf. At Wuthering Heights it always sounded on quiet days, following a great thaw or a season of steady rain; and of Wuthering Heights, Catherine was thinking as she listened—that is, if she thought, or listened, at all—but she had the vague, distant look I mentioned before, which expressed no recognition of material things either by ear or eye.

"There's a letter for you, Mrs. Linton," I said, gently inserting it in one hand that rested on her knee. "You must read it immediately, because it wants an answer. Shall I break the seal?"

"Yes," she answered, without altering the direction of her eyes.

I opened it—it was very short.

"Now," I continued, "read it."

She drew away her hand, and let it fall. I replaced it in her lap, and stood waiting till it should please her to glance down; but that movement was so long delayed that at last I resumed—

"Must I read it, ma'am? It is from Mr. Heathcliff."

There was a start, and a troubled gleam of recollection, and a struggle to arrange her ideas. She lifted the letter, and seemed to peruse it; and when she came to the signature she sighed; yet still I found she had not gathered its import, for, upon my desiring to hear her reply, she merely pointed to the name, and gazed at me with mournful and questioning eagerness.

"Well, he wishes to see you," said I, guessing her need of an interpreter. "He's in the garden by this time, and impatient to know what answer I shall bring."

As I spoke, I observed a large dog, lying on the sunny grass beneath, raise its ears, as if about to bark, and then smoothing them back, announce by a wag of the tail that some one approached whom it did not consider a stranger.

Mrs. Linton bent forward, and listened breathlessly. The minute after, a step traversed the hall; the open house was too tempting for Heathcliff to resist walking in: most likely he supposed that I was inclined to shirk my promise, and so resolved to trust to his own audacity.

With straining eagerness Catherine gazed towards the entrance of her chamber. He did not hit the right room directly; she motioned me to admit him; but he found it out, ere I could reach the door, and in a stride or two was at her side, and had her grasped in his arms.

He neither spoke, nor loosed his hold, for some five minutes, during which period he bestowed more kisses than ever he gave in his life before, I dare say; but then my mistress had kissed him first, and I plainly saw that he could hardly bear, for downright agony, to look into her face! The same conviction had stricken him as me, from the instant he beheld her, that there was no prospect of ultimate recovery there—she was fated, sure to die.

"Oh, Cathy! Oh, my life! how can I bear it?" was the first sentence he uttered, in a tone that did not seek to disguise his despair.

And now he stared at her so earnestly that I thought the very intensity of his gaze would bring tears into his eyes; but they burned with anguish, they did not melt.

"What now?" said Catherine, leaning back, and returning his look with a suddenly clouded brow: her humour was a mere vane for constantly varying caprices. "You and Edgar have broken my heart, Heathcliff! And you both come to bewail the deed to me, as if *you* were the people to be pitied! I shall not pity you, not I. You have killed me—and thriven on it, I think. How strong you are! How many years do you mean to live after I am gone?"

Heathcliff had knelt on one knee to embrace her; he attempted to rise, but she seized his hair, and kept him down.

"I wish I could hold you," she continued, bitterly, "till we were both dead! I shouldn't care what you suffered. I care nothing for your sufferings. Why shouldn't you suffer? I do! Will you forget me—will you be happy when I am in the earth? Will you say twenty years hence, 'That's the grave of Catherine Earnshaw. I loved her long ago, and was wretched to lose her; but it is past. I've loved many others since—my children are dearer to me than she was, and, at death, I shall not rejoice that I am going to her, I shall be sorry that I must leave them!' Will you say so, Heathcliff?"

"Don't torture me till I'm as mad as yourself," cried he, wrenching his head free, and grinding his teeth.

The two, to a cool spectator, made a strange and fearful picture. Well might Catherine deem that Heaven would be a land of exile to her, unless, with her mortal body, she cast away her mortal character also. Her present countenance had a wild vindictiveness in its white cheek, and a bloodless lip and scintillating eye; and she retained in her closed fingers a portion of the locks she had been grasping. As to her companion, while raising himself with one hand, he had taken her arm with the other; and so inadequate was his stock of gentleness to the requirements of her condition, that on his letting go, I saw four distinct impressions left blue in the colourless skin.

"Are you possessed with a devil," he pursued, savagely, "to talk in that manner to me, when you are dying? Do you reflect that all those words will be branded in my memory, and eating deeper eternally, after you have left me? You know you lie to say I have killed you; and, Catherine, you know that I could as soon forget you as my existence! Is it not sufficient for your infernal selfishness, that while you are at peace I shall writhe in the torments of hell?"

"I shall not be at peace," moaned Catherine, recalled to a sense of physical weakness by the violent, unequal throbbing of her heart, which beat visibly and audibly under this excess of agitation.

She said nothing further till the paroxysm was over; then she continued, more kindly—

"I'm not wishing you greater torment than I have, Heathcliff! I only wish us never to be parted—and should a word of mine distress you hereafter, think I feel the same distress underground, and for my own sake, forgive me! Come here and kneel down again! You never harmed me in your life. Nay, if you nurse anger, that will be worse to remember than my harsh words! Won't you come here again? Do!"

Heathcliff went to the back of her chair, and leant over, but not so far as to let her see his face, which was livid with emotion. She bent round to look at him; he would not permit it; turning abruptly, he walked to the fire-place, where he stood, silent, with his back towards us.

Mrs. Linton's glance followed him suspiciously: every movement woke a new sentiment in her. After a pause, and a prolonged gaze, she resumed, addressing me in accents of indignant disappointment—

"Oh, you see, Nelly! he would not relent a moment, to keep me out of the grave! *That* is how I'm loved! Well, never mind! That is not *my* Heathcliff. I shall love mine yet; and take him with me—he's in my soul. And," added she, musingly, "the thing that irks me most is this shattered prison, after all. I'm tired, tired of being enclosed here. I'm wearying to escape into that glorious world, and to be always there; not seeing it dimly through tears, and yearning for it through the walls of an aching heart; but really with it, and in it. Nelly, you think you are better and more fortunate than I; in full health and strength. You are sorry for me—very soon that will be altered. I shall be sorry for *you*. I shall be incomparably beyond and above you all. I *wonder* he won't be near me!" She went on to herself. "I thought he wished it. Heathcliff, dear! you should not be sullen now. Do come to me, Heathcliff."

In her eagerness she rose and supported herself on the arm of the chair. At that earnest appeal, he turned to her, looking absolutely desperate. His eyes wide, and wet at last, flashed fiercely on her; his breast heaved convulsively. An instant they held asunder; and then how they met I hardly saw, but Catherine made a spring, and he caught her, and they were locked in an embrace from which I thought my mistress would never be released alive. In fact, to my eyes, she seemed directly insensible. He flung himself into the nearest seat, and on my approaching hurriedly to ascertain if she had fainted, he gnashed at me, and foamed like a mad dog, and gathered her to him with greedy jealousy. I did not feel as if I were in the company of a creature of my own species; it appeared that he would not understand, though I spoke to him; so I stood off, and held my tongue, in great perplexity.

A movement of Catherine's relieved me a little presently: she put up her hand to clasp his neck, and bring her cheek to his, as he held her; while he, in return, covering her with frantic caresses, said wildly—

"You teach me now how cruel you've been—cruel and false. *Why* did you despise me? *Why* did you betray your own heart, Cathy? I have not one word of comfort. You deserve this. You have killed yourself. Yes, you may kiss me, and cry; and wring out my kisses and tears. They'll blight you—they'll damn you. You loved me—then what *right* had you to leave me? What right—answer me—for the poor fancy you felt for Linton? Because misery, and degradation, and death, and nothing that God or Satan could inflict would have parted us, *you*, of your own will, did it. I have not broken your heart—*you* have broken it—and in breaking it, you have broken mine. So much the worse for me, that I am strong. Do I want to live? What kind of living will it be when you—oh, God! would *you* like to live with your soul in the grave?"

"Let me alone. Let me alone," sobbed Catherine. "If I've done wrong, I'm dying for it. It is enough! You left me too; but I won't upbraid you! I forgive you. Forgive me!"

"It is hard to forgive, and to look at those eyes, and feel those wasted hands," he answered. "Kiss me again; and don't let me see your eyes! I forgive what you have done to me. I love *my* murderer—but *yours!* How can I?"

They were silent—their faces hid against each other, and washed by each other's tears. At least, I suppose the weeping was on both sides; as it seemed Heathcliff *could* weep on a great occasion like this.

I grew very uncomfortable, meanwhile; for the afternoon wore fast away, the man whom I had sent off returned from his errand, and I could distinguish, by the shine of the westering sun up the valley, a concourse thickening outside Gimmerton chapel porch.

"Service is over," I announced. "My master will be here in half-an-hour."

Heathcliff groaned a curse, and strained Catherine closer—she never moved.

Ere long I perceived a group of the servants passing up the road towards the kitchen wing. Mr. Linton was not far behind; he opened the gate himself, and sauntered slowly up, probably enjoying the lovely afternoon that breathed as soft as summer.

"Now he is here," I exclaimed. "For heaven's sake, hurry down! You'll not meet any one on the front stairs. Do be quick; and stay among the trees till he is fairly in."

"I must go, Cathy," said Heathcliff, seeking to extricate himself from his companion's arms. "But, if I live, I'll see you again before you are asleep. I won't stray five yards from your window."

"You must not go!" she answered, holding him as firmly as her strength allowed. "You shall not, I tell you."

"For one hour," he pleaded, earnestly.

"Not for one minute," she replied.

"I *must*—Linton will be up immediately," persisted the alarmed intruder.

He would have risen, and unfixed her fingers by the act—she clung fast, gasping; there was mad resolution in her face.

"No!" she shrieked. "Oh, don't, don't go. It is the last time! Edgar will not hurt us. Heathcliff, I shall die! I shall die!"

"Damn the fool. There he is," cried Heathcliff, sinking back into his seat. "Hush, my darling! Hush, hush, Catherine! I'll stay. If he shot me so, I'd expire with a blessing on my lips."

And there they were fast again. I heard my master mounting the stairs—the cold sweat ran from my forehead; I was horrified.

"Are you going to listen to her ravings?" I said, passionately. "She does not know what she says. Will you ruin her, because she has not wit to help herself? Get up! You could be free instantly. That is the most diabolical deed that ever you did. We are all done for —master, mistress, and servant."

I wrung my hands, and cried out; and Mr. Linton hastened his step at the noise. In the midst of my agitation, I was sincerely glad to observe that Catherine's arms had fallen relaxed, and her head hung down.

"She's fainted or dead," I thought, "so much the better. Far better that she should be dead, than lingering a burden and a misery-maker to all about her."

Edgar sprang to his unbidden guest, blanched with astonishment and rage. What he meant to do, I cannot tell; however, the other stopped all demonstrations, at once, by placing the lifeless-looking form in his arms.

"Look there," he said. "Unless you be a fiend, help her first—then you shall speak to me!"

He walked into the parlour, and sat down. Mr. Linton summoned me, and with great difficulty, and after resorting to many means, we managed to restore her to sensation; but she was all bewildered; she sighed, and moaned, and knew nobody. Edgar, in his anxiety for her, forgot her hated friend. I did not. I went at the earliest opportunity, and besought him to depart, affirming that Catherine was better, and he should hear from me in the morning, how she passed the night.

"I shall not refuse to go out of doors," he answered; "but I shall stay in the garden; and, Nelly, mind you keep your word tomorrow. I shall be under those larch trees. Mind! or I pay another visit, whether Linton be in or not."

He sent a rapid glance through the half-open door of the chamber, and ascertaining that what I stated was apparently true, delivered the house of his luckless presence.

Chapter XVI

About twelve o'clock that night was born the Catherine you saw at Wuthering Heights, a puny, seven months' child; and two hours after, the mother died, having never recovered sufficient consciousness to miss Heathcliff, or know Edgar.

The latter's distraction at his bereavement is a subject too painful to be dwelt on; its after effects showed how deep the sorrow sunk.

A great addition, in my eyes, was his being left without an heir. I bemoaned that, as I gazed on the feeble orphan; and I mentally abused old Linton for—what was only natural partiality—the securing his estate to his own daughter, instead of his son's.

An unwelcomed infant it was, poor thing! It might have wailed out of life, and nobody cared a morsel, during those first hours of existence. We redeemed the neglect afterwards; but its beginning was as friendless as its end is likely to be.

Next morning—bright and cheerful out of doors—stole softened in through the blinds of the silent room, and suffused the couch and its occupant with a mellow, tender glow.

Edgar Linton had his head laid on the pillow, and his eyes shut. His young and fair features were almost as death-like as those of the form beside him, and almost as fixed; but *his* was the hush of exhausted anguish, and *hers* of perfect peace. Her brow smooth, her lids closed, her lips wearing the expression of a smile. No angel in heaven could be more beautiful than she appeared; and I partook of the infinite calm in which she lay. My mind was never in a holier frame than while I gazed on that untroubled image of Divine rest. I instinctively echoed the words she had uttered, a few hours before. "Incomparably beyond, and above us all! Whether still on earth or now in heaven, her spirit is at home with God!"

I don't know if it be a peculiarity in me, but I am seldom otherwise than happy while watching in the chamber of death, should no frenzied or despairing mourner share the duty with me. I see a repose that neither earth nor hell can break; and I feel an assurance of the endless and shadowless hereafter—the Eternity they have entered—where life is boundless in its duration, and love in its sympathy, and joy in its fulness. I noticed on that occasion how much selfishness there is even in a love like Mr. Linton's, when he so regretted Catherine's blessed release!

To be sure, one might have doubted, after the wayward and impatient existence she had led, whether she merited a haven of peace at last. One might doubt in seasons of cold reflection, but not then, in the presence of her corpse. It asserted its own tranquillity, which seemed a pledge of equal quiet to its former inhabitant.

"Do you believe such people *are* happy in the other world, sir? I'd give a great deal to know."

I declined answering Mrs. Dean's question, which struck me as something heterodox. She proceeded—

"Retracing the course of Catherine Linton, I fear we have no right to think she is: but we'll leave her with her Maker."

The master looked asleep, and I ventured soon after sunrise to quit the room and steal out to the pure, refreshing air. The servants thought me gone to shake off the drowsiness of my protracted watch; in reality, my chief motive was seeing Mr. Heathcliff. If he had remained among the larches all night, he would have heard nothing of the stir at the Grange, unless, perhaps, he might catch the gallop of the messenger going to Gimmerton. If he had come nearer, he would probably be aware, from the lights flitting to and fro, and the opening and shutting of the outer doors, that all was not right within.

I wished, yet feared, to find him. I felt the terrible news must be told, and I longed to get it over, but *how* to do it I did not know.

He was there—at least a few yards further in the park; leant against an old ash tree, his hat off, and his hair soaked with the dew that had gathered on the budded branches, and fell pattering round him. He had been standing a long time in that position, for I saw a pair of ousels passing and repassing scarcely three feet from him, busy in building their nest, and regarding his proximity no more than that of a piece of timber. They flew off at my approach, and he raised his eyes and spoke—

"She's dead!" he said; "I've not waited for you to learn that. Put your handkerchief away—don't snivel before me. Damn you all! she wants none of *your* tears!"

I was weeping as much for him as her: we do sometimes pity creatures that have none of the feeling either for themselves or others; and when I first looked into his face, I perceived that he had got intelligence of the catastrophe; and a foolish notion struck me that his heart was quelled and he prayed, because his lips moved and his gaze was bent on the ground.

"Yes, she's dead!" I answered, checking my sobs and drying my cheeks. "Gone to heaven, I hope, where we may, everyone, join her, if we take due warning, and leave our evil ways to follow good!"

"Did *she* take due warning, then?" asked Heathcliff, attempting a sneer. "Did she die like a saint? Come, give me a true history of the event. How did—"

He endeavoured to pronounce the name, but could not manage it; and compressing his mouth, he held a silent combat with his inward agony, defying, meanwhile, my sympathy with an unflinching, ferocious stare.

"How did she die?" he resumed, at last—fain, notwithstanding his hardihood, to have a support behind him, for, after the struggle, he trembled, in spite of himself, to his very finger-ends.

"Poor wretch!" I thought; "you have a heart and nerves the same as your brother men! Why should you be so anxious to conceal them? Your pride cannot blind God! You tempt Him to wring them, till He forces a cry of humiliation!"

"Quietly as a lamb!" I answered, aloud. "She drew a sigh, and stretched herself, like a child reviving, and sinking again to sleep; and five minutes after I felt one little pulse at her heart, and nothing more!"

"And—and did she ever mention me?" he asked, hesitating, as if he dreaded the answer to his question would introduce details that he could not bear to hear.

"Her senses never returned—she recognised nobody from the time you left her," I said. "She lies with a sweet smile on her face; and her latest ideas wandered back to pleasant early days. Her life closed in a gentle dream—may she wake as kindly in the other world!"

"May she wake in torment!" he cried, with frightful vehemence, stamping his foot, and groaning in a sudden paroxysm of ungovernable passion. "Why, she's a liar to the end! Where is she? Not *there*—not in heaven—not perished—where? Oh! you said you cared nothing for my sufferings! And I pray one prayer—I repeat it till my tongue stiffens—Catherine Earnshaw, may you not rest, as long as I am living! You said I killed you—haunt me, then! The murdered *do* haunt their murderers, I believe—I know that ghosts *have* wandered on earth. Be with me always—take any form—drive me mad! only *do* not leave me in this abyss, where I cannot find you! Oh, God! it is unutterable! I *cannot* live without my life! I *cannot* live without my soul!"

He dashed his head against the knotted trunk; and, lifting up his eyes, howled, not like a man, but like a savage beast getting goaded to death with knives and spears.

I observed several splashes of blood about the bark of the tree, and his hand and forehead were both stained; probably the scene I witnessed was a repetition of others acted during the night. It hardly moved my compassion—it appalled me; still I felt reluctant to quit him so. But the moment he recollected himself enough to notice me watching, he thundered a command for me to go, and I obeyed. He was beyond my skill to quiet or console!

Mrs. Linton's funeral was appointed to take place on the Friday following her decease; and till then her coffin remained uncovered, and strewn with flowers and scented leaves, in the great drawing-room. Linton spent his days and nights there, a sleepless guardian; and—a circumstance concealed from all but me—Heathcliff spent his nights, at least, outside, equally a stranger to repose.

I held no communication with him; still I was conscious of his design to enter, if he could; and on the Tuesday, a little after dark, when my master, from sheer fatigue, had been compelled to retire a couple of hours, I went and opened one of the windows, moved by his perseverance to give him a chance of bestowing on the fading image of his idol one final adieu.

He did not omit to avail himself of the opportunity, cautiously and briefly—too cautiously to betray his presence by the slightest noise; indeed, I shouldn't have discovered that he had been there, except for the disarrangement of the drapery about the corpse's face, and for observing on the floor a curl of light hair, fastened with a silver thread, which, on examination, I ascertained to have been taken from a locket hung around Catherine's neck. Heathcliff had opened the trinket and cast out its contents, replacing them by a black lock of his own. I twisted the two, and enclosed them together.

Mr. Earnshaw was, of course, invited to attend the remains of his sister to the grave; he sent no excuse, but he never came; so that besides her husband, the mourners were wholly composed of tenants and servants. Isabella was not asked.

The place of Catherine's interment, to the surprise of the villagers, was neither in the chapel, under the carved monument of the Lintons, nor yet by the tombs of her own relations, outside. It was dug on a green slope, in a corner of the kirkyard, where the wall is so low that heath and bilberry plants have climbed over it from the moor; and peat mould almost buries it. Her husband lies in the same spot, now; and they have each a simple headstone above, and a plain grey block at their feet, to mark the graves.

Chapter XVII

That Friday made the last of our fine days, for a month. In the evening, the weather broke; the wind shifted from south to north-east, and brought rain first, and then sleet and snow.

On the morrow one could hardly imagine that there had been three weeks of summer: the primroses and crocuses were hidden under wintry drifts; the larks were silent, the young leaves of the early trees smitten and blackened. And dreary, and chill, and dismal that morrow did creep over! My master kept his room. I took possession of the lonely parlour, converting it into a nursery; and there I was sitting, with the moaning doll of a child laid on my knee, rocking it to and fro, and watching, meanwhile, the still driving flakes build up the uncurtained window, when the door opened, and some person entered, out of breath and laughing!

My anger was greater than my astonishment for a minute; I supposed it one of the maids, and I cried—

"Have done! How dare you show your giddiness here? What would Mr. Linton say if he heard you?"

"Excuse me!" answered a familiar voice, "but I know Edgar is in bed, and I cannot stop myself."

With that, the speaker came forward to the fire, panting and holding her hand to her side.

"I have run the whole way from Wuthering Heights!" she continued, after a pause. "Except where I've flown. I couldn't count the number of falls I've had. Oh, I'm aching all over! Don't be alarmed. There shall be an explanation as soon as I can give it—only just have the goodness to step out and order the carriage to take me on to Gimmerton, and tell a servant to seek up a few clothes in my wardrobe."

The intruder was Mrs. Heathcliff. She certainly seemed in no laughing predicament: her hair streamed on her shoulders, dripping with snow and water; she was dressed in the girlish dress she commonly wore, befitting her age more than her position—a low frock, with short sleeves, and nothing on either head or neck. The frock was of light silk, and clung to her with wet; and her feet were protected merely by thin slippers; add to this a deep cut under one ear, which only the cold prevented from bleeding profusely, a white face scratched and bruised, and a frame hardly able to support itself through fatigue, and you may fancy my first fright was not much allayed when I had leisure to examine her.

"My dear young lady," I exclaimed, "I'll stir nowhere, and hear nothing, till you have removed every article of your clothes, and put on dry things; and certainly you shall not go to Gimmerton to-night; so it is needless to order the carriage."

"Certainly, I shall," she said; "walking or riding; yet I've no objection to dress myself decently; and—ah, see how it flows down my neck now! The fire does make it smart."

She insisted on my fulfilling her directions, before she would let me touch her; and not till after the coachman had been instructed to get ready, and a maid set to pack up some necessary attire, did

I obtain her consent for binding the wound and helping to change her garments.

"Now, Ellen," she said, when my task was finished, and she was seated in an easy chair on the hearth, with a cup of tea before her, "you sit down opposite me, and put poor Catherine's baby away—I don't like to see it! You mustn't think I care little for Catherine, because I behaved so foolishly on entering. I've cried too, bitterly—yes, more than any one else has reason to cry. We parted unreconciled, you remember, and I shan't forgive myself. But for all that, I was not going to sympathise with him—the brute beast! O, give me the poker! This is the last thing of his I have about me." She slipped the gold ring from her third finger, and threw it on the floor. "I'll smash it!" she continued, striking with childish spite. "And then I'll burn it!" and she took and dropped the misused article among the coals. "There! he shall buy another, if he gets me back again. He'd be capable of coming to seek me, to tease Edgar—I dare not stay, lest that notion should possess his wicked head! And besides, Edgar has not been kind, has he? And I won't come suing for his assistance; nor will I bring him into more trouble. Necessity compelled me to seek shelter here; though, if I had not learnt he was out of the way, I'd have halted at the kitchen, washed my face, warmed myself, got you to bring what I wanted, and departed again to anywhere out of the reach of my accursed—of that incarnate goblin! Ah, he was in such a fury! If he had caught me! It's a pity Earnshaw is not his match in strength—I wouldn't have run till I'd seen him all but demolished, had Hindley been able to do it!"

"Well, don't talk so fast, Miss!" I interrupted, "you'll disorder the handkerchief I have tied round your face, and make the cut bleed again. Drink your tea, and take breath and give over laughing. Laughter is sadly out of place under this roof, and in your condition!"

"An undeniable truth," she replied. "Listen to that child! It maintains a constant wail—send it out of my hearing, for an hour; I shan't stay any longer."

I rang the bell, and committed it to a servant's care; and then I inquired what had urged her to escape from Wuthering Heights in such an unlikely plight, and where she meant to go, as she refused remaining with us.

"I ought, and I wish to remain," answered she, "to cheer Edgar and take care of the baby, for two things, and because the Grange is my right home. But I tell you, he wouldn't let me! Do you think he could bear to see me grow fat and merry; and could bear to think that we were tranquil, and not resolve on poisoning our comfort? Now, I have the satisfaction of being sure that he detests me to the point of its annoying him seriously to have me within ear-shot, or eye-sight. I notice, when I enter his presence, the muscles of his countenance are involuntarily distorted into an expression of hatred; partly arising from his knowledge of the good causes I have to feel that sentiment for him, and partly from original aversion. It is strong enough to make me feel pretty certain that he would not chase me over England, supposing I contrived a clear escape; and therefore I must get quite away. I've recovered from my first desire to be killed by him. I'd rather he'd kill himself! He has extinguished my love effectually, and so I'm at my ease. I can recollect yet how I loved him; and can dimly imagine that I could still be loving him, if—no, no! Even if he had doted on me, the devilish nature would have revealed its existence somehow. Catherine had an awfully perverted taste to esteem him so dearly, knowing him so well. Monster! would that he could be blotted out of creation, and out of my memory!"

"Hush, hush! He's a human being," I said. "Be more charitable; there are worse men than he is yet!"

"He's not a human being," she retorted; "and he has no claim on my charity. I gave him my heart, and he took and pinched it to death; and flung it back to me. People feel with their hearts, Ellen, and since he has destroyed mine, I have not power to feel for him, and I would not, though he groaned from this to his dying day, and wept tears of blood for Catherine! No, indeed, indeed, I wouldn't!" And here Isabella began to cry; but, immediately dashing the water from her lashes, she recommenced.

"You asked, what has driven me to flight at last? I was compelled to attempt it, because I had succeeded in rousing his rage a pitch above his malignity. Pulling out the nerves with red hot pincers requires more coolness than knocking on the head. He was worked up to forget the fiendish prudence he boasted of, and proceeded to murderous violence. I experienced pleasure in being able to exasperate him: the sense of pleasure woke my instinct of self-preservation, so I fairly broke free, and if ever I come into his hands again he is welcome to a signal revenge.

"Yesterday, you know, Mr. Earnshaw should have been at the funeral. He kept himself sober for the purpose—tolerably sober; not going to bed mad at six o'clock and getting up drunk at twelve. Consequently, he rose, in suicidal low spirits, as fit for the church as for a dance; and instead, he sat down by the fire and swallowed gin or brandy by tumblerfuls.

"Heathcliff—I shudder to name him!—has been a stranger in the house from last Sunday till to-day. Whether the angels have fed him, or his kin beneath, I cannot tell; but he has not eaten a meal with us for nearly a week. He has just come home at dawn, and gone upstairs to his chamber; locking himself in—as if anybody dreamt of coveting his company! There he has continued, praying like a Methodist; only the deity he implored is senseless dust and ashes; and God, when addressed, was curiously confounded with his own black father! After concluding these precious orisons—and they lasted generally till he grew hoarse, and his voice was strangled in his throat—he would be off again; always straight down to the Grange! I wonder Edgar did not send for a constable, and give him into custody! For me, grieved as I was about Catherine, it was impossible to avoid regarding this season of deliverance from degrading oppression as a holiday.

"I recovered spirits sufficient to hear Joseph's eternal lectures without weeping; and to move up and down the house, less with the foot of a frightened thief than formerly. You wouldn't think that I should cry at anything Joseph could say, but he and Hareton are detestable companions. I'd rather sit with Hindley, and hear his awful talk, than with 't' little maister,' and his staunch supporter, that odious old man!

"When Heathcliff is in, I'm often obliged to seek the kitchen and their society, or starve among the damp, uninhabited chambers; when he is not, as was the case this week, I establish a table and chair at one corner of the house fire, and never mind how Mr. Earnshaw may occupy himself; and he does not interfere with my arrangements. He is quieter now than he used to be, if no one provokes him; more sullen and depressed, and less furious. Joseph affirms he's sure he's an altered man; that the Lord has touched his heart, and he is saved 'so as by fire.' I'm puzzled to detect signs of the favourable change, but it is not my business.

"Yester-evening, I sat in my nook reading some old books till late on towards twelve. It seemed so dismal to go upstairs, with the wild snow blowing outside, and my thoughts continually reverting to the kirkyard and the new-made grave! I dared hardly lift my eyes from the page before me, that melancholy scene so instantly usurped its place.

"Hindley sat opposite, his head leant on his hand, perhaps meditating on the same subject. He had ceased drinking at a point below irrationality, and had neither stirred nor spoken during two or three hours. There was no sound through the house but the moaning wind which shook the windows every now and then, the faint crackling of the coals, and the click of my snuffers as I removed at intervals the long wick of the candle. Hareton and Joseph were probably fast asleep in bed. It was very, very sad, and while I read, I sighed, for it seemed as if all joy had vanished from the world, never to be restored.

"The doleful silence was broken at length by the sound of the kitchen latch. Heathcliff had returned from his watch earlier than usual, owing, I suppose, to the sudden storm.

"That entrance was fastened, and we heard him coming round to get in by the other. I rose with an irrepressible expression of what I felt on my lips, which induced my companion, who had been staring towards the door, to turn and look at me.

" 'I'll keep him out five minutes,' he exclaimed. 'You won't object?'

" 'No, you may keep him out the whole night, for me,' I answered. 'Do! put the key in the lock, and draw the bolts.'

"Earnshaw accomplished this ere his guest reached the front; he then came and brought his chair to the other side of my table, leaning over it, and searching in my eyes for a sympathy with the burning hate that gleamed from his: as he both looked and felt like an assassin, he couldn't exactly find that; but he discovered enough to encourage him to speak.

" 'You and I,' he said, 'have each a great debt to settle with the man out yonder! If we were neither of us cowards, we might combine to discharge it. Are you as soft as your brother? Are you willing to endure to the last, and not once attempt a repayment?'

" 'I'm weary of enduring now,' I replied, 'and I'd be glad of a retaliation that wouldn't recoil on myself; but treachery and violence are spears pointed at both ends—they wound those who resort to them, worse than their enemies.'

" 'Treachery and violence are a just return for treachery and violence!' cried Hindley. 'Mrs. Heathcliff, I'll ask you to do nothing but sit still and be dumb. Tell me now, can you? I'm sure you would have as much pleasure as I in witnessing the conclusion of the fiend's existence; he'll be *your* death unless you overreach him—and he'll be *my* ruin. Damn the hellish villain! He knocks at the door as if he were master here already! Promise to hold your tongue, and before that clock strikes—it wants three minutes of one—you're a free woman!"

"He took the implements which I described to you in my letter from his breast, and would have turned down the candle. I snatched it away, however, and seized his arm.

" 'I'll not hold my tongue!' I said; 'you mustn't touch him. Let the door remain shut and be quiet!'

" 'No! I've formed my resolution, and by God, I'll execute it!' cried the desperate being. 'I'll do you a kindness in spite of yourself, and Hareton justice! And you needn't trouble your head to screen me; Catherine is gone. Nobody alive would regret me, or be ashamed, though I cut my throat this minute—and it's time to make an end!'

"I might as well have struggled with a bear, or reasoned with a lunatic. The only resource left me was to run to a lattice, and warn his intended victim of the fate which awaited him.

" 'You'd better seek shelter somewhere else to-night!' I exclaimed in a rather triumphant tone. 'Mr. Earnshaw has a mind to shoot you, if you persist in endeavouring to enter.'

" 'You'd better open the door, you ——' he answered, addressing me by some elegant term that I don't care to repeat.

" 'I shall not meddle in the matter,' I retorted again. 'Come in, and get shot, if you please! I've done my duty.'

"With that I shut the window, and returned to my place by the fire, having too small a stock of hypocrisy at my command to pretend any anxiety for the danger that menaced him.

"Earnshaw swore passionately at me, affirming that I loved the villain yet, and calling me all sorts of names for the base spirit I evinced. And I, in my secret heart (and conscience never reproached me) thought what a blessing it would be for *him*, should Heathcliff put him out of misery; and what a blessing for *me*, should he send Heathcliff to his right abode! As I sat nursing these reflections, the casement behind me was banged on to the floor by a blow from the latter individual, and his black countenance looked blightingly through. The stanchions stood too close to suffer his shoulders to follow, and I smiled, exulting in my fancied security. His hair and clothes were whitened with snow, and his sharp cannibal teeth, revealed by cold and wrath, gleamed through the dark.

" 'Isabella, let me in, or I'll make you repent!' he 'girned,'[1] as Joseph calls it.

" 'I cannot commit murder,' I replied. 'Mr. Hindley stands sentinel with a knife and loaded pistol.'

" 'Let me in by the kitchen door!' he said.

" 'Hindley will be there before me,' I answered. 'And that's a poor love of yours that cannot bear a shower of snow! We were left at peace in our beds as long as the summer moon shone, but the moment a blast of winter returns, you must run for shelter! Heathcliff, if I were you, I'd go stretch myself over her grave and die like a faithful dog. The world is surely not worth living in now, is it? You had distinctly impressed on me the idea that Catherine was the whole joy of your life. I can't imagine how you think of surviving her loss.'

" 'He's there, is he?' exclaimed my companion, rushing to the gap. 'If I can get my arm out I can hit him!'

"I'm afraid, Ellen, you'll set me down as really wicked; but you don't know all, so don't judge! I wouldn't have aided or abetted an attempt on even *his* life, for anything. Wish that he were dead, I must, and therefore I was fearfully disappointed, and unnerved by

1. Snarled.

terror for the consequences of my taunting speech, when he flung himself on Earnshaw's weapon and wrenched it from his grasp.

"The charge exploded, and the knife, in springing back, closed into its owner's wrist. Heathcliff pulled it away by main force, slitting up the flesh as it passed on, and thrust it dripping into his pocket. He then took a stone, struck down the division between two windows, and sprung in. His adversary had fallen senseless with excessive pain and the flow of blood that gushed from an artery, or a large vein.

"The ruffian kicked and trampled on him, and dashed his head repeatedly against the flags, holding me with one hand, meantime, to prevent me summoning Joseph.

"He exerted preter-human self-denial in abstaining from finishing him completely; but getting out of breath, he finally desisted, and dragged the apparently inanimate body onto the settle.

"There he tore off the sleeve of Earnshaw's coat, and bound up the wound with brutal roughness, spitting and cursing during the operation, as energetically as he had kicked before.

"Being at liberty, I lost no time in seeking the old servant, who, having gathered by degrees the purport of my hasty tale, hurried below, gasping, as he descended the steps two at once.

" 'Whet is thur tuh do, nah? whet is thur tuh do, nah?'

" 'There's this to do,' thundered Heathcliff, 'that your master's mad; and should he last another month, I'll have him to an asylum. And how the devil did you come to fasten me out, you toothless hound? Don't stand muttering and mumbling there. Come, I'm not going to nurse him. Wash that stuff away; and mind the sparks of your candle—it is more than half brandy!'

" 'Und soa, yah been murthering on him!' exclaimed Joseph, lifting his hands and eyes in horror. 'If iver Aw seed a seeght loike this! May the Lord—'

"Heathcliff gave him a push onto his knees in the middle of the blood, and flung a towel to him; but instead of proceeding to dry it up, he joined his hands, and began a prayer which excited my laughter from its odd phraseology. I was in the condition of mind to be shocked at nothing; in fact, I was as reckless as some malefactors show themselves at the foot of the gallows.

" 'Oh, I forgot you,' said the tyrant. 'You shall do that. Down with you. And you conspire with him against me, do you, viper? There, that is work fit for you!'

"He shook me till my teeth rattled, and pitched me beside Joseph, who steadily concluded his supplications and then rose, vowing he would set off for the Grange directly. Mr. Linton was a magistrate, and though he had fifty wives dead, he should inquire into this.

"He was so obstinate in his resolution that Heathcliff deemed it expedient to compel from my lips a recapitulation of what had taken place; standing over me, heaving with malevolence, as I reluctantly delivered the account in answer to his questions.

"It required a great deal of labour to satisfy the old man that Heathcliff was not the aggressor; especially with my hardly wrung replies. However, Mr. Earnshaw soon convinced him that he was alive still; he hastened to administer a dose of spirits, and by their succour his master presently regained motion and consciousness.

"Heathcliff, aware that his opponent was ignorant of the treatment received while insensible, called him deliriously intoxicated; and said he should not notice his atrocious conduct further, but advised him to get to bed. To my joy, he left us after giving this judicious counsel, and Hindley stretched himself on the hearthstone. I departed to my own room, marvelling that I had escaped so easily.

"This morning, when I came down, about half-an-hour before noon, Mr. Earnshaw was sitting by the fire, deadly sick; his evil genius, almost as gaunt and ghastly, leant against the chimney. Neither appeared inclined to dine, and having waited till all was cold on the table, I commenced alone.

"Nothing hindered me from eating heartily; and I experienced a certain sense of satisfaction and superiority, as, at intervals, I cast a look towards my silent companions, and felt the comfort of a quiet conscience within me.

"After I had done, I ventured on the unusual liberty of drawing near the fire, going round Earnshaw's seat, and kneeling in the corner beside him.

"Heathcliff did not glance my way, and I gazed up and contemplated his features almost as confidently as if they had been turned to stone. His forehead, that I once thought so manly, and that I now think so diabolical, was shaded with a heavy cloud; his basilisk eyes were nearly quenched by sleeplessness, and weeping, perhaps, for the lashes were wet then; his lips devoid of their ferocious sneer, and sealed in an expression of unspeakable sadness. Had it been another, I would have covered my face in the presence of such grief. In *his* case, I was gratified; and ignoble as it seems to insult a fallen enemy, I couldn't miss this chance of sticking in a dart; his weakness was the only time when I could taste the delight of paying wrong for wrong."

"Fie, fie, Miss!" I interrupted. "One might suppose you had never opened a Bible in your life. If God afflict your enemies, surely that ought to suffice you.[2] It is both mean and presumptuous to add your torture to his!"

2. Psalms 55. 18–23 stresses trust in God to afflict one's enemies, and urges one to "Cast thy burden upon the Lord, and he shall sustain thee."

"In general, I'll allow that it would be, Ellen," she continued. "But what misery laid on Heathcliff could content me, unless I have a hand in it? I'd rather he suffered *less*, if I might cause his sufferings and he might *know* that I was the cause. Oh, I owe him so much. On only one condition can I hope to forgive him. It is, if I may take an eye for an eye, a tooth for a tooth; for every wrench of agony, return a wrench, reduce him to my level. As he was the first to injure, make him the first to implore pardon; and then—why then, Ellen, I might show you some generosity. But it is utterly impossible I can ever be revenged, and therefore I cannot forgive him. Hindley wanted some water, and I handed him a glass, and asked him how he was.

" 'Not as ill as I wish,' he replied. 'But leaving out my arm, every inch of me is as sore as if I had been fighting with a legion of imps!'

" 'Yes, no wonder,' was my next remark. 'Catherine used to boast that she stood between you and bodily harm: she meant that certain persons would not hurt you, for fear of offending her. It's well people don't *really* rise from their grave, or, last night, she might have witnessed a repulsive scene! Are not you bruised, and cut over your chest and shoulders?'

" 'I can't say,' he answered; 'but what do you mean? Did he dare to strike me when I was down?'

" 'He trampled on, and kicked you, and dashed you on the ground,' I whispered. 'And his mouth watered to tear you with his teeth; because he's only half a man—not so much.'

"Mr. Earnshaw looked up, like me, to the countenance of our mutual foe, who, absorbed in his anguish, seemed insensible to anything around him; the longer he stood, the plainer his reflections revealed their blackness through his features.

" 'Oh, if God would but give me strength to strangle him in my last agony, I'd go to hell with joy,' groaned the impatient man, writhing to rise, and sinking back in despair, convinced of his inadequacy for the struggle.

" 'Nay, it's enough that he has murdered one of you,' I observed aloud. 'At the Grange, every one knows your sister would have been living now, had it not been for Mr. Heathcliff. After all, it is preferable to be hated than loved by him. When I recollect how happy we were—how happy Catherine was before he came—I'm fit to curse the day.'

"Most likely, Heathcliff noticed more the truth of what was said, than the spirit of the person who said it. His attention was roused, I saw, for his eyes rained down tears among the ashes, and he drew his breath in suffocating sighs.

"I stared full at him, and laughed scornfully. The clouded windows of hell flashed a moment towards me; the fiend which usually looked out, however, was so dimmed and drowned that I did not fear to hazard another sound of derision.

" 'Get up, and begone out of my sight,' said the mourner.

"I guessed he uttered those words, at least, though his voice was hardly intelligible.

" 'I beg your pardon,' I replied. 'But I loved Catherine too; and her brother requires attendance which, for her sake, I shall supply. Now that she's dead, I see her in Hindley; Hindley has exactly her eyes, if you had not tried to gouge them out and made them black and red, and her—'

" 'Get up, wretched idiot, before I stamp you to death!' he cried, making a movement that caused me to make one also.

" 'But then,' I continued, holding myself ready to flee, 'if poor Catherine had trusted you, and assumed the ridiculous, contemptible, degrading title of Mrs. Heathcliff, she would soon have presented a similar picture! *She* wouldn't have borne your abominable behaviour quietly; her detestation and disgust must have found voice.'

"The back of the settle and Earnshaw's person interposed between me and him; so instead of endeavouring to reach me, he snatched a dinner knife from the table and flung it at my head. It struck beneath my ear, and stopped the sentence I was uttering; but, pulling it out, I sprang to the door and delivered another which I hope went a little deeper than his missile.

"The last glimpse I caught of him was a furious rush on his part, checked by the embrace of his host; and both fell locked together on the hearth.

"In my flight through the kitchen I bid Joseph speed to his master; I knocked over Hareton, who was hanging a litter of puppies from a chair-back in the doorway; and, blest as a soul escaped from purgatory, I bounded, leaped, and flew down the steep road; then, quitting its windings, shot direct across the moor, rolling over banks, and wading through marshes; precipitating myself, in fact, towards the beacon light of the Grange. And far rather would I be condemned to a perpetual dwelling in the infernal regions, than even for one night abide beneath the roof of Wuthering Heights again."

Isabella ceased speaking, and took a drink of tea; then she rose, and bidding me put on her bonnet and a great shawl I had brought, and turning a deaf ear to my entreaties for her to remain another hour, she stepped onto a chair, kissed Edgar's and Catherine's portraits, bestowed a similar salute on me, and descended to the carriage accompanied by Fanny, who yelped wild with joy at recovering her mistress. She was driven away, never to revisit this neighbourhood; but a regular correspondence was established between her and my master when things were more settled.

I believe her new abode was in the south, near London; there she had a son born, a few months subsequent to her escape. He was christened Linton, and, from the first, she reported him to be an ailing, peevish creature.

Mr. Heathcliff, meeting me one day in the village, inquired where she lived. I refused to tell. He remarked that it was not of any moment, only she must beware of coming to her brother; she should not be with him, if he had to keep her himself.

Though I would give no information, he discovered, through some of the other servants, both her place of residence and the existence of the child. Still he didn't molest her; for which forbearance she might thank his aversion, I suppose.

He often asked about the infant, when he saw me; and on hearing its name, smiled grimly, and observed—

"They wish me to hate it too, do they?"

"I don't think they wish you to know any thing about it," I answered.

"But I'll have it," he said, "when I want it. They may reckon on that!"

Fortunately, its mother died before the time arrived, some thirteen years after the decease of Catherine, when Linton was twelve, or a little more.

On the day succeeding Isabella's unexpected visit, I had no opportunity of speaking to my master: he shunned conversation, and was fit for discussing nothing. When I could get him to listen, I saw it pleased him that his sister had left her husband, whom he abhorred with an intensity which the mildness of his nature would scarcely seem to allow. So deep and sensitive was his aversion, that he refrained from going anywhere where he was likely to see or hear of Heathcliff. Grief, and that together, transformed him into a complete hermit: he threw up his office of magistrate, ceased even to attend church, avoided the village on all occasions, and spent a life of entire seclusion within the limits of his park and grounds, only varied by solitary rambles on the moors, and visits to the grave of his wife, mostly at evening, or early morning before other wanderers were abroad.

But he was too good to be thoroughly unhappy long. *He* didn't pray for Catherine's soul to haunt him. Time brought resignation, and a melancholy sweeter than common joy. He recalled her memory with ardent, tender love, and hopeful aspiring to the better world, where, he doubted not, she was gone.

And he had earthly consolation and affections, also. For a few days, I said, he seemed regardless of the puny successor to the departed: that coldness melted as fast as snow in April, and ere the tiny thing could stammer a word or totter a step, it wielded a despot's sceptre in his heart.

It was named Catherine, but he never called it the name in full, as he had never called the first Catherine short, probably because Heathcliff had a habit of doing so. The little one was always Cathy; it formed to him a distinction from the mother, and yet, a connection with her; and his attachment sprang from its relation to her, far more than from its being his own.

I used to draw a comparison between him and Hindley Earnshaw, and perplex myself to explain satisfactorily why their conduct was so opposite in similar circumstances. They had both been fond husbands, and were both attached to their children; and I could not see how they shouldn't both have taken the same road, for good or evil. But, I thought in my mind, Hindley, with apparently the stronger head, has shown himself sadly the worse and the weaker man. When his ship struck, the captain abandoned his post; and the crew, instead of trying to save her, rushed into riot and confusion, leaving no hope for their luckless vessel. Linton, on the contrary, displayed the true courage of a loyal and faithful soul: he trusted God; and God comforted him. One hoped, and the other despaired: they chose their own lots, and were righteously doomed to endure them.

But you'll not want to hear my moralizing, Mr. Lockwood: you'll judge as well as I can, all these things; at least, you'll think you will, and that's the same.

The end of Earnshaw was what might have been expected; it followed fast on his sister's: there were scarcely six months between them. We, at the Grange, never got a very succinct account of his state preceding it; all that I did learn was on occasion of going to aid in the preparations for the funeral. Mr. Kenneth came to announce the event to my master.

"Well, Nelly," said he, riding into the yard one morning, too early not to alarm me with an instant presentiment of bad news. "It's yours and my turn to go into mourning at present. Who's given us the slip now, do you think?"

"Who?" I asked in a flurry.

"Why, guess!" he returned, dismounting, and slinging his bridle on a hook by the door. "And nip up the corner of your apron; I'm certain you'll need it."

"Not Mr. Heathcliff, surely?" I exclaimed.

"What! would you have tears for him?" said the doctor. "No, Heathcliff's a tough young fellow; he looks blooming to-day—I've just seen him. He's rapidly regaining flesh since he lost his better half."

"Who is it, then, Mr. Kenneth?" I repeated impatiently.

"Hindley Earnshaw! Your old friend Hindley," he replied, "and my wicked gossip; though he's been too wild for me this long while. There! I said we should draw water. But cheer up! He died true to his character, drunk as a lord. Poor lad; I'm sorry, too. One can't help missing an old companion, though he had the worst tricks with him that ever man imagined, and has done me many a rascally turn. He's barely twenty-seven, it seems; that's your own age; who would have thought you were born in one year!"

I confess this blow was greater to me than the shock of Mrs. Linton's death: ancient associations lingered round my heart; I sat down in the porch and wept as for a blood relation, desiring Kenneth to get another servant to introduce him to the master.

I could not hinder myself from pondering on the question—"Had he had fair play?" Whatever I did, that idea would bother me: it was so tiresomely pertinacious that I resolved on requesting leave to go to Wuthering Heights, and assist in the last duties to the dead. Mr. Linton was extremely reluctant to consent, but I pleaded eloquently for the friendless condition in which he lay; and I said my old master and foster brother had a claim on my services as strong as his own. Besides, I reminded him that the child, Hareton, was his wife's nephew, and, in the absence of nearer kin, he ought to act as its guardian; and he ought to and must inquire how the property was left, and look over the concerns of his brother-in-law.

He was unfit for attending to such matters then, but he bid me speak to his lawyer; and at length permitted me to go. His lawyer had been Earnshaw's also: I called at the village, and asked him to accompany me. He shook his head, and advised that Heathcliff should be let alone, affirming, if the truth were known, Hareton would be found little else than a beggar.

"His father died in debt," he said; "the whole property is mortgaged, and the sole chance for the natural heir is to allow him an opportunity of creating some interest in the creditor's heart, that he may be inclined to deal leniently towards him."

When I reached the Heights, I explained that I had come to see everything carried on decently, and Joseph, who appeared in sufficient distress, expressed satisfaction at my presence. Mr. Heathcliff said he did not perceive that I was wanted, but I might stay and order the arrangements for the funeral, if I chose.

"Correctly," he remarked, "that fool's body should be buried at the cross-roads, without ceremony of any kind.[3] I happened to leave

3. Crossroads burial for criminals (particularly suicides) was permitted until 1823. See Robert Halliday, "Criminal Graves and Rural Crossroads," *British Archaeology* 27 (June 1997).

him ten minutes, yesterday afternoon; and, in that interval, he fastened the two doors of the house against me, and he has spent the night in drinking himself to death deliberately! We broke in this morning, for we heard him snorting like a horse; and there he was, laid over the settle: flaying and scalping would not have wakened him. I sent for Kenneth, and he came; but not till the beast had changed into carrion: he was both dead and cold and stark; and so you'll allow, it was useless making more stir about him!"

The old servant confirmed this statement, but muttered—

"Aw'd raything he'd goan hisseln fur t' doctor! Aw sud uh taen tent uh t' maister better nur him—un he warn't deead when Aw left, nowt uh t' soart!"[4]

I insisted on the funeral being respectable. Mr. Heathcliff said I might have my own way there too; only, he desired me to remember that the money for the whole affair came out of his pocket.

He maintained a hard, careless deportment, indicative of neither joy nor sorrow; if anything, it expressed a flinty gratification at a piece of difficult work successfully executed. I observed once, indeed, something like exultation in his aspect: it was just when the people were bearing the coffin from the house. He had the hypocrisy to represent a mourner; and previous to following with Hareton, he lifted the unfortunate child on to the table and muttered, with peculiar gusto—

"Now, my bonny lad, you are *mine!* And we'll see if one tree won't grow as crooked as another, with the same wind to twist it!"

The unsuspecting thing was pleased at this speech; he played with Heathcliff's whiskers, and stroked his cheek, but I divined its meaning and observed tartly—

"That boy must go back with me to Thrushcross Grange, sir. There is nothing in the world less yours than he is!"

"Does Linton say so?" he demanded.

"Of course—he has ordered me to take him," I replied.

"Well," said the scoundrel, "we'll not argue the subject now; but I have a fancy to try my hand at rearing a young one, so intimate to your master that I must supply the place of this with my own, if he attempt to remove it. I don't engage to let Hareton go, undisputed; but I'll be pretty sure to make the other come! Remember to tell him."

This hint was enough to bind our hands. I repeated its substance on my return, and Edgar Linton, little interested at the commencement, spoke no more of interfering. I'm not aware that he could have done it to any purpose, had he been ever so willing.

4. "I'd rather he'd gone himself for the doctor! I should have taken care of the master better than him—and he wasn't dead when I left, nothing of the sort!"

The guest was now the master of Wuthering Heights: he held firm possession, and proved to the attorney, who, in his turn, proved it to Mr. Linton, that Earnshaw had mortgaged every yard of land he owned for cash to supply his mania for gaming; and he, Heathcliff, was the mortgagee.

In that manner, Hareton, who should now be the first gentleman in the neighbourhood, was reduced to a state of complete dependence on his father's inveterate enemy; and lives in his own house as a servant deprived of the advantage of wages, and quite unable to right himself, because of his friendlessness, and his ignorance that he has been wronged.

Chapter XVIII

The twelve years, continued Mrs. Dean, following that dismal period, were the happiest of my life: my greatest troubles, in their passage, rose from our little lady's trifling illnesses, which she had to experience in common with all children, rich and poor.

For the rest, after the first six months, she grew like a larch, and could walk and talk too, in her own way, before the heath blossomed a second time over Mrs. Linton's dust.

She was the most winning thing that ever brought sunshine into a desolate house—a real beauty in face, with the Earnshaws' handsome dark eyes, but the Lintons' fair skin, and small features, and yellow curling hair. Her spirit was high, though not rough, and qualified by a heart sensitive and lively to excess in its affections. That capacity for intense attachments reminded me of her mother; still she did not resemble her, for she could be soft and mild as a dove, and she had a gentle voice, and pensive expression: her anger was never furious; her love never fierce; it was deep and tender.

However, it must be acknowledged, she had faults to foil her gifts. A propensity to be saucy was one; and a perverse will that indulged children invariably acquire, whether they be good tempered or cross. If a servant chanced to vex her, it was always: "I shall tell papa!" And if he reproved her, even by a look, you would have thought it a heart-breaking business: I don't believe he ever did speak a harsh word to her.

He took her education entirely on himself, and made it an amusement. Fortunately, curiosity and a quick intellect urged her into an apt scholar; she learnt rapidly and eagerly, and did honour to his teaching.

Till she reached the age of thirteen, she had not once been beyond the range of the park by herself. Mr. Linton would take her with him a mile or so outside, on rare occasions; but he trusted her to no one else. Gimmerton was an unsubstantial name in her ears;

the chapel, the only building she had approached or entered, except her own home. Wuthering Heights and Mr. Heathcliff did not exist for her; she was a perfect recluse, and, apparently, perfectly contented. Sometimes, indeed, while surveying the country from her nursery window, she would observe—

"Ellen, how long will it be before I can walk to the top of those hills? I wonder what lies on the other side—is it the sea?"

"No, Miss Cathy," I would answer, "it is hills again just like these."

"And what are those golden rocks like, when you stand under them?" she once asked.

The abrupt descent of Penistone Crags particularly attracted her notice, especially when the setting sun shone on it and the topmost heights, and the whole extent of landscape besides lay in shadow.

I explained that they were bare masses of stone, with hardly enough earth in their clefts to nourish a stunted tree.

"And why are they bright so long after it is evening here?" she pursued.

"Because they are a great deal higher up than we are," replied I; "you could not climb them, they are too high and steep. In winter the frost is always there before it comes to us; and, deep into summer, I have found snow under that black hollow on the north-east side!"

"Oh, you have been on them!" she cried, gleefully. "Then I can go, too, when I am a woman. Has papa been, Ellen?"

"Papa would tell you, Miss," I answered, hastily, "that they are not worth the trouble of visiting. The moors, where you ramble with him, are much nicer; and Thrushcross park is the finest place in the world."

"But I know the park, and I don't know those," she murmured to herself. "And I should delight to look round me from the brow of that tallest point—my little pony, Minny, shall take me some time."

One of the maids mentioning the Fairy cave quite turned her head with a desire to fulfil this project; she teased Mr. Linton about it; and he promised she should have the journey when she got older. But Miss Catherine measured her age by months, and—

"Now, am I old enough to go to Penistone Crags?" was the constant question in her mouth.

The road thither wound close by Wuthering Heights. Edgar had not the heart to pass it; so she received as constantly the answer—

"Not yet, love, not yet."

I said Mrs. Heathcliff lived above a dozen years after quitting her husband. Her family were of a delicate constitution: she and Edgar both lacked the ruddy health that you will generally meet in these parts. What her last illness was, I am not certain; I conjecture they died of the same thing, a kind of fever, slow at its commencement, but incurable, and rapidly consuming life towards the close.

She wrote to inform her brother of the probable conclusion of a four months' indisposition under which she had suffered; and entreated him to come to her, if possible, for she had much to settle, and she wished to bid him adieu, and deliver Linton safely into his hands. Her hope was, that Linton might be left with him, as he had been with her; his father, she would fain convince herself, had no desire to assume the burden of his maintenance or education.

My master hesitated not a moment in complying with her request; reluctant as he was to leave home at ordinary calls, he flew to answer this; commending Catherine to my peculiar vigilance in his absence, with reiterated orders that she must not wander out of the park, even under my escort: he did not calculate on her going unaccompanied.

He was away three weeks: the first day or two, my charge sat in a corner of the library, too sad for either reading or playing: in that quiet state she caused me little trouble; but it was succeeded by an interval of impatient, fretful weariness; and being too busy, and too old then, to run up and down amusing her, I hit on a method by which she might entertain herself.

I used to send her on her travels round the grounds—now on foot, and now on a pony; indulging her with a patient audience of all her real and imaginary adventures, when she returned.

The summer shone in full prime; and she took such a taste for this solitary rambling that she often contrived to remain out from breakfast till tea; and then the evenings were spent in recounting her fanciful tales. I did not fear her breaking bounds, because the gates were generally locked, and I thought she would scarcely venture forth alone, if they had stood wide open.

Unluckily, my confidence proved misplaced. Catherine came to me, one morning, at eight o'clock, and said she was that day an Arabian merchant, going to cross the Desert with his caravan; and I must give her plenty of provision for herself and beasts, a horse and three camels, personated by a large hound and a couple of pointers.

I got together good store of dainties, and slung them in a basket on one side of the saddle; and she sprang up as gay as a fairy, sheltered by her wide-brimmed hat and gauze veil from the July sun, and trotted off with a merry laugh, mocking my cautious counsel to avoid galloping, and come back early.

The naughty thing never made her appearance at tea. One traveler, the hound, being an old dog and fond of its ease, returned;

but neither Cathy, nor the pony, nor the two pointers were visible in any direction; and I despatched emissaries down this path, and that path, and, at last, went wandering in search of her myself.

There was a labourer working at a fence round a plantation, on the borders of the grounds. I enquired of him if he had seen our young lady.

"I saw her at morn," he replied; "she would have me to cut her a hazel switch, and then she leapt her galloway[1] over the hedge yonder, where it is lowest, and galloped out of sight."

You may guess how I felt at hearing this news. It struck me directly she must have started for Penistone Crags.

"What will become of her?" I ejaculated, pushing through a gap which the man was repairing, and making straight to the high road.

I walked as if for a wager, mile after mile, till a turn brought me in view of the Heights, but no Catherine could I detect, far or near.

The Crags lie about a mile and a half beyond Mr. Heathcliff's place, and that is four from the Grange, so I began to fear night would fall ere I could reach them.

"And what if she should have slipped in, clambering among them," I reflected, "and been killed, or broken some of her bones?"

My suspense was truly painful; and, at first, it gave me delightful relief to observe, in hurrying by the farm-house, Charlie, the fiercest of the pointers, lying under a window, with swelled head and bleeding ear.

I opened the wicket and ran to the door, knocking vehemently for admittance. A woman whom I knew, and who formerly lived at Gimmerton, answered: she had been servant there since the death of Mr. Earnshaw.

"Ah," said she, "you are come a seeking your little mistress! don't be frightened. She's here safe—but I'm glad it isn't the master."

"He is not at home then, is he?" I panted, quite breathless with quick walking and alarm.

"No, no," she replied, "both he and Joseph are off, and I think they won't return this hour or more. Step in and rest you a bit."

I entered, and beheld my stray lamb seated on the hearth, rocking herself in a little chair that had been her mother's, when a child. Her hat was hung against the wall, and she seemed perfectly at home, laughing and chattering, in the best spirits imaginable, to Hareton, now a great, strong lad of eighteen, who stared at her with considerable curiosity and astonishment; comprehending precious little of the fluent succession of remarks and questions which her tongue never ceased pouring forth.

1. A small but strong breed of horses peculiar to Galloway.

"Very well, Miss," I exclaimed, concealing my joy under an angry countenance. "This is your last ride, till papa comes back. I'll not trust you over the threshold again, you naughty, naughty girl."

"Aha, Ellen!" she cried gaily, jumping up, and running to my side. "I shall have a pretty story to tell to-night—and so you've found me out. Have you ever been here in your life before?"

"Put that hat on, and home at once," said I. "I'm dreadfully grieved at you, Miss Cathy, you've done extremely wrong! It's no use pouting and crying; that won't repay the trouble I've had, scouring the country after you. To think how Mr. Linton charged me to keep you in; and you stealing off so; it shows you are a cunning little fox, and nobody will put faith in you any more."

"What have I done?" sobbed she, instantly checked. "Papa charged me nothing: he'll not scold me, Ellen—he's never cross, like you!"

"Come, come!" I repeated. "I'll tie the riband. Now, let us have no petulance. Oh, for shame. You thirteen years old, and such a baby!"

This exclamation was caused by her pushing the hat from her head, and retreating to the chimney out of my reach.

"Nay," said the servant, "don't be hard on the bonny lass, Mrs. Dean. We made her stop—she'd fain have ridden forwards, afeard you should be uneasy. Hareton offered to go with her, and I thought he should. It's a wild road over the hills."

Hareton, during the discussion, stood with his hands in his pockets, too awkward to speak, though he looked as if he did not relish my intrusion.

"How long am I to wait?" I continued, disregarding the woman's interference. "It will be dark in ten minutes. Where is the pony, Miss Cathy? And where is Phoenix? I shall leave you, unless you be quick, so please yourself."

"The pony is in the yard," she replied, "and Phoenix is shut in there. He's bitten—and so is Charlie. I was going to tell you all about it; but you are in a bad temper, and don't deserve to hear."

I picked up her hat, and approached to reinstate it; but perceiving that the people of the house took her part, she commenced capering round the room; and, on my giving chase, ran like a mouse, over and under and behind the furniture, rendering it ridiculous for me to pursue.

Hareton and the woman laughed, and she joined them, and waxed more impertinent still; till I cried, in great irritation—

"Well, Miss Cathy, if you were aware whose house this is, you'd be glad enough to get out."

"It's *your* father's, isn't it?" said she, turning to Hareton.

"Nay," he replied, looking down, and blushing bashfully.

He could not stand a steady gaze from her eyes, though they were just his own.

"Whose, then—your master's?" she asked.

He coloured deeper, with a different feeling, muttered an oath, and turned away.

"Who is his master?" continued the tiresome girl, appealing to me. "He talked about 'our house,' and 'our folk.' I thought he had been the owner's son. And he never said, Miss; he should have done, shouldn't he, if he's a servant?"

Hareton grew black as a thunder-cloud, at this childish speech. I silently shook my questioner, and, at last, succeeded in equipping her for departure.

"Now, get my horse," she said, addressing her unknown kinsman as she would one of the stable-boys at the Grange. "And you may come with me. I want to see where the goblin hunter rises in the marsh, and to hear about the *fairishes*,[2] as you call them—but make haste! What's the matter? Get my horse, I say."

"I'll see thee damned, before I be *thy* servant!" growled the lad.

"You'll see me *what?*" asked Catherine in surprise.

"Damned—thou saucy witch!" he replied.

"There, Miss Cathy! you see you have got into pretty company," I interposed. "Nice words to be used to a young lady! Pray don't begin to dispute with him. Come, let us seek for Minny ourselves, and begone."

"But, Ellen," cried she, staring, fixed in astonishment. "How dare he speak so to me? Mustn't he be made to do as I ask him? You wicked creature, I shall tell papa what you said—Now then!"

Hareton did not appear to feel this threat; so the tears sprung into her eyes with indignation. "You bring the pony," she exclaimed, turning to the woman, "and let my dog free this moment!"

"Softly, Miss," answered the addressed. "You'll lose nothing by being civil. Though Mr. Hareton, there, be not the master's son, he's your cousin; and I was never hired to serve you."

"*He* my cousin!" cried Cathy with a scornful laugh.

"Yes, indeed," responded her reprover.

"Oh, Ellen! don't let them say such things," she pursued in great trouble. "Papa is gone to fetch my cousin from London—my cousin is a gentleman's son. That my—" she stopped, and wept outright; upset at the bare notion of relationship with such a clown.

"Hush, hush!" I whispered, "people can have many cousins and of all sorts, Miss Cathy, without being any the worse for it; only they needn't keep their company, if they be disagreeable and bad."

2. Hareton uses the West Yorkshire word for fairies. The *English Dialect Dictionary* cites one instance of this term in Charlotte Brontë's *Shirley* (1849).

"He's not, he's not my cousin, Ellen!" she went on, gathering fresh grief from reflection, and flinging herself into my arms for refuge from the idea.

I was much vexed at her and the servant for their mutual revelations; having no doubt of Linton's approaching arrival, communicated by the former, being reported to Mr. Heathcliff; and feeling as confident that Catherine's first thought on her father's return would be to seek an explanation of the latter's assertion concerning her rude-bred kindred.

Hareton, recovering from his disgust at being taken for a servant, seemed moved by her distress; and, having fetched the pony round to the door, he took, to propitiate her, a fine crooked-legged terrier whelp from the kennel, and putting it into her hand, bid her wisht[3] for he meant naught.

Pausing in her lamentations, she surveyed him with a glance of awe and horror, then burst forth anew.

I could scarcely refrain from smiling at this antipathy to the poor fellow, who was a well-made, athletic youth, good-looking in features, and stout and healthy, but attired in garments befitting his daily occupations of working on the farm, and lounging among the moors after rabbits and game. Still, I thought I could detect in his physiognomy a mind owning better qualities than his father ever possessed. Good things lost amid a wilderness of weeds, to be sure, whose rankness far over-topped their neglected growth; yet, notwithstanding, evidence of a wealthy soil that might yield luxuriant crops under other and favourable circumstances. Mr. Heathcliff, I believe, had not treated him physically ill; thanks to his fearless nature, which offered no temptation to that course of oppression; it had none of the timid susceptibility that would have given zest to ill-treatment, in Heathcliff's judgment. He appeared to have bent his malevolence on making him a brute: he was never taught to read or write; never rebuked for any bad habit which did not annoy his keeper; never led a single step towards virtue, or guarded by a single precept against vice. And from what I heard, Joseph contributed much to his deterioration by a narrow-minded partiality which prompted him to flatter and pet him, as a boy, because he was the head of the old family. And as he had been in the habit of accusing Catherine Earnshaw and Heathcliff, when children, of putting the master past his patience, and compelling him to seek solace in drink, by what he termed their "offald ways,"[4] so at present he laid the whole burden of Hareton's faults on the shoulders of the usurper of his property.

3. Hush.
4. Disreputable ways.

If the lad swore, he wouldn't correct him; nor however culpably he behaved. It gave Joseph satisfaction, apparently, to watch him go the worst lengths. He allowed that he was ruined; that his soul was abandoned to perdition; but then, he reflected that Heathcliff must answer for it. Hareton's blood would be required at his hands; and there lay immense consolation in that thought.

Joseph had instilled into him a pride of name, and of his lineage; he would, had he dared, have fostered hate between him and the present owner of the Heights, but his dread of that owner amounted to superstition; and he confined his feelings regarding him to muttered innuendoes and private comminations.

I don't pretend to be intimately acquainted with the mode of living customary in those days at Wuthering Heights. I only speak from hearsay; for I saw little. The villagers affirmed Mr. Heathcliff was *near*,[5] and a cruel hard landlord to his tenants; but the house, inside, had regained its ancient aspect of comfort under female management; and the scenes of riot common in Hindley's time were not now enacted within its walls. The master was too gloomy to seek companionship with any people, good or bad, and he is yet.

This, however, is not making progress with my story. Miss Cathy rejected the peace-offering of the terrier, and demanded her own dogs, Charlie and Phoenix. They came limping, and hanging their heads; and we set out for home, sadly out of sorts, every one of us.

I could not wring from my little lady how she had spent the day; except that, as I supposed, the goal of her pilgrimage was Penistone Crags; and she arrived without adventure to the gate of the farmhouse, when Hareton happened to issue forth, attended by some canine followers who attacked her train.

They had a smart battle, before their owners could separate them: that formed an introduction. Catherine told Hareton who she was, and where she was going; and asked him to show her the way, finally beguiling him to accompany her.

He opened the mysteries of the Fairy cave, and twenty other queer places; but, being in disgrace, I was not favoured with a description of the interesting objects she saw.

I could gather, however, that her guide had been a favourite till she hurt his feelings by addressing him as a servant; and Heathcliff's housekeeper hurt hers by calling him her cousin.

Then the language he had held to her rankled in her heart; she who was always "love," and "darling," and "queen," and "angel," with everybody at the Grange, to be insulted so shockingly by a stranger! She did not comprehend it; and hard work I had to obtain a promise that she would not lay the grievance before her father.

5. Miserly.

I explained how he objected to the whole household at the Heights, and how sorry he would be to find she had been there; but I insisted most on the fact, that if she revealed my negligence of his orders, he would perhaps be so angry that I should have to leave; and Cathy couldn't bear that prospect: she pledged her word, and kept it, for my sake—after all, she was a sweet little girl.

Chapter XIX

A letter, edged with black, announced the day of my master's return. Isabella was dead; and he wrote to bid me get mourning for his daughter, and arrange a room and other accommodations for his youthful nephew.

Catherine ran wild with joy at the idea of welcoming her father back, and indulged most sanguine anticipations of the innumerable excellencies of her "real" cousin.

The evening of their expected arrival came. Since early morning, she had been busy, ordering her own small affairs; and now, attired in her new black frock—poor thing! her aunt's death impressed her with no definite sorrow—she obliged me, by constant worrying, to walk with her down through the grounds to meet them.

"Linton is just six months younger than I am," she chattered, as we strolled leisurely over the swells and hollows of mossy turf, under shadow of the trees. "How delightful it will be to have him for a playfellow! Aunt Isabella sent papa a beautiful lock of his hair; it was lighter than mine—more flaxen, and quite as fine. I have it carefully preserved in a little glass box; and I've often thought what pleasure it would be to see its owner. Oh! I am happy—and papa, dear, dear papa! Come, Ellen, let us run! come run!"

She ran, and returned and ran again, many times before my sober footsteps reached the gate, and then she seated herself on the grassy bank beside the path, and tried to wait patiently, but that was impossible; she couldn't be still a minute.

"How long they are!" she exclaimed. "Ah, I see some dust on the road—they are coming! No! When will they be here? May we not go a little way—half a mile, Ellen, only just half a mile? Do say yes, to that clump of birches at the turn!"

I refused staunchly; and, at length, her suspense was ended: the travelling carriage rolled in sight.

Miss Cathy shrieked, and stretched out her arms, as soon as she caught her father's face, looking from the window. He descended, nearly as eager as herself; and a considerable interval elapsed ere they had a thought to spare for any but themselves.

While they exchanged caresses, I took a peep in to see after Linton. He was asleep in a corner, wrapped in a warm, fur-lined cloak, as if it had been winter. A pale, delicate, effeminate boy, who might have been taken for my master's younger brother, so strong was the resemblance; but there was a sickly peevishness in his aspect that Edgar Linton never had.

The latter saw me looking; and having shaken hands, advised me to close the door, and leave him undisturbed; for the journey had fatigued him.

Cathy would fain have taken one glance; but her father told her to come on, and they walked together up the park, while I hastened before to prepare the servants.

"Now, darling," said Mr. Linton, addressing his daughter, as they halted at the bottom of the front steps, "your cousin is not so strong or so merry as you are, and he has lost his mother, remember, a very short time since; therefore, don't expect him to play and run about with you directly. And don't harass him much by talking—let him be quiet this evening, at least, will you?"

"Yes, yes, papa," answered Catherine; "but I do want to see him; and he hasn't once looked out."

The carriage stopped; and the sleeper, being roused, was lifted to the ground by his uncle.

"This is your cousin Cathy, Linton," he said, putting their little hands together. "She's fond of you already; and mind you don't grieve her by crying to-night. Try to be cheerful now; the travelling is at an end, and you have nothing to do but rest and amuse yourself as you please."

"Let me go to bed, then," answered the boy, shrinking from Catherine's salute; and he put his fingers to his eyes to remove incipient tears.

"Come, come, there's a good child," I whispered, leading him in. "You'll make her weep too—see how sorry she is for you!"

I do not know whether it were sorrow for him, but his cousin put on as sad a countenance as himself, and returned to her father. All three entered, and mounted to the library, where tea was laid ready.

I proceeded to remove Linton's cap and mantle, and placed him on a chair by the table; but he was no sooner seated than he began to cry afresh. My master inquired what was the matter.

"I can't sit on a chair," sobbed the boy.

"Go to the sofa, then, and Ellen shall bring you some tea," answered his uncle, patiently.

He had been greatly tried during the journey, I felt convinced, by his fretful, ailing charge.

Linton slowly trailed himself off, and lay down. Cathy carried a foot-stool and her cup to his side.

At first she sat silent; but that could not last; she had resolved to make a pet of her little cousin, as she would have him to be; and she commenced stroking his curls, and kissing his cheek, and offering him tea in her saucer, like a baby. This pleased him, for he was not much better; he dried his eyes, and lightened into a faint smile.

"Oh, he'll do very well," said the master to me, after watching them a minute. "Very well, if we can keep him, Ellen. The company of a child of his own age will instil new spirit into him soon, and by wishing for strength he'll gain it."

"Aye, if we can keep him!" I mused to myself; and sore misgivings came over me that there was slight hope of that. And then, I thought, however will that weakling live at Wuthering Heights, between his father and Hareton? What playmates and instructors they'll be.

Our doubts were presently decided—even earlier than I expected. I had just taken the children upstairs, after tea was finished, and seen Linton asleep—he would not suffer me to leave him till that was the case. I had come down, and was standing by the table in the hall, lighting a bed-room candle for Mr. Edgar, when a maid stepped out of the kitchen and informed me that Mr. Heathcliff's servant, Joseph, was at the door, and wished to speak with the master.

"I shall ask him what he wants first," I said, in considerable trepidation. "A very unlikely hour to be troubling people, and the instant they have returned from a long journey. I don't think the master can see him."

Joseph had advanced through the kitchen, as I uttered these words, and now presented himself in the hall. He was donned in his Sunday garments, with his most sanctimonious and sourest face; and holding his hat in one hand and his stick in the other, he proceeded to clean his shoes on the mat.

"Good evening, Joseph," I said, coldly. "What business brings you here to-night?"

"It's Maister Linton Aw mun spake tull,"[1] he answered, waving me disdainfully aside.

"Mr. Linton is going to bed; unless you have something particular to say, I'm sure he won't hear it now," I continued. "You had better sit down in there, and entrust your message to me."

"Which is his rahm?" pursued the fellow, surveying the range of closed doors.

I perceived he was bent on refusing my mediation; so very reluctantly I went up to the library, and announced the unseasonable visitor, advising that he should be dismissed till next day.

1. Speak to.

Mr. Linton had no time to empower me to do so, for he mounted close at my heels, and, pushing into the apartment, planted himself at the far side of the table, with his two fists clapped on the head of his stick, and began in an elevated tone, as if anticipating opposition—

"Hathecliff has send me for his lad, un Aw munn't goa back 'baht him."[2]

Edgar Linton was silent a minute; an expression of exceeding sorrow overcast his features; he would have pitied the child on his own account; but, recalling Isabella's hopes and fears, and anxious wishes for her son, and her commendations of him to his care, he grieved bitterly at the prospect of yielding him up, and searched in his heart how it might be avoided. No plan offered itself: the very exhibition of any desire to keep him would have rendered the claimant more peremptory: there was nothing left but to resign him. However, he was not going to rouse him from his sleep.

"Tell Mr. Heathcliff," he answered, calmly, "that his son shall come to Wuthering Heights to-morrow. He is in bed, and too tired to go the distance now. You may also tell him that the mother of Linton desired him to remain under my guardianship; and, at present, his health is very precarious."

"Noa!" said Joseph, giving a thud with his prop on the floor, and assuming an authoritative air. "Noa! that manes nowt Hathecliff maks noa 'cahnt uh t' mother, nur yah norther—bud he'll hev his lad; und Aw mun tak him—soa nah yah knaw!"[3]

"You shall not to-night!" answered Linton, decisively. "Walk down stairs at once, and repeat to your master what I have said. Ellen, show him down. Go—"

And, aiding the indignant elder with a lift by the arm, he rid the room of him, and closed the door.

"Varrah weel!" shouted Joseph, as he slowly drew off. "Tuh morn, he's come hisseln, un' thrust *him* aht, if yah darr!"[4]

Chapter XX

To obviate the danger of this threat being fulfilled, Mr. Linton commissioned me to take the boy home early, on Catherine's pony, and, said he—

"As we shall now have no influence over his destiny, good or bad, you must say nothing of where he is gone to my daughter; she

2. ". . . and I mustn't go back without him."
3. "No, that means nothing. Heathcliff takes no account of the mother, nor of you either —but he'll have his lad; and I must take him—so now you know!"
4. "Very well . . . He'll come himself in the morning, and throw *him* out if you dare!"

cannot associate with him hereafter, and it is better for her to remain in ignorance of his proximity, lest she should be restless, and anxious to visit the Heights. Merely tell her, his father sent for him suddenly, and he has been obliged to leave us."

Linton was very reluctant to be roused from his bed at five o'clock, and astonished to be informed that he must prepare for further travelling; but I softened off the matter by stating that he was going to spend some time with his father, Mr. Heathcliff, who wished to see him so much, he did not like to defer the pleasure till he should recover from his late journey.

"My father?" he cried, in strange perplexity. "Mamma never told me I had a father. Where does he live? I'd rather stay with uncle."

"He lives a little distance from the Grange," I replied, "just beyond those hills—not so far but you may walk over here, when you get hearty. And you should be glad to go home, and to see him. You must try to love him, as you did your mother, and then he will love you."

"But why have I not heard of him before?" asked Linton; "why didn't mamma and he live together, as other people do?"

"He had business to keep him in the north," I answered; "and your mother's health required her to reside in the south."

"And why didn't mamma speak to me about him?" persevered the child. "She often talked of uncle, and I learnt to love him long ago. How am I to love papa? I don't know him."

"Oh, all children love their parents," I said. "Your mother, perhaps, thought you would want to be with him, if she mentioned him often to you. Let us make haste. An early ride on such a beautiful morning is much preferable to an hour's more sleep."

"Is *she* to go with us?" he demanded. "The little girl I saw yesterday?"

"Not now," replied I.

"Is uncle?" he continued.

"No, I shall be your companion there," I said.

Linton sank back on his pillow, and fell into a brown study.

"I won't go without uncle," he cried at length; "I can't tell where you mean to take me."

I attempted to persuade him of the naughtiness of showing reluctance to meet his father; still he obstinately resisted any progress towards dressing, and I had to call for my master's assistance in coaxing him out of bed.

The poor thing was finally got off with several delusive assurances that his absence should be short; that Mr. Edgar and Cathy would visit him; and other promises, equally ill-founded, which I invented and reiterated at intervals throughout the way.

The pure heather-scented air, and the bright sunshine, and the gentle canter of Minny relieved his despondency, after a while. He began to put questions concerning his new home, and its inhabitants, with greater interest and liveliness.

"Is Wuthering Heights as pleasant a place as Thrushcross Grange?" he inquired, turning to take a last glance into the valley, whence a light mist mounted and formed a fleecy cloud on the skirts of the blue.

"It is not so buried in trees," I replied, "and it is not quite so large, but you can see the country beautifully, all round; and the air is healthier for you—fresher and dryer. You will, perhaps, think the building old and dark at first—though it is a respectable house, the next best in the neighbourhood. And you will have such nice rambles on the moors! Hareton Earnshaw—that is Miss Cathy's other cousin, and so yours in a manner—will show you all the sweetest spots; and you can bring a book in fine weather, and make a green hollow your study; and, now and then, your uncle may join you in a walk: he does, frequently, walk out on the hills."

"And what is my father like?" he asked. "Is he as young and handsome as uncle?"

"He's as young," said I, "but he has black hair and eyes, and looks sterner, and he is taller and bigger altogether. He'll not seem to you so gentle and kind at first, perhaps, because it is not his way—still, mind you be frank and cordial with him; and naturally he'll be fonder of you than any uncle, for you are his own."

"Black hair and eyes!" mused Linton. "I can't fancy him. Then I am not like him, am I?"

"Not much," I answered. Not a morsel, I thought, surveying with regret the white complexion and slim frame of my companion, and his large languid eyes—his mother's eyes, save that, unless a morbid touchiness kindled them a moment, they had not a vestige of her sparkling spirit.

"How strange that he should never come to see mamma and me," he murmured. "Has he ever seen me? If he have, I must have been a baby—I remember not a single thing about him!"

"Why, Master Linton," said I, "three hundred miles is a great distance; and ten years seem very different in length to a grown up person, compared with what they do to you. It is probable Mr. Heathcliff proposed going, from summer to summer, but never found a convenient opportunity; and now it is too late. Don't trouble him with questions on the subject: it will disturb him for no good."

The boy was fully occupied with his own cogitations for the remainder of the ride, till we halted before the farm-house garden gate. I watched to catch his impressions in his countenance. He surveyed the carved front and low-browed lattices, the straggling gooseberry bushes and crooked firs, with solemn intentness, and then shook his head: his private feelings entirely disapproved of the exterior of his new abode; but he had sense to postpone complaining—there might be compensation within.

Before he dismounted, I went and opened the door. It was half-past six; the family had just finished breakfast; the servant was clearing and wiping down the table. Joseph stood by his master's chair telling some tale concerning a lame horse; and Hareton was preparing for the hay-field.

"Hallo, Nelly!" cried Mr. Heathcliff, when he saw me. "I feared I should have to come down and fetch my property myself. You've brought it, have you? Let us see what we can make of it."

He got up and strode to the door: Hareton and Joseph followed in gaping curiosity. Poor Linton ran a frightened eye over the faces of the three.

"Sure-ly," said Joseph after a grave inspection, "he's swopped wi' ye, maister, an' yon's his lass!"

Heathcliff, having stared his son into an ague of confusion, uttered a scornful laugh.

"God! what a beauty! what a lovely, charming thing!" he exclaimed. "Haven't they reared it on snails and sour milk, Nelly? Oh, damn my soul! but that's worse than I expected—and the devil knows I was not sanguine!"

I bid the trembling and bewildered child get down, and enter. He did not thoroughly comprehend the meaning of his father's speech, or whether it were intended for him: indeed, he was not yet certain that the grim, sneering stranger was his father; but he clung to me with growing trepidation, and on Mr. Heathcliff's taking a seat, and bidding him "come hither," he hid his face on my shoulder, and wept.

"Tut, tut!" said Heathcliff, stretching out a hand and dragging him roughly between his knees, and then holding up his head by the chin. "None of that nonsense! We're not going to hurt thee, Linton—isn't that thy name? Thou art thy mother's child, entirely! Where is *my* share in thee, puling chicken?"

He took off the boy's cap and pushed back his thick flaxen curls, felt his slender arms, and his small fingers; during which examination, Linton ceased crying, and lifted his great blue eyes to inspect the inspector.

"Do you know me?" asked Heathcliff, having satisfied himself that the limbs were all equally frail and feeble.

"No!" said Linton, with a gaze of vacant fear.

"You've heard of me, I dare say?"

"No," he replied again.

"No? What a shame of your mother, never to waken your filial regard for me! You are my son, then, I'll tell you; and your mother was a wicked slut to leave you in ignorance of the sort of father you possessed. Now, don't wince, and colour up! Though it *is* something to see you have not white blood. Be a good lad; and I'll do for you. Nelly, if you be tired you may sit down; if not get home again. I guess you'll report what you hear and see, to the cipher at the Grange; and this thing won't be settled while you linger about it."

"Well," replied I, "I hope you'll be kind to the boy, Mr. Heathcliff, or you'll not keep him long, and he's all you have akin in the wide world that you will ever know—remember."

"I'll be *very* kind to him, you needn't fear!" he said, laughing. "Only nobody else must be kind to him—I'm jealous of monopolizing his affection. And, to begin my kindness, Joseph! bring the lad some breakfast. Hareton, you infernal calf, begone to your work. Yes, Nell," he added when they were departed, "my son is prospective owner of your place, and I should not wish him to die till I was certain of being his successor. Besides, he's *mine*, and I want the triumph of seeing *my* descendent fairly lord of their estates; my child hiring their children to till their fathers' lands for wages. That is the sole consideration which can make me endure the whelp—I despise him for himself, and hate him for the memories he revives! But that consideration is sufficient; he's as safe with me, and shall be tended as carefully as your master tends his own. I have a room upstairs, furnished for him in handsome style; I've engaged a tutor, also, to come three times a week, from twenty miles distance, to teach him what he pleases to learn. I've ordered Hareton to obey him; and in fact I've arranged everything with a view to preserve the superior and the gentleman in him, above his associates. I do regret, however, that he so little deserves the trouble. If I wished any blessing in the world, it was to find him a worthy object of pride, and I'm bitterly disappointed with the whey-faced whining wretch!"

While he was speaking, Joseph returned, bearing a basin of milk-porridge, and placed it before Linton. He stirred round the homely mess with a look of aversion, and affirmed he could not eat it.

I saw the old man-servant shared largely in his master's scorn of the child, though he was compelled to retain the sentiment in his heart, because Heathcliff plainly meant his underlings to hold him in honour.

"Cannot ate it?" repeated he, peering in Linton's face, and subduing his voice to a whisper, for fear of being overheard. "But Maister Hareton nivir ate nowt else, when he wer a little un: und what wer gooid eneugh fur him's gooid eneugh fur yah, Aw's rayther think!"

"I *shan't* eat it!" answered Linton, snappishly. "Take it away."

Joseph snatched up the food indignantly, and brought it to us.

"Is there owt ails th' victuals?" he asked, thrusting the tray under Heathcliff's nose.

"What should ail them?" he said.

"Wah!" answered Joseph, "yon dainty chap says he cannut ate 'em. Bud Aw guess it's raight! His mother wer just soa—we wer a'most too mucky tuh sow t' corn fur makking her breead."

"Don't mention his mother to me," said the master, angrily. "Get him something that he can eat, that's all. What is his usual food, Nelly?"

I suggested boiled milk or tea; and the housekeeper received instructions to prepare some.

Come, I reflected, his father's selfishness may contribute to his comfort. He perceives his delicate constitution, and the necessity of treating him tolerably. I'll console Mr. Edgar by acquainting him with the turn Heathcliff's humour has taken.

Having no excuse for lingering longer, I slipped out, while Linton was engaged in timidly rebuffing the advances of a friendly sheep-dog. But he was too much on the alert to be cheated: as I closed the door, I heard a cry, and a frantic repetition of the words—

"Don't leave me! I'll not stay here! I'll not stay here!"

Then the latch was raised and fell: they did not suffer him to come forth. I mounted Minny, and urged her to a trot; and so my brief guardianship ended.

Chapter XXI

We had sad work with little Cathy that day: she rose in high glee, eager to join her cousin; and such passionate tears and lamentations followed the news of his departure, that Edgar himself was obliged to sooth her, by affirming he should come back soon; he added, however, "if I can get him"; and there were no hopes of that.

This promise poorly pacified her, but time was more potent; and though still, at intervals, she inquired of her father when Linton would return, before she did see him again, his features had waxed so dim in her memory that she did not recognise him.

When I chanced to encounter the housekeeper of Wuthering Heights, in paying business-visits to Gimmerton, I used to ask how the young master got on; for he lived almost as secluded as Catherine herself, and was never to be seen. I could gather from her that he continued in weak health, and was a tiresome inmate. She said Mr. Heathcliff seemed to dislike him ever longer and worse, though he took some trouble to conceal it. He had an antipathy to the sound of his voice, and could not do at all with his sitting in the same room with him many minutes together.

There seldom passed much talk between them; Linton learnt his lessons, and spent his evenings in a small apartment they called the parlour; or else lay in bed all day, for he was constantly getting coughs, and colds, and aches, and pains of some sort.

"And I never knew such a faint-hearted creature," added the woman; "nor one so careful of hisseln. He *will* go on, if I leave the window open, a bit late in the evening. Oh! it's killing, a breath of night air! And he must have a fire in the middle of summer; and Joseph's 'bacca pipe is poison; and he must always have sweets and dainties, and always milk, milk for ever—heeding naught how the rest of us are pinched in winter; and there he'll sit, wrapped in his furred cloak in his chair by the fire, and some toast and water, or other slop on the hob to sip at; and if Hareton, for pity, comes to amuse him—Hareton is not bad-natured, though he's rough—they're sure to part, one swearing and the other crying. I believe the master would relish Earnshaw's thrashing him to a mummy, if he were not his son; and I'm certain he would be fit to turn him out of doors, if he knew half the nursing he gives hisseln. But then, he won't go into danger of temptation; he never enters the parlour, and should Linton show those ways in the house where he is, he sends him upstairs directly."

I divined, from this account, that utter lack of sympathy had rendered young Heathcliff selfish and disagreeable, if he were not so originally; and my interest in him, consequently, decayed, though still I was moved with a sense of grief at his lot, and a wish that he had been left with us.

Mr. Edgar encouraged me to gain information; he thought a great deal about him, I fancy, and would have run some risk to see him; and he told me once to ask the housekeeper whether he ever came into the village?

She said he had only been twice, on horseback, accompanying his father; and both times he pretended to be quite knocked up for three or four days afterwards.

That housekeeper left, if I recollect rightly, two years after he came; and another, whom I did not know, was her successor: she lives there still.

Time wore on at the Grange in its former pleasant way, till Miss Cathy reached sixteen. On the anniversary of her birth we never manifested any signs of rejoicing, because it was also the anniversary of my late mistress's death. Her father invariably spent that day alone in the library; and walked, at dusk, as far as Gimmerton kirkyard, where he would frequently prolong his stay beyond midnight. Therefore Catherine was thrown on her own resources for amusement.

This twentieth of March was a beautiful spring day, and when her father had retired, my young lady came down dressed for going out, and said she had asked to have a ramble on the edge of the moors with me; and Mr. Linton had given her leave, if we went only a short distance and were back within the hour.

"So make haste, Ellen!" she cried. "I know where I wish to go; where a colony of moor game are settled. I want to see whether they have made their nests yet."

"That must be a good distance up," I answered; "they don't breed on the edge of the moor."

"No, it's not," she said. "I've gone very near with papa."

I put on my bonnet and sallied out, thinking nothing more of the matter. She bounded before me, and returned to my side, and was off again like a young greyhound; and, at first, I found plenty of entertainment in listening to the larks singing far and near, and enjoying the sweet, warm sunshine, and watching her, my pet and my delight, with her golden ringlets flying loose behind, and her bright cheek, as soft and pure in its bloom as a wild rose, and her eyes radiant with cloudless pleasure. She was a happy creature, and an angel, in those days. It's a pity she could not be content.

"Well," said I, "where are your moor-game, Miss Cathy? We should be at them—the Grange park-fence is a great way off now."

"Oh, a little further—only a little further, Ellen," was her answer, continually. "Climb to that hillock, pass that bank, and by the time you reach the other side, I shall have raised the birds."

But there were so many hillocks and banks to climb and pass, that, at length, I began to be weary, and told her we must halt, and retrace our steps.

I shouted to her, as she had outstripped me, a long way; she either did not hear or did not regard, for she still sprang on, and I was compelled to follow. Finally, she dived into a hollow; and before I came in sight of her again, she was two miles nearer Wuthering Heights than her own home; and I beheld a couple of persons arrest her, one of whom I felt convinced was Mr. Heathcliff himself.

Cathy had been caught in the fact of plundering, or, at least, hunting out the nests of the grouse.

The Heights were Heathcliff's land, and he was reproving the poacher.

"I've neither taken any nor found any," she said, as I toiled to them, expanding her hands in corroboration of the statement. "I didn't mean to take them; but papa told me there were quantities up here, and I wished to see the eggs."

Heathcliff glanced at me with an ill-meaning smile, expressing his acquaintance with the party, and, consequently, his malevolence towards it, and demanded who "papa" was?

"Mr. Linton of Thrushcross Grange," she replied. "I thought you did not know me, or you wouldn't have spoken in that way."

"You suppose papa is highly esteemed and respected then?" he said, sarcastically.

"And what are you?" inquired Catherine, gazing curiously on the speaker. "That man I've seen before. Is he your son?"

She pointed to Hareton, the other individual, who had gained nothing but increased bulk and strength by the addition of two years to his age: he seemed as awkward and rough as ever.

"Miss Cathy," I interrupted, "it will be three hours instead of one that we are out, presently. We really must go back."

"No, that man is not my son," answered Heathcliff, pushing me aside. "But I have one, and you have seen him before, too; and, though your nurse is in a hurry, I think both you and she would be the better for a little rest. Will you just turn this nab of heath,[1] and walk into my house? You'll get home earlier for the ease; and you shall receive a kind welcome."

I whispered Catherine that she mustn't, on any account, accede to the proposal; it was entirely out of the question.

"Why?" she asked, aloud. "I'm tired of running, and the ground is dewy—I can't sit here. Let us go, Ellen! Besides, he says I have seen his son. He's mistaken, I think; but I guess where he lives—at the farm-house I visited in coming from Penistone Crags. Don't you?"

"I do. Come, Nelly, hold your tongue—it will be a treat for her to look in on us. Hareton, get forwards with the lass. You shall walk with me, Nelly."

"No, she's not going to any such place," I cried, struggling to release my arm which he had seized; but she was almost at the door-stones already, scampering round the brow at full speed. Her appointed companion did not pretend to escort her; he shyed off by the road-side, and vanished.

"Mr. Heathcliff, it's very wrong," I continued; "you know you mean no good. And there she'll see Linton, and all will be told, as soon as ever we return; and I shall have the blame."

"I want her to see Linton," he answered; "he's looking better these few days; it's not often he's fit to be seen. And we'll soon persuade her to keep the visit secret—where is the harm of it?"

1. A *nab* is an abrupt termination of a range of uplands. Bronte may have had in mind the escarpment of Millstone Grit, from which the whole of the Haworth moorlands could be viewed. It was known as the "Nab."

"The harm of it is, that her father would hate me if he found I suffered her to enter your house; and I am convinced you have a bad design in encouraging her to do so," I replied.

"My design is as honest as possible. I'll inform you of its whole scope," he said. "That the two cousins may fall in love, and get married. I'm acting generously to your master; his young chit has no expectations, and should she second my wishes, she'll be provided for, at once, as joint successor with Linton."

"If Linton died," I answered, "and his life is quite uncertain, Catherine would be the heir."

"No, she would not," he said. "There is no clause in the will to secure it so; his property would go to me; but, to prevent disputes, I desire their union, and am resolved to bring it about."

"And I'm resolved she shall never approach your house with me again," I returned, as we reached the gate, where Miss Cathy waited our coming.

Heathcliff bid me be quiet; and, preceding us up the path, hastened to open the door. My young lady gave him several looks, as if she could not exactly make up her mind what to think of him; but now he smiled when he met her eye, and softened his voice in addressing her, and I was foolish enough to imagine the memory of her mother might disarm him from desiring her injury.

Linton stood on the hearth. He had been out walking in the fields, for his cap was on, and he was calling to Joseph to bring him dry shoes.

He had grown tall of his age, still wanting some months of sixteen. His features were pretty yet, and his eye and complexion brighter than I remembered them, though with merely temporary lustre borrowed from the salubrious air and genial sun.

"Now, who is that?" asked Mr. Heathcliff, turning to Cathy. "Can you tell?"

"Your son?" she said, having doubtfully surveyed first one and then the other.

"Yes, yes," answered he; "but is this the only time you have beheld him? Think! Ah! you have a short memory. Linton, don't you recall your cousin, that you used to tease us so with wishing to see?"

"What, Linton!" cried Cathy, kindling into joyful surprise at the name. "Is that little Linton? He's taller than I am! Are you Linton?"

The youth stepped forward, and acknowledged himself: she kissed him fervently, and they gazed with wonder at the change time had wrought in the appearance of each.

Catherine had reached her full height; her figure was both plump and slender, elastic as steel, and her whole aspect sparkling with health and spirits. Linton's looks and movements were very languid, and his form extremely slight; but there was a grace in his manner that mitigated these defects, and rendered him not unpleasing.

After exchanging numerous marks of fondness with him, his cousin went to Mr. Heathcliff, who lingered by the door, dividing his attention between the objects inside and those that lay without, pretending, that is, to observe the latter, and really noting the former alone.

"And you are my uncle, then!" she cried, reaching up to salute him. "I thought I liked you, though you were cross, at first. Why don't you visit at the Grange with Linton? To live all these years such close neighbours, and never see us, is odd; what have you done so for?"

"I visited it once or twice too often before you were born," he answered. "There—damn it! If you have any kisses to spare, give them to Linton—they are thrown away on me."

"Naughty Ellen!" exclaimed Catherine, flying to attack me next with her lavish caresses. "Wicked Ellen! to try to hinder me from entering. But I'll take this walk every morning in future. May I, uncle—and sometimes bring papa? Won't you be glad to see us?"

"Of course!" replied the uncle, with a hardly surpressed grimace, resulting from his deep aversion to both the proposed visitors. "But stay," he continued, turning towards the young lady. "Now I think of it, I'd better tell you. Mr. Linton has a prejudice against me; we quarrelled at one time of our lives, with unchristian ferocity; and, if you mention coming here to him, he'll put a veto on your visits altogether. Therefore, you must not mention it, unless you be careless of seeing your cousin hereafter. You may come, if you will, but you must not mention it."

"Why did you quarrel?" asked Catherine, considerably crestfallen.

"He thought me too poor to wed his sister," answered Heathcliff, "and was grieved that I got her. His pride was hurt, and he'll never forgive it."

"That's wrong!" said the young lady: "some time, I'll tell him so. But Linton and I have no share in your quarrel. I'll not come here, then; he shall come to the Grange."

"It will be too far for me," murmured her cousin; "to walk four miles would kill me. No, come here, Miss Catherine, now and then, not every morning, but once or twice a week."

The father launched towards his son a glance of bitter contempt.

"I am afraid, Nelly, I shall lose my labour," he muttered to me. "Miss Catherine, as the ninny calls her, will discover his value, and send him to the devil. Now, if it had been Hareton—do you know that, twenty times a day, I covet Hareton, with all his degradation? I'd have loved the lad had he been some one else. But I think he's safe from *her* love. I'll pit him against that paltry creature, unless it bestir itself briskly. We calculate it will scarcely last till it is eighteen. Oh, confound the vapid thing. He's absorbed in drying his feet, and never looks at her—Linton!"

"Yes, father," answered the boy.

"Have you nothing to show your cousin, anywhere about; not even a rabbit, or a weasel's nest? Take her into the garden, before you change your shoes; and into the stable to see your horse."

"Wouldn't you rather sit here?" asked Linton, addressing Cathy in a tone which expressed reluctance to move again.

"I don't know," she replied, casting a longing look to the door, and evidently eager to be active.

He kept his seat, and shrank closer to the fire.

Heathcliff rose, and went into the kitchen, and from thence to the yard, calling out for Hareton.

Hareton responded, and presently the two re-entered. The young man had been washing himself, as was visible by the glow on his cheeks, and his wetted hair.

"Oh, I'll ask *you*, uncle," cried Miss Cathy, recollecting the housekeeper's assertion. "That's not my cousin, is he?"

"Yes," he replied, "Your mother's nephew. Don't you like him?"

Catherine looked queer.

"Is he not a handsome lad?" he continued.

The uncivil little thing stood on tiptoe, and whispered a sentence in Heathcliff's ear.

He laughed; Hareton darkened; I perceived he was very sensitive to suspected slights, and had obviously a dim notion of his inferiority. But his master or guardian chased the frown by exclaiming—

"You'll be the favourite among us, Hareton! She says you are a —what was it? Well, something very flattering. Here! you go with her round the farm. And behave like a gentleman, mind! Don't use any bad words; and don't stare, when the young lady is not looking at you, and be ready to hide your face when she is; and, when you speak, say your words slowly, and keep your hands out of your pockets. Be off, and entertain her as nicely as you can."

He watched the couple walking past the window. Earnshaw had his countenance completely averted from his companion. He seemed studying the familiar landscape with a stranger's and an artist's interest.

Catherine took a sly look at him, expressing small admiration. She then turned her attention to seeking out objects of amusement for herself, and tripped merrily on, lilting a tune to supply the lack of conversation.

"I've tied his tongue," observed Heathcliff. "He'll not venture a single syllable, all the time! Nelly, you recollect me at his age—nay, some years younger. Did I ever look so stupid, so 'gaumless,'[2] as Joseph calls it?"

"Worse," I replied, "because more sullen with it."

"I've a pleasure in him," he continued reflecting aloud. "He has satisfied my expectations. If he were a born fool I should not enjoy it half so much. But he's no fool; and I can sympathise with all his feelings, having felt them myself. I know what he suffers now, for instance, exactly—it is merely a beginning of what he shall suffer, though. And he'll never be able to emerge from his bathos of coarseness and ignorance. I've got him faster than his scoundrel of a father secured me, and lower; for he takes a pride in his brutishness. I've taught him to scorn everything extra-animal as silly and weak. Don't you think Hindley would be proud of his son, if he could see him? almost as proud as I am of mine. But there's this difference; one is gold put to the use of paving stones, and the other is tin polished to ape a service of silver. *Mine* has nothing valuable about it; yet I shall have the merit of making it go as far as such poor stuff can go. *His* had first-rate qualities, and they are lost—rendered worse than unavailing. I have nothing to regret; he would have more than any, but I, are aware of. And the best of it is, Hareton is damnably fond of me! You'll own that I've outmatched Hindley there. If the dead villain could rise from his grave to abuse me for his offspring's wrongs, I should have the fun of seeing the said offspring fight him back again, indignant that he should dare to rail at the one friend he has in the world!"

Heathcliff chuckled a fiendish laugh at the idea; I made no reply, because I saw that he expected none.

Meantime, our young companion, who sat too removed from us to hear what was said, began to evince symptoms of uneasiness, probably repenting that he had denied himself the treat of Catherine's society for fear of a little fatigue.

His father remarked the restless glances wandering to the window, and the hand irresolutely extended towards his cap.

"Get up, you idle boy!" he exclaimed with assumed heartiness. "Away after them! they are just at the corner, by the stand of hives."

Linton gathered his energies, and left the hearth. The lattice was open, and, as he stepped out, I heard Cathy inquiring of her unsociable attendant, what was that inscription over the door?

Hareton stared up, and scratched his head like a true clown.

"It's some damnable writing," he answered. "I cannot read it."

"Can't read it?" cried Catherine; "I can read it: it's English. But I want to know why it is there."

Linton giggled—the first appearance of mirth he had exhibited.

2. Witless.

"He does not know his letters," he said to his cousin. "Could you believe in the existence of such a colossal dunce?"

"Is he all as he should be?" asked Miss Cathy seriously, "or is he simple—not right? I've questioned him twice now, and each time he looked so stupid I think he does not understand me; I can hardly understand *him*, I'm sure!"

Linton repeated his laugh, and glanced at Hareton tauntingly, who certainly did not seem quite clear of comprehension at that moment.

"There's nothing the matter but laziness, is there, Earnshaw?" he said. "My cousin fancies you are an idiot. There you experience the consequence of scorning 'book-larning,' as you would say. Have you noticed, Catherine, his frightful Yorkshire pronunciation?"

"Why, where the devil is the use on't?" growled Hareton, more ready in answering his daily companion. He was about to enlarge further, but the two youngsters broke into a noisy fit of merriment; my giddy Miss being delighted to discover that she might turn his strange talk to matter of amusement.

"Where is the use of the devil in that sentence?" tittered Linton. "Papa told you not to say any bad words, and you can't open your mouth without one. Do try to behave like a gentleman, now do!"

"If thou weren't more a lass than a lad, I'd fell thee this minute, I would; pitiful lath of a crater!" retorted the angry boor, retreating, while his face burnt with mingled rage and mortification; for he was conscious of being insulted, and embarrassed how to resent it.

Mr. Heathcliff, having overheard the conversation as well as I, smiled when he saw him go, but immediately afterwards cast a look of singular aversion on the flippant pair, who remained chattering in the door-way: the boy finding animation enough while discussing Hareton's faults and deficiencies, and relating anecdotes of his goings on; and the girl relishing his pert and spiteful sayings, without considering the ill-nature they evinced. But I began to dislike, more than to compassionate, Linton, and to excuse his father, in some measure, for holding him cheap.

We stayed till afternoon: I could not tear Miss Cathy away, before: but happily my master had not quitted his apartment, and remained ignorant of our prolonged absence.

As we walked home, I would fain have enlightened my charge on the characters of the people we had quitted; but she got it into her head that I was prejudiced against them.

"Aha!" she cried, "you take papa's side, Ellen—you are partial, I know, or else you wouldn't have cheated me so many years into the notion that Linton lived a long way from here. I'm really extremely angry, only I'm so pleased, I can't show it! But you must hold your tongue about my uncle: he's *my* uncle, remember, and I'll scold papa for quarrelling with him."

And so she ran on, till I dropped endeavouring to convince her of her mistake.

She did not mention the visit that night, because she did not see Mr. Linton. Next day it all came out, sadly to my chagrin; and still I was not altogether sorry: I thought the burden of directing and warning would be more efficiently borne by him than me, but he was too timid in giving satisfactory reasons for his wish that she would shun connection with the household of the Heights, and Catherine liked good reasons for every restraint that harassed her petted will.

"Papa!" she exclaimed, after the morning's salutations, "guess whom I saw yesterday, in my walk on the moors. Ah, papa, you started! you've not done right, have you, now? I saw—But listen, and you shall hear how I found you out, and Ellen, who is in league with you, and yet pretended to pity me so, when I kept hoping, and was always disappointed about Linton's coming back!"

She gave a faithful account of her excursion and its consequences; and my master, though he cast more than one reproachful look at me, said nothing till she had concluded. Then he drew her to him, and asked if she knew why he had concealed Linton's near neighbourhood from her? Could she think it was to deny her a pleasure that she might harmlessly enjoy?

"It was because you disliked Mr. Heathcliff," she answered.

"Then you believe I care more for my own feelings than yours, Cathy?" he said. "No, it was not because I disliked Mr. Heathcliff, but because Mr. Heathcliff dislikes me; and is a most diabolical man, delighting to wrong and ruin those he hates, if they give him the slightest opportunity. I knew that you could not keep up an acquaintance with your cousin, without being brought into contact with him; and I knew he would detest you, on my account; so, for your own good, and nothing else, I took precautions that you should not see Linton again—I meant to explain this some time as you grew older, and I'm sorry I delayed it!"

"But Mr. Heathcliff was quite cordial, papa," observed Catherine, not at all convinced; "and *he* didn't object to our seeing each other: he said I might come to his house when I pleased, only I must not tell you, because you had quarrelled with him, and would not forgive him for marrying Aunt Isabella. And you won't—*you* are the one to be blamed. He is willing to let *us* be friends—at least Linton and I—and you are not."

My master, perceiving that she would not take his word for her uncle-in-law's evil disposition, gave a hasty sketch of his conduct to Isabella, and the manner in which Wuthering Heights became his property. He could not bear to discourse long upon the topic, for though he spoke little of it, he still felt the same horror and detestation of his ancient enemy that had occupied his heart ever since Mrs. Linton's death. "She might have been living yet, if it had not been for him!" was his constant bitter reflection; and, in his eyes, Heathcliff seemed a murderer.

Miss Cathy, conversant with no bad deeds except her own slight acts of disobedience, in justice and passion, rising from hot temper and thoughtlessness, and repented of on the day they were committed, was amazed at the blackness of spirit that could brood on and cover revenge for years, and deliberately prosecute its plans, without a visitation of remorse. She appeared so deeply impressed and shocked at this new view of human nature—excluded from all her studies and all her ideas till now—that Mr. Edgar deemed it unnecessary to pursue the subject. He merely added—

"You will know hereafter, darling, why I wish you to avoid his house and family; now, return to your old employments and amusements, and think no more about them!"

Catherine kissed her father, and sat down quietly to her lessons for a couple of hours, according to custom; then she accompanied him into the grounds, and the whole day passed as usual: but in the evening, when she had retired to her room, and I went to help her to undress, I found her crying, on her knees by the bedside.

"Oh, fie, silly child!" I exclaimed. "If you had any real griefs, you'd be ashamed to waste a tear on this little contrariety. You never had one shadow of substantial sorrow, Miss Catherine. Suppose, for a minute, that master and I were dead, and you were by yourself in the world—how would you feel, then? Compare the present occasion with such an affliction as that, and be thankful for the friend you have, instead of coveting more."

"I'm not crying for myself, Ellen," she answered, "it's for him. He expected to see me again to-morrow, and there, he'll be so disappointed—and he'll wait for me, and I shan't come!"

"Nonsense!" said I, "do you imagine he has thought as much of you as you have of him? Hasn't he Hareton for a companion? Not one in a hundred would weep at losing a relation they had just seen twice, for two afternoons. Linton will conjecture how it is, and trouble himself no further about you."

"But may I not write a note to tell him why I cannot come?" she asked, rising to her feet. "And just send those books I promised to lend him? His books are not as nice as mine, and he wanted to have them extremely, when I told him how interesting they were. May I not, Ellen?"

"No, indeed, no, indeed!" replied I with decision. "Then he would write to you, and there'd never be an end of it. No, Miss Catherine, the acquaintance must be dropped entirely—so papa expects, and I shall see that it is done!"

"But how can one little note—" she recommenced, putting on an imploring countenance.

"Silence!" I interrupted. "We'll not begin with your little notes. Get into bed!"

She threw at me a very naughty look, so naughty that I would not kiss her good-night at first: I covered her up, and shut her door, in great displeasure; but, repenting half-way, I returned softly, and lo! there was Miss, standing at the table with a bit of blank paper before her and a pencil in her hand, which she guiltily slipped out of sight, on my re-entrance.

"You'll get nobody to take that, Catherine," I said, "if you write it; and at present I shall put out your candle."

I set the extinguisher on the flame, receiving as I did so a slap on my hand, and a petulant "cross thing!" I then quitted her again, and she drew the bolt in one of her worst, most peevish humours.

The letter was finished and forwarded to its destination by a milk-fetcher who came from the village, but that I didn't learn till some time afterwards. Weeks passed on, and Cathy recovered her temper, though she grew wondrous fond of stealing off to corners by herself, and often, if I came near her suddenly while reading, she would start, and bend over the book, evidently desirous to hide it; and I detected edges of loose paper sticking out beyond the leaves.

She also got a trick of coming down early in the morning, and lingering about the kitchen, as if she were expecting the arrival of something; and she had a small drawer in a cabinet in the library, which she would trifle over for hours, and whose key she took special care to remove when she left it.

One day, as she inspected this drawer, I observed that the play-things and trinkets, which recently formed its contents, were transmuted into bits of folded paper.

My curiosity and suspicions were roused; I determined to take a peep at her mysterious treasures; so, at night, as soon as she and my master were safe upstairs, I searched and readily found among my house keys, one that would fit the lock. Having opened, I emptied the whole contents into my apron, and took them with me to examine at leisure in my own chamber.

Though I could not but suspect, I was still surprised to discover that they were a mass of correspondence—daily almost, it must have been—from Linton Heathcliff, answers to documents forwarded by her. The earlier dated were embarrassed and short; gradually, however, they expanded into copious love letters, foolish as the age of the writer rendered natural, yet with touches, here and there, which I thought were borrowed from a more experienced source.

Some of them struck me as singularly odd compounds of ardour and flatness; commencing in strong feeling, and concluding in the affected, wordy way that a school-boy might use to a fancied, incorporeal sweetheart.

Whether they satisfied Cathy, I don't know, but they appeared very worthless trash to me.

After turning over as many as I thought proper, I tied them in a handkerchief and set them aside, re-locking the vacant drawer.

Following her habit, my young lady descended early, and visited the kitchen: I watched her go to the door, on the arrival of a certain little boy; and, while the dairy maid filled his can, she tucked something into his jacket pocket, and plucked something out.

I went round by the garden, and laid wait for the messenger, who fought valorously to defend his trust, and we spilt the milk between us; but I succeeded in abstracting the epistle, and, threatening serious consequences if he did not look sharp home, I remained under the wall, and perused Miss Cathy's affectionate composition. It was more simple and more eloquent than her cousin's—very pretty and very silly. I shook my head, and went meditating into the house.

The day being wet, she could not divert herself with rambling about the park; so, at the conclusion of her morning studies, she resorted to the solace of the drawer. Her father sat reading at the table; and I, on purpose, had sought a bit of work in some unripped fringes of the window curtain, keeping my eye steadily fixed on her proceedings.

Never did any bird flying back to a plundered nest which it had left brim-ful of chirping young ones, express more complete despair in its anguished cries and flutterings, than she by her single "Oh!" and the change that transfigured her late happy countenance. Mr. Linton looked up.

"What is the matter, love? Have you hurt yourself?" he said.

His tone and look assured her *he* had not been the discoverer of the hoard.

"No, papa—" she gasped. "Ellen! Ellen! come upstairs—I'm sick!"

I obeyed her summons, and accompanied her out.

"Oh, Ellen! you have got them," she commenced immediately, dropping on her knees, when we were enclosed alone. "O, give them to me, and I'll never never do so again! Don't tell papa—you have not told papa, Ellen, say you have not! I've been exceedingly naughty, but I won't do it any more!"

With a grave severity in my manner, I bid her stand up.

"So," I exclaimed, "Miss Catherine, you are tolerably far on, it seems—you may well be ashamed of them! A fine bundle of trash you study in your leisure hours, to be sure: why, it's good enough to be printed! And what do you suppose the master will think, when I display it before him? I haven't shown it yet, but you needn't imagine I shall keep your ridiculous secrets. For shame! And you must have led the way in writing such absurdities; he would not have thought of beginning, I'm certain."

"I didn't! I didn't!" sobbed Cathy, fit to break her heart. "I didn't once think of loving him till—"

"*Loving!*" cried I, as scornfully as I could utter the word. "*Loving!* Did anybody ever hear the like! I might just as well talk of loving the miller who comes once a year to buy our corn. Pretty loving, indeed, and both times together you have seen Linton hardly four hours in your life! Now here is the babyish trash. I'm going with it to the library; and we'll see what your father says to such *loving*."

She sprang at her precious epistles, but I held them above my head; and then she poured out further frantic entreaties that I would burn them—do anything rather than show them. And being really fully as inclined to laugh as scold, for I esteemed it all girlish vanity, I at length relented in a measure, and asked—

"If I consent to burn them, will you promise faithfully, neither to send nor receive a letter again, nor a book—for I perceive you have sent him books—nor locks of hair, nor rings, nor playthings?"

"We don't send playthings!" cried Catherine, her pride overcoming her shame.

"Nor anything at all, then, my lady!" I said. "Unless you will, here I go."

"I promise, Ellen!" she cried, catching my dress. "Oh, put them in the fire, do, do!"

But when I proceeded to open a place with the poker, the sacrifice was too painful to be borne. She earnestly supplicated that I would spare her one or two.

"One or two, Ellen, to keep for Linton's sake!"

I unknotted the handkerchief, and commenced dropping them in from an angle, and the flame curled up the chimney.

"I will have one, you cruel wretch!" she screamed, darting her hand into the fire, and drawing forth some half consumed fragments, at the expense of her fingers.

"Very well—and I will have some to exhibit to papa!" I answered, shaking back the rest into the bundle, and turning anew to the door.

She emptied her blackened pieces into the flames, and motioned me to finish the immolation. It was done; I stirred up the ashes, and interred them under a shovel-full of coals; and she mutely, and with a sense of intense injury, retired to her private apartment. I descended to tell my master that the young lady's qualm of sickness was almost gone, but I judged it best for her to lie down a while.

She wouldn't dine; but she re-appeared at tea, pale and red about the eyes, and marvellously subdued in outward aspect.

Next morning, I answered the letter by a slip of paper inscribed, "Master Heathcliff is requested to send no more notes to Miss Linton, as she will not receive them." And, thenceforth, the little boy came with vacant pockets.

Chapter XXII

Summer drew to an end, and early Autumn: it was past Michaelmas,[1] but the harvest was late that year, and a few of our fields were still uncleared.

Mr. Linton and his daughter would frequently walk out among the reapers; at the carrying of the last sheaves, they stayed till dusk, and the evening happening to be chill and damp, my master caught a bad cold, that, settling obstinately on his lungs, confined him indoors throughout the whole of the winter, nearly without intermission.

Poor Cathy, frightened from her little romance, had been considerably sadder and duller since its abandonment; and her father insisted on her reading less, and taking more exercise. She had his companionship no longer; I esteemed it a duty to supply its lack, as much as possible, with mine: an inefficient substitute, for I could only spare two or three hours, from my numerous diurnal occupations, to follow her footsteps, and then my society was obviously less desirable than his.

On an afternoon in October, or the beginning of November, a fresh watery afternoon, when the turf and paths were rustling with moist, withered leaves, and the cold, blue sky was half hidden by clouds, dark grey streamers, rapidly mounting from the west, and boding abundant rain—I requested my young lady to forego her ramble because I was certain of showers. She refused; and I unwillingly donned a cloak, and took my umbrella to accompany her on a stroll to the bottom of the park: a formal walk which she generally affected if low-spirited—and that she invariably was when Mr. Edgar had been worse than ordinary; a thing never known from his confession, but guessed both by her and me from his increased silence, and the melancholy of his countenance.

She went sadly on: there was no running or bounding now, though the chill wind might well have tempted her to a race. And often, from the side of my eye, I could detect her raising a hand, and brushing something off her cheek.

1. September 29, the feast of St. Michael, one of four quarter-days (with Christmas, Lady Day, and Midsummer Day) of the English business year. Tenancy of houses usually begins and ends on these days.

I gazed round for a means of diverting her thoughts. On one side of the road rose a high, rough bank, where hazels and stunted oaks, with their roots half exposed, held uncertain tenure: the soil was too loose for the latter; and strong winds had blown some nearly horizontal. In summer, Miss Catherine delighted to climb along these trunks, and sit in the branches, swinging twenty feet above the ground; and I, pleased with her agility, and her light, childish heart, still considered it proper to scold every time I caught her at such an elevation, but so that she knew there was no necessity for descending. From dinner to tea she would lie in her breeze-rocked cradle, doing nothing except singing old songs—my nursery lore—to herself, or watching the birds, joint tenants, feed and entice their young ones to fly, or nestling with closed lids, half thinking, half dreaming, happier than words can express.

"Look, Miss!" I exclaimed, pointing to a nook under the roots of one twisted tree. "Winter is not here yet. There's a little flower, up yonder, the last bud from the multitude of blue-bells that clouded those turf steps in July with a lilac mist. Will you clamber up, and pluck it to show to papa?"

Cathy stared a long time at the lonely blossom trembling in its earthy shelter, and replied, at length—

"No, I'll not touch it—but it looks melancholy, does it not, Ellen?"

"Yes," I observed, "about as starved and sackless[2] as you—your cheeks are bloodless; let us take hold of hands and run. You're so low, I dare say I shall keep up with you."

"No," she repeated, and continued sauntering on, pausing, at intervals, to muse over a bit of moss, or a tuft of blanched grass, or a fungus spreading its bright orange among the heaps of brown foliage; and, ever and anon, her hand was lifted to her averted face.

"Catherine, why are you crying, love?" I asked, approaching and putting my arm over her shoulder. "You mustn't cry because papa has a cold; be thankful it is nothing worse."

She now put no further restraint on her tears; her breath was stifled by sobs.

"Oh, it *will* be something worse," she said. "And what shall I do when papa and you leave me, and I am by myself? I can't forget your words, Ellen, they are always in my ear. How life will be changed, how dreary the world will be, when papa and you are dead."

"None can tell, whether you won't die before us," I replied. "It's wrong to anticipate evil. We'll hope there are years and years to come before any of us go: master is young, and I am strong, and

2. Feeble.

hardly forty-five. My mother lived till eighty, a canty[3] dame to the last. And suppose Mr. Linton were spared till he saw sixty, that would be more years than you have counted, Miss. And would it not be foolish to mourn a calamity above twenty years beforehand?"

"But Aunt Isabella was younger than papa," she remarked, gazing up with timid hope to seek further consolation.

"Aunt Isabella had not you and me to nurse her," I replied. "She wasn't as happy as master; she hadn't as much to live for. All you need do, is to wait well on your father, and cheer him by letting him see you cheerful; and avoid giving him anxiety on any subject—mind that, Cathy! I'll not disguise but you might kill him, if you were wild and reckless, and cherished a foolish, fanciful affection for the son of a person who would be glad to have him in his grave; and allowed him to discover that you fretted over the separation he has judged it expedient to make."

"I fret about nothing on earth except papa's illness," answered my companion. "I care for nothing in comparison with papa. And I'll never—never—oh, never, while I have my senses, do an act, or say a word to vex him. I love him better than myself, Ellen; and I know it by this: I pray every night that I may live after him, because I would rather be miserable than that he should be—that proves I love him better than myself."

"Good words," I replied. "But deeds must prove it also; and after he is well, remember you don't forget resolutions formed in the hour of fear."

As we talked, we neared a door that opened on the road; and my young lady, lightening into sunshine again, climbed up, and seated herself on the top of the wall, reaching over to gather some hips that bloomed scarlet on the summit branches of the wild rose trees, shadowing the highway side; the lower fruit had disappeared, but only birds could touch the upper, except from Cathy's present station.

In stretching to pull them, her hat fell off; and as the door was locked, she proposed scrambling down to recover it. I bid her be cautious lest she got a fall, and she nimbly disappeared.

But the return was no such easy matter; the stones were smooth and neatly cemented, and the rosebushes and blackberry stragglers could yield no assistance in re-ascending. I, like a fool, didn't recollect that till I heard her laughing, and exclaiming—

"Ellen! you'll have to fetch the key, or else I must run round to the porter's lodge. I can't scale the ramparts on this side!"

"Stay where you are," I answered, "I have my bundle of keys in my pocket; perhaps I may manage to open it; if not, I'll go."

3. Lively.

Catherine amused herself with dancing to and fro before the door, while I tried all the large keys in succession. I had applied the last, and found that none would do; so, repeating my desire that she would remain there, I was about to hurry home as fast as I could, when an approaching sound arrested me. It was the trot of a horse; Cathy's dance stopped, and in a minute the horse stopped also.

"Who is that?" I whispered.

"Ellen, I wish you could open the door," whispered back my companion, anxiously.

"Ho, Miss Linton!" cried a deep voice (the rider's). "I'm glad to meet you. Don't be in haste to enter, for I have an explanation to ask and obtain."

"I shan't speak to you, Mr. Heathcliff!" answered Catherine. "Papa says you are a wicked man, and you hate both him and me; and Ellen says the same."

"That is nothing to the purpose," said Heathcliff. (He it was.) "I don't hate my son, I suppose, and it is concerning him that I demand your attention. Yes! you have cause to blush. Two or three months since, were you not in the habit of writing to Linton? making love in play, eh? You deserved, both of you, flogging for that! You especially, the elder, and less sensitive, as it turns out. I've got your letters, and if you give me any pertness, I'll send them to your father. I presume you grew weary of the amusement, and dropped it, didn't you? Well, you dropped Linton with it, into a Slough of Despond. He was in earnest—in love—really. As true as I live, he's dying for you—breaking his heart at your fickleness, not figuratively, but actually. Though Hareton has made him a standing jest for six weeks, and I have used more serious measures, and attempted to frighten him out of his idiocy, he gets worse daily, and he'll be under the sod before summer, unless you restore him!"

"How can you lie so glaringly to the poor child!" I called from the inside. "Pray ride on! How can you deliberately get up such paltry falsehoods? Miss Cathy, I'll knock the lock off with a stone. You won't believe that vile nonsense. You can feel in yourself, it is impossible that a person should die for love of a stranger."

"I was not aware there were eaves-droppers," muttered the detected villain. "Worthy Mrs. Dean, I like you, but I don't like your double dealing," he added, aloud. "How could *you* lie so glaringly, as to affirm I hated the 'poor child'? And invent bugbear stories to terrify her from my door-stones? Catherine Linton (the very name warms me), my bonny lass, I shall be from home all this week; go and see if I have not spoken truth; do, there's a darling! Just imagine your father in my place, and Linton in yours; then think how you would value your careless lover, if he refused to stir a step to comfort you, when your father, himself, entreated him; and don't, from pure stupidity, fall into the same error. I swear, on my salvation, he's going to his grave, and none but you can save him!"

The lock gave way, and I issued out.

"I swear Linton is dying," repeated Heathcliff, looking hard at me. "And grief and disappointment are hastening his death. Nelly, if you won't let her go, you can walk over yourself. But I shall not return till this time next week; and I think your master himself would scarcely object to her visiting her cousin!"

"Come in," said I, taking Cathy by the arm and half forcing her to re-enter, for she lingered, viewing with troubled eyes, the features of the speaker, too stern to express his inward deceit.

He pushed his horse close, and, bending down, observed—

"Miss Catherine, I'll own to you that I have little patience with Linton—and Hareton and Joseph have less. I'll own that he's with a harsh set. He pines for kindness, as well as love; and a kind word from you would be his best medicine. Don't mind Mrs. Dean's cruel cautions, but be generous, and contrive to see him. He dreams of you day and night, and cannot be persuaded that you don't hate him, since you neither write nor call."

I closed the door, and rolled a stone to assist the loosened lock in holding it; and spreading my umbrella, I drew my charge underneath, for the rain began to drive through the moaning branches of the trees, and warned us to avoid delay.

Our hurry prevented any comment on the encounter with Heathcliff, as we stretched towards home; but I divined instinctively that Catherine's heart was clouded now in double darkness. Her features were so sad, they did not seem hers: she evidently regarded what she had heard as every syllable true.

The master had retired to rest before we came in. Cathy stole to his room to inquire how he was; he had fallen asleep. She returned, and asked me to sit with her in the library. We took our tea together; and afterwards she lay down on the rug, and told me not to talk, for she was weary.

I got a book, and pretended to read. As soon as she supposed me absorbed in my occupation, she recommenced her silent weeping: it appeared, at present, her favourite diversion. I suffered her to enjoy it a while; then I expostulated, deriding and ridiculing all Mr. Heathcliff's assertions about his son, as if I were certain she would coincide. Alas! I hadn't the skill to counteract the effect his account had produced; it was just what he intended.

"You may be right, Ellen," she answered; "but I shall never feel at ease till I know. And I must tell Linton it is not my fault that I don't write; and convince him that I shall not change."

What use were anger and protestations against her silly credulity? We parted that night hostile; but next day beheld me on the road to Wuthering Heights, by the side of my wilful young mistress's pony. I couldn't bear to witness her sorrow, to see her pale, dejected countenance, and heavy eyes; and I yielded in the faint hope that Linton himself might prove, by his reception of us, how little of the tale was founded on fact.

Chapter XXIII

The rainy night had ushered in a misty morning—half frost, half drizzle—and temporary brooks crossed our path, gurgling from the uplands. My feet were thoroughly wetted; I was cross and low, exactly the humour suited for making the most of these disagreeable things.

We entered the farm-house by the kitchen way to ascertain whether Mr. Heathcliff were really absent, because I put slight faith in his own affirmation.

Joseph seemed sitting in a sort of elysium alone, beside a roaring fire; a quart of ale on the table near him, bristling with large pieces of toasted oat cake, and his black, short pipe in his mouth.

Catherine ran to the hearth to warm herself. I asked if the master were in?

My question remained so long unanswered, that I thought the old man had grown deaf, and repeated it louder.

"Na—ay!" he snarled, or rather screamed through his nose. "Na—ay! yah muh goa back whear yah coom frough."

"Joseph!" cried a peevish voice, simultaneously with me, from the inner room. "How often am I to call you? There are only a few red ashes now. Joseph! come this moment."

Vigorous puffs, and a resolute stare into the grate, declared he had no ear for this appeal. The housekeeper and Hareton were invisible; one gone on an errand, and the other at his work, probably. We knew Linton's tones and entered.

"Oh, I hope you'll die in a garret! starved to death," said the boy, mistaking our approach for that of his negligent attendant.

He stopped, on observing his error; his cousin flew to him.

"Is that you, Miss Linton?" he said, raising his head from the arm of the great chair in which he reclined. "No—don't kiss me. It takes my breath—dear me! Papa said you would call," continued he, after recovering a little from Catherine's embrace, while she stood by looking very contrite. "Will you shut the door, if you please? you left it open, and those—those *detestable* creatures won't bring coals to the fire. It's so cold!"

I stirred up the cinders, and fetched a scuttle-full myself. The invalid complained of being covered with ashes; but he had a tiresome cough, and looked feverish and ill, so I did not rebuke his temper.

"Well, Linton," murmured Catherine, when his corrugated brow relaxed. "Are you glad to see me? Can I do you any good?"

"Why didn't you come before?" he said. "You should have come, instead of writing. It tired me dreadfully, writing those long letters. I'd far rather have talked to you. Now, I can neither bear to talk, nor anything else. I wonder where Zillah is! Will you (looking at me) step into the kitchen and see?"

I had received no thanks for my other service; and being unwilling to run to and fro at his behest, I replied—

"Nobody is out there but Joseph."

"I want to drink," he exclaimed, fretfully, turning away. "Zillah is constantly gadding off to Gimmerton since papa went. It's miserable! And I'm obliged to come down here—they resolved never to hear me upstairs."

"Is your father attentive to you, Master Heathcliff?" I asked, perceiving Catherine to be checked in her friendly advances.

"Attentive? He makes *them* a little more attentive, at least," he cried. "The wretches! Do you know, Miss Linton, that brute Hareton laughs at me. I hate him—indeed, I hate them all—they are odious beings."

Cathy began searching for some water; she lighted on a pitcher in the dresser, filled a tumbler, and brought it. He bid her add a spoonful of wine from a bottle on the table; and, having swallowed a small portion, appeared more tranquil, and said she was very kind.

"And are you glad to see me?" asked she, reiterating her former question, and pleased to detect the faint dawn of a smile.

"Yes, I am. It's something new to hear a voice like yours!" he replied, "but I *have* been vexed, because you wouldn't come. And papa swore it was owing to me; he called me a pitiful, shuffling, worthless thing; and said you despised me; and if he had been in my place, he would be more the master of the Grange than your father, by this time. But you don't despise me, do you, Miss—"

"I wish you would say Catherine, or Cathy!" interrupted my young lady. "Despise you? No! Next to papa, and Ellen, I love you better than anybody living. I don't love Mr. Heathcliff, though; and I dare not come when he returns; will he stay away many days?"

"Not many," answered Linton, "but he goes onto the moors frequently, since the shooting season commenced, and you might spend an hour or two with me, in his absence. Do! say you will! I think I should not be peevish with you; you'd not provoke me, and you'd always be ready to help me, wouldn't you?"

"Yes," said Catherine, stroking his long soft hair; "if I could only get papa's consent, I'd spend half my time with you. Pretty Linton! I wish you were my brother!"

"And then you would like me as well as your father?" observed he, more cheerfully. "But papa says you would love me better than him and all the world, if you were my wife—so I'd rather you were that!"

"No! I should never love anybody better than papa," she returned gravely. "And people hate their wives, sometimes; but not their sisters and brothers, and if you were the latter, you would live with us, and papa would be as fond of you as he is of me."

Linton denied that people ever hated their wives; but Cathy affirmed they did, and in her wisdom, instanced his own father's aversion to her aunt.

I endeavoured to stop her thoughtless tongue. I couldn't succeed till everything she knew was out. Master Heathcliff, much irritated, asserted her relation was false.

"Papa told me; and papa does not tell falsehoods!" she answered pertly.

"*My* papa scorns yours!" cried Linton. "He calls him a sneaking fool!"

"Yours is a wicked man," retorted Catherine, "and you are very naughty to dare to repeat what he says. He must be wicked, to have made Aunt Isabella leave him as she did!"

"She didn't leave him," said the boy; "you shan't contradict me!"

"She did!" cried my young lady.

"Well, I'll tell *you* something!" said Linton. "Your mother hated your father, now then."

"Oh!" exclaimed Catherine, too enraged to continue.

"And she loved mine!" added he.

"You little liar! I hate you now," she panted, and her face grew red with passion.

"She did! she did!" sang Linton, sinking into the recess of his chair, and leaning back his head to enjoy the agitation of the other disputant, who stood behind.

"Hush, Master Heathcliff!" I said; "that's your father's tale too, I suppose."

"It isn't—you hold your tongue!" he answered. "She did, she did, Catherine, she did, she did!"

Cathy, beside herself, gave the chair a violent push, and caused him to fall against one arm. He was immediately seized by a suffocating cough that soon ended his triumph.

It lasted so long that it frightened even me. As to his cousin, she wept with all her might, aghast at the mischief she had done, though she said nothing.

I held him till the fit exhausted itself. Then he thrust me away, and leant his head down, silently. Catherine quelled her lamentations also, took a seat opposite, and looked solemnly into the fire.

"How do you feel now, Master Heathcliff?" I inquired, after waiting ten minutes.

"I wish *she* felt as I do," he replied, "spiteful, cruel thing! Hareton never touches me, he never struck me in his life. And I was better to-day—and there—" his voice died in a whimper.

"*I* didn't strike you!" muttered Cathy, chewing her lip to prevent another burst of emotion.

He sighed and moaned like one under great suffering, and kept it up for a quarter of an hour, on purpose to distress his cousin, apparently, for whenever he caught a stifled sob from her, he put renewed pain and pathos into the inflexions of his voice.

"I'm sorry I hurt you, Linton!" she said at length, racked beyond endurance. "But *I* couldn't have been hurt by that little push; and I had no idea that you could, either—you're not much, are you, Linton? Don't let me go home thinking I've done you harm! Answer, speak to me."

"I can't speak to you," he murmured, "you've hurt me so, that I shall lie awake all night, choking with this cough! If you had it you'd know what it was; but *you'll* be comfortably asleep, while I'm in agony—and nobody near me! I wonder how you would like to pass those fearful nights!" And he began to wail aloud for very pity of himself.

"Since you are in the habit of passing dreadful nights," I said, "it won't be Miss who spoils your ease; you'd be the same, had she never come. However, she shall not disturb you again—and perhaps you'll get quieter when we leave you."

"Must I go?" asked Catherine dolefully, bending over him. "Do you want me to go, Linton?"

"You can't alter what you've done," he replied pettishly, shrinking from her, "unless you alter it for the worse, by teasing me into a fever."

"Well, then I must go?" she repeated.

"Let me alone, at least," said he; "I can't bear your talking!"

She lingered, and resisted my persuasions to departure, a tiresome while, but as he neither looked up nor spoke, she finally made a movement to the door and I followed.

We were recalled by a scream. Linton had slid from his seat on to the hearthstone, and lay writhing in the mere perverseness of an indulged plague of a child, determined to be as grievous and harassing as it can.

I thoroughly gauged his disposition from his behaviour, and saw at once it would be folly to attempt humouring him. Not so my companion: she ran back in terror, knelt down, and cried, and soothed, and entreated, till he grew quiet from lack of breath, by no means from compunction at distressing her.

"I shall lift him on to the settle," I said, "and he may roll about as he pleases; we can't stop to watch him. I hope you are satisfied, Miss Cathy, that *you* are not the person to benefit him, and that his condition of health is not occasioned by attachment to you. Now then, there he is! Come away; as soon as he knows there is nobody by to care for his nonsense, he'll be glad to lie still!"

She placed a cushion under his head, and offered him some water; he rejected the latter, and tossed uneasily on the former, as if it were a stone, or a block of wood.

She tried to put it more comfortably.

"I can't do with that," he said, "it's not high enough!"

Catherine brought another to lay above it.

"That's *too* high!" murmured the provoking thing.

"How must I arrange it, then?" she asked despairingly.

He twined himself up to her, as she half knelt by the settle, and converted her shoulder into a support.

"No, that won't do!" I said. "You'll be content with the cushion, Master Heathcliff! Miss has wasted too much time on you already; we cannot remain five minutes longer."

"Yes, yes, we can!" replied Cathy. "He's good and patient, now. He's beginning to think I shall have far greater misery than he will to-night, if I believe he is the worse for my visit; and then, I dare not come again. Tell the truth about it, Linton, for I mustn't come, if I have hurt you."

"You must come, to cure me," he answered. "You ought to come because you have hurt me. You know you have, extremely! I was not as ill when you entered, as I am at present—was I?"

"But you've made yourself ill by crying, and being in a passion."

"I didn't do it all," said his cousin. "However, we'll be friends now. And you want me—you would wish to see me sometimes, really?"

"I told you I did!" he replied impatiently. "Sit on the settle and let me lean on your knee. That's as mamma used to do, whole afternoons together. Sit quite still, and don't talk, but you may sing a song if you can sing, or you may say a nice, long interesting ballad—one of those you promised to teach me—or a story. I'd rather have a ballad, though: begin."

Catherine repeated the longest she could remember. The employment pleased both mightily. Linton would have another, and after that another, notwithstanding my strenuous objections; and so they went on until the clock struck twelve, and we heard Hareton in the court, returning for his dinner.

"And to-morrow, Catherine, will you be here to-morrow?" asked young Heathcliff, holding her frock, as she rose reluctantly.

"No!" I answered, "nor next day neither." She, however, gave a different response, evidently, for his forehead cleared as she stooped and whispered in his ear.

"You won't go to-morrow, recollect, Miss!" I commenced, when we were out of the house. "You are not dreaming of it, are you?"

She smiled.

"Oh, I'll take good care!" I continued; "I'll have that lock mended, and you can escape by no way else."

"I can get over the wall," she said, laughing. "The Grange is not a prison, Ellen, and you are not my jailer. And besides, I'm almost seventeen. I'm a woman—and I'm certain Linton would recover quickly if he had me to look after him. I'm older than he is, you know, and wiser, less childish, am I not? And he'll soon do as I direct him with some slight coaxing. He's a pretty little darling when he's good. I'd make such a pet of him, if he were mine. We should never quarrel, should we, after we were used to each other? Don't you like him, Ellen?"

"Like him?" I exclaimed. "The worst-tempered bit of a sickly slip that ever struggled into its teens! Happily, as Mr. Heathcliff conjectured, he'll not win twenty! I doubt whether he'll see spring, indeed—and small loss to his family, whenever he drops off; and lucky it is for us that his father took him. The kinder he was treated, the more tedious and selfish he'd be! I'm glad you have no chance of having him for a husband, Miss Catherine!"

My companion waxed serious at hearing this speech. To speak of his death so regardlessly wounded her feelings.

"He's younger than I," she answered, after a protracted pause of meditation, "and he ought to live the longest; he will—he must live as long as I do. He's as strong now as when he first came into the North, I'm positive of that! It's only a cold that ails him, the same as papa has. You say papa will get better, and why shouldn't he?"

"Well, well," I cried, "after all, we needn't trouble ourselves; for listen, Miss—and mind, I'll keep my word—if you attempt going to Wuthering Heights again, with or without me, I shall inform Mr. Linton, and, unless he allow it, the intimacy with your cousin must not be revived."

"It has been revived!" muttered Cathy sulkily.

"Must not be continued, then!" I said.

"We'll see!" was her reply, and she set off at a gallop, leaving me to toil in the rear.

We both reached home before our dinner-time; my master supposed we had been wandering through the park, and therefore he demanded no explanation of our absence. As soon as I entered, I hastened to change my soaked shoes and stockings; but sitting such a while at the Heights had done the mischief. On the succeeding morning, I was laid up; and during three weeks I remained incapacitated for attending to my duties—a calamity never experienced prior to that period, and never, I am thankful to say, since.

My little mistress behaved like an angel in coming to wait on me, and cheer my solitude: the confinement brought me exceedingly low. It is wearisome, to a stirring active body, but few have slighter reasons for complaint than I had. The moment Catherine left Mr. Linton's room, she appeared at my bed-side. Her day was divided between us; no amusement usurped a minute: she neglected her meals, her studies, and her play; and she was the fondest nurse that ever watched. She must have had a warm heart, when she loved her father so, to give so much to me!

I said her days were divided between us; but the master retired early, and I generally needed nothing after six o'clock, thus the evening was her own.

Poor thing, I never considered what she did with herself after tea. And though frequently, when she looked in to bid me good-night, I remarked a fresh colour in her cheeks, and a pinkness over her slender fingers; instead of fancying the hue borrowed from a cold ride across the moors, I laid it to the charge of a hot fire in the library.

Chapter XXIV

At the close of three weeks, I was able to quit my chamber, and move about the house. And on the first occasion of my sitting up in the evening, I asked Catherine to read to me, because my eyes were weak. We were in the library, the master having gone to bed: she consented, rather unwillingly, I fancied; and imagining my sort of books did not suit her, I bid her please herself in the choice of what she perused.

She selected one of her own favourites, and got forward steadily about an hour; then came frequent questions.

"Ellen, are not you tired? Hadn't you better lie down now? You'll be sick, keeping up so long, Ellen."

"No, no, dear, I'm not tired," I returned, continually.

Perceiving me immovable, she essayed another method of showing her dis-relish for her occupation. It changed to yawning, and stretching, and—

"Ellen, I'm tired."

"Give over then and talk," I answered.

That was worse: she fretted and sighed, and looked at her watch till eight; and finally went to her room, completely overdone with sleep, judging by her peevish, heavy look, and the constant rubbing she inflicted on her eyes.

The following night she seemed more impatient still; and on the third from recovering my company, she complained of a head-ache, and left me.

I thought her conduct odd; and having remained alone a long while, I resolved on going, and inquiring whether she were better, and asking her to come and lie on the sofa, instead of upstairs, in the dark.

No Catherine could I discover upstairs, and none below. The servants affirmed they had not seen her. I listened at Mr. Edgar's door—all was silence. I returned to her apartment, extinguished my candle, and seated myself in the window.

The moon shone bright; a sprinkling of snow covered the ground, and I reflected that she might, possibly, have taken it into her head to walk about the garden, for refreshment. I did detect a figure creeping along the inner fence of the park, but it was not my young mistress; on its emerging into the light, I recognised one of the grooms.

He stood a considerable period, viewing the carriage-road through the grounds; then started off at a brisk pace, as if he had detected something, and reappeared presently, leading Miss's pony; and there she was, just dismounted, and walking by its side.

The man took his charge stealthily across the grass towards the stable. Cathy entered by the casement-window of the drawing-room, and glided noiselessly up to where I awaited her.

She put the door gently to, slipped off her snowy shoes, untied her hat, and was proceeding, unconscious of my espionage, to lay aside her mantle, when I suddenly rose and revealed myself. The surprise petrified her an instant: she uttered an inarticulate exclamation, and stood fixed.

"My dear Miss Catherine," I began, too vividly impressed by her recent kindness to break into a scold, "where have you been riding out at this hour? And why should you try to deceive me, by telling a tale? Where have you been? Speak!"

"To the bottom of the park," she stammered. "I didn't tell a tale."

"And nowhere else?" I demanded.

"No," was the muttered reply.

"Oh, Catherine," I cried, sorrowfully. "You know you have been doing wrong, or you wouldn't be driven to uttering an untruth to me. That does grieve me. I'd rather be three months ill, than hear you frame a deliberate lie."

She sprang forward, and bursting into tears, threw her arms round my neck.

"Well, Ellen, I'm so afraid of you being angry," she said. "Promise not to be angry, and you shall know the very truth. I hate to hide it."

We sat down in the window-seat; I assured her I would not scold, whatever her secret might be, and I guessed it, of course; so she commenced—

"I've been to Wuthering Heights, Ellen, and I've never missed going a day since you fell ill; except thrice before, and twice after you left your room. I gave Michael books and pictures to prepare Minny every evening, and to put her back in the stable; you mustn't scold *him* either, mind. I was at the Heights by half-past six, and generally stayed till half-past eight, and then galloped home. It was not to amuse myself that I went; I was often wretched all the time. Now and then, I was happy, once in a week perhaps. At first, I expected there would be sad work persuading you to let me keep my word to Linton, for I had engaged to call again next day, when we quitted him; but, as you stayed upstairs on the morrow, I escaped that trouble; and while Michael was refastening the lock of the park door in the afternoon, I got possession of the key, and told him how my cousin wished me to visit him, because he was sick, and couldn't come to the Grange; and how papa would object to my going. And then I negotiated with him about the pony. He is fond of reading, and he thinks of leaving soon to get married, so he offered, if I would lend him books out of the library, to do what I wished; but I preferred giving him my own, and that satisfied him better.

"On my second visit, Linton seemed in lively spirits; and Zillah —that is their housekeeper—made us a clean room and a good fire, and told us that, as Joseph was out at a prayer-meeting and Hareton Earnshaw was off with his dogs—robbing our woods of pheasants, as I heard afterwards—we might do what we liked.

"She brought me some warm wine and gingerbread, and appeared exceedingly good-natured; and Linton sat in the arm-chair, and I in the little rocking chair on the hearthstone, and we laughed and talked so merrily, and found so much to say; we planned where we would go, and what we would do in summer. I needn't repeat that, because you would call it silly.

"One time, however, we were near quarrelling. He said the pleasantest manner of spending a hot July day was lying from morning till evening on a bank of heath in the middle of the moors, with the bees humming dreamily about among the bloom, and the larks singing high up over head, and the blue sky and bright sun shining steadily and cloudlessly. That was his most perfect idea of heaven's happiness. Mine was rocking in a rustling green tree, with a west wind blowing, and bright, white clouds flitting rapidly above; and not only larks, but throstles, and blackbirds, and linnets, and cuckoos pouring out music on every side, and the moors seen at a distance, broken into cool dusky dells; but close by, great swells of long grass undulating in waves to the breeze; and woods and sounding water, and the whole world awake and wild with joy. He wanted all to lie in an ecstacy of peace; I wanted all to sparkle, and dance in a glorious jubilee.

"I said his heaven would be only half alive, and he said mine would be drunk; I said I should fall asleep in his, and he said he could not breathe in mine, and began to grow very snappish. At last, we agreed to try both as soon as the right weather came; and then we kissed each other and were friends. After sitting still an hour, I looked at the great room with its smooth, uncarpeted floor, and thought how nice it would be to play in, if we removed the table; and I asked Linton to call Zillah in to help us, and we'd have a game at blind-man's buff—she should try to catch us; you used to, you know, Ellen. He wouldn't; there was no pleasure in it, he said, but he consented to play at ball with me. We found two in a cupboard, among a heap of old toys: tops, and hoops, and battledores, and shuttlecocks. One was marked C., and the other H.; I wished to have the C., because that stood for Catherine, and the H. might be for Heathcliff, his name; but the bran came out of H., and Linton didn't like it.

"I beat him constantly; and he got cross again, and coughed, and returned to his chair. That night, though, he easily recovered his good humour; he was charmed with two or three pretty songs—*your* songs, Ellen; and when I was obliged to go, he begged and entreated me to come the following evening, and I promised.

"Minny and I went flying home as light as air: and I dreamt of Wuthering Heights, and my sweet, darling cousin, till morning.

"On the morrow, I was sad; partly because you were poorly, and partly that I wished my father knew, and approved of my excursions: but it was beautiful moonlight after tea; and, as I rode on, the gloom cleared.

"I shall have another happy evening, I thought to myself, and what delights me more, my pretty Linton will.

"I trotted up their garden, and was turning round to the back, when that fellow Earnshaw met me, took my bridle, and bid me go in by the front entrance. He patted Minny's neck, and said she was a bonny beast, and appeared as if he wanted me to speak to him. I only told him to leave my horse alone, or else it would kick him.

"He answered in his vulgar accent.

" 'It wouldn't do mitch hurt if it did'; and surveyed its legs with a smile.

"I was half inclined to make it try; however, he moved off to open the door, and, as he raised the latch, he looked up to the inscription above, and said, with a stupid mixture of awkwardness and elation—

" 'Miss Catherine! I can read yon, nah.'

" 'Wonderful,' I exclaimed. 'Pray let us hear you—you *are* grown clever!'

"He spelt, and drawled over by syllables, the name—

" 'Hareton Earnshaw.'

" 'And the figures?' I cried, encouragingly, perceiving that he came to a dead halt.

" 'I cannot tell them yet,' he answered.

" 'Oh, you dunce!' I said, laughing heartily at his failure.

"The fool stared, with a grin hovering about his lips, and a scowl gathering over his eyes, as if uncertain whether he might not join in my mirth; whether it were not pleasant familiarity, or what it really was, contempt.

"I settled his doubts by suddenly retrieving my gravity, and desiring him to walk away, for I came to see Linton, not him.

"He reddened—I saw that by the moonlight—dropped his hand from the latch, and skulked off, a picture of mortified vanity. He imagined himself to be as accomplished as Linton, I suppose, because he could spell his own name; and was marvellously discomfited that I didn't think the same."

"Stop, Miss Catherine, dear!" I interrupted. "I shall not scold, but I don't like your conduct there. If you had remembered that Hareton was your cousin as much as Master Heathcliff, you would have felt how improper it was to behave in that way. At least, it was praiseworthy ambition for him to desire to be as accomplished as Linton; and probably he did not learn merely to show off; you had made him ashamed of his ignorance before, I have no doubt; and he wished to remedy it and please you. To sneer at his imperfect attempt was very bad breeding. Had *you* been brought up in his circumstances, would you be less rude? He was as quick and as intelligent a child as ever you were, and I'm hurt that he should be despised now, because that base Heathcliff has treated him so unjustly."

"Well, Ellen, you won't cry about it, will you?" she exclaimed, surprised at my earnestness. "But wait, and you shall hear if he conned his A B C to please me; and if it were worth while being civil to the brute. I entered; Linton was lying on the settle, and half got up to welcome me.

" 'I'm ill to-night, Catherine, love,' he said, 'and you must have all the talk, and let me listen. Come, and sit by me. I was sure you wouldn't break your word, and I'll make you promise again, before you go.'

"I knew now that I mustn't tease him, as he was ill; and I spoke softly and put no questions, and avoided irritating him in any way. I had brought some of my nicest books for him; he asked me to read a little of one, and I was about to comply, when Earnshaw burst the door open, having gathered venom with reflection. He advanced direct to us, seized Linton by the arm, and swung him off the seat.

" 'Get to thy own room!' he said in a voice almost inarticulate with passion, and his face looked swelled and furious. 'Take her there if she comes to see thee—thou shalln't keep me out of this. Begone, wi' ye both!'

"He swore at us, and left Linton no time to answer, nearly throwing him into the kitchen; and he clenched his fist, as I followed, seemingly longing to knock me down. I was afraid, for a moment, and I let one volume fall; he kicked it after me, and shut us out.

"I heard a malignant, crackly laugh by the fire, and turning, beheld that odious Joseph, standing rubbing his bony hands, and quivering.

" 'Aw wer sure he'd sarve ye eht! He's a grand lad! He's getten t' raight sperrit in him! *He* knaws—Aye, he knaws, as weel as Aw do, who sud be t' maister yonder. Ech, ech, ech! He mad ye skift properly![1] Ech, ech, ech!'

" 'Where must we go?' I said to my cousin, disregarding the old wretch's mockery.

"Linton was white and trembling. He was not pretty then, Ellen. Oh, no! he looked frightful! for his thin face and large eyes were wrought into an expression of frantic, powerless fury. He grasped the handle of the door, and shook it—it was fastened inside.

" 'If you don't let me in, I'll kill you! If you don't let me in, I'll kill you!' he rather shrieked than said. 'Devil! devil! I'll kill you, I'll kill you!'

"Joseph uttered his croaking laugh again.

" 'Thear, that's t' father!' he cried. 'That's father! We've allas summut uh orther side in us.[2] Niver heed Hareton, lad—dunnut be 'feard—he cannot get at thee!'

"I took hold of Linton's hands, and tried to pull him away; but he shrieked so shockingly that I dared not proceed. At last, his cries were choked by a dreadful fit of coughing; blood gushed from his mouth, and he fell on the ground.

"I ran into the yard, sick with terror; and called for Zillah, as loud as I could. She soon heard me; she was milking the cows in a shed

1. "I was sure he would so serve you . . . He's getting the right spirit in him! *He* knows—Yes, he knows, as well as I do, who should be the master yonder . . . He made you move properly!"
2. "We've always something of the other side [of the family; e.g. Heathcliff] in us."

behind the barn, and hurrying from her work, she inquired what there was to do?

"I hadn't breath to explain; dragging her in, I looked about for Linton. Earnshaw had come out to examine the mischief he had caused, and he was then conveying the poor thing upstairs. Zillah and I ascended after him; but he stopped me at the top of the steps, and said I shouldn't go in, I must go home.

"I exclaimed that he had killed Linton and I *would* enter.

"Joseph locked the door, and declared I should do 'no sich stuff,' and asked me whether I were 'bahn[3] to be as mad as him.'

"I stood crying, till the housekeeper re-appeared; she affirmed he would be better in a bit, but he couldn't do with that shrieking and din, and she took me, and nearly carried me into the house.

"Ellen, I was ready to tear my hair off my head! I sobbed and wept so that my eyes were almost blind; and the ruffian you have such sympathy with stood opposite, presuming every now and then to bid me 'wisht,' and denying that it was his fault; and finally, frightened by my assertions that I would tell papa, and that he should be put in prison and hanged, he commenced blubbering himself, and hurried out to hide his cowardly agitation.

"Still, I was not rid of him: when at length they compelled me to depart, and I had got some hundred yards off the premises, he suddenly issued from the shadow of the road-side, and checked Minny and took hold of me.

" 'Miss Catherine, I'm ill grieved,' he began, 'but it's raything too bad—'

"I gave him a cut with my whip, thinking perhaps he would murder me. He let go, thundering one of his horrid curses, and I galloped home more than half out of my senses.

"I didn't bid you good-night, that evening; and I didn't go to Wuthering Heights, the next. I wished to, exceedingly; but I was strangely excited, and dreaded to hear that Linton was dead, sometimes; and sometimes shuddered at the thoughts of encountering Hareton.

"On the third day I took courage; at least, I couldn't bear longer suspense and stole off once more. I went at five o'clock, and walked, fancying I might manage to creep into the house, and up to Linton's room, unobserved. However, the dogs gave notice of my approach: Zillah received me, and saying 'the lad was mending nicely,' showed me into a small, tidy, carpeted apartment, where, to my inexpressible joy, I beheld Linton laid on a little sofa, reading one of my books. But he would neither speak to me nor look at me, through a whole hour, Ellen. He has such an unhappy temper—and what

3. Born.

quite confounded me, when he did open his mouth it was to utter the falsehood that I had occasioned the uproar, and Hareton was not to blame!

"Unable to reply, except passionately, I got up and walked from the room. He sent after me a faint 'Catherine!' He did not reckon on being answered so, but I wouldn't turn back; and the morrow was the second day on which I stayed at home, nearly determined to visit him no more.

"But it was so miserable going to bed, and getting up, and never hearing anything about him, that my resolution melted into air before it was properly formed. It *had* appeared wrong to take the journey once; now it seemed wrong to refrain. Michael came to ask if he must saddle Minny; I said 'Yes,' and considered myself doing a duty as she bore me over the hills.

"I was forced to pass the front windows to get to the court; it was no use trying to conceal my presence.

" 'Young master is in the house,' said Zillah, as she saw me making for the parlour.

"I went in; Earnshaw was there also, but he quitted the room directly. Linton sat in the great arm chair half asleep; walking up to the fire, I began in a serious tone, partly meaning it to be true—

" 'As you don't like me, Linton, and as you think I come on purpose to hurt you, and pretend that I do so every time, this is our last meeting—let us say good-bye; and tell Mr. Heathcliff that you have no wish to see me, and that he mustn't invent any more falsehoods on the subject.'

" 'Sit down and take your hat off, Catherine,' he answered. 'You are so much happier than I am, you ought to be better. Papa talks enough of my defects, and shows enough scorn of me, to make it natural I should doubt myself. I doubt whether I am not altogether as worthless as he calls me, frequently; and then I feel so cross and bitter, I hate everybody! I *am* worthless, and bad in temper, and bad in spirit, almost always—and if you choose, you *may* say good-bye. You'll get rid of an annoyance. Only, Catherine, do me this justice; believe that if I might be as sweet, and as kind, and as good as you are, I would be, as willingly, and more so, than as happy and as healthy. And believe that your kindness has made me love you deeper than if I deserved your love, and though I couldn't, and cannot help showing my nature to you, I regret it and repent it, and shall regret and repent it, till I die!'

"I felt he spoke the truth; and I felt I must forgive him; and, though he should quarrel the next moment, I must forgive him again. We were reconciled, but we cried, both of us, the whole time I stayed. Not entirely for sorrow, yet I *was* sorry Linton had that distorted nature. He'll never let his friends be at ease, and he'll never be at ease himself!

"I have always gone to his little parlour, since that night; because his father returned the day after. About three times, I think, we have been merry and hopeful, as we were the first evening; the rest of my visits were dreary and troubled—now, with his selfishness and spite; and now, with his sufferings: but I've learnt to endure the former with nearly as little resentment as the latter.

"Mr. Heathcliff purposely avoids me. I have hardly seen him at all. Last Sunday, indeed, coming earlier than usual, I heard him abusing poor Linton, cruelly, for his conduct of the night before. I can't tell how he knew of it, unless he listened. Linton had certainly behaved provokingly; however, it was the business of nobody but me; and I interrupted Mr. Heathcliff's lecture by entering and telling him so. He burst into a laugh, and went away, saying he was glad I took that view of the matter. Since then, I've told Linton he must whisper his bitter things.

"Now, Ellen, you have heard all; and I can't be prevented from going to Wuthering Heights, except by inflicting misery on two people; whereas, if you'll only not tell papa, my going need disturb the tranquillity of none. You'll not tell, will you? It will be very heartless if you do."

"I'll make up my mind on that point by to-morrow, Miss Catherine," I replied. "It requires some study; and so I'll leave you to your rest, and go think it over."

I thought it over aloud, in my master's presence; walking straight from her room to his, and relating the whole story, with the exception of her conversations with her cousin, and any mention of Hareton.

Mr. Linton was alarmed and distressed more than he would acknowledge to me. In the morning, Catherine learnt my betrayal of her confidence, and she learnt also that her secret visits were to end.

In vain she wept and writhed against the interdict, and implored her father to have pity on Linton: all she got to comfort her was a promise that he would write, and give him leave to come to the Grange when he pleased; but explaining that he must no longer expect to see Catherine at Wuthering Heights. Perhaps, had he been aware of his nephew's disposition and state of health, he would have seen fit to withhold even that slight consolation.

Chapter XXV

"These things happened last winter, sir," said Mrs. Dean; "hardly more than a year ago. Last winter, I did not think, at another twelve months' end, I should be amusing a stranger to the family with relating them! Yet, who knows how long you'll be a stranger? You're too young to rest always contented, living by yourself; and I some way fancy no one could see Catherine Linton, and not love her. You smile; but why do you look so lively and interested, when I talk about her? and why have you asked me to hang her picture over your fireplace? and why—"

"Stop, my good friend!" I cried. "It may be very possible that *I* should love her; but would she love me? I doubt it too much to venture my tranquillity by running into temptation; and then my home is not here. I'm of the busy world, and to its arms I must return. Go on. Was Catherine obedient to her father's commands?"

"She was," continued the housekeeper. "Her affection for him was still the chief sentiment in her heart; and he spoke without anger. He spoke in the deep tenderness of one about to leave his treasures amid perils and foes, where his remembered words would be the only aid that he could bequeath to guide her.

He said to me, a few days afterwards—

"I wish my nephew would write, Ellen, or call. Tell me, sincerely, what you think of him—is he changed for the better, or is there a prospect of improvement, as he grows a man?"

"He's very delicate, sir," I replied; "and scarcely likely to reach manhood; but this I can say, he does not resemble his father; and if Miss Catherine had the misfortune to marry him, he would not be beyond her control, unless she were extremely and foolishly indulgent. However, master, you'll have plenty of time to get acquainted with him, and see whether he would suit her: it wants four years and more to his being of age."

Edgar sighed; and, walking to the window, looked out towards Gimmerton Kirk. It was a misty afternoon, but the February sun shone dimly, and we could just distinguish the two fir trees in the yard, and the sparely scattered gravestones.

"I've prayed often," he half soliloquized, "for the approach of what is coming; and now I begin to shrink, and fear it. I thought the memory of the hour I came down that glen a bridegroom would be less sweet than the anticipation that I was soon, in a few months, or, possibly, weeks, to be carried up, and laid in its lonely hollow! Ellen, I've been very happy with my little Cathy. Through winter nights and summer days she was a living hope at my side. But I've been as happy musing by myself among those stones, under that old church—lying, through the long June evenings, on the green mound of her mother's grave, and wishing, yearning for the time when I might lie beneath it. What can I do for Cathy? How must I quit her? I'd not care one moment for Linton being Heathcliff's son; nor for his taking her from me, if he could console her for my loss. I'd not care that Heathcliff gained his ends, and triumphed in robbing me of my last blessing! But should Linton be unworthy—only a feeble tool to his father—I cannot abandon her to him! And, hard though it be to crush her buoyant spirit, I must persevere in making her sad while I live, and leaving her solitary when I die. Darling! I'd rather resign her to God, and lay her in the earth before me."

"Resign her to God, as it is, sir," I answered, "and if we should lose you—which may He forbid—under His providence, I'll stand her friend and counsellor to the last. Miss Catherine is a good girl; I don't fear that she will go willfully wrong; and people who do their duty are always finally rewarded."

Spring advanced; yet my master gathered no real strength, though he resumed his walks in the grounds with his daughter. To her inexperienced notions, this itself was a sign of convalescence; and then his cheek was often flushed, and his eyes were bright: she felt sure of his recovering.

On her seventeenth birthday, he did not visit the churchyard; it was raining, and I observed—

"You'll surely not go out to-night, sir?"

He answered—

"No, I'll defer it this year, a little longer."

He wrote again to Linton, expressing his great desire to see him; and, had the invalid been presentable, I've no doubt his father would have permitted him to come. As it was, being instructed, he returned an answer, intimating that Mr. Heathcliff objected to his calling at the Grange; but his uncle's kind remembrance delighted him, and he hoped to meet him, sometimes, in his rambles, and personally to petition that his cousin and he might not remain long so utterly divided.

That part of his letter was simple, and probably his own. Heathcliff knew he could plead eloquently enough for Catherine's company, then—

"I do not ask," he said, "that she may visit here; but am I never to see her, because my father forbids me to go to her home, and you forbid her to come to mine? Do, now and then, ride with her towards the Heights; and let us exchange a few words, in your presence! We have done nothing to deserve this separation; and you are not angry with me—you have no reason to dislike me, you allow, yourself. Dear uncle! send me a kind note to-morrow; and leave to join you anywhere you please, except at Thrushcross Grange. I believe an interview would convince you that my father's character is not mine; he affirms I am more your nephew than his son; and though I have faults which render me unworthy of Catherine, she has excused them, and, for her sake, you should also. You inquire after my health—it is better; but while I remain cut off from all hope, and doomed to solitude, or the society of those who never did, and never will like me, how can I be cheerful and well?"

Edgar, though he felt for the boy, could not consent to grant his request; because he could not accompany Catherine.

He said, in summer, perhaps, they might meet: meantime, he wished him to continue writing at intervals, and engaged to give him what advice and comfort he was able by letter; being well aware of his hard position in his family.

Linton complied; and had he been unrestrained, would probably have spoiled all by filling his epistles with complaints and lamentations; but his father kept a sharp watch over him; and, of course, insisted on every line that my master sent being shown; so, instead of penning his peculiar personal sufferings and distresses, the themes constantly uppermost in his thoughts, he harped on the cruel obligation of being held asunder from his friend and love; and gently intimated that Mr. Linton must allow an interview soon, or he should fear he was purposely deceiving him with empty promises.

Cathy was a powerful ally at home; and, between them, they at length persuaded my master to acquiesce in their having a ride or a walk together, about once a week, under my guardianship, and on the moors nearest the Grange, for June found him still declining; and, though he had set aside, yearly, a portion of his income for my young lady's fortune, he had a natural desire that she might retain—or, at least, return in a short time to—the house of her ancestors; and he considered her only prospect of doing that was by a union with his heir; he had no idea that the latter was failing almost as fast as himself; nor had any one, I believe: no doctor visited the Heights, and no one saw Master Heathcliff to make report of his condition, among us.

I, for my part, began to fancy my forebodings were false, and that he must be actually rallying, when he mentioned riding and walking on the moors, and seemed so earnest in pursuing his object.

I could not picture a father treating a dying child as tyrannically and wickedly as I afterwards learnt Heathcliff had treated him, to compel this apparent eagerness; his efforts redoubling the more imminently his avaricious and unfeeling plans were threatened with defeat by death.

Chapter XXVI

Summer was already past its prime, when Edgar reluctantly yielded his assent to their entreaties, and Catherine and I set out on our first ride to join her cousin.

It was a close, sultry day, devoid of sunshine, but with a sky too dappled and hazy to threaten rain; and our place of meeting had been fixed at the guide-stone, by the crossroads. On arriving there, however, a little herd-boy, despatched as a messenger, told us that—

"Maister Linton wer just ut this side th' Heights: and he'd be mitch obleeged to us to gang on a bit further."

"Then Master Linton has forgot the first injunction of his uncle," I observed: "he bid us keep on the Grange land, and here we are, off at once."

"Well, we'll turn our horses' heads round, when we reach him," answered my companion; "our excursion shall lie towards home."

But when we reached him, and that was scarcely a quarter of a mile from his own door, we found he had no horse, and we were forced to dismount, and leave ours to graze.

He lay on the heath, awaiting our approach, and did not rise till we came within a few yards. Then he walked so feebly, and looked so pale, that I immediately exclaimed—

"Why, Master Heathcliff, you are not fit for enjoying a ramble this morning. How ill you do look!"

Catherine surveyed him with grief and astonishment; she changed the ejaculation of joy on her lips, to one of alarm, and the congratulation on their long postponed meeting, to an anxious inquiry, whether he were worse than usual?

"No—better—better!" he panted, trembling, and retaining her hand as if he needed its support, while his large blue eyes wandered timidly over her; the hollowness round them, transforming to haggard wildness the languid expression they once possessed.

"But you have been worse," persisted his cousin, "worse than when I saw you last—you are thinner, and—"

"I'm tired," he interrupted, hurriedly. "It is too hot for walking, let us rest here. And, in the morning, I often feel sick—papa says I grow so fast."

Badly satisfied, Cathy sat down, and he reclined beside her.

"This is something like your paradise," said she, making an effort at cheerfulness. "You recollect the two days we agreed to spend in the place and way each thought pleasantest? This is nearly yours, only there are clouds; but then, they are so soft and mellow, it is nicer than sunshine. Next week, if you can, we'll ride down to the Grange Park, and try mine."

Linton did not appear to remember what she talked of; and he had evidently great difficulty in sustaining any kind of conversation. His lack of interest in the subjects she started, and his equal incapacity to contribute to her entertainment, were so obvious that she could not conceal her disappointment. An indefinite alteration had come over his whole person and manner. The pettishness that might be caressed into fondness, had yielded to a listless apathy; there was less of the peevish temper of a child which frets and teases on purpose to be soothed, and more of the self-absorbed moroseness of a confirmed invalid, repelling consolation, and ready to regard the good-humoured mirth of others as an insult.

Catherine perceived, as well as I did, that he held it rather a punishment, than a gratification, to endure our company; and she made no scruple of proposing, presently, to depart.

That proposal, unexpectedly, roused Linton from his lethargy, and threw him into a strange state of agitation. He glanced fearfully towards the Heights, begging she would remain another half-hour, at least.

"But, I think," said Cathy, "you'd be more comfortable at home than sitting here; and I cannot amuse you to-day, I see, by my tales, and songs, and chatter; you have grown wiser than I, in these six months; you have little taste for my diversions now; or else, if I could amuse you, I'd willingly stay."

"Stay to rest yourself," he replied. "And, Catherine, don't think, or say that I'm *very* unwell—it is the heavy weather and heat that make me dull; and I walked about, before you came, a great deal, for me. Tell uncle, I'm in tolerable health, will you?"

"I'll tell him that *you* say so, Linton. I couldn't affirm that you are," observed my young lady, wondering at his pertinacious assertion of what was evidently an untruth.

"And be here again next Thursday," continued he, shunning her puzzled gaze. "And give him my thanks for permitting you to come—my best thanks, Catherine. And—and if you *did* meet my father, and he asked you about me, don't lead him to suppose that I've been extremely silent and stupid; don't look sad and downcast, as you *are* doing—he'll be angry."

"I care nothing for his anger," exclaimed Cathy, imagining she would be its object.

"But I do," said her cousin, shuddering. "*Don't* provoke him against me, Catherine, for he is very hard."

"Is he severe to you, Master Heathcliff?" I inquired. "Has he grown weary of indulgence, and passed from passive, to active hatred?"

Linton looked at me, but did not answer; and, after keeping her seat by his side another ten minutes, during which his head fell drowsily on his breast, and he uttered nothing except suppressed moans of exhaustion or pain, Cathy began to seek solace in looking for bilberries, and sharing the produce of her researches with me: she did not offer them to him, for she saw further notice would only weary and annoy.

"Is it half an hour now, Ellen?" she whispered in my ear, at last. "I can't tell why we should stay. He's asleep, and papa will be wanting us back."

"Well, we must not leave him asleep," I answered; "wait till he wakes and be patient. You were mighty eager to set off, but your longing to see poor Linton has soon evaporated!"

"Why did *he* wish to see me?" returned Catherine. "In his crossest humours, formerly, I liked him better than I do in his present curious mood. It's just as if it were a task he was compelled to perform—this interview—for fear his father should scold him. But I'm hardly going to come to give Mr. Heathcliff pleasure, whatever reason he may have for ordering Linton to undergo this penance. And, though I'm glad he's better in health, I'm sorry he's so much less pleasant, and so much less affectionate to me."

"You think *he is* better in health, then?" I said.

"Yes," she answered; "because he always made such a great deal of his sufferings, you know. He is not tolerably well, as he told me to tell papa, but he's better, very likely."

"Then you differ with me, Miss Cathy," I remarked; "I should conjecture him to be far worse."

Linton here started from his slumber in bewildered terror, and asked if any one had called his name.

"No," said Catherine; "unless in dreams. I cannot conceive how you manage to doze, out of doors, in the morning."

"I thought I heard my father," he gasped, glancing up to the frowning nab above us. "You are sure nobody spoke?"

"Quite sure," replied his cousin. "Only Ellen and I were disputing concerning your health. Are you truly stronger, Linton, than when we separated in winter? If you be, I'm certain one thing is not stronger—your regard for me—speak, are you?"

The tears gushed from Linton's eyes as he answered—

"Yes, yes, I am!"

And, still under the spell of the imaginary voice, his gaze wandered up and down to detect its owner.

Cathy rose.

"For to-day we must part," she said. "And I won't conceal that I have been sadly disappointed with our meeting, though I'll mention it to nobody but you—not that I stand in awe of Mr. Heathcliff!"

"Hush," murmured Linton; "for God's sake, hush! He's coming." And he clung to Catherine's arm, striving to detain her; but, at that announcement, she hastily disengaged herself, and whistled to Minny, who obeyed her like a dog.

"I'll be here next Thursday," she cried, springing to the saddle. "Good-bye. Quick, Ellen!"

And so we left him, scarcely conscious of our departure, so absorbed was he in anticipating his father's approach.

Before we reached home, Catherine's displeasure softened into a perplexed sensation of pity and regret largely blended with vague, uneasy doubts about Linton's actual circumstances, physical and social; in which I partook, though I counselled her not to say much, for a second journey would make us better judges.

My master requested an account of our ongoings: his nephew's offering of thanks was duly delivered, Miss Cathy gently touching on the rest: I also threw little light on his inquiries, for I hardly knew what to hide, and what to reveal.

Chapter XXVII

Seven days glided away, every one marking its course by the henceforth rapid alteration of Edgar Linton's state. The havoc that months had previously wrought was now emulated by the inroads of hours.

Catherine, we would fain have deluded yet, but her own quick spirit refused to delude her. It divined, in secret, and brooded on the dreadful probability, gradually ripening into certainty.

She had not the heart to mention her ride, when Thursday came round; I mentioned it for her, and obtained permission to order her out of doors; for the library, where her father stopped a short time daily—the brief period he could bear to sit up—and his chamber had become her whole world. She grudged each moment that did not find her bending over his pillow, or seated by his side. Her countenance grew wan with watching and sorrow, and my master gladly dismissed her to what he flattered himself would be a happy change of scene and society, drawing comfort from the hope that she would not now be left entirely alone after his death.

He had a fixed idea, I guessed by several observations he let fall, that as his nephew resembled him in person, he would resemble him in mind; for Linton's letters bore few or no indications of his defective character. And I, through pardonable weakness, refrained from correcting the error; asking myself what good there would be in disturbing his last moments with information that he had neither power nor opportunity to turn to account.

We deferred our excursion till the afternoon; a golden afternoon of August—every breath from the hills so full of life, that it seemed whoever respired it, though dying, might revive.

Catherine's face was just like the landscape—shadows and sunshine flitting over it, in rapid succession; but the shadows rested longer and the sunshine was more transient, and her poor little heart reproached itself for even that passing forgetfulness of its cares.

We discerned Linton watching at the same spot he had selected before. My young mistress alighted, and told me that as she was resolved to stay a very little while, I had better hold the pony and remain on horseback; but I dissented; I wouldn't risk losing sight of the charge committed to me a minute; so we climbed the slope of heath together.

Master Heathcliff received us with greater animation on this occasion; not the animation of high spirits though, nor yet of joy; it looked more like fear.

"It is late!" he said, speaking short, and with difficulty. "Is not your father very ill? I thought you wouldn't come."

"*Why* won't you be candid?" cried Catherine, swallowing her greeting. "Why cannot you say at once, you don't want me? It is strange, Linton, that for the second time, you have brought me here on purpose, apparently, to distress us both, and for no reason besides!"

Linton shivered, and glanced at her, half supplicating, half ashamed, but his cousin's patience was not sufficient to endure this enigmatical behaviour.

"My father *is* very ill," she said, "and why am I called from his bedside—why didn't you send to absolve me from my promise, when you wished I wouldn't keep it? Come! I desire an explanation; playing and trifling are completely banished out of my mind, and I can't dance attendance on your affectations, now!"

"My affectations!" he murmured; "what are they? For heaven's sake, Catherine, don't look so angry! Despise me as much as you please; I am a worthless, cowardly wretch—I can't be scorned enough! but I'm too mean for your anger—hate my father, and spare me, for contempt!"

"Nonsense!" cried Catherine in a passion. "Foolish, silly boy! And there! he trembles, as if I were really going to touch him! You needn't bespeak contempt, Linton; anybody will have it spontaneously, at your service. Get off! I shall return home; it is folly dragging you from the hearth-stone, and pretending—what do we pretend? Let go my frock! If I pitied you for crying and looking so very frightened, you should spurn such pity. Ellen, tell him how disgraceful this conduct is. Rise, and don't degrade yourself into an abject reptile—*don't*."

With streaming face and an expression of agony, Linton had thrown his nerveless frame along the ground; he seemed convulsed with exquisite terror.

"Oh!" he sobbed, "I cannot bear it! Catherine, Catherine, I'm a traitor too, and I dare not tell you! But leave me and I shall be killed! *Dear* Catherine, my life is in your hands; and you have said you loved me—and if you did, it wouldn't harm you. You'll not go, then? kind, sweet, good Catherine! And perhaps you *will* consent—and he'll let me die with you!"

My young lady, on witnessing his intense anguish, stooped to raise him. The old feeling of indulgent tenderness overcame her vexation, and she grew thoroughly moved and alarmed.

"Consent to what?" she asked. "To stay? Tell me the meaning of this strange talk, and I will. You contradict your own words, and distract me! Be calm and frank, and confess at once all that weighs on your heart. You wouldn't injure me, Linton, would you? You wouldn't let any enemy hurt me, if you could prevent it? I'll believe you are a coward, for yourself, but not a cowardly betrayer of your best friend."

"But my father threatened me," gasped the boy, clasping his attenuated fingers, "and I dread him—I dread him! I *dare* not tell!"

"Oh well!" said Catherine, with scornful compassion, "keep your secret, *I'm* no coward—save yourself, I'm not afraid!"

Her magnanimity provoked his tears; he wept wildly, kissing her supporting hands, and yet could not summon courage to speak out.

I was cogitating what the mystery might be, and determined Catherine should never suffer to benefit him or any one else, by my good will; when hearing a rustle among the ling,[1] I looked up, and saw Mr. Heathcliff almost close upon us, descending the Heights. He didn't cast a glance towards my companions, though they were sufficiently near for Linton's sobs to be audible; but hailing me in the almost hearty tone he assumed to none besides, and the sincerity of which I couldn't avoid doubting, he said—

"It is something to see you so near to my house, Nelly! How are you at the Grange? Let us hear! The rumour goes," he added in a lower tone, "that Edgar Linton is on his death-bed—perhaps they exaggerate his illness?"

"No; my master is dying," I replied; "it is true enough. A sad thing it will be for us all, but a blessing for him!"

"How long will he last, do you think?" he asked.

"I don't know," I said.

"Because," he continued, looking at the two young people, who were fixed under his eye—Linton appeared as if he could not venture to stir, or raise his head, and Catherine could not move, on his account—"Because that lad yonder seems determined to beat me—and I'd thank his uncle to be quick, and go before him. Hallo!

1. Heather.

Has the whelp been playing that game long? I *did* give him some lessons about snivelling. Is he pretty lively with Miss Linton generally?"

"Lively? no—he has shown the greatest distress," I answered. "To see him, I should say, that instead of rambling with his sweetheart on the hills, he ought to be in bed, under the hands of a doctor."

"He shall be, in a day or two," muttered Heathcliff. "But first—get up, Linton! Get up!" he shouted. "Don't grovel on the ground, there—up this moment!"

Linton had sunk prostrate again in another paroxysm of helpless fear, caused by his father's glance towards him, I suppose: there was nothing else to produce such humiliation. He made several efforts to obey, but his little strength was annihilated for the time, and he fell back again with a moan.

Mr. Heathcliff advanced, and lifted him to lean against a ridge of turf.

"Now," said he with curbed ferocity, "I'm getting angry—and if you don't command that paltry spirit of yours—*Damn* you! Get up, directly!"

"I will, father!" he panted. "Only, let me alone, or I shall faint! I've done as you wished, I'm sure. Catherine will tell you that—that I—have been cheerful. Ah! keep by me, Catherine; give me your hand."

"Take mine," said his father; "stand on your feet! There now—she'll lend you her arm. That's right, look at *her*. You would imagine I was the devil himself, Miss Linton, to excite such horror. Be so kind as to walk home with him, will you? He shudders, if I touch him."

"Linton, dear!" whispered Catherine, "I can't go to Wuthering Heights—papa has forbidden me. He'll not harm you, why are you so afraid?"

"I can never re-enter that house," he answered. "I am *not* to re-enter it without you!"

"Stop!" cried his father. "We'll respect Catherine's filial scruples. Nelly, take him in, and I'll follow your advice concerning the doctor, without delay."

"You'll do well," replied I, "but I must remain with my mistress. To mind your son is not my business."

"You are very stiff!" said Heathcliff; "I know that—but you'll force me to pinch the baby, and make it scream, before it moves your charity. Come then, my hero. Are you willing to return, escorted by me?"

He approached once more, and made as if he would seize the fragile being; but shrinking back, Linton clung to his cousin, and implored her to accompany him, with a frantic importunity that admitted no denial.

However I disapproved, I couldn't hinder her; indeed, how could she have refused him herself? What was filling him with dread, we had no means of discerning, but there he was, powerless under its gripe, and any addition seemed capable of shocking him into idiocy.

We reached the threshold; Catherine walked in; and I stood waiting till she had conducted the invalid to a chair, expecting her out immediately; when Mr. Heathcliff, pushing me forward, exclaimed—

"My house is not stricken with the plague, Nelly; and I have a mind to be hospitable to-day; sit down, and allow me to shut the door."

He shut and locked it also. I started.

"You shall have tea, before you go home," he added. "I am by myself. Hareton is gone with some cattle to the Lees—and Zillah and Joseph are off on a journey of pleasure. And, though I'm used to being alone, I'd rather have some interesting company, if I can get it. Miss Linton, take your seat by *him*. I give you what I have; the present is hardly worth accepting; but I have nothing else to offer. It is Linton, I mean. How she does stare! It's odd what a savage feeling I have to anything that seems afraid of me! Had I been born where laws are less strict, and tastes less dainty, I should treat myself to a slow vivisection of those two, as an evening's amusement."

He drew in his breath, struck the table, and swore to himself—

"By hell! I hate them."

"I'm not afraid of you!" exclaimed Catherine, who could not hear the latter part of his speech.

She stepped close up, her black eyes flashing with passion and resolution.

"Give me that key—I will have it!" she said. "I wouldn't eat or drink here, if I were starving."

Heathcliff had the key in his hand that remained on the table. He looked up, seized with a sort of surprise at her boldness, or, possibly, reminded by her voice and glance, of the person from whom she inherited it.

She snatched at the instrument, and half succeeded in getting it out of his loosened fingers; but her action recalled him to the present; he recovered it speedily.

"Now, Catherine Linton," he said, "stand off, or I shall knock you down; and that will make Mrs. Dean mad."

Regardless of this warning, she captured his closed hand and its contents again.

"We *will* go!" she repeated, exerting her utmost efforts to cause the iron muscles to relax; and finding that her nails made no impression, she applied her teeth pretty sharply.

Heathcliff glanced at me a glance that kept me from interfering a moment. Catherine was too intent on his fingers to notice his face. He opened them suddenly, and resigned the object of dispute; but, ere she had well secured it, he seized her with the liberated hand, and, pulling her on his knee, administered with the other a shower of terrific slaps on both sides of the head, each sufficient to have fulfilled his threat, had she been able to fall.

At this diabolical violence, I rushed on him furiously.

"You villain!" I began to cry, "you villain!"

A touch on the chest silenced me; I am stout, and soon put out of breath; and, what with that and the rage, I staggered dizzily back, and felt ready to suffocate, or to burst a blood-vessel.

The scene was over in two minutes; Catherine, released, put her two hands to her temples, and looked just as if she were not sure whether her ears were off or on. She trembled like a reed, poor thing, and leant against the table perfectly bewildered.

"I know how to chastise children, you see," said the scoundrel, grimly, as he stooped to repossess himself of the key, which had dropped to the floor. "Go to Linton now, as I told you; and cry at your ease! I shall be your father to-morrow—all the father you'll have in a few days—and you shall have plenty of that—you can bear plenty—you're no weakling—you shall have a daily taste, if I catch such a devil of a temper in your eyes again!"

Cathy ran to me instead of Linton, and knelt down, and put her burning cheek on my lap, weeping aloud. Her cousin had shrunk into a corner of the settle, as quiet as a mouse, congratulating himself, I dare say, that the correction had lighted on another than him.

Mr. Heathcliff, perceiving us all confounded, rose, and expeditiously made the tea himself. The cups and saucers were laid ready. He poured it out, and handed me a cup.

"Wash away your spleen," he said. "And help your own naughty pet and mine. It is not poisoned, though I prepared it. I'm going out to seek your horses."

Our first thought, on his departure, was to force an exit somewhere. We tried the kitchen door, but that was fastened outside, we looked at the windows—they were too narrow for even Cathy's little figure.

"Master Linton," I cried, seeing we were regularly imprisoned, "you know what your diabolical father is after, and you shall tell us, or I'll box your ears, as he has done your cousin's."

"Yes, Linton; you must tell," said Catherine. "It was for your sake I came; and it will be wickedly ungrateful if you refuse."

"Give me some tea, I'm thirsty, and then I'll tell you," he answered. "Mrs. Dean, go away. I don't like you standing over me.

Now, Catherine, you are letting your tears fall into my cup! I won't drink that. Give me another."

Catherine pushed another to him, and wiped her face. I felt disgusted at the little wretch's composure, since he was no longer in terror for himself. The anguish he had exhibited on the moor subsided as soon as ever he entered Wuthering Heights; so I guessed he had been menaced with an awful visitation of wrath if he failed in decoying us there; and, that accomplished, he had no further immediate fears.

"Papa wants us to be married," he continued, after sipping some of the liquid. "And he knows your papa wouldn't let us marry now; and he's afraid of my dying, if we wait; so we are to be married in the morning, and you are to stay here all night; and, if you do as he wishes, you shall return home next day, and take me with you."

"Take you with her, pitiful changeling?" I exclaimed. "*You* marry? Why, the man is mad, or he thinks us fools, every one. And do you imagine that beautiful young lady, that healthy, hearty girl, will tie herself to a little perishing monkey like you? Are you cherishing the notion that *anybody*, let alone Miss Catherine Linton, would have you for a husband? You want whipping for bringing us in here at all, with your dastardly, puling tricks; and—don't look so silly now! I've a very good mind to shake you severely, for your contemptible treachery, and your imbecile conceit."

I did give him a slight shaking, but it brought on the cough, and he took to his ordinary resource of moaning and weeping, and Catherine rebuked me.

"Stay all night? No!" she said, looking slowly round. "Ellen, I'll burn that door down, but I'll get out."

And she would have commenced the execution of her threat directly, but Linton was up in alarm, for his dear self, again. He clasped her in his two feeble arms, sobbing—

"Won't you have me, and save me? Not let me come to the Grange? Oh! darling Catherine! you mustn't go, and leave me, after all. You *must* obey my father, you *must!*"

"I must obey my own," she replied, "and relieve him from this cruel suspense. The whole night! What would he think? he'll be distressed already. I'll either break or burn a way out of the house. Be quiet! You're in no danger—but, if you hinder me—Linton, I love papa better than you!"

The mortal terror he felt of Mr. Heathcliff's anger restored to the boy his coward's eloquence. Catherine was near distraught; still, she persisted that she must go home, and tried entreaty, in her turn, persuading him to subdue his selfish agony.

While they were thus occupied, our jailer re-entered.

"Your beasts have trotted off," he said, "and—Now, Linton! snivelling again? What has she been doing to you? Come, come—have done, and get to bed. In a month or two, my lad, you'll be able to pay her back her present tyrannies, with a vigorous hand. You're pining for pure love, are you not? nothing else in the world—and she shall have you! There, to bed! Zillah won't be here to-night; you must undress yourself. Hush! hold your noise! Once in your own room, I'll not come near you, you needn't fear. By chance, you've managed tolerably. I'll look to the rest."

He spoke these words, holding the door open for his son to pass; and the latter achieved his exit exactly as a spaniel might, which suspected the person who attended on it of designing a spiteful squeeze.

The lock was re-secured. Heathcliff approached the fire, where my mistress and I stood silent. Catherine looked up, and instinctively raised her hand to her cheek: his neighbourhood revived a painful sensation. Anybody else would have been incapable of regarding the childish act with sternness, but he scowled on her, and muttered—

"Oh, you are not afraid of me? Your courage is well disguised—you *seem* damnably afraid!"

"I *am* afraid now," she replied; "because if I stay, papa will be miserable; and how can I endure making him miserable—when he—when he—Mr. Heathcliff, *let* me go home! I promise to marry Linton—papa would like me to, and I love him—and why should you wish to force me to do what I'll willingly do of myself?"

"Let him dare to force you!" I cried. "There's law in the land, thank God, there is! though we *be* in an out-of-the-way place. I'd inform, if he were my own son, and it's felony without benefit of clergy!"

"Silence!" said the ruffian. "To the devil with your clamour! I don't want *you* to speak. Miss Linton, I shall enjoy myself remarkably in thinking your father will be miserable; I shall not sleep for satisfaction. You could have hit on no surer way of fixing your residence under my roof, for the next twenty-four hours, than informing me that such an event would follow. As to your promise to marry Linton, I'll take care you shall keep it, for you shall not quit the place till it is fulfilled."

"Send Ellen then, to let papa know I'm safe!" exclaimed Catherine, weeping bitterly. "Or marry me now. Poor papa! Ellen, he'll think we're lost. What shall we do?"

"Not he! He'll think you are tired of waiting on him, and run off, for a little amusement," answered Heathcliff. "You cannot deny that you entered my house of your own accord, in contempt of his injunctions to the contrary. And it is quite natural that you should desire amusement at your age; and that you should weary of nursing a sick man, and that man *only* your father. Catherine, his happiest days were over when your days began. He cursed you, I dare say, for coming into the world (I did, at least). And it would just do if he cursed you as *he* went out of it. I'd join him. I don't love you! How should I? Weep away. As far as I can see, it will be your chief diversion hereafter, unless Linton make amends for other losses; and your provident parent appears to fancy he may. His letters of advice and consolation entertained me vastly. In his last, he recommended my jewel to be careful of his; and kind to her when he got her. Careful and kind—that's paternal! But Linton requires his whole stock of care and kindness for himself. Linton can play the little tyrant well. He'll undertake to torture any number of cats if their teeth be drawn, and their claws pared. You'll be able to tell his uncle fine tales of his *kindness*, when you get home again, I assure you."

"You're right there!" I said; "explain your son's character. Show his resemblance to yourself; and then, I hope, Miss Cathy will think twice before she takes the cockatrice!"

"I don't much mind speaking of his amiable qualities now," he answered, "because she must either accept him, or remain a prisoner, and you along with her, till your master dies. I can detain you both, quite concealed, here. If you doubt, encourage her to retract her word, and you'll have an opportunity of judging!"

"I'll not retract my word," said Catherine. "I'll marry him, within this hour, if I may go to Thrushcross Grange afterwards. Mr. Heathcliff, you're a cruel man, but you're not a fiend; and you won't, from *mere* malice, destroy, irrevocably, all my happiness. If papa thought I had left him on purpose, and if he died before I returned, could I bear to live? I've given over crying; but I'm going to kneel here, at your knee; and I'll not get up, and I'll not take my eyes from your face, till you look back at me! No, don't turn away! *do* look! You'll see nothing to provoke you. I don't hate you. I'm not angry that you struck me. Have you never loved *anybody*, in all your life, uncle? *never?* Ah! you must look once—I'm so wretched—you can't help being sorry and pitying me."

"Keep your eft's[1] fingers off; and move, or I'll kick you!" cried Heathcliff, brutally repulsing her. "I'd rather be hugged by a snake. How the devil can you dream of fawning on me? I *detest* you!"

He shrugged his shoulders—shook himself, indeed, as if his flesh crept with aversion, and thrust back his chair, while I got up, and

1. "Lizzard's."

opened my mouth, to commence a downright torrent of abuse; but I was rendered dumb in the middle of the first sentence, by a threat that I should be shown into a room by myself, the very next syllable I uttered.

It was growing dark—we heard a sound of voices at the garden gate. Our host hurried out, instantly; *he* had his wits about him; *we* had not. There was a talk of two or three minutes, and he returned alone.

"I thought it had been your cousin Hareton," I observed to Catherine. "I wish he would arrive! Who knows but he might take our part?"

"It was three servants sent to seek you from the Grange," said Heathcliff, overhearing me. "You should have opened a lattice and called out; but I could swear that chit is glad you didn't. She's glad to be obliged to stay, I'm certain."

At learning the chance we had missed, we both gave vent to our grief without control, and he allowed us to wail on till nine o'clock; then he bid us go upstairs, through the kitchen, to Zillah's chamber, and I whispered my companion to obey; perhaps we might contrive to get through the window there, or into a garret, and out by its skylight.

The window, however, was narrow like those below, and the garret trap was safe from our attempts; for we were fastened in as before.

We neither of us lay down: Catherine took her station by the lattice, and watched anxiously for morning—a deep sigh being the only answer I could obtain to my frequent entreaties that she would try to rest.

I seated myself in a chair, and rocked, to and fro, passing harsh judgment on my many derelictions of duty; from which, it struck me then, all the misfortunes of all my employers sprang. It was not the case, in reality, I am aware; but it was, in my imagination, that dismal night, and I thought Heathcliff himself less guilty than I.

At seven o'clock he came, and inquired if Miss Linton had risen.

She ran to the door immediately, and answered—

"Yes."

"Here, then," he said, opening it, and pulling her out.

I rose to follow, but he turned the lock again. I demanded my release.

"Be patient," he replied; "I'll send up your breakfast in a while."

I thumped on the panels, and rattled the latch angrily; and Catherine asked why I was still shut up? He answered, I must try to endure it another hour, and they went away.

I endured it two or three hours; at length, I heard a footstep, not Heathcliff's.

"I've brought you something to eat," said a voice; "oppen t' door!"

Complying eagerly, I beheld Hareton, laden with food enough to last me all day.

"Tak it," he added, thrusting the tray into my hand.

"Stay one minute," I began.

"Nay!" cried he, and retired, regardless of any prayers I could pour forth to detain him.

And there I remained enclosed, the whole day, and the whole of the next night; and another, and another. Five nights and four days I remained, altogether, seeing nobody but Hareton, once every morning, and he was a model of a jailer—surly, and dumb, and deaf to every attempt at moving his sense of justice or compassion.

Chapter XXVIII

On the fifth morning, or rather afternoon, a different step approached—lighter and shorter—and, this time, the person entered the room. It was Zillah, donned in her scarlet shawl, with a black silk bonnet on her head, and a willow basket swung to her arm.

"Eh, dear! Mrs. Dean," she exclaimed. "Well! there is a talk about you at Gimmerton. I never thought but you were sunk in the Blackhorse marsh, and Missy with you, till master told me you'd been found, and he'd lodged you here! What, and you must have got on an island, sure? And how long were you in the hole? Did master save you, Mrs. Dean? But you're not so thin—you've not been so poorly, have you?"

"Your master is a true scoundrel!" I replied. "But he shall answer for it. He needn't have raised that tale—it shall all be laid bare!"

"What do you mean?" asked Zillah. "It's not his tale: they tell that in the village—about your being lost in the marsh; and I calls to Earnshaw, when I come in—"

" 'Eh, they's queer things, Mr. Hareton, happened since I went off. It's a sad pity of that likely young lass, and cant[1] Nelly Dean.'

"He stared. I thought he had not heard aught, so I told him the rumour.

"The master listened, and he just smiled to himself, and said—

" 'If they have been in the marsh, they are out now, Zillah. Nelly Dean is lodged, at this minute, in your room. You can tell her to flit, when you go up; here is the key. The bog-water got into her head, and she would have run home, quite flighty, but I fixed her, till she came round to her senses. You can bid her go to the Grange, at once, if she be able, and carry a message from me, that her young lady will follow in time to attend the Squire's funeral."

1. Brisk or lively.

"Mr. Edgar is not dead?" I gasped. "Oh! Zillah, Zillah!"

"No, no—sit you down, my good mistress," she replied; "you're right sickly yet. He's not dead: Doctor Kenneth thinks he may last another day. I met him on the road and asked."

Instead of sitting down, I snatched my outdoor things, and hastened below, for the way was free.

On entering the house, I looked about for some one to give information of Catherine.

The place was filled with sunshine, and the door stood wide open, but nobody seemed at hand.

As I hesitated whether to go off at once, or return and seek my mistress, a slight cough drew my attention to the hearth.

Linton lay on the settle, sole tenant, sucking a stick of sugar-candy, and pursuing my movements with apathetic eyes.

"Where is Miss Catherine?" I demanded, sternly, supposing I could frighten him into giving intelligence, by catching him thus, alone.

He sucked on like an innocent.

"Is she gone?" I said.

"No," he replied; "she's upstairs—she's not to go; we won't let her."

"You won't let her, little idiot!" I exclaimed. "Direct me to her room immediately, or I'll make you sing out sharply."

"Papa would make you sing out, if you attempted to get there," he answered. "He says I'm not to be soft with Catherine; she's my wife, and it's shameful that she should wish to leave me! He says, she hates me, and wants me to die, that she may have my money, but she shan't have it; and she shan't go home! She never shall! she may cry, and be sick as much as she pleases!"

He resumed his former occupation, closing his lids, as if he meant to drop asleep.

"Master Heathcliff," I resumed, "have you forgotten all Catherine's kindness to you, last winter, when you affirmed you loved her, and when she brought you books, and sung you songs, and came many a time through wind and snow to see you? She wept to miss one evening, because you would be disappointed; and you felt then, that she was a hundred times too good to you; and now you believe the lies your father tells, though you know he detests you both! And you join him against her. That's fine gratitude, is it not?"

The corner of Linton's mouth fell, and he took the sugar-candy from his lips.

"Did she come to Wuthering Heights, because she hated you?" I continued. "Think for yourself! As to your money, she does not even know that you will have any. And you say she's sick; and yet, you leave her alone, up there in a strange house! *You*, who have felt what it is to be so neglected! You could pity your own sufferings, and she pitied them, too, but you won't pity hers! I shed tears, Master Heathcliff, you see—an elderly woman, and a servant merely—and you, after pretending such affection, and having reason to worship her almost, store every tear you have for yourself, and lie there quite at ease. Ah! you're a heartless, selfish boy!"

"I can't stay with her," he answered crossly. "I'll not stay, by myself. She cries so I can't bear it. And she won't give over, though I say I'll call my father. I did call him once; and he threatened to strangle her, if she was not quiet, but she began again, the instant he left the room; moaning and grieving, all night long, though I screamed for vexation that I couldn't sleep."

"Is Mr. Heathcliff out?" I inquired, perceiving that the wretched creature had no power to sympathise with his cousin's mental tortures.

"He's in the court," he replied, "talking to Doctor Kenneth, who says uncle is dying, truly, at last. I'm glad, for I shall be master of the Grange after him—and Catherine always spoke of it as *her* house. It isn't hers! It's mine—papa says everything she has is mine. All her nice books are mine; she offered to give me them, and her pretty birds, and her pony Minny, if I would get the key of our room, and let her out; but I told her she had nothing to give, they were all, all mine. And then she cried, and took a little picture from her neck, and said I should have that—two pictures in a gold case, on one side her mother, and on the other, uncle, when they were young. That was yesterday—I said *they* were mine, too; and tried to get them from her. The spiteful thing wouldn't let me; she pushed me off, and hurt me. I shrieked out—that frightens her—she heard papa coming, and she broke the hinges, and divided the case and gave me her mother's portrait; the other she attempted to hide; but papa asked what was the matter and I explained it. He took the one I had away; and ordered her to resign hers to me; she refused, and he—he struck her down, and wrenched it off the chain, and crushed it with his foot."

"And were you pleased to see her struck?" I asked, having my designs in encouraging his talk.

"I winked," he answered. "I wink to see my father strike a dog, or a horse, he does it so hard. Yet I was glad at first—she deserved punishing for pushing me: but when papa was gone, she made me come to the window and showed me her cheek cut on the inside, against her teeth, and her mouth filling with blood; and then she gathered up the bits of the picture, and went and sat down with her face to the wall, and she has never spoken to me since, and I sometimes think she can't speak for pain. I don't like to think so! but she's a naughty thing for crying continually; and she looks so pale and wild, I'm afraid of her!"

"And you can get the key if you choose?" I said.

"Yes, when I am upstairs," he answered; "but I can't walk upstairs now."

"In what apartment is it?" I asked.

"Oh," he cried, "I shan't tell *you* where it is! It is our secret. Nobody, neither Hareton, nor Zillah are to know. There! you've tired me—go away, go away!" And he turned his face onto his arm, and shut his eyes, again.

I considered it best to depart without seeing Mr. Heathcliff; and bring a rescue for my young lady, from the Grange.

On reaching it, the astonishment of my fellow servants to see me, and their joy also, was intense; and when they heard that their little mistress was safe, two or three were about to hurry up, and shout the news at Mr. Edgar's door: but I bespoke the announcement of it, myself.

How changed I found him, even in those few days! He lay an image of sadness, and resignation, waiting his death. Very young he looked: though his actual age was thirty-nine, one would have called him ten years younger, at least. He thought of Catherine, for he murmured her name. I touched his hand, and spoke.

"Catherine is coming, dear master!" I whispered; "she is alive, and well; and will be here I hope to-night."

I trembled at the first effects of this intelligence: he half rose up, looked eagerly round the apartment, and then sunk back in a swoon.

As soon as he recovered, I related our compulsory visit, and detention at the Heights. I said Heathcliff forced me to go in, which was not quite true; I uttered as little as possible against Linton; nor did I describe all his father's brutal conduct, my intentions being to add no bitterness, if I could help it, to his already overflowing cup.

He divined that one of his enemy's purposes was to secure the personal property, as well as the estate, to his son, or rather himself; yet why he did not wait till his decease, was a puzzle to my master, because ignorant how nearly he and his nephew would quit the world together.

However, he felt his will had better be altered. Instead of leaving Catherine's fortune at her own disposal, he determined to put it in the hands of trustees, for her use during life, and for her children, if she had any, after her. By that means, it could not fall to Mr. Heathcliff should Linton die.

Having received his orders, I despatched a man to fetch the attorney, and four more, provided with serviceable weapons, to demand my young lady of her jailer. Both parties were delayed very late. The single servant returned first.

He said Mr. Green, the lawyer, was out when he arrived at his house, and he had to wait two hours for his re-entrance: and then Mr. Green told him he had a little business in the village that must be done, but he would be at Thrushcross Grange before morning.

The four men came back unaccompanied, also. They brought word that Catherine was ill, too ill to quit her room, and Heathcliff would not suffer them to see her.

I scolded the stupid fellows well, for listening to that tale, which I would not carry to my master; resolving to take a whole bevy up to the Heights, at daylight, and storm it, literally, unless the prisoner were quietly surrendered to us.

Her father *shall* see her, I vowed, and vowed again, if that devil be killed on his own doorstones in trying to prevent it!

Happily, I was spared the journey, and the trouble.

I had gone downstairs at three o'clock to fetch a jug of water; and was passing through the hall with it in my hand, when a sharp knock at the front door made me jump.

"Oh! it is Green," I said, recollecting myself, "—only Green," and I went on, intending to send somebody else to open it; but the knock was repeated, not loud, and still importunately.

I put the jug on the banister, and hastened to admit him myself.

The harvest moon shone clear outside. It was not the attorney. My own sweet little mistress sprung on my neck sobbing—

"Ellen! Ellen! Is papa alive?"

"Yes!" I cried, "yes, my angel, he is! God be thanked, you are safe with us again!"

She wanted to run, breathless as she was, upstairs to Mr. Linton's room; but I compelled her to sit down on a chair, and made her drink, and washed her pale face, chafing it into a faint colour with my apron. Then I said I must go first, and tell of her arrival; imploring her to say, she should be happy with young Heathcliff. She stared, but soon comprehending why I counselled her to utter the falsehood, she assured me she would not complain.

I couldn't abide to be present at their meeting. I stood outside the chamber-door a quarter of an hour, and hardly ventured near the bed, then.

All was composed, however; Catherine's despair was as silent as her father's joy. She supported him calmly, in appearance; and he fixed on her features his raised eyes, that seemed dilating with ecstasy.

He died blissfully, Mr. Lockwood; he died so. Kissing her cheek, he murmured—

"I am going to her, and you, darling child, shall come to us"; and never stirred or spoke again, but continued that rapt, radiant gaze, till his pulse imperceptibly stopped, and his soul departed. None could have noticed the exact minute of his death, it was so entirely without a struggle.

Whether Catherine had spent her tears, or whether the grief were too weighty to let them flow, she sat there dry-eyed till the sun rose; she sat till noon, and would still have remained, brooding over that death-bed, but I insisted on her coming away, and taking some repose.

It was well I succeeded in removing her, for at dinner-time appeared the lawyer, having called at Wuthering Heights to get his instructions how to behave. He had sold himself to Mr. Heathcliff, and that was the cause of his delay in obeying my master's summons. Fortunately, no thought of worldly affairs crossed the latter's mind, to disturb him, after his daughter's arrival.

Mr. Green took upon himself to order everything and everybody about the place. He gave all the servants but me, notice to quit. He would have carried his delegated authority to the point of insisting that Edgar Linton should not be buried beside his wife, but in the chapel, with his family. There was the will, however, to hinder that, and my loud protestations against any infringement of its directions.

The funeral was hurried over; Catherine, Mrs. Linton Heathcliff now, was suffered to stay at the Grange, till her father's corpse had quitted it.

She told me that her anguish had at last spurred Linton to incur the risk of liberating her. She heard the men I sent, disputing at the door, and she gathered the sense of Heathcliff's answer. It drove her desperate. Linton, who had been conveyed up to the little parlour soon after I left, was terrified into fetching the key before his father re-ascended.

He had the cunning to unlock, and re-lock the door, without shutting it; and when he should have gone to bed, he begged to sleep with Hareton, and his petition was granted, for once.

Catherine stole out before break of day. She dare not try the doors, lest the dogs should raise an alarm; she visited the empty chambers, and examined their windows; and, luckily, lighting on her mother's, she got easily out of its lattice, and onto the ground, by means of the fir tree, close by. Her accomplice suffered for his share in the escape, notwithstanding his timid contrivances.

Chapter XXIX

The evening after the funeral, my young lady and I were seated in the library; now musing mournfully, one of us despairingly, on our loss, now venturing conjectures as to the gloomy future.

We had just agreed the best destiny which could await Catherine, would be a permission to continue resident at the Grange, at least during Linton's life: he being allowed to join her there, and I to remain as housekeeper. That seemed rather too favourable an arrangement to be hoped for, and yet I did hope, and began to cheer up under the prospect of retaining my home, and my employment, and, above all, my beloved young mistress, when a servant—one of the discarded ones, not yet departed—rushed hastily in, and said, "that devil Heathcliff" was coming through the court: should he fasten the door in his face?

If we had been mad enough to order that proceeding, we had not time. He made no ceremony of knocking, or announcing his name; he was master, and availed himself of the master's privilege to walk straight in, without saying a word.

The sound of our informant's voice directed him to the library; he entered, and motioning him out, shut the door.

It was the same room into which he had been ushered, as a guest, eighteen years before: the same moon shone through the window; and the same autumn landscape lay outside. We had not yet lighted a candle, but all the apartment was visible, even to the portraits on the wall—the splendid head of Mrs. Linton, and the graceful one of her husband.

Heathcliff advanced to the hearth. Time had little altered his person either. There was the same man, his dark face rather sallower, and more composed, his frame a stone or two heavier, perhaps, and no other difference.

Catherine had risen with an impulse to dash out, when she saw him.

"Stop!" he said, arresting her by the arm. "No more runnings away! Where would you go? I'm come to fetch you home; and I hope you'll be a dutiful daughter, and not encourage my son to further disobedience. I was embarrassed how to punish him, when I discovered his part in the business—he's such a cobweb, a pinch would annihilate him—but you'll see by his look that he has received his due! I brought him down one evening, the day before yesterday, and just set him in a chair, and never touched him afterwards. I sent Hareton out, and we had the room to ourselves. In two hours, I called Joseph to carry him up again; and, since then, my presence is as potent on his nerves as a ghost; and I fancy he sees me often, though I am not near. Hareton says he wakes and shrieks in the night by the hour together; and calls you to protect him from me; and, whether you like your precious mate or not, you must come—he's your concern now; I yield all my interest in him to you."

"Why not let Catherine continue here?" I pleaded, "and send Master Linton to her. As you hate them both, you'd not miss them; they *can* only be a daily plague to your unnatural heart."

"I'm seeking a tenant for the Grange," he answered; "and I want my children about me, to be sure—besides, that lass owes me her services for her bread; I'm not going to nurture her in luxury and idleness after Linton is gone. Make haste and get ready now. And don't oblige me to compel you."

"I shall," said Catherine. "Linton is all I have to love in the world, and, though you have done what you could to make him hateful to me, and me to him, you *cannot* make us hate each other! and I defy you to hurt him when I am by, and I defy you to frighten me."

"You are a boastful champion!" replied Heathcliff; "but I don't like you well enough to hurt him: you shall get the full benefit of the torment, as long as it lasts. It is not I who will make him hateful to you—it is his own sweet spirit. He's as bitter as gall at your desertion, and its consequences; don't expect thanks for this noble devotion. I heard him draw a pleasant picture to Zillah of what he would do, if he were as strong as I. The inclination is there, and his very weakness will sharpen his wits to find a substitute for strength."

"I know he has a bad nature," said Catherine; "he's your son. But I'm glad I've a better, to forgive it; and I know he loves me and for that reason I love him. Mr. Heathcliff, *you* have *nobody* to love you; and, however miserable you make us, we shall still have the revenge of thinking that your cruelty rises from your greater misery! You *are* miserable, are you not? Lonely, like the devil, and envious like him? *Nobody* loves you—*nobody* will cry for you, when you die! I wouldn't be you!"

Catherine spoke with a kind of dreary triumph: she seemed to have made up her mind to enter into the spirit of her future family, and draw pleasure from the griefs of her enemies.

"You shall be sorry to be yourself presently," said her father-in-law, "if you stand there another minute. Begone, witch, and get your things."

She scornfully withdrew.

In her absence, I began to beg for Zillah's place at the Heights, offering to resign her mine; but he would suffer it on no account. He bid me be silent, and then, for the first time, allowed himself a glance round the room, and a look at the pictures. Having studied Mrs. Linton, he said—

"I shall have that at home. Not because I need it, but—"

He turned abruptly to the fire, and continued, with what, for lack of a better word, I must call a smile—

"I'll tell you what I did yesterday! I got the sexton, who was digging Linton's grave, to remove the earth off her coffin lid, and I opened it. I thought, once, I would have stayed there, when I saw her face again—it is hers yet—he had hard work to stir me; but he said it would change, if the air blew on it, and so I struck one side of the coffin loose, and covered it up—not Linton's side, damn him! I wish he'd been soldered in lead—and I bribed the sexton to pull it away, when I'm laid there, and slide mine out too. I'll have it made so, and then, by the time Linton gets to us, he'll not know which is which!"

"You were very wicked, Mr. Heathcliff!" I exclaimed; "were you not ashamed to disturb the dead?"

"I disturbed nobody, Nelly," he replied; "and I gave some ease to myself. I shall be a great deal more comfortable now; and you'll have a better chance of keeping me underground, when I get there. Disturbed her? No! she has disturbed me, night and day, through eighteen years—incessantly—remorselessly—till yesternight—and yesternight, I was tranquil. I dreamt I was sleeping the last sleep, by that sleeper, with my heart stopped, and my cheek frozen against hers."

"And if she had been dissolved into earth, or worse, what would you have dreamt of then?" I said.

"Of dissolving with her, and being more happy still!" he answered. "Do you suppose I dread any change of that sort? I expected such a transformation on raising the lid, but I'm better pleased that it should not commence till I share it. Besides, unless I had received a distinct impression of her passionless features, that strange feeling would hardly have been removed. It began oddly. You know, I was wild after she died, and eternally, from dawn to dawn, praying her to return to me—her spirit—I have a strong faith in ghosts; I have a conviction that they can, and do exist, among us!

"The day she was buried there came a fall of snow. In the evening I went to the churchyard. It blew bleak as winter—all round was solitary: I didn't fear that her fool of a husband would wander up the den[1] so late—and no one else had business to bring them there.

"Being alone, and conscious two yards of loose earth was the sole barrier between us, I said to myself—

" 'I'll have her in my arms again! If she be cold, I'll think it is this north wind that chills *me*; and if she be motionless, it is sleep.'

1. Up the valley.

"I got a spade from the toolhouse, and began to delve with all my might—it scraped the coffin; I fell to work with my hands; the wood commenced cracking about the screws, I was on the point of attaining my object, when it seemed that I heard a sigh from some one above, close at the edge of the grave, and bending down—'if I can only get this off,' I muttered, 'I wish they may shovel in the earth over us both!' and I wrenched at it more desperately still. There was another sigh, close at my ear. I appeared to feel the warm breath of it displacing the sleet-laden wind. I knew no living thing in flesh and blood was by—but as certainly as you perceive the approach to some substantial body in the dark, though it cannot be discerned, so certainly I felt that Cathy was there, not under me, but on the earth.

"A sudden sense of relief flowed from my heart through every limb. I relinquished my labour of agony, and turned consoled at once, unspeakably consoled. Her presence was with me; it remained while I re-filled the grave, and led me home. You may laugh, if you will, but I was sure I should see her there. I was sure she was with me, and I could not help talking to her.

"Having reached the Heights, I rushed eagerly to the door. It was fastened; and, I remember, that accursed Earnshaw and my wife opposed my entrance. I remember stopping to kick the breath out of him, and then hurrying upstairs, to my room, and hers. I looked round impatiently—I felt her by me—I could *almost* see her, and yet I *could not!* I ought to have sweat blood then, from the anguish of my yearning, from the fervour of my supplications to have but one glimpse! I had not one. She showed herself, as she often was in life, a devil to me! And, since then, sometimes more, and sometimes less, I've been the sport of that intolerable torture! Infernal —keeping my nerves at such a stretch, that, if they had not resembled catgut, they would, long ago, have relaxed to the feebleness of Linton's.

"When I sat in the house with Hareton, it seemed that on going out, I should meet her; when I walked on the moors I should meet her coming in. When I went from home, I hastened to return; she *must* be somewhere at the Heights, I was certain! And when I slept in her chamber—I was beaten out of that—I couldn't lie there; for the moment I closed my eyes, she was either outside the window, or sliding back the panels, or entering the room, or even resting her darling head on the same pillow as she did when a child. And I must open my lids to see. And so I opened and closed them a hundred times a night—to be always disappointed! It racked me! I've often groaned aloud, till that old rascal Joseph no doubt believed that my conscience was playing the fiend inside of me.

"Now since I've seen her, I'm pacified—a little. It was a strange way of killing, not by inches, but by fractions of hair-breadths, to beguile me with the spectre of a hope, through eighteen years!"

Mr. Heathcliff paused and wiped his forehead. His hair clung to it, wet with perspiration; his eyes were fixed on the red embers of the fire; the brows not contracted, but raised next the temples, diminishing the grim aspect of his countenance, but imparting a peculiar look of trouble, and a painful appearance of mental tension towards one absorbing subject. He only half addressed me, and I maintained silence—I didn't like to hear him talk!

After a short period, he resumed his meditation on the picture, took it down, and leant it against the sofa to contemplate it at better advantage; and while so occupied Catherine entered, announcing that she was ready, when her pony should be saddled.

"Send that over to-morrow," said Heathcliff to me, then turning to her he added, "You may do without your pony; it is a fine evening, and you'll need no ponies at Wuthering Heights, for what journeys you take, your own feet will serve you—Come along."

"Good-bye, Ellen!" whispered my dear little mistress. As she kissed me, her lips felt like ice. "Come and see me, Ellen, don't forget."

"Take care you do no such thing, Mrs. Dean!" said her new father. "When I wish to speak to you I'll come here. I want none of your prying at my house!"

He signed her to precede him; and casting back a look that cut my heart, she obeyed.

I watched them from the window walk down the garden. Heathcliff fixed Catherine's arm under his, though she disputed the act, at first, evidently, and with rapid strides, he hurried her into the alley, whose trees concealed them.

Chapter XXX

I have paid a visit to the Heights, but I have not seen her since she left; Joseph held the door in his hand, when I called to ask after her, and wouldn't let me pass. He said Mrs. Linton was "thrang,"[1] and the master was not in. Zillah has told me something of the way they go on, otherwise I should hardly know who was dead, and who living.

She thinks Catherine haughty, and does not like her, I can guess by her talk. My young lady asked some aid of her, when she first came, but Mr. Heathcliff told her to follow her own business, and

1. Busy.

let his daughter-in-law look after herself, and Zillah willingly acquiesced, being a narrow-minded, selfish woman. Catherine evinced a child's annoyance at this neglect; repaid it with contempt, and thus enlisted my informant among her enemies, as securely as if she had done her some great wrong.

I had a long talk with Zillah, about six weeks ago, a little before you came, one day when we foregathered on the moor; and this is what she told me.

"The first thing Mrs. Linton did," she said, "on her arrival at the Heights, was to run upstairs without even wishing good-evening to me and Joseph; she shut herself into Linton's room, and remained till morning. Then, while the master and Earnshaw were at breakfast, she entered the house and asked all in a quiver if the doctor might be sent for? her cousin was very ill."

" 'We know that!' answered Heathcliff, 'but his life is not worth a farthing, and I won't spend a farthing on him.'

" 'But I cannot tell how to do,' she said, 'and if nobody will help me, he'll die!'

" 'Walk out of the room!' cried the master, 'and let me never hear a word more about him! None here care what becomes of him; if you do, act the nurse; if you do not, lock him up and leave him.'

"Then she began to bother me, and I said I'd had enough plague with the tiresome thing; we each had our tasks, and hers was to wait on Linton; Mr. Heathcliff bid me leave that labour to her.

"How they managed together, I can't tell. I fancy he fretted a great deal, and moaned hisseln,[2] night and day; and she had precious little rest, one could guess by her white face, and heavy eyes. She sometimes came into the kitchen all wildered like, and looked as if she would fain beg assistance: but I was not going to disobey the master. I never dare disobey him, Mrs. Dean, and though I thought it wrong that Kenneth should not be sent for, it was no concern of mine, either to advise or complain; and I always refused to meddle.

"Once or twice, after we had gone to bed, I've happened to open my door again, and seen her sitting crying, on the stairs' top; and then I've shut myself in, quick, for fear of being moved to interfere. I did pity her then, I'm sure; still, I didn't wish to lose my place, you know!

"At last, one night she came boldly into my chamber, and frightened me out of my wits, by saying—

" 'Tell Mr. Heathcliff that his son is dying—I'm sure he is, this time. Get up, instantly, and tell him!'

2. Moaned to himself.

"Having uttered this speech, she vanished again. I lay a quarter of an hour listening and trembling. Nothing stirred—the house was quiet.

" 'She's mistaken,' I said to myself. 'He's got over it. I needn't disturb them.' And I began to doze. But my sleep was marred a second time, by a sharp ringing of the bell—the only bell we have, put up on purpose for Linton; and the master called to me, to see what was the matter, and inform them that he wouldn't have that noise repeated.

"I delivered Catherine's message. He cursed to himself, and in a few minutes, came out with a lighted candle, and proceeded to their room. I followed. Mrs. Heathcliff was seated by the bedside, with her hands folded on her knees. Her father-in-law went up, held the light to Linton's face, looked at him, and touched him; afterwards he turned to her.

" 'Now—Catherine,' he said, 'how do you feel?'

"She was dumb.

" 'How do you feel, Catherine?' he repeated.

" 'He's safe, and I'm free,' she answered, 'I should feel well—but,' she continued with a bitterness she couldn't conceal, 'you have left me so long to struggle against death, alone, that I feel and see only death! I feel like death!'

"And she looked like it, too! I gave her a little wine. Hareton and Joseph, who had been wakened by the ringing and the sound of feet, and heard our talk from outside, now entered. Joseph was fain, I believe, of the lad's removal: Hareton seemed a thought bothered, though he was more taken up with staring at Catherine than thinking of Linton. But the master bid him get off to bed again—we didn't want his help. He afterwards made Joseph remove the body to his chamber, and told me to return to mine, and Mrs. Heathcliff remained by herself.

"In the morning, he sent me to tell her she must come down to breakfast. She had undressed, and appeared going to sleep, and said she was ill; at which I hardly wondered. I informed Mr. Heathcliff, and he replied—

" 'Well, let her be till after the funeral; and go up now and then to get her what is needful; and as soon as she seems better, tell me.' "

Cathy stayed upstairs a fortnight, according to Zillah, who visited her twice a day, and would have been rather more friendly, but her attempts at increasing kindness were proudly and promptly repelled.

Heathcliff went up once, to show her Linton's will. He had bequeathed the whole of his, and what had been her, moveable property to his father. The poor creature was threatened, or coaxed, into that act during her week's absence, when his uncle died. The lands, being a minor, he could not meddle with. However, Mr. Heathcliff has claimed and kept them in his wife's right, and his also, I suppose legally. At any rate Catherine, destitute of cash and friends, cannot disturb his possession.

"Nobody," said Zillah, "ever approached her door, except that once, but I; and nobody asked anything about her. The first occasion of her coming down into the house, was on a Sunday afternoon.

"She had cried out, when I carried up her dinner, that she couldn't bear any longer being in the cold; and I told her the master was going to Thrushcross Grange; and Earnshaw and I needn't hinder her from descending; so, as soon as she heard Heathcliff's horse trot off, she made her appearance, donned in black, and her yellow curls combed back behind her ears, as plain as a Quaker;[3] she couldn't comb them out.

"Joseph and I generally go to chapel on Sundays," (the Kirk, you know, has no minister now, explained Mrs. Dean, and they call the Methodists' or Baptists' place, I can't say which it is, at Gimmerton, a chapel[4]). "Joseph had gone," she continued, "but I thought proper to bide at home. Young folks are always the better for an elder's over-looking, and Hareton, with all his bashfulness, isn't a model of nice behaviour. I let him know that his cousin would very likely sit with us, and she had been always used to see the Sabbath respected, so he had as good leave his guns and bits of in-door work alone, while she stayed.

"He coloured up at the news, and cast his eyes over his hands and clothes. The train-oil[5] and gunpowder were shoved out of sight in a minute. I saw he meant to give her his company; and I guessed, by his way, he wanted to be presentable; so, laughing, as I durst not laugh when the master is by, I offered to help him, if he would, and joked at his confusion. He grew sullen, and began to swear.

"Now, Mrs. Dean," she went on, seeing me not pleased by her manner, "you happen think your young lady too fine for Mr. Hareton, and happen you're right; but, I own, I should love well to bring her pride a peg lower. And what will all her learning and her daintiness do for her, now? She's as poor as you or I—poorer, I'll be bound; you're saving, and I'm doing my little all, that road."[6]

Hareton allowed Zillah to give him her aid; and she flattered him into a good humour; so, when Catherine came, half forgetting her

3. Members of the Religious Society of Friends (which Catherine is not) practiced plainness of dress and speech. Jane Eyre, when offered jewels, refuses, telling Rochester she is his "plain, Quakerish governess" (*Jane Eyre*, Ch. XXIV).
4. In distinction from "Kirk," which here could refer to the state church of either Scotland or England, "chapel" was the term used for dissenters' places of worship.
5. Oil from whales or seals, here used for gun-cleaning.
6. That way.

former insults, he tried to make himself agreeable, by the housekeeper's account.

"Missis walked in," she said, "as chill as an icicle, and as high as a princess. I got up and offered her my seat in the arm-chair. No, she turned up her nose at my civility. Earnshaw rose too, and bid her come to the settle, and sit close by the fire; he was sure she was starved.

" 'I've been starved a month and more,' she answered, resting on the word, as scornful as she could.

"And she got a chair for herself, and placed it at a distance from both of us.

"Having sat till she was warm, she began to look round, and discovered a number of books in the dresser; she was instantly upon her feet again, stretching to reach them, but they were too high up.

"Her cousin, after watching her endeavours a while, at last summoned courage to help her; she held her frock, and he filled it with the first that came to hand.

"That was a great advance for the lad. She didn't thank him; still, he felt gratified that she had accepted his assistance, and ventured to stand behind as she examined them, and even to stoop and point out what struck his fancy in certain old pictures which they contained; nor was he daunted by the saucy style in which she jerked the page from his finger; he contented himself with going a bit farther back, and looking at her instead of the book.

"She continued reading, or seeking for something to read. His attention became, by degrees, quite centred in the study of her thick, silky curls; her face he couldn't see, and she couldn't see him. And, perhaps, not quite awake to what he did, but attracted like a child to a candle, at last he proceeded from staring to touching; he put out his hand and stroked one curl, as gently as if it were a bird. He might have stuck a knife into her neck, she started round in such a taking.

" 'Get away, this moment! How dare you touch me? Why are you stopping there?' she cried, in a tone of disgust. 'I can't endure you! I'll go up stairs again, if you come near me.'

"Mr. Hareton recoiled, looking as foolish as he could do; he sat down in the settle, very quiet, and she continued turning over her volumes, another half hour; finally, Earnshaw crossed over, and whispered to me—

" 'Will you ask her to read to us, Zillah? I'm stalled of doing naught; and I do like—I could like to hear her! Dunnot say I wanted it, but ask of yourseln.'

" 'Mr. Hareton wishes you would read to us, ma'am,' I said, immediately. 'He'd take it very kind—he'd be much obliged.'

"She frowned; and, looking up, answered—

" 'Mr. Hareton, and the whole set of you, will be good enough to understand that I reject any pretence at kindness you have the hypocrisy to offer! I despise you, and will have nothing to say to any of you! When I would have given my life for one kind word, even to see one of your faces, you all kept off. But I won't complain to you! I'm driven down here by the cold, not either to amuse you, or enjoy your society.'

" 'What could I ha' done?' began Earnshaw. 'How was I to blame?'

" 'Oh! you are an exception,' answered Mrs. Heathcliff. 'I never missed such a concern as you.'

" 'But I offered more than once, and asked,' he said, kindling up at her pertness, 'I asked Mr. Heathcliff to let me wake for[7] you—'

" 'Be silent! I'll go out of doors, or anywhere, rather than have your disagreeable voice in my ear!' said my lady.

"Hareton muttered, she might go to hell, for him! and unslinging his gun, restrained himself from his Sunday occupations no longer.

"He talked now, freely enough; and she presently saw fit to retreat to her solitude: but the frost had set in, and, in spite of her pride, she was forced to condescend to our company, more and more. However, I took care there should be no further scorning at my good nature. Ever since, I've been as stiff as herself; and she has no lover, or liker among us—and she does not deserve one—for, let them say the least word to her, and she'll curl back without respect of any one! She'll snap at the master himself, and as good as dares him to thrash her; and the more hurt she gets, the more venomous she grows."

At first, on hearing this account from Zillah, I determined to leave my situation, take a cottage, and get Catherine to come and live with me; but Mr. Heathcliff would as soon permit that, as he would set up Hareton in an independent house; and I can see no remedy, at present, unless she could marry again; and that scheme, it does not come within my province to arrange.

Thus ended Mrs. Dean's story. Notwithstanding the doctor's prophecy, I am rapidly recovering strength, and, though it be only the second week in January, I propose getting out on horseback, in a day or two, and riding over to Wuthering Heights, to inform my landlord that I shall spend the next six months in London; and, if he likes, he may look out for another tenant to take the place, after October—I would not pass another winter here, for much.

7. Watch for, guard.

Chapter XXXI

Yesterday was bright, calm, and frosty. I went to the Heights as I proposed; my housekeeper entreated me to bear a little note from her to her young lady, and I did not refuse, for the worthy woman was not conscious of anything odd in her request.

The front door stood open, but the jealous gate was fastened, as at my last visit; I knocked and invoked Earnshaw from among the garden beds; he unchained it, and I entered. The fellow is as handsome a rustic as need be seen. I took particular notice of him this time; but then he does his best, apparently, to make the least of his advantages.

I asked if Mr. Heathcliff were at home? He answered, no; but he would be in at dinner-time. It was eleven o'clock, and I announced my intention of going in, and waiting for him, at which he immediately flung down his tools and accompanied me, in the office of watchdog, not as a substitute for the host.

We entered together; Catherine was there, making herself useful in preparing some vegetables for the approaching meal; she looked more sulky, and less spirited than when I had seen her first. She hardly raised her eyes to notice me, and continued her employment with the same disregard to common forms of politeness, as before; never returning my bow and good morning by the slightest acknowledgment.

"She does not seem so amiable," I thought, "as Mrs. Dean would persuade me to believe. She's a beauty, it is true; but not an angel."

Earnshaw surlily bid her remove her things to the kitchen.

"Remove them yourself," she said, pushing them from her, as soon as she had done, and retiring to a stool by the window, where she began to carve figures of birds and beasts, out of the turnip parings in her lap.

I approached her, pretending to desire a view of the garden; and, as I fancied, adroitly dropped Mrs. Dean's note onto her knee, unnoticed by Hareton—but she asked aloud—

"What is that?" And chucked it off.

"A letter from your old acquaintance, the housekeeper at the Grange," I answered, annoyed at her exposing my kind deed, and fearful lest it should be imagined a missive of my own.

She would gladly have gathered it up at this information, but Hareton beat her; he seized, and put it in his waistcoat, saying Mr. Heathcliff should look at it first.

Thereat, Catherine silently turned her face from us, and, very stealthily, drew out her pocket-handkerchief and applied it to her eyes; and her cousin, after struggling a while to keep down his softer feelings, pulled out the letter and flung it on the floor beside her as ungraciously as he could.

Catherine caught and perused it eagerly; then she put a few questions to me concerning the inmates, rational and irrational, of her former home; and gazing towards the hills, murmured in soliloquy—

"I should like to be riding Minny down there! I should like to be climbing up there—Oh! I'm tired—I'm *stalled*, Hareton!"

And she leant her pretty head back against the sill, with half a yawn and half a sigh, and lapsed into an aspect of abstracted sadness, neither caring nor knowing whether we remarked her.

"Mrs. Heathcliff," I said, after sitting some time mute, "you are not aware that I am an acquaintance of yours? so intimate, that I think it strange you won't come and speak to me. My housekeeper never wearies of talking about and praising you; and she'll be greatly disappointed if I return with no news of, or from you, except that you received her letter, and said nothing!"

She appeared to wonder at this speech and asked—

"Does Ellen like you?"

"Yes, very well," I replied unhesitatingly.

"You must tell her," she continued, "that I would answer her letter, but I have no materials for writing, not even a book from which I might tear a leaf."

"No books!" I exclaimed. "How do you contrive to live here without them, if I may take the liberty to inquire? Though provided with a large library, I'm frequently very dull at the Grange; take my books away, and I should be desperate!"

"I was always reading, when I had them," said Catherine, "and Mr. Heathcliff never reads; so he took it into his head to destroy my books. I have not had a glimpse of one, for weeks. Only once, I searched through Joseph's store of theology, to his great irritation; and once, Hareton, I came upon a secret stock in your room—some Latin and Greek, and some tales and poetry; all old friends. I brought the last here—and you gathered them, as a magpie gathers silver spoons, for the mere love of stealing! They are of no use to you; or else you concealed them in the bad spirit, that as you cannot enjoy them, nobody else shall. Perhaps *your* envy counselled Mr. Heathcliff to rob me of my treasures? But I've most of them written on my brain and printed in my heart, and you cannot deprive me of those!"

Earnshaw blushed crimson, when his cousin made this revelation of his private literary accumulations, and stammered an indignant denial of her accusations.

"Mr. Hareton is desirous of increasing his amount of knowledge,"

I said, coming to his rescue. "He is not *envious* but *emulous* of your attainments. He'll be a clever scholar in a few years!"

"And he wants *me* to sink into a dunce, meantime," answered Catherine. "Yes, I hear him trying to spell and read to himself, and pretty blunders he makes! I wish you would repeat Chevy Chase, as you did yesterday; it was extremely funny! I heard you—and I heard you turning over the dictionary, to seek out the hard words, and then cursing, because you couldn't read their explanations!"

The young man evidently thought it too bad that he should be laughed at for his ignorance, and then laughed at for trying to remove it. I had a similar notion, and, remembering Mrs. Dean's anecdote of his first attempt at enlightening the darkness in which he had been reared, I observed—

"But, Mrs. Heathcliff, we have each had a commencement, and each stumbled and tottered on the threshold, and had our teachers scorned, instead of aiding us, we should stumble and totter yet."

"Oh!" she replied, "I don't wish to limit his acquirements. Still, he has no right to appropriate what is mine, and make it ridiculous to me with his vile mistakes and mis-pronunciations! Those books, both prose and verse, were consecrated to me by other associations, and I hate to have them debased and profaned in his mouth! Besides, of all, he has selected my favourite pieces that I love the most to repeat, as if out of deliberate malice!"

Hareton's chest heaved in silence a minute; he laboured under a severe sense of mortification and wrath, which it was no easy task to suppress.

I rose, and, from a gentlemanly idea of relieving his embarrassment, took up my station in the door-way, surveying the external prospect, as I stood.

He followed my example, and left the room, but presently reappeared, bearing half-a-dozen volumes in his hands, which he threw into Catherine's lap, exclaiming—

"Take them! I never want to hear, or read, or think of them again!"

"I won't have them, now!" she answered. "I shall connect them with you, and hate them."

She opened one that had obviously been often turned over, and read a portion in the drawling tone of a beginner; then laughed, and threw it from her.

"And listen!" she continued provokingly, commencing a verse of an old ballad in the same fashion.

But his self-love would endure no further torment. I heard, and not altogether disapprovingly, a manual check given to her saucy tongue. The little wretch had done her utmost to hurt her cousin's sensitive though uncultivated feelings, and a physical argument was the only mode he had of balancing the account and repaying its effects on the inflicter.

He afterwards gathered the books and hurled them on the fire. I read in his countenance what anguish it was to offer that sacrifice to spleen. I fancied that as they consumed, he recalled the pleasure they had already imparted, and the triumph and ever increasing pleasure he had anticipated from them; and, I fancied, I guessed the incitement to his secret studies, also. He had been content with daily labour and rough animal enjoyments, till Catherine crossed his path. Shame at her scorn, and hope of her approval were his first prompters to higher pursuits; and instead of guarding him from one, and winning him the other, his endeavours to raise himself had produced just the contrary result.

"Yes, that's all the good that such a brute as you can get from them!" cried Catherine, sucking her damaged lip, and watching the conflagration with indignant eyes.

"You'd *better* hold your tongue, now!" he answered fiercely.

And his agitation precluding further speech, he advanced hastily to the entrance, where I made way for him to pass. But, ere he had crossed the door-stones, Mr. Heathcliff, coming up the causeway, encountered him and laying hold of his shoulder, asked—

"What's to do now, my lad?"

"Naught, naught!" he said, and broke away, to enjoy his grief and anger in solitude.

Heathcliff gazed after him, and sighed.

"It will be odd, if I thwart myself!" he muttered, unconscious that I was behind him. "But, when I look for his father in his face, I find *her* every day more! How the devil is he so like? I can hardly bear to see him."

He bent his eyes to the ground, and walked moodily in. There was a restless, anxious expression in his countenance I had never remarked there before, and he looked sparer in person.

His daughter-in-law, on perceiving him through the window, immediately escaped to the kitchen, so that I remained alone.

"I'm glad to see you out of doors again, Mr. Lockwood," he said in reply to my greeting, "from selfish motives partly; I don't think I could readily supply your loss in this desolation. I've wondered, more than once, what brought you here."

"An idle whim, I fear, sir," was my answer, "or else an idle whim is going to spirit me away. I shall set out for London next week, and I must give you warning, that I feel no disposition to retain Thrushcross Grange, beyond the twelvemonths I agreed to rent it. I believe I shall not live there any more."

"Oh, indeed! you're tired of being banished from the world, are you?" he said. "But, if you be coming to plead off paying for a place you won't occupy, your journey is useless. I never relent in exacting my due, from any one."

"I'm coming to plead off nothing about it!" I exclaimed, considerably irritated. "Should you wish it, I'll settle with you now," and I drew my notebook from my pocket.

"No, no," he replied coolly; "you'll leave sufficient behind, to cover your debts, if you fail to return. I'm not in such a hurry—sit down and take your dinner with us; a guest that is safe from repeating his visit, can generally be made welcome. Catherine! bring the things in—where are you?"

Catherine re-appeared, bearing a tray of knives and forks.

"You may get your dinner with Joseph," muttered Heathcliff aside, "and remain in the kitchen till he is gone."

She obeyed his directions very punctually; perhaps she had no temptation to transgress. Living among clowns and misanthropists, she probably cannot appreciate a better class of people, when she meets them.

With Mr. Heathcliff, grim and saturnine, on one hand, and Hareton, absolutely dumb, on the other, I made a somewhat cheerless meal, and bid adieu early. I would have departed by the back way to get a last glimpse of Catherine, and annoy old Joseph; but Hareton received orders to lead up my horse, and my host himself escorted me to the door, so I could not fulfil my wish.

"How dreary life gets over in that house!" I reflected, while riding down the road. "What a realization of something more romantic than a fairy tale it would have been for Mrs. Linton Heathcliff, had she and I struck up an attachment, as her good nurse desired, and migrated together into the stirring atmosphere of the town!"

Chapter XXXII

1802.—This September, I was invited to devastate the moors of a friend,[1] in the North; and, on my journey to his abode, I unexpectedly came within fifteen miles of Gimmerton. The hostler at a roadside public-house was holding a pail of water to refresh my horses, when a cart of very green oats, newly reaped, passed by, and he remarked—

"Yon's frough Gimmerton, nah! They're allas three wick' after other folk wi' ther harvest."

"Gimmerton?" I repeated—my residence in that locality had already grown dim and dreamy. "Ah! I know! How far is it from this?"

"Happen fourteen mile' o'er th' hills, and a rough road," he answered.

1. He had been invited to hunt and speaks with the jocular affection of "sportsmen" who killed great numbers of birds.

A sudden impulse seized me to visit Thrushcross Grange. It was scarcely noon, and I conceived that I might as well pass the night under my own roof, as in an inn. Besides, I could spare a day easily, to arrange matters with my landlord, and thus save myself the trouble of invading the neighbourhood again.

Having rested a while, I directed my servant to inquire the way to the village; and, with great fatigue to our beasts, we managed the distance in some three hours.

I left him there, and proceeded down the valley alone. The grey church looked greyer, and the lonely churchyard lonelier. I distinguished a moor sheep cropping the short turf on the graves. It was sweet, warm weather—too warm for travelling; but the heat did not hinder me from enjoying the delightful scenery above and below; had I seen it nearer August, I'm sure it would have tempted me to waste a month among its solitudes. In winter, nothing more dreary, in summer, nothing more divine, than those glens shut in by hills, and those bluff, bold swells of heath.

I reached the Grange before sunset, and knocked for admittance; but the family had retreated into the back premises, I judged by one thin, blue wreath curling from the kitchen chimney, and they did not hear.

I rode into the court. Under the porch, a girl of nine or ten sat knitting, and an old woman reclined on the horse-steps, smoking a meditative pipe.

"Is Mrs. Dean within?" I demanded of the dame.

"Mistress Dean? Nay!" she answered, "shoo doesn't bide here; shoo's up at th' Heights."

"Are you the housekeeper, then?" I continued.

"Eea, Aw keep th' hause," she replied.

"Well, I'm Mr. Lockwood, the master. Are there any rooms to lodge me in, I wonder? I wish to stay here all night."

"T' maister!" she cried in astonishment. "Whet, whoiver knew yah wur coming? Yah sud ha' send word! They's nowt norther dry, nor mensful abaht t' place—nowt there isn't!"[2]

She threw down her pipe and bustled in, the girl followed, and I entered too; soon perceiving that her report was true, and, moreover, that I had almost upset her wits by my unwelcome apparition.

I bid her be composed—I would go out for a walk; and, meantime, she must try to prepare a corner of a sitting-room for me to sup in, and a bed-room to sleep in. No sweeping and dusting, only good fires and dry sheets were necessary.

2. "What, whoever knew you were coming? You should have sent word! There's nothing dry or properly ready about the place—no there isn't!"

She seemed willing to do her best; though she thrust the hearth-brush into the grates in mistake for the poker, and mal-appropriated several other articles of her craft; but I retired, confiding in her energy for a resting-place against my return.

Wuthering Heights was the goal of my proposed excursion. An after-thought brought me back, when I had quitted the court.

"All well at the Heights?" I enquired of the woman.

"Eea, f'r owt Ee knaw!" she answered, skurrying away with a pan of hot cinders.

I would have asked why Mrs. Dean had deserted the Grange; but it was impossible to delay her at such a crisis, so I turned away and made my exit, rambling leisurely along with the glow of a sinking sun behind, and the mild glory of a rising moon in front—one fading, and the other brightening, as I quitted the park, and climbed the stony by-road branching off to Mr. Heathcliff's dwelling.

Before I arrived in sight of it, all that remained of day was a beamless, amber light along the west; but I could see every pebble on the path, and every blade of grass by that splendid moon.

I had neither to climb the gate, nor to knock—it yielded to my hand.

That is an improvement! I thought. And I noticed another, by the aid of my nostrils; a fragrance of stocks and wall flowers, wafted on the air, from amongst the homely fruit trees.

Both doors and lattices were open; and yet, as is usually the case in a coal district, a fine, red fire illumined the chimney; the comfort which the eye derives from it, renders the extra heat endurable. But the house of Wuthering Heights is so large, that the inmates have plenty of space for withdrawing out of its influence; and, accordingly, what inmates there were had stationed themselves not far from one of the windows. I could both see them and hear them talk before I entered, and looked and listened in consequence, being moved thereto by a mingled sense of curiosity and envy that grew as I lingered.

"Con-*trary!*" said a voice, as sweet as a silver bell—"That for the third time, you dunce! I'm not going to tell you, again—Recollect, or I pull your hair!"

"Contrary, then," answered another, in deep, but softened tones. "And now, kiss me, for minding so well."

"No, read it over first correctly, without a single mistake."

The male speaker began to read. He was a young man, respectably dressed, and seated at a table, having a book before him. His handsome features glowed with pleasure, and his eyes kept impatiently wandering from the page to a small white hand over his shoulder, which recalled him by a smart slap on the cheek, whenever its owner detected such signs of inattention.

Its owner stood behind; her light shining ringlets blending, at intervals, with his brown locks, as she bent to superintend his studies; and her face—it was lucky he could not see her face, or he would never have been so steady. I could, and I bit my lip, in spite, at having thrown away the chance I might have had of doing something besides staring at its smiting beauty.

The task was done, not free from further blunders, but the pupil claimed a reward, and received at least five kisses, which, however, he generously returned. Then, they came to the door, and from their conversation, I judged they were about to issue out and have a walk on the moors. I supposed I should be condemned in Hareton Earnshaw's heart, if not by his mouth, to the lowest pit in the infernal regions if I showed my unfortunate person in his neighbourhood then, and feeling very mean and malignant, I skulked round to seek refuge in the kitchen.

There was unobstructed admittance on that side also; and, at the door, sat my old friend, Nelly Dean, sewing and singing a song, which was often interrupted from within, by harsh words of scorn and intolerance, uttered in far from musical accents.

"Aw'd rayther, by th' haulf, hev 'em swearing i' my lugs frough morn tuh neeght, nur hearken yah, hahsiver!" said the tenant of the kitchen, in answer to an unheard speech of Nelly's. "It's a blazing shaime, ut Aw cannut oppen t' Blessed Book, bud yah set up them glories tuh Sattan, un' all t' flaysome wickednesses ut iver wer born intuh t' warld! Oh! yah're a raight nowt; un' shoo's another; un' that poor lad 'ull be lost, atween ye. Poor lad!" he added, with a groan; "he's witched, Aw'm sartin on't! O, Lord, judge 'em, for they's norther law nur justice amang wer rullers!"[3]

"No! or we should be sitting in flaming fagots, I suppose," retorted the singer. "But wisht, old man, and read your Bible, like a Christian, and never mind me. This is 'Fairy Annie's Wedding'—a bonny tune—it goes to a dance."

Mrs. Dean was about to recommence, when I advanced, and recognising me directly, she jumped to her feet, crying—

"Why, bless you, Mr. Lockwood! How could you think of returning in this way? All's shut up at Thrushcross Grange. You should have given us notice!"

"I've arranged to be accommodated there, for as long as I shall stay," I answered. "I depart again to-morrow. And how are you transplanted here, Mrs. Dean? tell me that."

3. "I'd rather, by half, have him swearing in my ears from morning till night, than listen to you, whatsoever! . . . It's a blazing shame I cannot open the Blessed Book, but that you sing irreligious songs, and all the terrible wickednesses that ever were born into the world! Oh! You're all right now; and she's another; and that poor lad will be lost, between you . . . he's cursed, I am certain of it! Oh, Lord, judge them, for there is neither law nor justice among our rulers!"

"Zillah left, and Mr. Heathcliff wished me to come, soon after you went to London, and stay till you returned. But, step in, pray! Have you walked from Gimmerton this evening?"

"From the Grange," I replied; "and, while they make me lodging room there, I want to finish my business with your master, because I don't think of having another opportunity in a hurry."

"What business, sir?" said Nelly, conducting me into the house. "He's gone out, at present, and won't return soon."

"About the rent," I answered.

"Oh! then it is with Mrs. Heathcliff you must settle," she observed, "or rather with me. She has not learnt to manage her affairs yet, and I act for her; there's nobody else."

I looked surprised.

"Ah! you have not heard of Heathcliff's death, I see!" she continued.

"Heathcliff dead?" I exclaimed, astonished. "How long ago?"

"Three months since—but, sit down, and let me take your hat, and I'll tell you all about it. Stop, you have had nothing to eat, have you?"

"I want nothing. I have ordered supper at home. You sit down too. I never dreamt of his dying! Let me hear how it came to pass. You say you don't expect them back for some time—the young people?"

"No—I have to scold them every evening, for their late rambles, but they don't care for me. At least, have a drink of our old ale—it will do you good—you seem weary."

She hastened to fetch it, before I could refuse, and I heard Joseph asking whether "it warn't a crying scandal that she should have fellies at her time of life? And then, to get them jocks out uh t' Maister's cellar! He fair shaamed to 'bide still and see it."[4]

She did not stay to retaliate, but re-entered, in a minute, bearing a reaming, silver pint, whose contents I lauded with becoming earnestness. And afterwards she furnished me with the sequel of Heathcliff's history. He had a "queer" end, as she expressed it.

I was summoned to Wuthering Heights, within a fortnight of your leaving us, she said; and I obeyed joyfully, for Catherine's sake.

My first interview with her grieved and shocked me! she had altered so much since our separation. Mr. Heathcliff did not explain his reasons for taking a new mind about my coming here; he only told me he wanted me, and he was tired of seeing Catherine; I must make the little parlour my sitting room, and keep her with me. It was enough if he were obliged to see her once or twice a day.

4. *Fellies*: fellows; *jocks*: jugs.

She seemed pleased at this arrangement; and, by degrees, I smuggled over a great number of books and other articles, that had formed her amusement at the Grange; and flattered myself we should get on in tolerable comfort.

The delusion did not last long. Catherine, contented at first, in a brief space grew irritable and restless. For one thing, she was forbidden to move out of the garden, and it fretted her sadly to be confined to its narrow bounds, as Spring drew on; for another, in following the house, I was forced to quit her frequently, and she complained of loneliness; she preferred quarrelling with Joseph in the kitchen, to sitting at peace in her solitude.

I did not mind their skirmishes; but Hareton was often obliged to seek the kitchen also, when the master wanted to have the house to himself; and, though, in the beginning, she either left it at his approach, or quietly joined in my occupations, and shunned remarking, or addressing him—and though he was always as sullen and silent as possible—after a while, she changed her behaviour, and became incapable of letting him alone: talking at him; commenting on his stupidity and idleness; expressing her wonder how he could endure the life he lived—how he could sit a whole evening staring into the fire, and dozing.

"He's just like a dog, is he not, Ellen?" she once observed, "or a cart-horse? He does his work, eats his food, and sleeps, eternally! What a blank, dreary mind he must have! Do you ever dream, Hareton? And, if you do, what is it about? But you can't speak to me!"

Then she looked at him; but he would neither open his mouth, nor look again.

"He's perhaps dreaming now," she continued. "He twitched his shoulder as Juno twitches hers. Ask him, Ellen."

"Mr. Hareton will ask the master to send you upstairs, if you don't behave!" I said. He had not only twitched his shoulder, but clenched his fist, as if tempted to use it.

"I know why Hareton never speaks, when I am in the kitchen," she exclaimed, on another occasion. "He is afraid I shall laugh at him. Ellen, what do you think? He began to teach himself to read once; and, because I laughed, he burned his books, and dropped it—was he not a fool?"

"Were not you naughty?" I said; "answer me that."

"Perhaps I was," she went on, "but I did not expect him to be so silly. Hareton, if I gave you a book, would you take it now? I'll try!"

She placed one she had been perusing on his hand; he flung it off, and muttered, if she did not give over, he would break her neck.

"Well, I shall put it here," she said, "in the table drawer, and I'm going to bed."

Then she whispered me to watch whether he touched it, and departed. But he would not come near it, and so I informed her in the morning, to her great disappointment. I saw she was sorry for his persevering sulkiness and indolence. Her conscience reproved her for frightening him off improving himself; she had done it effectually.

But her ingenuity was at work to remedy the injury; while I ironed, or pursued other stationary employments I could not well do in the parlour, she would bring some pleasant volume, and read it aloud to me. When Hareton was there, she generally paused in an interesting part, and left the book lying about—that she did repeatedly; but he was as obstinate as a mule, and, instead of snatching at her bait, in wet weather he took to smoking with Joseph, and they sat like automatons, one on each side of the fire, the elder happily too deaf to understand her wicked nonsense, as he would have called it, the younger doing his best to seem to disregard it. On fine evenings the latter followed his shooting expeditions, and Catherine yawned and sighed, and teased me to talk to her, and ran off into the court or garden, the moment I began; and, as a last resource, cried and said she was tired of living, her life was useless.

Mr. Heathcliff, who grew more and more disinclined to society, had almost banished Earnshaw out of his apartment. Owing to an accident, at the commencement of March, he became for some days a fixture in the kitchen. His gun burst while out on the hills by himself; a splinter cut his arm, and he lost a good deal of blood before he could reach home. The consequence was, that, perforce, he was condemned to the fire-side and tranquillity, till he made it up again.

It suited Catherine to have him there: at any rate, it made her hate her room upstairs more than ever; and she would compel me to find out business below, that she might accompany me.

On Easter Monday, Joseph went to Gimmerton fair with some cattle; and, in the afternoon, I was busy getting up linen in the kitchen. Earnshaw sat, morose as usual, at the chimney corner, and my little mistress was beguiling an idle hour with drawing pictures on the window panes, varying her amusement by smothered bursts of songs, and whispered ejaculations, and quick glances of annoyance and impatience in the direction of her cousin, who steadfastly smoked, and looked into the grate.

At a notice that I could do with her no longer intercepting my light, she removed to the hearthstone. I bestowed little attention on her proceedings, but, presently, I heard her begin—

"I've found out, Hareton, that I want—that I'm glad—that I should like you to be my cousin, now, if you had not grown so cross to me, and so rough."

Hareton returned no answer.

"Hareton, Hareton, Hareton! do you hear?" she continued.

"Get off wi' ye!" he growled, with uncompromising gruffness.

"Let me take that pipe," she said, cautiously advancing her hand, and abstracting it from his mouth.

Before he could attempt to recover it, it was broken, and behind the fire. He swore at her and seized another.

"Stop," she cried, "you must listen to me, first; and I can't speak while those clouds are floating in my face."

"Will you go to the devil!" he exclaimed, ferociously, "and let me be!"

"No," she persisted, "I won't—I can't tell what to do to make you talk to me, and you are determined not to understand. When I call you stupid, I don't mean anything—I don't mean that I despise you. Come, you shall take notice of me, Hareton—you are my cousin, and you shall own me."

"I shall have naught to do wi' you, and your mucky pride, and your damned, mocking tricks!" he answered. "I'll go to hell, body and soul, before I look sideways after you again! Side out of t' gait,[5] now; this minute!"

Catherine frowned, and retreated to the window-seat, chewing her lip, and endeavouring, by humming an eccentric tune, to conceal a growing tendency to sob.

"You should be friends with your cousin, Mr. Hareton," I interrupted, "since she repents of her sauciness! It would do you a great deal of good—it would make you another man, to have her for a companion."

"A companion!" he cried; "when she hates me, and does not think me fit to wipe her shoon! Nay, if it made me a king, I'd not be scorned for seeking her good will any more."

"It is not I who hate you, it is you who hate me!" wept Cathy, no longer disguising her trouble. "You hate me as much as Mr. Heathcliff does, and more."

"You're a damned liar," began Earnshaw; "why have I made him angry, by taking your part then, a hundred times? and that, when you sneered at, and despised me, and—Go on plaguing me, and I'll step in yonder, and say you worried me out of the kitchen!"

"I didn't know you took my part," she answered, drying her eyes; "and I was miserable and bitter at everybody; but, now I thank you and beg you to forgive me, what can I do besides?"

She returned to the hearth, and frankly extended her hand.

He blackened, and scowled like a thunder cloud, and kept his fists resolutely clenched, and his gaze fixed on the ground.

5. Get out of the way.

Catherine, by instinct, must have divined it was obdurate perversity, and not dislike, that prompted this dogged conduct; for, after remaining an instant undecided, she stooped, and impressed on his cheek a gentle kiss.

The little rogue thought I had not seen her, and, drawing back, she took her former station by the window, quite demurely.

I shook my head reprovingly; and then she blushed, and whispered—

"Well! what should I have done, Ellen? He wouldn't shake hands, and he wouldn't look. I must show him some way that I like him, that I want to be friends."

Whether the kiss convinced Hareton, I cannot tell; he was very careful, for some minutes, that his face should not be seen; and when he did raise it, he was sadly puzzled where to turn his eyes.

Catherine employed herself in wrapping a handsome book neatly in white paper; and having tied it with a bit of riband, and addressed it to "Mr. Hareton Earnshaw," she desired me to be her ambassadress, and convey the present to its destined recipient.

"And tell him, if he'll take it, I'll come and teach him to read it right," she said, "and, if he refuse it, I'll go upstairs, and never tease him again."

I carried it, and repeated the message, anxiously watched by my employer. Hareton would not open his fingers, so I laid it on his knee. He did not strike it off either. I returned to my work. Catherine leaned her head and arms on the table, till she heard the slight rustle of the covering being removed; then she stole away, and quietly seated herself beside her cousin. He trembled, and his face glowed. All his rudeness and all his surly harshness had deserted him—he could not summon courage, at first, to utter a syllable, in reply to her questioning look, and her murmured petition.

"Say you forgive me, Hareton, do! You can make me so happy, by speaking that little word."

He muttered something inaudible.

"And you'll be my friend?" added Catherine, interrogatively.

"Nay! you'll be ashamed of me every day of your life," he answered. "And the more, the more you know me, and I cannot bide it."

"So, you won't be my friend?" she said, smiling as sweet as honey, and creeping close up.

I overheard no further distinguishable talk; but, on looking round again, I perceived two such radiant countenances bent over the page of the accepted book, that I did not doubt the treaty had been ratified on both sides, and the enemies were, thenceforth, sworn allies.

The work they studied was full of costly pictures; and those, and their position, had charm enough to keep them unmoved, till Joseph came home. He, poor man, was perfectly aghast at the spectacle of Catherine seated on the same bench with Hareton Earnshaw, leaning her hand on his shoulder; and confounded at his favourite's endurance of her proximity. It affected him too deeply to allow an observation on the subject that night. His emotion was only revealed by the immense sighs he drew, as he solemnly spread his large Bible on the table, and overlaid it with dirty bank-notes from his pocket-book, the produce of the day's transactions. At length, he summoned Hareton from his seat.

"Tak' these in tuh t' maister, lad," he said, "un' bide theare; Aw's gang up tuh my awn rahm. This hoile's norther mensful, nor seemly fur us—we mun side aht, and search another!"[6]

"Come, Catherine," I said, "we must 'side out,' too—I've done my ironing, are you ready to go?"

"It is not eight o'clock!" she answered, rising unwillingly, "Hareton, I'll leave this book upon the chimney-piece, and I'll bring some more to-morrow."

"Ony books ut yah leave, Aw suall tak' intuh th' hahse," said Joseph, "un' it 'ull be mitch if yah find 'em agean; soa, yah muh plase yourseln!"[7]

Cathy threatened that his library should pay for hers; and, smiling as she passed Hareton, went singing upstairs, lighter of heart, I venture to say, than ever she had been under that roof before, except, perhaps, during her earliest visits to Linton.

The intimacy, thus commenced, grew rapidly, though it encountered temporary interruptions. Earnshaw was not to be civilized with a wish; and my young lady was no philosopher, and no paragon of patience; but both their minds tending to the same point—one loving and desiring to esteem, and the other loving and desiring to be esteemed—they contrived in the end to reach it.

You see, Mr. Lockwood, it was easy enough to win Mrs. Heathcliff's heart; but now, I'm glad you did not try. The crown of all my wishes will be the union of those two; I shall envy no one on their wedding-day—there won't be a happier woman than myself in England!

6. "Take these in to the master . . . and wait there. I am going up to my own room. This room is neither proper, nor seemly for us—we must get out, and find another."
7. "Any books that you leave, I shall take into the house . . . and it will be a marvel if you find them again; so, you may please yourself."

Chapter XXXIII

On the morrow of that Monday, Earnshaw being still unable to follow his ordinary employments, and, therefore, remaining about the house, I speedily found it would be impracticable to retain my charge beside me, as heretofore.

She got downstairs before me, and out into the garden, where she had seen her cousin performing some easy work; and when I went to bid them come to breakfast, I saw she had persuaded him to clear a large space of ground from currant and gooseberry bushes, and they were busy planning together an importation of plants from the Grange.

I was terrified at the devastation which had been accomplished in a brief half hour; the black currant trees were the apple of Joseph's eye, and she had just fixed her choice of a flower bed in the midst of them!

"There! That will be all shewn to the master," I exclaimed, "the minute it is discovered. And what excuse have you to offer for taking such liberties with the garden? We shall have a fine explosion on the head of it: see if we don't! Mr. Hareton, I wonder you should have no more wit, than to go and make that mess at her bidding!"

"I'd forgotten they were Joseph's," answered Earnshaw, rather puzzled, "but I'll tell him I did it."

We always ate our meals with Mr. Heathcliff. I held the mistress's post in making tea and carving; so I was indispensable at table. Catherine usually sat by me; but to-day, she stole nearer to Hareton, and I presently saw she would have no more discretion in her friendship, than she had in her hostility.

"Now, mind you don't talk with and notice your cousin too much," were my whispered instructions as we entered the room. "It will certainly annoy Mr. Heathcliff, and he'll be mad at you both."

"I'm not going to," she answered.

The minute after, she had sidled to him, and was sticking primroses in his plate of porridge.

He dared not speak to her, there; he dared hardly look, and yet she went on teasing, till he was twice on the point of being provoked to laugh; and I frowned, and then she glanced towards the master, whose mind was occupied on other subjects than his company, as his countenance evinced, and she grew serious for an instant, scrutinizing him with deep gravity. Afterwards she turned, and recommenced her nonsense; at last, Hareton uttered a smothered laugh.

Mr. Heathcliff started; his eye rapidly surveyed our faces. Catherine met it with her accustomed look of nervousness, and yet defiance, which he abhorred.

"It is well you are out of my reach"; he exclaimed. "What fiend possesses you to stare back at me, continually, with those infernal eyes? Down with them! and don't remind me of your existence again. I thought I had cured you of laughing!"

"It was me," muttered Hareton.

"What do you say?" demanded the master.

Hareton looked at his plate, and did not repeat the confession.

Mr. Heathcliff looked at him a bit, and then silently resumed his breakfast, and his interrupted musing.

We had nearly finished, and the two young people prudently shifted wider asunder, so I anticipated no further disturbance during that sitting, when Joseph appeared at the door, revealing by his quivering lip and furious eyes, that the outrage committed on his precious shrubs was detected.

He must have seen Cathy and her cousin about the spot before he examined it, for while his jaws worked like those of a cow chewing its cud, and rendered his speech difficult to understand, he began—

"Aw mun hev my wage, and Aw mun goa! Aw *hed* aimed tuh dee, wheare Aw'd sarved fur sixty year; un' Aw thowt Aw'd lug my books up intuh t' garret, un' all my bits uh stuff, un' they sud hev t' kitchen tuh theirseln; fur t' sake uh quietness. It wur hard tuh gie up my awn hearthstun, bud Aw thowt Aw *could* do that! Bud nah, shoo's taan my garden frough me, un' by th' heart, Maister, Aw cannot stand it! Yah muh bend tuh th' yoak, an ye will—*Aw'* noan used to 't and an ow'd man doesn't sooin get used tuh new barthens. Aw'd rayther arn my bite an' my sup, wi' a hammer in th' road!"[1]

"Now, now, idiot!" interrupted Heathcliff, "cut it short! What's your grievance? I'll interfere in no quarrels between you and Nelly. She may thrust you into the coal-hole for anything I care."

"It's noan Nelly!" answered Joseph. "Aw sudn't shift fur Nelly—nasty, ill nowt as shoo is. Thank God! *shoo* cannot stale t' sowl uh nob'dy! Shoo wer niver soa handsome, bud whet a body mud look at her 'baht winking. It's yon flaysome, graceless quean, ut's witched ahr lad, wi' her bold een, un' her forrard ways till—Nay! It fair brusts my heart! He's forgetten all E done for him, un made on him, un' goan un' riven up a whole row ut t' grandest currant trees

1. "I must have my pay, and I must go! I *had* planned to die, where I had served for sixty years; and I thought I'd haul my books up into the garret, and all my things, and they should have the kitchen to themselves; for the sake of quietness. It was hard to give up my place by the hearth, but I thought I *could* do that! But no, she's taken my garden from me, and by the heart, Master, I cannot stand it! You may bend the yoke, and you will—*I'm* not used to it and an old man doesn't soon get used to new surroundings [literally, to other warm places for cattle]. I'd rather earn my meal and my soup, with a hammer [working] in the road."

i' t' garden!"[2] And here he lamented outright, unmanned by a sense of his bitter injuries, and Earnshaw's ingratitude and dangerous condition.

"Is the fool drunk?" asked Mr. Heathcliff. "Hareton, is it you he's finding fault with?"

"I've pulled up two or three bushes," replied the young man, "but I'm going to set 'em again."

"And why have you pulled them up?" said the master.

Catherine wisely put in her tongue.

"We wanted to plant some flowers there," she cried. "I'm the only person to blame, for I wished him to do it."

"And who the devil gave *you* leave to touch a stick about the place?" demanded her father-in-law, much surprised. "And who ordered *you* to obey her?" he added, turning to Hareton.

The latter was speechless; his cousin replied—

"You shouldn't grudge a few yards of earth for me to ornament, when you have taken all my land!"

"Your land, insolent slut? you never had any!" said Heathcliff.

"And my money," she continued, returning his angry glare, and, meantime, biting a piece of crust, the remnant of her breakfast.

"Silence!" he exclaimed. "Get done, and begone!"

"And Hareton's land, and his money," pursued the reckless thing. "Hareton and I are friends now; and I shall tell him all about you!"

The master seemed confounded a moment; he grew pale, and rose up, eyeing her all the while, with an expression of mortal hate.

"If you strike me, Hareton will strike you!" she said; "so you may as well sit down."

"If Hareton does not turn you out of the room, I'll strike him to hell," thundered Heathcliff. "Damnable witch! dare you pretend to rouse him against me? Off with her! Do you hear? Fling her into the kitchen! I'll kill her, Ellen Dean, if you let her come into my sight again!"

Hareton tried under his breath to persuade her to go.

"Drag her away!" he cried savagely. "Are you staying to talk?" And he approached to execute his own command.

"He'll not obey you, wicked man, any more!" said Catherine, "and he'll soon detest you, as much as I do!"

"Wisht! wisht!" muttered the young man reproachfully. "I will not hear you speak so to him. Have done!"

2. "It's not Nelly . . . I shouldn't move for Nelly—nasty, bad nobody that she is. Thank God! *She* cannot steal the soul of anyone! She was never so beautiful, but that someone might look at her without winking. It's yon dreadful, graceless queen, who's bewitched our lad, with her bold eyes, and her forward ways till—No! It nearly bursts my heart! He's forgotten all I did for him, and made of him, and gone and dug up the whole row of currant trees in the garden."

"But you won't let him strike me?" she cried.

"Come then!" he whispered earnestly.

It was too late—Heathcliff had caught hold of her.

"Now *you* go!" he said to Earnshaw. "Accursed witch! this time she has provoked me, when I could not bear it; and I'll make her repent it for ever!"

He had his hand in her hair; Hareton attempted to release the locks, entreating him not to hurt her that once. His black eyes flashed; he seemed ready to tear Catherine in pieces, and I was just worked up to risk coming to the rescue, when of a sudden, his fingers relaxed, he shifted his grasp from her head to her arm, and gazed intently in her face. Then, he drew his hand over his eyes, stood a moment to collect himself apparently, and turning anew to Catherine, said with assumed calmness—

"You must learn to avoid putting me in a passion, or I shall really murder you, some time! Go with Mrs. Dean, and keep with her, and confine your insolence to her ears. As to Hareton Earnshaw, if I see him listen to you, I'll send him seeking his bread where he can get it! Your love will make him an outcast, and a beggar. Nelly, take her, and leave me, all of you! Leave me!"

I led my young lady out; she was too glad of her escape, to resist; the other followed, and Mr. Heathcliff had the room to himself, till dinner.

I had counselled Catherine to get her upstairs; but, as soon as he perceived her vacant seat, he sent me to call her. He spoke to none of us, ate very little, and went out directly afterwards, intimating that he should not return before evening.

The two new friends established themselves in the house, during his absence, where I heard Hareton sternly check his cousin, on her offering a revelation of her father-in-law's conduct to his father.

He said he wouldn't suffer a word to be uttered to him, in his disparagement; if he were the devil, it didn't signify; he would stand by him; and he'd rather she would abuse himself, as she used to, than begin on Mr. Heathcliff.

Catherine was waxing cross at this; but he found means to make her hold her tongue, by asking, how she would like *him* to speak ill of her father? and then she comprehended that Earnshaw took the master's reputation home to himself, and was attached by ties stronger than reason could break—chains, forged by habit, which it would be cruel to attempt to loosen.

She showed a good heart, thenceforth, in avoiding both complaints and expressions of antipathy concerning Heathcliff, and confessed to me her sorrow that she had endeavoured to raise a bad spirit between him and Hareton; indeed, I don't believe she had ever breathed a syllable, in the latter's hearing, against her oppressor, since.

When this slight disagreement was over, they were thick again, and as busy as possible, in their several occupations, of pupil and teacher. I came in to sit with them, after I had done my work, and I felt so soothed and comforted to watch them, that I did not notice how time got on. You know, they both appeared, in a measure, my children: I had long been proud of one, and now, I was sure, the other would be a source of equal satisfaction. His honest, warm, and intelligent nature shook off rapidly the clouds of ignorance and degradation in which it had been bred; and Catherine's sincere commendations acted as a spur to his industry. His brightening mind brightened his features, and added spirit and nobility to their aspect. I could hardly fancy it the same individual I had beheld on the day I discovered my little lady at Wuthering Heights, after her expedition to the Crags.

While I admired, and they laboured, dusk drew on, and with it returned the master. He came upon us quite unexpectedly, entering by the front way, and had a full view of the whole three, ere we could raise our heads to glance at him.

Well, I reflected, there was never a pleasanter, or more harmless sight; and it will be a burning shame to scold them. The red firelight glowed on their two bonny heads, and revealed their faces, animated with the eager interest of children; for, though he was twenty-three, and she eighteen, each had so much of novelty to feel and learn, that neither experienced nor evinced the sentiments of sober disenchanted maturity.

They lifted their eyes together, to encounter Mr. Heathcliff. Perhaps you have never remarked that their eyes are precisely similar, and they are those of Catherine Earnshaw. The present Catherine has no other likeness to her, except a breadth of forehead, and a certain arch of the nostril that makes her appear rather haughty, whether she will or not. With Hareton the resemblance is carried farther; it is singular, at all times—then, it was particularly striking, because his senses were alert, and his mental faculties wakened to unwonted activity.

I suppose this resemblance disarmed Mr. Heathcliff: he walked to the hearth in evident agitation, but it quickly subsided, as he looked at the young man; or, I should say, altered its character, for it was there yet.

He took the book from his hand, and glanced at the open page, then returned it without any observation, merely signing Catherine away. Her companion lingered very little behind her, and I was about to depart also, but he bid me sit still.

"It is a poor conclusion, is it not," he observed, having brooded a while on the scene he had just witnessed. "An absurd termination to my violent exertions? I get levers and mattocks to demolish the two houses, and train myself to be capable of working like Hercules, and when everything is ready, and in my power, I find the will to lift a slate off either roof has vanished! My old enemies have not beaten me; now would be the precise time to revenge myself on their representatives: I could do it; and none could hinder me. But where is the use? I don't care for striking, I can't take the trouble to raise my hand! That sounds as if I had been labouring the whole time, only to exhibit a fine trait of magnanimity. It is far from being the case—I have lost the faculty of enjoying their destruction, and I am too idle to destroy for nothing.

"Nelly, there is a strange change approaching—I'm in its shadow at present. I take so little interest in my daily life, that I hardly remember to eat, and drink. Those two, who have left the room, are the only objects which retain a distinct material appearance to me; and that appearance causes me pain, amounting to agony. About *her* I won't speak; and I don't desire to think; but I earnestly wish she were invisible—her presence invokes only maddening sensations. *He* moves me differently; and yet if I could do it without seeming insane, I'd never see him again! You'll perhaps think me rather inclined to become so," he added, making an effort to smile, "if I try to describe the thousand forms of past associations and ideas he awakens, or embodies—But you'll not talk of what I tell you, and my mind is so eternally secluded in itself, it is tempting, at last, to turn it out to another.

"Five minutes ago, Hareton seemed a personification of my youth, not a human being. I felt to him in such a variety of ways, that it would have been impossible to have accosted him rationally.

"In the first place, his startling likeness to Catherine connected him fearfully with her. That, however, which you may suppose the most potent to arrest my imagination, is actually the least, for what is not connected with her to me? and what does not recall her? I cannot look down to this floor, but her features are shaped on the flags! In every cloud, in every tree—filling the air at night, and caught by glimpses in every object by day, I am surrounded with her image! The most ordinary faces of men and women—my own features—mock me with a resemblance. The entire world is a dreadful collection of memoranda that she did exist, and that I have lost her!

"Well, Hareton's aspect was the ghost of my immortal love, of my wild endeavours to hold my right, my degradation, my pride, my happiness, and my anguish—

"But it is frenzy to repeat these thoughts to you; only it will let you know why, with a reluctance to be always alone, his society is no benefit, rather an aggravation of the constant torment I suffer; and it partly contributes to render me regardless how he and his cousin go on together. I can give them no attention, any more."

"But what do you mean by a *change*, Mr. Heathcliff?" I said, alarmed at his manner, though he was neither in danger of losing his senses, nor dying; according to my judgment he was quite strong and healthy; and, as to his reason, from childhood he had a delight in dwelling on dark things, and entertaining odd fancies. He might have had a monomania on the subject of his departed idol; but on every other point his wits were as sound as mine.

"I shall not know that, till it comes," he said, "I'm only half conscious of it now."

"You have no feeling of illness, have you?" I asked.

"No, Nelly, I have not," he answered.

"Then, you are not afraid of death?" I pursued.

"Afraid? No!" he replied. "I have neither a fear, nor a presentiment, nor a hope of death. Why should I? With my hard constitution, and temperate mode of living, and unperilous occupations, I ought to, and probably *shall* remain above ground, till there is scarcely a black hair on my head. And yet I cannot continue in this condition! I have to remind myself to breathe—almost to remind my heart to beat! And it is like bending back a stiff spring; it is by compulsion that I do the slightest act not prompted by one thought, and by compulsion, that I notice anything alive, or dead, which is not associated with one universal idea. I have a single wish, and my whole being and faculties are yearning to attain it. They have yearned towards it so long, and so unwaveringly, that I'm convinced it *will* be reached—and *soon*—because it has devoured my existence. I am swallowed in the anticipation of its fulfilment.

"My confessions have not relieved me, but they may account for some otherwise unaccountable phases of humour, which I show. O, God! It is a long fight, I wish it were over!"

He began to pace the room, muttering terrible things to himself, till I was inclined to believe, as he said Joseph did, that conscience had turned his heart to an earthly hell. I wondered greatly how it would end.

Though he seldom before had revealed this state of mind, even by looks, it was his habitual mood, I had no doubt: he asserted it himself; but not a soul, from his general bearing, would have conjectured the fact. You did not, when you saw him, Mr. Lockwood; and at the period of which I speak, he was just the same as then, only fonder of continued solitude, and perhaps still more laconic in company.

Chapter XXXIV

For some days after that evening, Mr. Heathcliff shunned meeting us at meals; yet he would not consent, formally, to exclude Hareton and Cathy. He had an aversion to yielding so completely to his feelings, choosing rather to absent himself; and eating once in twenty-four hours seemed sufficient sustenance for him.

One night, after the family were in bed, I heard him go downstairs, and out at the front door: I did not hear him re-enter and, in the morning, I found he was still away.

We were in April then: the weather was sweet and warm, the grass as green as showers and sun could make it, and the two dwarf apple trees, near the southern wall, in full bloom.

After breakfast, Catherine insisted on my bringing a chair, and sitting with my work under the fir trees at the end of the house; and she beguiled Hareton, who had perfectly recovered from his accident, to dig and arrange her little garden, which was shifted to that corner by the influence of Joseph's complaints.

I was comfortably revelling in the spring fragrance around, and the beautiful soft blue overhead, when my young lady, who had run down near the gate to procure some primrose roots for a border, returned only half laden, and informed us that Mr. Heathcliff was coming in.

"And he spoke to me," she added with a perplexed countenance.

"What did he say?" asked Hareton.

"He told me to begone as fast as I could," she answered. "But he looked so different from his usual look that I stopped a moment to stare at him."

"How?" he enquired.

"Why, almost bright and cheerful—No, almost nothing—*very much* excited, and wild and glad!" she replied.

"Night-walking amuses him, then," I remarked, affecting a careless manner. In reality, as surprised as she was, and, anxious to ascertain the truth of her statement, for to see the master looking glad would not be an every day spectacle, I framed an excuse to go in.

Heathcliff stood at the open door; he was pale, and he trembled; yet, certainly, he had a strange joyful glitter in his eyes that altered the aspect of his whole face.

"Will you have some breakfast?" I said, "You must be hungry rambling about all night!"

I wanted to discover where he had been; but I did not like to ask directly.

"No, I'm not hungry," he answered, averting his head, and speaking rather contemptuously, as if he guessed I was trying to divine the occasion of his good humour.

I felt perplexed; I didn't know whether it were not a proper opportunity to offer a bit of admonition.

"I don't think it right to wander out of doors," I observed, "instead of being in bed: it is not wise, at any rate, this moist season. I dare say you'll catch a bad cold, or a fever—you have something the matter with you now!"

"Nothing but what I can bear," he replied, "and with the greatest pleasure, provided you'll leave me alone. Get in, and don't annoy me."

I obeyed; and, in passing, I noticed he breathed as fast as a cat.

"Yes!" I reflected to myself, "we shall have a fit of illness. I cannot conceive what he has been doing!"

That noon, he sat down to dinner with us, and received a heaped-up plate from my hands, as if he intended to make amends for previous fasting.

"I've neither cold, nor fever, Nelly," he remarked, in allusion to my morning's speech. "And I'm ready to do justice to the food you give me."

He took his knife and fork, and was going to commence eating, when the inclination appeared to become suddenly extinct. He laid them on the table, looked eagerly towards the window, then rose and went out.

We saw him walking, to and fro, in the garden, while we concluded our meal; and Earnshaw said he'd go and ask why he would not dine; he thought we had grieved him some way.

"Well, is he coming?" cried Catherine, when her cousin returned.

"Nay," he answered, "but he's not angry; he seemed rare and pleased[1] indeed; only, I made him impatient by speaking to him twice; and then he bid me be off to you; he wondered how I could want the company of any body else."

I set his plate, to keep warm, on the fender; and after an hour or two, he re-entered, when the room was clear, in no degree calmer: the same unnatural—it was unnatural—appearance of joy under his black brows; the same bloodless hue, and his teeth visible, now and then, in a kind of smile; his frame shivering, not as one shivers with chill or weakness, but as a tight-stretched cord vibrates—a strong thrilling, rather than trembling.

I will ask what is the matter, I thought, or who should? And I exclaimed—

"Have you heard any good news, Mr. Heathcliff? You look uncommonly animated."

"Where should good news come from, to me?" he said. "I'm animated with hunger; and, seemingly, I must not eat."

1. Very pleased.

"Your dinner is here," I returned; "why won't you get it?"

"I don't want it now," he muttered, hastily. "I'll wait till supper. And, Nelly, once for all, let me beg you to warn Hareton and the other away from me. I wish to be troubled by nobody—I wish to have this place to myself."

"Is there some new reason for this banishment?" I inquired. "Tell me why you are so queer, Mr. Heathcliff? Where were you last night? I'm not putting the question through idle curiosity, but—"

"You are putting the question through very idle curiosity," he interrupted with a laugh. "Yet, I'll answer it. Last night, I was on the threshold of hell. To-day, I am within sight of my heaven. I have my eyes on it—hardly three feet to sever me! And now you'd better go. You'll neither see nor hear anything to frighten you, if you refrain from prying."

Having swept the hearth and wiped the table, I departed more perplexed than ever.

He did not quit the house again that afternoon, and no one intruded on his solitude, till, at eight o'clock, I deemed it proper, though unsummoned, to carry a candle and his supper to him.

He was leaning against the ledge of an open lattice, but not looking out; his face was turned to the interior gloom. The fire had smouldered to ashes; the room was filled with the damp, mild air of the cloudy evening, and so still, that not only the murmur of the beck down Gimmerton was distinguishable, but its ripples and its gurgling over the pebbles, or through the large stones which it could not cover.

I uttered an ejaculation of discontent at seeing the dismal grate, and commenced shutting the casements, one after another, till I came to his.

"Must I close this?" I asked, in order to rouse him, for he would not stir.

The light flashed on his features, as I spoke. Oh, Mr. Lockwood, I cannot express what a terrible start I got, by the momentary view! Those deep black eyes! That smile, and ghastly paleness! It appeared to me, not Mr. Heathcliff, but a goblin; and, in my terror, I let the candle bend towards the wall, and it left me in darkness.

"Yes, close it," he replied, in his familiar voice. "There, that is pure awkwardness! Why did you hold the candle horizontally? Be quick, and bring another."

I hurried out in a foolish state of dread, and said to Joseph—

"The master wishes you to take him a light, and rekindle the fire." For I dared not go in myself again just then.

Joseph rattled some fire into the shovel, and went; but he brought it back, immediately, with the supper tray in his other hand, explaining that Mr. Heathcliff was going to bed, and he wanted nothing to eat till morning.

We heard him mount the stairs directly; he did not proceed to his ordinary chamber, but turned into that with the panelled bed. Its window, as I mentioned before, is wide enough for anybody to get through, and it struck me that he plotted another midnight excursion, which he had rather we had no suspicion of.

"Is he a ghoul, or a vampire?" I mused. I had read of such hideous, incarnate demons. And then I set myself to reflect how I had tended him in infancy; and watched him grow to youth; and followed him almost through his whole course; and what absurd nonsense it was to yield to that sense of horror.

"But where did he come from, the little dark thing, harboured by a good man to his bane?" muttered superstition, as I dozed into unconsciousness. And I began, half dreaming, to weary myself with imaging some fit parentage for him; and repeating my waking meditations, I tracked his existence over again, with grim variations; at last, picturing his death and funeral; of which, all I can remember is, being exceedingly vexed at having the task of dictating an inscription for his monument, and consulting the sexton about it; and, as he had no surname, and we could not tell his age, we were obliged to content ourselves with the single word, "Heathcliff." That came true; we were. If you enter the kirkyard, you'll read on his headstone only that, and the date of his death.

Dawn restored me to common sense. I rose, and went into the garden, as soon as I could see, to ascertain if there were any footmarks under his window. There were none.

"He has stayed at home," I thought, "and he'll be all right, today!"

I prepared breakfast for the household, as was my usual custom, but told Hareton and Catherine to get theirs ere the master came down, for he lay late. They preferred taking it out of doors, under the trees, and I set a little table to accommodate them.

On my re-entrance, I found Mr. Heathcliff below. He and Joseph were conversing about some farming business; he gave clear, minute directions concerning the matter discussed, but he spoke rapidly, and turned his head continually aside, and had the same excited expression, even more exaggerated.

When Joseph quitted the room, he took his seat in the place he generally chose, and I put a basin of coffee before him. He drew it nearer, and then rested in his arms on the table, and looked at the opposite wall, as I supposed, surveying one particular portion, up and down, with glittering, restless eyes, and with such eager interest, that he stopped breathing, during half a minute together.

"Come now," I exclaimed, pushing some bread against his hand. "Eat and drink that, while it is hot. It has been waiting near an hour."

He didn't notice me, and yet he smiled. I'd rather have seen him gnash his teeth than smile so.

"Mr. Heathcliff! master!" I cried. "Don't, for God's sake, stare as if you saw an unearthly vision."

"Don't, for God's sake, shout so loud," he replied. "Turn round, and tell me, are we by ourselves?"

"Of course," was my answer, "of course, we are!"

Still, I involuntarily obeyed him, as if I were not quite sure.

With a sweep of his hand, he cleared a vacant space in front among the breakfast things, and leant forward to gaze more at his ease.

Now, I perceived he was not looking at the wall, for when I regarded him alone, it seemed exactly that he gazed at something within two yards distance. And, whatever it was, it communicated, apparently, both pleasure and pain, in exquisite extremes; at least, the anguished, yet raptured expression of his countenance suggested that idea.

The fancied object was not fixed, either; his eyes pursued it with unwearied vigilance, and, even in speaking to me, were never weaned away.

I vainly reminded him of his protracted abstinence from food; if he stirred to touch anything in compliance with my entreaties, if he stretched his hand out to get a piece of bread, his fingers clenched, before they reached it, and remained on the table, forgetful of their aim.

I sat, a model of patience, trying to attract his absorbed attention from its engrossing speculation, till he grew irritable, and got up, asking why I would not allow him to have his own time in taking his meals? and saying that, on the next occasion, I needn't wait; I might set the things down, and go.

Having uttered these words, he left the house, slowly sauntered down the garden path, and disappeared through the gate.

The hours crept anxiously by: another evening came. I did not retire to rest till late, and when I did, I could not sleep. He returned after midnight, and, instead of going to bed, shut himself into the room beneath. I listened, and tossed about; and, finally, dressed and descended. It was too irksome to lie up there, harassing my brain with a hundred idle misgivings.

I distinguished Mr. Heathcliff's step, restlessly measuring the floor; and he frequently broke the silence by a deep inspiration, resembling a groan. He muttered detached words also; the only one

I could catch was the name of Catherine, coupled with some wild term of endearment or suffering, and spoken as one would speak to a person present—low and earnest, and wrung from the depth of his soul.

I had not courage to walk straight into the apartment; but I desired to divert him from his reverie, and, therefore fell foul of the kitchen fire, stirred it, and began to scrape the cinders. It drew him forth sooner than I expected. He opened the door immediately, and said—

"Nelly, come here—is it morning? Come in with your light."

"It is striking four," I answered; "you want a candle to take upstairs—you might have lit one at this fire."

"No, I don't wish to go upstairs," he said. "Come in, and kindle *me* a fire, and do anything there is to do about the room."

"I must blow the coals red first, before I can carry any," I replied, getting a chair and the bellows.

He roamed to and fro, meantime, in a state approaching distraction; his heavy sighs succeeding each other so thick as to leave no space for common breathing between.

"When day breaks, I'll send for Green," he said; "I wish to make some legal inquiries of him while I can bestow a thought on those matters, and while I can act calmly. I have not written my will yet, and how to leave my property, I cannot determine! I wish I could annihilate it from the face of the earth."

"I would not talk so, Mr. Heathcliff," I interposed. "Let your will be, a while—you'll be spared to repent of your many injustices, yet! I never expected that your nerves would be disordered: they are, at present, marvellously so, however; and, almost entirely, through your own fault. The way you've passed these three last days might knock up a Titan. Do take some food, and some repose. You need only look at yourself in a glass to see how you require both. Your cheeks are hollow, and your eyes blood-shot, like a person starving with hunger, and going blind with loss of sleep."

"It is not my fault, that I cannot eat or rest," he replied. "I assure you it is through no settled designs. I'll do both, as soon as I possibly can. But you might as well bid a man struggling in the water, rest within arms-length of the shore! I must reach it first, and then I'll rest. Well, never mind Mr. Green; as to repenting of my injustices, I've done no injustice, and I repent of nothing—I'm too happy, and yet I'm not happy enough. My soul's bliss kills my body, but does not satisfy itself."

"Happy, master?" I cried. "Strange happiness! If you would hear me without being angry, I might offer some advice that would make you happier.

"What is that?" he asked. "Give it."

"You are aware, Mr. Heathcliff," I said, "that from the time you were thirteen years old, you have lived a selfish, unchristian life; and probably hardly had a Bible in your hands during all that period. You must have forgotten the contents of the book, and you may not have space to search it now. Could it be hurtful to send for some one—some minister of any denomination, it does not matter which, to explain it, and show you how very far you have erred from its precepts, and how unfit you will be for its heaven, unless a change takes place before you die?"

"I'm rather obliged than angry, Nelly," he said, "for you remind me of the manner that I desire to be buried in. It is to be carried to the churchyard, in the evening. You and Hareton may, if you please accompany me—and mind, particularly, to notice that the sexton obeys my directions concerning the two coffins! No minister need come; nor need anything be said over me. I tell you, I have nearly attained *my* heaven; and that of others is altogether unvalued and uncoveted by me!"

"And supposing you persevered in your obstinate fast, and died by that means, and they refused to bury you in the precincts of the Kirk?" I said, shocked at his godless indifference. "How would you like it?"

"They won't do that," he replied; "if they did, you must have me removed secretly; and if you neglect it, you shall prove, practically, that the dead are not annihilated!"

As soon as he heard the other members of the family stirring he retired to his den, and I breathed freer. But in the afternoon, while Joseph and Hareton were at their work, he came into the kitchen again, and with a wild look, bid me come, and sit in the house—he wanted somebody with him.

I declined, telling him plainly that his strange talk and manner frightened me, and I had neither the nerve nor the will to be his companion, alone.

"I believe you think me a fiend!" he said, with his dismal laugh, "something too horrible to live under a decent roof!"

Then turning to Catherine, who was there, and who drew behind me at his approach, he added, half sneeringly—

"Will *you* come, chuck? I'll not hurt you. No! to you, I've made myself worse than the devil. Well, there is *one* who won't shrink from my company! By God! she's relentless. Oh, damn it! It's unutterably too much for flesh and blood to bear, even mine."

He solicited the society of no one more. At dusk, he went into his chamber. Through the whole night, and far into the morning, we heard him groaning, and murmuring to himself. Hareton was anxious to enter, but I bid him fetch Mr. Kenneth, and he should go in and see him.

When he came, and I requested admittance and tried to open the door, I found it locked; and Heathcliff bid us be damned. He was better, and would be left alone; so the doctor went away.

The following evening was very wet; indeed it poured down, till day-dawn; and, as I took my morning walk round the house, I observed the master's window swinging open, and the rain driving straight in.

He cannot be in bed, I thought; those showers would drench him through! He must either be up, or out. But I'll make no more ado, I'll go boldly and look!

Having succeeded in obtaining entrance with another key, I ran to unclose the panels, for the chamber was vacant; quickly pushing them aside, I peeped in. Mr. Heathcliff was there—laid on his back. His eyes met mine so keen and fierce, I started; and then he seemed to smile.

I could not think him dead, but his face and throat were washed with rain; the bedclothes dripped, and he was perfectly still. The lattice, flapping to and fro, had grazed one hand that rested on the sill; no blood trickled from the broken skin, and when I put my fingers to it, I could doubt no more—he was dead and stark!

I hasped the window; I combed his black long hair from his forehead; I tried to close his eyes—to extinguish, if possible, that frightful, life-like gaze of exultation, before any one else beheld it. They would not shut; they seemed to sneer at my attempts, and his parted lips and sharp, white teeth sneered too! Taken with another fit of cowardice, I cried out for Joseph. Joseph shuffled up and made a noise, but resolutely refused to meddle with him.

"Th' divil's harried off his soul," he cried, "and he muh hev his carcass intuh t' bargin, for ow't Aw care! Ech! what a wicked un he looks girnning[2] at death!" and the old sinner grinned in mockery.

I thought he intended to cut a caper round the bed; but suddenly composing himself, he fell on his knees, and raised his hands, and returned thanks that the lawful master and the ancient stock were restored to their rights.

I felt stunned by the awful event; and my memory unavoidably recurred to former times with a sort of oppressive sadness. But poor Hareton, the most wronged, was the only one that really suffered much. He sat by the corpse all night, weeping in bitter earnest. He pressed its hand, and kissed the sarcastic, savage face that every one else shrank from contemplating; and bemoaned him with that strong grief which springs naturally from a generous heart, though it be tough as tempered steel.

2. *Harried*: hurried; *girnning*: grinning scornfully.

Kenneth was perplexed to pronounce of what disorder the master died. I concealed the fact of his having swallowed nothing for four days, fearing it might lead to trouble, and then, I am persuaded he did not abstain on purpose; it was the consequence of his strange illness, not the cause.

We buried him, to the scandal of the whole neighbourhood, as he had wished. Earnshaw, and I, the sexton and six men to carry the coffin, comprehended the whole attendance.

The six men departed when they had let it down into the grave: we stayed to see it covered. Hareton, with a streaming face, dug green sods, and laid them over the brown mould himself. At present it is as smooth and verdant as its companion mounds—and I hope its tenant sleeps as soundly. But the country folks, if you asked them, would swear on their Bible that he *walks*. There are those who speak to having met him near the church, and on the moor, and even within this house. Idle tales, you'll say, and so say I. Yet that old man by the kitchen fire affirms he has seen two on 'em looking out of his chamber window, on every rainy night, since his death—and an odd thing happened to me about a month ago.

I was going to the Grange one evening—a dark evening threatening thunder—and, just at the turn of the Heights, I encountered a little boy with a sheep and two lambs before him; he was crying terribly, and I supposed the lambs were skittish, and would not be guided.

"What is the matter, my little man?" I asked.

"They's Heathcliff and a woman, yonder, under t' Nab," he blubbered, "un' Aw darnut pass 'em."

I saw nothing; but neither the sheep nor he would go on, so I bid him take the road lower down.

He probably raised the phantoms from thinking, as he traversed the moors alone, on the nonsense he had heard his parents and companions repeat—yet still, I don't like being out in the dark, now; and I don't like being left by myself in this grim house—I cannot help it—I shall be glad when they leave it, and shift to the Grange!

"They are going to the Grange, then?" I said.

"Yes," answered Mrs. Dean, "as soon as they are married; and they will be on New Year's day."

"And who will live here then?"

"Why, Joseph will take care of the house, and, perhaps, a lad to keep him company. They will live in the kitchen, and the rest will be shut up."

"For the use of such ghosts as choose to inhabit it," I observed.

"No, Mr. Lockwood," said Nelly, shaking her head. "I believe the dead are at peace, but it is not right to speak of them with levity."

At that moment the garden gate swung to; the ramblers were returning.

"*They* are afraid of nothing," I grumbled, watching their approach through the window. "Together they would brave Satan and all his legions."

As they stepped onto the door-stones, and halted to take a last look at the moon, or, more correctly, at each other, by her light, I felt irresistibly impelled to escape them again; and, pressing a remembrance into the hand of Mrs. Dean, and disregarding her expostulations at my rudeness, I vanished through the kitchen, as they opened the house-door, and so should have confirmed Joseph in his opinion of his fellow-servant's gay indiscretions, had he not, fortunately, recognised me for a respectable character by the sweet ring of a sovereign at his feet.

My walk home was lengthened by a diversion in the direction of the Kirk. When beneath its walls, I perceived decay had made progress, even in seven months—many a window showed black gaps deprived of glass; and slates jutted off, here and there, beyond the right line of the roof, to be gradually worked off in coming autumn storms.

I sought, and soon discovered, the three head-stones on the slope next the moor—the middle one, grey, and half buried in heath—Edgar Linton's only harmonized by the turf, and moss creeping up its foot—Heathcliff's still bare.

I lingered round them, under that benign sky; watched the moths fluttering among the heath and hare-bells; listened to the soft wind breathing through the grass; and wondered how any one could ever imagine unquiet slumbers for the sleepers in that quiet earth.

THE END

BACKGROUNDS AND CONTEXTS

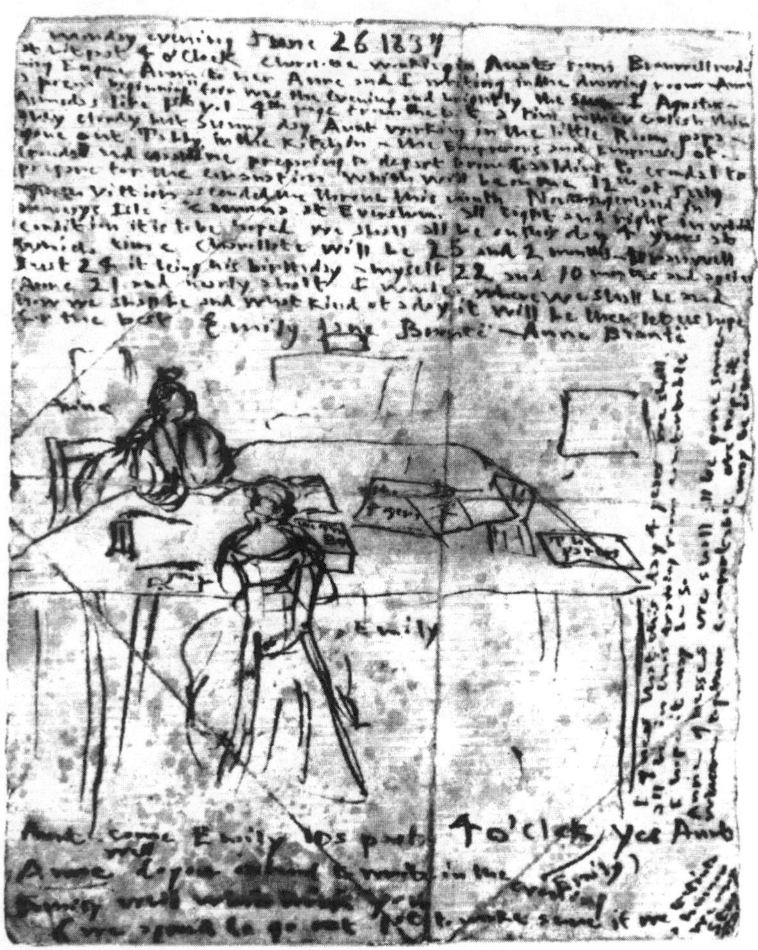

A page from Emily's diary, with her sketch of herself and Anne writing. Photocopy courtesy of the Brontë Society.

The 1847 *Wuthering Heights*

Emily Brontë's Diary†

Apart from her novel and poems, few writings by Emily Brontë survive, but there are brief diary entries from 1834, 1837, 1841, and 1845. The last three are all birthday reflections, one written on her brother Branwell's birthday, the other two on her twenty-third and twenty-seventh birthdays. The diaries give glimpses of life at the Haworth parsonage and describe Emily's ongoing involvement with the imaginary world of Gondal. The diary pages are on display at the Brontë Parsonage.

November 24, 1834

November the 24 1834 Monday
Emily Jane Brontë
Anne Brontë

I fed Rainbow. Diamond Snowflake Jasper pheasant (alias) this morning Branwell went down to Mr. Driver's and brought news that Sir Robert Peel was going to be invited to stand for Leeds Anne and I have been peeling apples for Charlotte to make us an apple pudding and for Aunt nuts and apples Charlotte said she made puddings perfectly and she was of a quick but limited intellect. Tabby said just now Come Anne pilloputate (i.e. pill a potato) Aunt has come into the kitchen just now and said where are your feet Anne Anne answered On the floor Aunt papa opened the parlour door and gave Branwell a letter saying here Branwell read this and show it to your Aunt and Charlotte—the Gondals are discovering the interior of Gaaldine Sally Mosley is washing in the back kitchen

It is past Twelve o'clock Anne and I have not tidied ourselves, done our bedwork or done our lessons and we want to go out to play we are goin to have for Dinner Boiled Beef, Turnips, potatoes and applepudding. The Kitchin is in a very untidy state Anne and I have not done our music exercise which consists of b major Taby said on my putting a pen in her face Ya pitter pottering there instead of pilling a potate I answered O Dear, O Dear, O dear I will directly

† Diary entries are reprinted with the permission of the Brontë Society.

with that I get up, take a knife and begin pilling (finished pilling the potatoes) papa going to walk Mr. Sunderland expected

Anne and I say I wonder what we shall be like and what we shall be and where we shall be if all goes well in the year 1874—in which year I shall be in my 54th year Anne will be going in her 55th year Branwell will be going in his 58th year And Charlotte in her 57th year hoping we shall all be well at that time we close our paper[1]

* * *

June 26, 1837

Monday evening June 26th 1837

A bit past 4 o'clock Charlotte working in Aunt's room, Branwell reading *Eugene Aram* to her—Anne and I writing in the drawing-room—Anne a poem beginning "Fair was the evening and brightly the sun"—I Augusta Almeda's life 1st V. 1–4th page from the last—fine rather coolish thin grey cloudy but sunny day Aunt working in the little room the old nursery Papa gone out Tabby in the kitchen—the Emperors and Empresses of Gondal and Gaaldine preparing to depart from Gaaldine to Gondal to prepare for the coronation which will be on the 12th July Queen Vittoria ascended the throne this month. Northangerland in Monkey's Isle—Zamora at Eversham. All tight and right in which condition it is hoped we shall all be this day 4 years at which time Charlotte will be 25 and 2 months—Branwell just 24 it being his birthday—myself 22 and 10 months and a piece [*sic*] Anne 21 and nearly a half I wonder where we shall be and how we shall be and what kind of a day it will be then—let us hope for the best

Emily Jane Brontë—Anne Brontë

I guess that this day 4 years we shall all be in this drawing-room comfortable I hope it may be so. Anne guesses we shall all be gone somewhere comfortable We hope it may be so indeed.

Aunt: Come Emily it's past 4 o'clock
Emily: Yes, Aunt Exit Aunt
Ann: Well, do you intend to write in the evening
Emily: Well, what think you
(We agreed to go out 1st to make sure if we got into the humour. We may stay in—)

* * *

1. Emily miscalculates: Charlotte was born in 1816, Branwell in 1817, Emily in 1818, and Anne in 1820.

July 30, 1841

A PAPER to be opened
when Anne is
25 years old,
or my next birthday after
if
all be well.
Emily Jane Brontë. July the 30th, 1841

It is Friday evening, near 9 o'clock—wild rainy weather. I am seated in the dining-room alone, having just concluded tidying our desk boxes, writing this document. Papa is in the parlour—aunt upstairs in her room. She has been reading *Blackwood's Magazine* to papa. Victoria and Adelaide [the geese] are ensconced in the peat-house. Keeper [the dog] is in the kitchen—Hero [a hawk] in his cage. We are all stout and hearty, as I hope is the case with Charlotte, Branwell, and Anne, of whom the first is at John White, Esq., Upperwood House, Rawdon; the second is at Luddended Foot; and the third is, I believe, at Scarborough, inditing perhaps a paper corresponding to this.

A scheme is at present in agitation for setting us up in a school of our own; as yet nothing is determined, but I hope and trust it may go on and prosper and answer our highest expectations. This day four years I wonder whether we shall still be dragging on in our present condition or established to our hearts' content. Time will show.

I guess that at the time appointed for the opening of this paper we i.e. Charlotte, Anne, and I, shall be all merrily seated in our own sitting-room in some pleasant and flourishing seminary, having just gathered in for the midsummer holyday. Our debts will be paid off, and we shall have cash in hand to a considerable amount. Papa, aunt, and Branwell will either have been or will be coming to visit us. It will be a fine warm summer evening, very different from this bleak look-out, and Anne and I will perchance slip out into the garden for a few minutes to peruse our papers. I hope either this or something better will be the case.

The Gondalians are at present in a threatening state, but there is no open rupture as yet. All the princes and princesses of the Royalty are at the Palace of Instruction. I have a good many books on hand, but I am sorry to say that as usual I make small progress with any. However, I have just made a new regularity paper! and I mean *verb sap* to do great things. And now I must close, sending from far an exhortation, "Courage, courage," to exiled and harassed Anne, wishing she was here.

* * *

July 30, 1845

Haworth, Thursday, July 30th, 1845

My birthday—showery, breezy, cool. I am twenty-seven years old today. This morning Anne and I opened the papers we wrote four years since, on my twenty-third birthday. This paper we intend, if all be well, to open on my thirtieth—three years hence, in 1848. Since the 1841 paper the following events have taken place. Our school scheme has been abandoned, and instead Charlotte and I went to Brussels on the 8th February 1842.

Branwell left his place at Luddenden Foot. C. and I returned from Brussels, November 8th, 1842, in consequence of aunt's death.

Branwell went to Thorp Green as a tutor, where Anne still continued. January 1843.

Charlotte returned to Brussels the same month, and after staying a year, came back again on New Year's Day 1844.

Anne left her situation at Thorp Green of her own accord, June 1845.

"The Butterfly"†

As Sue Lonoff notes in her edition of the Brontës' Belgian essays, the nine essays Emily composed in French while a student at the Pensionnat Heger in Brussels in 1842 "make a difference" to the scant record that remains of Emily's writing. Although composed as assigned tasks for learning the French language, these essays (*devoirs*), were not ordinary schoolgirl work, because at ages 25 and 23, Charlotte and Emily were prolific writers with a considerable body of juvenilia behind them. Lonoff further notes that the Brontës "encountered a professor who also broke the mold, a man whose energy to teach matched theirs to learn. So despite the evident restrictions—composing under orders and in a foreign language—they wrote some extraordinary essays" (p. xiii).

"The Butterfly," like a number of Emily Brontë's poems, has interested readers searching for the personal vision and the counterforces of creation and destruction in her work, but Lonoff asks that we regard it and the other school essays according to what was most immediate in Emily's life, the six months of intense learning in Belgium. Lonoff notes that in this essay Emily characteristically constructed an argument by working through a series of antitheses. Whatever clues "The Butterfly" may provide about the author's mind and art, its formal tensions anticipate those of *Wuthering Heights*, as do such reflections as

† From *The Belgian Essays: Charlotte Brontë and Emily Brontë*, ed. and trans. by Sue Lonoff (New Haven: Yale UP, 1996) 176–79. Reprinted by permission of Yale University Press.

those concerning the "principle of destruction in nature" countered by the concept of "this globe [as] the embryo of a new heaven and a new earth."

Emily J. Brontë August 11th, 1842

[Devoir]

The Butterfly.

In one of those moods that everyone falls into sometimes, when the world of the imagination suffers a winter that blights its vegetation; when the light of life seems to go out and existence becomes a barren desert where we wander, exposed to all the tempests that blow under heaven, without hope of rest or shelter—in one of these black humors, I was walking one evening at the edge of a forest. It was summer; the sun was still shining high in the west and the air resounded with the songs of birds. All appeared happy, but for me, it was only an appearance. I sat at the foot of an old oak, among whose branches the nightingale had just begun its vespers. "Poor fool," I said to myself, "is it to guide the bullet to your breast or the child to your brood that you sing so loud and clear? Silence that untimely tune, perch yourself on your nest; tomorrow, perhaps, it will be empty." But why address myself to you alone? All creation is equally mad. Behold those flies playing above the brook; the swallows and fish diminish their number every minute. These will become, in their turn, the prey of some tyrant of the air or water; and man for his amusement or his needs will kill their murderers. Nature is an inexplicable problem; it exists on a principle of destruction. Every being must be the tireless instrument of death to others, or itself must cease to live, yet nonetheless we celebrate the day of our birth, and we praise God for having entered such a world.

During my soliloquy I picked a flower at my side; it was fair and freshly opened, but an ugly caterpillar had hidden itself among the petals and already they were shriveling and fading. "Sad image of the earth and its inhabitants!" I exclaimed. "This worm lives only to injure the plant that protects it. Why was it created, and why was man created? He torments, he kills, he devours; he suffers, dies, is devoured—there you have his whole story. It is true that there is a heaven for the saint, but the saint leaves enough misery here below to sadden him even before the throne of God.

I threw the flower to earth. At that moment the universe appeared to me a vast machine constructed only to produce evil. I almost doubted the goodness of God, in not annihilating man on the day he first sinned. "The world should have been destroyed," I said, "crushed as I crush this reptile which has done nothing in its life but render all that it touches as disgusting as itself." I had scarcely removed my foot from the poor insect when, like a censoring angel sent from heaven, there came fluttering through the trees a butterfly with large wings of lustrous gold and purple. It shone but a moment before my eyes; then, rising among the leaves, it vanished into the height of the azure vault. I was mute, but an inner voice said to me, "Let not the creature judge his Creator; here is a symbol of the world to come. As the ugly caterpillar is the origin of the splendid butterfly, so this globe is the embryo of a new heaven and a new earth whose poorest beauty will infinitely exceed your mortal imagination. And when you see the magnificent result of that which seems so base to you now, how you will scorn your blind presumption, in accusing Omniscience for not having made nature perish in her infancy.

God is the god of justice and mercy; then surely, every grief that he inflicts on his creatures, be they human or animal, rational or irrational, every suffering of our unhappy nature is only a seed of that divine harvest which will be gathered when, Sin having spent its last drop of venom, Death having launched its final shaft, both will perish on the pyre of a universe in flames and leave their ancient victims to an eternal empire of happiness and glory.

EDWARD CHITHAM

Sculpting the Statue: A Chronology of the Process of Writing *Wuthering Heights*†

During the past twenty years great strides have been taken in understanding the ways in which Emily Brontë worked. There has also been a re-evaluation of her poetry, which has shown that her best poems stand comparison with any written in the nineteenth century, by male or female poets. These poems are as important a part of her *oeuvre* as *Wuthering Heights*, and are coherent with the novel. The Brontë scholar, therefore, is entitled to use the evidence of Emily Brontë's working methods in her poetry (of which many manuscripts survive) to understand her methods of working on her unique novel (of which unfortunately there is no manuscript, and not a single note about its composition remains).

† For this Norton Critical Edition, Chitham has provided brief additional commentary to excerpts from his *The Birth of Wuthering Heights: Emily Brontë at Work* (London: Macmillan, 1998), chapters 14, 15. Reprinted by permission of the author and publisher.

There is a certain amount of external evidence which can also be used. In the following article, I shall present what appears to be a neat and homogeneous chronology of the novel's production. Like the novel itself, this chronology has had to be worked at over a period of time, and some parts of it are stronger than others. Emily Brontë is one of the most secretive of nineteenth-century writers, and her sister Charlotte largely respected that secrecy. Much contemporary evidence for Brontë lives stems from Charlotte's letters to her close friend Ellen Nussey, and to the publishers with whom she gradually became friends. She did not feel free to discuss Emily's work unreservedly with either of these two kinds of correspondent. Ellen knew nothing of the Brontës' early attempts at publishing their work. Between Charlotte and her two sisters there was strong disagreement about the merits of Thomas Newby, who published the novels of Emily and Anne. This restricted Charlotte's freedom to discuss their work with her own publisher until after their deaths.

Once her sisters had died, Charlotte, grief stricken, felt both a literary and family duty to present their work and to edit it in such a way as to aid communication between the two sisters and a public which might misunderstand. She added a "Biographical Notice" and an "Editor's Preface." Among the points she made in these concerning *Wuthering Heights* are the following: "Neither Anne nor Emily was learned; . . . they always wrote from the impulse of nature" ("Biographical Notice"); "Having formed these beings, she did not know what she had done" ("Preface"); "the creative gift . . . sets to work on statue hewing" ("Preface"); "Wuthering Heights was hewn in a wild workshop, with simple tools, out of homely materials. The statuary found a granite rock on a solitary moor; . . . He wrought with a crude chisel, and from no model but the vision of his meditations. With time and labour, the crag took shape" ("Preface"). In fact, Emily was probably more learned than Charlotte, and all three sisters were avid for learning, but we can see Charlotte's line of defence. Unfortunately part of the tone of this apologia has caused some critics over the years to see Emily Brontë as "wild," "simple," and "crude" to the point of imagining that all her output must have come simply to her, by some form of supernatural inspiration, rather than as a balanced result of inspiration and labour. The other aspect of these quotes, though, forbids us to think that the novel was written speedily and without angst.

It has gradually become apparent that *Wuthering Heights* as eventually published cannot be the novel as originally submitted. Dr. Tom Winnifrith set out the arguments as long ago as 1983 in *Brontë Facts and Brontë Problems*. In *The Birth of Wuthering Heights*, I filled in the detail, working from an understanding of Emily Brontë's methods of composition and from such external sources as we can find. The chronology now presented therefore rests on different types of evidence, and it does need to be stressed that while some of this chronology is absolutely certain, other parts have to be inferred. The dates of Emily's poems are usually given by her in the manuscripts, and these dates can be shown on external grounds in the majority of cases to be composition dates, not, for example, copying dates. There are some dates to be gathered from Charlotte's letters; there are dates to be found in the so-called diary papers. Other dates and events are probable rather than certain, such as, for example, my suggestion that it was Newby, the eventual publisher of *Wuthering Heights* and *Agnes Grey*, who rejected the original package of the three Brontë novels in August 1846. In the chronology presented I have tried to make clear how firm the dating is.

Finally, I should like to summarize a few points from *The Birth of Wuthering Heights* in which detailed argument stretches over many pages and cannot be fully reproduced here.

First, the question of the form of the novel as submitted in 1846. There may be objectors who wish to argue that we have no precise knowledge of what that submission was like, and it could have been the novel as we now know it. In answer to this, I have tried to lay out exact details of the numbers of pages involved in the final three-volume presentation of *Agnes Grey* and *Wuthering Heights*. The question has to be asked how three novels, *The Master*, *Agnes Grey* and *Wuthering Heights*, in which one was almost as long as the others put together, would have been acceptable either to a publisher or to the Brontës, having regard to Charlotte's careful balancing of length in the published poem edition. Her letter to Colburn is very specific: '. . . three tales, each occupying a volume . . .' If the novel of 1847 was the same as that submitted in 1846, how is it that it occupied two volumes when finally issued?

In proposing this piecemeal planning of the novel, it may seem that I have set the clock back to before Sanger's discoveries of 1926 about the tight chronology of *Wuthering Heights*. This aspect of the book is rightly pointed out as evidence of Emily Brontë's intellectual control of the material. In reply, I should agree that Sanger is quite right to discern this chronological underpinning, but note that almost all the chronological clues are given in the parts of the book I see as added in October 1846 to June 1847. Much chronology is found in Chapters 18–33 and the apostrophes to Lockwood by Nelly Dean which interrupt her story. I do not deny that chronology is very important in the novel, and that the shifts and references back and forth across a period of time are crucial, and were inherent even in the first version, but this whole element was accentuated and systematised in the revision.

The third objection might be the radical one that by throwing doubt on Emily Brontë's forward planning of the novel, I am undermining its status. As I have suggested, much of this status derives according to critics from its compactness, its intensity, its drama, its poetry, its daring, its depth of treatment, its range in raising issues both social and psychological. Critics mainly concentrate on part one. Those who go on to part two see different virtues in the book, interpreting it as a dialogue, an attempt to domesticate the wild, a logical extension and meditation on issues raised in part one. Sanger's evidence of chronological control has possibly misled some commentators to see more order in the structure than is actually present, and an emphasis placed on Emily Brontë's preplanning which overvalues this element of the novel. Sanger's discovery is quite valid, the chronological control adds to the book, and the second version is better than the first would have been, but that does not mean we have to argue against the implication in much critical work that the first part is more essential than much of part two.

Emily Brontë has been compared to Beethoven: both stormy geniuses whose work has great resonance in a Romantic mode. The knowledge that Beethoven worked furiously at his compositions, revising and changing his plans, does not diminish him. If it is accepted that Emily Brontë's work was revised and altered out of recognition as a result of rejection by a publisher, leading to a dialogue with her sister Anne (and probably also Charlotte) and a change of mind concerning the main aims of the book, this does not diminish or invalidate in any way our respect for the composition and production of this unique book.

* * *

December 1844

All three Brontë sisters are at home for Christmas. It had become obvious by about October that the school scheme which Charlotte had been pursuing for some years was not feasible. Emily and Anne, possibly with Charlotte, began to consider whether their stories could be turned into saleable commodities. The evidence of Anne's poem 'Call me away' written on her return to Thorp Green in January suggests that the two younger sisters had been involved in Gondal, but this is also the last occasion on which they could have met to discuss writing fiction, and we have sufficient basis for an opinion that Anne was writing *Agnes Grey* during the middle of the year. Though *Agnes Grey* and *Wuthering Heights* appear so different, they both begin with scenes related to the emergence of the two sisters into the world of teaching, Anne at Blake Hall in 1839, and Emily at Law Hill in 1838.

An agreement to adopt this as a starting point meant for Emily a willingness to abandon Gondal or at least to alter it in such a way that any public which could be coaxed to read their books would recognise an English scenario. It should not be supposed that she was necessarily unwilling to do this, since she herself had favoured realistic settings on earlier occasions.

January 1845

Once Anne had returned to Thorp Green, it is likely that Emily began work on recreating the scene at High Sunderland, which she had evidently visited during the winter of 1838–9. There are no poems recorded for January 1845, and it is into this gap that the first and parts of the second chapter of *Wuthering Heights* can be fitted.

February 1845

The poem 'Enough of Thought, Philosopher' is dated 3 February 1845. A complex poem of 56 lines, it is likely to have taken several days to complete. It is likely to have provided a diversion from the novel, still in its early stages.

March 1845

During a period of snowy weather the poem 'Cold in the earth' was written and dated 3 March. The pervasive snow made a strong appearance in this first part of *Wuthering Heights*, especially Chapter 3, where Lockwood is lodged in the chamber with the strange closet for a bed. Here he dreams of a figure (Jabes Branderham) naturalised from Gondal, and of Catherine Earnshaw, a recreation at this stage of one of Emily's lost sisters, but merging with elements of Gondal and Law Hill. She does not know how to explain this ghost child, and no clear solution is forthcoming. At this point, then, it seems likely that the novel is allowed to lapse. It is possible to speculate on letters from Anne at Thorp Green, though there is no trace of such letters. Emily seems unaccountably buoyed up this spring, possibly in contrast to what she hears about Anne and Branwell.

April–June 1845

This is an amazingly fruitful period in Emily Brontë's poetry, leading to the production of over 200 lines of poetry of highest quality: 'Death' (10 April); 'Stars' (14 April); 'A thousand sounds of happiness' (22 April); 'Heavy hangs the raindrop' (28 May) with its counterpart 'Child of Delight! with sunbright hair'; and 'Anticipation' (2 June). The poems suggest much increased confidence, but they may be seen as another interlude in the composition of *Wuthering Heights*, which at this stage must have consisted of the bulk of present Chapters 1 and 3 with some of Chapter 2 and possibly other material not present in the finished version.

June and July 1845

Brontë biography shows a summer of turmoil, with Anne finally leaving Thorp Green, Branwell losing his post there, Charlotte going on holiday with Ellen Nussey, and Emily and Anne going on a 'journey' which should have taken them to Scarborough but which ended in York. The diary papers written by the two youngest sisters do not mention the novels, though 'Passages in the Life of an Individual' is often thought to be *Agnes Grey*. Emily is writing the story of the Emperor Julius, whose characteristics become merged with those of Heathcliff. On the journey to York the pair act out parts of the Gondal story, but Anne (according to her diary paper) is much less involved in the saga than Emily.

August 1845

Emily wrote a rather uninspired poem about a Gondal prison on an unknown date this month. But for some reason the novel began to take hold of her again. It seems likely that it was now that she discovered the voice of Nelly Dean (Emily Jane) and began the story of Heathcliff's arrival from the beginning. This 'very beginning' was the 'very beginning' of Emily Brontë or Prunty, an outcast's story in Liverpool. This part of the story is located in time by the promise to bring apples and pears home. The first of a series of theatrical scenes shows the arrival of Heathcliff. This part of the novel will proceed in a sustained series of such scenes, made up with one eye on the distant precepts of Horace about events on stage and events reported. Novel writing will not be uninterrupted, however.

September 1845

Emily's imagination returns to the topography of Shibden and High Sunderland. She begins to see the contrast between the windy heights and the rich lowland as integral to her story. Always acutely interested in contrasts and dialectic, she develops Lockwood's position as a tenant of the wooded park in the valley and finds that her Gondal character Gerald can be turned into Edgar L., the prosperous squire's son. Several Gondal characters are turned into Yorkshire people. The girl ghost of the winter begins to subsume traits from Geraldine.

As Catherine and Heathcliff escape from their washhouse prison, prisons and their constraints are strongly in Emily's mind, and she assembles fragments for a poem, 'Silent is the house' which she copies into her Gondal notebook early next month.

October 1845

It is not clear why Charlotte is searching for poetry to edit and form the basis of an attempt at publication, but this is evidently the case. If she knew of the fiction being produced by the two younger sisters it is not easy to see why she decided to interrupt the flow of writing. It is clear that her discovery of Emily's poetry, generally agreed to be the B (Gondal) notebook, has to do with the school failure and the need to earn money by writing, but it is surprising that Charlotte did not prefer fiction. One possible explanation is that her own attempts to draft the book which eventually became *The Professor* were proving difficult. The evidence is that having discovered the poetry, possibly with 'Silent is the House' the final poem copied into the booklet, she tried to interest Emily in editing it and met with reluctance. It is generally thought that this reluctance was because of the personal nature of the poetry, but an additional point may be that Emily was by now very involved in her novel and was unwilling to be drawn away from it.

There is still dispute about the degree to which Emily collaborated in the editing of her poems, but Derek Roper has shown that she did at least play some part in the process, presumably laying aside her work on *Wuthering Heights*.

November and December 1845

Assuming the poetry editing to be perfunctory or speedy, Emily Brontë was ready to resume consistent work on the novel by some time in November. She took the story from the Sunday on which the two children escaped to watch their neighbours at Thrushcross Grange on to Christmas. Edgar's rivalry with Heathcliff was recapitulating Gondal episodes but the tone and locale of the novel was releasing a new power and intensity in Emily which may have been accentuated by the increased confidence aroused by re-reading and editing her strongest poems.

January–April 1846

Emily's strong poem 'No coward soul' was written on 2 January. The tone of this poem accords with the next section of *Wuthering Heights*. The weather at Boston, Lincs, a county adjacent to Yorkshire, was warmer than usual for the time of year (January an average of 5°F above normal, February an average of 4°F above normal, March a little above normal). There was no snow in January. Thus Emily Brontë was able to write summer scenes in weather that was 'unusually fine' (February). There was a patch of snow from 9–13 February and a little snow on 19 March. The thunder on 26 March may have influenced the storm scene in Chapter 9, though this seems a little late for this chapter to be under construction.

It must be remembered that there is no poetry being written in these confident months, and that is surely because *Wuthering Heights* is currently an obsession. The white heat of this section of the novel is very noticeable, and it seems likely that it gave rise to such remarks of Charlotte's concerning her sister as that 'she never lingered' over a task.

It is on 20 March that Catherine the younger is born, and a possibility that the date is chosen to reflect the actual date; however, this does not accord with the date of the storm mentioned above. The tense and inspired writing begins at this point to calm and it may be that Emily was discussing with Charlotte and Anne how near they were to offering their tales to the public.

April–May 1846

6 April 1846 is the date of Charlotte's letter announcing the preparation of the three novels. Emily Brontë now had to complete the story of Heathcliff's love for Catherine and his revenge. She did this in Chapter 16 and parts of 17, and perhaps early versions of parts of Chapters 32 and 33, with a substantial part of Chapter 34, relating Heathcliff's death.

June–July 1846

The completed first version was copied and perhaps somewhat revised ready for despatch to Henry Colburn.

4 July 1846

This is the date of Charlotte's letter requesting permission to send the three 'tales' to Henry Colburn. A note suggests that Colburn asked to know the nature of the tales, and it is assumed but not proved that the three novels were then sent to him. We do not have any letter in which he rejected the novels and we have no idea why he did so. Such decisions were made quickly in the mid-nineteenth century, and we can be fairly certain this process could have taken place by the end of July.

July and August 1846

It is an open question whether there were two more rejections during late July and August or only one. I have argued above that the August rejection was perhaps by Newby himself.

24/25 August 1846

Emily and Anne, at Haworth, received the rejected novels back from this publisher. It can perhaps be inferred from what happened later that *Agnes Grey* was substantially accepted, while Charlotte's book, then called *The Master*, was rejected outright. *Wuthering Heights* was neither praised nor damned. It is likely that the changes introduced by Emily were intended to answer the objections raised, and there are probably further echoes of these objections in Charlotte's later comments on the book and perhaps also her editing of 1850. The two sisters at Haworth sent on *The Master* to Manchester, where Charlotte was attending their father while his eyes were operated on. Mrs Gaskell records the return of the novel.

August and September 1846

We can reasonably infer a discussion between the three sisters when Charlotte returned from Manchester. At the end of it, Charlotte withdrew completely from the consortium and began work on *Jane Eyre*. This left the three-volume set short of a volume. Initially, as we can see from what happened in September, it was not clear what could be done to save the situation, and it must have seemed as though Anne's contribution to the set, which must have been approved, would have to be abandoned.

14 September 1846

Both Anne and Emily wrote narrative poems with Gondal or part-Gondal reference. It is notable that Anne's poem is a gain in strength from her earlier Gondal work, reflecting the acceptance of her novel and the growing confidence that brought, while Emily's casts about for some time, beginning with a question and indicating changes of mind and attitude. In the first part of 'Why ask to know . . . ?' we see Emily writing to distract herself and in a context which reflected the civil war in the Brontë household.

September 1846

On the evidence of *Wildfell Hall* we can suppose that Anne disliked the tone of *Wuthering Heights* in its first version. This is amply supported by Charlotte's later remarks. Anne's objections were now underlined by the qualified rejection by publishers. She took exception to the way in which violence and drunkenness were portrayed in *Wuthering Heights*, and the way in which Emily had allowed events to occur without probing the psychological and moral consequences. The way in which Isabella ran away from Heathcliff may have been a major point.

If Anne's novel had been accepted and *Wuthering Heights* criticised as unsuitable but not irremediable, so long as Emily refused to remedy it she was standing in Anne's light. Anne must have announced her intention to write a new novel which would comment on *Wuthering Heights* and take over some of the situations. However, Emily finally agreed to change and expand the rejected book so that it could fill two volumes and still be issued with *Agnes Grey*. These changes would have the effect of tempering the harshness of the book, showing Emily relenting as her mercenary would relent in the contemporary narrative poem. Anne was wishing to expand her diary style which had been at the edge of the method in *Agnes Grey*. The two sisters agreed to use almanacks from the 1820s. This focused Emily's mind on the precise time-scale of *Wuthering Heights*. If one objection of the publisher had been the confusing narrative approach, tightening the time-scale would give sound indicators to the public. Hence we have tighter time control introduced in part one and a flood of time references in part two.

September and October 1846

Emily wrote the chapter now known as 32 and in previous editions as Volume II, Chapter 18. This includes September weather based on that of September 1846, and mirrored in the weather of the narrative poem contemporary with this part of *Wuthering Heights*. It may be that Lockwood's second visit was originally to have been located at the centre of the book and was later transferred to its present position. The dates 1801 and 1802 also seem to be provided at this point, matching Anne's attention to dates in the 1820s. The construction of Emily's time-scale would be more difficult than Anne's and it must surely have been produced on a chart at this stage. A few anomalies escaped Emily during the imposition of the time-scale, but the original ghost girl's cry did not, causing some fluffing in what is now Chapter 12.

November 1846–about June 1847

During this period Emily Brontë added her new chapters and revised the rest of the book, giving Lockwood and Nelly more to say by way of explanation, inserting the 'apostrophes' we have noted, and tightening the time-scale. Nevertheless, there is evidence of haste in the final preparation, such as the speedy writing which allowed numbers 3 and 5 to be confused, and the careless accumulation of housekeepers. Two reasons for this could be pressure from Charlotte and Anne as they finished *Jane Eyre* and *Wildfell Hall* and Emily's self-doubt or impatience. Spellings of Peniston and the transformation of Gimmerden into Gimmerton were not even noticed by her as she sped to complete the book. Nor did she pick these points up later at proof stage.

August 1847

Proofs arrive at Haworth. There are some manuscript corrections in a copy of *Agnes Grey* but nothing corresponding to this is known for *Wuthering Heights*, and we do not know the precise status of Anne's corrections. It is not a proof copy.

December 1847

The three-volume set is published in the early part of the month. A review in *The Spectator* is dated 18 December.

* * *

Publishing the 1847 *Wuthering Heights*

The only surviving documentation of the Brontës' efforts to place their fiction with publishers is in a few of Charlotte's letters. In his study of the chronology of the writing of *Wuthering Heights*, Edward Chitham discusses the complications that arose when Charlotte's manuscript was not taken by Newby, the publisher willing to go forward with her sisters' stories. Assuming that the initial submission was of three works that would comprise the usual three-volume format, the publisher needed a work of greater length, and Chitham and others have regarded this as the occasion for Emily's expansion of the original *Wuthering*

Heights. But with neither manuscript nor proofs, the precise nature of the changes cannot be determined.

There are several interesting points to note beyond the dating these letters provide of the year or more it took to place the manuscripts. In April of 1846, made wary by having had to underwrite the publication of the volume of poetry, Charlotte was firm about the authors' unwillingness to "publish these tales on their own account." But by July of that year, while reminding Henry Colburn that "the authors of these tales have already appeared before the public," she says nothing about assuming any share of publication costs.

The letters to her own publisher's representative, W. S. Williams, reveal their distrust of Newby, who "shuffles, gives his word and breaks it." Less than a month after her sisters' novels finally appeared, Charlotte expressed the opinion that "few authors would like to have him for their publisher a second time." Nonetheless, Newby would publish Anne's *The Tenant of Wildfell Hall* in 1848, and he was interested in a second work from Emily, one we now cannot be sure was even started. After her sisters' deaths, Charlotte did succeed in having her publisher, Smith, Elder, reissue the poems of 1846 and her 1850 edition of *Wuthering Heights* and *Agnes Grey*.

To Messrs Aylott and Jones, 6 April 1846†

[Haworth]

Gentlemen

C. E & A Bell are now preparing for the Press a work of fiction —consisting of three distinct and unconnected tales[1] which may be published either together as a work of 3 vols. of the ordinary novel-size, or separately as single vols—as shall be deemed most advisable.

It is not their intention to publish these tales on their own account.

They direct me to ask you whether you would be disposed to undertake the work—after having of course by due inspection of the M.S. ascertained that its contents are such as to warrant an expectation of success.

An early answer will oblige as in case of your negativing the proposal—inquiry must be made of other Publishers—

I am Gentlemen
Yrs truly
C Brontë

† From *The Letters of Charlotte Brontë*, ed. Margaret Smith (Oxford: Clarendon Press, 1995, 2000). The first five of the letters here excerpted are from vol. I; the final letter of this section is from vol. II. Reprinted by permission of the editor and the publisher.

1. Emily's and Anne's novels would be published together as three volumes in December 1847, with *Agnes Grey* being the third volume. Charlotte's *The Professor* was not published until after 1857, two years after her death.

To Henry Colburn, 4 July 1846

[Haworth]

Sir

I request permission to send for your inspection the M.S of a work of fiction in 3 vols. It consists of three tales, each occupying a volume and capable of being published together or separately, as thought most advisable. The authors of these tales have already appeared before the public.

Should you consent to examine the work, would you, in your reply, state at what period after transmission of the M.S. to you, the authors may expect to receive your decision upon its merits—

I am Sir
Yours respectfully
C Bell

Address Mr Currer Bell
Parsonage.
Haworth
Bradford
Yorkshire.

To W. S. Williams, 10 November 1847

[Haworth]

Dear Sir,

* * *

Your account of the various surmises respecting the identity of the brothers Bell, amused me much: were the enigma solved, it would probably be found not worth the trouble of solution; but I will let it alone; it suits ourselves to remain quiet and certainly injures no one else.

The Reviewer, who noticed the little book of poems, in the "Dublin Magazine," conjectured that the soi-disant three personages were in reality but one, who, endowed with an unduly prominent organ of self-esteem, and consequently impressed with a somewhat weighty notion of his own merits, thought them too vast to be concentrated in a single individual, and accordingly divided himself into three, out of consideration, I suppose, for the nerves of the much-to-be-astounded public! This was an ingenious thought in the Reviewer; very original and striking, but not accurate. We are three.

A prose work by Ellis and Acton will soon appear: it should have been out, indeed, long since, for the first proof-sheets were already in the press at the commencement of last August, before Currer

Bell had placed the M.S. of "Jane Eyre" in your hands. Mr N⟨ewby⟩, however, does not do business like Messrs. Smith and Elder; a different spirit seems to preside at 72. Mortimer Street to that which guides the helm at 65. Cornhill. Mr. N⟨ewby⟩ shuffles, gives his word and breaks it; Messrs. Smith and Elder's performance is always better than their promise. My relatives have suffered from exhausting delay and procrastination, while I have to acknowledge the benefits of a management, at once business-like and gentlemanlike, energetic and considerate.

I should like to know if Mr. N⟨ewby⟩ often acts as he has done to my relatives, or whether this is an exceptional instance of his method. Do you know, and can you tell me anything about him? You must excuse me for going to the point at once, when I want to learn anything; if my questions are importunate, you are, of course, at liberty to decline answering them.—I am yours respectfully,

C. Bell.

To W. S. Williams, 14 December 1847

[Haworth]

Dear Sir

* * *

"Wuthering Heights" is, I suppose, at ⟨last⟩ 'length' published—at least Mr. Newby has sent the authors their six copies—I wonder how it will be received. I should say it merits the epithets of "vigorous" and "original" much more decidedly than "Jane Eyre" did. "Agnes Grey" should please such critics as Mr. Lewes—for it is "true" and "unexaggerated" enough.

The books are not well got up—they abound in errors of the press. On a former occasion I expressed myself with perhaps too little reserve regarding Mr. Newby—yet I cannot but feel, and feel painfully that Ellis and Acton have not had the justice at his hands that I have had at those of Messrs. Smith & Elder

Believe me, dear Sir,
Yours respectfully
C. Bell—

To W. S. Williams, 21 December 1847

[Haworth]

Dear Sir

* * *

You are not far wrong in your judgment respecting "Wuthering Heights" & "Agnes Grey". Ellis has a strong, original mind, full of strange though sombre power: when he writes poetry that power speaks in language at once condensed, elaborated and refined—but in prose it breaks forth in scenes which shock more than they attract—Ellis will improve, however, because he knows his defects. "Agnes Grey" is the mirror of the mind of the writer. The orthography & punctuation of the books are mortifying to a degree—almost all the errors that were corrected in the proof-sheets appear intact in what should have been the fair copies. If Mr. Newby always does business in this way, few authors would like to have him for their publisher a second time.

T. C. Newby to ?Emily J. Brontë ['Ellis Bell'], 15 February 1848

Dear Sir,

I am much obliged by your kind note & shall have great pleasure in making arrangements for your next novel. I would not ?hurry its completion, for I think you are quite right not to let it go before the world until well satisfied with it, for much depends on your next work if it be an improvement on your first you will have established yourself as a first rate novelist, but if it fall short the Critics will be too apt to say that you have expended your talent in your first novel. I shall therefore, have pleasure in accepting it upon the understanding that its completion be at your own time.

Believe me
my dear Sir
Yrs. sincerely
T C Newby

REVIEWS OF THE 1847 *WUTHERING HEIGHTS*

Emily Brontë saved portions of five reviews, which eventually found their way into the Brontë Parsonage Museum as part of the contents of her writing desk. Four have been identified as having appeared in the January 1848 numbers of the *Atlas*, *Douglas Jerrold's Weekly Newspaper*, the *Examiner*, and the *Britannia*. Neither the date nor the source has been located for the fifth review. To reflect the range of speculation and opinion about *Wuthering Heights*, it is helpful also to read one of the first reviews, that by H. F. Chorley in December 1847, and also a brief *New Monthly Magazine* notice which took a line from Lockwood's first impression of Wuthering Heights to characterize the book itself as "a perfect misanthropist's heaven." From Charlotte Brontë's 1850 biographical notice, it is evident that Sydney Dobell's remarks earlier that year in the *Palladium* had impressed her as rare recognition of Emily's powers. The final review reprinted in this section is E. P. Whipple's of an 1848 American edition of *Wuthering Heights*, included because it was one Charlotte brought to Emily's attention and because it is another to which Charlotte took strong exception. The grounds for her sweeping attacks on Emily's critics can best be assayed after sampling all of these reviews.

Athenaeum

[*H. F. Chorley*]

December 25, 1847

'Jane Eyre,' it will be recollected, was *edited* by Mr. Currer Bell. Here are two tales so nearly related to 'Jane Eyre' in cast of thought, incident, and language as to excite some curiosity. All three might be the work of one hand,—but the first issued remains the best. In spite of much power and cleverness; in spite of its truth to life in the remote nooks and corners of England, 'Wuthering Heights' is a disagreeable story. The Bells seem to affect painful and exceptional subjects:—the misdeeds and oppressions of tyranny—the eccentricities of "woman's fantasy." They do not turn away from dwelling upon those physical acts of cruelty which we know to have their warrant in the real annals of crime and suffering,—but the contemplation of which true taste rejects. The brutal master of the lonely house on "Wuthering Heights"—a prison which might be pictured from life—has doubtless had his prototype in those ungenial and remote districts where human beings, like the trees, grow gnarled and dwarfed and distorted by the inclement climate; but he might have been indicated with far fewer touches, in place of so entirely filling the canvas that there is hardly a scene untainted by his presence. It was a like dreariness—a like unfortunate selection of objects—which cut short the popularity of Charlotte Smith's novels,[1]—rich though they be in true pathos and faithful descriptions of Nature. Enough of what is mean and bitterly painful and degrading gathers round us during the course of his pilgrimage

1. Charlotte Smith (1749–1806) wrote gothic romances, with her best-known being *The Old Manor House* (1793).

through this vale of tears to absolve the Artist from choosing his incidents and characters out of such a dismal catalogue; and if the Bells, singly or collectively, are contemplating future or frequent utterances in Fiction, let us hope that they will spare us further interiors so gloomy as the one here elaborated with such dismal minuteness. * * * In both these tales [*Wuthering Heights* and *Agnes Grey*] there is so much feeling for character, and nice marking of scenery, that we cannot leave them without once again warning their authors against what is eccentric and unpleasant. Never was there a period in our history of Society when we English could so ill afford to dispense with sunshine.

Atlas

January 1848

About two years ago a small volume of poems by "Currer, Acton, and Ellis Bell" was given to the world. The poems were of varying excellence; those by Currer Bell, for the most part, exhibiting the highest order of merit; but, as a whole, the little work produced little or no sensation, and was speedily forgotten. Currer, Acton, and Ellis Bell have now all come before us as novelists, and all with so much success as to make their future career a matter of interesting speculation in the literary world.

Whether, as there is little reason to believe, the names which we have written are the genuine names of actual personages—whether they are, on the other hand, mere publishing names, as is our own private conviction—whether they represent three distinct individuals, or whether a single personage is the actual representative of the "three gentlemen at once" of the title-pages—whether the authorship of the poems and the novels is to be assigned to one gentleman or to one lady, to three gentlemen or three ladies, or to a mixed male and female triad of authors—are questions over which the curious may puzzle themselves, but are matters really of little account. One thing is certain; as in the poems, so in the novels, the signature of "Currer Bell" is attached to pre-eminently the best performance. We were the first to welcome the author of *Jane Eyre* as a new writer of no ordinary power. A new edition of that singular work had been called for, and we do not doubt that its success has done much to ensure a favourable reception for the volumes which are now before us.

Wuthering Heights is a strange, inartistic story. There are evidences in every chapter of a sort of rugged power—an unconscious strength—which the possessor seems never to think of turning to the best advantage. The general effect is inexpressibly painful. We know nothing in the whole range of our fictitious literature which presents such shocking pictures of the worst forms of humanity. *Jane Eyre* is a book which affects the reader to tears; it touches the most hidden sources of emotion. *Wuthering Heights* casts a gloom over the mind not easily to be dispelled. It does not soften; it harasses, it extenterates [*sic*]. There are passages in it which remind us of the *Nowlans* of the late John Banim; but of all pre-existent works the one which it most recalls to our memory is the *History of Mathew Wald*.[2] It has not, however, the unity and concentration of that fiction; but is a *sprawling* story, carrying us, with no mitigation of anguish, through two generations of sufferers—though one presiding evil genius sheds a grim shadow over the whole and imparts a singleness of malignity to the somewhat disjointed tale. A more natural unnatural story we do not remember to have read. Inconceivable as are the combinations of human degradation which are here to be found moving within the circle of a few miles, the *vraisemblance* is so admirably preserved; there is so much truth in what we may call the *costumery* (not applying the word in its narrow acceptation)—the general mounting of the entire piece—that we readily identify the scenes and personages of the fiction; and when we lay aside the book it is some time before we can persuade ourselves that we have held nothing more than imaginary intercourse with the ideal creations of the brain. The reality of unreality has never been so aptly illustrated as in the scenes of almost savage life which Ellis Bell has brought so vividly before us.

The book wants relief. A few glimpses of sunshine would have increased the reality of the picture and given strength rather than weakness to the whole. There is not in the entire *dramatis personae* a single character which is not utterly hateful or thoroughly contemptible. If you do not detest the person, you despise him; and if you do not despise him, you detest him with your whole heart. Hindley, the brutal, degraded sot, strong in the desire to work all mischief, but impotent in his degradation; Linton Heathcliff, the miserable, drivelling coward, in whom we see selfishness in its most abject form; and Heathcliff himself, the presiding evil genius of the piece, the tyrant father of an imbecile son, a creature in whom every evil passion seems to have reached a gigantic excess—form a group of deformities such as we have rarely seen gathered together on the same canvas. The author seems to have designed to throw some redeeming touches into the character of the brutal Heathcliff by portraying him as one faithful to the "idol of his boyhood"—loving

2. *Nowlans* was part of Banim's *Tales by the O'Hara Family* (1826). *The History of Matthew Wald* (1824) was by J. G. Lockhart.

to the very last—long, long after death had divided them, the unhappy girl who had cheered and brightened up the early days of his wretched life. Here is the touch of nature which makes the whole world kin—but it fails of the intended effect. There is a selfishness—a ferocity in the love of Heathcliff, which scarcely suffer it, in spite of its rugged constancy, to relieve the darker parts of his nature. Even the female characters excite something of loathing and much of contempt. Beautiful and loveable in their childhood, they all, to use a vulgar expression, "turn out badly." Catherine the elder—wayward, impatient, impulsive—sacrifices herself and her lover to the pitiful ambition of becoming the wife of a gentleman of station. Hence her own misery—her early death—and something of a brutal wickedness of Heathcliff's character and conduct; though we cannot persuade ourselves that even a happy love would have tamed down the natural ferocity of the tiger. Catherine the younger is more sinned against than sinning, and in spite of her moral defects, we have some hope of her at the last.

Douglas Jerrold's Weekly Newspaper

January 1848

Two of these volumes contain a tale by Mr. Ellis Bell, called *Wuthering Heights*, and the third volume is devoted to another story told in an autobiographical form by Mr. Acton Bell, and is entitled *Agnes Grey*.

Dissimilar as they are in many respects, there is a distinct family likeness between these two tales; and, if our organ of comparison be not out of order, we are not far wrong is asserting that they are not so much like each other, as they are both like a novelty recently published under the editorship of Mr. Currer Bell, viz., *Jane Eyre*. We do not mean to say that either of the tales now before us is equal in merit to that novel, but they have somewhat of the same fresh, original, and uncoventional spirit; while the style of composition is, undoubtedly, of the same north-country, Doric school; it is simple, energetic, and apparently disdainful of prettinesses and verbal display.

* * *

Wuthering Heights is a strange sort of book—baffling all regular criticism; yet, it is impossible to begin and not finish it; and quite as impossible to lay it aside afterwards and say nothing about it. In the midst of the reader's perplexity the ideas predominant in his mind concerning this book are likely to be—brutal cruelty, and semi-savage love. What may be the moral which the author wishes the reader to deduce from his work, it is difficult to say; and we refrain from assigning any, because to speak honestly, we have discovered none but mere glimpses of hidden morals or secondary meanings. There seems to us great power in this book but a purposeless power, which we feel a great desire to see turned to better account. We are quite confident that the writer of *Wuthering Heights* wants but the practised skill to make a great artist; perhaps, a great dramatic artist. His qualities are, at present, excessive; a far more promising fault, let it be remembered, than if they were deficient. He may tone down, whereas the weak and inefficient writer, however carefully he may write by rule and line, will never work up his productions to the point of beauty in art. In *Wuthering Heights* the reader is shocked, disgusted, almost sickened by details of cruelty, inhumanity, and the most diabolical hate and vengeance, and anon come passages of powerful testimony to the supreme power of love—even over demons in the human form. The women in the book are of a strange fiendish-angelic nature, tantalizing, and terrible, and the men are indescribable out of the book itself. Yet, towards the close of the story occurs the following pretty, soft picture, which comes like the rainbow after a storm.[3] * * *

We strongly recommend all our readers who love novelty to get this story, for we can promise them that they never have read anything like it before. It is very puzzling and very interesting; and if we had but space we would willingly devote a little more time to the analysis of this remarkable story, but we must leave it to our readers to decide what sort of a book it is.

Examiner

January 1848

This is a strange book. It is not without evidences of considerable power: but, as a whole, it is wild, confused; disjointed, and improbable; and the people who make up the drama, which is tragic enough in its consequences, are savages ruder than those who lived before the days of Homer. With the exception of Heathcliff, the story is confined to the family of Earnshaw, who intermarry with the Lintons; and the scene of their exploits is a rude old-fashioned house, at the top of one of the high moors or fells in the north of England. Whoever has traversed the bleak heights of Hartside or Cross Fell, on his road from Westmoreland to the dales of York-

3. The "soft picture" is the account of Cathy teaching Hareton to read.

shire, and has been welcomed there by the winds and rain on a 'gusty day', will know how to estimate the comforts of Wuthering Heights in wintry weather. But it may be as well to give the author's own sketch of the spot, taken, it should be observed at a more genial season.

* * *

This Heathcliff may be considered as the hero of the book, if a hero there be. He is an incarnation of evil qualities; implacable hate, ingratitude, cruelty, falsehood, selfishness, and revenge. He exhibits, moreover, a certain stoical endurance in early life, which enables him to 'bide his time', and nurse up his wrath till it becomes mature and terrible; and there is one portion of his nature, one only, wherein he appears to approximate to humanity. Like the Corsair, and other such melodramatic heroes, he is

Linked to one virtue and a thousand crimes;[4]

and it is with difficulty that we can prevail upon ourselves to believe in the appearance of such a phenomenon, so near our own dwellings as the summit of a Lancashire or Yorkshire moor.

It is not easy to disentangle the incidents and set them forth in chronological order. The tale if confused, as we have said, notwithstanding that the whole drama takes place in the house that we have described, and that the sole actors are the children of Earnshaw, by birth or adoption, and their servants.

* * *

We are not disposed to ascribe any particular intention to the author in drawing the character of Heathcliff, nor can we perceive any very obvious moral in the story. There are certain good rough dashes at character; some of the incidents look like real events; and the book has the merit, which must not be undervalued, of avoiding common-place and affectation. The language, however, is not always appropriate and we entertain great doubts as to the truth, or rather the *vraisemblance* of the main character. The hardness, selfishness and cruelty of Heathcliff are in our opinion inconsistent with the romantic love that he is stated to have felt for Catherine Earnshaw. As Nelly Dean says, "he is as hard as a whinstone." He has no gratitude, no affection, no liking for anything human except for one person, and that liking is thoroughly selfish and ferocious. He hates the son of Hindley, which is intelligible enough; but he

4. The final lines of Byron's *The Corsair* (1814) declare that the pirate title-character has disappeared: "He left a Corsair's name to other times, / Linked with one virtue, and a thousand crimes."

also hates and tyrannizes over his own son and the daughter of his beloved Catherine, and this we cannot understand.

We have said that there are some good dashes at character. The first Catherine is sketched thus.

* * *

From what we have said, the reader will imagine that the book is full of grim pictures. Here is one.[5] It should be premised that Heathcliff has manifested symptoms of restlessness and trouble for some time past.

* * *

If this book be, as we apprehend it is, the first work of the author, we hope that he will produce a second, —giving himself more time in its composition than in the present case, developing his incidents more carefully, eschewing exaggeration and obscurity, and looking steadily at human life, under all its moods, for those pictures of the passions that he may desire to sketch for our public benefit. It may be well also to be sparing of certain oaths and phrases, which do not materially contribute to any character, and are by no means to be reckoned among the evidences of a writer's genius. We detest the affectation and effeminate frippery which is but too frequent in the modern novel, and willingly trust ourselves with an author who goes at once fearlessly into the moors and desolate places, for his heroes; but we must at the same time stipulate with him that he shall not drag into light all that he discovers, of coarse and loathsome, in his wanderings, but simply so much good and ill as he may find necessary to elucidate his history—so much only as may be interwoven inextricably with the persons whom he professes to paint. It is the province of an artist to modify and in some cases refine what he beholds in the ordinary world. There never was a man whose daily life (that is to say, *all* his deeds and sayings, entire and without exception) constituted fit materials for a book of fiction. Even the figures of the Greeks (which are

In old marbles ever beautiful)[6]

were without doubt selected from the vistors in the ancient games, and others, by Phidias and his scholars, and their forms and countenances made perfect before they were thought worthy to adorn the temple of the wise Athena.

The only book which occurs to us as resembling *Wuthering*

5. Heathcliff's telling of his opening of Catherine's grave.
6. The quoted line is from John Keats, *Endymion*, I, 319, in respect to the heroes of the battle of Thermopylae.

Heights is a novel of the late Mr. Hooton's,[7] a work of very great talent, in which the hero is a tramper or beggar, and the *dramatis personae* all derived from humble and middle life; but which, notwithstanding its defects, we remember thinking better in its peculiar kind than anything that had been produced since the days of Fielding.

Britannia

January 1848

There are scenes of savage wildness in nature which, though they inspire no pleasurable sensation, we are yet well satisfied to have seen. In the rugged rock, the gnarled roots which cling to it, the dark screen of overhanging vegetation, the dank, moist ground and tangled network of weeds and bushes,—even in the harsh cry of solitary birds, the cries of wild animals, and the startling motion of the snake as it springs away scared by the intruder's foot,—there is an image of primeval rudeness which has much to fascinate, though nothing to charm, the mind. The elements of beauty are round us in the midst of gloom and danger, and some forms are the more picturesque from their distorted growth amid so many obstacles. A tree clinging to the side of a precipice may more attract the eye than the pride of a plantation.

The principle may, to some extent, be applied to life. The uncultured freedom of native character presents more rugged aspects than we meet with in educated society. Its manners are not only more rough but its passions are more violent. It knows nothing of those breakwaters to the fury of tempest which civilized training establishes to subdue the harsher workings of the soul. Its wrath is unrestrained by reflection; the lips curse and the hand strikes with the first implulse of anger. It is more subject to brutal instinct than to divine reason.

It is humanity in this wild state that the author of *Wuthering Heights* essays to depict. His work is strangely original. It bears a resemblance to some of those irregular German tales in which the writers, giving the reins to their fancy, represent personages as swayed and impelled to evil by supernatural influences. But they give spiritual identity to evil impulses, while Mr. Bell more naturally shows them as the natural offspring of the unregulated heart. He displays considerable power in his creations. They have all the an-

7. Charles Hooton (1813–1847): novelist and journalist, best known for his writings and travels in the United States and Canada. The reviewer may have in mind *Lancelot Wedge*, which was serialized in 1847.

gularity of misshapen growth, and form in this respect a striking contrast to those regular forms we are accustomed to meet with in English fiction. They exhibit nothing of the composite character. There is in them no trace of ideal models. They are so new, so wildly grotesque, so entirely without art, that they strike us as proceeding from a mind of limited experience, but of original energy, and of a singular and distinctive cast.

In saying this we indicate both the merits and faults of the tale. It is in parts very unskilfully constructed: many passages in it display neither the grace of art nor the truth of nature, but only the vigour of one positive idea,—that of passionate ferocity. It blazes forth in the most unsuitable circumstances and from persons the least likely to be animated by it. The author is a Salvator Rosa[8] with his pen. He delineates forms of savage grandeur when he wishes to represent sylvan beauty. His Griseldas are furies and his swains Polyphemi. For this reason his narrative leaves an unpleasant effect on the mind. There are no green spots in it on which the mind can linger with satisfaction. The story rushes onwards with impetuous force, but it is the force of a dark and sullen torrent, flowing between high and rugged rocks.

It is permitted to painting to seize one single aspect of nature, and, the pleasure arising from its contemplation proceeds partly from love of imitation, objects unattractive in themselves may be made interesting on canvas. But in fiction this kind of isolation is not allowed. The exhibition of one quality or passion is not sufficient for it. So far as the design extends it must present a true image of life, and if it takes in many characters it must show them animated by many motives. There may be a predominant influence of one strong emotion, perhaps that is necessary to unity of effect, but it should be relieved by contrasts, and set off by accessories. *Wuthering Heights* would have been a far better romance if Heathcliff alone had been a being of stormy passions, instead of all the other characters being nearly as violent and destructive as himself. In fiction, too, as the imitation of nature can never be so vivid and exact as in painting, that imitation is insufficient of itself to afford pleasure, and when it deals with brutal subjects it becomes positively disgusting. It is of course impossible to prescribe rules for either the admission or the rejection of what is shocking and dreadful. It is nothing to say that reality is faithfully followed. The aim of fiction is to afford some sensation of delight. We admit we cannot rejoice in the triumph of goodness—that triumph which consists in the superiority of spirit to body—without knowing its trials and

8. Seventeenth-century Italian painter and poet, known for the wild beauty of his landscapes.

sufferings. But the end of fictitious writings should always be kept in view; and that end is not merely mental excitement, for a very bad book may be very exciting. Generally we are satisfied there is some radical defect in those fictions which leave behind them an impression of pain and horror. It would not be difficult to show why this is, and must be, the case, but it would lead us into deeper considerations than are appropriate to this article.

Mr. Ellis Bell's romance is illuminated by some gleams of sunshine towards the end which serve to cast a grateful light on the dreary path we have travelled. Flowers rise over the grave of buried horrors. The violent passions of two generations are closed in death, yet in the vision of peace with which the tale closes we almost fear their revival in the warped nature of the young survivors.

* * *

It is difficult to pronounce any decisive judgment on a work in which there is so much rude ability displayed, yet in which there is so much matter for blame. The scenes of brutality are unnecessarily long and unnecessarily frequent; and as an imaginative writer the author has to learn the first principles of his art. But there is a singular power in his portraiture of strong passion. He exhibits it as convulsing the whole frame of nature, distracting the intellect to madness, and snapping the heart-strings. The anguish of Heathcliff on the death of Catherine approaches to sublimity.

We do not know whether the author writes with any purpose; but we can speak of one effect of his production. It strongly shows the brutalizing influence of unchecked passion. His characters are a commentary on the truth that there is no tyranny in the world like that which thoughts of evil exercise in the daring and reckless breast.

Another reflection springing from the narrative is, that temper is often spoiled in the years of childhood. "The child is the father of the man."[9] The pains and crosses of its youthful years are engrafted in its blood, and form a sullen and a violent disposition. Grooms know how often the tempers of horses are irremediably spoiled in training. But some parents are less wise regarding their children. The intellect in its growth has the faculty of accommodating itself to adverse circumstances. To violence it sometimes opposes violence, sometimes dogged obstinacy. The consequence in either case is fatal to the tranquility of life. Young Catherine Linton is represented as a naturally sensitive, high-spirited girl; subjected to the

9. The line is from Wordsworth, first in "My heart leaps up"; reappearing as the first line of the epigraph in "Ode: Intimations of Immortality from Recollections of Early Childhood."

cruel usage of her brutal stepfather, she is roused to resistance, and answers his curses with taunts, and his stripes with threatenings. Released from his tyranny, a more gracious spirit comes over her, and she is gentle and peaceful.

There are some fine passages scattered through the pages. Here is a thought on the tranquility of death:—

"I don't know if it be a peculiarity in me, but I am seldom otherwise than happy while watching in the chamber of death, should no frenzied or despairing mourner share the duty with me. I see a repose that neither earth nor hell can break, and I feel an assurance of the endless and shadowless hereafter—the eternity they have entered—where life is boundless in its duration, and love in its sympathy, and joy in its fulness."

Of Joseph, the old sullen servant of Heathcliff, it is quaintly said that he was "the sourest-hearted pharisee that ever searched a Bible to rake all the blessings to himself and fling all the curses to his neighbours."

The third volume of the book is made up of a separate tale[1] relating to the fortunes of a governess. Some characters and scenes are nicely sketched in it, but it has nothing to call for special notice. The volumes abound in provincialisms. In many respects they remind us of the recent novel of *Jane Eyre*. We presume they proceed from one family, if not from one pen.

The tale to which we have more particularly alluded is but a fragment, yet of colossal proportion, and bearing evidence of some great design.

With all its power and originality, it is so rude, so unfinished, and so careless, that we are perplexed to pronounce an opinion on it, or to hazard a conjecture on the future career of the author. As yet it belongs to the future to decide whether he will remain a rough hewer of marble or become a great and noble sculptor.

Unidentified Review

This is a work of great ability, and contains many chapters, to the production of which talent of no common order has contributed. At the same time, the materials which the author has placed at his own disposal have been but few. In the resources of his own mind, and in his own manifestly vivid perceptions of the peculiarities of character—in short, in his knowledge of human nature—has he found them all. An antiquated farm-house, and a neighbouring residence of a somewhat more pretending description, to-

1. *Agnes Grey*.

gether with their respective inmates, amounting to some half a dozen souls in each, constitute the material and the personal components of one of the most interesting stories we have read for many a long day. The comfortable cheerfulness of the one abode, and the cheerless discomfort of the other—the latter being less the result of a cold and bleak situation, old and damp rooms, and (if we may use the term) of a sort of "haunted house" appearance, than of the strange and mysterious character of its inhabitants—the loves and marriages, separations and hatreds, hopes and disappointments, of two or three generations of the gentle occupants of the one establishment, and the ruder tenants of the other, are brought before us at one moment with a tenderness, at another with a fearfulness, which appeals to our sympathies with the truest tones of the voice of nature; and it is quite impossible to read the book—and this is no slight testimony to the merits of a work of the kind—without feeling that, if placed in the same position as any one of the characters in any page of it, the chances would be twenty to one in favour of our conduct in that position being precisely such as the author has assigned to the personages he has introduced into his domestic drama. But we must at once impose upon ourselves a task—and we confess it is a hard one—we must abstain (from a regard to the space at our disposal) from yielding to the temptation by which we are beset to enter into that minute description of the plot of this very dramatic production to which such a work has an undoubted claim. It is not every day that so good a novel makes its appearance; and to give its contents in detail would be depriving many a reader of half the delight he would experience from the perusal of the work itself. To its pages we must refer him, then; there will he have ample opportunity of sympathising—if he has one touch of nature that "makes the whole world kin"—with the feelings of childhood, youth, manhood, and age, and all the emotions and passions which agitate the restless bosom of humanity. May he derive from it the delight we have ourselves experienced, and be equally grateful to its author for the genuine pleasure he has afforded him.

New Monthly Magazine

January 1848

WUTHERING HEIGHTS

Ellis Bell and Acton Bell appear in the light of two names borrowed to represent two totally different styles of composition and two utterly opposed modes of treatment of the novel, rather than to indicate two real personages.

They are names coupled together as mysteriously in the literary, as the sons of Leda[2] are in the asterial world; and there is something at least gained by being mysterious at starting. "Wuthering Heights," by Ellis Bell, is a terrific story, associated with an equally fearful and repulsive spot. It should have been called *Withering* Heights, for any thing from which the mind and body would more instinctively shrink, than the mansion and its tenants, cannot be easily imagined. "Wuthering," however, as expressive in provincial phraseology of "the frequency of atmospheric tumults out of doors" must do, however much the said tumults may be surpassed in frequency and violence by the disturbances that occur in doors. Our novel reading experience does not enable us to refer to any thing to be compared with the personages we are introduced to at this desolate spot—a perfect misanthropist's heaven.

Palladium†

September 1850

[SYDNEY DOBELL]

* * * Who is Currer Bell? is a question which has been variously answered, and has lately, we believe, received in well-informed quarters, a satisfactory reply. A year or two ago, we mentally solved the problem thus: Currer Bell is a woman. Every word she utters is female. Not feminine, but female. There is a sex about it which cannot be mistaken, even in its manliest attire. Though she translated the manuscript of angels—every thought neutral and every feeling cryptogamous—her *voice* would betray her.

* * * For her most perfect work the world is still waiting, and will be content for some years to wait; and placing in an assumed order of production (though not of publication) the novels called *Wuthering Heights*, *Wildfell Hall*, *Jane Eyre* and *Shirley*, as the works of one author under sundry disguises, we should have deemed, a few days since, that an analysis of the first (and, by our

2. Castor and Pollux were the twin sons of Leda and Zeus, and they compose the constellation Gemini. The mystery of their "asterial" coupling may refer to Castor also being known as the phenomenon of "corposant" (St. Elmo's fire), and when two such balls of fire were in conjunction, they were thought to portend the end of a storm.

† An extract from an essay entitled "Currer Bell," reprinted from *The Life and Letters of Sydney Dobell*, ed. Jolly (London, 2 vols. 1878), I.165–71. It originally appeared in the *Palladium* for September 1850.

theory, the earliest) of these was the amplest justice she could at present receive. Opening, however, the third edition of *Jane Eyre*, published before the appearance of *Shirley*, we find a preface in which all other works are disclaimed. A *nom de guerrist*[3] has many privileges, and we are willing to put down to a *double entendre* all that is serious in this disclaimer. That any hand but that which shaped *Jane Eyre* and *Shirley* cut out the rougher earlier statues, we should require more than the evidence of our senses to believe. That the author of *Jane Eyre* need fear nothing in acknowledging these yet more immature creations of one of the most vigorous of modern idiosyncrasies, we think we shall shortly demonstrate.

Laying aside *Wildfell Hall*, we open *Wuthering Heights*, as at once the earlier in date and ruder in execution. We look upon it as the flight of an impatient fancy fluttering in the very exultation of young wings; sometimes beating against its solitary bars, but turning, rather to exhaust, in a circumscribed space, the energy and agility which it may not yet spend in the heavens—a youthful story, written for oneself in solitude, and thrown aside till other successes recall the eyes to it in hope. In this thought let the critic take up the book; lay it down in what thought he will, there are some things in it he can lay down no more.

That Catherine Earnshaw—at once so wonderfully fresh, so fearfully natural—new, 'as if brought from other spheres,' and familiar as the recollection of some woeful experience—what can surpass the strange compatibility of her simultaneous loves; the involuntary art with which her two natures are so made to co-exist, that in the very arms of her lover we dare not doubt her purity; the inevitable belief with which we watch the oscillations of the old and new elements in her mind, and the exquisite truth of the last victory of nature over education, when the past returns to her as a flood, sweeping every modern landmark from within her, and the soul of the child, expanding, fills the woman?

Found at last, by her husband, insensible on the breast of her lover, and dying of the agony of their parting, one looks back upon her, like that husband, without one thought of accusation or absolution; her memory is chaste as the loyalty of love, pure as the air of the Heights on which she dwelt.

Heathcliff *might* have been as unique a creation. The conception in his case was as wonderfully strong and original, but he is spoilt in detail. The authoress has too often disgusted, where she should have terrified, and has allowed us a familiarity with her fiend which had ended in unequivocal contempt. If *Wuthering Heights* had been written as lately as *Jane Eyre*, the figure of Heathcliff, symmetrised

3. Person using a pseudonym.

and elevated, might have been one of the most natural and most striking portraits in the gallery of fiction.

Not a subordinate place or person in this novel but bears more or less the stamp of high genius. Ellen Dean is the ideal of the peasant playmate and servant of 'the family.' The substratum in which her mind moves is finely preserved. Joseph, as a specimen of the sixty years' servitor of 'the house,' is worthy a museum case. We feel that if Catherine Earnshaw bore her husband a child, it must be that Cathy Linton, and no other. The very Jane Eyre, of quiet satire, peeps out in such a paragraph as this:—'He told me to put on my cloak, and run to Gimmerton for the doctor and the parson. I went through wind and rain, and brought one, the doctor, back with me: the other said, *he would come in the morning*.' What terrible truth, what nicety of touch, what 'uncanny' capacity for mental aberration in the first symptoms of Catherine's delirium. 'I'm not wandering; you're mistaken, or else I should believe you really *were* that withered hag, and I should think I *was* under Penistone Crags: and I'm conscious it's night, and there are two candles on the table making the black press shine like jet.' What an unobtrusive, unexpected sense of *keeping*[4] in the hanging of Isabella's dog.

The book abounds in such things. But one looks back at the whole story as to a world of brilliant figures in an atmosphere of mist; shapes that come out upon the eye, and burn their colours into the brain, and depart into the enveloping fog. It is the unformed writing of a giant's hand: the 'large utterance' of a baby god. In the sprawling of the infant Hercules, however, there must have been attitudes from which the statuary might model. In the early efforts of unusual genius, there are not seldom unconscious felicities which maturer years may look back upon with envy. The child's hand wanders over the strings. It cannot combine them in the chords and melodies of manhood; but its separate notes are perfect in themselves, and perhaps sound all the sweeter for the Æolian discords from which they come.

We repeat, that there are passages in this book of *Wuthering Heights* of which any novelist, past or present, might be proud. Open the first volume at the fourteenth page, and read to the sixty-first. There are few things in modern prose to surpass these pages for native power. We cannot praise too warmly the brave simplicity, the unaffected air of intense belief, the admirable combination of extreme likelihood with the rarest originality, the nice provision of the possible even in the highest effects of the supernatural, the easy strength and instinct of keeping with which the accessory circum-

4. "Proper subserviency of tone and colour in every part of a picture, so that the general effect is harmonious to the eye." *OED*.

stances are grouped, the exquisite but unconscious art with which the chiaroscuro of the whole is managed, and the ungenial frigidity of place, time, weather, and persons, is made to heighten the unspeakable pathos of one ungovernable outburst.

The *thinking out* of some of these pages * * * is the masterpiece of a poet, rather than the hybrid creation of the novelist. The mass of readers will probably yawn over the whole; but, in the memory of those whose remembrance makes *fame*, the images in these pages will live—when every word that conveyed them is forgotten—as a recollection of *things heard and seen*. This is the highest triumph of description; and perhaps every creation of the fancy is more or less faulty, so long as, in a mind fitted to reproduce them, the images co-exist only with the words that called them up. The spiritual structure is not complete till the scaffolding can be safely struck away. That which thou sowest is not quickened except it die. This mortal must put on the immortality of the mind. Ideas should be permanent, words evanescent. Whoever has watched a trowel in the hands of a skillful mason, has seen an example of a very high excellence of authorship. The mortar is laid, but the trowel is already withdrawn. * * *

* * * We are at a loss to find anywhere in modern prose a less residuum from the fiery ordeal; or to discover, in the same space, such wealth and such economy, such apparent ease, such instinctive art. *Instinctive* art; for to the imaginative writer, all art that is not instinctive is dangerous. All art that is the application of principles, however astutely those principles be applied * * * smacks not of the artist, but the artisan. Let no man think to improve in his working by any knowledge that can be taken up or laid down at will, any means or appliances from without. All improvement in the creation must first exist in the creator. Say not to the artist, write, paint, play, by such and such a rule, but *grow* by it. Have you literary principles?—write them in your leisure hours on the fleshly tables of the heart. Have you theories of taste?—set your brain in idle time to their tune. Is there a virtue you would emulate, or a fault you would discard?—gaze on spare days upon the one till your soul has risen under it as the tide under the moon, or scourge the other in the sight of all your faculties till every internal sense recoils from its company. Then, when your error is no longer a trespass to be condemned by judgment, but an impiety at which feeling revolts—when your virtue is no more obedience to a formula, but the natural action of a reconstructed soul—strike off the clay mould from the bronze Apollo, throw your critics to one wind and their sermons to the other, let Self be made absolute as you take up your pen and write, like a god, in a sublime egotism, to which your own likes and dislikes are unquestioned law. * * * What is true of the

poet, the creator, the intellectual viceregent of God, is true, in different degrees, of all who in any grade share the creative spirit—of every one of the apostlehood and priesthood through whom genius evangelises, sanctifies, and regenerates the world. And the higher in the scale, the more imperative is the duty of autocracy, and the more fatal any 'tempering of the iron with the clay.'

These truths supply us with the great secret of success and failure in the works of Currer Bell; and there is no admission we could make which could be a higher testimony to her powers as a creative artist. If this authoress had *published* any novel before *Jane Eyre*, *Jane Eyre* would not have been the moral wonder which it is, and will for many years remain. If *Jane Eyre* had met with a less triumphant *furore* of review, *Shirley* would have been a worthier successor.

To say that an artist is *spoilt* by criticism, is to disprove his right to the title; to say that he is, for the present, maimed and disabled by it, may be to bear the highest witness to his intrinsic genius—and this witness we bear to Currer Bell. When Currer Bell writes her next novel, let her remember, as far as possible, the frame of mind in which she sat down to her first. She cannot now commit the faults of that early effort; it will be well for her if she be still capable of the virtues. She will never sin so much against consistent keeping as to draw another Heathcliff; she is too much *au fait* of her profession to make again those sacrifices to machinery which deprive her early picture of any claim to be ranked as a work of art. Happy she, if her next book demonstrate the unimpaired possession of those powers of insight, that instinctive obedience to the nature within her, and those occurrences of infallible inspiration which astound the critic in the young author of *Wuthering Heights*. She will not let her next dark-haired hero babble away the respect of her reader and the awe of his antecedents; nor will she find another housekeeper who remembers two volumes *literatim*. Let her rejoice if she can again give us such an elaboration of a rare and fearful form of mental disease—so terribly strong, so exquisitely subtle—with such nicety in its transitions, such intimate symptomatic truth in its details, as to be at once a psychological and medical study. It has been said of Shakespeare, that he drew cases which the physician might study; Currer Bell has done no less. She will not, again, employ her wonderful pencil on a picture so destitute of moral beauty and human worth. Let her exult, if she can still invest such a picture with such interest. We stand painfully before her portraits; but our eyes are drawn towards them by the irresistible ties of blood relationship. Let her exult, if she can still make us weep with the simple pathos of that fading face, which looked from the golden crocuses on her pillow to the hills which concealed the old home and the churchyard of Gimmerton. 'These are the earliest flowers at the Heights,' she exclaimed. 'They remind me of thaw-winds, and warm sunshine, and nearly-melted snow. Edgar, is there not a south wind, and is not the snow almost gone?'—'The snow is quite gone down here, darling,' replied her husband; 'and I only see two white spots on the whole range of moors. The sky is blue, and the larks are singing, and the becks and brooks are all brimful. Catherine, last spring, at this time, I was longing to have you under this roof; now, I wish you were a mile or two up those hills: the air blows so sweetly, I feel that it would cure you.'—'I shall never be there but once more,' said the invalid, 'and then you'll leave me, and I shall remain for ever. Next spring, you'll long again to have me under this roof, and you'll look back, and think you were happy to-day.'

Let Currer Bell prize the young intuition of character which dictated Cathy's speech to Ellen. There is a deep, unconscious philosophy in it. There are minds whose crimes and sorrows are not so much the result of intrinsic evil as of a false position in the scheme of things, which clashes their energies with the arrangements of surrounding life. It is difficult to cure such a soul from *within*. The point of view, not the eye or the landscape, is in fault. Move *that*, and as at the changing of a stop, the mental machine assumes its proper relative place, and the powers of discord become, in the same measure, the instruments of harmony. It was a fine instinct which saw this. Let Currer Bell be passing glad if it is as vigorous now as then; and let her thank God if she can now draw the apparition of the 'Wanderer of the Moor.'

North American Review

October 1848

"NOVELS OF THE SEASON"

[E. P. WHIPPLE][5]

There was a time when the appearance of a clever novel would justify its separate examination in a Review. * * * But in this age

5. In this unsigned review of American editions of eight English novels, Whipple includes *Jane Eyre, an Autobiography*. Edited by Currer Bell. Boston: Wilkins, Carter, & Co. 1848; *Wuthering Heights*. By the Author of *Jane Eyre*. New York: Harper & Brothers. 1848; *The Tenant of Wildfell Hall*. By Acton Bell, Author of *Wuthering Heights*. This misattribution of authorship may reflect the efforts of Emily's and Anne's publisher, Thomas Newby, to benefit from the success of *Jane Eyre*, which Smith, Elder had published in London shortly before the first British edition of her sisters' novels. See Charlotte Brontë's comments on this review, p. 309.

of ready writers, romances must be reviewed in battalions, or allowed to pass unchallenged. Every week beholds a new irruption of emigrants into the sunny land of fiction, sadly disturbing the old balance of power, and introducing a fearful confusion of names and habits.* * * Another evil is the comparative absence of individualities, amid all the increase of population. Opinions have nearly supplanted characters. We look for men, and discern propositions, —for women, and are favored with woman's rights. Theologians, metaphysicians, politicians, reformers, philanthropists, prophets of the general overturn and the good time coming, the march-of-intellect boys in a solid phalanx, have nearly pushed the novelist aside. The dear old nonsense, which has delighted the heart for so many centuries, is so mixed up with nonsense of another kind, that it cannot be recognized either in drawing-room or kitchen. The sacred flame still burns in some sixpenny or ninepenny novellettes, the horror of the polite and the last hope of the sentimental; but it burns in a battered copper lamp, and among ruins.

Accordingly, in the novels whose titles grace the head of the present article, our readers must not expect to find, in its full perfection, that peculiar aspect of human weakness of which the novelist is the legitimate exponent. They must be content with a repast of matters and things in general, among which may be named some good philosophy, several dishes of controversial theology, much spicy satire, a little passable morality, a little impertinent immorality, and a good deal of the philosophy of history and the science of the affections.

The first three novels on our list are those which have proceeded from the firm of Bell & Co. Not many months ago, the New England States were visited by a distressing mental epidemic, passing under the name of the "Jane Eyre fever," which defied all the usual nostrums of the established doctors of criticism. Its effects varied with different constitutions, in some producing a soft ethical sentimentality, which relaxed all the fibres of conscience, and in others exciting a general fever of moral and religious indignation. It was to no purpose that the public were solemnly assured, through the intelligent press, that the malady was not likely to have any permanent effect either on the intellectual or moral constitution. The book which caused the distemper would probably have been inoffensive, had not some sly manufacturer of mischief hinted that it was a book which no respectable man should bring into his family circle. Of course, every family soon had a copy of it, and one edition after another found eager purchasers. The hero, Mr. Rochester * * * became a great favorite in the boarding-schools and in the worshipful society of governesses. That portion of Young America known as ladies' men began to swagger and swear in the presence of the gentler sex, and to allude darkly to events in their lives which excused impudence and profanity.

While fathers and mothers were much distressed at this strange conduct of their innocents, and with a pardonable despair were looking for the dissolution of all the bonds of society, the publishers of Jane Eyre announced Wuthering Heights, by the same author. When it came, it was purchased and read with universal eagerness; but, alas! it created disappointment almost as universal. It was a panacea for all the sufferers under the epidemic. Society returned to its old condition, parents were blessed in hearing once more their children talk common sense, and rakes and battered profligates of high and low degree fell instantly to their proper level. Thus ended the last desperate attempt to corrupt the virtue of the sturdy descendants of the Puritans.

The novel of Jane Eyre, which caused this great excitement, purports to have been edited by Currer Bell, and the said Currer divides the authorship, if we are not misinformed, with a brother and sister. The work bears the marks of more than one mind and one sex, and has more variety than either of the novels which claim to have been written by Acton Bell. The family mind is strikingly peculiar, giving a strong impression of unity, but it is still male and female. From the masculine tone of Jane Eyre, it might pass altogether as the composition of a man, were it not for some unconscious feminine peculiarities, which the strongest-minded woman that ever aspired after manhood cannot suppress. * * * There are also scenes of passion, so hot, emphatic, and condensed in expression, and so sternly masculine in feeling, that we are almost sure we observe the mind of the author of Wuthering Heights at work in the text. * * * The truth is, that the whole firm of Bell & Co. seem to have a sense of the depravity of human nature peculiarly their own. It is the yahoo, not the demon, that they select for representation; their Pandemonium is of mud rather than fire.

This is especially the case with Acton Bell, the author of Wuthering Heights, The Tenant of Wildfell Hall, and, if we mistake not, of certain offensive but powerful portions of Jane Eyre. Acton, when left altogether to his own imaginations, seems to take a morose satisfaction in developing a full and complete science of human brutality. In Wuthering Heights he has succeeded in reaching the summit of this laudable ambition. He appears to think that spiritual wickedness is a combination of animal ferocities, and has accordingly made a compendium of the most striking qualities of tiger, wolf, cur, and wild-cat, in the hope of framing out of such elements a suitable brute-demon to serve as the hero of his novel. Compared with Heathcote [*sic*], Squeers is considerate and Quilp humane.[6] He is a deformed monster, whom the Mephistopheles of Goethe would have nothing to say to, whom the Satan of Milton would consider as an object of simple disgust, and to whom Dante would hesitate in awarding the honor of a place among those whom he has consigned to the burning pitch. This epitome of brutality, disavowed by man and devil, Mr. Acton Bell attempts in two whole volumes to delineate, and certainly he is to be congratulated on his success. As he is a man of uncommon talents, it is needless to say that it is to his subject and his dogged manner of handling it that we are to refer the burst of dislike with which the novel was received. His mode of delineating a bad character is to narrate every offensive act and repeat every vile expression which are characteristic. Hence, in Wuthering Heights, he details all the ingenuities of animal malignity, and exhausts the whole rhetoric of stupid blasphemy, in order that there may be no mistake as to the kind of person he intends to hold up to the popular gaze. Like all spendthrifts of malice and profanity, however, he overdoes the business. Though he scatters oaths as plentifully as sentimental writers do interjections, the comparative parsimony of the great novelists in this respect is productive of infinitely more effect. It must be confessed that this coarseness, though the prominent, is not the only characteristic of the writer. His attempt at originality does not stop with the conception of Heathcote, but he aims further to exhibit the action of the sentiment of love on the nature of the being whom his morbid imagination has created. This is by far the ablest and most subtile portion of his labors, and indicates that strong hold upon the elements of character, and that decision of touch in the delineation of the most evanescent qualities of emotion, which distinguish the mind of the whole family. For all practical purposes, however, the power evinced in Wuthering Heights is power thrown away. Nightmares and dreams, through which devils dance and wolves howl, make bad novels.

6. Wackford Squeers, the brutal boarding school master in Dickens's *Nicholas Nickleby*; Daniel Quilp, the diabolical dwarf in Dickens's *The Old Curiosity Shop*.

WUTHERING HEIGHTS

AND

AGNES GREY.

BY

ELLIS AND ACTON BELL.

A NEW EDITION REVISED, WITH

A BIOGRAPHICAL NOTICE OF THE AUTHORS,
A SELECTION FROM THEIR LITERARY REMAINS,
AND A PREFACE,

BY CURRER BELL.

LONDON:
SMITH, ELDER AND CO., 65, CORNHILL.

1850.

The 1850 *Wuthering Heights*

After the success of *Jane Eyre*, Charlotte Brontë urged her sisters to offer their future work to Smith, Elder and Company, her publisher, rather than to continue with the unscrupulous T. C. Newby. However, by mid-February 1848, Newby had obtained agreements from both Emily and Anne for their next novels. No manuscript of a second novel by Emily has survived, but Newby did publish Anne's *The Tenant of Wildfell Hall* later that year. Meanwhile, the sisters chose Smith, Elder for republication of *Poems by Acton, Currer, and Ellis Bell* in 1848. Emily died in December 1848 and Anne the following May.

Charlotte's publisher suggested a reprint of *Wuthering Heights* and *Agnes Grey*, "with a prefatory and explanatory notice of the authors." Spurred no doubt by the coincident appearance in September 1850 of Sydney Dobell's favorable comments about *Wuthering Heights*, Charlotte welcomed the opportunity to "prepare a Preface comprising a brief and simple notice of the authors—such as might set at rest all erroneous conjectures concerning their identity—and adding a few poetical remains of each."[1] She expressed concern that Newby might claim rights to these works, noting that after promising 350 copies he had printed only 250. Thus her conclusion "from the whole of Mr. Newby's conduct to my sisters—was that he is a man with whom it is desirable to have little to do: I think he must be needy as well as tricky—and if he is, one would not distress him, even for one's rights."[2] Smith, Elder determined that Newby had no copyright interest and proceeded with the new edition. In December 1850 she sent Dobell a copy of the new edition, thanking him for "the noble justice" of his remarks about Emily, and asking him to let her know whether the new introduction left any lingering doubts "respecting the authorship of *Wuthering Heights*."[3] Her 1850 biographical notice was the first public statement by a Brontë "to explain briefly the origin and authorship of the books written by Currer, Ellis, and Acton Bell."

Charlotte's judgments of *Wuthering Heights*, both in the "Biographical Notice" and her "Editor's Preface" to the new edition, echo earlier comments in letters and respond directly to the reviewers' failures to recognize the "very real powers revealed in *Wuthering*

1. Margaret Smith, ed., *The Letters of Charlotte Brontë*, vol. II (Oxford: Clarendon Press, 2000) 465. All citations from these letters are reprinted by permission of the editor and Clarendon Press.
2. *Letters*, p. 465.
3. *Letters*, p. 526.

Heights" or to understand "its import and nature." Rereading the novel for the first time after her sister's death produced a mixed reaction by Charlotte: "Its power fills me with renewed admiration—but yet I am oppressed—the reader scarcely ever permitted a taste of unalloyed pleasure—every beam of sunshine is poured down through black bars of threatening cloud—every page is surcharged with a sort of moral electricity; and the writer was unconscious of this—nothing could make her conscious of it. And this makes me reflect—perhaps I too am incapable of perceiving the faults and peculiarities of my own style."[4]

The 1850 *Wuthering Heights* in Progress

To W. S. Williams, 5 September 1850[1]

I should much like to carry out your suggestion respecting a reprint of "Wuthering Heights" and "Agnes Grey" in 1 vol. With a prefatory and explanatory notice of the authors—but the question occurs—would Newby claim it? I could not bear to commit it to any other hands than those of Mr. Smith. * * *

To James Taylor, 5 September 1850

The article in the "Palladium" is one of those notices over which an author rejoices with trembling. He rejoices to find his work finely, fully, fervently appreciated—and trembles under the responsibility such appreciation seems to devolve upon him. I am counselled to wait watch. D. V. I will do so. Yet it is harder work to wait with the hands bound and the observant and reflective faculties ⟨only⟩, at their silent unseen work, than to labour mechanically.

I need not say how I felt the remarks on "Wuthering Heights": they woke the saddest yet most grateful feelings; they are true, they are discriminating; they are full of late justice—but it is very late—alas! In one sense—too late. Of this, however, and of the pang of regret for a light prematurely extinguished—it is not wise to speak much. Whoever the author of this article may be—I remain his debtor.

To W. S. Williams, 13 September 1850

Mr. Newby undertook first to print 350 copies of "Wuthering Heights", but he afterwards declared he had only printed 250.

4. *Letters*, p. 479.

1. This and the following excerpts are from Margaret Smith, ed., *The Letters of Charlotte Brontë*, vol. II (Oxford: Clarendon Press, 2000). Reprinted by permission of the editor and Clarendon Press.

I doubt whether he could be induced to return the £50 without a good deal of trouble—much more than I should feel justified in delegating to Mr. Smith. For my own part, the conclusion I drew from the whole of Mr. Newby's conduct to my sisters—was that he is a man with whom it is desirable to have little to do; I think he must be needy as well as tricky—and if he is, one would not distress him, even for one's rights.

If Mr. Smith thinks proper to reprint "Wuthering Heights & Agnes Grey", I would prepare a Preface comprising a brief and simple notice of the authors—such as might set at rest all erroneous conjectures respecting their identity—and adding a few poetical remains of each

In case this arrangement is approved—you will kindly let me know—and I will commence the task—(a sad but, I believe—a necessary one)—and send it when finished

To W. S. Williams, 20 September 1850

I herewith send you a very roughly written copy of what I have to say about my sisters. When you have read it, you can better judge whether the word "Notice" or "Memoir" is the most appropriate. I think—the former. Memoir seems to me to express a more circumstantial and different sort of account. My aim is to give a just idea of their identity, not to write any narrative of their simple, uneventful lives. I depend on you for faithfully pointing out whatever may strike you as faulty. I could not write it in the conventional form—that I found impossible.

To W. S. Williams, 27 September 1850

It is my intention to write a few lines of remark on "W. Heights" which however I proposed to place apart as a brief preface before the tale—I am likewise compelling myself to read it over for the first time of opening the book since my sister's death. Its power fills me with renewed admiration—but yet I am oppressed—the reader is scarcely ever permitted a taste of unalloyed pleasure—every beam of sunshine is poured down through black bars of threatening cloud—every page is surcharged with a sort of moral electricity; and the writer was unconscious of all this—nothing could make her conscious of it. And this makes me reflect—perhaps I too am incapable of perceiving the faults and peculiarities of my own style.

I should wish to revise the proofs, if it be not too great an inconvenience to send them. It seems to me advisable to modify the orthography of the old servant Joseph's speeches—for though—as it stands—it exactly renders the Yorkshire accent to a Yorkshire ear—yet I am sure Southerns must find it unintelligible—and thus one of the most graphic characters in the book is lost on them.

What the probable quantity of new matter will be, I cannot say exactly—but I think it will not exceed ⟨30 or⟩ thirty or, at the most forty pages—since it is so inconsiderable, would it not be better to place the title thus

Wuthering Heights & Agnes Grey by
E & A Bell
With a Notice of the Authors by Currer Bell
and a Selection from their literary Remains?

I only suggest this—if there are reasons ⟨for⟩ rendering the other title preferable—adopt it.

I will prepare and send some extracts from reviews.

I grieve to say that I possess no portrait of either of my sisters. Believe me

To W. S. Williams, [*?c.19 November 1850*]

I have to thank you for the care and kindness with which you have assisted me throughout in correcting these "Remains."

Whether—when they are published—they will appear to others as they do to me—I cannot tell—I hope not—and indeed I suppose what to me is bitter pain will only be soft pathos to the general reader.

To Sydney Dobell, 8 December 1850

I offer this little book[2] to my critic in the "Palladium", and he must believe it accompanied by a tribute of the sincerest gratitude, not so much for anything he has said of myself, as for the noble justice he has rendered to one dear to me as myself—perhaps dearer, and perhaps one kind word spoken for her awakens a deeper, tenderer sentiment of thankfulness than eulogies heaped on my own head.

As you will see when you have read the biographical notice, my sister cannot thank you herself; she is gone out of your sphere and mine, and human blame and praise are nothing to her now; but to me—for her sake—they are something still; it revived me for many a day to find that ⟨the⟩ dead as she was—the work of her genius had at last met with worthy appreciation.

Tell me—when you have read the introduction, whether any doubts still linger in your mind respecting the authorship of "Wuthering Heights," "Wildfell Hall" &c. Your mistrust did me some in-

2. The 1850 *Wuthering Heights* was published on December 7.

justice; it proved a general conception of character such as I should be sorry to call mine—but these false ideas will naturally arise when we only judge an author from his works. In fairness, I must also disclaim the flattering side of the portrait: I am no "young 'Penthesilea mediis in millibus' ",[3] but a plain country parson's daughter.

[CHARLOTTE BRONTË]

Biographical Notice of Ellis and Acton Bell (1850)

It has been thought that all the works published under the names of Currer, Ellis, and Acton Bell, were, in reality, the production of one person. This mistake I endeavoured to rectify by a few words of disclaimer prefixed to the third edition of *Jane Eyre*. These, too, it appears, failed to gain general credence, and now, on the occasion of a reprint of *Wuthering Heights* and *Agnes Grey*, I am advised distinctly to state how the case really stands.

Indeed, I feel myself that it is time the obscurity attending those two names—Ellis and Acton—was done away. The little mystery, which formerly yielded some harmless pleasure, has lost its interest; circumstances are changed. It becomes, then, my duty to explain briefly the origin and authorship of the books written by Currer, Ellis, and Acton Bell.

About five years ago, my two sisters and myself, after a somewhat prolonged period of separation, found ourselves reunited, and at home. Resident in a remote district where education had made little progress, and where, consequently, there was no inducement to seek social intercourse beyond our own domestic circle, we were wholly dependent on ourselves and each other, on books and study, for the enjoyments and occupations of life. The highest stimulus, as well as the liveliest pleasure we had known from childhood upwards, lay in attempts at literary composition; formerly we used to show each other what we wrote, but of late years this habit of communication and consultation had been discontinued: hence it ensued, that we were mutually ignorant of the progress we might respectively have made.

One day, in the autumn of 1845, I accidentally lighted on a MS. volume of verse in my sister Emily's handwriting. Of course, I was not surprised, knowing that she could and did write verse: I looked it over, and something more than surprise seized me,—a deep conviction that these were not common effusions, nor at all like the

3. A reference to a depiction of a queen of the Amazons (one in the midst of thousands) in *Aeneid*, 1.491.

poetry women generally write. I thought them condensed and terse, vigorous and genuine. To my ear, they had also a peculiar music—wild, melancholy, and elevating.

My sister Emily was not a person of demonstrative character, nor one, on the recesses of whose mind and feelings, even those nearest and dearest to her could, with impunity, intrude unlicensed; it took hours to reconcile her to the discovery I had made, and days to persuade her that such poems merited publication. I knew, however, that a mind like hers could not be without some latent spark of honourable ambition, and refused to be discouraged in my attempts to fan that spark to flame.

Meantime, my younger sister quietly produced some of her own compositions, intimating that since Emily's had given me pleasure, I might like to look at hers. I could not but be a partial judge, yet I thought that these verses too had a sweet sincere pathos of their own.

We had very early cherished the dream of one day becoming authors. This dream, never relinquished even when distance divided and absorbing tasks occupied us, now suddenly acquired strength and consistency: it took the character of a resolve. We agreed to arrange a small selection of our poems, and, if possible, get them printed. Averse to personal publicity, we veiled our own names under those of Currer, Ellis, and Acton Bell; the ambiguous choice being dictated by a sort of conscientious scruple at assuming Christian names, positively masculine, while we did not like to declare ourselves women, because—without at that time suspecting that our mode of writing and thinking was not what is called "feminine"—we had a vague impression that authoresses are liable to be looked on with prejudice; we had noticed how critics sometimes use for their chastisement the weapon of personality, and for their reward, a flattery, which is not true praise.

The bringing out of our little book was hard work. As was to be expected, neither we nor our poems were at all wanted; but for this we had been prepared at the outset; though inexperienced ourselves, we had read the experience of others. The great puzzle lay in the difficulty of getting answers of any kind from the publishers to whom we applied. Being greatly harassed by this obstacle, I ventured to apply to the Messrs. Chambers, of Edinburgh, for a word of advice; *they* may have forgotten the circumstance, but *I* have not, for from them I received a brief and business-like but civil and sensible reply, on which we acted, and at last made a way.

The book was printed: it is scarcely known, and all of it that merits to be known are the poems of Ellis Bell. The fixed conviction I held, and hold, of the worth of these poems has not indeed received the confirmation of much favourable criticism; but I must retain it notwithstanding.

Ill-success failed to crush us: the mere effort to succeed had given a wonderful zest to existence; it must be pursued. We each set to work on a prose tale: Ellis Bell produced *Wuthering Heights*. Acton Bell *Agnes Grey*, and Currer Bell also wrote a narrative in one volume. These MSS. were perseveringly obtruded upon various publishers for the space of a year and a half; usually, their fate was an ignominious and abrupt dismissal.

At last *Wuthering Heights* and *Agnes Grey* were accepted on terms somewhat impoverishing to the two authors: Currer Bell's book found acceptance nowhere, nor any acknowledgment of merit, so that something like the chill of despair began to invade his heart. As a forlorn hope, he tried one publishing house more—Messrs. Smith and Elder. Ere long, in a much shorter space than that on which experience had taught him to calculate—there came a letter, which he opened in the dreary expectation of finding two hard hopeless lines, intimating that Messrs. Smith and Elder "were not disposed to publish the MS." and, instead, he took out of the envelope a letter of two pages. He read it trembling. It declined, indeed, to publish that tale, for business reasons, but it discussed its merits and demerits so courteously, so considerately, in a spirit so rational, with a discrimination so enlightened, that this very refusal cheered the author better than a vulgarly-expressed acceptance would have done. It was added, that a work in three volumes would meet with careful attention.

I was then just completing *Jane Eyre*, at which I had been working while the one volume tale was plodding its weary round in London: in three weeks I sent it off; friendly and skilful hands took it in. This was in the commencement of September 1847; it came out before the close of October following, while *Wuthering Heights* and *Agnes Grey*, my sisters' works, which had already been in the press for months, still lingered under a different management.[1]

They appeared at last. Critics failed to do them justice. The immature but very real powers revealed in *Wuthering Heights* were scarcely recognised; its import and nature were misunderstood; the identity of its author was misrepresented; it was said that this was an earlier and ruder attempt of the same pen which had produced *Jane Eyre*. Unjust and grievous error! We laughed at it at first, but I deeply lament it now. Hence, I fear, arose a prejudice against the book. That writer who could attempt to palm off an inferior and

1. *Jane Eyre* was published on October 19, 1847; *Wuthering Heights* and *Agnes Grey* were published during the week ending December 15, 1847.

immature production under cover of one successful effort, must indeed be unduly eager after the secondary and sordid result of authorship, and pitiably indifferent to its true and honourable meed. If reviewers and the public truly believed this, no wonder that they looked darkly on the cheat.

Yet I must not be understood to make these things subject for reproach or complaint; I dare not do so; respect for my sister's memory forbids me. By her any such querulous manifestation would have been regarded as an unworthy, and offensive weakness.

It is my duty, as well as my pleasure, to acknowledge one exception to the general rule of criticism. One writer,[2] endowed with the keen vision and fine sympathies of genius, has discerned the real nature of *Wuthering Heights*, and has, with equal accuracy, noted its beauties and touched on its faults. Too often do reviewers remind us of the mob of Astrologers, Chaldeans, and Soothsayers gathered before the "writing on the wall," and unable to read the characters or make known the interpretation. We have a right to rejoice when a true seer comes at last, some man in whom is an excellent spirit, to whom have been given light, wisdom, and understanding; who can accurately read the "Mene, Mene, Tekel, Upharsin"[3] of an original mind (however unripe, however inefficiently cultured and partially expanded that mind may be); and who can say with confidence, "This is the interpretation thereof."

Yet even the writer to whom I allude shares the mistake about the authorship, and does me the injustice to suppose that there was equivoque in my former rejection of this honour (as an honour, I regard it). May I assure him that I would scorn in this and in every other case to deal in equivoque; I believe language to have been given us to make our meaning clear, and not to wrap it in dishonest doubt.

The Tenant of Wildfell Hall by Acton Bell, had likewise an unfavourable reception. At this I cannot wonder. The choice of subject was an entire mistake. Nothing less congruous with the writer's nature could be conceived. The motives which dictated this choice were pure, but, I think, slightly morbid. She had, in the course of her life, been called on to contemplate, near at hand and for a long time, the terrible effects of talents misused and faculties abused; hers was naturally a sensitive, reserved, and dejected nature; what she saw sank very deeply into her mind; it did her harm. She brooded over it till she believed it to be a duty to reproduce every detail (of course with fictitious characters, incidents, and situations)

2. Sydney Dobell. See the *Palladium* for September 1850.
3. Figuratively, the writing on the wall; literally, in Daniel 5.25–28, the interpretation of these words ["numbered, numbered, weighed, divided"] foretold the doom of Belshazzar's kingdom.

as a warning to others. She hated her work, but would pursue it. When reasoned with on the subject, she regarded such reasonings as a temptation to self-indulgence. She must be honest; she must not varnish, soften, or conceal. This well-meant resolution brought on her misconstruction and some abuse, which she bore, as it was her custom to bear whatever was unpleasant, with mild, steady patience. She was a very sincere and practical Christian, but the tinge of religious melancholy communicated a sad shade to her brief, blameless life.

Neither Ellis nor Acton allowed herself for one moment to sink under want of encouragement; energy nerved the one, and endurance upheld the other. They were both prepared to try again; I would fain think that hope and the sense of power was yet strong within them. But a great change approached: affliction came in that shape which to anticipate is dread; to look back on, grief. In the very heat and burden of the day, the labourers failed over their work.

My sister Emily first declined. The details of her illness are deep-branded in my memory, but to dwell on them, either in thought or narrative, is not in my power. Never in all her life had she lingered over any task that lay before her, and she did not linger now. She sank rapidly. She made haste to leave us. Yet, while physically she perished, mentally, she grew stronger than we had yet known her. Day by day, when I saw with what a front she met suffering, I looked on her with an anguish of wonder and love. I have seen nothing like it; but, indeed, I have never seen her parallel in anything. Stronger than a man, simpler than a child, her nature stood alone. The awful point was, that, while full of ruth for others, on herself she had no pity; the spirit was inexorable to the flesh; from the trembling hand, the unnerved limbs, the faded eyes, the same service was exacted as they had rendered in health. To stand by and witness this, and not dare to remonstrate, was a pain no words can render.

Two cruel months of hope and fear passed painfully by, and the day came at last when the terrors and pains of death were to be undergone by this treasure, which had grown dearer and dearer to our hearts as it wasted before our eyes. Towards the decline of that day, we had nothing of Emily but her mortal remains as consumption left them. She died December 19, 1848.

We thought this enough; but we were utterly and presumptuously wrong. She was not buried ere Anne fell ill. She had not been committed to the grave a fortnight, before we received distinct intimation that it was necessary to prepare our minds to see the younger sister go after the elder. Accordingly, she followed in the same path with slower step, and with a patience that equalled the other's fortitude. I have said that she was religious, and it was by leaning on those Christian doctrines in which she firmly believed, that she found support through her most painful journey. I witnessed their efficacy in her latest hour and greatest trial, and must bear my testimony to the calm triumph with which they brought her through. She died May 28, 1849.

What more shall I say about them? I cannot and need not say much more. In externals, they were two unobtrusive women; a perfectly secluded life gave them retiring manners and habits. In Emily's nature the extremes of vigour and simplicity seemed to meet. Under an unsophisticated culture, inartificial tastes, and an unpretending outside, lay a secret power and fire that might have informed the brain and kindled the veins of a hero; but she had no worldly wisdom; her powers were unadapted to the practical business of life; she would fail to defend her most manifest rights, to consult her most legitimate advantage. An interpreter ought always to have stood between her and the world. Her will was not very flexible, and it generally opposed her interest. Her temper was magnanimous, but warm and sudden; her spirit altogether unbending.

Anne's character was milder and more subdued; she wanted the power, the fire, the originality of her sister, but was well-endowed with quiet virtues of her own. Long-suffering, self-denying, reflective, and intelligent, a constitutional reserve and taciturnity placed and kept her in the shade, and covered her mind, and especially her feelings, with a sort of nun-like veil, which was rarely lifted. Neither Emily nor Anne was learned; they had no thought of filling their pitchers at the well-spring of other minds; they always wrote from the impulse of nature, the dictates of intuition, and from such stores of observation as their limited experience had enabled them to amass. I may sum up all by saying, that for strangers they were nothing, for superficial observers less than nothing; but for those who had known them all their lives in the intimacy of close relationship, they were genuinely good and truly great.

This notice has been written, because I felt it a sacred duty to wipe the dust off their gravestones, and leave their dear names free from soil.

Currer Bell

September 19, 1850.

[CHARLOTTE BRONTË]

Editor's Preface to the New Edition of *Wuthering Heights* (1850)[1]

I have just read over "Wuthering Heights," and, for the first time, have obtained a clear glimpse of what are termed (and, perhaps, really are) its faults; have gained a definite notion of how it appears to other people—to strangers who knew nothing of the author; who are unacquainted with the locality where the scenes of the story are laid; to whom the inhabitants, the customs, the natural characteristics of the outlying hills and hamlets in the West-Riding of Yorkshire are things alien and unfamiliar.

To all such "Wuthering Heights" must appear a rude and strange production. The wild moors of the north of England can for them have no interest: the language, the manners, the very dwellings and household customs of the scattered inhabitants of those districts, must be to such readers in a great measure unintelligible, and—where intelligible—repulsive. Men and women who, perhaps, naturally very calm, and with feelings moderate in degree, and little marked in kind, have been trained from their cradle to observe the utmost evenness of manner and guardedness of language, will hardly know what to make of the rough, strong utterance, the harshly manifested passions, the unbridled aversions, and headlong partialities of unlettered moorland hinds and rugged moorland squires, who have grown up untaught and unchecked, except by mentors as harsh as themselves. A large class of readers, likewise, will suffer greatly from the introduction into the pages of this work of words printed with all their letters, which it has become the custom to represent by the initial and final letter only—a blank line filling the interval. I may as well say at once that, for this circumstance, it is out of my power to apologize; deeming it, myself, a rational plan to write words at full length. The practice of hinting by single letters those expletives with which profane and violent persons are wont to garnish their discourse, strikes me as a proceeding which, however well meant, is weak and futile. I cannot tell what good it does—what feeling it spares—what horror it conceals.

With regard to the rusticity of "Wuthering Heights," I admit the charge, for I feel the quality. It is rustic all through. It is moorish, and wild, and knotty as a root of heath. Nor was it natural that it

1. For a commentary on the lasting impact of this Preface on *Wuthering Heights* criticism, see J. Hillis Miller, p. 365.

should be otherwise; the author being herself a native and nursling of the moors. Doubtless, had her lot been cast in a town, her writings, if she had written at all, would have possessed another character. Even had chance or taste led her to choose a similar subject, she would have treated it otherwise. Had Ellis Bell been a lady or a gentleman accustomed to what is called "the world," her view of a remote and unreclaimed region, as well as of the dwellers therein, would have differed greatly from that actually taken by the home-bred country girl. Doubtless it would have been wider—more comprehensive: whether it would have been more original or more truthful is not so certain. As far as the scenery and locality are concerned, it could scarcely have been so sympathetic: Ellis Bell did not describe as one whose eye and taste alone found pleasure in the prospect; her native hills were far more to her than a spectacle; they were what she lived in, and by, as much as the wild birds, their tenants, or as the heather, their produce. Her descriptions, then, of natural scenery, are what they should be, and all they should be.

Where delineation of human character is concerned, the case is different. I am bound to avow that she had scarcely more practical knowledge of the peasantry amongst whom she lived, then a nun has of the country people who sometimes pass her convent gates. My sister's disposition was not naturally gregarious; circumstances favoured and fostered her tendency to seclusion; except to go to church or take a walk on the hills, she rarely crossed the threshold of home. Though her feeling for the people round was benevolent, intercourse with them she never sought; nor, with very few exceptions, ever experienced. And yet she knew them: knew their ways, their language, their family histories; she could hear of them with interest, and talk of them with detail, minute, graphic, and accurate; but *with* them, she rarely exchanged a word. Hence it ensued that what her mind had gathered of the real concerning them, was too exclusively confined to those tragic and terrible traits of which, in listening to the secret annals of every rude vicinage, the memory is sometimes compelled to receive the impress. Her imagination, which was a spirit more sombre than sunny, more powerful than sportive, found in such traits material whence it wrought creations like Heathcliff, like Earnshaw, like Catherine. Having formed these beings, she did not know what she had done. If the auditor of her work when read in manuscript, shuddered under the grinding influence of natures so relentless and implacable, of spirits so lost and fallen; if it was complained that the mere hearing of certain vivid and fearful scenes banished sleep by night, and disturbed mental peace by day, Ellis Bell would wonder what was meant, and suspect the complainant of affectation. Had she but lived, her mind would of itself have grown like a strong tree, loftier, straighter, wider-spreading, and its matured fruits would have attained a mellower ripeness and sunnier bloom; but on that mind time and experience alone could work: to the influence of other intellects, it was not amenable.

Having avowed that over much of "Wuthering Heights" there broods "a horror of great darkness;" that, in its storm-heated and electrical atmosphere, we seem at times to breathe lightning, let me point to those spots where clouded daylight and the eclipsed sun still attest their existence. For a specimen of true benevolence and homely fidelity, look at the character of Nelly Dean; for an example of constancy and tenderness, remark that of Edgar Linton. (Some people will think these qualities do not shine so well incarnate in a man as they would do in a woman, but Ellis Bell could never be brought to comprehend this notion: nothing moved her more than any insinuation that the faithfulness and clemency, the long-suffering and loving-kindness which are esteemed virtues in the daughers of Eve, become foibles in the sons of Adam. She held that mercy and forgiveness are the divinest attributes of the Great Being who made both man and woman, and that what clothes the Godhead in glory, can disgrace no form of feeble humanity.) There is a dry saturnine humour in the delineation of old Joseph, and some glimpses of grace and gaiety animate the younger Catherine. Nor is even the first heroine of the name destitute of a certain strange beauty in her fierceness, or of honesty in the midst of perverted passion and passionate perversity.

Heathcliff, indeed, stands unredeemed; never once swerving in his arrow-straight course to perdition, from the time when "the little black-haired, swarthy thing, as dark as if it came from the Devil," was first unrolled out of the bundle and set on its feet in the farmhouse kitchen, to the hour when Nelly Dean found the grim, stalwart corpse laid on its back in the panel-enclosed bed, with wide-gazing eyes that seemed "to sneer at her attempt to close them, and parted lips and sharp white teeth that sneered too."

Heathcliff betrays one solitary human feeling, and that is *not* his love for Catherine; which is a sentiment fierce and inhuman: a passion such as might boil and glow in the bad essence of some evil genius; a fire that might form the tormented centre—the ever-suffering soul of a magnate of the infernal world: and by its quenchless and ceaseless ravage effect the execution of the decree which dooms him to carry Hell with him wherever he wanders. No; the single link that connects Heathcliff with humanity is his rudely confessed regard for Hareton Earnshaw—the young man whom he has ruined; and then his half-implied esteem for Nelly Dean. These solitary traits omitted, we should say he was child neither of Lascar nor gipsy, but a man's shape animated by demon life—a Ghoul—an Afreet.[2]

Whether it is right or advisable to create beings like Heathcliff, I do not know: I scarcely think it is. But this I know; the writer who possesses the creative gift owns something of which he is not always master—something that at times strangely wills and works for itself. He may lay down rules and devise principles, and to rules and principles it will perhaps for years lie in subjection; and then, haply without any warning of revolt, there comes a time when it will not longer consent "to harrow the vallies, or be bound with a band in the furrow"—when it "laughs at the multitude of the city, and regards not the crying of the driver"—when, refusing absolutely to make ropes out of sea-sand any longer, it sets to work on statue-hewing, and you have a Pluto or a Jove, a Tisiphone or a Psyche, a Mermaid or a Madonna, as Fate or Inspiration direct. Be the work grim or glorious, dread or divine, you have little choice left but quiescent adoption. As for you—the nominal artist—your share in it has been to work passively under dictates you neither delivered nor could question—that would not be uttered at your prayer, nor suppressed nor changed at your caprice. If the result be attractive, the World will praise you, who little deserve praise; if it be repulsive, the same World will blame you, who almost as little deserve blame.

"Wuthering Heights" was hewn in a wild workshop, with simple tools, out of homely materials. The statuary found a granite block on a solitary moor: gazing thereon, he saw how from the crag might be elicited a head, savage, swart, sinister; a form moulded with at least one element of grandeur—power. He wrought with a rude chisel, and from no model but the vision of his meditations. With time and labour, the crag took human shape: and there it stands colossal, dark, and frowning, half statue, half rock in the former sense, terrible and goblin-like; in the latter, almost beautiful, for its colouring is of mellow grey, and moorland moss clothes it; and heath, with its blooming bells and balmy fragrance, grows faithfully close to the giant's foot.

Currer Bell

2. Two years earlier, Charlotte had called Heathcliff "quite another creation. He exemplifies the effects which a life of continued injustice and hard usage may produce on a naturally perverse, vindictive and inexorable disposition. Carefully trained and kindly treated, the black gipsey-cub [*sic*] might possibly have been reared into a human being, but tyranny and ignorance made of him a mere demon. The worst of it is, some of his spirit seems breathed through the whole narrative in which he figures; it haunts every moor and glen, and beckons in every fir-tree of the 'Heights'." Margaret Smith, ed., *The Letters of Charlotte Brontë*, vol. II (Oxford: Clarendon Press, 2000), 99.

EMILY BRONTË'S POEMS FOR THE 1850 *WUTHERING HEIGHTS*

The sisters' first effort at publication was the largely ignored 1846 *Poems*, by Currer, Ellis and Acton Bell, for which the authors had shared Aylott and Jones's cost of publication. After the success of *Jane Eyre*, Charlotte's publisher, Smith, Elder and Company, in 1848 reissued the 1846 volume. When Charlotte selected poetry to present as the literary remains of her sisters she did not reprint work that had been in the earlier collection. Her objective in honoring their memory was to provide a reliable edition as she responded to unfounded speculations about authorship of the several works. As her brief preface put it, she was bound by "the scruples and the wishes of those whose written thoughts these papers held." She noted that some of the poetry originated in childhood writing, and she did not want "to expose in print the crude thoughts of the unripe mind, the rude efforts of the unpractised hand." This may account for a number of Charlotte's editorial changes, but she well understood how much Emily had protected her privacy and how much she would have resented any revelation about Gondal, the imaginary world of her juvenilia or any comment concerning her beliefs and feelings. Thus, as we can see by comparison of manuscripts with the 1850 poems, Charlotte detatched them from Gondal contexts, provided titles and headnotes, substituted wording and even added stanzas. For several of the poems she printed only a small part of the original. Mid-nineteenth-century readers had no indication of how heavy Charlotte's hand was as she claimed to have "culled from the mass only a little poem here and there."

However well justified by conscience and sisterly concern, Charlotte in the 1850 editorial work set out to acknowledge the unique nature of Emily's character and talent and to make that life and work more accessible to mid-Victorian readers. The consequence has been well recognized by Brontë biographer Winifred Gérin: "Interpret Emily to the world as Charlotte constantly attempted to do, she did not allow the authentic voice of Emily to be heard, except in the already published works."[1] Charlotte's editorial changes to the text of *Wuthering Heights* in 1850 were largely ones of correcting many of the sloppy errors she and her sisters found in the Newby first edition, matters of paragraphing, spelling, and punctuation. Nowhere in her editing of the novel did Charlotte change the original text to the extent she did with the poetry. Because there was no authoritative text for Emily's poems before well into the twentieth century and because only the ones published first in 1846 along with these in 1850 were generally available, Charlotte's editorial choices long prevailed.

With the most recent and scrupulously edited new edition of her poems, Emily's achievements as poet and the ties between her verse and fiction can be recognized and assessed. Thanks particularly to

1. Winifred Gérin, *Emily Brontë* (Oxford: Clarendon Press, 1971) 263.

Derek Roper, with the assistance of Edward Chitham, in *The Poems of Emily Brontë* (1995), the relationship of published poems to manuscripts has been clearly documented. For example, these editors show how Charlotte combined separate poems (120A and 120B), and she added one (201) for which there is no surviving manuscript and whose authorship thus has been questioned. But even though Gérin characterized Charlotte's editorial work as an "altering and shortening of texts, suppressing their original Gondal titles, eliminating, in fact, the key to their inspiration and confusing their sense," Roper and Chitham conclude otherwise. They think the impact of Charlotte's work on the interpretation of Emily's poems has been exaggerated, and suggest that she often made the poems more accessible as she made minor local verbal improvements (Gérin, p. 451; Roper and Chitham, p. 24). Certainly the Roper-Chitham texts for the 1850 poems, reprinted here, allow readers to see them in ways not previously possible, because we can read them both as Emily wrote them and as Charlotte changed them. Here and there we find obvious scenes, themes, and character types that recur in *Wuthering Heights*, and here, too, the author masks or otherwise distances her voice. Even her sister seemed unable always to distinguish when Emily the poet was speaking as herself or as a fictional being more or less like herself.

[CHARLOTTE BRONTË]

Selections

It would not have been difficult to compile a volume out of the papers left by my sisters, had I, in making the selection, dismissed from my consideration the scruples and the wishes of those whose written thoughts these papers held. But this was impossible: an influence, stronger than could be exercised by any motive of expediency, necessarily regulated the selection. I have, then, culled from the mass only a little poem here and there. The whole makes but a tiny nosegay, and the colour and perfume of the flowers are not such as fit them for festal uses.

It has been already said that my sisters wrote much in childhood and girlhood. Usually, it seems a sort of injustice to expose in print the crude thoughts of the unripe mind, the rude efforts of the unpractised hand; yet I venture to give three little poems of my sister Emily's, written in her sixteenth year,[1] because they illustrate a point in her character.

At that period she was sent to school. Her previous life, with the exception of a single half-year, had been passed in the absolute

1. The Roper edition of the poems shows that the manuscript for the three poems dates their composition in Emily's twentieth year.

retirement of a village parsonage, amongst the hills bordering Yorkshire and Lancashire. The scenery of these hills is not grand—it is not romantic; it is scarcely striking. Long low moors, dark with heath, shut in little valleys, where a stream waters, here and there, a fringe of stunted copse. Mills and scattered cottages chase romance from these valleys; it is only higher up, deep in amongst the ridges of the moors, that Imagination can find rest for the sole of her foot: and even if she finds it there, she must be a solitude-loving raven—no gentle dove. If she demand beauty to inspire her, she must bring it inborn: these moors are too stern to yield any product so delicate. The eye of the gazer must *itself* brim with a 'purple light,' intense enough to perpetuate the brief flower-flush of August on the heather, or the rare sunset-smile of June; out of his heart must well the freshness, that in latter spring and early summer brightens the bracken, nurtures the moss, and cherishes the starry flowers that spangle for a few weeks the pasture of the moor-sheep. Unless that light and freshness are innate and self-sustained, the drear prospect of a Yorkshire moor will be found as barren of poetic as of agricultural interest: where the love of wild nature is strong, the locality will perhaps be clung to with the more passionate constancy, because from the hill-lover's self comes half its charm.

My sister Emily loved the moors. Flowers brighter than the rose bloomed in the blackest of the heath for her; out of a sullen hollow in a livid hillside her mind could make an Eden. She found in the bleak solitude many and dear delights; and not the least and best loved was—liberty.

Liberty was the breath of Emily's nostrils; without it, she perished. The change from her own home to a school, and from her own very noiseless, very secluded, but unrestricted and inartificial mode of life, to one of disciplined routine (though under the kindliest auspices) was what she failed in enduring. Her nature proved here too strong for her fortitude. Every morning when she woke, the vision of home and the moors rushed on her, and darkened and saddened the day that lay before her. Nobody knew what ailed her but me—I knew only too well. In this struggle her health was quickly broken: her white face, attenuated form, and failing strength threatened rapid decline. I felt in my heart she would die, if she did not go home, and with this conviction obtained her recall. She had only been three months at school; and it was some years before the experiment of sending her from home was again ventured on. After the age of twenty, having meantime studied alone with diligence and perseverance, she went with me to an establishment on the Continent: the same suffering and conflict ensued, heightened by the strong recoil of her upright, heretic and English spirit from the gentle Jesuitry of the foreign and Romish system. Once more she seemed sinking, but this time she rallied through the mere force of resolution: with inward remorse and shame she looked back on her former failure, and resolved to conquer in this second ordeal. She did conquer: but the victory cost her dear. She was never happy till she carried her hard-won knowledge back to the remote English village, the old parsonage-house, and desolate Yorkshire hills. A very few years more, and she looked her last on those hills, and breathed her last in that house, and under the aisle of that obscure village church found her last lowly resting-place. Merciful was the decree that spared her when she was a stranger in a strange land, and guarded her dying bed with kindred love and congenial constancy.

The following pieces[2] were composed at twilight, in the schoolroom, when the leisure of the evening play-hour brought back in full tide the thoughts of home.

POEMS†

40[1]

December 4th 1838

A little while, a little while
The noisy crowd are barred away;[2]
And I can sing and I can smile—
A little[3] while I've holyday!

Where wilt thou go my harassed heart?
Full many a land[4] invites thee now;
And places near, and far apart
Have[5] rest for thee, my weary brow—

There is a spot mid barren hills
Where winter howls and driving rain
But if the dreary tempest chills
There is a light that warms again

2. Charlotte refers to the first three reprinted poems.

† These selections are from Derek Roper, ed., with Edward Chitham, *The Poems of Emily Brontë* (Oxford: Clarendon Press, 1995), and are reprinted with permission of Clarendon Press. For this Norton Critical Edition, the poems are reproduced as they appeared in Emily's manuscripts, and the footnotes record the changes Charlotte made for publication in 1850.

1. 1850 title: "Stanzas"
2. "The weary task is put"
3. "Alike" (possibly a misreading of "A little")
4. "What thought, what scene"
5. "Has"

The house is old, the trees are bare
And moonless bends the misty dome[6]
But what on earth is half so dear—
So longed for as the hearth of home?

The mute bird sitting on the stone,
The dank moss dripping from the wall,[7]
The garden-walk with weeds o'e'r-grown
I love them—how I love them all!

Shall I go there? or shall I seek[8]
Another clime, another sky—
Where tongues familiar music speak
In accents dear to memory?

Yes,[9] as I mused, the naked room,
The flickering[1] firelight died away
And from the midst of cheerless gloom
I passed to bright, unclouded day—

A little and a lone green lane
That opened on a common wide
A distant, dreamy, dim blue chain
Of mountains[2] circling every side—

A heaven so clear, an earth so calm,
So sweet, so soft, so hushed an air
And, deepening still the dreamlike charm,
Wild moor sheep feeding every where—

That[3] was the scene—I knew it well
I knew the pathways far and near[4]
That winding o'er each billowy swell
Marked out the tracks of wandering deer[5]

Could I have lingered but an hour
It well had paid a week of toil

6. "Moonless above bends twilight's dome"
7. "The thorn-trees gaunt, the walks"
8. Lines 21–24 omitted
9. "Still"
1. "alien"
2. "moorland"
3. "*That*"
4. "turfy pathway's sweep"
5. "sheep"

But truth has banished fancy's power
I hear my dungeon bars recoil—[6]

Even as I stood with raptured eye
Absorbed in bliss so deep and dear
My hour of rest had fleeted by
And given me back to weary care—[7]

42[1]

December 18th 1838

The bluebell is the sweetest flower
That waves in summer air
Its blossems have the mightest power
To soothe my spirit's care

There is a spell in purple heath
Too wildly, sadly dear
The violet has a fragrant breath
But fragrence will not cheer

The trees are bare, the sun is cold
And seldom, seldom seen—
The heavens have lost their zone of gold
The earth its robe of green

And ice upon the glancing stream
Has cast its[2] sombre shade
And distant hills and valleys seem
In frozen mist arrayed—

The blue bell cannot charm me now
The heath has lost its bloom
The violets in the glen below
They yeild no sweet perfume

But though I mourn the heather-bell[3]
'Tis better far, away
I know how fast my tears would swell
To see it smile to day

6. "Restraint & heavy task recoil"
7. "And back came labour, bondage, care"
1. 1850 title: "The Bluebell"
2. "her"
3. "sweet Bluebell"

And that wood flower that hides so shy[4]
Beneath the mossy stone
Its balmy scent and dewy eye
Tis not for them I moan

It is the slight and stately stem
The blossem's silvery blue
The buds hid like a sapphire gem
In sheathes of emerald hue

'Tis these that breathe upon my heart
A calm and softening spell
That if it makes the tear-drop start
Has power to soothe as well

For these I weep, so long devided
Through winter's dreary day
In longing weep—but most when guided
On withered banks to stray

If chilly then the light should fall[5]
Adown the[6] dreary sky
And gild the[7] dank and darkened wall
With transient brilliency

How do I yearn,[8] how do I pine
For the time of flowers to come
And turn me from that fading shine
To mourn the fields of home—

39[1]

November 11th 1838

Loud without the wind was roaring
Through the waned autumnal[2] sky,

4. Lines 25–40 omitted
5. "For, oh! When chill the sunbeams fall!"
6. "that"
7. "yon"
8. "weep"
1. Titling this "Stanzas," Charlotte stated that this and the previous two poems had been written in her sister's sixteenth year, "composed at twilight, in the schoolroom, when the leisure of the evening play-hour brought back in full tide the thoughts of home." Roper points out that the composition dates indicate Emily, aged twenty, wrote them during her period of teaching at Law Hill in 1838–39. Some of Charlotte's alterations remove fictional touches that might relate to Gondal or Scotland.
2. "th' autumnal"

Drenching wet, the cold rain pouring
Spoke of stormy winters[3] nigh.

All Too like that dreary eve
Sighed within repining greif—[4]
Sighed at first—but sighed not long[5]
Sweet—How softly sweet it came!
Wild words of an ancient song—
Undefined, without a name—

"It was spring, for[6] the skylark was singing."
Those words they awakened a spell—
They unlocked a deep fountain whose springing
Nor Absence nor Distance can quell.

In the gloom of a cloudy November
They uttered the music of May—
They kindled the perishing ember
Into fervour that could not decay

Awaken on all my dear moorlands
The wind in its glory and pride!
O call me from valleys and highlands
To walk by the hill-rivers side![7]

It is swelled with the first snowy weather;
The roaks they are icy and hoar
And darker waves round[8] the long heather
And the firn-leaves are sunny no more

There are no yellow-stars on the mountain
The blue-bells have long died away
From the brink of the moss-bedded fountain,
From the side of the wintery[9] brae—

But lovlier than corn-fields all waving
In emerald and scarlet[1] and gold

3. "of winter"
4. "Did my exiled spirit grieve"
5. "Grieved at first—but grieved not long"
6. "and"
7. "Awaken, o'er all my dear moorland,
West-wind, in thy glory and pride!
O! call me from valley and lowland,
To walk by the hill-torrent's side!"
8. "sullenly waves"
9. "wintry"
1. "vermeil"

Are the slopes[2] where the north-wind is raving
And the glens[3] where I wandered of old—

"[4]It was morning, the bright sun was beaming—"
How sweetly that[5] brought back to me
The time when nor labour nor dreaming
Broke the sleep of the happy and free

But blithely we rose as the dusk heaven[6]
Was melting to amber and blue
And swift were the wings to our feet given
While[7] we traversed the meadows of dew.

For the moors, for the moors where the short grass
Like velvet beneath us should lie!
For the moors, for the moors where each high pass
Rose sunny against the clear sky!

For the moors, where the linnet was trilling
Its song on the old granite stone—
Where the lark—the wild sky-lark was filling
Every breast with delight like its own.

What language can utter the feeling
That[8] rose when, in exile afar,
On the brow of a lonely hill kneeling
I saw the brown heath growing there:

It was scattered and stunted, and told me
That soon even that would be gone
It wispered; "The grim walls enfold me
"I have bloomed in my last summer's sun—"

But not the loved music whose waking
Makes the soul of the swiss die away
Has a spell—more adored and heart-breaking
Than in its half-blighted bells lay—[9]

2. "heights"
3. "crags"
4. No quotation marks.
5. "it"
6. "dawn-heaven"
7. "As"
8. "Which"
9. "Than, for me, in that blighted heath lay"

The spirit that[1] bent 'neath its power
How it longed, how it burned to be free!
If I could have wept in that hour
Those tears had been heaven to me—

Well, well the sad minutes are moving
Though loaded with trouble and pain—
And sometime the loved and the loving
Shall meet on the mountains again—

84[1]

May 16th 1841

Shall Earth no more inspire thee,
Thou lonely dreamer now?
Since passion may not fire thee
Shall Nature cease to bow?

Thy mind is ever moving
In regions dark to thee;
Recall its usless roving—
Come back and dwell with me—

I know my mountain breezes
Enchant and soothe thee still—
I know my sunshine pleases
Despite thy wayward will—

When day with evening blending
Sinks from the summer sky,
I've seen thy spirit bending
In fond idolatry—

I've whached thee every hour—
I know my mighty sway—
I know my magic power
To drive thy greifs away—

Few hearts to mortals given
On earth so wildly pine

1. "which"
1. Charlotte titled this "Shall Earth no more inspire thee," and provided a prefatory sentence: "The following little piece has no title; but in it the Genius of a solitary region seems to address his wandering and wayward votary, and to recall within his influence the proud mind which rebelled at times even against what it most loved." Roper observes that "the speaker seems in fact to be Earth, or Nature."

Yet none[2] would ask a Heaven
More like the[3] Earth than thine—

Then let my winds caress thee—
Thy comrade let me be—
Since nought beside can bless thee—
Return and dwell with me—

79[1]

September 11th 1840

The night wind

In summer's mellow midnight
  A cloudless moon shone through
Our open parlour window
And rosetrees wet with dew—

I sat in silent musing—
  The soft wind waved my hair
It told me Heaven was glorious
And sleeping Earth was fair—

I needed not its breathing
To bring such thoughts to me
But still it wispered lowly
"How dark the woods will be!—

"The thick leaves in my murmer
"Are rustling like a dream,
"And all their myriad voices
"Instinct with spirit seem"

I said, "go gentle singer,
"Thy wooing voice is kind
"But do not think its music
"Has power to reach my mind—

"play with the scented flower,
"The young tree's supple bough—
"And leave my human feelings
"In their own course to flow"

2. "few"
3. "this"
1. 1850 title: "The Night Wind."

The Wanderer would not leave[2] me
Its kiss grew warmer still—
"O come," it sighed so sweetly
"I'll win thee 'gainst thy will—

"Have we not been from childhood friends?[3]
"Have I not loved thee long?
"As long as thou hast loved the night[4]
"Whose silence wakes my song?

"And when thy heart is resting
"Beneath the churcheyard[5] stone
"I[6] shall have time for mourning
"And thou[7] for being alone"—

85[1]

July 6th 1841

Aye there it is! It wakes to night
Sweet thoughts that will not die
And feeling's fires flash all as bright
As in the years gone by!—[2]

And[3] I can tell by thine altered cheek
And by thy kindled[4] gaze
And by the words thou scearce dost speak,
How wildly fancy plays—

2. "heed"
3. "Were we not friends from childhood?"
4. "the solemn night"
5. "church-aisle"; Roper notes that Emily was buried in the family vault under the chancel in Haworth church.
6. "*I*"
7. "*thou*"
1. Titling this "Aye, there it is!" Charlotte provided a prefatory sentence: "In these stanzas a louder gale has roused the sleeper on her pillow: the wakened soul struggles to blend with the storm by which it is swayed." Roper notes that "the speaker is not necessarily in bed, and a basic problem is to decide who is speaking and to whom. CB presents 1–4 as spoken by EB, 5–24 as spoken to her by a being such as the Night Wind . . . or Earth or Nature. . . . It is easier to read the poem as one speech: conceivably addressed by EB to some real or imagined person sharing her response to the wind, but more likely addressed to an EB figure, either by this person or by a spirit of nature."
2. "Aye there it is! It wakes to night
Deep feelings I thought dead;
Strong in the blast—quick gathering light—
The heart's flame kindles red"
3. "Now"
4. "thine eyes' full"

Yes I could swear that glorious wind
Has swept the world aside
Has dashed its memory from thy mind
Like foam-bells from the tide—

And thou art now a spirit pouring
Thy presence into all—
The essence[5] of the Tempest's roaring
And of the Tempest's fall—[6]

A universal influence
From Thine own influence free—
A principle of life intense
Lost to mortality—

Thus truely when that breast is cold
Thy prisoned soul shall rise
The Dungeon mingle with the mould—
The captive with the skies—[7]

128[1]

Love is like the wild rose briar,
Friendship, like the holly tree
The holly is dark when the rose briar blooms,
But which will bloom most constantly?

The wild rose briar is sweet in spring,
Its summer blossems scent the air
yet wait till winter comes again
And who will call the wild-briar fair

Then scorn the silly rose-wreath now
And deck thee with the holly's sheen
That when December blights thy brow
He still may leave thy garland green—

5. "thunder"
6. "The whisper of its fall:"
7. Without a stanza break, 1850 adds:
"Nature's deep being, thine shall hold,
Her spirit all thy spirit fold,
Her breath absorb thy sighs.
Mortal! Though soon life's tale is told;
Who once lives, never dies!"
1. Charlotte's title: "Love and Friendship."

112[1]

Nov 11th 1844

From a Dungeon Wall in the Southern College—
J B Sept. 1825

"Listen! when your hair like mine
"Takes a tint of silver grey,
"When your eyes, with dimmer shine,
"Whach life's bubbles float away,

"When you, young man, have borne like me
"The weary weight of sixty three
"Then shall penance sore be paid
"For these[2] hours so wildly squandered
"And the words that now fall dead
"On your ears[3] be deeply pondered
"pondered and approved at last
"But their virtue will be past!

"Glorious is the prize of Duty
"Though she be a serious power[4]
"Treacherous all the lures of Beauty
"Thorny bud and poisonous flower!

"Mirth is but a mad beguiling
"Of the golden gifted Time—
"Love—a demon meteor wiling
"Heedless feet to gulfs of crime—

"Those who follow earthly pleasure
"Heavenly knowledge will not lead
"Wisdom hides from them her treasure,
"Virtue bids them evil speed!

"Vainly may their hearts, repenting,
"Seek for aid in future years—
"Wisdom scorned knows no relenting—
"Virtue is not won by tears[5]

1. Charlotte's title: "The Elder's Rebuke."
2. "those"
3. "ear"
4. " 'a serious power' "; Roper suggests Charlotte may have used quotation marks because she recalled "awful Power" in Wordsworth's "Ode to Duty."
5. "fears"

"Fain would we your steps reclaim[6]
"Waken fear and holy shame
"And to this end, our council well
"And kindly doomed you to a cell
"Whose darkness, may perchance, disclose
"A beacon-guide from sterner woes—"

So spake my Judge—then seized his lamp
And left me in the dungeon damp.
A vault-like place whose stagnant air
Suggests and nourishes dispair!

Rosina, this had never been
Except for you, my despot queen
Except for you the billowy sea
Would now be tossing under me
The winds' wild voice my bosom thrill
And my glad heart bound wilder still

Flying before the rapid gale
Those wonderous southern isles to hail
Which wait for my companions free
But thank your passion—not for me!

You know too well—and so do I
Your haughty beauty's soveriegnty
Yet have I read those falcon eyes—
Have dived into their mysteries—
Have studied long their glance and feel
It is not love those eyes reveal—

They Flash—they burn with lightening shine
But not with such fond fire as mine;
The tender star fades faint and wan
Before Ambition's scorching sun—
So deem I now—and Time will prove
If I have wronged Rosina's love—

6. Lines 29–60 replaced with:
"Thus spake the ice-blooded elder gray;
The young man scoffed as he turned away,
Turned to the call of a sweet lute's measure,
Waked by the lightsome touch of pleasure:
Had he ne'er met a gentler teacher,
Woe had been wrought by that pitiless preacher"

106[1]

E.W. to A.G.A.[2] *March 11th 1844*

How few, of all the hearts that loved,
are greiveing for thee now!
And why should mine, to night, be moved
With such a sense of woe?

Too often, thus, when left alone
Where none my thoughts can see,
Comes back a word, a passing tone
From thy strange history—

Sometimes I seem to see thee rise
A glorious child again—
All virtues beaming from thine eyes
That ever honoured men—

Courage and Truth, a generous breast
Where Love and Gladness[3] lay;
A being whose very Memory[4] blest
And made the mourner gay—[5]

O, fairly spread thy early sail
And fresh and pure and free
Was the first impulse of the gale
That[6] urged life's wave for thee!

Why did the pilot, too confiding
Dream oe'r that Oacens foam?
And trust in Pleasure's careless guiding
To bring his vessel home?

For, well, he knew what dangers frowned,
What mists would gather dim,
What roaks and shelves and sands lay round
Between his port and him—

1. Charlotte's title: "The Wanderer from the Fold."
2. Omitted in 1850.
3. "sinless sunshine"
4. "presence"
5. "Like gladsome summer-day"
6. "Which"

The very brightness of the sun,
The splendor of the main,
The wind that bore him wildly on
Should not have warned in vain

An anxious gazer from the shore,
I marked the whitening wave
And wept above thy fate the more
Because I could not save—

It recks not now, when all is over,
But, yet my heart will be
A mourner still, though freind and lover
Have both forgotten thee!

98[1]

September 6th 1843

In the earth, the earth thou shalt be laid
A grey stone standing over thee;
Black mould beneath thee spread
And black mould to cover thee—

"Well, there is rest there
"So fast come thy prophecy—
"The time when my sunny hair
"Shall with grass roots twined[2] be"

But cold, cold is that resting place
Shut out from Joy and Liberty
And all who loved thy living face
Will shrink from its gloom and thee[3]

"Not so, *here* the world is chill
"And sworn friends fall from me
"But *there*, they'll[4] own me still
"And prize my memory"

Farewell then, all that love
All that deep sympathy;
Sleep on, heaven laughs above—
Earth never misses thee

1. Charlotte's title: "Warning and Reply."
2. "entwined"
3. "Will shrink from it shudderingly"
4. "they will"

Turf-sod and tombstone drear
Part human company
One heart broke,[5] only, there[6]
That heart[7] was worthy thee!—

35[1]

October 17th 1838

Song by J. Brenzaida to G.S.

I knew not 't was so dire a crime
To say the word, Adieu—
But, this shall be the only time
My slighted heart[2] shall sue.[3]

The wild moorside,[4] the winter morn,
The gnarled and ancient tree—
If in your breast they waken scorn
Shall wake the same in me.

I can forget black eyes and brows
And lips of rosey[5] charm
If you forget the sacred vows
Those faithless lips could form—

If hard commands can tame your love,
Or prison[6] walls can hold
I would not wish to greive above
A thing so false and cold—

And there are bosoms bound to mine
With links both tried and strong;
And there are eyes, whose lightening shine
Has warmed and blessed me long:

Those eyes shall make my only day,
Shall set my spirit free

5. "breaks"
6. "—here,"
7. "But that heart"
1. Charlotte's title: "Last Words."
2. "lips or heart"
3. Although other readers have found parallels in these lines and Heathcliff's reproaching Catherine for leaving him, Roper points out that "the tone is quite different."
4. "hill-side"
5. "falsest"
6. "strongest"

And chase the foolish thoughts away
That mourn your memory!

32[1]

A. G. A. *August 30th 1838*

For him who struck thy foreign string
I ween this heart hath ceased to care
Then why dost thou such feelings bring
To my sad spirit, Old guitar?

It is as if the warm sunlight
In some deep glen should lingering stay
When cloudes of tempest and of night[2]
Had wrapt the parent Orb away—

It is as if the glassy brook
Should image still its willows fair
Though years ago, the woodman's stroke
Laid low in dust their gleaming[3] hair:

Even so, guitar, thy majic tone
Hath moved the tear and woke[4] the sigh
Hath bid the ancient torrent flow[5]
Although its very source is dry!

120a[1]

A.E. and R.C.[2] *May 28th 1845*

Heavy hangs the raindrop
From the burdened spray;
Heavy broods the damp mist
On Uplands far away;

Heavy looms the dull sky,
Heavy rolls the sea—

1. Charlotte's title: "The Lady to her guitar."
2. "When clouds of storm, or shades of night"
3. "dryad"
4. "waked"
5. "moan"
1. This and the following poem (120B) appeared in 1850 without a break and with Charlotte's title: "The Two Children."
2. Omitted in 1850.

And heavy beats[3] the young heart
Beneath that lonely Tree—

Never has a blue streak
Cleft the clouds since morn—
Never has his grim Fate
Smiled since he was born—

Frowning on the infant,
Shadowing childhood's joy;
Gardian angel knows not
That melancholy boy.

Day is passing swiftly
Its sad and sombre prime;
Youth is fast invading[4]
Sterner[5] manhood's time—

All the flowers are praying
For sun before they close
And he prays too, unknowing,[6]
That sunless human rose!

Blossems,[7] that the westwind
Has never wooed to blow
Scentless are your[8] petals,
Your dew as[9] cold as snow—

Soul, where kindred kindness
No early promise woke
Barren is your[1] beauty
As weed upon the[2] roak—

Wither, Brothers, wither,[3]
You[4] were vainly given—
Earth reserves no blessing
For the unblessed of Heaven!

3. "throbs"
4. "Boyhood sad is merging"
5. "In sadder"
6. "unconscious"
7. "Blossom"
8. "thy"
9. "Thy dew is"
1. "thy"
2. "a"
3. "Wither, soul and blossom"
4. "You both"

120b[1]

Child of Delight! with sunbright hair
And seablue, sea-deep eyes
Spirit of Bliss, what brings thee here
Beneath these sullen skies?

Thou shouldest[2] live in eternal spring
Where endless day is never dim
Why, seraph, has thy[3] erring wing
Borne[4] thee down to weep with him?

"Ah, not from heaven am I decended
"And I do not[5] come to mingle tears
"But sweet is day though with shadows blended
"And though clouded, sweet are youthful years—

"I, the image of light and gladness
"Saw and pitied that mournful boy
"And I swore to take his gloomy sadness[6]
"And give to him my beamy[7] joy—

"Heavy and dark the night is closing
"Heavy and dark may its biding be
"Better for all from greif reposing
"And better for all who whach like me—[8]

"Guardian angel, he lacks no longer;
"Evil fortune he need not fear;
"Fate is strong—but Love is stronger
"And more unsleeping than angel's care—"[9]

1. See 120a, which Charlotte combined with 120b.
2. "shouldst"
3. "thine"
4. "Wafted"
5. "Nor do I"
6. "And I vowed—if need were—to share his sadness"
7. "sunny"
8. Charlotte inserted the following stanza:
   "Watch in love by a fevered pillow,
   Cooling the fever with pity's balm;
   Safe as the petrel on tossing billow,
   Safe in mine own soul's golden calm!"
9. "And *my* love is truer than angel-care"

123[1]

Julian M——and A. G. Rochelle—[2] *October 9th 1845*

Silent is the House—all are laid asleep;
One, alone, looks out o'er the snow-wreaths deep;
Watching every cloud, dreading every breeze
That whirls the wildering drifts and bends the groaning trees—

Cheerful is the hearth, soft the matted floor
Not one shivering gust creeps through pane or door
The little lamp burns straight; its rays shoot strong and far
I trim it well to be the Wanderers guiding star—

Frown my haughty sire, chide my angry Dame;
Set your slaves to spy, threaten me with shame;
But neither sire nor dame, nor prying serf shall know
What angel nightly tracks that waste of winter[3] snow.[4]

In the dungeon crypts idly did I stray
Reckless of the lives wasteing there away;
"Draw the ponderous bars, open Warder stern!"
He dare not say me nay—the hinges harshly turn—

"Our guests are darkly lodged" I whispered gazing through
The vault whose grated eye showed heaven more grey than blue;
(—This was when glad Spring laughed in awaking pride.)
"Aye, darkly lodged enough!" returned my sullen guide.

Then, God forgive my youth, forgive my careless tongue—!
I scoffed as the chill chains on the damp flagstones rung;
"Confined in triple walls, art thou so much to fear,
"That we must bind thee down and clench thy fetters here?"

1. This complete poem was first published in 1938. For the 1846 volume, Emily extracted lines 13–44 and 65–92 together with a new final stanza under the title "The Prisoner." In 1850, Charlotte published lines 1–12 plus two additional stanzas which were probably her own. She titled this work "The Visionary."
2. Omitted in 1850.
3. "frozen"
4. In place of the rest of Emily's poem, here Charlotte added her stanzas:

   What I love shall come like visitant of air,
   Safe in secret power from lurking human snare;
   What love's me, no word of mine shall e'er betray,
   Though for faith unstained my life must forfeit pay.

   Burn, then, little lamp; glimmer straight and clear—
   Hush! a rustling wing stirs, methinks, the air:
   He for whom I wait, thus ever comes to me;
   Strange Power! I trust thy might; trust thou my constancy.

The captive raised her face; it was as soft and mild
As sculptured marble saint or slumbering, unweaned child
It was so soft and mild, it was so sweet and fair
Pain could not trace a line nor greif a shadow there!

The captive raised her hand and pressed it to her brow
"I have been struck, she said, and I am suffering now
"Yet these are little worth, your bolts and irons strong
"And were they forged in steel they could not hold me long—"

Hoarse laughed the jailor grim, "Shall I be won to hear
"Doest think fond, dreaming wretch that *I* shall grant thy prayer?
"Or better still, wilt melt my master's heart with groans?
"Ah sooner might the sun thaw down these granite stones!—

"My master's voice is low, his aspect bland and kind
"But hard as hardest flint the soul that lurks behind:
"And I am rough and rude, yet, not more rough to see
"Than is the hidden ghost which has its home in me!"

About her lips there played a smile of almost scorn
"My friend, she gently said, you have not heard me mourn
"When you, my parent's lives—*my* lost life can restore
"Then may I weep and sue, but, never, Friend, before!"

Her head sank on her hands its fair curls swept the ground
The Dungeon seemed to swim in strange confusion round—
"Is she so near to death?" I murmered half aloud
And kneeling, parted back the floating golden cloud

Alas, how former days upon my heart were borne,
How Memory mirrored then the prisoners joyous morn—
Too blithe, too loving child, too warmly, wildly gay!
Was that the wintry close of thy celestial May?

She knew me and she sighed "Lord Julian, can it be,
"Of all my playmates, you, alone, remember me?
"Nay start not at my words, unless you deem it shame
"To own from conquered foe, a once familiar name—

"I can not wonder now at aught the world will do
"And insult and contempt I lightly brook from you,
"Since those who vowed away their souls to win my love
"Around this living grave like utter strangers move!

"Nor has one voice been raised to plead that I might die
"Not buried under earth but in the open sky;

"By ball or speedy knife or headsman's skillful blow—
"A quick and welcome pang instead of lingering woe!

"Yet, tell them, Julian, all, I am not doomed to wear
"Year after year in gloom and desolate despair;
"A messenger of Hope comes every night to me
"And offers, for short life, eternal liberty—

"He comes with western winds, with evening's wandering airs,
"With that clear dusk of heaven that brings the thickest stars;
"Winds take a pensive tone and stars a tender fire
"And visions rise and change which kill me with desire—

"Desire for nothing known in my maturer years
"When joy grew mad with awe at counting future tears;
"When, if my spirit's sky was full of flashes warm,
"I knew not whence they came from sun or thunder storm;

"But first a hush of peace, a soundless calm descends;
"The struggle of distress and feirce impatience ends;
"Mute music sooths my breast—unuttered harmony
"That I could never dream till earth was lost to me.

"Then dawns the Invisible, the Unseen its truth reveals;
"My outward sense is gone, my inward essence feels—
"Its wings are almost free, its home, its harbour found;
"Measuring the gulf it stoops and dares the final bound!

"O, dreadful is the check—intense the agony
"When the ear begins to hear and the eye begins to see;
"When the pulse begins to throb, the brain to think again,
"The soul to feel the flesh and the flesh to feel the chain!

"Yet I would lose no sting, would wish no torture less;
"The more that anguish racks the earlier it will bless;
"And robed in fires of Hell, or bright with heavenly shine
"If it but herald Death, the vision is divine—"

She ceased to speak and I, unanswering watched her there
Not daring now to touch one lock of silken hair—
As I had knelt in scorn, on the dank floor I knelt still,
My fingers on the links of that iron hard and chill—

I heard and yet heard not the surly keeper growl;
I saw, yet did not see, the flagstones damp and foul;
The keeper, to and fro, paced by the bolted door
And shivered as he walked and as he shivered, swore—

While my cheek glowed in flame, I marked that he did rave
Of air that froze his blood and moisture like the grave—
"We have been Two hours good!" he muttered peevishly,
Then, losing off his belt the rusty dungeon key,

He said, "you may be pleased, Lord Julian, still to stay
"But duty will not let me linger here all day;
"If I might go, I'd leave this badge of mine with you
"Not doubting that you'd prove a jailor stern and true"

I took the proffered charge; the captive's drooping lid
Beneath its shady lash a sudden lightening hid
Earth's hope was not so dead heavens home was not so dear
I read it in that flash of longing quelled by fear

Then like a tender child whose hand did just enfold
Safe in its eager grasp a bird it wept to hold
When peirced with one wild glance from the troubled hazle eye
It gushes into tears and lets its treasure fly

Thus ruth and selfish love together striving tore
The heart all newly taught to pity and adore;
If I should break the chain I felt my bird would go
Yet I must break the chain or seal the prisoner's woe.

Short strife what rest could soothe—what peace could visit me
While she lay pining there for Death to set her free?
"Rochelle, the dungeons teem with foes to gorge our hate—
"Thou art too young to die by such a bitter fate!"

With hurried blow on blow I struck the fetters through
Regardless how that deed my after hours might rue
Oh, I was over-blest by the warm unasked embrace—
By the smile of grateful joy that lit her angel face!

And I was overblest—aye, more than I could dream
When, faint, she turned aside from noon's unwonted beam;
When though the cage was wide—the heaven around it lay—
Its pinion would not waft my wounded dove away—

Through thirteen anxious weeks of terror-blent delight
I guarded her by day and guarded her by night
While foes were prowling near and Death gazed greedily
And only Hope remained a faithful friend to me—

Then oft with taunting smile, I heard my kindred tell
"How Julian loved his hearth and sheltering rooftree well;
"How the trumpet's voice might call the battle-standard wave
"But Julian had no heart to fill a patriot's grave."

And I, who am so quick to answer sneer with sneer;
So ready to condemn to scorn a coward's fear—
I held my peace like one whose conscience keeps him dumb
And saw my kinsmen go—and lingered still at home—

Another hand than mine, my rightful banner held
And gathered my renown on Freedom's crimson field
Yet I had no desire the glorious prize to gain—
It needed braver nerve to face the world's disdain—

And by the patient strength that could that world defy;
By suffering with calm mind, contempt and calumny;
By never-doubting love, unswerving constancy,
Rochelle, I earned at last an equal love from thee!

89[1]

A S to G S[2] *December 19th 1841*

I do not weep, I would not weep;
Our Mother needs no tears:
Dry thine eyes too, 'tis vain to keep
This causless greif for years

What though her brow be changed and cold,
Her sweet eyes closed for ever?
What though the stone—the darksome mould
Our mortal bodies sever?

What though her hand smoothe ne'er again
Those silken locks of thine—
Nor through long hours of future pain
Her kind face o'er thee shine?

Remember still she is not dead
She sees us Gerald[3] now
Laid where her angel spirit fled
Mid heath and frozen snow

1. Charlotte's title: "Encouragement."
2. Omitted in 1850.
3. "sister"

And from that world of heavenly light
Will she not always bend,
To guide us in our lifetimes night
And guard us to the end?

Thou knowst[4] she will and well[5] mayst mourn
That we[6] are left below
But not that she can ne'er return
To share our earthly woe—

201[1]

Stanzas

Often rebuked, yet always back returning
To those first feelings that were born with me,
And leaving busy chase of wealth and learning
For idle dreams of things which cannot be:

To-day, I will seek not the shadowy region,
Its unsustaining vastness waxes drear;
And visions rising, legion after legion,
Bring the unreal world too strangely near.

I'll walk, but not in old heroic traces,
And not in paths of high morality,
And not among the half-distinguished faces,
The clouded forms of long-past history.

I'll walk where my own nature would be leading:
It vexes me to choose another guide:
Where the grey flocks in ferny glens are feeding;
Where the wild wind blows on the mountain side.

What have those lonely mountains worth revealing?
More glory and more grief than I can tell:
The earth that wakes *one* human heart to feeling
Can centre both the worlds of Heaven and Hell.

4. "knowest"
5. "thou"
6. "*we*"
1. Titled "Stanzas." Because there is no extant manuscript, the authorship of this poem has been questioned, and Roper remarks: "In view of CB's revisions and expansions of EB's poems in 1850, there is nothing improbable about her producing a complete poem on her sister's behalf to set her in a desired light. This 201 would have done by bringing EB out on the side of truth and nature as against the 'shadowy region' of romance, in a conflict which seems to have disturbed CB more than her sister. . . . [S]ome reasons for accepting the poem as authentic are set out by [Edward] Chitham in ' "Often Rebuked": Emily's After All,' *Brontë Society Transactions*, 18/93 (1983), 222–6."

125[1]

Jan 2d 1846

No coward soul is mine
No trembler in the world's storm troubled sphere
I see Heaven's glories shine
And Faith shines equal arming me from Fear

O God within my breast
Almighty ever-present Deity
Life, that in me hast[2] rest
As I,—Undying Life, have power in thee

Vain are the thousand creeds
That move men's hearts, unutterably vain,
Worthless as withered weeds
Or idlest froth amid the boundless main

To waken doubt in one
Holding so fast by thy[3] infinity
So surely anchored on
The steadfast rock of Immortality

With wide-embracing love
Thy Spirit animates eternal years
Pervades and broods above,
Changes, sustains, dissolves, creates and rears

Though Earth and moon[4] were gone
And suns and universes ceased to be
And Thou wert[5] left alone
Every Exsistance would exsist in thee

1. Providing the title, "No Coward Soul," Charlotte declared that, "The following are the last lines my sister Emily ever wrote," a claim which has been questioned by the early 1846 date of the manuscript, but as Roper notes in his introduction, during the final two years of her life Emily is known to have written only this poem and a long unfinished narrative poem. In the autumn of 1845, "Charlotte discovered and read some of Emily's poems, and by doing so caused, at first, great resentment. Perhaps having her poetry brought into the open inhibited Emily from writing more, though the effect need not have been so traumatic as it has appeared to some biographers. The failure of *Poems by Currer, Ellis, and Acton Bell* (1846) which included twenty-one of Emily's best poems, cannot have increased her confidence in her verse. In late 1845 and early 1846 most of her creative energies went into *Wuthering Heights.*"
2. "has"
3. "thine"
4. "man"
5. "were"

There is not room for Death
Nor atom that his might could render void
Since Thou art Being and Breath[6]
And what thou art may never be destroyed

REVIEWS OF THE 1850 *WUTHERING HEIGHTS*

By early 1851 the only notices Charlotte Brontë had seen of the new edition of *Wuthering Heights* were those of the *Examiner*, *Leader*, and *Athenaeum*. These had little new or different to say about the novel, but all responded to Charlotte's biographical and prefatory comments. The *Examiner* defended its earlier critical judgments, noting that Currer Bell herself had discussed "what was faulty as well as excellent" in her late sister's writing. The *Leader* noted Charlotte's points about the book's rustic truth and moral force, and wondered that such coarseness of expression had been produced by "two girls living almost alone." We know now that the author of the *Athenaeum* reviews of 1848 and 1850 was H. F. Chorley, who concluded his second review with the observation that the "volume, with its preface, [was] a more than unusually interesting contribution to the whole history of female authorship in England." But the *Eclectic Review* remarked that the issues of authorship addressed in the Biographical Notice "avail little against the general complexion and air of the works in question."

Examiner

December 21, 1850

In a preface to this volume the author of *Jane Eyre* partially lifts the veil from a history and mystery of authorship which has occupied the Quidnuncs of literature for the past two years. * * *

* * * The reception of *Jane Eyre* is known to all. The other books also made appearance at last, but, according to Currer Bell, had a very different reception. "Critics," she says, "failed to do them justice. The immature but very real powers revealed in *Wuthering Heights* were scarcely recognized: its import and nature were misunderstood; the identity of its author was misrepresented; it was said that this was an earlier and ruder attempt of the same pen which produced *Jane Eyre*. Unjust and grievous error! We laughed at it at first, but I deeply lament it now. Hence, I fear, arose a prejudice against the book." This somewhat grave charge is advanced with but one exception to be shortly noticed; when we shall at the same time see what justice there is in the accusation.

6. "Thou—THOU art Being and Breath"—Charlotte's misreading of manuscript.

The writer proceeds to describe the reception of Acton Bell's *Tenant of Wildfell Hall* as not more favourable, but more justly founded, than that of Ellis Bell's *Wuthering Heights*; but she adds that neither Ellis nor Acton suffered herself for one moment to sink under this want of encouragement. Energy nerved the one, endurance upheld the other, and both were prepared to try again; when there approached a more fell assailant than even unjust criticism. Both sisters were doomed to perish by rapid consumption. The illness of Emily is described in language steeped and interpenetrated with bleeding recollections. * * *

* * * So ends their brief, sad story. And if the sister who shared with them in these struggles and disappointments of genius, and excelled them in its instant manifestation and acceptance, may not thus lift their names to the level of her own success, she has at least fairly challenged for them dead, more honourable recognition than she believes to have fallen to them living. She has done her best to reverse what she holds to have been the unjust judgment of the critics who coldly disapproved or harshly misrepresented their productions. She has wiped off this dust, and freed them from this soil.

But let us not overstate Currer Bell's censure of the critical neglect by which her sisters suffered. She makes one exception.

> It is my duty, as well as my pleasure, to acknowledge one exception to the general rule of criticism. One writer, endowed with the keen vision and fine sympathies of genius, has discerned the real nature of *Wuthering Heights*, and has, with equal accuracy, noted its beauties and touched on its faults. Too often do reviewers remind us of the mob of Astrologers, Chaldeans, and Soothsayers gathered before the "writing on the wall," and unable to read the characters or make known the interpretation. We have a right to rejoice when a true seer comes at last, some man in whom is an excellent spirit, to whom have been given light, wisdom, and understanding; who can accurately read the "Mene, Mene, Tekel, Upharisin" of an original mind (however unripe, however inefficiently cultured and partially expanded that mind may be); and who can say with confidence, "This is the interpretation thereof."

The "general rule of criticism" is a phrase somewhat startling in connection with the wondrous unanimity of critical judgments on *Jane Eyre*; and there is another passage in the preface, where Currer Bell speaks of the assumed names of herself and her sisters, in which a yet stonger feeling of the same sort perhaps unconsciously escapes. "We had a vague impression that authoresses are liable to be looked on with prejudice; we had noticed how critics sometimes use for their chastisement the weapon of personality, *and for their reward, a flattery which is not true praise*." Poor hapless critics! But nothing of this kind should surprise a writer who has had the most moderate experience of the thankless vocation. Whether it be censure contemptuously rejected as unworthy, or praise condescendingly received as not worthy enough, the reviewer's fate knows very little variation. Nor be it ours to say that he may not for the most part be worthy of it, and find himself justly in the position of the old lady in the fable whose ear was bitten off by her son at the gallows, for having refused to hear the truth of him, encouraged him in his extravagant courses, and (as Currer Bell expresses it) rewarded him with a flattery which was not true praise. But to the particular case recorded in this volume we have a word or two, on our own poor behalf, to plead in arrest of judgment.

The authors of *Wuthering Heights* and the *Tenant of Wildfell Hall* were not unjustly or contemptuously treated in the columns [*sic*] of the *Examiner*. We do not lay claim to the mene-tekel-upharsin powers assigned to the critic of "keen vision and fine sympathies" singled out by Currer Bell as having alone done justice to her sister, and who appears to have done his somewhat tardy justice so recently as last September in a journal called the *Palladium*. We dare say, judging from the tone of the extracted criticism prefixed to the volume, that our style of handling these things would seldom come up to the mark of Currer Bell's rejoicing. But it is right to mention notwithstanding, that reviews of the works in question by no means depreciatory appeared in this journal almost instantly on the appearance of the tales respectively named, and that we did not wait till

> "deaf the closed ear and mute the tuneful tongue,"[1]

before we gave expression to the praise which both Ellis and Acton Bell seemed fairly to challenge at our hands. Lengthy reviews with very copious extracts were given of both, at the opening of 1848 and in the summer of the same year.

Wuthering Heights we characterized as a strange but powerful book, containing good "rough dashes at character," the impress of "real events," and "no commonplace or affectation." We said that it had forcibly reminded us of a book which we remembered thinking "better in its peculiar kind than anything that had been produced since the days of Fielding." * * *

1. The quoted line is from Alexander Pope, "Elegy to the Memory of an Unfortunate Lady": "Poets themselves must fall like those they sung, / Deaf the prais'd ear and mute the tuneful tongue."

Was this scant or grudging praise? Did it refuse to recognize the "immature but very real powers" of these young and struggling authors? Did it "misunderstand" or "misrepresent" them?

If so, Currer Bell must herself share the reproach, for the language in which she speaks of her sister Emily's early habits and associations, as explaining what was faulty as well as was excellent in her writings, does not materially differ from this which has just been quoted. For ourselves we have nothing to add to it—neither praise to retract, nor censure to explain. We have only most unfeignedly to deplore the blight which fell prematurely on sure rich intellectual promise, and to regret that natures so rare and noble should so early have passed away.

Leader

December 28, 1850

There are various points of interest in this republication, some arising from the intrinsic excellence of the works themselves, other from the lustre reflected on them by *Jane Eyre*. The biographical notice of her two sisters is plainly and touchingly written by Currer Bell * * *

Critics, we are told, failed to do them justice. But to judge from the extracts given of articles in the *Britannia* and *Atlas*, the critics were excessively indulgent, and we take it the great public was the most recalcitrant, and would *not* be amused with these strange wild pictures of incult humanity, painted as if by lurid torchlight, though painted with unmistakeable power—the very power only heightening their repulsiveness. The visions of madmen are not more savage, or more remote from ordinary life. The error committed is an error in art—the excessive predominance of shadows darkening the picture. One cannot dine off condiments, nor sup off horrors without an indigestion.

And yet, although there is a want of air and light in the picture we cannot deny its truth: sombre, rude, brutal, yet true. The fierce ungoverned instincts of powerful organizations, bred up amidst violence, revolt, and moral apathy, are here seen in operation; such brutes we should all be, or the most of us, were our lives as insubordinate to law; were our affections and sympathies as little cultivated, our imaginations as undirected. And herein lies the moral of the book, though most people will fail to draw the moral from very irritation at it.

Curious enough it is to read *Wuthering Heights* and *The Tenant of Wildfell Hall*, and remember that the writers were two retiring, solitary, consumptive girls! Books, coarse even for men, coarse in language and coarse in conception, the coarseness apparently of violent and uncultivated men—turn out to be the productions of two girls living almost alone, filling their loneliness with quiet studies, and writing these books from a sense of duty, hating the pictures they drew, yet drawing them with austere conscientiousness! There is matter here for the moralist or critic to speculate on.

That it was no caprice of a poor imagination wandering in search of an "exciting" subject we are most thoroughly convinced. The three sisters have been haunted by the same experience. Currer Bell throws more humanity into her picture; but Rochester belongs to the Earnshaw and Heathcliff family. Currer Bell's riper mind enables her to paint with a freer hand; nor can we doubt but that her two sisters, had they lived, would also have risen into greater strength and clearness, retaining the extraordinary power of vigorous delineation which makes their writings so remarkable.

The power, indeed, is wonderful. Heathcliff, devil though he may be, is drawn with a sort of dusky splendour which fascinates, and we feel the truth of his burning and impassioned love for Catherine, and of her inextinguishable love for him. It was a happy thought to make her love the kind, weak, elegant Edgar, and yet without lessening her passion for Heathcliff. Edgar appeals to her love of refinement, and goodness, and culture; Heathcliff clutches her soul in his passionate embrace. Edgar is the husband she has chosen, the man who alone is fit to call her wife; but although she is ashamed of her early playmate she loves him with a passionate abandonment which sets culture, education, the world, at defiance. It is in the treatment of this subject that Ellis Bell shows real mastery, and it shows more genius, in the highest sense of the word, than you will find in a thousand novels.

Creative power is so rare and so valuable that we should accept even its caprices with gratitude. Currer Bell, in a passage on this question, doubts whether the artist can control his power; she seems to think with Plato (see his argument in the *Ion*), that the artist does not possess, but is possessed. * * *

This is so true that we suppose every writer will easily recall his sensations of being "carried away" by the thoughts which in moments of exaltation possessed his soul—will recall the headlong feeling of letting the reins slip—being himself as much astonished at the result as any reader can be. There is at such time a *momentum* which propels the mind into regions inaccessible to calculation, unsuspected in our calmer moods.

The present publication is decidedly an interesting one. Besides the two novels of *Wuthering Heights* and *Agnes Grey* it contains the biographical notices already spoken of, and a selection from the poems left by both sisters. We cannot share Currer Bell's partiality for them; in no one quality distinguishing poetry from prose are they remarkable; but although their poetic interest is next to nought they have a biographical interest which justifies their publication. The volume is compact, and may be slipped into a coat pocket for the railway, so that the traveller may wile away with it the long hours of his journey in grim pleasure.

Athenaeum

[*H. F. Chorley*]

December 28, 1850

Female genius and female authorship may be said to present some peculiarities of aspect and circumstance in England, which we find associated with them in no other country. Among the most daring and original manifestations of invention by Englishwomen,—some of the most daring and original have owed their parentage, not to defying *Britomarts*[1] at war with society, who choose to make their literature match with their lives,—not to brilliant women figuring in the world, in whom every gift and faculty has been enriched, and whetted sharp and encouraged into creative utterance, by perpetual communication with the most distinguished men of the time,—but to writers living retired lives in retired places, stimulated to activity by no outward influence, driven to confession by no history that demands apologetic parable or subtle plea. This, as a characteristic of English female genius, we have long noticed:—but it has rarely been more simply, more strongly, some will add more strangely, illustrated than in the volume before us.

The lifting of that veil which for a while concealed the authorship of *Jane Eyre* and its sister-novels, excites in us no surprise. It seemed evident from the first prose pages bearing the signatures of Currer, Ellis, and Acton Bell, that these were *Rosalinds*—or a *Rosalind*[2]—in masquerade—some doubt as to the plurality of persons being engendered by a certain uniformity of local colour and resemblance in choice of subject, which might have arisen either from identity, or from joint peculiarities of situation and of circumstance.—It seemed no less evident * * * that the writers described from personal experience the wild and rugged scenery of the northern parts of this kingdom; and no assertion or disproval,

1. Britomart was the female knight in Spenser's *Faerie Queene*.
2. Rosalind was the Duke's daughter who posed as a man in Shakespeare's *As You Like It*.

no hypothesis or rumour, which obtained circulation after the success of *Jane Eyre*, could shake convictions that had been gathered out of the books themselves. In similar cases, guessers are too apt to raise plausible arguments on some point of detail,—forgetting that this may have been thrown in *ex proposito* to mislead the bystander; and hence the most ingenious discoverers become so pertinaciously deluded as to lose eye and ear for those less obvious indications of general tone of style, colour of incident, and form of fable on which more phlegmatic persons base measurement and comparison. Whatever of truth there may or may not be generally in the above remarks,—certain it is, that in the novels now in question instinct or divination directed us aright. In the prefaces and notices before us, we find that the Bells were three sisters:—two of whom are no longer amongst the living.

* * *

Though the above particulars be little more than the filling-up of an outline already clearly traced and constantly present whenever those characteristic tales recurred to us,—by those who have held other ideas with regard to the authorship of *Jane Eyre* they will be found at once curious and interesting from the plain and earnest sincerity of the writer. She subsequently enters on an analysis and discussion of *Wuthering Heights* as a work of Art:—in the closing paragraph of her preface to that novel, insinuating an argument, if not a defence, the urgency of which is not sufficiently admitted by the bulk of the world of readers. * * *

It might have been added, that to those whose experience of men and manners is neither extensive nor various, the construction of a self-consistent monster is easier than the delineation of an imperfect or inconsistent reality—with all its fallings-short, its fitful aspirations, its mixed enterprises, and its interrupted dreams. But we must refrain from further speculation and illustration:—enough having been given to justify our characterizing this volume, with its preface, as a more than usually interesting contribution to the history of female authorship in England.

Eclectic Review

February 1851

We purpose dealing rather with the Biographical Notice prefixed to this volume, than with the two works which it contains. There are various reasons for this. It is sufficient to say that the former interests us deeply, which the latter do not; and that the present is its first appearance, whereas the *Fictions* it prefaces are already somewhat known to the public. Not that we shall wholly omit to record our judgment, more particularly on 'Wuthering Heights'; but our special business is with the 'Notice' now supplied by Currer, rather than with the productions of Ellis and Acton Bell. Our readers are, doubtless, aware of the questions which have been raised respecting the authorship of 'Jane Eyre' and 'Shirley,' with that of their predecessors reprinted in the volume on our table. Whether these works were the productions of a gentleman or a lady, and whether their authorship was single or threefold, have been mooted with considerable interest in some literary circles, and have sometimes been pronounced on with a dogmatism which would have been amusing, had it not indicated a sad lack of modesty and intelligence. Though the internal evidence of the works is strongly favorable to the hypothesis of a female authorship, there is, nevertheless, a certain masculine air about their style, a repudiation of conventionalisms, and a bold, nervous, cast of thought and action, which suggests the presence of the other sex. Slight inaccuracies in some matters of female dress are, moreover, alleged in proof of their being the production of a masculine pen.

These considerations, however, avail little against the general complexion and air of the works in question. It appears to us impossible to read them without feeling that their excellences and faults, their instinctive attachments and occasional exaggerations, the depths of their tenderness and their want of practical judgment, all betoken the authorship of a lady. In their perusal, we are in the company of an intelligent, free-spoken, and hearty woman, who feels deeply, can describe with power, has seen some of the rougher sides of life, and, though capable of strong affection, is probably wanting in the 'sweet attractive grace' which Milton so beautifully ascribes to Eve.

As to the other point which had been mooted, it is marvellous, we confess, that a doubt should ever have existed. That either of the works now before us should be attributed to the same writer as 'Jane Eyre' and 'Shirley,' is one of the strangest blunders of criticism with which we ever met. It is true there is talent in them, and that too of an order—we refer more particularly to 'Wuthering Heights'—similar in its general character to what those works display. Yet the points of distinction are numerous, and of a character which ought to have precluded doubt. But we may now dispense with conjecture, for one of the sisterhood has kindly withdrawn the curtain, and invited us to look upon the *terra incognita* about which we have been contending. The revelation is deeply, yet painfully, interesting. The scene we behold, though partially illumined, is shaded by some deep clouds. We hear sighs and groans, look upon faded forms and weeping eyes, and turn from the spectacle with a painful conviction that sorrow, in some form or other, is the heritage of man. Well, be it so. The mystery of life will soon be disclosed, and we shall then see the intimate connexion that subsists between the afflictions of this world and the higher and nobler interests of the human soul.

About five years since, Currer Bell, and her two sisters—for we doubt not that *Currer* is a lady, though she does not plainly say so—after a long separation were reunited at home. They resided in a remote northern district, and were entirely dependent on each other and on books 'for the enjoyments and occupations of life.' In the autumn of 1845, a volume of poetry in the handwriting of one of the sisters was accidentally discovered, which, being approved, Currer Bell informs us, 'My younger sister quietly produced some of her own compositions, intimating that since Emily's had given me pleasure, I might like to look at hers. I could not but be a partial judge, yet I thought that these verses too had a sweet sincere pathos of their own.' * * *

* * * Their effort to succeed had aroused faculties of which they were previously unconscious, and the mere exercise of these faculties ministered delight infinitely superior to the frivolous and evanescent enjoyments of the gay. They resolved, therefore, to persevere, and each set vigorously to work at the production of a prose tale. Ellis Bell wrote 'Wuthering Heights,' Acton Bell 'Agnes Grey,' and Currer a narrative, the title of which is not given. These manuscripts were offered to various publishers, but their usual fate was 'an ignominious and abrupt dismissal.' Still the sisters persevered * * *

'Jane Eyre' was instantaneously popular; but not so the productions of Ellis and Acton Bell. We are not surprised at this. The fact is easily solved. A single perusal of the three will explain the mystery. The successful work was attractive as well as talented, while 'Wuthering Heights'—we know little of 'Agnes Grey'—is one of the most repellent books we ever read. With all its talent—and it has much—we cannot imagine its being read through from any fascination in the tale itself. The powers it displays are not only premature, but are misdirected. The characters sketched are, for the most part, dark and loathsome, while a gloomy and sombre air rests on the whole scene, which renders it anything but pleasing. But to our narrative. 'Neither Ellis nor Acton allowed herself, for one moment, to sink under want of encouragement; energy nerved the one, and endurance upheld the other. They resolved on another trial—Hope and the sense of power were yet strong within them.' But a fearful change was at hand. Their domestic circle was obtruded on by one whose might they could not resist. In the midst of labour their strength failed them. * * *

Such, in brief, is the sorrowful tale unfolded in this biographical notice. It has much literary interest, but to us it is yet far more interesting in the picture it exhibits of domestic harmony and love, broken in upon and shaded by the presence of 'the king of terrors.' Such scenes are of frequent occurrence, though it rarely happens that a sisterhood is linked by such mental sympathies and literary engagements as distinguished Ellis, Acton, and Currer Bell. May the survivor combine, with her intellectual occupations, the faith and devotion which stand in intimate connexion with 'joys unspeakable and divine!'

Of 'Wuthering Heights' we must say a word before closing. We have already indicated our opinion; but it is due to our readers and to ourselves that we should state somewhat more fully the grounds of our judgment. That the work has considerable merit we admit. The scenery is laid in the North, the bleak, moorish, wild, character of which is admirably preserved. Ellis Bell was evidently attached to her native hills. She was at home amongst them; and there is, therefore, a vividness and graphic power in her sketches which present them actually before us. So far we prefer no complaint, but the case is different with the *dramatis personæ*. Such a company we never saw grouped before; and we hope never to meet with its like again. Heathcliff is a perfect monster, more demon than human. Hindley Earnshaw is a besotted fool, for whom we scarce feel pity; while his son Hareton is at once ignorant and brutish, until, as by the wand of an enchanter, he takes polish in the last scene of the tale, and retires a docile and apt scholar. The two Catherines, mother and daughter, are equally exaggerations, more than questionable in some parts of their procedure, and absurdly unnatural in the leading incidents of their life. Isabella Linton is one of the silliest and most credulous girls that fancy ever painted; and the enduring affection and tenderness of her brother Edgar are so exhibited as to produce the impression of a feeble rather than of a virtuous character. Of the minor personages we need say nothing, save that, with slight exceptions, they are in keeping with their superiors.

As the characters of the tale are unattractive, so the chief incidents are sadly wanting in probability. They are devoid of truthfulness, are not in harmony with the actual world, and have, therefore, but little more power to move our sympathies than the romances of the middle ages, or the ghost stories which made our granddames tremble.

CRITICISM

A. STUART DALEY†

A Chronology of *Wuthering Heights*

This chronology both amplifies and silently corrects the 1926 chronology by C. P. Sanger.[1] As I have explained in "The Moons and Almanacs of *Wuthering Heights*," the novel years 1784 and 1802 conform to the Easter, weekdays, and ephemeris of the calendar for 1826, and the novel years 1800 and 1801 conform to 1827.[2] The source of calculation is the more than six hundred temporal allusions in the novel. Some day-dates may, however, be qualified as "on or about." Critics have placed Heathcliff's death variously between April and, even, June. But the reasons for taking April 15 as the latest possibility appear in my "The Date of Heathcliff's Death: April, 1802," *Brontë Society Transactions* 17 (1976): 15–17. The 1826 and 1827 "Almanack for Yorkshire, Durham, Northumberland, Westmorland, and Cumberland" were consulted for astronomical data and special days, e.g., the Quarter Sessions in West Riding.

Year	Season/Month/Day	Event (by chapter)
1757	Before September	Hindley Earnshaw born
1762	Before September	Edgar Linton born
c. 1764		Heathcliff born
1765	Summer	Catherine Earnshaw born
1765	Late in year	Isabella Linton born (6, 10)

† Daley prepared this for the Third Norton Critical Edition of *Wuthering Heights*, and it is reprinted with his permission, adding Sanger's genealogy of the Earnshaws and Lintons.

1. The family genealogy further clarifies the chronology and provides ready reference to the relationships and generations of the two principal families:

Mr Earnshaw	*m.*	Mrs Earnshaw	Mr Linton	*m.*	Mrs Linton
d. Oct. 1777.		*d.* Spring 1773.	*d.* Autumn 1780.		*d.* Autumn 1780.

Hindley	*m.*	*Frances*	Catherine	*m.*	Edgar	*Heathcliff*	*m.*	Isabella
b. Summer *d.* Sept. 1784.	1777.	*b.* 1757. *d.* late 1778.	*b.* Summer 1765. *d.* Mar. 20, 1784.	April 1783.	*b.* 1762. *d.* Sept. 1801.	*b.* 1764. *d.* April 1802.	Jan. 1784.	*b.* late 1765. *d.* June 1797.

Hareton	*m.*	Catherine	*m.*	Linton
b. June 1778.	Jan. 1, 1803.	*b.* Mar. 20, 1784.	Aug. 1801.	*b.* Sept. 1784. *d.* Oct. 1801.

2. *Huntington Library Quarterly* 37 (1974): 337–53.

1771	September, start of harvest	Mr. Earnshaw brings Heathcliff home (4)
1773	Spring/early summer	Mrs. Earnshaw dies (4)
1774	October	Hindley Earnshaw sent to college (5)
1777	Before mid-September	Hindley Earnshaw marries (5)
1777	An October evening	Mr. Earnshaw dies (5); Hindley is master of the Heights (6)
1777	Sunday, November 19	Catherine and Heathcliff rebel against Sabbath discipline (3); they are caught intruding at Thrushcross (6)
1777	Sunday, December 24	Catherine returns from Thrushcross (7)
1777	Monday, December 25	Earnshaws visit the Heights; Heathcliff excluded from the Christmas party (7)
1778	June, start of haying	Hareton Earnshaw born; later in year or in early 1779, Frances Earnshaw dies
1780	Two days in early summer, full moon	Major episode, beginning with Edgar Linton's visit, climaxed by Heathcliff's disappearance, and ending with Catherine's coming down with a fever (8–9)
1780	Autumn	Catherine convalesces at Thrushcross; senior Lintons catch her infection and die (9)
1783	Spring or early summer	Edgar and Catherine marry; Ellen joins Catherine at Thrushcross (9)
1783	Thursday, September 11, Harvest moon	Heathcliff returns (10)
1783	October	Isabella in love with Heathcliff (Edgar at Quarter Sessions sitting of October 24) (10)
1783	December/early January 1784	Ellen sees Hareton; Heathcliff kisses Isabella (11)
1784	Monday, January 9, Plough Monday	Quarrel between Edgar and Heathcliff; Catherine locks herself in bedroom, refuses to eat (11)

1784	Friday, January 13	Catherine delirious; at 2 A.M. Isabella elopes with Heathcliff (12)
1784	Monday, March 13	The Heathcliffs return to the Heights (13)
1784	Wednesday, March 15	Ellen brings letter from the Heights to Catherine (11)
1784	Sunday, March 19, Palm Sunday	Heathcliff visits Catherine; passionate leave-taking (15);
1784	Monday, March 20	Catherine II born about midnight; 2 A.M., her mother dies (16, date given in 21)
1784	Tuesday, March 21, Vernal Equinox	Heathcliff puts lock of his hair in Catherine's locket (16)
1784	Friday, March 24, Good Friday	Catherine is buried (16); Hindley attempts to kill Heathcliff (17)
1784	Saturday, March 25, Lady Day	Isabella runs away (17)
1784	September	Linton Heathcliff born about eight months after his parents elope (17, 19)
1784	September	Hindley Earnshaw dies; Heathcliff acquires Heights (17, 19)
1797	July	Cathy Linton meets Hareton, who shows her around Penistone Crags (18)
1797	Beginning of August	Edgar brings Linton Heathcliff home following Isabella's death; Heathcliff takes Linton to Heights (19, 20)
1800	March 20	Cathy Linton and Ellen meet Hareton and go to Heights to see Linton Heathcliff; Edgar forbids Cathy's correspondence with Linton (21)
1800	Tuesday, October 30	Heathcliff induces Cathy to visit Linton at Heights (22)
1800	Wednesday, October 31, Almanack for 1827 forecasts "cold with rain"	Cathy and Ellen visit Linton; Ellen ill after getting wet (23)
1800	Thursday and Friday, November 1 and 2	Cathy disobeys Edgar and sees Linton at Heights (29)

1800	Saturday, November 3, Full Moon	Hareton reads in moonlight the inscription above Heights entrance (29)
1800	Wednesday, November 21	Ellen leaves her sickroom (24)
1800	Sunday, November 25, First Quarter moon, 6 P.M.	Ellen surprises Cathy returning from Heights at about 9 P.M. (24)
1801	February—June	Edgar in failing health (25)
1801	March 20	Edgar too ill to keep remembrance vigil at Catherine's grave (25)
1801	Thursday, August 23	Cathy and Ellen meet Linton (26)
1801	Thursday, August 30	They meet again; Heathcliff confines Cathy and Ellen at Heights (27)
1801	Friday, August 31	Marriage of Cathy and Linton (27)
1801	Tuesday, September 4	Ellen released, returns to Thrushcross to find Edgar dying (28)
1801	Wednesday, September 5, Harvest Moon	Cathy escapes, reaches Thrushcross at 3 A.M.; Edgar dies before sunrise, intestate (28)
1801	September, "evening after the funeral"	Heathcliff takes Cathy to Heights (29)
1801	Autumn	Linton Heathcliff dies; Hareton friendly to Cathy (30)
1801	October 10, old Michaelmas, observed as a quarter day	Lockwood rents Thrushcross
1801	November	Lockwood calls at Heights (1)
1801	November, next day	Lockwood calls again, is snowbound, spends night at Heights (2, 3)
1801	November, next day	Lockwood takes ill and Ellen Dean begins her story (4)
1801	December, about the tenth and three weeks later	Heathcliff sends Lockwood the last grouse of the season (10)
1801	December, one week later	Heathcliff calls (10)

1802	January, one week later	Lockwood continues Ellen's tale (15)
1802	January, second week	Before leaving next week, Lockwood calls at Heights (31)
1802	Beginning of February	Ellen moves to Heights (32)
1802	Early March	Hareton housebound after hunting accident (32)
1802	Monday, March 27, Easter Monday cattle fair at Haworth	Cathy kisses Hareton (32)
1802	Tuesday, March 28	Heathcliff experiences "a strange change approaching" (33)
1802	Beginning of April	Heathcliff "swallows nothing for four days" (34)
1802	Before April 15 (for week of tenth, forecast for "Windy, with rain or sleet")	Heathcliff dies on windy, rainy night and is buried beside Catherine (34)
1802	Saturday, September 16, Splendid Harvest Moon	Lockwood returns and Ellen updates story; concluding scene in light of full moon (32–34)
1802	October 9, Michaelmas Quarter Day Eve	Last day of Lockwood's tenure of Thrushcross
1803	January 1	Cathy and Hareton to marry (34)

J. HILLIS MILLER

Wuthering Heights: Repetition and the "Uncanny"†

"I don't care—I will get in!"
Emily Brontë, *Wuthering Heights*

* * *

Lockwood's "ejaculation," as Brontë calls it, when he tries to get back into the Heights a second time, might be taken as an emblem of the situation of the critic of *Wuthering Heights*. This novel has

† Excerpted by permission of the author and publishers from pp. 42–49, 50–53, 60–68, and 70–72 of *Fiction and Repetition: Seven English Novels*, by J. Hillis Miller. Cambridge, Massachusetts: Harvard University Press, Copyright © 1982 by J. Hillis Miller.

been a strong enticement for readers. It exerts great power over its readers in its own violence, and in its presentation of striking psychological, sociological, and natural detail. It absorbs the reader, making him enwrapped or enrapt by the story. In spite of its many peculiarities of narrative technique and theme, it is, in its extreme vividness of circumstantial detail, a masterwork of "realistic" fiction. It obeys most of the conventions of Victorian realism, though no reader can miss the fact that it gives these conventions a twist. The reader is persuaded that the novel is an accurate picture of the material and sociological conditions of life in Yorkshire in the early nineteenth century. The novel to an unusual degree gives that pleasure appropriate to realistic fiction, the pleasure of yielding to the illusion that one is entering into a real world by way of the words on the page.

Another way the novel entices the reader is by presenting abundant material inviting interpretation. Like *Lord Jim*, it overtly invites the reader to believe that there is some secret explanation which will allow him to understand the novel wholly. Such an interpretation would integrate all the details perspicuously. It is in this way chiefly that the first, grounded form of repetition is present in this novel. The details, the reader is led to believe, are the repetition of a hidden explanatory source. They are signs of it. By "materials inviting interpretation" I mean all those passages in the novel which present something evidently meaning more than what is simply present. The surface of "literal representation" is rippled throughout not only by overtly figurative language but also by things literally represented which at the same time are signs of something else or can be taken as such signs. Examples would be the three gravestones by which Lockwood stands at the end of the novel, or the "moths fluttering among the heath, and hare-bells" and the "soft wind breathing through the grass" as he stands there. Such things are evidently emblematic, but of what? Passages of this sort lead the reader further and further into the novel in his attempt to get in, to reach the inside of the inside where a full retrospective explanation of all the enigmatic details will be possible. Nor is this feature of style intermittent. Once the reader catches sight of this wavering away from the literal in one detail, he becomes suspicious of every detail. He must reinterrogate the whole, like a detective of life or of literature on whom nothing is lost. The text itself, in its presentation of enigmas in the absence of patent totalizing explanation, turns him into such a detective.

The reader is also coaxed into taking the position of an interpreting spectator by the presentation in the novel of so many models of this activity. Lockwood, the timid and civilized outsider, who "shrunk icily into [himself], like a snail" at the first sign of warm response demanding warmth from him, is the reader's delegate in the novel. He is that familiar feature of realistic fiction, the naive and unreliable narrator. Like the first readers of the novel, like modern readers, in spite of all the help they get from the critics, Lockwood is confronted with a mass of fascinating but confusing data which he must try to piece together to make a coherent pattern. I say "must" not only because this is what we as readers have been taught to do with a text, but also because there are so many examples in the novel, besides Lockwood, of texts with interpretation or commentary, or of the situation of someone who is attempting to make sense of events by narrating them.

Lockwood establishes the situation of many characters in the novel and of its readers as interpreting witnesses in a passage near the start of the novel. He first boasts of his ability to understand Heathcliff instinctively, and then withdraws this to say he may be merely projecting his own nature: "I know, by instinct, his reserve springs from an aversion to show displays of feeling—to manifestations of mutual kindliness . . .—No, I'm running on too fast—I bestow my own attributes over liberally on him. Mr. Heathcliff may have entirely dissimilar reasons for keeping his hand out of the way, when he meets a would be acquaintance, to those which actuate me." The second chapter gives additional examples of Lockwood's ineptness as a reader of signs or as a gatherer of details into a pattern. He mistakes a heap of dead rabbits for cats, thinks Catherine Linton is Mrs. Heathcliff, and so on. His errors are a warning to the over-confident reader.

Lockwood is of course by no means the only interpreter or reader in the novel. Catherine's diary is described by Lockwood as "a pen and ink commentary—at least, the appearance of one—covering every morsel of blank that the printer had left" in all the books of her "select" library. That library includes a Testament and the printed sermon of the Reverend Jabes Branderham. Catherine's diary is written in the margin of the latter. Branderham's sermon is an interpretation of a text in the New Testament. That text is itself an interpretation by Jesus of his injunction to forgiveness as well as a reading of certain Old Testament phrases which are echoed, just as Jesus's interpretation (or that of the Gospel-maker) comes accompanied, characteristically, by a parable. A parable is an interpretation by means of a story "thrown beside" that which is to be interpreted, as in fact all of *Wuthering Heights* might be said to be, since Lockwood's narration is adjacent to or at the margin of the enigmatic events he attempts to understand. Branderham's sermon is "interpreted" by Lockwood's dream of the battle in the chapel, in which "every man's hand [is] against his neighbor." The sound of rapping in the dream, in turn, is rationally "read," when Lockwood wakes, as the fir-branch scratching against the window, like a pen scratching on paper. That scratching is reinterpreted once more, in Lockwood's next dream, as the sound of Catherine's ghost trying to get through the window. Lockwood, when he wakens again, and Heathcliff, when he comes running in response to Lockwood's yell, of course interpret the dream differently. Lockwood sees Heathcliff's frantic calling out the window to Catherine (" 'Come in! come in!' he sobbed. 'Cathy, do come.' ") as "a piece of superstition."

These few pages present a sequence of interpretations and of interpretations within interpretations. This chain establishes, at the beginning, the situation of the reader as one of gradual penetration from text to text, just as Lockwood moves from room to room of the house, each inside the other, until he reaches the paneled bed inside Catherine's old room. There he finds himself confronting the Chinese boxes of texts within texts I have just described. The reader of *Wuthering Heights* must thread his or her way from one interpretative narrative to another—from Lockwood's narrative to Nelly's long retelling (which is also a rationalizing and conventionally religious explanation), to Isabella's letter, or to Catherine's dream of being thrown out of heaven, to her interpretation of this in the "I am Heathcliff" speech, and so on.

The novel keeps before the reader emblems of his own situation by showing so many characters besides Lockwood reading or learning to read.[1] The mystery Lockwood tries to understand is the "same" mystery as that which confronts the reader of the novel: How have things got the way they are at Wuthering Heights when Lockwood first goes there? What is the original cause lying behind this sad disappearance of civility? Why is it that the novel so resists satisfactory reasonable explanation? Lockwood, at the point of his deepest penetration spatially into the house and temporally back near the "beginning," encounters not an event or a presence open to his gaze, but Catherine's diary, another text to read. Catherine and Heathcliff, in their turns, are shown, in the diary, condemned to read two religious pamphlets, "The Helmet of Salvation" and "The Broad Way to Destruction," on the "awful Sunday" when they escape for their "scamper on the moors" under the dairy-woman's cloak. Edgar Linton reads in his study while Catherine is willing her own death. He tries to keep her in life by enticing her to read: "A book lay spread on the sill before her, and the scarcely perceptible wind fluttered its leaves at intervals. I believe Linton had laid it there, for she never endeavoured to divert herself with reading, or occupation of any kind." Much later, the taming of Hareton is

1. See Robert C. McKibben, "The Image of the Book in *Wuthering Heights*," *Nineteenth-Century Fiction*, 15 (1960), 159–169.

signaled by his patiently learning to read under the second Catherine's tutelage. Reading seems to be opposed to the wind on the moors, to death, and to sexual experience. Yet all the readers, in the novel and of the novel, can have as a means of access to these is a book, or some other mediating emblem.

Brontë's problem, once she had agreed with her sisters to try her hand at a novel, was to bend the vision she had been expressing more directly and privately in the Gondal poems to the conventions of nineteenth-century fiction, or to bend those conventions to accommodate the vision. Each technical device contributing to the celebrated complexity of narration in *Wuthering Heights* has its precedents in modern fictional practice from Cervantes down to novelists contemporary with Brontë. The time shifts, the multiplication of narrators and narrators within narrators, the double plot, the effacement of the author, and the absence of any trustworthy and knowing narrator who clearly speaks for the author are used strategically in *Wuthering Heights* to frustrate the expectations of a reader such as Lockwood. They are used to invite the reader to move step by step, by way of a gradual unveiling, room by room, into the "penetralium" of Brontë's strange vision of life.

The first who accepted this invitation was Brontë's sister Charlotte, or rather one should say almost the first, since the first reviews of *Wuthering Heights* precede Charlotte's essay. Charlotte Brontë's two prefaces, the "Biographical Notice of Ellis and Acton Bell" and the "Editor's Preface to the New [1850] Edition of *Wuthering Heights*," are often the first thing the modern reader of the novel encounters, with the exception of some twentieth-century critic's introductory essay. The novel comes to the reader wrapped in layers of prefatory material. It is difficult to be sure where the margin of the introductions ends and where the novel "proper" begins. Where does the reader step over the threshold into the novel itself? If the modern critical essay is definitely outside, a kind of alien presence within the covers of the book, Charlotte's prefaces would seem to have privileged access to the house. They seem to be the last layer before entrance, the inside outside, or perhaps the first region actually within, the outside inside, an entrance room. Perhaps they should be thought of as liminal, as the threshold itself. In any case, the language of Charlotte's prefaces is often continuous with Emily's language, for example in its use of figures of speech drawn from Yorkshire scenery, though whether or not Charlotte's language distorts Emily's language by misusing it is another question.

Charlotte's prefaces establish the rhetorical stance which has been characteristic of criticism of this novel. This stance involves dismissing most previous critics and claiming one has oneself solved the enigma, cracked the code. Charlotte's prefaces also establish the situation of a reader confronting an enigmatic text as the appropriate emblem for those both inside and outside the novel:

> Too often do reviewers remind us of the mob of Astrologers, Chaldeans, and Soothsayers gathered before the "writing on the wall," and unable to read the characters or make known the interpretation. We have a right to rejoice when a true seer comes at last, some man in whom is an excellent spirit, to whom have been given light, wisdom, and understanding; who can accurately read the "Mene, Mene, Tekel, Upharsin" of an original mind (however unripe, however inefficiently cultured and partially expanded that mind may be); and who can say, with confidence, "This is the interpretation thereof."

Charlotte is here ostensibly praising the one previous review of which she approves, that by Sydney Dobell in the *Palladium* for September 1850. Dobell was persuaded that Charlotte Brontë had written *Wuthering Heights*. His review is by no means unintelligent, for example in what he says of Catherine Earnshaw: "in the very arms of her lover we dare not doubt her purity." In the end, however, Dobell only restates the enigma rather than solving it: "one looks back at the whole story as to a world of brilliant figures in an atmosphere of mist; shapes that come out upon the eye, and burn their colours into the brain, and depart into the enveloping fog. It is the unformed writing of a giant's hand; the 'large utterance' of a baby god." Charlotte, in spite of her praise of Dobell, means to present herself as the first genuine reader of this "unformed writing," the first true interpreter of the "Mene, Mene, Tekel, Upharsin."

Charlotte's preface of 1850 confidently tells the reader, before he has even read the novel, what the text is to mean. The difficulty is that she presents in fact at least four incompatible readings, citing chapter and verse for each interpretation she proposes, without apparent awareness that they differ from one another. Her readings, moreover, function to throw the reader off the track. They attempt to shift the blame for the novel away from Emily by reducing its meaning to something Charlotte imagines Victorian readers will accept.

Emily Brontë was in *Wuthering Heights*, says Charlotte in the first reading she proposes, simply following nature. She was warbling her native wood-notes wild. The novel is not Emily speaking, but nature speaking through her. The novel "is rustic all through. It is moorish, and wild, and knotty as a root of health. Nor was it natural that it should be otherwise; the author being herself a native and nursling of the moors."

This reading is immediately qualified and replaced by a new one.

The true source of the novel, says Charlotte now, is the actual wild way of life of the peasants of Yorkshire. The novel is sociologically accurate. Emily is merely the innocent transcriber of fact: "She knew them; knew their ways, their language, their family histories; she could hear of them with interest, and talk of them with detail, minute, graphic, and accurate . . . Her imagination, which was a spirit more sombre than sunny, more powerful than sportive, found in such traits material whence it wrought creations like Heathcliff, like Earnshaw, like Catherine. Having formed these beings, she did not know what she had done."

No, after all, this is not it either, Charlotte in effect says in proposing yet another reading. In fact Emily Brontë was a Christian. The novel is a religious allegory, with Heathcliff, for example, an incarnation of the Devil: "Heathcliff, indeed, stands unredeemed; never once swerving in his arrow-straight course to perdition." His love for Catherine is "a passion such as might boil and glow in the bad essence of some evil genius; a fire that might form the tormented centre—the ever-suffering soul of a magnate of the infernal world: and by its quenchless and ceaseless ravage effect the execution of the decree which dooms him to carry Hell with him wherever he wanders."

No, says Charlotte finally, this is not the true explanation or excuse. In fact, whatever the nature of the work, Emily is not to be blamed for it because she was not responsible for it. She was the passive medium through which something or someone else spoke, just as, for Rimbaud, in "les lettres du voyant," the metal is not to blame if it finds itself a trumpet ("Je est un autre."); and just as the speaker in some of Brontë's poems is subject to a "God of visions" who speaks through her without her volition. "But this, I know," says Charlotte; "the writer who possesses the creative gift owns something of which he is not always master—something that at times strangely wills and works for itself . . . Be the work grim or glorious, dread or divine, you have little choice left but quiescent adoption. As for you—the nominal artist—your share in it has been to work passively under dictates you neither delivered not could question—that would not be uttered at your prayer, nor suppressed nor changed at your caprice."

Charlotte's prefaces, with their multiple interpretations, each based on some aspect of the actual text of *Wuthering Heights*, establish a program for all the hundreds of essays and books on *Wuthering Heights* which were to follow. They do this both in the sense that most readings could be lined up under one or another of Charlotte's four readings. They do it also in the sense that all these books and essays are also empirically based on the text. Each tends to be plausible, but demonstrably partial, though each also, like Charlotte's prefaces, tends to be presented with confident certainty. Each critic presents himself as the Daniel who can at last decipher the writing on the wall. Though the many essays on the novel do not exist on a common axis of judgment, that is, though they do not even raise the same questions about the novel, much less give the same answers, each critic tends to claim that he has found something of importance which will indicate the right way to read the novel as a whole.

* * *

* * * The literature on *Wuthering Heights* is abundant and its incoherence striking. Even more than some other great works of literature this novel seems to have an inexhaustible power to call forth commentary and more commentary. All literary criticism tends to be the presentation of what claims to be the definitive rational explanation of the text in question. The criticism of *Wuthering Heights* is characterized by the unusual degree of incoherence among the various explanations and by the way each takes some one element in the novel and extrapolates it toward a total explanation. The essays tend not to build on one another according to some ideal of progressive elucidation. Each is exclusive.

All these interpretations are, I believe, wrong. This is not because each does not illuminate something in *Wuthering Heights*. Each brings something to light, even though it covers something else up in the act of doing so. * * *

My argument is not that criticism is a free-for-all in which one reading is as good as another. No doubt there would be large areas of agreement among competent readers even of this manifestly controversial novel. It is possible to present a reading of *Wuthering Heights* which is demonstrably wrong, not even partially right, though I believe all the readings listed above are in one way or another partially right. They are right because they arise from responses determined by the text. The error lies in the assumption that the meaning is going to be single, unified, and logically coherent. My argument is that the best readings will be the ones which best account for the heterogeneity of the text, its presentation of a definite group of possible meanings which are systematically interconnected, determined by the text, but logically incompatible. The clear and rational expression of such a system of meanings is difficult, perhaps impossible. The fault of premature closure is intrinsic to criticism. The essays on *Wuthering Heights* I have cited seem to me insufficient, not because what they say is demonstrably mistaken, but rather because there is an error in the assumption that there *is* a single secret truth about *Wuthering Heights*. This secret truth would be something formulable as a univocal principle of explanation which would account for everything in the novel. The secret truth about *Wuthering Heights*, rather, is that there is no secret truth which criticism might formulate in this way. No hidden identifiable ordering principle which will account for everything stands at the head of the chain or at the back of the back. Any formulation of such a principle is visibly reductive. It leaves something important still unaccounted for. This is a remnant of opacity which keeps the interpreter dissatisfied, the novel still open, the process of interpretation still able to continue. One form or another of this openness may characterize all works of literature, but * * * this resistance to a single definitive reading takes different forms in different works. In *Wuthering Heights* this special form is the invitation to believe that there is a supernatural transcendent "cause" for all events, while certain identification of this cause, or even assurance of its existence, is impossible.

Wuthering Heights produces its effect on its reader through the way it is made up of repetitions of the same in the other which permanently resist rational reduction to some satisfying principle of explanation. The reader has the experience, in struggling to understand the novel, that a certain number of the elements which present themselves for explanation can be reduced to order. This act of interpretation always leaves something over, something just at the edge of the circle of theoretical vision which that vision does not encompass. This something left out is clearly a significant detail. There are always in fact a group of such significant details which have been left out of any reduction to order. The text is over-rich.

This resistance to theoretical domination, both in the sense of clear-seeing and in the sense of conceptual formulation, is not accidental, nor is it without significance. It is not a result of Brontë's inexperience or of the fact that she overloaded her novel with elements which can be taken as having meaning beyond their realistic references. The novel is not incoherent, confused, or flawed. It is a triumph of the novelist's art. It uses the full resources of that art against the normal assumptions about character and about human life which are built into the conventions of realistic fiction. The difficulties of interpreting *Wuthering Heights* and the superabundance of possible (and actual) interpretations do not mean that the reader is free to make the novel mean anything he wants to make it mean. The fact that no demonstrable single meaning or principle of meaningfulness can be identified does not mean that all meanings are equally good. Each good reader of *Wuthering Heights* is subject to the text, coerced by it. The best readings, it may be, are those, like Charlotte Brontë's, which repeat in their own alogic the text's failure to satisfy the mind's desire for logical order with a demonstrable base. *Wuthering Heights* incorporates the reader in the process of understanding which the text mimes in Lockwood's narration. It forces him to repeat in his own way an effort of understanding that the text expresses, and to repeat also the baffling of that effort.

* * *

The celebrated circumstantiality of *Wuthering Heights* is the circumstantiality of this constant encounter with new signs. The reader of *Wuthering Heights*, like the narrator, is led deeper and deeper into the text by the expectation that sooner or later the last veil will be removed. He will then find himself face to face not with the emblem of something missing but with the right real thing at last. This will be truly original, the bona fide starting place. It will therefore be possessed of full explanatory power over the whole network of signs which it has generated and which it controls, giving each sign its deferred meaning. Through this labyrinth of linkages the reader has to thread his way. He is led from one to another in the expectation of reaching a goal, as Heathcliff leads Lockwood from marker to marker down that snowcovered road.

A further feature of this web of signs behind signs is that they tend to be presented in paired oppositions. Each element of these pairs is not so much the opposite of its mate as another form of it. It is a differentiated form, born of some division within the same, as the different Catherines in the passage discussed above are forms of the same Catherine; or as Heathcliff and Lockwood are similar in their exclusion from the place where Catherine is, as well as opposite in temperament, sexual power, and power of volition; or as Cathy says of Heathcliff not that he is her opposite, other than she is, but that "He's more myself than I am"; or as, in the passage describing the three graves, Edgar on one side of Catherine or Heathcliff on the other each represents one aspect of her double nature. The novel everywhere organizes itself according to such patterns of sameness and difference, as in the opposition between stormy weather and calm weather; or between the roughness of the Heights and the civilized restraint of Thrushcross Grange, or between inside and outside, domestic interior and wild nature outside, beyond the window or over the wall; or between the stories of the two Catherines, or between those who read and those who scorn books as weak intermediaries, or between people of strong will like Heathcliff, who is "a fierce, pitiless, wolfish man" and people of weak will like Lockwood.

These apparently clear oppositions have two further properties. The reader is nowhere given access to the generative unity from which the pairs are derived. The reader never sees directly, for example, the moment in childhood when Cathy and Heathcliff slept in the same bed and were joined in a union which was prior to sexual differentiation. This union was prior to any sense of separate selfhood, prior even to language, figurative or conceptual, which might express that union. As soon as Cathy can say, "I *am* Heathcliff," or "My love for Heathcliff resembles the eternal rocks beneath," they are already divided. This division has always already occurred as soon as there is consciousness and the possibility of retrospective storytelling. Storytelling is always after the fact, and it is always constructed over a loss. What is lost in the case of *Wuthering Heights* is the "origin" which would explain everything.

Another characteristic of the oppositions follows from this loss of the explanatory source. The separated pairs, differentiations of the same rather than true opposites, have a tendency to divide further, and then subdivide again, endlessly proliferating into various nuances and subsets. Once the "primal" division has occurred, and for Brontë as soon as there is a story to tell it has already occurred, there seems to be no stopping a further division. Once this primitive cell is self-divided it divides and subdivides perpetually in an effort to achieve reunification which only multiplies it in new further-divided life cells.

The sequence of generations in *Wuthering Heights*, for example, began long before the three presented in the novel. The name Hareton Earnshaw and the date 1500 carved in stone above the front door of the Heights testify to that. The marriage of the second Cathy and the new Hareton at the end of the novel will initiate a new generation. The deaths of Heathcliff, Edgar Linton, and the first Catherine have by no means put a stop to the reproductive power of the two families. This force finds its analogue in the power of the story to reproduce itself. It is told over and over by the sequence of narrators, and it is reproduced again in each critical essay, or each time it is followed through by a new reader. The words on the page act like a genetic pattern able to program the minds of those who encounter it. It induces them to take, for a time at least, the pattern of the experience of those long-dead imaginary protagonists. The emblem for this might be that concluding scene in which Lockwood stands by the triple grave prolonging the lives of Edgar, Catherine, and Heathcliff by his meditation on the names inscribed on their tombstones. In this act and in the narration generated by it he prevents them from dying wholly. Many Victorian novels stress this double form of repetitive extension beyond the deaths of the protagonists, for example *Tess of the d'Urbervilles*. *Wuthering Heights* gives this familiar pattern a special form by relating it to the question of whether Cathy and Heathcliff are to be thought of as surviving their deaths or whether they survive only in the narrations of those who have survived them.

Any of the oppositions which may be taken as a means of interpreting *Wuthering Heights* has this property of reproducing itself in proliferating divisions and subdivisions. Just as, for example, the name of the maiden Catherine caught between her two possible married names becomes an air "swarming" with Catherines, so the neat opposition within Christianity between good and evil, salvation and damnation, "The Helmet of Salvation" and "The Broad Way to Destruction," becomes the separation of sins into seven distinctions, and this in turn, in the Reverend Jabes Branderham's sermon, becomes a monstrous division and subdivision of sins, a dividing of the text, as Protestantism has multiplied sects and set each man's hand against his neighbor. Two becomes seven becomes seventy times seven, in a grotesque parody of a sermon: "he preached—good God! what a sermon: divided into *four hundred and ninety* parts—each fully equal to an ordinary address from the pulpit—and each discussing a separate sin!"

Wuthering Heights is perhaps best read by taking one or more of its emblematic oppositions as an interpretative hypothesis and pushing it to the point where the initial distinction no longer clearly holds. Only by this following of a track as far as possible, until it peters out into the trackless snow, can the reader get inside this strange text and begin to understand why he cannot ever lucidly understand it or ever have rational mastery over it. The limitation of many critical essays on the novel lies not in any error in the initial interpretative hypothesis (that storm and calm are opposed in the novel, or that windows, walls, and doors are used emblematically, for example). The limitation lies rather in the failure to push the given schematic hypothesis far enough. It must be pushed to the point where it fails to hypothecate the full accounting for the novel which is demanded in the critical contract. At that point the mortgage on *Wuthering Heights* is foreclosed and the reader, it may be, confronts his mortality as reader, that vanishing of lucid understanding which his critical reason, the reason that divides and discriminates in order to master, has done everything to evade.

Why is it that, with this novel, the logical mind so conspicuously fails? What does this have to do with the gage or promissory note that both holds off death and risks death, puts one's death on the line, as a kind of mortgage insurance? Why is it that an interpretative origin, *logos* in the sense of ground, measure, chief word, or accounting reason, cannot be identified for *Wuthering Heights*? If such an origin could be found, all obscurity could be cleared up. Everything could be brought out in the open where it might be clearly seen, added up, paid off, and evened out. What forbids this accounting?

An economic metaphor of course pervades *Wuthering Heights*.

Heathcliff uses his mysteriously acquired wealth to take possession of the Heights and the Grange. He takes possession of them because each thing and person in each household reminds him of Catherine. By appropriating all and then destroying them, he can take revenge on the enemies who have stood between him and Catherine. At the same time he can reach Catherine through them, in their demolition. This is a violently incarnated way to experience a paradoxical logic of signs:

> "What is not connected with her to me? and what does not recall her? I cannot look down to this floor, but her features are shaped on the flags! In every cloud, in every tree—filling the air at night, and caught by glimpses in every object by day, I am surrounded with her image! The most ordinary faces of men and women—my own features mock me with a resemblance. The entire world is a dreadful collection of memoranda that she did exist, and that I have lost her!"

In this strange numismatics, each thing is stamped with the same image, the face of the person who is Queen to Heathcliff's Jack. In this novel no man is King or Ace. The Queen's countenance makes everything have value and pass current. There are problems with this coinage, however. For one thing, no one of these stamped images has a distinct number which indicates its worth in relation to other images or its exchange value in relation to goods or services. No orderly economic system of substitution and circulation is set up by this mint. Neither Heathcliff, nor Lockwood, nor the reader can buy anything with this money. There is, in fact, nothing left to buy, since there is nothing which is not coin stamped with the same image, of infinite value and so of no value.

The entire world is a dreadful collection of memoranda. Memoranda of what? Here is the second problem with this coinage. Each thing stands not for the presence of Catherine as the substance behind the coin, the standard guaranteeing its value, the thing both outside the money system and dispersed everywhere in delegated form within it. In this case, each thing stands rather for the absence of Catherine. All things are memoranda, written or inscribed memorials, like a note I write myself to remind me of something. They are memoranda that she did exist and that Heathcliff has lost her, that she is dead, vanished from the face of the earth. Everything in the world is a sign indicating Catherine, but also indicating, by its existence, his failure to possess her and the fact that she is dead. Each sign is both an avenue to the desired unity with her and also the barrier standing in the way of it.

From this follows the double bind of Heathcliff's relation to Hareton and to the second Cathy, both of whom he detests and loves because they look so much like the first Catherine. From this also follows the double bind of his relation to the Heights and to the Grange. He has taken much trouble to obtain them, manipulating the property laws of Yorkshire to do this as C. P. Sanger has shown. If he possesses the two households, he can take possession of Catherine through them, since they are her property, stamped with her image, proper to her, as much hers as her proper name. But to possess her image, like appropriating her by uttering her name ("Cathy, do come. Oh do—*once* more! Oh! my heart's darling! hear me *this* time—Catherine, at last!") is to possess only a sign for her, not Catherine herself. He must therefore destroy the things he has made his own in order to reach what they signify. He must destroy Hareton and the second Cathy, as well as the two houses. If he destroys them, however, he will of course reach not Catherine but her absence, the vacancy which stands behind every sign that she once existed and that he has lost her. In the same way, his goal of "dissolving with her, and being more happy still!" is blocked, in the coffin-opening scene, by the vision of Catherine's spirit not in the grave, "not under me, but on the earth." To merge with her body, like merging with his new possessions by destroying them, is to join only a sign and to destroy its function as sign. When Heathcliff recognizes this, he abandons his goal of destroying the Heights and the Grange. This leaves him as far from his goal as ever. He will be an infinite distance from it as long as he is alive:

> "It is a poor conclusion, is it not," he observed, having brooded a while on the scene he had just witnessed [the second Catherine and Hareton reading a book together, a sign of their growing intimacy]. "An absurd termination to my violent exertions? I get levers and mattocks to demolish the two houses, and train myself to be capable of working like Hercules, and when everything is ready, and in my power, I find the will to lift a slate off either roof has vanished! My old enemies have not beaten me—now would be the precise time to revenge myself on their representatives—I could do it; and none could hinder me—But where is the use? I don't care for striking, I can't take the trouble to raise my hand! . . . I have lost the faculty of enjoying their destruction, and I am too idle to destroy for nothing."

"But where is the use?" This extraordinary passage defines a complex economy of substitution and exchange which has broken down in an infinite inflation which has made the money worthless. The manipulation of the system is therefore of no use. Each element in this system is now without value either in relation to other elements it "represents" or in relation to what it stands for outside the system, since the standard behind the system has vanished, leaving it supported by nothing. It is like a paper currency which has no gold or silver, or no more credit, behind it, and so becomes again mere paper. The two houses and their land have represented Heathcliff's enemies. His enemies are those who stood between him and Catherine, forbidding their union. To destroy the houses is to destroy the enemies. His enemies, Hindley, Earnshaw, and Edgar Linton, are now dead. He must get at them through their living representatives, Hareton and the second Catherine, the scions of the two families, last of each stock. What these have always stood for is Catherine herself. To put this more exactly, they have stood for the infinite distance between Heathcliff and Catherine. This distance always exists as long as there are still signs for her. Everything resembles her, even Heathcliff's own features, but this resemblance is the sign that she is gone. To leave these signs in existence is to be tormented by the absence they all point to, but of which they also block the filling. To destroy them is to be left with nothing, not even with any signs of the fact that Cathy once existed and that he has lost her. There is no "use" in either destroying or not destroying. Within that situation Heathcliff remains poised, destroying himself in the tension of it, so that breathing or doing any slightest act is for him "like bending back a stiff spring."

The critic's conceptual or figurative scheme of interpretation, including my own here, is up against the same blank wall as the totalizing emblems within the novel, or up against the same impasse that blocks Heathcliff's enterprise of reaching Cathy by taking possession of everything that carries her image and then destroying it. If "something" is incompatible with any sign, if it cannot be seen, signified, or theorized about, it is, in our tradition, no "thing." It is nothing. The trace of such an absence therefore retraces nothing. It can refer only to another trace, in that relation of incongruity which leads the reader of *Wuthering Heights* from one such emblematic design to another. Each passage stands for another passage, in the way Branderham's sermon, as I have said, is a commentary on Jesus's words, themselves a commentary on an Old Testament passage, and so on. Such a movement is a constant passage from one place to another without ever finding the original literal text of which the others are all figures. This missing center is the head referent which would still the wandering movement from emblem to emblem, from story to story, from generation to generation, from Catherine to Catherine, from Hareton to Hareton, from narrator to narrator. There is no way to see or name this head referent because it cannot exist as present event, as a past which once was present, or as a future which will be present. It is something which has always already occurred and been forgotten. It has become immemorial, remembered only veiled in figure, however far back one goes. In the other temporal direction, it is always about to occur, as an end which never quite comes, or when it comes to another, leaving only another dead sign, like the corpse of Heathcliff at the end of the novel with its "frightful, life-like gaze of exultation." "It" leaps suddenly from the always not yet of the future to the always already of the unremembered past. This loss leaves the theorizing spectator once more standing in meditation by a grave reading an epitaph, impelled again to tell another story, which will once more fail to bring the explanatory cause into the open. Each emblematic passage in the novel is both a seeming avenue to the desired unity and also a barrier forbidding access to it. Each means the death of experience, of consciousness, of seeing, and of theory by naming the "state" or "place" that lies always outside the words of the novel and therefore can never be experienced as such, and at the same time, in itself and in its intrinsic tendency to repeat itself, each emblematic passage holds off that death.

This "death" may be called an "it" in order not to prejudge the question of whether it is a thing, a place, a person, a state, a relationship, or a supernatural being. The various narrations and emblematic schemas of the novel presuppose an original state of unity. This ghostly glimpse is a projection outward of a oneness from a state of twoness within. This duality is within the self, within the relation of the self to another, within nature, within society, and within language. The sense that there must at some time have been an original state of unity is generated by the state of division as a haunting insight, always at the corner or at the blind center of vision, where sight fails. This insight can never be adequately expressed in language or in other signs, nor can it be "experienced directly," since experience, language, and signs exist only in one thing set against another, one thing divided from another. The insight nevertheless exists for us only in language. The sense of "something missing" is an effect of the text itself, and of the critical texts which add themselves to the primary text. This means it may be a performative effect of language, not a referential object of language. The language of narration in *Wuthering Heights* is this originating performative enacted by Lockwood, Nelly, and the rest. This narrative creates both the intuition of unitary origin and the clues, in the unresolvable heterogeneity of the narration, to the fact that the origin may be an effect of language, not some preexisting state or some "place" in or out of the world. The illusion is created by figures of one sort or another—substitutions, equivalences, representative displacements, synecdoches, emblematic invitations to totalization. The narrative sequence, in its failure ever to become transparent, in the incongruities of its not-quite-matching repetitions, demonstrates the inadequacy of any one of those figures.

* * *

* * * The situation of the reader of *Wuthering Heights* is inscribed within the novel in the situations of all those characters who are readers, tellers of tales, most elaborately in Lockwood. The lesson for the reader is to make him aware that he has by reading the novel incurred a responsibility like that of the other spectator-interpreters.

"Thou art the man!"—this applies as much to the reader as to Lockwood or to the other narrators. The double guilt of Lockwood's narration as of any critic's discourse is the following. If he does not penetrate all the way to the innermost core of the story he tells, he keeps the story going, repeating itself interminably in its incompletion. This is like the guilt of the one who keeps a grave open, or like the guilt of a sexual failure. On the other hand, to pierce all the way in is to be guilty of the desecration of a grave, to be guilty, like Heathcliff when he opens Cathy's grave, of necrophilia. The punishment for that is to be condemned to go where the vanished protagonists are. Really to penetrate, to get inside the events, rather than seeing them safely from the outside, would be to join Cathy and Heathcliff wherever they now are. The reader's sense of guilt is systematically connected to the swarm of other emotions aroused in any good reader of *Wuthering Heights* as he makes his way through the book: affection for the two Catherines, though in a different way for each, and mixed with some fear of her intransigence in the case of the first Catherine; scorn for Lockwood, but some pity for his limitations; awe of Heathcliff's suffering; and so on.

The line of witnesses who feel one or another form of this complex of emotions goes from the reader-critic to Charlotte Brontë to Emily Brontë to that pseudonymous author "Ellis Bell" to Lockwood to Nelly to Heathcliff to Cathy, the inside of the inside, or it moves the other way around, from Cathy out to the reader. The reader is the last surviving consciousness enveloping all these other consciousnesses, one inside the other. The reader is condemned, like all the others, to be caught by a double contradictory demand: to bring it all out in the open and at the same time to give it decent burial, to keep the book open and at the same time to close its covers once and for all, so it may be forgotten, or so it may be read once more, this time definitively. The guilt of the reader is the impossibility of doing either of these things, once he has opened the book and begun to read: "1801—I have just returned from a visit to my landlord."

The reading of the first present-tense words of the novel performs a multiple act of resurrection, an opening of graves or a raising of ghosts. In reading those first words and then all the ones that follow to the end, the reader brings back from the grave first the fictive "I" who is supposed to have written them or spoken them, that Lockwood who has and had no existence outside the covers of the book. With that "I" the reader brings back also the moment in the fall of 1801 when his "I have just returned" is supposed to have been written or spoken. By way of that first "I" and first present moment the reader then resurrects from the dead, with Lockwood's help, in one direction Hindley, Nelly, Joseph, Hareton, the two Catherines, Heathcliff, and the rest, so that they walk the moors once again and live once again at the Heights and the Grange. In the other direction are also evoked first Ellis Bell, the pseudonymous author, who functions as a ghostly name on the title page. Ellis Bell is a male name veiling the female author, but it is also the name of a character in the book: someone who has survived Lockwood, an "editor" into whose hands Lockwood's diary has fallen and who presents it to the public, or, more likely, the consciousness surrounding Lockwood's consciousness, overhearing what he says to himself, what he thinks, feels, sees, and presenting it again to the reader as though it were entirely the words of Lockwood. In doing this Ellis Bell effaces himself, but he is present as a ghostly necessity of the narrative behind Lockwood's words. The name Ellis Bell functions to name a spectator outside Lockwood, who is the primary spectator. Ellis Bell is another representative of the reader, overhearing, overseeing, overthinking, and overfeeling what Lockwood says, sees, thinks, feels, and writing it down so we can in our turns evoke Lockwood again and raise also that thin and almost invisible ghost, effaced presupposition of the words of the novel, Ellis Bell himself. Behind Ellis Bell, finally, is Brontë, who, the reader knows, actually wrote down those words, "1801—I have just returned . . . " at Haworth on some day probably in 1846. Brontë too, in however indirect fashion, is brought back to life in the act of reading.

If in Lockwood's dream the air swarms with Catherines, so does this book swarm with ghosts who walk the Yorkshire moors inside the covers of any copy of *Wuthering Heights*, waiting to be brought back from the grave by anyone who chances to open the book and read. The most powerful form of repetition in fiction, it may be, is not the echoes of one part of the book by another, but the way even the simplest, most representational words in a novel ("1801—I have just returned . . . ") present themselves as already a murmuring repetition, something which has been repeating itself incessantly there in the words on the page waiting for me to bring it back to life as the meaning of the words forms itself in my mind. Fiction is possible only because of an intrinsic capacity possessed by ordinary words in grammatical order. Words no different from those we use in everyday life, "I have just returned," may detach themselves or be detached from any present moment, any living "I," any immediate perception of reality, and go on functioning as the creators of the fictive world repeated into existence, to use the verb transitively, whenever the act of reading those words is performed. The words themselves, there on the page, both presuppose the deaths of that long line of personages and at the same time keep them from dying wholly, as long as a single copy of *Wuthering Heights* survives to be reread.

SANDRA M. GILBERT

Looking Oppositely: Emily Brontë's Bible of Hell†

* * *

Is it coincidental that the author of *Wuthering Heights* was the sister of the authors of *Jane Eyre* and *Agnes Grey*? Did the parents, especially the father, bequeath a frustrated drive toward literary success to their children? These are interesting though unanswerable questions, but they imply a point that is crucial in any consideration of the Brontës, just as it was important in thinking about Mary Shelley: it was the habit in the Brontë family, as in the Wollstonecraft-Godwin-Shelley family, to approach reality through the mediating agency of books, to read one's relatives, and to feel related to one's reading. Thus the transformation of three lonely yet ambitious Yorkshire governesses into the magisterially androgynous trio of Currer, Ellis, and Acton Bell was a communal act, an assertion of family identity. And significantly, even the games these writers played as children prepared them for such a literary mode of self-definition. As most Brontë admirers know, the four young inhabitants of Haworth Parsonage began producing extended narratives at an early age, and these eventually led to the authorship of a large library of miniature books which constitutes perhaps the most famous juvenilia in English. Though in subject matter these works are divided into two groups—one, the history of the imaginary kingdom of Gondal, written by Emily and Anne, and the other, stories of the equally imaginary land of Angria, written by Charlotte

† From Sandra M. Gilbert and Susan Gubar, *The Madwoman in the Attic* (New Haven: Yale University Press, 1979), pp. 248–308. Reprinted by permission of the publisher.

and Branwell—all four children read and discussed all the tales, and even served as models for characters in many. Thus the Brontës' deepest feelings of kinship appear to have been expressed first in literary collaboration and private childish attempts at fictionalizing each other, and then, later, in the public collaboration the sisters undertook with the ill-fated collection of poetry that was their first "real" publication. Finally Charlotte, the last survivor of these prodigious siblings, memorialized her lost sisters in print, both in fiction and in non-fiction (*Shirley*, for instance, mythologizes Emily). Given the traditions of her family, it was no doubt inevitable that, for her, writing—not only novel-writing but the writing of prefaces to "family" works—would replace tombstone-raising, hymn-singing, maybe even weeping.

That both literary activity and literary evidence were so important to the Brontës may be traced to another problem they shared with Mary Shelley. Like the anxious creator of *Frankenstein*, the authors of *Wuthering Heights*, *Jane Eyre*, and *The Tenant of Wildfell Hall* lost their mother when they were very young. Like Shelley, indeed, Emily and Anne Brontë were too young when their mother died even to know much about her except through the evidence of older survivors and perhaps through some documents. Just as *Frankenstein*, with its emphasis on orphans and beggars, is a motherless book, so all the Brontë novels betray intense feelings of motherlessness, orphanhood, destitution. And in particular the problems of literary orphanhood seem to lead in *Wuthering Heights*, as in *Frankenstein*, not only to a concern with surviving evidence but also to a fascination with the question of origins. Thus if all women writers, metaphorical orphans in patriarchal culture, seek literary answers to the questions "How are we fal'n, / Fal'n by mistaken rules . . . ?" motherless orphans like Mary Shelley and Emily Brontë almost seem to seek literal answers to that question, so passionately do their novels enact distinctive female literary obsessions.

Finally, that such a psychodramatic enactment is going on in both *Wuthering Heights* and *Frankenstein* suggests a similarity between the two novels which brings us back to the tension between dramatic surfaces and metaphysical depths. * * * For just as one of *Frankenstein*'s most puzzling traits is the symbolic ambiguity or fluidity its characters display when they are studied closely, so one of *Wuthering Heights*'s key elements is what Leo Bersani calls its "ontological slipperiness."[1] In fact, because it is a *metaphysical* romance (just as *Frankenstein* is a *metaphysical* thriller) *Wuthering Heights* seems at times to be about forces or beings rather than

1. Leo Bersani, *A Future for Astyanax: Character and Desire in Literature* (Boston: Little, Brown, 1976), p. 203.

people, which is no doubt one reason why some critics have thought if generically problematical, maybe not a novel at all but instead an extended exemplum, or a "prosified" verse drama. And just as all the characters in *Frankenstein* are in a sense the same two characters, so "everyone [in *Wuthering Heights*] is finally related to everyone else and, in a sense, repeated in everyone else," as if the novel, like an illustration of Freud's "Das Unheimlische," were about "the danger of being haunted by alien versions of the self."[2] But when it is created by a woman in the misogynistic context of Western literary culture, this sort of anxiously philosophical, problem-solving, myth-making narrative must—so it seems—inevitably come to grips with the countervailing stories told by patriarchal poetry, and specifically by Milton's patriarchal poetry.

* * *

That *Wuthering Heights* is about heaven and hell, for instance, has long been seen by critics, partly because all the narrative voices, from the beginning of Lockwood's first visit to the Heights, insist upon casting both action and description in religious terms, and partly because one of the first Catherine's major speeches to Nelly Dean raises the questions "What is heaven? Where is hell?" perhaps more urgently than any other speech in an English novel:

> "If I were in heaven, Nelly, I should be extremely miserable. . . . I dreamt once that I was there [and] that heaven did not seem to be my home, and I broke my heart with weeping to come back to earth; and the angels were so angry that they flung me out into the middle of the heath on the top of Wuthering Heights, where I woke sobbing for joy." (Chap. 9)

Satan too, however—at least Satan as Milton's prototypical Byronic hero—has long been considered a participant in *Wuthering Heights*, for "that devil Heathcliff," as both demon lover and ferocious natural force, is a phenomenon critics have always studied. Isabella's "Is Mr. Heathcliff a man? If so, is he mad? And if not is he a devil?" (chap. 13) summarizes the traditional Heathcliff problem most succinctly, but Nelly's "I was inclined to believe . . . that conscience had turned his heart to an earthly hell" (Chap. 33) more obviously echoes *Paradise Lost*.

Again, that *Wuthering Heights* is in some sense about a fall has frequently been suggested, though critics from Charlotte Brontë to Mark Schorer, Q. D. Leavis, and Leo Bersani have always disputed its exact nature and moral implications. Is Catherine's fall the archetypal fall of the *Bildungsroman* protagonist? Is Heathcliff's fall,

2. Ibid., pp. 203, 208–9.

his perverted "moral teething," a shadow of Catherine's? Which of the two worlds of *Wuthering Heights* (if either) does Brontë mean to represent the truly "fallen" world? These are just some of the controversies that have traditionally attended this issue. Nevertheless, that the story of *Wuthering Heights* is built around a central fall seems indisputable, so that a description of the novel as in part a *Bildungsroman* about a girl's passage from "innocence" to "experience" (leaving aside the precise meaning of those terms) would probably also be widely accepted. And that the fall in *Wuthering Heights* has Miltonic overtones is no doubt culturally inevitable. But even if it weren't, the Miltonic implications of the action would be clear enough from the "mad scene" in which Catherine describes herself as "an exile, and outcast . . . from what had been my world," adding "Why am I so changed? Why does my blood rush into a hell of tumult at a few words?" (Chap. 12). Given the metaphysical nature of *Wuthering Heights*, Catherine's definition of herself as "an exile and outcast" inevitably suggests those trail-blazing exiles and outcasts Adam, Eve, and Satan. And her Romantic question—"Why am I so changed?"—with its desperate straining after the roots of identity, must ultimately refer back to Satan's hesitant (but equally crucial) speech to Beelzebub, as they lie stunned in the lake of fire: "If thou be'est he; But O . . . how chang'd" (*PL* 1.84).

Of course, *Wuthering Heights* has often, also, been seen as a subversively visionary novel. Indeed, Brontë is frequently coupled with Blake as a practitioner of mystical politics. Usually, however, as if her book were written to illustrate the enigmatic religion of "No coward soul is mine," this visionary quality is related to Catherine's assertion that she is tired of "being enclosed" in "this shattered prison" of her body, and "wearying to escape into that glorious world, and to be always there" (Chap. 15). Many readers define Brontë, in other words, as a ferocious pantheist/transcendentalist, worshipping the manifestations of the One in rock, tree, cloud, man and woman, while manipulating her story to bring about a Romantic *Liebestod* in which favored characters enter "the endless and shadowless hereafter." And certainly such ideas, like Blake's *Songs of Innocence*, are "something heterodox," to use Lockwood's phrase. At the same time, however, they are soothingly rather than disquietingly neo-Miltonic, like fictionalized visions of *Paradise Lost*'s luminous Father God. They are, in fact, the ideas of "steady, reasonable" Nelly Dean, whose denial of the demonic in life, along with her commitment to the angelic tranquility of death, represents only one of the visionary alternatives in *Wuthering Heights*. And, like Blake's metaphor of the lamb, Nelly's pious alternative has no real meaning for Brontë outside of the context provided by its tigerish opposite.

The tigerish opposite implied by *Wuthering Heights* emerges most dramatically when we bring all the novel's Miltonic elements together with its author's personal concerns in an attempt at a single formulation of Brontë's metaphysical intentions: the sum of this novel's visionary parts is an almost shocking revisionary whole. Heaven (or its rejection), hell, Satan, a fall, mystical politics, metaphysical romance, orphanhood, and the question of origins—disparate as some of these matters may seem, they all cohere in a rebelliously topsy-turvy retelling of Milton's and Western culture's central tale of the fall of woman and her shadow self, Satan. This fall, says Brontë, is not a fall *into* hell. It is a fall *from* "hell" into "heaven," not a fall from grace (in the religious sense) but a fall into grace (in the cultural sense). Moreover, for the heroine who falls it is the loss of Satan rather than the loss of God that signals the painful passage from innocence to experience. Emily Brontë, in other words, is not just Blakeian in "double" mystical vision, but Blakeian in a tough, radically political commitment to the belief that the state of being patriarchal Christianity calls "hell" is eternally, energetically delightful, whereas the state called "heaven" is rigidly hierarchical, Urizenic, and "kind" as a poison tree. But because she was metaphorically one of Milton's daughters, Brontë differs from Blake, that powerful son of a powerful father, in reversing the terms of Milton's Christian cosmogony for specifically feminist reasons.

* * *

Because Emily Brontë was looking oppositely not only for heaven (and hell) but for her own female origins, *Wuthering Heights* is one of the few authentic instances of novelistic myth-making, myth-making in the functional sense of problem-solving. Where writers from Charlotte Brontë and Henry James to James Joyce and Virginia Woolf have used mythic material to give point and structure to their novels, Emily Brontë uses the novel form to give substance—plausibility, really—to her myth. It is urgent that she do so because, as we shall see, the feminist cogency of this myth derives not only from its daring corrections of Milton but also from the fact that it is a distinctively nineteenth-century answer to the question of origins: It is the myth of how culture came about, and specifically of how nineteenth-century society occurred, the tale of where tea-tables, sofas, crinolines, and parsonages like the one at Haworth came from.

Because it is so ambitious a myth, *Wuthering Heights* has the puzzling self-containment of a *mystery* in the old sense of that word—the sense of mystery plays and Eleusinian mysteries. Locked in by Lockwood's uncomprehending narrative, Nelly Dean's story, with its baffling duplication of names, places, events, seems endlessly to reenact itself, like some ritual that must be cyclically repeated in order to sustain (as well as explain) both nature and culture. At the same time, because it is so prosaic a myth—a myth about crinolines!—*Wuthering Heights* is not in the least portentous or self-consciously "mythic." On the contrary, like all true rituals and myths, Brontë's "cuckoo's tale" turns a practical, casual, humorous face to its audience. For as Lévi-Strauss's observations suggest, true believers gossip by the prayer wheel, since that modern reverence which enjoins solemnity is simply the foster child of modern skepticism.[3]

Gossipy but unconventional true believers were rare, even in the pious nineteenth century, as Arnold's anxious meditations and Carlyle's angry sermons note. But Brontë's paradoxically matter-of-fact imaginative strength, her ability to enter a realistically freckled fantasy land, manifested itself early. One of her most famous adolescent diary papers juxtaposes a plea for culinary help from the parsonage housekeeper, Tabby—"Come Anne pilloputate"—with "The Gondals are discovering the interior of Gaaldine" and "Sally Mosely is washing in the back kitchen." Significantly, no distinction is made between the heroic exploits of the fictional Gondals and Sally Mosely's real washday business. The curiously childlike voice of the diarist records all events without commentary, and this reserve suggests an implicit acquiescence in the equal "truth" of all events. Eleven years later, when the sixteen-year-old reporter of "pilloputate" has grown up and is on the edge of *Wuthering Heights*, the naive, uninflected surface of her diary papers is unchanged:

> . . . Anne and I went our first long journey by ourselves together, leaving home on the 30th of June, Monday, sleeping at York, returning to Keighley Tuesday evening . . . during our excursion we were Ronald Mcalgin, Henry Angora, Juliet Angusteena, Rosabella Esmalden, Ella and Julian Egremont, Catharine Navarre, and Cordilia Fitzaphnold, escaping from the palaces of instruction to join the Royalists who are hard driven at present by the victorious Republicans. . . . I must hurry off now to my turning and ironing. I have plenty of work on hands, and writing; and am altogether full of business.

Psychodramatic "play," this passage suggests, is an activity at once as necessary and as ordinary as housework: ironing and the explo-

3. See Claude Lévi-Strauss, *Tristes Topiques* (New York: Atheneum, 1965), pp. 214–16: "There is something almost scandalous, to a European observer, in the ease with which the (as it seems to us) almost incompatible activities of the men's house are harmonized. Few people are as deeply religious as the Bororo. . . . But their spiritual beliefs and their habits of every day are so intimately mingled that they seem not to have any sensation of passing from one to the other."

ration of alternative lives are the same kind of "business"—a perhaps uniquely female idea of which Anne Bradstreet and Emily Dickinson, those other visionary housekeepers, would have approved.

* * *

The world of *Wuthering Heights*, in other words, like the world of Brontë's diary papers, is one where what seem to be the most unlikely opposites coexist without, apparently, any consciousness on the author's part that there is anything unlikely in their coexistence. The ghosts of Byron, Shakespeare, and Jane Austen haunt the same ground. People with decent Christian names (Catherine, Nelly, Edgar, Isabella) inhabit a landscape in which also dwell people with strange animal or nature names (Hindley, Hareton, Heathcliff). Fairy-tale events out of what Mircea Eliade would call "great time" are given a local habitation and a real chronology in just that historical present Eliade defines as great time's opposite.[4] Dogs and gods (or goddesses) turn out to be not opposites but, figuratively speaking, the same words spelled in different ways. Funerals are weddings, weddings funerals. And of course, most important for our purposes here, hell is heaven, heaven hell, though the two are not separated, as Milton and literary decorum would prescribe, by vast cons of space but by a little strip of turf, for Brontë was rebelliously determined to walk

> . . . not in old heroic traces
> And not in paths of high morality.
> And not among the half-distinguished faces,
> The clouded forms of long-past history.

On the contrary, surveying that history and its implications, she came to the revisionary conclusion that "the earth that wakes *one* human heart to feeling / Can centre both the worlds of Heaven and Hell."[5]

* * *

Why is Wuthering Heights so Miltonically hellish? And what happened to Catherine Earnshaw? Why has she become a demonic, storm-driven ghost? The "real" etiological story of *Wuthering Heights* begins, as Lockwood learns from his "human fixture" Nelly Dean, with a random weakening of the fabric of ordinary human society. Once upon a time, somewhere in what mythically speaking qualifies as pre-history or what Eliade calls "illo tempore," there

4. Mircea Eliade, *The Myth of the Eternal Return* (New York: Pantheon, 1954).
5. C. W. Hatfield, ed., *The Complete Poems of Emily Jane Brontë* (New York: Columbia University Press, 1941), pp. 255–56.

is/was a primordial family, the Earnshaws, who trace their lineage back at least as far as the paradigmatic Renaissance inscription "1500 Hareton Earnshaw" over their "principal doorway." And one fine summer morning toward the end of the eighteenth century, the "old master" of the house decides to take a walking tour of sixty miles to Liverpool (Chap. 4). His decision, like Lear's decision to divide his kingdom, is apparently quite arbitrary, one of those mystifying psychic *données* for which the fictional convention of "once upon a time" was devised. Perhaps it means, like Lear's action, that he is half-consciously beginning to prepare for death. In any case, his ritual questions to his two children—an older son and a younger daughter—and to their servant Nelly are equally stylized and arbitrary, as are the children's answers. "What shall I bring you?" the old master asks, like the fisherman to whom the flounder gave three wishes. And the children reply, as convention dictates, by requesting their heart's desires. In other words, they reveal their true selves, just as a father contemplating his own ultimate absence from their lives might have hoped they would.

Strangely enough, however, only the servant Nelly's heart's desire is sensible and conventional: she asks for (or, rather, accepts the promise of) a pocketful of apples and pears. Hindley, on the other hand, the son who is destined to be next master of the household, does not ask for a particularly masterful gift. His wish, indeed, seems frivolous in the context of the harsh world of the Heights. He asks for a fiddle, betraying both a secret, soft-hearted desire for culture and an almost decadent lack of virile purpose. Stranger still is Catherine's wish for a whip. "She could ride any horse in the stable," says Nelly, but in the fairy-tale context of this narrative that realistic explanation hardly seems to suffice,[6] for, symbolically, the small Catherine's longing for a whip seems like a powerless younger daughter's yearning for power.

Of course, as we might expect from our experience of fairy tales, at least one of the children receives the desired boon. Catherine gets her whip. She gets it figuratively—in the form of a "gypsy brat"—rather than literally, but nevertheless "it" (both whip and brat) functions just as she must unconsciously have hoped it would, smashing her rival-brother's fiddle and making a desirable third

6. The realistically iconoclastic nature of Catherine's interest in riding, however, is illuminated by this comment from a nineteenth-century conduct book: "[Horseback riding] produces in ladies a coarseness of voice, a weathered complexion, and unnatural consolidation of the bones of the lower part of the body, ensuring a frightful impediment to future functions which need not here be dwelt upon; by overdevelopment of the muscles equitation produces an immense increase in the waist and is, in short, altogether masculine and unwomanly." (Donald Walker, *Exercises for Ladies*, 1837, quoted in C. W. Cunnington, *Feminine Attitudes in the Nineteenth Century* [London: W. Heinemann, 1935]).

among the children in the family so as to insulate her from the pressure of her brother's domination. (That there should always have been three children in the family is clear from the way other fairytale rituals of three are observed, and also from the fact that Heathcliff is given the name of a dead son, perhaps even the true oldest son, as if he were a reincarnation of the lost child.)

Having received her deeply desired whip, Catherine now achieves, as Hillis Miller and Leo Bersani have noticed, an extraordinary fullness of being.[7] * * *

In part Catherine's new wholeness results from a very practical shift in family dynamics. Heathcliff as a fantasy replacement of the dead oldest brother does in fact supplant Hindley in the old master's affections, and therefore he functions as a tool of the dispossessed younger sister whose "whip" he is. Specifically, he enables her for the first time to get possession of the kingdom of Wuthering Heights, which under her rule threatens to become, like Gondal, a queendom. In addition to this, however, Heathcliff's presence gives the girl a fullness of being that goes beyond power in household politics, because as Catherine's whip he is (and she herself recognizes this) an alternative self or double for her, a complementary addition to her being who fleshes out all her lacks the way a bandage might staunch a wound. Thus in her union with him she becomes, like Manfred in his union with his sister Astarte, a perfect androgyne. As devoid of sexual awareness as Adam and Eve were in the prelapsarian garden, she sleeps with her whip, her other half, every night in the primordial fashion of the countryside. Gifted with that innocent, unselfconscious sexual energy which Blake saw as eternal delight, she has "ways with her," according to Nelly, "such as I never saw a child take up before" (Chap. 5). And if Heathcliff's is the body that does her will—strong, dark, proud, and a native speaker of "gibberish" rather than English—she herself is an "unfeminine" instance of transcendently vital spirit. For she is never docile, never submissive, never ladylike. On the contrary, her joy—and the Coleridgean word is not too strong—is in what Milton's Eve is never allowed: a tongue "always going—singing, laughing, and plaguing everybody who would not do the same," and "ready words: turning Joseph's religious curses into ridicule . . . and doing just what her father hated most" (Chap. 5).

Perverse as it may seem, this paradise into which Heathcliff's advent has transformed Wuthering Heights for the young Catherine is as authentic a fantasy for women as Milton's Eden was for men. * * *

7. See Bersani, *A Future for Astyanax*, and J. Hillis Miller, *The Disappearance of God* (Cambridge, Mass.: Harvard UP, 1963), pp. 155–211.

Nevertheless, her personal heaven is surrounded, like Milton's Eden, by threats from what she would define as "hell." If, for instance, she had in some part of herself hoped that her father's death would ease the stress of that shadowy patriarchal yoke which was the only cloud on her heaven's horizon, Catherine was mistaken. For paradoxically old Earnshaw's passing brings with it the end to Catherine's Edenic "half savage and hardy and free" girlhood. It brings about a divided world in which the once-androgynous child is to be "laid alone" for the first time. And most important it brings about the accession to power of Hindley, by the patriarchal laws of primogeniture the real heir and thus the new father who is to introduce into the novel the proximate causes of Catherine's (and Heathcliff's) fall and subsequent decline.

* * *

Catherine's fall, however, is caused by a patriarchal past and present, besides being associated with a patriarchal future. It is significant, then, that her problems begin—violently enough—when she literally falls down and is bitten by a male bulldog, a sort of guard/god from Thrushcross Grange. Though many readers overlook this point, Catherine does not *go* to the Grange when she is twelve years old. On the contrary, the Grange seizes her and "holds [her] fast," a metaphoric action which emphasizes the turbulent and inexorable nature of the psychosexual *rites de passage Wuthering Heights* describes, just as the ferociously masculine bull/dog—as a symbolic representative of Thrushcross Grange—contrasts strikingly with the ascendancy at the Heights of the hellish female bitch goddess alternately referred to as "Madam" and "Juno."[8]

Realistically speaking, Catherine and Heathcliff have been driven in the direction of Thrushcross Grange by their own desire to escape not only the pietistic tortures Joseph inflicts but also, more urgently, just that sexual awareness irritatingly imposed by Hindley's romantic paradise. Neither sexuality nor its consequences can be evaded, however, and the farther the children run the closer they come to the very fate they secretly wish to avoid. Racing "from the top of the Heights to the park without stopping," they plunge from the periphery of Hindley's paradise (which was transforming their heaven into a hell) to the boundaries of a place that at first seems authentically heavenly, a place full of light and softness and color, a "splendid place carpeted with crimson . . . and [with] a pure white ceiling bordered by gold, a shower of glass-drops hanging in silver chains from the centre, and shimmering with little soft tapers"

8. Terry Eagleton discusses the Lintons' dogs from a Marxist perspective; see *Myths of Power: A Marxist Study of the Brontës* (Basingstoke: Macmillan, 1975), pp. 106–7.

(Chap. 6). Looking in the window, the outcasts speculate that if they were inside such a room "we should have thought ourselves in heaven!" From the outside, at least, the Lintons' elegant haven appears paradisaical. But once the children have experienced its Urizenic interior, they know that in their terms this heaven is hell.

* * *

To say that Thrushcross Grange is genteel or cultured and that it therefore seems "heavenly" is to say, of course, that it is the opposite of Wuthering Heights. And certainly at every point the two houses are opposed to each other, as if each in its self-assertion must absolutely deny the other's being. Like Milton and Blake, Emily Brontë thought in polarities. Thus, where Wuthering Heights is essentially a great parlorless room built around a huge central hearth, a furnace of dark energy like the fire of Los, Thrushcross Grange has a parlor notable not for heat but for light, for "a pure white ceiling bordered by gold" with "a shower of glass-drops" in the center that seems to parody the "sovran vital Lamp" (*PL* 3.22) which illuminates Milton's heaven of Right Reason. Where Wuthering Heights, moreover, is close to being naked or "raw" in Lévi-Strauss' sense—its floors uncarpeted, most of its inhabitants barely literate, even the meat on its shelves open to inspection—Thrushcross Grange is clothed and "cooked": carpeted in crimson, bookish, feeding on cakes and tea and negus. It follows from this, then, that where Wuthering Heights is functional, even its dogs working sheepdogs or hunters, Thrushcross Grange (though guarded by bulldogs) appears to be decorative or aesthetic, the home of lapdogs as well as ladies. And finally, therefore, Wuthering Heights in its stripped functional rawness is essentially anti-hierarchical and egalitarian as the aspirations of Eve and Satan, while Thrushcross Grange reproduces the hierarchical chain of being that Western culture traditionally proposes as heaven's decree.

* * *

It has often been argued that Catherine's anxiety and uncertainty about her own identity represents a moral failing, a fatal flaw in her character which leads to her inability to choose between Edgar and Heathcliff. * * * To talk of morality in connection with Catherine's fall—and specifically in connection with her self-deceptive decision to marry Edgar—seems pointless, however, for morality only becomes a relevant term where there are meaningful choices.

As we have seen, Catherine has no meaningful choices. Driven from Wuthering Heights to Thrushcross Grange by her brother's marriage, seized by Thrushcross Grange and held fast in the jaws of reason, education, decorum, she cannot do otherwise than as she does, must marry Edgar because there is no one else for her to marry and a lady must marry. Indeed, her self-justifying description of her love for Edgar—"I love the ground under his feet, and the air over his head, and everything he touches, and every word he says" (Chap. 9)—is a bitter parody of a genteel romantic declaration which shows how effective her education has been in indoctrinating her with the literary romanticism deemed suitable for young ladies, the swooning "femininity" that identifies all energies with the charisma of fathers/lovers/husbands. Her concomitant explanation that it would "degrade" her to marry Heathcliff is an equally inevitable product of her education, for her fall into ladyhood has been accompanied by Heathcliff's reduction to an equivalent position of female powerlessness, and Catherine has learned, correctly, that if it is degrading to be a woman it is even more degrading to be *like* a woman. Just as Milton's Eve, therefore, being already fallen, had no meaningful choice despite Milton's best efforts to prove otherwise, so Catherine has no real choice. Given the patriarchal nature of culture, women must fall—that is, they are already fallen because doomed to fall.

* * *

Catherine Earnshaw Linton's decline follows Catherine Earnshaw's fall. Slow at first, it is eventually as rapid, sickening, and deadly as the course of Brontë's own consumption was to be. And the long slide toward death of the body begins with what appears to be an irreversible death of the soul—with Catherine's fatalistic acceptance of Edgar's offer and her consequent self-imprisonment in the role of "Mrs. Linton, the lady of Thrushcross Grange." It is, of course, her announcement of this decision to Nelly, overheard by Heathcliff, which leads to Heathcliff's self-exile from the Heights and thus definitively to Catherine's psychic fragmentation. And significantly, her response to the departure of her true self is a lapse into illness which both signals the beginning of her decline and foreshadows its mortal end. Her words to Nelly the morning after Heathcliff's departure are therefore symbolically as well as dramatically resonant: "Shut the window, Nelly, I'm starving!" (Chap. 9).

As Dorothy van Ghent has shown, windows in *Wuthering Heights* consistently represent openings into possibility, apertures through which subversive otherness can enter, or wounds out of which respectability can escape like flowing blood. It is, after all, on the window ledge that Lockwood finds Catherine's different names obsessively inscribed, as if the girl had been trying to decide which self to let in the window or in which direction she ought to fly after making her own escape down the branches of the neighboring pine. It is through the same window that the ghost of Catherine Linton extends her icy fingers to the horrified visitor. And it is a window at the Grange that Catherine, in her "madness," begs Nelly to open so that she can have one breath of the wind that "comes straight down the moor" (Chap. 12). "Open the window again wide, fasten it open!" she cries, then rises and, predicting her own death, seems almost ready to start on her journey homeward up the moor. ("I could not trust her alone by the gaping lattice," Nelly comments wisely.) But besides expressing a general wish to escape from "this shattered prison" of her body, her marriage, her self, her life, Catherine's desire now to *open* the window refers specifically back to that moment three years earlier when she had chosen instead to close it, chosen to inflict on herself the imprisonment and starvation that as part of her education had been inflicted on her double, Heathcliff.

Imprisonment leads to madness, solipsism, paralysis, as Byron's *Prisoner of Chillon*, some of Brontë's Gondal poems, and countless other gothic and neo-gothic tales suggest. Starvation—both in the modern sense of malnutrition and the archaic Miltonic sense of freezing ("to starve in ice")—leads to weakness, immobility, death. During her decline, starting with both starvation and imprisonment, Catherine passes through all these grim stages of mental and physical decay. At first she seems (to Nelly anyway) merely somewhat "head-strong." Powerless without her whip, keenly conscious that she has lost the autonomy of her hardy and free girlhood, she gets her way by indulging in tantrums, wheedling, manipulating, so that Nelly's optimistic belief that she and Edgar "were really in possession of a deep and growing happiness" contrasts ironically with the housekeeper's simultaneous admission that Catherine "was never subject to depression of spirits before" the three interlocking events of Heathcliff's departure, her "perilous illness," and her marriage (Chap. 10). But Heathcliff's mysterious reappearance six months after her wedding intensifies rather than cures her symptoms. For his return does not in any way suggest a healing of the wound of femaleness that was inflicted at puberty. Instead, it signals the beginning of "madness," a sort of feverish infection of the wound. Catherine's marriage to Edgar has now inexorably locked her into a social system that denies her autonomy, and thus, as psychic symbolism, Heathcliff's return represents the return of her true self's desires without the rebirth of her former powers. And desire without power, as Freud and Blake both knew, inevitably engenders disease.

If we understand all the action that takes place at Thrushcross Grange between Edgar, Catherine, and Heathcliff from the moment of Heathcliff's reappearance until the time of Catherine's death to be ultimately psychodramatic, a grotesque playing out of Catherine's emotional fragmentation on a "real" stage, then further discussion of her sometimes genteelly Victorian, sometimes fiercely Byronic decline becomes almost unnecessary, its meaning is so obvious. Edgar's autocratic hostility to Heathcliff—that is, to Catherine's desirous self, her independent will—manifests itself first in his attempt to have her entertain the returned "gipsy" or "ploughboy" in the kitchen because he doesn't belong in the parlor. But soon Edgar's hatred results in a determination to expel Healthcliff entirely from his house because he fears the effects of this demonic intruder, with all he signifies, not only upon his wife but upon his sister. His fear is justified because, as we shall see, the Satanic rebellion Heathcliff introduces into the parlors of "heaven" contains the germ of a terrible dis-ease with patriarchy that causes women like Catherine and Isabella to try to escape their imprisonment in roles and houses by running away, by starving themselves, and finally by dying.

* * *

Joseph's important remark about the restoration of the lawful master and the ancient stock, together with the dates—1801/1802—which surround Nelly's tale of a pseudo-mythic past, confirm the idea that *Wuthering Heights* is somehow etiological. More, the famous care with which Brontë worked out the details surrounding both the novel's dates and the Earnshaw-Linton lineage suggests she herself was quite conscious that she was constructing a story of origins and renewals. Having arrived at the novel's conclusion, we can now go back to its beginning, and try to summarize the basic story *Wuthering Heights* tells. Though this may not be the book's only story, it is surely a crucial one. As the names on the windowsill indicate, *Wuthering Heights* begins and ends with Catherine and her various avatars. More specifically, it studies the evolution of Catherine Earnshaw into Catherine Heathcliff and Catherine Linton, and then her return through Catherine Linton II and Catherine Heathcliff II to her "proper" role as Catherine Earnshaw II. More generally, what this evolution and de-evolution conveys is the following parodic, anti-Miltonic myth:

There was an Original Mother (Catherine), a daughter of nature whose motto might be "Thou, Nature, art my goddess; to thy law / My services are bound." But this girl fell into a decline, at least in part through eating the poisonous cooked food of culture. She fragmented herself into mad or dead selves on the one hand (Catherine, Heathcliff) and into lesser, gentler/genteeler selves on the other (Catherine II, Hareton). The fierce primordial selves disappeared into nature, the perversely hellish heaven which was their home.

The more teachable and docile selves learned to read and write, and moved into the fallen cultured world of parlors and parsonages, the Miltonic heaven which, from the Original Mother's point of view, is really hell. Their passage from nature to culture was facilitated by a series of teachers, preachers, nurses, cooks, and model ladies or patriarchs (Nelly, Joseph, Frances, the Lintons), most of whom gradually disappear by the end of the story, since these lesser creations have been so well instructed that they are themselves able to become teachers or models for other generations. Indeed, so model are they that they can be identified with the founders of ancestral houses (Hareton Earnshaw, 1500) and with the original mother redefined as the patriarch's wife (Catherine Linton Heathcliff Earnshaw).

* * *

Emily Brontë seems to have believed that Eve had become tragically separated from her fiery original self, and that therefore she had "lost her Virgin Eagle Body . . . and so been sown into a slumbering Death, in Folly, Weakness, and Dishonor."[9]

Her slumbering death, however, was one from which Eve might still arise. Elegiac as it is, mournfully definitive as its myth of origin seems, *Wuthering Heights* is nevertheless haunted by the ghost of a lost gynandry, a primordial possibility of power now only visible to children like the ones who see Heathcliff and Catherine.

> No promised Heaven, these wild Desires
> Could all or half fulfil,
> No threatened Hell, with quenchless fire
> Subdue this quenchless will!

Emily Brontë declares in one of her poems. The words may or may not be intended for a Gondalian speech, but it hardly matters, since in any case they characterize the quenchless and sardonically impious will that stalks through *Wuthering Heights*, rattling the windowpanes of ancient houses and blotting the pages of family bibles. Exorcised from the hereditary estate of the ancient stock, driven to the sinister androgyny of their *Liebestod*, Catherine and Heathcliff nevertheless linger still at the edge of the estate, as witch and goblin, Eve and Satan. Lockwood's two dreams, presented as prologues to Nelly's story, are also, then, necessary epilogues to that tale. In the first, "Jabes Branderham," Joseph's nightmare fellow, tediously thunders Miltonic curses at Lockwood, enumerating the four hundred and ninety sins of which erring nature and the quenchless will

9. Jane Lead, *A Fountain of Gardens* (London, 1697–1701), II:105–7.

are guilty. In the second, nature, personified as the wailing witch child "Catherine Linton," rises willfully in protest, and gentlemanly Lockwood's unexpectedly violent attack upon her indicates his terrified perception of the danger she represents.

* * *

MARTHA NUSSBAUM

Wuthering Heights: the Romantic Ascent†

I

> "If I were in heaven, Nelly, I should be extremely miserable. I dreamt, once, that I was there. . . . [H]eaven did not seem to be my home; and I broke my heart with weeping to come back to earth; and the angels were so angry that they flung me out, into the middle of the heath on the top of Wuthering Heights; where I woke sobbing for joy." (Ch. IX)

Cathy's soul cannot live in the Christian heaven. For her soul, she explains, is the same as Heathcliff's soul, and the heavenly soul of Linton is as different from theirs "as a moonbeam from lightning, or frost from fire." Much later, as she lies on her deathbed, now the wife of Edgar Linton, thinking the Linton thought that what she wants is an escape into "that glorious world" of paradise and peace, Heathcliff watches her with burning eyes. At last she calls to him:

> In her eagerness she rose and supported herself on the arm of the chair. At that earnest appeal, he turned to her, looking absolutely desperate. His eyes wide, and wet at last, flashed fiercely on her; his breast heaved convulsively. An instant they held asunder; and then how they met I hardly saw, but Catherine made a spring, and he caught her, and they were locked in an embrace from which I thought my mistress would never be released alive. In fact, to my eyes, she seemed directly insensible. He flung himself into the nearest seat, and on my approaching hurriedly to ascertain if she had fainted, he gnashed at me, and foamed like a mad dog, and gathered her to him with greedy jealousy. I did not feel as if I were in the company of a creature of my own species; it appeared that he

† From *Philosophy and Literature* 20 (1996): 362–82. Reprinted by permission of Johns Hopkins University Press and the author.

> would not understand, though I spoke to him; so I stood off, and held my tongue, in great perplexity. (Ch. XV)

Brontë's description alludes to the imagery of the Christian ascent tradition. As in Augustine and Dante, love is a flame that animates the eyes, a lightning bolt that pierces the fog of our obtuse daily condition; as in that tradition, love's energy causes the lover to leap away from the petty egoism of the daily into an ecstatic and mutually loving embrace. But we know we are far from the world of the Christian ascent, even its erotic Augustinian form. Cathy's spring is not an upward, but a horizontal movement—not toward heaven, but toward her beloved moors and winds, severed from which she would find heaven miserable; not toward God but toward Heathcliff, the lover of her soul. Nor is there redemption into heaven in this work; there is, if anything, a redemption *from* a world dominated by the imagination of heaven, into a world that the pious Ellen Dean can recognize only as an animal world, a world inhabited by creatures of a different species, who probably do not understand language, so thoroughly are they identified with the energy of the body. A few hours after Cathy's death Heathcliff, as Ellen Dean tells us, in a sudden "paroxysm of ungovernable passion," dashes his head against the knotted trunk of a tree, splashing the bark with blood, "and, lifting up his eyes, howled, not like a man, but like a savage beast being goaded to death with knives and spears" (Ch. XVI). It is in his world alone, it would seem, that flame is truly found. As Cathy said to Edgar Linton, "Your cold blood cannot be worked into a fever: your veins are full of ice-water, but mine are boiling, and the sight of such chillness makes them dance" (Ch. XI).

Brontë's novel situates itself within a long tradition of writing about love and its ascent or purification. This tradition, inaugurated by Socrates' description of the ladder of love in Plato's *Symposium*, is continued by later Platonists, and radically reformulated by Christian thinkers, who stress, against Plato, the soul's receptivity and vulnerability to the inscrutable operations of grace. In both the Platonic and the Christian pictures, however, love's ascent leads ultimately—whether in this life or the next—to a resting-place in which there is no more longing and striving. Desire, propelling itself upward, seeks, and finds, its own extinction. The vulnerability that gave birth to desire is for all time removed—and, with it, the body seen as a seat of vulnerability and therefore an object of shame.[1] In Romantic conceptions of love's ascent, striving itself, and the

1. The body that will join the soul at the last judgment is a purified and perfected body, no longer vulnerable to disease or unchaste desire.

peculiarly human movements of embodied erotic effort, become an ascent and an end in themselves, in no need of redemption by a static and extra-temporal telos. Indeed, redemption is found in the very depth of exposure in erotic effort—redemption from the clutter of everyday life and its superficial cares, which obscure from the self its own true being. In the very extent of the lovers' exposure to pain and risk in love, a risk so profound that it courts death, there is the most authentic expression of pure and purified life; and there is an expression of both agency and particularity in love that is, so it would seem, unavailable to any less reckless passion.

The Platonic lover and the Christian lover had to be redeemed from the ordinary world to a purer world; so too here. But the direction of redemption is not from striving and temporality and embodiment toward peace and stasis; it is, rather, from a hollow simulacrum of peace to the vibrant energy of the committed soul; striving is now given full value as an end. Romantic lovers will still, like the Christian lover, cast aspersions on false attachments to worldly status and worldly goods, which are still seen as impediments to authentic personal love. But their heaven is not Edgar Linton's static paradise, it is the vibrant realm of earthly passion, in which nature and the body become the very essence of the loving soul. They will still have the Christian lover's concern for free agency and for particular perception in love. But this concern can no longer be housed, it would seem, within a conventional system of religious authority; agency must find its own direction from within itself, and its way looks to the conventional Christian like the way to hell.

The Romantic ascent of love takes more than one form. Within a general commitment to striving as an end in itself, one may find versions that attempt to reconcile romantic goals with the Christian ascent; but one may also discover a bleaker vision. In examining the dark world of *Wuthering Heights*, we must ask whether it proposes an ascent at all, and whether its critique of the Christian ascent is valid as a critique of Augustine and Dante, or only as a commentary on degenerate instances of Christian piety that such thinkers would also find prideful and dead. Finally, we must ask whether this love can stand in any fruitful relationship to community and to general compassion. Romantic love will claim that it uncovers deep sources of spiritual richness and personal authenticity without which any morality of human concern is dead. But the question must be what happens next—whether love can find a way back to compassion, or whether its absorption in the particular is so deep that it must simply depart from the world.

As she addresses these questions, Brontë issues a defiant challenge to all systems of conventional social virtue, suggesting that the Christian ascent is doomed in its very nature to produce chilly and inauthentic human relations. This is so, she will suggest, because of its relationship to the deep reasons why human beings shroud themselves in egoism and refuse true love. Up to a point, as we shall see, Brontë expresses a radical Augustinian Christian sensibility, convicting the conventional Christian world of self-protectiveness and pride. But her challenge ultimately reaches beyond the conventional, to challenge the roots of Augustinian Christianity itself. The novel is therefore structured around an opposition between Christian pity and authentic love, in which Heathcliff cannot see out of his love to a general concern for others, and in which the conventionally compassionate gaze of Ellen Dean cannot "see into" his passion, though its intensity lures and fascinates her. (Seeing Heathcliff staining the tree trunk with his own blood, she remarks, "It hardly moved my compassion—it appalled me; still, I felt reluctant to quit him so.")

In short: the Romantic lover claims to bring to the Christian world an energy and a depth of commitment that it has lost. Can it do so without forfeiting Christian pity and turning us into animals?

A preliminary observation. In a number of works in the post-Dantean ascent tradition, we discover the figure of an outsider or alien—closely linked with the point of view of the implied author of the work. These aliens are of dark complexion, suspiciously soft and sensuous, of ambiguous gender or sexuality. They are mocked and hated by the Christian world around them, which shrinks from their too intimate, too penetrating gaze. The dark-skinned gypsy Heathcliff is both male and, as double of Cathy, female; in the self-exposure of his passion he defies conventional norms of manly control. * * *

II

We must begin with two features of the novel that are likely to be forgotten by readers who have read the novel years ago, or whose memory is colored by the Hollywood film version. These are: the character of the work's narrator, Mr. Lockwood, and the ubiquity in the text of hatred and revenge. * * *

The work opens * * * with the refusal of community. The city man has come to the country to avoid, it seems, the "stir" and bustle of superficial social forms. But what attracts Mr. Lockwood to Thrushcross Grange is not simply its wildness, its promise of intensity. It is, at the same time, its desolation, its emptiness of love. It is, at the same time, retentiveness and self-sufficiency.

The man through whose eyes this strange world is described for us is a city man, a refined society man, a man of means. His usual occupation in the country is hunting—which he calls "devastat[ing] the moors." His usual milieu is "the stirring atmosphere of the town." His usual vacation choice is "a month of fine weather at the seacoast." His choice of the desolate isolation of Thrushcross Grange is, however, not accidental: it grows from the "peculiar constitution" that led his mother to predict that he "should never have a comfortable home." This constitution is shortly revealed as an inability to accept the reciprocation of love:

> While enjoying a month of fine weather at the sea-coast, I was thrown into the company of a most fascinating creature, a real goddess in my eyes, as long as she took no notice of me. I "never told my love" vocally; still, if looks have language, the merest idiot might have guessed I was over head and ears: she understood me at last, and looked a return—the sweetest of all imaginable looks. And what did I do? I confess it with shame—shrunk icily into myself, like a snail; at every glance retired colder and farther; till, finally, the poor innocent was led to doubt her own senses, and, overwhelmed with confusion at her supposed mistake, persuaded her mamma to decamp.
>
> By this curious turn of disposition I have gained the reputation of deliberate heartlessness, how undeserved, I alone can appreciate. (Ch. I)

The entire story, then, is made possible because Lockwood is afraid and ashamed of love. In a gesture that parallels Cathy's refusal of Heathcliff, he pretends that he does not have feelings that he evidently does—why? Because to him the reciprocation of love is more terrifying than its non-reciprocation, because the gaze of desire, seeing into his own desire, makes him passive and ashamed of his own softness, the snail without its shell. Because a life of watching and romantic narration is manageable, and a life of passion is not. His name is significantly chosen: he locks his vulnerability away behind the wooden exterior of conventional social forms.

Nor is this locking without its clear psychic cost. The first night he spends under the roof of Wuthering Heights, stranded by a snowstorm, Lockwood is tormented by a dream. He falls asleep reading Cathy Linton's journal, in which she has been describing her brother Hindley's cruelty to Heathcliff. He now has a dream that he is in a chapel, where the Reverend Jabes Branderham is delivering a sermon divided into four hundred ninety parts, each discussing a separate sin. * * *

Lockwood's dream reveals a depth of guilt and anxiety that can only be discharged, it seems, in ferocious aggression against anyone who sees into his situation. What is the four hundred ninety-first sin, the sin that no Christian need pardon? Is it the erotic love he has felt, or is it his snail-like shame, his inability to express and reciprocate love? We do not know: we know only that Lockwood wants to murder the eye that sees him, to wipe out the reminder of his nakedness. We know only that he is haunted by the piteous voice of an unknown woman, trying to force her frozen arm through a crack in the casement. He longs so intensely to open the casement that he is forced to adopt three stratagems to prevent himself from yielding. He stops his ears; he piles up books, the armory of the intellect; he bloodies the arm that has reached too far inside. As he says: terror made me cruel.

By framing the narrative in this way, Brontë makes us consider from the start that the obstacles to deep love are not only obstacles created by superficial social deadness and hypocrisy—though, as we shall see, they do include these. The obstacle to Lockwood's love is in his own shame and fear, which make him flee the nakedness of reciprocated passion. He is both kin to Heathcliff and his opposite pole—fascinated by his darkness, drawn to his gloomy integrity and depth, to the depth of life in the countryside, where people live "more in earnest, more in themselves, and less in surface, change, and frivolous external things." But at the same time he is ice to Heathcliff's fire, the self-protective snail to Heathcliff's total exposure, shame to his almost bestial shamelessness, observation and narration to his total immersion. Self-protection has exacted a price in his inner world: for the effort required to repel the objects that ask to be let in is so great that it produces a poisonous cruelty and envy directed at all in the world who are not locked up: at the dark alien above all, whose gaze reveals to him his own fear of penetration. Later, having lost the chance to court the younger Cathy out of fear of danger, thus repeating the refusal of love that led him to the moors, Lockwood can only watch Cathy and Hareton with "a mingled sense of curiosity and envy," and, "feeling very mean and malignant," "skul[k] round to seek refuge in the kithen."

The famous Olivier film of the novel had one great virtue: the nobility and clarity of Olivier's Heathcliff, who has an evident greatness of soul, a towering generosity of passion and thought, that the other inhabitants of this dark world all lack. In another way, however, the film is a disastrous distortion. For it makes the world of the novel if dark, still "romantic" in an acceptable and even pretty way. It more or less completely omits one of the novel's most striking characteristics: the obsession of its narrators and almost all of its other characters with anger, revenge, even cruelty. The story, as recollected by the internal narrator, Ellen Dean, begins with an act of Christian charity. Mr. Earnshaw comes home from Liverpool with a gypsy child, "a dirty, ragged, black-haired child." "You must e'en take it as a gift of God," says Mr. Earnshaw to his wife, "though it's as dark almost as if it came from the devil." The child was homeless and starving in the streets. He inquired for its owner, and, getting no reply, refused to leave it as he had found it. Earnshaw takes the alien into his home, determined to treat it as the equal of his own children.

From this auspicious beginning, however, we soon move on to a world dominated by envy, prejudice, and violence. The children refuse to allow Heathcliff in their room. Ellen Dean exiles him to the stair landing. Hindley and Ellen come increasingly to hate him, and they torment him without cease, both physically and psychologically. Heathcliff, all the while, endures Hindley's blows without retaliation; he "said precious little, and generally the truth." Because Mr. Earnshaw favors Heathcliff, "all hated, and longed to do him an ill turn." The torture accelerates at Mr. Earnshaw's death. Heathcliff is relegated to servant status, mocked and humiliated. When at last he turns against his oppressors, throwing a dish of applesauce at Edgar Linton, the pattern of the violent plot is set. Envy and retribution dominate the novel, in scene after scene of brutal and uncontrolled physical violence in which every character partakes. Cathy pinches her devoted servant Ellen "with a prolonged wrench, very spitefully on the arm." She slaps her on the cheek, shakes little Hareton until he is white, and hits her suitor Edgar on the ear. Hindley takes a knife to his own son and threatens to cut off the little boy's ears. Heathcliff and Cathy talk with pleasure of how Isabella Linton's face might be turned black and blue "every day or two." Edgar Linton, overcome by "mingled anger and humiliation," strikes Heathcliff "full on the throat a blow that would have levelled a slighter man." Cathy dashes her own head against the sofa until she lies as if dead, with "blood on her lips." The marriage of Heathcliff and Isabella contains, it appears, both physical violence and sexual sadomasochism.[2] Heathcliff holds the dying Cathy's arm so fiercely that Ellen sees "four distinct impressions left blue in the colorless skin." Heathcliff dashes his head against the knotted tree-trunk, splashing it with his blood, and throws a knife at Ellen, who mocks his grief. Little Hareton is observed

2. This aspect is veiled in obscurity. Isabella breaks off—"But I'll not repeat his language, nor describe his habitual conduct: he is ingenious and unresting in seeking to gain my abhorrence! I sometimes wonder at him with an intensity that deadens my fear: yet, I assure you, a tiger or a venomous serpent could not rouse terror in me equal to that which he wakens." It is compatible with these lines that Heathcliff's sadism consists in mockery and humiliation, rather than in physical sexual cruelty. But the intent to cause suffering and humiliation of some painful sort is central to Heathcliff's plan: "he told me . . . that I should be Edgar's proxy in suffering, till he could get hold of him." Isabella's narration of the marriage does not acknowledge any pleasure in Heathcliff's cruelty; but Heathcliff sees it: "But no brutality disgusted her: I suppose she has an innate admiration of it. . . ."

"hanging a litter of puppies from a chair-back in the doorway"—as Heathcliff once hanged Isabella Linton's little dog.

As Lockwood says: terror and shame produce cruelty. From the petty quarrels and the petty revenge of Edgar and Isabella to the grand obsessive sweep of Heathcliff's entire life, the desire to retaliate for a slight or humiliation produces most of the action of the book, until every love is mingled with disdain or hatred. Hindley hates Heathcliff and avenges on him his own father's deficient love. Later, reduced to a drunken shadow of his former self, his eyes gleaming with "burning hate," he contemplates a final act of violence against the man who has robbed him of his property. Isabella hates the Heathcliff who abuses her. Edgar "abhors" Heathcliff "with an intensity which the mildness of his nature would scarcely seem to allow." Heathcliff, from the beginning mocked and humiliated for his dark skin, his poverty, and his unknown origins, devotes his entire life to revenge against Hindley and the Lintons, making himself master of Hindley's fortune, leading Isabella into a life of misery. Just as he can play the gentleman better than the gentlemen, just as he can play the money maker better than the money makers, so too he can play at envy and violence—although his heart is altogether elsewhere, although he could do no harm to his beloved Cathy, although he would and does give her his entire life. The others torment out of fear; only Heathcliff torments out of love.

III

The novel sets up a central opposition between the Christian world of the Lintons, a world of Christian "pity," "charity," and "humanity," and the world of Heathcliff, a world of love from the point of view of which the Linton sentiments appear watery and self-serving. Isabella Linton, writing home to Ellen after her marriage to Heathcliff: "How did you contrive to preserve the common sympathies of human nature when you resided here? I cannot recognize any sentiment which those around share with me." Ellen is moved to compassion for Heathcliff's loss, but she cannot really feel compassion for him—so far has he, in her view, put himself outside the common behavior of human beings. " 'Do you understand what the word pity means?' " she asked him long before. " 'Did you ever feel a touch of it in your life?' " It would appear that the Linton world is the world of compassion and the moral virtues, whereas Heathcliff's world is amoral and impervious to sympathy.

But things are not so simple. We have seen already that the world of the Christian characters is portrayed as the source of poisonous cruelty against the alien. Heathcliff can give back what he gets—but he is not the initiator of violence, nor is it clear that his refusal of the Linton moral sentiments is to be simply condemned. For the world of the Lintons, the heavenly world, is also depicted as a shallow world: an indoor world, by contrast to the wild and passionate world of the moors, a world of stasis by contrast to Heathcliff and Cathy's restless motion, a world of ungenerous and spiteful social judgments, by contrast to the sweep and size of all of Heathcliff's passions. When Cathy announces her plan to marry Edgar, Ellen Dean asks her where the obstacle is: " '*Here!* and *here!*' replied Catherine, striking one hand on her forehead, and the other on her breast: 'in whichever place the soul lives. In my soul and in my heart, I'm convinced I'm wrong' " (Ch. IX).

She is wrong, she continues, because heaven is not a place in which her soul could ever be happy. She dreamed that she was in heaven, and wept for the earth; and "the angels were so angry that they flung me out into the middle of the heath on the top of Wuthering Heights; where I woke sobbing for joy. Heathcliff's soul, she continues, is made of the same stuff that hers is, he is "more myself than I am," while Linton's soul "is as different as a moonbeam from lightning, or frost from fire." And after Heathcliff's angry rejection of pity, he insists that these heavenly sentiments, in the Linton world, produce a kind of hell, the absence of real passion: "Oh, I've no doubt she's in hell among you! . . . You say she is often restless, and anxious-looking—is that a proof of tranquillity? . . . And that insipid, paltry creature attending her from *duty* and *humanity*! From *pity* and *charity*! He might as well plant an oak in a flowerpot, and expect it to thrive, as imagine he can restore her to vigour in the soil of his shallow cares!" (Ch. XIV). Where is, then, the real heaven of emotion, and where its hell?

There is a doubleness, then, in the novel's treatment of Christian charity. On the one hand, it shows Heathcliff as demonic and scarcely human; on the other hand, it stands accused, itself, of shallowness, fearfulness, and self-protection. There is a corresponding ambiguity in the imagery used of Heathcliff, who is depicted as bestial and demonic—but also as a figure of authentic Christian love. * * * Clearly, it is not a minor devil that he is seen to resemble; it is Lucifer himself, whose pride leads him to rebel against all religion, all moral authority. When he refuses Ellen Dean's compassion after Cathy's death, she cries, "Your pride cannot blind God! You tempt Him to wring them [his nerves], till He forces a cry of humiliation."

On the other hand, it is only Heathcliff, in this novel who gives his life for another. All the other characters hold something back, insist on control and calculation, insist on seeing all round about them, their mind and eyes not fixed on any one. And this means that in a very real sense they are already half dead. What the devil's spies of Heathcliff's countenance see in their faces is avoidance, eyes deflected away from the world and those whom they are alleged to love. When Edgar Linton dies, his "rapt, radiant gaze" on the heavenly world, "none could have noticed the exact minute of his death, it was so entirely without a struggle." The love of Heathcliff for Cathy contains the total exposure of self to other from which Lockwood shrank in fear and in shame. Only Heathcliff permits his very soul to be at risk. The other is in him and is him. In her death he dies, in a surrender, incomprehensible to the narrators, of reason and of boundaries. At Cathy's death, the blood of Heathcliff's head is spattered on the bark of the tree, "a repetition of other [scenes] acted during the night."

The dead sentiments of Linton are linked with social morality, and both of these with self-protective control and calculation. Heathcliff's entirely unguarded love is linked, by contrast, with a deeper sort of generosity and the roots of a truer altruism. There is no character but Heathcliff in this novel who really sacrifices his life for the life of another, none who acts against his own interests with sincere and uncompromised altruism. For he refrains from doing any harm to Edgar for fear that Cathy would suffer by his loss, and sacrifices his own interests at every turn to hers, both before and after her death. The capacity to throw away all self-centered calculation is at the heart of real altruism and authentic (Christian) morality. And in this sense Heathcliff—despite the vindictiveness forced into his character by abuse and humiliation—is not only the only living person among the dead, the only civilized man among savages, he is in a genuine if peculiar sense, the only Christian among the Pharisees, and—with respect to the one person he loves—a sacrificial figure of Christ himself, the only one who sheds his own blood for another. The novel suggests that only in this deep exposure is there true sacrifice and true redemption. At the novel's end, only Heathcliff's tombstone is uncovered by moss; and a child tells Lockwood that he has seen Heathcliff and Cathy walking on the moors. "They are afraid of nothing," Lockwood grumbles—referring ambiguously to the ghostly couple and to the younger living couple who have just returned from a loving walk. "Together they would brave Satan and all his legions."

IV

What, then, is the novel's critique of the Christian ascent? It works at two distinct levels. The first level is a critique of the Christianity depicted in the novel, and up to a point we may suppose that it is a critique of a degenerate imperfect Christianity. At this level four grave charges are made. First, the Christian sentiments of the pious characters are shown to be in large part hypocritical. The Lintons, Joseph, Ellen Dean, all pay lip service to pity and charity, but—as Ellen Dean at least has the grace to admit—all behave selfishly and vindictively most of the time. Joseph's rigid piety is a way of tyrannizing over the house; Edgar and Isabella are vain and "petted" children whose love is contaminated by vanity. All engage in vindictive actions, all seek to humiliate their enemies. And whereas Heathcliff's revenge is grand and caused by love, theirs is petty and self-serving. These degenerate sentiments, however, do derive nourishment from the institutionalized Christianity the characters know: for they have all learned to justify their acts using images of divine anger and retribution. Heathcliff's pride, says Ellen, tempts God to wring his nerves "till He forces a cry of humiliation." So the first charge is that institutionalized Christianity does too little to discourage vindictiveness and hatred.

Second, institutionalized Christianity is charged with supporting a world of social hierarchy that excludes the poor and the strange, the dark-skinned and the nameless. For the Linton world, Heathcliff's dark looks and lower-class manners must keep him apart from a Cathy who is taught that to marry him would "degrade" her. The good Christians are too prompt, we feel, to baptize Heathcliff as fiend and devil; it is an all too convenient way of repudiating a look that they do not like, a sexuality that frightens them. From the perspective of Christian piety, Cathy sees Heathcliff as terribly unlike herself, his love as unworthy. From the perspective of her love, these distinctions of rank vanish, and he is "more myself than I am." To him as well, she is his life, his soul; and nothing but her refusal can divide them. The second charge, then, is that Christianity will only realize its true potential if it embraces these differences and teaches a truly universal love.

Third, conventional Christianity, it is charged, teaches people to look to a static paradise in which all movement and striving cease. It thus teaches them to denigrate their own movement and striving, to cultivate the small Linton virtues rather than the large risk-taking virtues. This is a point made much later by Nietzsche; it emerges here in the contrast between Edgar, who dies before his death, and Heathcliff, who has no interest in any static telos. Cathy, torn between the two conceptions of the end, at last prefers the this-worldly striving of Heathcliff, the "ramble at liberty" that was always hers and Heathcliff's delight. The love of earth is an end in itself. An obsessive theme in Emily Brontë's poems and essays, it is often, as here, associated with the theme of personal liberty. The heavenly world is depicted as one in which agency has been surrendered, at last, to authority, a world in which one's place is fixed for all eternity. The world of nature and the earth, by contrast, is a world in which the heart can roam freely, and its agency is whole: "Give we the hills our equal prayer," Emily wrote in a poem of 1841, "Earth's breezy hills and heaven's blue sea; / We ask for nothing further here / But our own hearts and liberty." As Charlotte Brontë wrote, describing Emily's physical breakdown when she was sent to a boarding school where she could not roam around on the moors: "Liberty was the breath of Emily's nostrils; without it, she perished."[3]

* * *

In this third critique Emily, known to many acquaintances as the most philosophical and rigorous of the Brontë children, goes straight to the heart of the question of agency and freedom in the Christian ascent. The directedness of longing toward a static telos, she suggests, diminishes the significance of human agency and its liberty. The provisional character of all earthly relations squeezes them into small Linton sentiments. As Heathcliff says, it is like planting an oak in a flowerpot. This world, the suggestion is, will always remain a hell if we are allowed to aim at redemption from it, rather than at the amelioration of life within it, and led to anticipate the end of striving, rather than to respect the dignity of the striving itself.

Finally, the Christian world of the novel is charged with a neglect of one of the greatest of the human faculties, the imagination. None of the Christian characters imagines the life of another with vivid sympathy. Lockwood and Ellen Dean skulk round the edges of the world of the novel watching and waiting; their damaged inner lives call out to the characters with a mysterious longing; but this longing is distorted by malice. Only Heathcliff, from the beginning, knows how to imagine the hearts of his fellows. Only he consoles Cathy on her father's death; only he can inhabit her soul, and move so close to her that their two souls are as one. Heathcliff's heart, by contrast, is treated obtusely from the start by all the Christian characters around him, who can penetrate no deeper than the color of his skin, so little have their faculties of wonder been cultivated. What is called Christian pity is but a shell, until it is infused and given life by the visitation of that "sterner power"—as Emily writes in another early poem.

How far do these four charges touch the Christian ascent itself, and how far are they merely indictments of a lifeless and degenerate Christianity? Would a keenly alive, surgingly erotic Augustinian Christianity contain all that Brontë calls for here? (In asking these questions I do not step outside the world of the text itself; for Emily was an extremely learned classical scholar whose education in-

3. Juliet Barker, *The Brontës* (London: Orion, 1994), pp. 346–47.

cluded much essay-writing on just such Christian themes.) Indeed, her teacher in Brussels, M. Heger, expressed the view that Emily ought to become a philosopher: she had "a head for logic, and a capability of argument, unusual in a man, and rare indeed in a woman."[4] So: what is this philosophical mind expressing, and how far does it cut into the views we have studied?

We had already had questions for both Dante and Augustine about anger and intolerance, and about the hierarchies created by them. Christianity will need to become more inclusive of the alien and the stranger than either of these two ascents has yet been, in order to satisfy her demand. A still deeper challenge lies in the Romantic defense of liberty and imagination, values that are difficult to accommodate fully within a universe in which desire points insistently toward heaven. Dante * * * took up this challenge to at least some extent, restoring dignity to the this-worldly will and denying that earthly relations and acts are merely provisional. But there remained questions about the freedom of the mind within a context of authority, and about the significance of this-worldly striving within a universe that points toward eternity. One can imagine a romantic reformulation of the Thomistic Christian universe. * * * But it does require a serious reformulation of the ideal, not just a criticism of people who fail to live up to the norm.

V

We must now move, however, to the deeper level of the novel's critique. For the novel's critique of Christian charity does not address itself only to these elements, revisable in principle. Indeed, it traces all of these defects—especially cruelty to and hatred of the alien—to deeper human motives that are not only not cured but very much nourished by Christian teaching.

The love of Heathcliff and Cathy requires, we said, a total exposure of self to another's touch and gaze. In this way it courts a risk so total that it verges toward death. To one who loves totally, no defenses can exist. The other is in oneself and is oneself. For to allow one's boundaries to be porous in this way is not to be the self that one was and in society is. It is, indeed, to be an alien and a gypsy, to give up on the hard shell of self-sufficiency with which all these characters protect themselves.

The real question of the novel, we must now see, is not why Heathcliff cannot have Cathy. That is a material and social and political question, and in the end a superficial one. The deeper question is, why Cathy cannot accept Heathcliff, why she must be

4. Barker, p. 392.

false to him, and to her own soul. Why she is driven to choose someone who cannot truly love her over someone who sees and loves and *is* her, a civilized but superficial sexual flirtation * * * over a profound passion of the body and the spirit, the conventions of stable public married life over a life that contains and acknowledges her real self. "The sea could be as readily contained in that horse-trough, as her whole affection be monopolised by him!" And yet she chooses that "love" over the love that is the identity of her own soul.

It is not enough to say that the situation Heathcliff can offer her involves pain and adversity and social exclusion. This is true, but it is no explanation. As Heathcliff says, "Because misery and degradation, and death, and nothing that God or Satan could inflict would have parted us, *you*, of your own will, did it. I have not broken your heart—*you* have broken it; and in breaking it, you have broken mine. . . . *Why* did you betray your own heart, Cathy?"

Why indeed. Cathy's story, I think, is another version of the story of Mr. Lockwood. The extreme exposure of true passion, and its links with pain and death, are as intolerable, ultimately, to her as they were to our narrator. A part of her is Heathcliff. But she cannot bear the nakedness of that part; she is driven to cover it over with the clothing of the Linton life, with marriage and children, with social form and hierarchy, with a life that is a revenge against both her and him, against the naked self that he calls forth in her. In seeking to protect herself from the risk of death, however, she kills not only him but also her own soul, and forces him to hate as well as love her. He says, holding her, "Kiss me again; and don't let me see your eyes! I forgive what you have done to me. I love *my* murderer—but *yours*! How can I?" They draw close only then, in the grief of impending death, "their faces hid against each other, and washed by each other's tears." Heathcliff, who lives in and fully acknowledges the depth of his passion, is by this very act of acknowledgment placed outside the human species. For it is most human to avoid being seen with the eyes of love.

What are these people ashamed of? What do they fear, in fearing love? They fear and are ashamed of being given to and for others, which means that they fear following the image of Christ. But at the same time, the fear and shame take the body and its erotic passions as their object. Lockwood thinks of himself as a snail, curling up inside his shell to avoid encountering the gaze of passion. The snail without the shell is what he is ashamed to be. This is a deep image of the nakedness of the body, seen as an emblem of our helplessness, our penetrability, our givenness to the world's influences and to death. The object of shame and fear is not sexuality in and of itself, but sexuality experienced as a sign of our helpless insufficiency. Love, Brontë suggests—including and especially true Christian love—requires us to be in our insufficiency, given to the world and to others. Christianity, however, reacts to our shame by telling us to cover ourselves—with a fig leaf, with a snail's shell, with the hope of heaven, the submission to authority, the flame of chastity. It tells us that yes, we should be ashamed of our nakedness, we should shrink from the powerful gaze of love. So there is ultimately, she suggests, a deep inconsistency between radical Augustinian openness to grace and the Augustinian attitude to the body and the worldly person. We cannot give our bodies to the world like Christ if we cannot manage, first, to inhabit them and make them ourselves.

The Christian response to primal shame—no easily eliminable aspect of Christian teaching—is thus seen to be in league with the refusal of love. But the refusal of love is, we said, at the root of the hatred of the gaze of the woman, or the alien, the alien's all too fleshy dark presence, the woman's all too palpable embodiment. It is then Brontë's somewhat obscure suggestion that Christian morality is more than accidentally linked with racial hatred and misogyny.

But it is not as if she offers a practical alternative. The life of Heathcliff is unlivable in the world. It will not be tolerated by human beings, who have a deep need to be or become snails and to inflict pain upon those who are not. Nor is it, perhaps, even livable in itself, for already it wears its death upon its face. She offers us, then, a powerful dream of a love that is permitted to enter in at the casement, a love that wears the nobility of true humanity—only to show us that we all will scrape the arm against the pane of broken glass, and pile our books against the opening, and shout, "I'll never let you in, not if you beg for twenty years."

VI

Is there a heaven buried within this novel's hell? Does the love of young Cathy and Hareton, whose development occupies the entire second half of the novel, show possibilities for the harmonious reconciliation of Edgar Linton's pity and Heathcliff's passion? Cathy is introduced as a hopeful fusion of the best elements of the two lines: "Her spirit was high, though not rough, and qualified by a heart sensitive and lively to excess in its affections. That capacity for intense attachments reminded me of her mother: still she did not resemble her; for she could be soft and mild as a dove, and she had a gentle voice and pensive expression: her anger was never furious; her love never fierce: it was deep and tender." And there are hopeful signs in her relationship with Hareton—as she eventually shows him gentle compassion, teaching him to read, and as his sexual strength evokes in her an intensity that Linton Heathcliff could not even perceive.

And yet there is something unconvincing in the union. The most hopeful point is the manly vulnerability of Hareton, whose willingness to risk humiliation and shame for the sake of passion show the potential for real love. But there is an obstacle in the character of his lover. For young Cathy, her father's daughter, spoiled and petulant, has none of the first Cathy's demonic intensity of spirit. Just as she plays at loving a Linton who cannot possibly offer her any real emotion, so later she plays at being the civilizing force who will bring Hareton into line. She seeks him out more because she is bored than because she loves or needs him, and the very notion of deep erotic and spiritual vulnerability seems foreign to her. As she bends over her reading lover, teasing him for his mispronunciation with a "voice as sweet as a silver bell," saying "Recollect, or I'll pull your hair!", we know that we have here but a pale shadow of the woman who clings to Heathcliff with an embrace that was her death. Hareton, following her flirtatious pretty lead, will soon, we feel, be as dead as she.

Is there ascent and reconciliation, then, in the act of narration itself, in the perspectives of Ellen Dean and Lockwood, the riveted onlookers, who see and are moved by the depth of love without being drawn altogether away from general social concerns? We have no reason to think so. The self-protective snail-like character of Lockwood that keeps him in the world also prevents his heart from admitting anything closer to love than envy and spite, its twisted shadows. He sees enough of Heathcliff that we may see him too. But in the end Lockwood does not acknowledge the part of Heathcliff that is in himself. Nor does Ellen Dean show herself capable of real love, in her self-protective avoidance of risk—from the time when she is punished by old Mr. Earnshaw for callously making Heathcliff sleep on the stairs, to her passive collaboration with cruelty years later, as she pities young Cathy but shuts her door for fear of being moved to risk danger. "I didn't wish to lose my place, you know." What she says of the whole world is surely true of her, at least: "we *must* be for ourselves in the long run; the mild and generous are only more justly selfish than the domineering."

There is no final summation to be given here, because there is no positive proposal. The sensibility of this work tragically refuses all solutions, finding the roots of social degeneration deep in the human being's very way of being in the world. It imagines a Christianity reformed so as to remove hierarchy and revenge, so as to validate the claims of this-worldly striving and of the imagination. Then it takes the vision away, leaving us only with an image that haunts our dreams, a hand groping at the casement. We think that we are people of sympathy and charity; we think that we love and permit ourselves to be loved. Chances are we really don't. Chances are that we, like so many, are cleverly hedging our bets. And there is no social justice, just as there is no love, that can come from that.

Three headstones rest side by side on a slope next to the moor near Wuthering Heights. Edgar Linton's is "harmonised by the turf and moss creeping up its foot." Cathy's is "grey, and half buried in heath." Only Heathcliff's is bare. Lockwood the observer "lingered around them, under the benign sky," watching "the moths fluttering among the heath and the harebells," listening to "the soft wind breathing through the grass." He wonders "how any one could ever imagine unquiet slumbers for the sleepers in that quiet earth." A small boy tells Lockwood that he has seen Heathcliff and a woman walking on the moors together. "He probably raised the phantoms from thinking, as he traversed the moors alone." These phantoms of thought persist, to haunt any lover who has made compromises with life.

LIN HAIRE-SARGEANT

Sympathy for the Devil: The Problem of Heathcliff in Film Versions of *Wuthering Heights*†

When Emily Brontë created the pivotal character Heathcliff, she set herself a daunting challenge; how to tell the story of a brutal, calculating sadist, the bane of two families over two generations, in such a way that by the end the reader's horror is overwhelmed by sympathy. At first, critical reaction lacked such sympathy: most reviewers attacked the brutality of the book, saving their worst condemnation for Heathcliff. The *North American Review*'s pronouncement was typical: Heathcliff was a brute "whom the Mephistopheles of Goethe would have nothing to say to, whom the Satan of Milton would consider an object of singular disgust." Eventually the allure of his evil was recognized as part of the power of Brontë's book, and in the next century when *Wuthering Heights* was made into a movie, the stakes for a favorable response to Heathcliff grew

† Revised and expanded by Haire-Sargeant from her essay of the same title in Barbara Tepa Lupack, ed., *Nineteenth-Century Women at the Movies* (Bowling Green, KY: Bowling Green UP, 1999), pp. 167–91. Reprinted by permission of the publisher.

higher. It was not only sympathy for the devil that was required of us; it was love—a necessary generic condition of the feature film, where characters project as gods, the movie screen irresistibly our Olympus, our Sinai. There, even our darkest demons must show as angels dancing bright. Historically the films of *Wuthering Heights* have met this challenge in two ways: either by changing the story so that Heathcliff's evil deeds are lessened or mitigated, or straight on, as Emily Brontë does, directing the reader/viewer to absorb the totality of Heathcliff's evil and good within his human situation.

* * *

Brontë's means to greatness were linguistic; the filmmaker's must be visual. Inevitable differences follow. Where the novelist's words spark individual, intimate mind pictures in each reader, the filmmaker must define the image on the screen, the same for all viewers, and in doing so ground the story in time and space—the time and space in which the movie is filmed, not that in which the story is set. In these ways and others, the filmmaker creates a work of art separate from its "original" yet connected in an intimate way. So we should not judge a movie made from a book as a copy. Rather, we should evaluate whether the movie communicates something of the book's particular art. Then we should ask by what means that art is communicated, since it must be communicated by analog. Finally, we should tender the most important question: does the film succeed as a work of art in its own right? If it does, it creates its own sufficient reason for being. If it does not, it can be criticized not only as a failed film but as a failed adaptation: every departure from the novel becomes a fault. And even a great movie based on a novel has one irredeemable flaw: it is not the novel.

The four film versions of *Wuthering Heights* discussed here vary in mood and meaning, following shifts in time, national origin, and the artists' interpretations. My analysis proceeds chronologically, beginning with William Wyler's *Wuthering Heights*, filmed in the United States in 1939.

In his adaptation, Wyler goes a long way towards solving the problem of Heathcliff with his casting: Laurence Olivier plays Heathcliff like Heathcliff playing Laurence Olivier. The young Olivier delivers a bravura turn as an anesthetized brute whose intelligence takes him on forays into psychologizing sympathy ("You're lonely," he comforts Isabella [Geraldine Fitzgerald]. "It's lonely sitting like an outsider in so happy a household as your brother's. . . . You won't be lonely any more"). On the page this is almost laughably far from Brontë's Heathcliff, but paradoxically, of all the

Heathcliffs, the Wyler/Olivier version gives the strongest analog of Heathcliff's felt emotion, the injustices endured and absorbed, the repressed passion and rage.

This is accomplished partly through Olivier's performance (of which more later), and partly through Wyler's brilliantly conceptualized and realized artistic direction. The film is holographic; every frame, in narrative content and composition, contains the whole story. Wyler controls a black-and-white palette of exquisitely shaded tonality; even on a TV screen the numinously glowing whites, the engulfing blacks, and the shimmering grays eloquently express emotional and spiritual nuance.

The story is considerably truncated in this 103-minute version. It begins with Lockwood's arrival: "A stranger lost in a storm." Lockwood (Leo G. Carroll) runs the gamut of snarling dogs and unanswered knocks to finally gain shelter in Wuthering Heights. The family he encounters is not second generation Earnshaws and Lintons—that story has been cut. Rather it is Isabella, Nelly Dean (Flora Robson), Joseph, and a softened Heathcliff—who, when, reminded of his manners, responds with urbane irony: "I hardly know how to treat a guest—I and my *dog*" and himself offers Lockwood lodging. After Heathcliff, galvanized by Lockwood's dream of Cathy (Merle Oberon), bursts out into the blizzard to seek her, Nelly tells Lockwood the tale of the first generation of Earnshaws and Lintons. The conventional voice-over ("It began forty years ago when I was young") along with the track into a tight close-up of Nelly's face anticipate the dissolve to the long-ago scene of the boy Heathcliff's arrival at Wuthering Heights. The story of the entanglements of Heathcliff, Cathy, Edgar (David Niven), and Isabella, with occasional voice-over commentary by Nelly, is followed through to Cathy's death. Then there is a return to the frame story. As Nelly concludes her tale, Dr. Kenneth comes in out of the blizzard. He has found Heathcliff's body by Penistone Crag after first having seen a vision of him with Cathy. The film ends with a long shot of Heathcliff and Cathy ascending Penistone Crag together.

Paradoxically, Wyler and cinematographer Gregg Toland tell this tale of tightly caged violence through visuals that emphasize open space. In contrast to the description of a disorderly, cramped household in the novel, Wyler's Heights interiors, filmed deep focus, open an airy palatial zone behind the viewing screen. When Lockwood arrives, the camera follows him across uneasy expanses of floor while the family, huddled at the fireside, stare. Eventually Joseph leads Lockwood to his lodging for the night, Cathy's old bedroom. To get from Joseph's presentation—"the bridal chamber"—to Lockwood's reaction, the camera pans across what seems an immense expanse of dingy, candle-lit wall. The meaning of this emphasis on space is not the claustrophobia of the interlocking narratives and the closed worlds of the Heights and the Grange that really exist in Brontë's pages, but rather an edgy agoraphobia that at once contains its opposite and suggests its transcendence.

Another paradox: in the novel, Heathcliff and Cathy are characterized by violent movement—motion equals emotion. In the film, Cathy and Heathcliff, most tempestuous of lovers, are portrayed through the poetics of immobility. Olivier moves through much of the film with his trunk and arms stiff, his eyes fixed and unfocused, like a somnambulist who does not dream. This of course makes his occasional outbreaks of movement—two slaps across faithless Cathy's face, a plunge of bare knuckles through window glass—the more violently emotive, though ultimately we are taught to experience Heathcliff's giant rage most intensely in its tethering. Similarly, Merle Oberon's snow-queen Cathy, herself motionless, with each unmoving second builds charged emotion like a dynamo. She sits frozen at table while Hindley abuses Heathcliff, then flies from the house, over a wall, and up Penistone Crag to a tryst with Heathcliff impelled by a blast of primal desire usually confined by this Cathy's strong proprietary and propertarian good sense.

There is one scene in the film that brilliantly deploys the narrative's two lines of emotional symbolism, the agoraphobic use of space and the burning paralysis of the lovers. In a scene that does not appear in Brontë's book, Edgar and Cathy give a ball at Thrushcross Grange. The scene begins with dance music, then a fade to a moving shot as the camera pans up over a stone wall for an exterior view of Thrushcross Grange, recalling an earlier scene where prelapsarian Heathcliff and Cathy spied on just such a ball. With Cathy's marriage to Edgar she has become part of this world, while Heathcliff, though mysteriously transformed into a gentleman, remains shut out. Through brilliantly lit windows we can glimpse dancing couples. Then there is a fade to the interior scene shown through an ornate mirror. The restless camera pans rather jerkily away from the mirror, across expanses of mechanistically dancing couples, other mirrors, crystal chandeliers. The effect is of a giant music box; artifice, not humanity, is the key. The camera roves nervously above the dancers, a questing, disembodied point of view. Lighting is high key, focus is deep. The camera fixes its gaze on the entrance door; the footmen admit Heathcliff, in impeccable evening dress, a tall black column against the hard white surfaces of the ballroom. A bit later he stands immobile behind a seated Isabella; a harpsichordist begins to play a Mozart sonata. A crane shot circles above the frenetically pounding harpsichordist, surveys the immobilized audience. There is an extended close-up of a somber Heathcliff; we know where his unswerving gaze is directed. Cut to a close-up of Cathy. She is a snow woman with her white bared shoulders, and her apparel might as well be ice. The dress is highly polished white satin; diamonds sparkle from necklace, earrings, and tiara. She is like an ice sculpture, especially when Heathcliff's gaze freezes her. Then, though she struggles against it, her eyes are drawn to him. Such is the force of his gaze that it draws not only Cathy's notice but the notice of the crowd. The resulting voyeuristic heat is extraordinary. Will Cathy melt? Cut to an extreme close-up of the harpsichordist's hands banging away at the coda like jackhammers, invoking the brutal mocking mechanism of the social trap caging the lovers.

In Wyler's rationale for fabricating this scene we see his genius as a filmmaker. In the book *Wuthering Heights*, writing and reading, inscription and its decoding—the carving of Cathy's name on the wooden shelf in her bedroom, her palimpsistic writings in the book of sermons—these are the channels into the text, for the inside reader Lockwood, then for us outside readers. Part of the peculiar power of this device is that the medium doubles the message. For the book, the act of reading is an act of power and connection. First Lockwood's reading, then ours, becomes a process of spying on these distant lives; we catch ourselves brushing Lockwood's shoulder as we lean over to make sense of the words, and the distant lives become not so distant. For the film, Wyler translates this participatory mechanism to the visual. Passion, for Wyler's Cathy and Heathcliff, is always ocular, their gaze a conduit for voyeuristically charged eroticism—as is our gaze when we watch theirs. Our complicity must give us sympathy for the devil—except that under Wyler's gentlemanly direction Heathcliff is no devil, but a great heart more sinned against than sinning.

After the dancing resumes, Heathcliff's continued gaze compels Cathy to turn to him. They walk out to the veranda, a zone halfway between the Grange's caging civilization and the freedom of the natural world. Cathy chides Heathcliff for his somber air. "Don't pretend life hasn't improved for you." "Life has ended for me," he replies. As he leans toward Cathy with words of love, she turns away, and the howl of a cold wind from the moors overtakes the waltz music. The camera retreats through the leaves of the trees into darkness. By freezing his actors within open, uneasily shifting space, Wyler has shown both the spiritual connection of Cathy and Heathcliff and the terrifying emptiness of the universe for the one without the other.

In 1954, a quarter century after *Un Chien Andalou* and a decade before he was to father his second generation of great surrealist films, Luis Buñuel made a low-budget black-and-white adaptation of *Wuthering Heights* called *Abismos de Pasion*. Buñuel has no problem buying sympathy for Heathcliff, in this version called Alejandro (Jorge Mistral). He makes him a much better person than Emily Brontë did, and he makes the Edgar Linton character (Eduardo, played by Ernesto Alonso) much worse. But these are among the least of the departures from Brontë's text: *Wuthering Heights'* Yorkshire moor is here transformed to a Mexican desert, with corresponding changes in climate, architecture, costume, local color, even codes of behavior.

Abismos de Pasion covers a narrower time span than any other version of *Wuthering Heights*. Dispensing with frame narratives, the second generation's tale, and even with the childhood of the principals (except as backstory developed through dialogue), the film begins at the point of Alejandro's return and ends in Catalina's (Catherine's) tomb, a few days after her death. This gives Buñuel space to explore what clearly interests him most: the mesh of emotions among the five love-and-hate entangled siblings and lovers Alejandro, Catalina (Iraseme Dilian), Isabella (Lilia Prado), Eduardo, and the Hindley character Ricardo (Luis Aceves Casteneda). Buñuel's version is unique in that the latter three characters are as fully developed as the first two. The five-character ensemble is at times presented operatically: static camera and total depth of field that replicates an audience's view of a stage; groupings and regroupings of characters in confrontational "duets," "trios," and "quartets"; impassioned extended speeches like arias; even declamatory physical stances of divas presenting themselves to best advantage. As if to underline the operatic connection, Buñuel borrows leitmotifs from Wagner's *Tristan and Isolde*. Most strikingly, Buñuel's conception of the characters is operatic. He both simplifies and moralizes their stories (in such a way as to remind us that opera's conventions are more in tune with Buñuel's Spanish culture than Brontë's Anglo-Celtic roots), valorizing the heroic instinctual masculinity of Alejandro on one hand, the faithfulness of the wronged wife Isabella on the other.

The opening of the film sets Buñuel's simplifying moral tone. As the titles scroll, there is a long shot of a gnarled tree silhouetted against the sky. We are offered this introduction: "These characters are at the mercy of their own instincts and passions. They are unique beings for whom the so-called social conventions do not exist. Alejandro's love for Catalina is a fierce and inhuman feeling that can only be fulfilled through death." A gunshot rings out, and a flock of buzzards flaps from the tree.

"Inhuman," "instinct," and "fierce" are key words here, for the pervading trope in this movie is animal. All the principal characters are identified both as animal predators and as prey—visual correlatives of their cruelty to each other. Catalina is the hunter whose shot scatters the buzzards. "I kill them with one shot," she says in the discussion of cruelty that introduces the characters. "They pass to death's liberty without feeling anything." This in contrast to Eduardo's manner of killing a butterfly, shown to us in close-up—he crushes its body with his fingers. Catalina keeps a bird in a cage. Eduardo asks why she doesn't release it—or kill it. She coos to the bird, "Isn't my love enough so you won't mind being locked up?" In the meantime, dogs are barking. "It must be those buzzards again." In fact, the dogs bark at Alejandro, whose association with the dog ("Canaille!" Eduardo calls him) and the buzzard (scavenger, death) is established here to be used later.

Animal imagery follows human interaction throughout the story, glossing the characters' increasing cruelty: the buzzards' quick death followed by the crushing of the butterfly, and a bit later, the leisurely piercing of the insect with a pin (we are reminded that in Aztec lore, butterflies were souls of the dead). Still later, Ricardo's primitive old manservant tries to exorcise an evil spirit (Alejandro) from the house by immolating live frogs in a smoking charcoal brazier (another Aztec custom). The climax of cruelty occurs at the moment when Catalina swears to Eduardo that she will never again seek out Alejandro. Close-up of her proud smile; cut to the grimace of a terrified pig being roughly dragged to the slaughter. We escape its screams only as its throat is slit.

Less pointed, but equally effective, is the creepy display of Eduardo's insect collections in the background of various interior shots as silent commentary on Eduardo's and Catalina's marriage. First we see only panels of butterflies and moths, neatly ordered, hundreds and hundreds of them. Later we are shown a wall of flying beetles and wasps, and finally, with the household in crisis, the camera pans over ranks of scorpions and spiders. Periodically we see Eduardo handling his collection and his jars of anesthetizing gas with dreamy orgasmic absorption. All this takes place in Eduardo's house. At "The Farm" (Wuthering Heights), the collections come to life; Ricardo feeds flies to a spider that lives in a crack in the wall. Sooner or later, all characters in this story emerge red in tooth and claw.

If Buñuel's staging is operatic, if his use of animal symbolism is essentially literary, still his most masterful effects are achieved through purely cinematic means. Through subtle manipulation of light and the repetition of similarly composed shots, he builds up our sense of the transcendent relation of Catalina and Alejandro, and in doing so gains sympathy for Alejandro.

Catalina, in close-up, is often cocooned by gauzy light shading to dark toward the edge of the frame. Depending on context, this suggests either her anesthetized entrapment in the marriage with Eduardo or a spirituality that transcends worldly situations. That such spiritual transcendence is, for Catalina, linked to Alejandro is also shown by the symbolism of light. After Alejandro's return, Catalina stands at her open bedroom window to gaze out over the night-enshrouded valley. The next shot reveals Alejandro's answering gaze from the opposite side of the frame, at dawn. He raises his ecstatic face towards the luminous clouds of sunrise, and towards Catalina. For each of these lovers, the source of light, and life is the other.

From the start Alejandro is associated with thresholds; there are repeated shots of him entering or looking through passageways, doorways, staircases, windows, arches. After barking dogs disturb Eduardo's household early in the film, there is a tracking shot away from the building—in this and all other film versions of *Wuthering Heights*, a signal of demonic presence. And now Alejandro comes —in night rain and shadow, passing silhouetted through a lit stone archway. The next day, Catalina and Alejandro set out to revisit their childhood haunts, running hand-in-hand through a sun-streamed archway toward "places only the two of them know about." At "The Farm," on several occasions Alejandro walks up a dark staircase with a light at the top, as though drawn like a moth. The last such incident follows his fight with Ricardo after Catalina's death, when he disappears up the arched stairway with the demented concentration of one entering his own mind. In none of these threshold shots do we see Alejandro arriving. He is in shadow, seeking the light. What is his luminous destination?

After grieving for Catalina for three days, Alejandro goes to the cemetery where she has been interred. It is night. He wanders among crosses and tombs, searching for her grave. He is weak and faltering. We are shown a gun training upon him. Clearly now he is the prey of a yet unidentified predator. Alejandro finds the tomb, a raised catafalque with a large metal lock. With difficulty, he breaks the lock, raises the stone lid, and sees a staircase leading down to an underground tomb. There is a shotgun blast and Alejandro falls. We see that it is Ricardo, Catalina's brother, who is the hunter.

But Alejandro is only wounded. The staircase before him is lit by a dim radiance. He staggers down steps like those he has climbed before and reaches the inner tomb where the coffin of Catalina lies. There is Catalina in an earth-covered veil. He lifts her stiffened hand; when he lets go it snaps back. Then, as he raises the veil and kisses her dead face, Catalina in a glowing white wedding dress appears behind him at the bottom of the stairs. It is she, of course, who is the source of light; it is her radiance pouring through archways, from stair tops, that Alejandro has always been seeking, hers the sacred presence on the other side of the threshold. She holds out her arms. Alejandro raises his face joyously. But in a flash Catalina transforms into Ricardo, with an aimed gun. There is an explosion, and Alejandro's body falls over Catalina's in the coffin.

There is a cluster of images and associations here: Catalina equals light, and light stands for absolute union with the beloved, the kind of union that is impossible except in memories of a shared childhood paradise, and in death. This equation holds true in Brontë's book too. In the spirit, if emphatically not in the letter, Buñuel has been true to Brontë.

Robert Fuest's version of *Wuthering Heights* came out in 1970, less than two decades after Buñuel's, but there is more than a generation's worth of difference in the look of the two. Where Wyler had filmed mostly in Hollywood studios, and Buñuel shot his version in Mexico, Fuest was part of a growing trend to film on location, in this case, the Yorkshire moors. Add candy-colored, careening tracks and zooms and television-influenced longshot-closeup pulses, and Fuest would seem at first to blast slow, subtle Buñuel along with the restrained Wyler into sepia-tinged storage. But a more measured response would teach us the danger of undue haste, both in film pacing and in critical judgment.

Perhaps the most strikingly contemporary note is struck by Fuest's treatment of Heathcliff. He cast a very young Timothy Dalton, creating the handsomest Heathcliff in the Pantheon and in some ways the most appealing, though not as nuanced psychologically as any of the other Heathcliffs. Dalton strikes two character notes. Early in the movie, before he leaves, teenaged Heathcliff is vulnerable, affectionate, direct. He lays his head trustingly on old Earnshaw's knee, nuzzles Cathy with innocent ecstasy in their Penistone Crag's hideaway. Though this is only one aspect of the complicated creature Emily Brontë presents to us in her novel, it is an authentic aspect, and Dalton portrays it strongly. But in the balance of the film, the Fuest/Dalton Heathcliff is made to exude the menace and cynicism of a rock star. There is no doubt about it: this Heathcliff, with his high-decibel sexuality, seduces not only Anna Calder-Marshall's Cathy (in a stunning departure from Brontë's text!) but his audience as well. If this handily solves Heathcliff's negative appeal problem, it creates others, perhaps more serious.

Like Wyler and Buñuel. Fuest limits the story to the first generation of Earnshaws and Lintons, and like Buñuel cuts out Lockwood, his visit to the Heights, his visitation by the ghost of Cathy, etc. Nelly Dean's narration survives only in an introductory voiceover, soon abandoned. There are plot, character, and motivational changes as well, mainly resulting from the sexualization of the story. For instance, Nelly Dean (Judy Cornwall) is a simpering big-haired flirt who is in love with Hindley (Julian Glover); she is ridiculously (for a farm worker) squeezed into a breast-billowing corset. Then there is Heathcliff and Cathy's sex scene, which takes place in Thrushcross Grange Park right after Heathcliff's return from his mysterious three-year absence. A little later, Edgar (Ian Ogilvy) is comically surprised when the doctor informs him that Cathy is with child; it has been implied before that Edgar is impotent, so Cathy's baby is probably Heathcliff's ("Edgar's waitin' to see the color of its eyes," Joseph [Aubrey Woods] tells Heathcliff with a leer, as Heathcliff leers back). In keeping with this plot twist, Edgar cuts a pathetic figure all around. He seems more interested in his books than he does in his young wife. When Cathy goes on her hunger strike, Edgar cruelly refuses Nelly's pleadings for her. He is portrayed as cold, selfish, pompous, and not too bright—a fool made dangerous with power.

If in nothing else, Fuest follows his predecessors in his ending for the film. After Cathy's funeral, a drunken and furious Hindley lies in wait for Heathcliff inside Wuthering Heights, gun ready. In the cemetery, Heathcliff flings himself on Cathy's grave, plunges his hands into the soil, and curses her: "Catherine Earnshaw, may you not rest while I am living!" He hears her call teasingly, "Heathcliff!" When he looks up, he sees her ghost beckoning him to run after her. She draws him toward the Heights, where Isabella (Hilary Dwyer) connives with Hindley for Heathcliff's destruction. Cathy's ghost, with a come-on smile, lures Heathcliff to a shuttered window, where Hindley waits with his gun. As in Buñuel, the image of Cathy is replaced by that of the gun's barrel just as it blasts. And as in Wyler, the film leaves us with the image of apparitional Cathy and Heathcliff together on the moors.

Perhaps because of its privileging of the physical over the spiritual, visually this film is more grounded in the time of its making than are the Wyler or Buñuel versions. Male and female characters alike are bodied forth smooth surfaced and hard edged. Make-up style favors a rubbery Halloween-mask look, with high '60s magic-marker eyes and bubble gum lips. The women's hair is ratted up and varnished smooth. Men's coiffures are early Beatles. Costumes—solid-colored, generally clean, always unwrinkled—are probably polyester.

The set design extends the cartoon-like hard edges. Fuest's physical rendering of the house Wuthering Heights is the cleanest on record. Departing from the other sets' homespun look, this one abounds with straight lines, 90-degree angles, and gleaming, unmarred surfaces. Even Hindley's drunken roisterings seem to leave no mark; food and liquor spills disappear overnight, as though the Heights had been sprayed with Scotchguard. The general tidiness is literally highlighted by predominantly high-key illumination, even of Heights interiors, traditionally so murky. One example: the scene in the kitchen when Cathy tells Nelly of Edgar's proposal as Heathcliff eavesdrops. Other directors invoke the pathetic fallacy with prophetic shadows, a passionately flaring kitchen hearth, eureka lightning flashes ("Nelly, I *am* Heathcliff!"). But here the kitchen is suffused with a steady yellow glow, not quite the sunlight of reason banishing the storm clouds of Romanticism, more an assertion of reality and relevance and, above all, physical presence—yes, these are real people, looking three-dimensional and solid in the familiar light of every day.

Fuest's insistence on physicality may have governed his casting. Anna Calder-Marshall's Cathy is against type: she is cute, pert, short, and chunky—not in the least like almost anybody else's idea of Catherine Earnshaw. But the very wrongness of her looks makes her the more emphatically present to the audience. And somehow her eager, clumsy, boyish movements communicate Cathy's mercurial intensity perfectly; she is human, flawed, accessible. Oddly, the sketchiness of her beauty gives her an appeal that airbrush-perfect Merle Oberon and Juliette Binoche lack.

Physicality is also emphasized by dynamic camera movement, with many panning, zooming, and tracking shots. The film's signature shot pattern starts with an extreme close-up of an object, then pulls back to reveal a whole scene. For example, we are shown Heathcliff's dung-crusted boots, then (pull back, pan) Joseph towering up on a hill, enforcing labor from resentful, muddy, abject Heathcliff, low man on the class totem. A similarly managed shot a half-hour later fills the screen with impeccably groomed leather boots, pans suspensefully up the column of spanking new black suit and brilliant linen, then pulls back to reveal Heathcliff asking Hindley and his fellow wastrels what has happened to Cathy. Now Heathcliff has risen far above Joseph to Hindley's class level, and perhaps beyond—as he looms contemptuously above the carousers and tosses his fat bag of money onto the sordid gaming table. Significantly, Fuest's is the only version in which the audience experiences the shock of Heathcliff's return and class apotheosis from Hindley's point of view. In this film, the magic triangle of sex is all male—Heathcliff, Hindley, Edgar—with females Cathy, Isabella, and Nelly often sidelined as trophies in the males' strutting competitions for alpha position.

Of course Heathcliff wins, here and elsewhere, but Fuest/Dalton diverge from their forerunners in physical signals for his victory. Where Olivier's passion vibrates out of stillness, Dalton's emotion is all motion; where Mistral's Alejandro weakens and falters for love,

Dalton is ever puissant. In fact, decades before *The Living Daylights* and *The Rocketeer*, in Heathcliff Dalton was playing an action hero. We can see this in the spirited orchestration of Heathcliff's escape from the Grange after a confrontation with Edgar. In the space of a few seconds Heathcliff smashes a lock with a poker, knocks down two attacking manservants, chases a flurry of maidservants out of the house, vaults over a balustrade, smashes a greenhouse, evades Edgar's pistol fire, and (in one breathless take) runs into the orchard, leaps over a fence, kisses a fortuitously-placed Isabella, and bounds onto his horse. This is the sort of thing that Fuest does well, and so does Dalton. But the scene's James Bondish self-congratulation—the masculine mastery of time and motion to the end of dominance—cheapens not only Romance, but even romance.

For, in the balance, Dalton's Heathcliff is not only cruel; he is a smooth-talking rough-sex schemer. Worse, he turns both sex and violence against Cathy, first in the stable when, reproaching her for visiting the Lintons, he smacks her down into the muck and kisses her roughly; then, when after his return he again knocks her to the ground before having sex with her. This goes beyond the formal duel-like slaps Olivier delivered to Oberon into something more like rape; it is unequivocally wrong. Part of the essence and the genius of *Wuthering Heights* is that Heathcliff's overt violence is always deflected away from Cathy to her surrogates—to Isabella, to Hindley, to Cathy II, to Linton Heathcliff, to Hareton—as overt sex is displaced to Isabella. Fuest and Dalton degrade Heathcliff with their reading of his character.

Though Robert Fuest's *Wuthering Heights* tells its story with economy and clarity, through effective visual means, it is not the story Emily Brontë wrote. That is true of all the versions, but Fuest's distortions are the most disturbing of all. They trivialize Brontë's chief metaphysic: the uncanny, incorporeal love between Cathy and Heathcliff. Furthermore, Fuest shrinks or altogether dismisses subplots that in Brontë add their own metaphysical overtones: the story-within-story repetitions that teach and suggest so much about the nature of narrative, the second generation's reworking of their parents' drama that mimes the regenerating tragicomedy of the human condition. Finally, what Fuest's version does best is show us how Brontë's great story has become the type for a debased though appealing genre: the Gothic romance, with Dalton's Heathcliff a triumphant example of its menacing swashbuckling hero.

In the early '90s, Peter Kosminsky directed *Emily Brontë's Wuthering Heights*, a 104-minute British production. A 1992 release in the U.S. was hyped, then canceled; the film had been trashed in England, perhaps in part because of the unpopular casting of French film star Juliette Binoche as the quintessentially English Cathy. A few years later the film was shown on American cable TV, then released in video stores.

The problem of Heathcliff was turned on its head by another controversial casting: Ralph Fiennes. With his fair coloring, refined features, and lithe, well-proportioned body, Fiennes looks more an Edgar than a Heathcliff. He has to work hard at being bad—luckily a specialty of his. The virtuosic cosmic evil of *Schindler's List*, the all-for-love moral myopia of *The English Patient*—both are anticipated here. Yet evil as Fiennes gets, he never loses his appeal. The more pertinent question becomes, not how we are made to like him at all, but rather, why don't we hate him more thoroughly? The answer perhaps reflects more luster on the movie's psychology than on the moral soundness of its audience.

Sadism is the keynote of the Kosminsky/Fiennes Heathcliff. He is neither the leering, rough-sex artist of Fuest/Dalton, nor the sad, half-mad sufferer of Wyler/Olivier, but a quiet, smiling torturer at play. This is a character strand clearly present in Brontë: Kosminsky pulls a quote from the book when he has Heathcliff tell Cathy that while she was staying with the Lintons he put a wire mesh over a brood of fledgling lapwings and starved them. This neatly sets up Heathcliff's signature M.O.: when Cathy hurts him, he'll hurt, and hurt worse, something or someone Cathy loves.

This is daring. The cruelty of the Fiennes Heathcliff cannot be excused as an act of operatic fidelity to passion, as in Buñuel's Alejandro, nor seen as one part of a complex pattern of personality, as in the Olivier Heathcliff. Fiennes's harshness does not move with the tidal pulls of sex or heroism, as do Dalton's and Mistral's. Watching a smiling, controlled Fiennes jerk a puffy-lipped Isabella (Sophie Ward) by the wrist as he tells her how much he detests her, we see how this Heathcliff's sadism freezes hotter emotions. The production bets on Fiennes's ability to project, from his essence, an ironic, depressed, bitter, modern intelligence, one with which the audience must feel complicity, however uneasily.

But the audience is likely to be looking elsewhere. More than in any other version, it is Cathy, not Heathcliff, who carries the film. First, the script gives her more development and power, in a balance with Heathcliff more closely reflective of Brontë's intentions. But the more important factor is the strong charisma of Binoche, who plays both Cathys, mother and daughter. When she is on a screen she owns it, though her characterizations are almost annoyingly eccentric. Binoche as Cathy I laughs, charmingly and shockingly, at everything. Somehow this distracting tic is a fit psychological aberration to put beside Heathcliff's controlling sadism. Binoche's Cathy just laughs it off.

Binoche's smile, so defiantly merry, eerily mirrors Heathcliff's sadistic grin; in fact by nature or artifice in this film these two actors look very much alike. This resemblance brings out the submerged incest theme in their love affair, for Heathcliff and Cathy were brought up as brother and sister, and may in fact have been so. It is a fault of this version that it slides too quickly over the shared childhood that grounds their love. Their early paradisiacal relationship, young Cathy and Heathcliff in Eden, should be well established using plausible child actors, as in Wyler and Fuest, but Kosminsky dispatches his youngsters in seconds. Instead, suddenly we are confronted with the undisguisably adult Binoche and Fiennes essaying kiddie roles. They giggle through a scripture lesson, then, reprimanded, scamper off to their shared bed to play (of all things!) a guessing game about flowers and trees. These scenes are so obviously wrong that their inclusion seems like wanton sabotage, but Kosminsky won't give screen time to peripheral actors. He wants to immediately drench us with the glorious light of his big stars, and he wants to keep us in that light without distraction.

Sometimes that light is very beautiful. The most engaging scene in the movie (not to be found in Brontë's book) is one of the few that allows Cathy and Heathcliff to be happy. Early in the film, we are shown the two standing in a strange blasted landscape: a lava field serrated like the folds of the brain, with here and there a gnarled tree growing up out of it. Heathcliff enfolds Cathy in his arms. He's boasting, making himself out to be some kind of wizard. "I'll send your spirit into the tree. Listen!" Birds fly out, squawking.

She laughs. "How did you do that?"

"I can do a lot of things," he says. Squinting up at the rays of sun pouring out of a bright cloud, Heathcliff tells Cathy to close her eyes. "If when you open your eyes the day is sunny and bright, so shall your future be. But if the day is for storms, so shall be your life."

When Cathy looks, she laughs to see sun. But thunder growls behind them. They turn to find a horizon of roiling thunderheads. "What have you done?" Cathy breathes. Then she shouts defiantly to the sky, "I don't care! Do you hear? I don't care."

Here we have the visual analog for the animistic magic so vital to the metaphysic of Brontë's book, as voiced by Cathy speaking of Heathcliff, "If all else perished, and he remained, I should still continue to be; and, if all else remained, and he were annihilated, the Universe would turn to a mighty stranger. . . . my love for Heathcliff resembles the eternal rocks" (Ch. 9), and Heathcliff of Cathy, "In every cloud, in every tree—filling the air at night, and caught by glimpses in every object by day, I am surrounded with her image!" (Ch. 33). Their lives, too large to require nuance or explanation, are inscribed in rocks, in trees, in clouds. They are nature gods.

Kosminsky's essentialism, his emphasis on painting the right strokes very broad, is his greatest strength—when he can pull it off. His stubborn concentration on the spine of his story makes for marvelous efficiency. Unlike Wyler (103 minutes), Buñuel (90 minutes), and Fuest (105 minutes), Kosminsky includes both Lockwood *and* the second generation, all in 104 minutes. In fact, as indicated by his title, Kosminsky adds another frame story—a bold stroke that unfortunately goes wrong. Emily Brontë herself wanders catatonically through opening credits into the ruins of Wuthering Heights, wondering who lived there. "My pen creates stories of a world that might have been, and here is one that I will tell," she mutters. Her puzzlingly monotone narration intrudes several times during the action, and the film closes with a shot of her wandering out of the house again, still robotic. While this framing does remind a viewer/reader of the Chinese box narratives-within-narratives of the book, it proves at best a distraction and at worst an undercutting of the "reality" of the film world. Perhaps Kosminsky's motive was to save time with Brontë's strategically placed voice-over explanations. On the contrary: her presence scatters time along with viewer concentration.

But often Kosminsky's chic streamlining works brilliantly. Early in the film Kosminsky sets up an association between the first Catherine and a burning candle when Cathy II gives a candle to Lockwood at the door of the haunted bedchamber and tells him not to set it in the window. Of course he does, unwittingly summoning the ghost of the first Catherine. Thereafter, living and dead, she is recalled by a candle flame; in one scene late in the movie the effect is particularly stunning. It begins with a closeup of Heathcliff at Cathy's window, staring at a candle. He speaks slowly and intensely: "Catherine—Why have you not come back to me? Every day I wait for you. My one waking thought has been of you." Then cut to Cathy II at the Grange reading a letter as Heathcliff's words continue in voice-over, and we realize that Heathcliff is dictating a love letter to his son Linton, sadistically forcing Linton's courtship of his cousin as Heathcliff works toward final revenge. But of course more strongly Heathcliff is calling out to Cathy I to come back to him as a ghost—which at the climax of the film she will, at that very window. Viewing this scene, we feel pleasure, the pleasure that comes from the concentration, then release of emotion and understanding. Kosminsky has built meaning through the careful repetition of tropes (candle, window), and now deployed them in a scene that does double duty for two generations. This is accomplished visual story telling.

Another practice of sound filmic economy: where expression of a character's emotion can be intensified by condensing a scene. For negative proof one has only to go back to Fuest, a prodigy of motion compared to Wyler and Buñuel. Recall Fuest's version of the confrontation between Heathcliff and Edgar in the kitchen of the Grange. There the Dalton Heathcliff's escape was choreographed as swashbuckling action, all flash and dash, its emotion squandered in gaudy, expansive display. In Kosminsky this is condensed to a few quiet seconds: when Edgar hits Heathcliff, Heathcliff lifts a poker. He's frozen by one shake of Cathy's head. Icy eyes narrowing, Heathcliff brings the poker down on the lock of the door instead of the skull of his enemy. He walks out quietly, his anger compact as a fist.

But Kosminsky's less-is-more philosophy works against as much as for him. The story reads like shorthand; events pass so swiftly that we can scarcely comprehend some of them. Several five-second shots may be sufficient to remind a Brontë scholar of the ins and outs of an incident that takes twenty pages to develop in the book (i.e., Heathcliff's courtship of Isabella and their subsequent elopement), but they can hardly do more than sketch a plot point for even the most alert non-literary filmgoer. Furthermore, the movie's rapid pace does not allow character development for anyone but the two principals. Why does Nelly Dean keep turning up? You can't tell from this movie. Frances, Hindley's wife, dies before we are sure just who she is, and Hindley fades away off-screen without our caring. Even Heathcliff and Cathy are moved along too fast. Kosminsky gives us little chance to plant our emotions.

But, having said all that, fast is the way we want our stories told these days. Leisurely examination, lingering mood pieces, careful development of complexity—these are too often read as boring, pompous, and—worst of all—plain slow. Now condensation, implication, collage are preferred in all story telling, visual or written. In film, snappy, economic editing is favored—group-bursts of split-second takes swinging into sequences of longer takes, cuts for point-of-view switches in the middle of gestures or words. These Kosminsky gives us, in a treatment that also manages a flowing lyricism. It is altogether a chic, stylish production. In fact, Kosminsky's cinematography is so much of the moment and *in* the moment that it is hard to isolate its most significant elements. Their kinship to the prevailing ideology—the hot quick fix of the '90s, the cool rush onward into the next millennium—renders them almost transparent.

Ralph Fiennes's Heathcliff, then, is a Heathcliff for our age. Not only his taut physical grace, but the edge of irony to his sadism, his emotional aloofness, even his depressive personality—all these mark him as our own. In him these latter supposedly negative aspects of masculinity are redrawn as positive. In fact the film Heathcliff has always had permeable boundaries. He projects as a voyeuristic object, a spectacle. He's a trap for the fleeting animus, a shadow man showing viewers, female and male, what it is we need of darkness. Looking back, we can catch the shade of the male Zeitgeist behind each screen Heathcliff. In 1939, from a world playing out a relentless historical tragedy, the Wyler/Olivier Heathcliff, driven by fate, asserted the noble necessity of causing pain and enduring it. Buñuel's reactionary 1954 post-war Alejandro sought to escape the rigors of civilization by turning back nostalgically to a more personal, primitive code of masculine honor, where wildness and elementalism conquered refinement. Riding the boom-time '60s, Dalton's 1970 expansionist Heathcliff reveled in his command of screen spatials and erotics, defying the limitations of evil. Most recently, in the '90s, Fiennes's Heathcliff displaced authenticity from Knowledge and Action into Being; evil justified itself; in its existential energy it became an object of desire. Paradoxically given its distance in time, this film Heathcliff may be the one closest to Brontë's intentions—so far, anyway.

We are left to speculate on the nature of the next cinematic interpretation of *Wuthering Heights*—and of Heathcliff. Of one thing we can be sure: with the screen acting less like a window to the past than a mirror to our desires, it will show us what we want to know of evil.

List of Film Versions of Wuthering Heights

[*]Wuthering Heights. Dir. A. V. Bramble. With Milton Rosmer, Colette Brettel, Warwick Ward, and Anne Trevor. Six reels. British production, 1920.

Wuthering Heights. Dir. William Wyler. With Laurence Olivier and Merle Oberon. U.S.A.: Samuel Goldwyn, 1939.

Abismos de Pasion. Dir. Luis Buñuel. With Jorge Mistral and Iraseme Dilian. Mexico: Producciones Tepeyac, 1954.

Wuthering Heights. Dir. Robert Fuest. With Timothy Dalton and Anna Calder-Marshall. G.B.: American International Pictures, 1970.

[*]Wuthering Heights. Dir. Peter Hammond. With Ken Hutchison and Kay Adshead. G.B.: BBC, 1978.

[*] Not discussed here.

**Hurlevent*. Dir. Jacques Rivette. With Lucas Belvaux and Fabienne Babe. French production, 1985.

Emily Brontë's Wuthering Heights. Dir. Peter Kosminsky. With Ralph Fiennes and Juliette Binoche. British production, 1992.

**Wuthering Heights*. Dir. David Skynner. With Robert Cavanah and Orla Brady. Co-production of London Weekend Television and WGBH/Boston, 1998.

Emily Brontë: A Chronology

1818 Emily Jane Brontë is born on July 30. The family then included Maria (1814), Elizabeth (1815), Charlotte (1816), Branwell (1817). Her youngest sister, Anne, was born in 1820.

1821 Emily's mother, Maria Branwell Brontë, dies, and her aunt, Elizabeth Branwell, moves to join the family at Haworth.

1824 On November 25 Emily joins her three older sisters at the Cowen Bridge school for clergymen's daughters. The school records note that at age 5 3/4 she "Reads very prettily, and works a little. Left June 1, 1825. Subsequent career—Governess."

1825 Emily's ill sisters, Maria and Elizabeth, return home to die; Charlotte and Emily withdraw from Cowan Bridge school.

1831 Emily and Anne begin to write about the Kingdom of Gondal (in distinction from the Kingdom of Angria which had been the imaginary province for Charlotte's and Branwell's writing since at least 1825).

1835 Emily briefly attends Miss Wooler's school at Roe Head, where Charlotte was a teacher, and soon leaves because of homesickness. She remains, often in close company with Branwell, at Haworth for the next two years, a period of much reading and writing (particularly poetry) and learning of French and German.

1836 In October, Emily takes a teaching position at Law Hill, near Halifax, where the Misses Patchett had a school for some forty pupils. Charlotte reports receiving from Emily "an appalling account of her duties—hard labour from six in the morning until near eleven at night," and she fears her sister will not stand it. Emily leaves the school and returns home after teaching only six months.

1842 In February, Emily and Charlotte begin their residence as students (and with some responsibility for English instruction) at Pensionnat Heger in Brussels. They return to

Haworth in November after their aunt's death, and although Charlotte goes back and remains in Brussels until 1844, Emily remains at home.

1846 A selection of Emily's poems is published in *Poems by Currer, Ellis and Acton Bell.*

1847 Thomas Newby publishes, together, *Wuthering Heights* and Anne's *Agnes Grey* in December; two months earlier Smith, Elder had published Charlotte's *Jane Eyre.*

1848 Smith, Elder reprints *Poems by Currer, Ellis and Acton Bell.* Unauthorized American editions of the sisters' novels further confuse readers about the identity of their authors. Branwell Brontë dies on September 24. Emily dies on December 19.

1849 Anne Brontë dies on May 28.

1850 Charlotte edits *Wuthering Heights* and selects poems to include among her sisters' literary remains for the Smith, Elder editions of Emily's novel and Anne's *Agnes Grey.*

Selected Bibliography

• indicates works reprinted or excerpted in this Norton Critical Edition.

THE BRONTËS

Barker, Juliet. *The Brontës*. London: Weidenfeld and Nicolson, 1994.

• Lonoff, Sue, ed. and trans. *The Belgian Essays: Charlotte Brontë and Emily Brontë*. New Haven: Yale UP, 1996.

• Smith, Margaret, ed. *The Letters of Charlotte Brontë: With a Selection of Letters by Family and Friends*. Oxford: Clarendon Press, Vol I, 1995; Vol II, 2000.

EMILY BRONTË

Alexander, Christine. "The Art of Emily Brontë." In Christine Alexander and Jane Sellars, *The Art of the Brontës*. Cambridge: Cambridge UP, 1995. 100–128.

Davies, Stevie. *Emily Brontë: The Artist As a Free Woman*. Manchester: Carcanet, 1983.

Davies, Stevie. *Emily Brontë*. Hemel Hempstead: Harvester Wheatsheaf, 1988.

Gérin, Winifred. *Emily Brontë: A Biography*. Oxford: Clarendon Press, 1971.

Pykett, Lyn. *Emily Brontë*. London: Macmillan, 1989.

• Roper, Derek. ed., with Edward Chitham. *The Poems of Emily Brontë*. Oxford: Clarendon Press, 1995.

Stoneman, Patsy. *Brontë Transformations: The Cultural Dissemination of Jane Eyre and Wuthering Heights*. London: Prentice Hall Harvester Wheatsheaf, 1996.

Wallace, Robert K. *Emily Brontë and Beethoven: Romantic Equilibrium in Fiction and Music*. Athens: U of Georgia P, 1986.

WUTHERING HEIGHTS

Armstrong, Nancy. "Emily Brontë In and Out of Her Time." *Genre* 15 (1982): 243–64.

Cecil, David. "Emily Brontë." *Early Victorian Novelists*. London: Constable, 1934. 147–59.

• Chitham, Edward. *The Birth of Wuthering Heights: Emily Brontë at Work*. London: Macmillan, 1998.

Daley, A. Stuart. "The Moons and Almanacs of *Wuthering Heights*." *Huntington Library Quarterly* 37 (1974): 337–53.

• Daley, A. Stuart. "A Revised Chronology of *Wuthering Heights*." *Brontë Society Transactions* 21 (1995): 169–73. Reprint from 3d Norton Critical Edition of *Wuthering Heights*, 1990.

Eagleton, Terry. "*Wuthering Heights*." *Myths of Power: A Marxist Study of the Brontës*. London: Macmillan, 1975. 97–121.

• Gilbert, Sandra, and Susan Gubar. "Looking Oppositely: Emily Brontë's Bible of Hell." *The Madwoman in the Attic: The Woman Writer and the Nineteenth-Century Imagination*. New Haven: Yale UP, 1979. 248–308.

• Haire-Sargeant, Lin. "Sympathy for the Devil: The Problem of Heathcliff in Film Versions of *Wuthering Heights*." *Nineteenth-Century Women at the Movies: Adapt-*

ing Classic Women's Fiction to Film. Ed. Barbara Tepa Lupack. Bowling Green: Bowling Green State UP, 1999. 167–91.

Homans, Margaret. "The Name of the Mother in *Wuthering Heights*." *Bearing the Word: Language and Female Experience in Nineteenth-Century Women's Writing*. Chicago: U of Chicago P, 1989. 68–99.

Jacobs, Carol. "*Wuthering Heights*: At the Threshold of Interpretation." *Uncontainable Romanticism: Shelley, Brontë, Kleist*. Baltimore: Johns Hopkins UP, 1989.

Kermode, Frank. "A Modern Way with the Classic." *New Literary History* 5 (1974): 415–34.

Leavis, Q. D. "A Fresh Approach to *Wuthering Heights*." In F. R. Leavis and Q. D. Leavis, *Lectures in America*. London: Chatto and Windus, 1969. 85–138.

Mathison, John K. "Nelly Dean and the Power of *Wuthering Heights*." *Nineteenth-Century Fiction* 11 (1956): 106–29.

McCarthy, Terence. "The Incompetent Narrator of *Wuthering Heights*." *Modern Language Quarterly* 42 (1981): 48–64.

Miller, J. Hillis. "Emily Brontë." *The Disappearance of God: Five Nineteenth-Century Writers*. Cambridge: Harvard UP, 1963. 157–211.

• Miller, J. Hillis. "*Wuthering Heights*: Repetition and the 'Uncanny'." *Fiction and Repetition: Seven English Novels*. Cambridge: Harvard UP, 1982. 42–72.

Newman, Beth. " 'The Situation of the Looker-On:' Gender, Narration and Gaze in *Wuthering Heights*." *PMLA* 105 (1990): 1029–41.

• Nussbaum, Martha. "*Wuthering Heights*: The Romantic Ascent." *Philosophy and Literature* 20 (1996): 362–82.

Polhemus, Robert M. "The Passionate Calling: Emily Brontë's *Wuthering Heights*." *Erotic Faith: Being in Love from Jane Austen to D. H. Lawrence*. Chicago: U of Chicago P, 1990. 79–107.

Sabol, C. Ruth, and Todd K. Bender. *A Concordance to Brontë's Wuthering Heights*. New York: Garland, 1984.

Shannon, Edgar F. "Lockwood's Dreams and the Exegesis of *Wuthering Heights*." *Nineteenth-Century Fiction* 14 (1959): 95–109.

Stoneman, Patsy, ed. *Wuthering Heights* [Essays, Articles, Reviews]. New York: Columbia UP, 1998.

Van Ghent, Dorothy. "On *Wuthering Heights*." *The English Novel: Form and Function*. New York: Rinehart, 1953. 153–70.

Yeager, Patricia. "Violence in the Sitting Room: *Wuthering Heights* and the Woman's Novel." *Genre* 21 (1988): 203–29.